# About the Author

Mark G. Wentling was born in Wichita, Kansas, and raised in nearby small towns. He has lived most of his adult life in Africa, working for the U.S. government. He has published seven novels related to Africa, one book based on his experiences in Honduras and another related to his Kansas upbringing. He has also published numerous professional articles. He resides in Lubbock, Texas, with his Ethiopian wife and one of his seven grown children.

# Jackleg Boys

# Mark G. Wentling

## Jackleg Boys

Vanguard Press

*Vanguard Press is an imprint of*
*Pegasus Elliot Mackenzie Publishers Ltd.*
www.pegasuspublishers.com

First Published in 2024

**Vanguard Press**
**Sheraton House  Castle Park**
**Cambridge  England**

Printed & Bound in Great Britain

# Dedication

This book was inspired by the true-life story of my maternal great-grandfather, Henry Harrison Read (a.k.a. Charles Bonard) and his younger brother, Peyton Randolph Read.

They fled at a young age their multi-generation Virginia plantation during the U.S. Civil War in 1863 and went to Texas and ended up in Florida.

This is about all that is known about them and their tumultuous lives.

This book of historical fiction tries to fill in the gaps of their remarkable adventures.

Dedicated to my mother, Leah Deborah 'Georgia' Read.

Born on September 13, 1916, in Lawton, Oklahoma, and died on October 13, 2012, in Bronx, New York.

She was the daughter of Sudie Belle Bonard Read, who was born in Arcadia, Florida, on June 30, 1894, and died in El Dorado, Kansas, on March 21, 1939, and is buried in the Billings family plot in the Belle Vista Cemetery of El Dorado.

The ashes of Georgia are buried atop Sudie's grave.

Merriam-Webster definition of jackleg: 'Characterized by unscrupulousness, dishonesty, or lack of professional standards; lacking skills and training.'

# Contents

# Part I: Going West

# Chapter One
# Fleeing Old Virginie

Their horses were hungry. They were famished, but they needed their horses alive and well if they wanted to live. They did not know what to do or where to go. All they knew was that they needed to get as fast and far away as they could from their birthplace.

The Civil War had destroyed the privileged life they had known. Nothing was left of their family's historic Virginia plantation. All had been burnt to the ground, looted, and their slaves had fled to the four winds. The glory days of one of America's founding families had been reduced to ashes.

They were lucky to have survived by hiding in the thick woods. Their blue-blood father and older brothers had fled south in the hopes of joining southern Confederate troops, leaving his wife and two teenage sons behind to fend for themselves. He referred to his sons as 'jackleg boys' because they had not benefitted from his high level of education. He had obtained his law degree when he was eighteen years of age. He was proud to call himself an eleventh-generation American and could trace his lineage back to 1620 and the beginnings of America. He belonged to the elitist land-owning class of aristocratic Virginians.

The war had prevented his sons, Henry and Randolph, from completing their schooling. But more upsetting to them was that their beloved mother had decided to stay behind in her house and be burnt alive. She loved her youngest sons and demonstrated her love by making the ultimate sacrifice. She gave them all the money and the little food she had to them. Her last advice to her sons was to head west and stay hidden from all warring factions.

Her sons tried to leave her some food, but she said forthrightly, "Dead people don't eat."

She knew she was too weak to run and was determined to stay with her ancestral house. She was aware that her decision to stay was a fatal one, but it was one that she had to make. She steeled herself to the fact that she would go up in flames with her cherished house.

All the outbuildings were in flames, and the fire was flirting with igniting the back of the big house. The smoke was becoming thicker, and the crazed, terrified look on their mom's face intensified. Tears were streaming down her contorted face when she screamed, "Get going. Save yourselves. Forget me and the past. If you survive, there is nothing ahead for you except a starkly different and much more difficult life full of hardship. I will pray for you with my last breath. Now go before the oppressors get you! Go west. Go to Texas."

Henry and Randy were only two years apart, ages fourteen and sixteen when the fratricidal war decimated their lives in 1863. They did not know what to do but hold on to life as long as they could. They had fled their nightmarish situation during the previous night with their two horses and guns, and the packets of food their mother had given them, riding until daylight through the woods as far as their horses could take them. They decided they could best avoid danger by traveling off the main roads and paths at night.

Their young bodies were smarting fiercely as they had been whipped repeatedly by the branches of prickly bushes and thorny trees that they forced their way past. Their bodies were also suffering from their frequent tumbles in the moonless spring night. However, the ache of their bodies was dominated by their need for more food and water for them and their horses.

They had no idea of where to find the sustenance they needed to survive. They realized now they had consumed the food their mother gave them too quickly. They ate some tree leaves and a few mushrooms they found growing from a rotten log. They pulled up some sparse grass clumps and fed them to their horses. But that was not enough. They had to find food!

Henry softly suggested, "Maybe we kill one horse and eat it. I would do that before starving to death."

A tearful and frightful Randy replied, "That's crazy talk. Let's scout around while we still can for something to eat."

Then, out of nowhere, they heard a light coughing sound. They both grabbed their Springfield rifles and pointed them in the direction of the muffled noise. To their surprise, out came a young, half-dressed, barefooted, darkie teenage boy who had been hiding in the brush nearby. They were stunned by the words that came out of his mouth. "Shoot me, Massa. Kill me dead and put me out of my mis'ry. I'm goin' to die anyway, so kill'in me now wud be a relief."

Henry and Randy had no intention of killing the young black man in front of them. They asked him where he had come from, and he replied hesitantly with his eyes staring at the ground. "Read Plantation."

"Good God. That was our home. That means you were one of our slaves."

"Yes, Massa. I seen you's before."

The black boy went on to say, "If you's not kill'in me, do you's have somethin' to eat? I'm dyin' of hungra."

Henry and Randy did not have the strength to even laugh at the darkie's words. Henry quietly said, "We were hoping you would have some food because we, too, are almost dead from hunger."

Henry and Randy lowered their guns, and after a long silence, Henry asked, "Any idea where we can get some food? By the way, what's your name?"

The darkie immediately responded, "Me is called Jo. There's a farmhouse right over there. Maybe we get some vituals there."

United by the deep ache in their stomachs to find something to eat, they left their small riding horses tethered behind and walked furtively together through the dark woods to the edge of the pasture surrounding the farmhouse. They thought all the houses in this area would have already been raided by armed forces and looters. To their great surprise, this old wooden frame house and its outbuildings were still standing and intact.

They hid on the edge of the woods. Henry led the way and said in a hushed voice, "At first light, I'll just stagger innocently up to the front door, knock, and see what happens. If things go all right, Randy will follow me, and if we get in, Jo, you see what you can find in the barn."

Randy immediately popped up, "What about our guns?"

Henry replied, "After I'm in, you come and hide the guns under the front stoop, and then I'll invite you in if all is well."

Daylight was snaking its way through the woods, and their surroundings were slowly becoming visible. Henry sauntered weakly up to the house's front door and softly knocked. He waited a while, but there was no answer. He knocked a second time more loudly. Still, there was no answer. The profound silence accentuated his hunger pangs. He struggled to not cry out.

He was about to bust the front door down when it suddenly opened a crack, and he was staring down the barrel of a gun. He immediately cried out, "Don't shoot. I mean no harm."

At the other end of the long rifle stood an elderly woman dressed in a soiled calico dress, shaking and perspiring profusely. It was obvious that she was almost ready to collapse. She lowered her gun and managed to say, "Come on in. Anyone who speaks the King's English is welcome. But you'll need to change the way you talk to survive in these parts."

As Henry stepped into the house, he realized he would have to change not only the educated way he talked but his entire behavior if he were to make it to his destination… wherever that may be. But his stomach told him there was no time to think or make small talk, so his first words were, "Thanks, Ma'am. My little brother and I are starving. Do you have anything to eat?"

The old skinny woman laughed aloud like a mad woman at his words. She replied, "Food. What's that? All I got is some stale grits. Do you want some?"

"Sure. Let me call my younger brother."

While Henry went outside to call Randy, the old woman went into her kitchen to warm on her wood stove a pot of grits. When the boys came into the house, she told them to sit at the dining table. They did so but were tempted to follow the smell of hot grits wafting into the dining room from the kitchen. They struggled to control their basic instincts, which urged them to rush into the kitchen and gobble up the steaming grits.

The gray-haired woman came carrying a pot of cooked grits and sat it down in the middle of the rough wooden table. They wasted no time in dishing out onto their chipped white porcelain plates small heaps of grits, devouring them in spite of burning their mouths. The frail woman sat at the end of the table, watching the two boys ravishingly eat their grits. When they were scraping their plates and the serving bowl of every grit bit, she feebly said, "I can see you boys are terribly hungry, but where to you go from here? When and where will be your next meal?"

Of course, they had no answers to her questions. All Henry could say was, "Don't know. All I know is we have to keep heading west no matter what."

The woman scoffed. "West? Nothing but wilderness to the west. But I guess you have no choice 'cause there is war to the east."

Randy continued to scrape for more grits, hoping his scraping would cause the woman to bring more. The woman saw what he was doing and caustically said, "Sorry, there is no more. We'll see what comes first for me. Either I starve to death or get killed when the oppressors attack. For sure, I'm too old and weak to run anywhere."

Her words made Henry and Randy think of their own mother, who found herself trapped in similar circumstances. Henry broke the silence by speaking up, "Ma'am, we are mighty grateful for the food you gave us. We need to be going on our way in the woods. So, we have to say goodbye. By the way, my name is John, and my brother is named William."

"It has been a pleasure to meet you, John and William. My name is Margaret Evelyn Roberts."

Henry and Randy quickly got up from the table and, without looking back, headed for the door and left. As soon as they were outside, Henry asked Randy where he had put the guns. Randy showed him, and he strapped on the belt with two leather holsters holding the trusty big Colt .44 caliber pistols. He took one pistol and checked the chamber to see if there was a bullet ready to fire. He cocked the pistol and knocked gently on the door. The old lady answered, and without hesitation, he shot her in the face and yelled to Randy, "Come in and ransack the house; take what we need and can carry. Be quick."

Randy was in shock. He was horrified at what his brother had just done and tearfully moaned, "Why did you kill her? She was nice to us! What did she do to deserve being killed? Why give her phony names for us if you were going to kill her?"

The mild-mannered Henry looked at his little brother and said in no uncertain terms, "Look. You got to understand and change everything about you. We are no longer pampered rich schoolboys. We have to become like the worst kind of savages to survive. You have to accept that the odds are against our survival, but we have to do anything it takes to survive, even if that means lying, cheating, stealing, and killing. Now, get on with your search of the house."

Randy whimpered, "But you didn't have to kill her."

Ron replied softly but firmly, "Yes, I did. To be on the safe side, she had to die. She would have died eventually, anyhow. If she had lived, she would have talked, and the oppressors would have been on our trail. Now hurry along and see what you can find while I torch the house and outbuildings."

"What? You going to burn down the place, too?"

"It will be burnt to the ground anyway. Best we burn the place down around her body so it looks like the oppressors have already been this way."

Randy reluctantly accepted Henry's warped logic. He stepped carefully over the dead body and made sure he did not step in the blood that had flowed from her head. He then hustled to search the one-story house for anything that would be of use to their onward journey toward the unknown west. Henry poured the little tallow oil remaining in the plain glass lamp all about the sitting room and then smashed the lamp against the wall. The room quickly went up in flames, obliging Henry to call out to Randy, "Be quick. Grab what you can. We got to go."

Henry picked up the guns and stood in front of the house, waiting for Randy to exit. Soon, Randy came out carrying all he could, and Henry told him, "Go to the horses in the woods while I set fire to the barn. Jo should be in the woods by now."

Randy trotted toward the woods, and Henry took a piece of burning wood from the house and ran to set the barn on fire. Once the barn was sufficiently in flames, Henry joined Randy and their horses in the hiding place in the woods. The first words out of his mouth were, "Where's Jo?"

Randy harshly said, "Like a savage, you probably burnt him to death in the barn."

At that instant, a voice came out of the dense woods, "No, Massa. I's alive right here with this old nag I found in the barn with three old skinny chickins. Can I eat one now?"

Henry answered with a big grin on his face. "You sure can. Glad you made it back. Start a small fire to cook your chicken. But be quick. We have to get far away from this place."

Randy could not resist saying, "Why are you glad he's back while the old white woman who helped us lay dead?"

Henry swiftly retorted, "Our lives depend upon Jo being alive with us and that woman being dead."

He could see that Randy did not understand, so he grasped him by the shoulders and said sternly, "Little brother, listen to me. If we're going to live, we have to learn to be like Jo. He can teach us how to survive. He knows everything we need to know, and he wants to go west, too. And never use your real name or let on that you can read and write. We must act like poor white trash to survive. Now let's see what you got?"

Randy unpacked the blanket bundle of stuff he had rummaged from the house. There were small packets of coffee and salt, friction matches, some hard biscuits and beef jerky, and a flask full of water. Not much. The old woman had been living off the little she had for months.

Randy said, "I also got her old single-shot rifles, but there is only one bullet, and that is in the barrel."

"I was hoping you could find some clothes for us. We have to get rid of these fancy plantation riding outfits. I guess her husband and sons took all their clothes with them when they went off to war."

There was one item that interested Henry. He opened an antique brass-encased pocket compass, and saw that it worked, and showed them true west. He slipped the compass into his side pocket and said, "This is useful as it tells us if we are on the right track or not."

"Let's go on for a piece and then rest for a while. Be checking for any grass to feed our horses. Let's look for a creek to water our horses and camp out for the day at the nearest creek before forging ahead all night. Wait for me while I check on Jo."

Henry found Jo sitting in front of a small fire, munching on the crispy chicken that he had just killed, plucked, gutted, and roasted over his fire. The first question Henry asked him was, "How did you start your fire?"

Jo showed him the flint pieces he had and said, "Massa, this' wat we use when we can't snitch a piece of fire from a nebur. Massa, youse want a piece of chicken?"

"No, we had some grits. That chicken is for you. Put out your fire as soon as you can. We don't want anyone spotting it."

"Danks, Massa. I so hungra I can eat chicken bones and all. Massa, there was nothin in the barn except for two more skinny chickens and that old nag, which is more ded than alive."

"You did good, Jo. We'll be moving on soon before camping out for the day and moving at night. I guess you can ride that old gray nag bareback."

"I sur'can, Massa, but fo sur she cain't make it to Texas."

"Don't worry, we'll all have to find new mounts before getting to Texas. Our two riding ponies are not raised for this. We wanted to get regular quarter horses, but they had all been taken by the Confederate Army. By the way, why do you want to go to Texas?"

"I heard a black man can be free as the wind on the open range in Texas."

"I hope that is true. For sure, there will be new lives for all of us in Texas, if we ever get there. It will take us months, if we are lucky, to see what Texas looks like."

"Massa, excus, but you have to find new clothes. Those clothes you have are a ded giveaway dat you come from rich folk."

"You're right, Jo. There's a lot we need to change, and we're counting on you to tell us what we need to do."

Jo smiled. He was happy to be on the road to freedom with a belly full of roasted chicken and leaving cold winter weather behind him. He was also feeling good because he had never had a white man talk to him like a friend.

Henry uttered under his breath as he walked off. "Thank God for sending us Jo."

# Chapter Two
# Old Nag Meat

The creek was almost dry. The spring rains had been light so far. Jo dug a hole with his bare hands in the creek bed. A slow trickle created a clear pool of drinkable water. They drank directly from the pool and filled their jugs. When they finished, their horses drank their fill. The horses were then tethered to small trees in opposite directions so they could graze on any grass within their reach. The old nag preferred laying down while the two ponies calmly stood looking at Henry, wondering when they would return to the easy life they once lived.

The trio looked for individual places near the creek to lay down to take a nap before getting up at nightfall and trying to walk westward to unknown destinations. They wrapped up in their blankets to ward off the cool spring air. Randy gave Jo the blanket in which he had wrapped items stolen from the old lady's house.

Before dosing off, Henry said softly, "Try to get some rest. We have a long night of forging through the dense woods ahead of us."

The only sounds surrounding their camping spot near the creek were the chirps of a few night birds and the gurgling sound made by the low-water creek. Randy was sound asleep when a brusque tap on the sole of his right boot caused him to open his eyes to see the towering silhouette of his older brother, who whispered, "Time to go. It is almost dark."

Jo was already up and readying the horses. He wondered which way they would go as all sides of their camp were curtained by impenetrable woods. Henry looked around and said, "There is no good way to forge ahead. We'll go the way the compass says is west."

Henry snapped open the compass and pointed it in the direction that it indicated was west. He commanded Jo to take the lead, saying, "You go first with your big nag; she'll help clear the way. Break any branches in the way. We'll follow you with our smaller ponies. I'll bring up the rear."

The nag was hesitant to move ahead, and Jo had to gently whip her with the reins to get her to go where there was no place to go. Henry and Randy followed on foot with their frightened steeds. It was slow going, and at times, they could not force their way ahead and felt trapped in the woods. They found they could not go straight west but would have to meander in the woods in a general westward direction to get anywhere. The darkness of night added to their woes. Before long, they became lost in the woods with no way to go in any direction.

Randy moaned, "At this pace, it will take us forever to get to Texas or anywhere else between here and there."

Henry grudgingly agreed by saying, "We'll have to take the risk of following a path already forged in a westerly direction if we are to get anywhere."

Jo reluctantly said, "Yes'em, Massa. We's plum lost, and I feelin' bad hungra."

"Okay. Let's get out of this mess and follow the first path we come across. I say we head south and hope to find a path heading west. Try to go left, Jo."

Jo headed in the direction indicated by Henry, weaving his way around big trees, clumps of bushes, and tangles of underbrush. He could not see farther than an arm's length. They walked all night and only got a few miles from where they started. They forded a few creeks and kept going until the dawn's light made it clear how lost they were. Despite their physical exhaustion, they had only managed to go a short distance. Hunger pains were once again getting the best of them.

A worried Henry uttered, "Let's stop here to rest and eat some of the little we have. I got to have something to eat so I can think straight about what we can do next."

They all plopped down, and Randy removed from his horse a packet of hard biscuits and passed them around with a jug of water. They each had one biscuit to munch on, and they washed down the rancid biscuits with the creek water they had collected. Henry was served first and, after a few swallows of water, passed the jug to Randy. Although Randy was reluctant to pass the jug to Jo, he did so after Henry vigorously motioned for him to do so.

Henry gave Randy stern verbal advice. "You got to treat Jo as an equal and drop all your qualms about accepting him as a full team member. We're lucky to have Jo with us. He could be the difference between living or dying."

"Wat the horses goin' to eat?" Jo asked loudly.

"That's a good question. They got to eat. Looks like grass is scarce around this spot. Maybe we can try to go a little farther and search for a grassy patch."

They slowly trudged south through the woods and were pleasantly surprised to find, after a couple of miles, an open spot covered with little bluestem grass. They let their horses eat all they wanted and laid down at the edge of the woods to rest until nightfall obliged them to try again to make some progress in the start of their long journey.

Jo was the first to hear in the distance the sound of creaky wagon wheels. He could hear the sound moving closer, so he woke up Henry and whispered, "Massa, ther's a wagen a comin."

Henry immediately got up and strapped on his pistols, and told Jo, "Get our stuff and horses and hide in the woods with Randy while I deal with whatever is coming."

While Randy, Jo, and the horses hid in the woods, Henry walked across the grassy patch to see what was happening on the other side. He was surprised to see a two-track wagon cutting through the wilderness road. He dropped to the ground and hid himself in the tall grass and waited for the noisy wagon to approach.

He held his breath as the wagon came into view. He could now make out an elderly man in black attire sitting in the rein holder's seat conducting two old mules. Next to him was a bonneted woman. In the wagon bed, he spotted two children. He suppressed an impulse to attack and kill them all. He did not know what to do. In the end, he decided against his inner feelings and ran up to the wagon with his hands in the air to greet its occupants, saying clearly, "I mean no harm."

Upon hearing and seeing Henry, the man driving the wagon pulled his reins, and the wagon came to a stop. All eyes were on Henry. Nobody (even him) knew what he would do next. After a couple of minutes of pause, the man in the black suit said, "Greetings, friend. I'm Pastor Richard Ratherford, and this is my wife, Agnes, and our two children, Ester and Abraham. What are you doing alone in these parts?"

Henry was taken aback by the civilized, polite words of the man. He thought the world had gone crazy and become uncivilized. He hesitated to open his mouth but said as he walked closer to the wagon, "Pleased to meet you. My name is John, and I'm here with my younger brother, William, and our slave, Jo. We fled the destruction of our home in Virginia and all the dangers of the war. Where you headed?"

"Good to meet you, John. We're like you, fleeing the war. Our house and church were burnt to the ground by the oppressors, and we thought it best to try to go as far west as possible so we can get out of the way of the war. We don't have any guns. I see that you do, so maybe you would like to join us as our security guards?"

Henry hesitated with his reply, but he finally accepted the offer to join Pastor Ratherford and his family, saying, "Yes, we have guns and some ammunition, but we do not have much more. Let me signal to my brother and Jo to come out of hiding so they can join us."

Henry signaled for his brother and Jo to come with the horses and then asked, "Do you know where we are?"

"Like you, we're coming from Southern Virginia. I believe we're now in what they call Tennessee. Lots of people fleeing the war, so I would not be surprised to run into more people, but we have no choice but to stay on the road. We just have to take our risks and go as far as we can. We are thankful for the added protection you can provide us."

Henry was surprised to hear they were already in Tennessee. He did not think they had come that far. Anyway, they should make better time now that they were on the open road. The risks were higher, but they had no choice. He was worried about running into groups of other desperate people fleeing the war and asked the pastor, "Have you seen any other travelers on this road?"

"At the beginning of our journey, we saw hordes of people who were, for the most part, headed south to Chattanooga, where they hoped to find refuge or take a train or riverboat farther south. Seeing so many people in turmoil scared us, so we got off the main road and took this less-traveled road. We've been on this road for a few hours, and you are the first soul we have come across."

Curiosity got the best of Henry, and he asked, "How do you know where you're going?"

"We don't. We prayed about it and asked God to guide us to a safe place in these perilous times. But one idea we had was to try to find where we can hook up with the trail the army created years ago to move injuns to a new reservation out west. The Lord willing."

Henry did not know about divine guidance, but he thought the plan to find the westward Indian removal trail was a good one. At least it was better than any idea they had.

The pastor was also curious. "You guys must have stumbled through the Cumberland Gap without knowing it 'cause you could have never made it over the ridge. The Grace of God must have been on you."

Henry replied sardonically, "I don't know anything about gaps or ridges. It was pitch dark, and we struggled to forge through the densest of woods."

"Well, thank God there are no longer Indians in these parts, or we would all be already dead."

Randy and Jo joined Henry and tied their horses to the back of the wagon. Henry respectfully introduced Randy as his younger brother William and Jo simply as their remaining slave. Jo took his subordinate place at the back side of the wagon while Henry and Randy shook hands with the elderly preacher man. They noticed that his wife turned her head away to hide her sobbing, and the two children had deadpan looks on their sallow faces. Their actions communicated they had experienced the worst and expected that this journey would be the end of them. It appeared that only their Christian faith was keeping them alive.

Pastor Ratherford solemnly said, "Before we go on, let's say a few words of prayer."

They all bowed heads as the pastor delivered in a weak voice a short prayer: "Almighty God, bless those who join us in our efforts to find a new place to settle. We ask that you continue to guide, lead, and direct us. In Jesus' name, we pray. Amen."

They all mumbled, "Amen." And Randy felt compelled to ask the pastor, "What kind of preacher are you?"

"I'm an ordained Presbyterian minister. I have overseen several churches at different places in Virginia and was just founding a new church in the town of Merrill in Lee County when the war forced us to leave as fast as we could. We left with only the clothes on our backs and our Bibles."

Randy could see etched in the faces of the pastor and his family the depths of the terror they suffered. He appreciated that, but the ache deep in his stomach overrode all sentiments and prompted him to ask, "Do you have anything to eat?"

His words brought tears to the pastor's eyes as he replied, "No. We did not have time to gather any food. But the Lord will provide. Man does not live by bread alone."

The quotation of this Bible verse did not relieve Randy's hunger pains, and he gave a dreadful look at Henry and blurted out, "I need food now!"

Randy was on the verge of succumbing to hysterics when Henry grabbed him and said firmly, "Settle down. You'll have food soon. Just hold on a little while longer."

Henry told the pastor to keep heading down the road for as long as he could while he went ahead and looked for a place for them to camp for the night. He noted, "My brother, William, and our slave are armed in case you are bothered by any mischievous intruders. I won't be too far away. Just holler if you need me."

The pastor nodded in the affirmative, and Henry mounted his horse and rode off. The creaky wagon moved ahead at a slow and noisy pace. The wagon made so much noise that Randy asked, "Do you have any grease? We have to do something to reduce the noise your wheels are making."

"No, we got nothing for that, but for sure, the wheel could use some grease."

They had only gone a few miles when they spotted Henry ahead on the road, waving his arms above his head. Evidently, he had found a good place to camp. He waited for the wagon to arrive and said, "Just off the road is a good place next to a creek to pass the night. I can see that it has been used before as a campsite, but it seems safe. Follow me."

Henry showed them a beautiful spot underneath a huge black oak with a creek running through it. There was lots of space for their animals to graze on little bluestem grass, and new springtime shoots were sprouting everywhere. The field of grass was also full of a wide variety of colorful wildflowers. Henry thought this idyllic spot was definitely a place to settle in, but it was eliminated from consideration because it was too near a war zone.

Henry indicated to the pastor where he should park his wagon. When the pastor climbed down from the old wooden wagon, Henry got a measure of him. He was tall, thin, and visibly worn down by age and worry. Henry gently pulled the pastor aside and said, "I see no choice but to kill the old nag. We can stay alive by eating her meat. What do you think?"

"I knew the Lord would provide. The old nag is a true blessing."

"Okay. That settles it. I'll tell my brother and get Jo to help. Do you have pots or pans we can use? I have my huntin' knife to slit its throat, but any knives you have may also be useful. Maybe you can help William start a fire so we cook as much meat as we can before it gets dark. I'll go now and talk to William and our slave."

Henry informed the almost delirious Randy of his plan to butcher and eat the nag. He then walked over to Jo and told him about killing the nag and eating its meat. Jo joyfully said, "Gud, Massa. Dat's the only thing de old hors is gud fer."

Jo began to walk to a secluded place near the campsite when he turned and said in earnest to Henry, "I kno you got to say dat I be ur slave, but you kno I aim to be free."

Henry replied honestly, "I know, Jo. Calling you our slave is for your own protection. Even though the warfighting is north of us, we're still in the south. As soon as we get out of the South, you're free as you want to be. I figure it could take us a year or two, if we are lucky, for all of us to be free of the violent divisions in our country."

Jo led the nag to a clearing on the edge of their campsite. Henry unsheathed his hunting knife. The pastor came with a few pots and pans. Jo lay the nag down and stroked it while he hummed softly. Henry handed his knife to Jo. In a deliberate fashion, Jo cut the nag's jugular vein. They tried to catch as much blood as they could in the metal pots the pastor had brought, but most of the blood flowed into the ground. The nag struggled a bit at first, but the constant loss of blood slowly drained all resistance from her body, and death quieted her forever.

It was sad to see the nag bleed to death, but their survival depended upon her death. Jo took the pastor's knives and said he would butcher the nag like he assisted with the butchering of steers on the farm. He proceeded with the skinning and gutting of the old nag. And then sliced off big chunks of meat and handed them to the pastor and Henry to cook over the fire the pastor's wife was building in the nearby campsite with the piles of dead wood collected by her children.

Randy assisted the pastor's wife with spearing chunks of horse meat with sharpened tree stakes and balancing them over the smoky fire. The pastor's wife cut the meat into portions she thought were readily edible once the roasted meat was cooled. She first cut small slices of meat for her two children and carefully cooked it over the open fire. The children were the first to taste old nag meat. They gobbled it up as quickly as it was given to them.

Jo sliced the remaining good parts of meat into thin strips to hang over sapling limbs supported by forked uprights implanted in the ground to dry near the blazing fire. These strips would be cooked and dried and kept for chewing on later. All the meat should keep them nourished for several days. They cooked and ate on the spot as much meat as they could. The meat they could not eat now they would carry with them for as long as they could. When any remaining meat was too rotten to eat, they would throw it away.

Henry feasted on the nag's roasted meat and playfully said, "We used to say that we're so hungry we could eat a horse. Now, we have eaten a horse, and we are no longer hungry. Horse meat tasted mighty fine to me. I now know that when you are hungry, all food tastes good."

Jo sat on a log behind the group, which sat in a circle on the ground around the blazing fire. Jo raised his hand. After he was recognized by Henry, he said, "I got idee. Why not use nag fat so wagon wheels be quiet?"

Randy was feeling much better after gorging himself with cooked horsemeat, and he quickly replied to Jo's suggestion by saying. "Good idea. As soon as we have digested our meat, we'll use the fat to grease the wheels before nightfall."

The horse fat worked as well or better than real grease, and in the days ahead, they felt the nag's spirit with them by the silence made by the wagon wheels. It was no longer a creaky old wagon but a well-oiled nag four-wheeler. Nothing like full stomachs to put happier faces on everyone and everything. It was now westward ho with a smile and greater hope.

# Chapter Three
# Flash Flood

Circling high above their campsite was a band of buzzards readying their early morning descent to devour the old nag's bloody carcass. The flies had already been attracted in voracious swarms to the dead horse's remains. The nag's body had not only fed humans but would also feed many of nature's critters. Henry thought that maybe the old nag was more useful in death than in life, particularly under the circumstances.

The pastor and his family were doing their morning prayers. Randy was getting their two ponies ready for another day's travel. Jo had brought the mules to the wagon and hitched them up. Henry took a last look at their lovely camping spot and yelled, "Let's start making tracks. Daylight is burning."

Henry rode his horse ahead, and Randy brought up the rear. Jo plodded close behind the wagon to tend to the meat, making sure it got all the sunlight needed to help it cure as much as possible. The two children were quietly snuggled under a blanket in the front of the wagon bed. The pastor's wife sat next to her husband with a stony face, looking straight forward. The pastor sat bolt upright, holding the reins lightly as he coaxed his two old mules forward on the narrow dirt road. He was happy that an application of fat from the old nag had eliminated the screeches coming from his wagon's wheels.

The wagon caught up to Henry, and he reported, "The way looks clear. We should make good time today. The main obstacles are the crossing of creeks, but they should not pose much of a problem. How many days do you reckon it will take to reach the westward leading Indian removal path?"

The pastor hesitated before responding, "I figure at this pace, we are making ten to twelve miles a day. Barring any mishaps, this should have us at the Indian trail in ten days, give or take a day or two."

They continued their trek south, passing through unknown territory while keeping an eye out for any other people or signs of trouble. For several days, they were blessed by good sunny weather and a good stock of meat to fight off any hunger pains. Henry found that by eating only meat, he became constipated, so he asked the pastor, "What are we going to do? I've already lost a lot of weight, and all this meat is stopping me up completely."

"Yep. We need to eat some greens. When we come across another grassy field, I'll stop and have the wife and children look for edible wild greens that we can boil and eat with our evening meal of meat."

Henry rode ahead, stopping at a grassy spot near a creek and waiting for the wagon to arrive and come to a halt so that the pastor's wife and children could collect greens. The animals could also graze and drink from the creek.

The pastor's wife and children filled their cloth bags with an assortment of greens. They were pleased that so many edible greens thrived in these isolated grasslands. They could not wait to boil them into a wild spinach stew. The children did not normally like to eat greens, but these greens would be welcomed into their empty stomachs.

The successful collection of wild greens made everyone happy. For the first time, Henry saw the pastor's wife crack a little smile. He could see that the greens would not only provide them with a more balanced diet but also improve their outlook. Of course, they could not wait to devour the greens the pastor's wife would cook up for them to eat as part of their supper.

They traveled until it was almost nightfall and made camp at a spot that Henry had found. They did their usual routine and found places in which to fall fast asleep. As usual, Henry checked on everyone else and the animals before bedding down himself, keeping his rifle and pistols at the ready in case they had any unwanted intruders… two or four-legged.

His last stop in his pre-sleep rounds was to make sure the pastor and his family were okay. The pastor softly said, "Son, it is a real blessing to have run into you. In two or three days, we should cross the old Indian trail and then turn westward. May God continue to guide and protect us."

Henry was not interested in all this talk about God. For him, God had abandoned him and his family when their plantation was burnt to the ground, and history was forever changed. If God were truly all-powerful and good, He would have not allowed the destruction of his country. For him, God had nothing to do with whether he and his brother lived or died.

God died in Virginia, and he did not know if God would ever return.

The next day, they continued to make good progress, but dark skies cast a shadow over any optimism they harbored for better times ahead. The windy heavens brought forth a heavy rain, which added considerably to their misery. They made an early campsite beneath a big oak tree, but the tree provided little shelter for the deluge that fell from the sky all night. They all sat through the night shivering in the wagon with their blankets wrapped tightly around themselves. Even though they were high above the standing ground water, they were soaked to the bone. The depths of their wetness doused any hopes they had possessed before the calamitous rainfall.

The pastor and his family prayed for a letup in downpour, but none was forthcoming, and when dawn was near, the pastor proclaimed, "The rainfall is a sign from God. We need to pray in order to decipher His message."

For Henry, all the prayers in the world would not lead to an improvement in their soaked condition. They needed lots of sunlight to dry themselves and their animals. The early morning sun rays provided him with all the hope he needed, but he was afraid the rain would make the creeks ahead impassable.

Jo was worried about salvaging the meat and spread what he could on low-hanging tree limbs to dry out. Randy was even more worried about the delays in their journey the rain would cause by muddying the road paths. They all agreed that no matter what, they should try to move toward their destination.

They waited a couple of hours to dry out a bit and satisfy any calls of nature before getting ready to try to make progress on the muddy road. They wanted to see if the wagon could move even at a slower speed on the muddy tracks. It was slow going, but the wagon wheels turned, and the mules were able to plod through the water-saturated tracks.

There were clear skies and no signs of more rain. However, Henry worried about fording the creeks they would inevitably have to cross. They were able to maneuver across the first small creek they encountered. Its solid rocky bed helped them with their crossing. The second creek they had to cross was wider and deeper. About midway across this creek, a wagon wheel fell into an underwater hole, stopping the wagon from moving forward no matter how much the pastor whipped his mules.

Henry, Randy, and Jo waded into the water and grabbed ahold of the wheel and tried to push it forward while the pastor attempted to get the mules to pull with all their strength. Their repeated efforts to get the wagon moving failed. At the same time, those in the water noticed the creek was rising rapidly, and the depth of the water prevented them from pushing forward on the wheel and lifting high enough the wagon so it would become unstuck.

The water was rising above Henry's waist and was up to the chests of Randy and Jo. Henry yelled to everyone, "Get out of the wagon and go to higher ground far from the south bank of the creek. We'll get what we can from the wagon and carry it with us."

The pastor and his family scrambled to get out of the wagon. The pastor helped his wife and kids keep their heads above water as they struggled to get to the south creek bank. When he reached the bank, he hollered, "Can you unhitch the mules so they can be free to save themselves?"

Henry yelled back, "Too late for that. It's going to take all we can do to save ourselves."

They all swam back to the creek bank, losing much of what they had gathered from the wagon bed in the currents of the fast-rising water. They had just begun to dry out, and now they were thoroughly soaked again. The pastor and Henry both looked upstream and saw a wall of water coming at them. They all picked what they could and ran to higher ground. The pastor turned to Henry and said, "The Lord works in mysterious ways, but I wonder why He has created a flash flood just as we were crossing the creek. We'll have to wait a bit to see if the Lord has seen fit to save our mules."

The mountain of flood water roared by, demolishing everything in its path. Evidently, it had rained even more somewhere upstream, and they were the victims of a flash flood. The pastor bowed his head and struggled to say, "This is beautiful country, but its ruggedness makes it hard to tame. Maybe what happened to us is part of the revenge of the Indians who were wrongfully removed from these lands."

Henry did not know anything about that. For him, they had had the bad luck to be in wrong place at the wrong time, and they were lucky to be still alive. He had never heard of any forceful removal of the Indians and said, "Pastor, with all due respect, I've been to school, and nothing was ever said about forcing the Indians out of these lands."

"Son, I'm sorry to contradict you, but my church campaigned about twenty-five years ago against the decision by the U.S. Government to forcibly move all the Indians in these parts to a reservation somewhere west of the Mississippi River. It was a terrible scene. Thousands were herded like a bunch of animals and marched west. Several thousand died of disease and starvation. Many froze to death. Only twenty years earlier, they had signed a treaty with the government, which gave them rights to their ancestral lands forever. Because of greedy politicians and crooked land grabbers, these Indians were condemned to lasting suffering. The fact that you know nothing about this tragic event is a testament to some kind of cover-up of this nasty chapter in our history."

Henry, Randy, and Jo listened to this mini-sermon and shook their heads in disbelief. They could see that the pastor had much more to say about this subject and others, but they had no time for the kind of long-winded sermons that the pastor was used to giving, and Henry interrupted by saying, "Look. The water in the creek is going down. Let's go search for the mules and the wagon and see what we can salvage."

They all walked timidly to the edge of the water and began following the creek bank downstream, keeping a watch out over the water for any sign of the mules and wagon. They walked a long way but saw nothing. Henry finally turned to the pastor and sympathetically said, "It's of no use. The wagon is gone for good, and the mules are drowned and hidden in the depths of the water. Let's return to the road and decide what to do."

The pastor was too depressed for words. All he did was cry and mumble, "I had those two mules, Dolly and Willy, for years. They were like part of the family. It's tough to accept that they are gone for good."

They slowly walked back to the southward road tracks, and while the pastor gave something of a sermon to his family in an effort to boost their spirits, Henry huddled with Randy and Jo to take stock of their situation and plan their next move.

Randy said, "The first thing I want to do is go into the woods and remove all my clothes and hang them on tree limbs to dry. I can't do anything right in these wet clothes."

Henry replied, "Good idea. We should all do the same. I will tell the pastor to take a break and dry off as much as he and his family can."

While Henry was undressing in a secluded spot in the woods and hanging out his tattered clothing to dry, he was thinking that no matter what, they must keep moving. Their own survival depended on the distance they were able to cover each day. He met with Randy and Jo on the muddy road and told them, "We have to keep going. We'll leave one of our ponies with the pastor and some of the meat we were able to salvage. I'll tell them we'll walk ahead and look for a campsite."

Randy interjected, "Why don't we walk together?"

"They walk too slow for us. No way an old man, woman, and children can keep up with us. We have to move on."

Henry walked up to where the pastor and his family were standing and gently said, "We've decided to walk ahead and look for a campsite. We'll leave behind one of our ponies for you to take turns riding and carry any things you still have."

The pastor expressed sincerely, "We're thankful for all you're doing for us, and we ask God to protect you as you forge ahead. Don't worry about us. We'll follow you at our own pace. We've got God on our side, and we're always on the side of God. I will pray for all of us."

Henry felt bad about leaving the pastor and his family behind, but he saw no choice to do otherwise. "Take good care of my pony. He's not used to such rigors and misses his daily ration of grain, but he should be of help to you. If nothing else, he provides you with a possible source of food. Take good care of yourselves. We have to go now. Goodbye."

Henry, Randy, and Jo disappeared on foot down the trail with their fully loaded pony. They could not bear to look back at the pastor and his family. They could only look forward and struggle with their own fate.

Randy wanted to tell Henry to wait for the pastor, but the words stuck in his mouth. He knew that their survival depended on their arrival at unknown destinations. He missed his mother and the happy life he had before the war. He hated the war and all those who caused it. He realized he could not go back to his old life, but he was not sure of the new life, if any, awaited him. He felt like he was stuck between a rock and hard place, and there was no escape except death.

# Chapter Four
# Manna from Heaven

The sun went down, and the moon rose to cast a shadowy light on the land. The moonlight encouraged Henry to keep walking as far as he could. Randy and Jo were forcing themselves to keep up. Their legs were about to give out. Their persistent nocturnal walking discarded any notion of finding a campsite and waiting for the pastor and his family.

Randy called to Henry to tell him that his pony had stopped and refused to go any farther. The pony was exhausted and in a poor state of health. Henry was surprised the pony had made it this far. He had expected the pony to drop dead long ago. No living creature was made for these kinds of harsh conditions, let alone a pampered plantation pony.

Henry stopped and turned to take a good look of all that was behind him before saying, "Okay. Let's find a spot alongside the road to rest and eat for a few hours, but we must forge ahead to the Indian trail crossing. We should be getting close.

They ate a few strips of dried meat, wrapped themselves in their blanket, and fell fast asleep on the lumpy and wet ground. They were so tired that nothing else mattered. They could have been robbed and killed, but they had to sleep. After a few hours of shuteye, Henry was calling to Randy and Jo to get up so they could continue walking south. Jo responded, "Massa, your pony sleepin' for gud."

Henry rushed to the pony's side and saw immediately that he had died in his sleep. He assumed that without his companion, he was not willing to muster the strength needed to keep moving on. While Randy and Jo looked on, Henry said, "Damn. This was unexpected. I've known this pony all my life, and I did not expect he would leave us like this. I thought at the very least he could serve us as a supply of food."

Henry did not know what to do. Should they wait for daylight and butcher the pony and prepare its meat for eating on the onward journey? Henry figured that process would take the whole day. Losing a day was not an option he was willing to take. So, he told Randy and Jo, "Help me drag the dead pony into the dense roadside woods so nobody who might come along can see him. Sadly, he'll be our sacrifice to the varmints which live in these parts."

They took as much as their gear as they could on their backs, giving priority to their guns, ammunition, and the little dried meat they had left. Henry said, "Let's go. We're not stopping until we come to the Indian trail."

Randy and Jo doubted they had the physical power to go as far as Henry wanted, but they kept their thoughts to themselves. They were beginning to think that without horses, they were already dead. And when their food ran out, they would not be able to do anything but lie down and die.

They walked all day, and night fell. The moon was obscured by an overcast sky, so they had difficulty staying on the road south. Their steps were slower as they struggled to stay focused on the tracks. Then, all of a sudden, Henry cursed. He had bumped hard into something. At first, he thought a tree had fallen across the road and reached down to see if he could remove it. He was surprised that his hand did not touch a tree but the cold iron of a railroad rail.

The moon peeked for an instant through the cloud cover to reveal railroad tracks that stretched as far as the eye could see in east and west directions. Randy and Jo drew close to Henry to hear his words. "Where there is a railroad, there are people. We need to be more vigilant from here on out. We got to try hard to stay away from people, whether they be from the north or the south. They all represent trouble for us and our efforts to get to Texas."

Randy and Jo nodded and looked at Henry to see what they would be told to do next. Henry looked at them, trying to hide any doubts about what they should do next by saying, "Let's hide in the woods by the train tracks to see if any train passes. The kind of train that may go by will tell us a lot about what is going on in these parts."

They hid in a nearby clump of bushes and rested their legs. Dawn broke, and no train had passed. They were beginning to think that the rail line was not being used. Then Jo excitedly popped up, "Massa, listn' up. Train a comin'."

They were all ears as the noise of an approaching train grew. In a flash, the train was barreling fast eastward right in front of them. They could see that it was filled with Union troops and arms. The clattering train quickly passed at a high speed. They could not believe their eyes. Their ears stung by the silence that occurred after the loud noise of the train had subsided. Henry was the first to speak, "My God. Yankees are this far south! I can't believe it. Does that mean the South is losing the war? We've had no news for weeks of what's going on. I thought the South would have won weeks ago."

After hearing Henry's words, Jo said, "Massa, wat side we on?"

Without hesitation, Henry replied, "We are on the side of our survival. We are for any side that improves our chances of making it to Texas."

Randy added his penny's worth, "Whatever it takes to stay alive."

Henry got up and said, "Let's move quickly across the tracks. The Indian trail should not be far."

With fear in their hearts, they walked slowly across the tracks and farther south. They had not gone too far when there appeared to be a wide path going west. Henry raised his right hand, signaling to Randy and Jo to come to a halt. Henry walked a bit down the path and returned back to his companions to say, "This has got to be the old Indian removal path."

Randy could not believe what Henry was saying and asked, "How can you be sure? Maybe if we follow this path, we are goin' on a wild goose chase."

Henry tried to calm down his brother by pointing to small earthen mounds on the side of the path, saying, "You see those mounds. I'm thinking they're Indian graves."

Randy and Jo were left speechless. Henry said, "We have no choice but to go west on this path until we can go no more."

Henry did not say that he could see the path had been recently used by large bands of people and their horses. He could see that branches had been broken on both sides of the path by fast-moving mounted groups. He surmised that the armies of both the South and North were using this passage to wage war. These thoughts prompted him to turn and tell Randy and Jo and say, "At the slightest noise, get quickly off the path and hide in the woods."

They walked a while, and then Jo mumbled, "Massa, I got to rest. My feet are hurting me somthin' terrible."

Henry had forgotten that Jo was barefoot. He had come this far on well-calloused soles, but even his well-worn feet were not used to walking so far. Henry could see now that Jo's feet would be a problem. Even if, by some miracle, they were able to find some shoes for him, he would have difficulty wearing them because his feet were so rough.

Then a tearful Jo hesitantly said, "Massa, I'll need somethin' to cover my feet to go more."

Henry mulled over Jo's words for a few minutes before saying, "I understand, Jo. We got to find something for your feet and ourselves. Our clothes are in tatters, but you can still see that they are the remnants of pretty plantation boy clothes. Our meat supply is low. And we can't get anywhere without horses. We have no choice but to scavenge for some new duds, grub, and horses. But where can we do that?"

After a long silence, Randy opined, "You said it. Where there is a train, there are people. We have to move away from the path and follow the train tracks until we come across a settlement."

Henry reacted quickly to Randy's words. "You're right, brother. Let's cover Jo's feet by tearing off pieces of our blankets and head through the woods to be near the tracks and follow them westward."

They ripped apart their blankets and tore strips from them to cover Jo's painful and swollen feet. They then carefully moved toward the rail line and followed it at a safe distance. Stumbling through the dark at a slow pace, they came upon several old houses next to the rail line. Upon spying the houses, Henry motioned to them to get down to hide. They watched the houses for a long while and saw no lights or any evidence of human activity. Henry whispered that he was going to get closer to check things out.

Henry kept low as he stepped over the rails to approach the houses. He moved in a zigzag pattern, stopping frequently to look in all directions for signs of life. There was nothing to observe. All seemed dead and quiet. The wind was not even blowing. Moonlight filtered through partly cloudy skies. He eventually got close to the front of one of the small houses. He could see the front door wide open. For him, that was a sign that the place was no longer occupied. He returned to join Randy and Jo, telling them of what he had seen. He suggested, "I think we should go in the old house and see what we can find."

Randy and Jo nodded in agreement, and off they went, following Henry as he returned to the old house. This time, Henry told Randy and Jo to hide by the front stoop while he gingerly entered the open front door. It was so dark inside that he could not make out anything, so he quietly exited and softly told Randy and Jon, "It's too dark to see anything. Let's rest here in the shadows until there's some daylight. If you like, we can eat the last of our dried meat. We'll need to keep our strength to deal with this place and the settlement in broad daylight."

They ate some meat and drifted off into a deep sleep. Henry slept with his had gripping one of his .44 pistols. At the first sign of dawn, Henry's eyes sprung open, and he promptly got his bearings before kicking Randy and Jo to wake up. Once he saw they were awake, he said in a low voice, "Be alert and have your guns ready. There's enough light for me to see what is in this house. Keep your eyes peeled."

Henry gently walked through the front door with both of his .44 pistols ready. He tried not to make a sound, but what he saw revolted him, and his innards wanted to come out his mouth. There were two dead, bloated bodies riddled with bullets lying on the floor. The entire house had been ransacked, and everything of value taken. Henry assumed this had been the nasty work of northern troops, but it could have also been done by ruffians who were out to profit as much as they could from the war. Nonetheless, he wanted to search the house and see if he could find anything they could use.

Henry stepped out on the front stoop and asked, "Randy and Jo, come and help me remove two dead bodies. Their unholy stink is the nastiest thing I've ever smelled."

They covered their faces with their shirts and lifted the bodies one by one and dumped them some distance from the house. The male bodies had obviously put up a fight and paid with their lives. They wanted to dig them a shallow grave or cover them with stones, but there was nothing available, and even if there were, they did not have the energy or the time to give them proper burials.

Henry looked around himself and said, "Let's search the houses to see if anything is left that we can use. Let's do it quickly and quietly and get out of here as fast as possible."

They searched each house from top to bottom and found nothing of value. Henry could not bring himself to believe there was nothing left for them, so he began to search the house again. This time, he removed some floorboards and looked for a false room in the house's closet. He knocked on the closet's back wall and heard a hollow sound. He ripped a board off the wall and, saw the glint of a long gun, and fell to the ground. A loud shotgun blast flew over his head.

He was afraid of another shot killing him, and he cried out, "For Christ's sake. I mean no harm. I'm here to help."

There was no more shooting. All was quiet. "Let's talk."

Henry waited for a long while, and there was no response. He then risked saying, "I'm a young southern boy fleeing the war. Please let me help you."

Again, Henry was met with silence. He could hear Randy and Jo entering the house to see what was wrong. Henry lifted his left foot as a signal for them to be quiet and stay away. Whoever was hidden on the other side of the wall he would deal with himself, and he wanted this person to think he was alone.

Henry slowly rolled over to the edge of the closet and stood up. He then heard from the other side of the wall the low moaning of a person in distress. This sound prompted him to tear away another board on the closet back wall. There was not much light, but he was surprised by what little he could see. He could barely make out the image of an ancient woman seated, holding a double-barrel shotgun on her lap. He tore off some more boards, and he could see more clearly now an old woman near death.

He calmed her by showing her she had nothing to fear from him. He lifted gently the shotgun from her lap and checked the chambers to see that she had fired the only shell she had. She had a sheaf of paper sheets and a sharp piece of charcoal and scratched the words 'Take out' and looked straight forward to the sitting room.

Henry could see she was an old age invalid who was deaf and dumb. He called to Randy to come and give him a hand. They gently lifted her wooden kitchen chair and carried her into the room. She smelled bad as she had soiled herself. They could see that she was very weak. She feebly pointed to the paper where she had scribbled the words, 'Take out.'

Henry and Randy interpreted her gesture as wanting to go outside and carefully carried her on her chair to a spot in front of the house. When they placed her in her chair on the ground, she looked up and raised a finger in the direction of the surrounding woods. They interpreted her finger signal as indicating that she wanted them to carry her into the woods. Jo stood at some distance away, trying to block her view of the two dead bodies dumped in front of the house. She did not see anything except the nearby woods.

They kept an eye on the forefinger of her right hand as they wove their way through the woods and all the underbrush. They set down her chair to rest a while and discuss why they were carrying the old lady into the woods. Every time they set down the chair, she would point her finger again in the direction they should take. They followed her, pointing finger the best they could, winding through the woods to avoid becoming tangled up in the brush.

Jo tagged along, thinking this was sheer madness, then heard something that propelled him to catch up with the group, saying, "Massa. I herd somthin'. It like hose hooves."

Henry and Randy thought Jo was hearing things until they turned around a big tree, and there was an open place with two fine horses tethered to long ropes. They could not believe that there were still two horses the fighting armies had not confiscated. They stood still for a moment to admire these two fine equine examples. Then, they looked down at the old woman. Her finger was pointing to a spot in the surrounding woods.

Jo followed Henry and Randy to the spot her finger pointed. They did not see anything. They looked back at the woman, and her pointed finger was moving back and forth. Jo stepped up to look more closely into a clump of underbrush, pulling away some dead limbs, and another miracle occurred. He could see through a hole in the brush part of a big leather trunk. "Massa, I tink we find somthin gud."

Henry and Randy joined Jo in pulling away the brush, and they were pleased to see a large brown leather trunk. The woman and her family had obviously hidden the trunk and horses to keep them from falling into the hands of raiders. They assumed the bodies were of two young men who refused to reveal their secret hiding place. They assumed these young men were her sons and her husband was dead or a soldier in the Confederate army.

They opened the trunk and were teary-eyed with they saw it was full of many of the things they needed. It also contained saddles, saddle blankets, bridle, and reins… all the things they would need to ride these big horses. Jo became excited when he spotted a pair of boots and socks. They were too big for him, but any foot covering was more than welcome. "Massa, I wud be mity thanks for boots for my bad feet."

Henry handed him the boots and socks. "Massa yu a gud man," mumbled Jo.

Henry and Randy spread the contents of the trunk on the ground so they could see what there was. Henry said, "We'll take all we can carry that will be of use. I'm particularly interested in taking all the tinned goods to see what we can eat. The clothes will not fit us, but we should change into them. The same applies to the hats. We got to use as much as we can."

The old woman sat contently in the knowledge that what she and her sons had hidden in the woods would go to some good use. Henry turned to the old woman to gesture his happiness for all the gifts to which she had led them. He could see the smallest smile on the old lady's face, expressing satisfaction that all her things could go to people who desperately needed them. Henry walked over to her to mark on her paper a big thank you. She sat so still, and her eyes were closed.

He touched her hand, and it was cold as an icicle. He could see that she had died, and bringing them to this secret spot was done with her last breath. He could barely make out the words she had last written on her writing paper. These words were simply, 'Leave me.'

Randy said as he rummaged through the trunk items. "Shouldn't we carry her back to her house?"

Henry dourly replied, "Forget her. She's dead. Get the horses saddled up and load all the needful. We got to be going west."

Jo was waiting to see how he would go. He stood there with his old new boots and waited for Henry's orders. Henry and Randy were mounted on the fully loaded horses, and Jo was unsure of what would happen to him. Henry looked at Jo and said, "Well, you can stop standing there and hop on behind me."

# Chapter Five
# Nothing to Live For

They rode through the spooky moonless night as far west as they could. About every hour, they stopped to listen for any noises which would cause them to get off the trail and hide in the adjoining woods. They forded several creeks, but the body of water in front of them now was a big river, and they were trying to figure out how to cross it.

Henry said, "Let's walk the horses along the riverbank upstream until we come to a narrower spot that we all can swim across."

Jo became alarmed and said in a distressed voice, "Massa, I dunno swim."

Henry grinned and replied, "That's all right, Jo. We'll do something for you when we find a spot we think we can cross."

At a bend in the river, they found a narrower section they thought they could cross to the other side. Henry acted brave, although he had never swum across such a wide river before. He was worried about the horses and all the gear they carried. He thought he could make it with Jo holding on to him, but first, they needed to eat a few tins of their beans. This would not only lighten the load on the horses but would give them the added nourishment they needed to swim across the fast-flowing river.

Henry was particularly concerned about their ammunition getting wet. He and Randy unloaded all their guns and, wrapped the bullets in their shirts, and tied them around their necks. They also tied their boots around their necks. They stood shivering at the water's edge in their bare feet and naked torsos. With no time to lose, he told Randy, "You go first with the horses. Once you have reached the other side, I'll come with Jo. I'll be watching the horses and encouraging them to cross to the other side."

Randy knew he had to attempt the crossing, but he hesitated for the longest time. Finally, Henry walked over to him and pushed him into the water, saying, "It's now or never."

Randy battled fiercely the current which was dragging him down river.

His arms flailed as he tried as hard as he could to cross the murky river. He had no time to see how the horses were doing. He was focused on arriving alive on the opposite bank. There were moments he thought he would drown, but his feet started to touch the riverbed. He was relieved to know he would reach the other side. He struggled to walk up the slippery bank. When he reached the top of the bank, he looked around to see that the horses had also made it. He spied Henry, standing in the same spot, pointing to a place downstream. He thought that he was indicating that the horses had made it across, too. He waited for Henry to cross before doing anything about the horses.

Henry called for Jo to come and put his arms around him so they could begin their crossing. When Jo did not show up behind him, he looked around, and there was no sign of Jo. Evidently, Jo had fled rather than hold on to Henry to cross the river. Henry thought his fear of the water had caused him to go his own way. He was surprised by the loneliness he felt by the disappearance of Jo, but he was thankful he no longer had to worry about swimming across the river with Jo hanging on him.

He called softly to Jo a few more times, but he was met only by silence. The sudden departure of Jo disturbed Henry profoundly, but no matter what, he had to get across the river. He walked into the water, and when his feet could no longer feel the river bottom, he did his best to keep his head above water as he swam with all his might toward the opposite bank.

He arrived at the other side of the river and was glad to see his younger brother waiting for him. Randy gave him a hand so he could plant his soggy body onto the flat and dry top of the bank. Randy immediately asked, "Where's Jo?"

Once he caught his breath and brought his shivering under control, Henry emotionally replied, "I don't know. When it came time for us to swim across, he was nowhere to be found. I guess he was too afraid to cross the water and thought he was better off on his own."

After a brief pause, Henry continued, "Let's look for the horses and find somewhere nearby to camp and dry off."

They found their two horses grazing on a few clumps of grass not too far downstream. They found nearby a spot for drying off and resting. They took off all their clothes and hung them on tree branches. They unsaddled the horses and placed the saddles and other gear on the top of bushes. They checked their guns and ammunition, spreading them on a dry spot on the ground. Everything they had was wet. They spent the night huddled together, hoping their fatigue would bring some reprieve from the misery caused by their wetness.

At the first crack of dawn, they were up. Their clothes were only partially dry, but they dressed in them anyway. They checked the horses, and they seemed to be okay, although they were growing skinnier by the day. They ate some more beans and prepared to leave, but they were stopped from traveling farther west by a heavy rain. They huddled again with their blankets under a thick-branched tree. They tethered their horses nearby and gathered up all their meager belongings and put them at their sides.

It rained hard for two days. They thought the deluge would be the end of them. Their horses and everything they possessed were soaked. Henry tried to look on the bright side of the disaster that had befallen them by saying, "Good thing we crossed the river when we did because now it's running over its banks."

On the third day of their watery isolation, the sun peaked out from dissipating storm clouds, giving them the courage they needed to continue their journey west. They moved to a nearby location that was fully bathed in the spring sunshine. They began again, trying to dry as much as they could their horses, themselves, and their stuff.

They were not in good physical condition, and their morale was low. They were not sure they could go on. But the only thing they knew was to keep heading west, as their mother instructed. Going west may take their last breath, but they were determined to go as far west as they could.

While they were sunning themselves and their things, Randy stopped what he was doing to listen. He signaled to Henry to lend an ear to the distant sounds he was hearing. After a short while, Randy came over to Henry and said excitedly, "What is that?"

"I think we're hearing the sound of gunfire. Lots of guns and cannons. Maybe we are closer to the war than we thought. From now on, we have to be mighty careful. I hope Jo is safe. Best we wait here as long as we hear gunfire."

Randy nodded his agreement and asked, "Can we try to make a small fire to help get the chill out of our bones and dry better our stuff?"

"If you can get a fire going, go ahead. Too bad Jo is not here. He was our fire-starting wizard."

47

They stayed put for two days before the distant sounds of gunfire subsided. When the sounds had finished, Henry jumped up and said, "Let's get going. I don't hear anything any more."

They slowly rode through the woods. After going a couple of miles, they came to an opening that revealed a horrific sight. They stopped their horses at the woods' edge. They could not believe their eyes, and the awful new smell irritated their nostrils. There were dead and mutilated bodies of men and horses everywhere as far as they could see. The unbelievable horror of this sight choked them up and caused them to rapidly withdraw to a secluded spot in the woods.

Henry was uncharacteristically perspiring. The terrible sight also deeply affected Randy. If they were not scared before, they were mortified now. After a long silence, Henry softly said, "I can't believe the war has come so far south. I never imagined it would be this bloody. Thousands of dead men of both sides is too much to bear. I thought the South would have the won the war by now. But it is obvious from the bloody carnage we just saw that the war has just begun."

Randy was only fourteen years old, but he sensed they were as good as dead. He said with much sadness in his eyes, "If we're caught by the Northern troops, we'll be treated as Southerners, and if we're caught by Southern troops, we'll be treated like traitors. Either way, we lose."

Henry nodded and whispered, "Let's sneak away from this place as quietly as we can."

They backtracked and were beginning to turn in a southwest direction into wilderness when two gruffy men jumped from the woods in front of them with long guns aimed straight at them. One red-bearded man said angrily in a southern drawl, "Git your hands up. We need wat yu got."

Henry could see they were Southern adherents as they still had Confederate pants and caps. Henry and Randy raised their hands, and Henry said earnestly, "We just po white southern boys tryin' to git mo' south and out of the war."

The other shorter man with a scraggly beard said, "So, maybe yu ar kin and shud come with us. We goin' south to help the Confederacy load cotton bales on boats in the Missip. Yu kno cotton sales to Mexico is wat is I' money for the confederacy. With a little mo money, the federals won't have a chance. Yep, cotton is still king for the south."

Henry said, "I didn't kno dat. Sounds for sure like we shud join yu.

Can we take our hans' down now?"

"Okay. Now that we're all together and stuff, put yur hans down. Where yu boys from? Aren't you a little young to be so far from home?"

Henry replied quickly, "Virginie and we goin'to Memphis so we can head to Texas and be far from the war and the kind of sickening bloody battle scenes we just saw."

"You've come a long ways. Sorry yu had to see the Shiloh slaughter. We saw it, too. Made us sick to our stomachs. Not sur which side won, but the South needs more money to continue fighting against the federals, and dat is why we're headed to New Orlins to help send cotton to Mexico."

Henry thought he should say something, so he said, "I didn't kno the south was sellin'cotton to Mexico. I guess ther're boats goin' that way."

"We hear most of the cotton goes overland by oxen wagon to the Gulf Coast and then is taken by Mr. Ford and company and loaded on his shallow bottom boats on the Rio Grande River and sold to the Mexican side for payment in gold."

"Sounds like quite an operation. We'll be happy to help."

Henry tried to talk like these two low-class, ignorant white men, but his high level of education and refined habits rebelled against him talking like such riffraff.

"Glad to hear yu say that. There's just one thing. We'll ride yur horses, and yu walk behind."

"I guess we have no choice but to do as you ask. No problem. Why don't we eat some beans first? We got some tins of beans in our saddlebacks. All right if I go get them?"

"Go and git them. We ar mity hungry. But no funny business."

Henry left Randy standing quietly about six yards in front the two scruffy armed men and reached into his saddle bags. He rapidly pulled out his two .44's and shot both men and then walked closer to finish them off with two more shots. There was blood in his eyes and venom in his voice when he said, "Nobody takes our horses. We're goin' to Memphis."

Randy was shocked by what Henry had just done in the most cold-hearted manner, but deep down, he understood that it was something that needed to be done, no matter how brutal an act it was. He knew they could not trust anyone, especially in times of a war which pitted brother against brother.

Henry told Randy, "Quick. Look through their pockets to see if there is anything we can use."

Randy did as he was told. All he found was a wad of old Confederate bills. He also saw that their rifles were not loaded. Evidently, they were two deserters down on their luck. He reported back to Henry. "They got nothing except this worthless Confederate currency. Even their rifles were without bullets. Who knows what their true intentions were?"

Henry replied, "Exactly. Save the paper currency as it may be good to help start fires. Let's go now before the sound of my pistols may draw the attention of other no-goods. For better or worse, let's keep going to Memphis. Leave those two as they lie."

They rode westward, following the old trail and stopping from time to time to listen if there were others using the trail to go to Memphis on the western edge of Tennessee or Chattanooga on its far eastern side. They had gone but a few miles when they heard a large group of mounted men riding hard toward the east on the trail. They quickly hid in the woods some distance from the trail, peering out of their hideaway to see who was passing.

They did not have to wait long before they spied hundreds of mounted blue uniformed troops moving toward the east at a gallop. They remained motionless with their hands over their horses' mouths. The last contingent of this fast-moving Union cavalry battalion was made up of black soldiers. Maybe Henry was mistaken, but he thought he saw someone who looked like Jo.

The dust from the passing Union troops had barely subsided when Henry signaled that they had to keep going to Memphis. Henry quietly said, "I don't know which side is in control of Memphis. Whatever side it is, I'm thinking the worst they can do to us is put us in a prisoner of war or refugee camp. We just got to get to Memphis and find a way to cross the Mississippi River so we can keep heading west until we get to Texas. We got to do this or die trying."

They rode their horses westward until almost nightfall, and Henry said, "Let's go into the woods and find a resting spot. We should be rested and alert, as we could arrive in Memphis tomorrow. I don't know what to expect, but let's try to play our cards right."

After saying these words, Henry handed Randy a tin of beans and said in French with a grin on his face, "Bon appetit."

Randy took the tin and said pleasantly, "Merci."

They both knew that their pampered elitist upbringing and the fancy education they had received would do them no good on the road ahead. Randy accepted to follow Henry's aberrant behavior and became another person. He knew his survival required abandoning all civilized notions and becoming tough as nails in mind and body. He did not like how he would have to change to stay alive, but it was better than death, even though there was nothing to live for.

Henry sat with his back leaning on a tree, checking and reloading his two big .44 pistols. He withdrew from his pocket the knife from the old lady's trunk and started carving notches on the walnut handles of his .44's. One notch for each person he had killed so far. He said to Randy, who was sitting next to him, "If I'm to be a killer, I need to act like one. You know, you need to be a little crazy to survive in this new, chaotic world."

# Chapter Six
# Mississippi Crossing

They rode their emaciated horses until they could go no more. They led their horses gently down the worn road to Memphis. They marshaled all the strength they had left in their tired bodies to put one foot in front of another. They were in a daze and at the point of collapsing when Henry looked around and saw fellow travelers worse off than they were. The countryside was being drained of people seeking refuge from the war in Memphis.

Henry and Randy were too debilitated to talk, but they realized they had become part of a chaotic crowd headed toward Memphis. Some of the people in the crowd were Unionists hoping to be cared for by Union troops when they took over Memphis. A larger number of people were Southern sympathizers, hoping the Confederacy would hold off the inevitable attack by Union troops on Memphis. Most people wanted to cross the Mississippi River and keep going west until they were out of the war and the terrible bitterness and suffering it was causing.

The dirt roadway was overflowing with people on foot, horses, and wagons. They were all headed for the security they perceived Memphis offered. They came from all walks of life, but the majority were poor white farmers. Old women and children were sobbing, and strong men had tears in their eyes. They all felt trapped and had no idea of what their onward lives would be like. Many felt like lying down and dying. They had no hope for a better future. Henry and Randy were caught up in this reckless mayhem. They were also afraid their end was nigh. Randy wished more than ever that he could go back to the home he had and the embrace of his loving mother.

They arrived at the outskirts of Memphis and were stopped at a checkpoint manned by Confederate soldiers. A burly sergeant stepped in front of them and barked an inquiry. "Are you deserters?"

Henry quickly said, "No, sir, we po' farmers running from the Yankees."

The sergeant looked at them up and down and snarled. "Okay. You look too weak to fight. But we'll take your skinny horses. Take all out of your saddle bags. Keep your guns and ammunition. Maybe you'll find good use for them when the Yankees attack Memphis."

Henry was too weak to resist. He knew he could not win by disagreeing with the sergeant. He and Randy did as the sergeant wanted and bundled up their few belongings in their blankets. Henry asked the sergeant, "We need food. Any help you can give us?"

"Everybody needs foods. There are thousands of hungry strangers in Memphis now. I have no idea of what is going to happen to them. I'm almost more afraid of this large crowd of desperate people than I'm of the invading army."

Henry and Randy trudged on through the crowded streets of Memphis. On the lips of many was the constant refrain. "The Yankees are coming."

The calamity of the crowded streets of Memphis defied description. People did not know if they were safer staying at home or fleeing across the river. A crazed atmosphere reigned throughout the city. Henry thought the throngs of people had been pushed over the edge, and they had lost their minds. He could not see one stable and sane person to ask anything. He and Randy moved slowly in what they thought was the direction of the riverboat port. All they wanted was to get to the west side of the river.

They could not think straight. Their stomachs were stuck to their backbones. The depths of their hunger got the best of them. The had finished days ago their last tin of beans. They needed food now. Their steps slowed down. They could no longer go on without some food. They staggered to the side of the street and sat down. Suddenly, there was a scuffle in front of them. Famished people had resorted to an act of desperation and attacked a passing wagon carrying bags of grain.

The armed guards protecting the wagon fired their guns into the air, but this did not stop the ravenous crowd from pillaging the wagon. Then they fired into the crowd, wounding and killing a few people. The crowd partially backed off, but the hunger of a good number of people caused them to scramble madly to steal the contents of the grain bags. There was no way the two-armed guards could hold off such a hungry and unruly mob. They jumped off the wagon and fled for their lives.

The frantic crowd overwhelmed the wagon, carrying off the bags of grain in all directions. This chaotic scene resulted in the splitting of bags and the spilling of their contents onto the paving stones. Henry and Randy were among those crawling on their hands and knees to scoop up as much of the spilt grain as possible. When they had stuffed in their bundles as much grain as they could safely carry, they backed off to a nearby alleyway to begin devouring handfuls of grain. They slowly chewed the grain and washed the pasty substance in their mouths down with water from their trusty pouch.

They were enjoying the taste of this food even though they never had eaten before raw wheat grain. They sat still for a while, feeling the nourishment flow through their veins and slowly give new life to their increasingly fragile bodies. Henry said, "Now that we have re-gained some life, let's continue working our way toward the river and see what's required to cross it."

Henry paused a moment to scrutinize his brother. He spotted drops of perspiration on Randy's forehead. Henry took his brother's hand and softly said, "Don't get sick on me. You can't get sick with the fever. I've heard people here say that some yellow fever cases have been reported."

A troubled and weak Randy made the effort to utter quietly, "Yes, I'm sick, but I don't think it's serious. I think that after the wheat grain takes hold, my body will be better, and I'll stop running this fever."

They joined the stream of pedestrians of all types on the crowded street. It was slow going as they were constantly jostled. The crowd thickened as they approached the riverport. They thought they were within a hundred yards of the river, but the crowd had become so tight they could not move forward. They stood their ground and inched forward when the crowd moved. They assumed the crowd moved forward when some of them in the front were loaded onto boats for the crossing.

It took hours before they arrived in the front ranks, and the day was almost gone. They were hungry again, but they did not dare expose their grain to others. After all, they did not want to cause a panic when they were so near the front. Night fell, but the crowd kept moving forward. There were so many people that the boats were operating around the clock.

They finally arrived near the front row and could hear one of the men managing the boats say, "That'll be two Yankee dollars apiece."

Henry and Randy gulped. They did not have any money except for the wad of worthless Confederate bills. Their turn came, and Henry shamefully said, "We don't have any money."

The dowdy man in charge replied, "No money, no passage. Sorry."

Henry and Randy did not know what to do. They could not go backward as the huge crowd behind them was pressing forward. So, they had no choice but to stand there and wait. To their surprise, the man said to them, "I see you have guns. Do you know how to use them? I suppose you have ammunition for them."

Henry was afraid that he wanted to confiscate their guns, but he replied in a civil tone, "Yes, sir. We can shoot if need be."

The man looked at them intensely, trying to size up their character. He then said, "Well, maybe we can hire you to be nighttime guards so our regular armed guards can have the night off. What do you say? We can't pay you anything, but you'll get free passage. What do you say?"

Henry wasted no time in replying, "You got yourself two armed guards."

"Step this way. I'll let the next boat to the Arkansas side of the river know you are the guards."

"Thanks," said a sincere and relieved Henry.

Henry and Randy walked to the dock and spotted a riverboat jammed with people. A man on the boat yelled, "Are you the new guards?"

Henry responded, "At your service."

"One of you get in the front, and the other get in the back. Stay standing with your guns ready and fire away if there is any ruckus."

Henry and Randy did as they had been told and boarded the boat, stepping gently through the motley group of passengers. On shaky legs, they positioned themselves and tried to look grown-up and menacing. Neither of them had ever been on a boat. The moon was almost full, so they could see from one end to another of the medium size flatbottom boat. Henry estimated there were over hundred people sitting on the boat bottom, but it was hard to see small children. The wide river spread before them in the moonlight, but they had no idea of how much time it would take to cross such a big river. They bit their lips and hoped for the best.

The man operating the boat said in a loud voice, "Prepare yourselves. Hold tight. We're shoving off."

The man on the dock untied the boat, and they drifted in the water for a while. Two men sitting on the sides of the converted rectangular commercial flatboat began pushing it with long poles toward the other side. When the water became too deep, they began paddling with long oars.

Black slaves normally did this work, but these were far from normal times, and most of the slaves have fled toward the Union side. There was a widespread rumor that Henry and Randy were hearing that President Lincoln was planning to proclaim all the slaves free. There were so many rumors going around that you did not know what to believe.

Henry and Randy did not talk to anyone, and even if they did, they were not sure as to where they stood on the slavery issue. They did wonder who would do all the work if there were not slaves. They just wanted to survive and be free of the war for good. The war had torn their lives to shreds, and they wanted no more of it. It was everybody for themselves, and God bless those who could save themselves. This was no time to allow any sentiment to outweigh doing what you had to do to survive.

The shadowy man operating the boat reminded everyone. "Sit still. Don't panic. The crossing will take an hour or so."

They were about halfway across when a male passenger suddenly stood up and proclaimed loudly, "I can't wait any longer. I have to relieve myself."

Henry and Randy raised their guns and pointed them in the direction of the man. They kept an eye on the steersman for any sign that they should shoot the man.

The delirious man stepped to the side and, dropped his pants, and sat on the side railing with his buttocks protruding over the water. His movements caused the boat to rock wildly, and many of the other passengers screamed for him to stop moving. After relieving himself, he stood up, and when he used both hands to pull up his pants, he lost his footing and fell overboard into the water, making only a small splash.

There was no effort to save the man. The two men handling the big oars just kept rowing, concentrating on not being caught by the river's strong currents and being carried farther downstream. The steersman spit tobacco into the water as he held a steady course with a heavy hand on the rudder and said in an unperturbed matter, "I guess he got relieved of more than he bargained for. He done relieved himself of life."

The boat crowd quieted, and the oarsmen kept rowing without any let up in their rhythm. The western bank of the river was now visible. Henry estimated the width of the river at this point was about three thousand feet. The dock on the Arkansas side was now in view. The oarsmen stopped rowing and began using the long poles in the shallower water to maneuver the boat alongside the wooden dock.

They docked quietly in the moonlit night. Randy tried to count the passengers as they deboarded. Just as he had thought there were about a hundred people. At two dollars a head, the total came to 200 dollars. He told himself that for profit of one crossing, several cheap flatboats could be built. For him, this was outrageous price gauging and just one example at how some people were profiting from the war. He was disgusted by this conclusion, but he admitted that he would not hesitate in doing the same if it meant making money.

They deboarded along with the steersman and the oarsman. Another man on the dock saw them and said, "You the temporary security guards?"

Henry replied, "Yes, me and my brother."

"Well, I can make that permanent if you like."

"No, that's not possible. We going to Texas."

"You don't say. Everybody is going to Texas. I guess it is a big enough place for everyone. Well, get out of here and join the hundreds of others goin' to Texas."

After hearing the man say these words, Henry turned to Randy and said, "Let's go find a place to make camp and get some rest. I need to rest my head before we decide our next move."

# Chapter Seven
# Conscripted

They staggered to a dry spot beneath the nearest tree and collapsed into a deep sleep. At dawn, Henry awakened slowly and had to think for a moment about where they were. He looked around and could see many small groupings of people camped, trying to recover from getting out of calamitous Memphis and their tense crossing of the Mississippi River. Everyone who had crossed the river knew they had to find the strength to keep heading west along the military road.

Henry stood up and cleared his head before waking Randy. "Let's go and see how we can keep going west. Much depends on finding a source of food. Let's dig around this old pecan tree to see if we can find buried any nuts from last year."

They found a few nuts to shell and munch. But they were bitter and far from sufficient to satisfy their insatiable hunger. Randy said, "This is not going to cut it. Let's go back to the riverbank and wash off our faces and rinse out our mouths. We can also fill our water pouch."

Henry nodded his agreement, and they organized their bundles. Henry carefully wrapped in his blanket his two old .44 pistols. They kept their loaded long rifles at their sides. They found a secluded spot at the river's edge to wash up and relieve themselves. They were not alone. Scattered along the river were other people doing their morning toilet.

They had to find something to eat before they could think about how they would cross Arkansas. Hunger gnawed ferociously at their stomachs. The hunger pangs were so deep they could not think straight. Henry cut a couple of twigs from a maple tree and peeled the bark with his pocketknife. He gave one to Randy and said, "Sucking on this might relieve a bit your hunger. Also, you can use it to clean the scum off your teeth, keeping them from rotting."

Henry and Randy were twig scrubbing their teeth when a man dressed in a partial Confederate uniform rode up to them and sputtered. "You boys, deserters?"

"No, suh. We just po' farm boys who lost their family and farm in the war, and we be fleeing for our lives."

"Well, you don't look like much. You're so young, but we need anyone who can fire a rifle. I'm sure you'll do just fine once you're fed up and mounted. Follow me. We'll get you ready to join our militia."

Henry and Randy had little choice, so they followed behind the man on the horse. They were hoping there was food in the deal he was obliging them to accept. They came alongside a wagon train, and the man stopped his horse and dismounted, saying, "This is our quartermaster. He'll outfit you for the long ride to Ft. Smith."

Henry and Randy were happy to hear the reference to Ft. Smith because they knew that was in the direction they were headed. The short, crusty old quartermaster looked at the new recruits and shook his head, saying, "I guess this is the best that can be done given the circumstances, but we can't win a war with skin-and-bone boys."

With their heads hanging low, they remained silent, but they hoped they would be given some sort of food. The quartermaster said, "First, you need some good repeating rifles and lots of ammunition. Here's two new Henry rifles and four boxes of bullets. With these repeating rifles, you can outshoot anyone. That should do you for now. I'll take your old rifles."

Henry and Randy were reluctant to give up their old rifles for ones they did not know. They did as he asked, but getting some food overrode all else in their lives. They were almost ready to faint when the quartermaster passed them a couple of slouch hats, frock coats, and high-top shoes. After giving them these items, the quartermaster said, "That's all I got for you boys. You'll have to do like most militia men and get along with the baggy old clothes you got. Go to the next supply wagon to see if there is anything for you."

After a quick "Thank you, suh," they rushed to see what they could get from the next wagon. They were greeted with a laugh and a stream of words. "I can see the Confederacy is really scraping the bottom to find new recruits. Here, take a bag of cornmeal and some hardtack. Not much. but eating these army victuals should keep hunger at bay."

Henry and Randy greedily took the food items and were ready to run off and begin gorging themselves, but the man on the wagon said, "Wait. I got more for you. Here's a small bag of rice, a pinch of salt, and a few tins of beans. This should hold you for a few days. Now go get some hot food and coffee from the chuck wagon in front of me."

The smell of hot food penetrated their bodies and locked them in an involuntary trance. "Welcome boys to a cooked meal," said the jolly rotund man as he dished out to them some hot grits on tin plates, saying, "Here's what you git. If there is more, come back and get it. When this morning's ration is finished, that is all she wrote until tomorrow? I'll have a little coffee for you later."

Henry and Randy could not wait to find a spot to begin eating. They had trouble moving with all they had been given. They awkwardly plopped down at the first dry, shady spot they came across and began devouring like the starving young men they were the readily edible food items. In his haste to eat the hardtack biscuits, Henry thought he had broken a tooth on these metallic biscuits.

They had never drunk coffee, but Henry thought it was time to try the stimulating hot beverage when the cook man hollered, "Coffee ready."

Henry told Randy, "Stay here and watch our stuff while I get us some coffee."

Henry grabbed his new rifle and walked at a brisk pace back to the chuck wagon. There were a number of men jostling to get to the front of the line to get a cup of coffee. Henry could hear the chuckwagon master say, "Give me your plates, and I'll give you some coffee."

Henry had forgotten their plates and went back to Randy to fetch them. Then he rejoined the line and moved forward to get his hot coffee. He could hear the men before him ask the chuckwagon master. "Where did you get coffee? I haven't had coffee in the longest time."

The wagon master answered. "Well, I'll tell you a little secret. When things were quiet, our scouts traded with Union troops some tobacco for coffee. The Union got coffee, but it ain't got tobacco. Seems like a fair trade for two sides at war."

Henry got close and handed in his two tin plates and was poured from a metal kettle a full tin cup of boiling hot black coffee. The coffee was so hot that he could not hold the cup and had to keep changing hands as he tried to not spill any as he walked back to Randy. He set the cup on the ground and said to Randy. "Voila. Our first cup of Union coffee. We'd better wait for a while so it can cool off."

Randy was curious and asked Henry why he called it Union coffee.

Henry explained to him what he had overheard at the chuckwagon. Randy commented, "Odd that southern troops would have such contact with Northerners. I hope that both sides got to enjoy their trade before they killed each other."

The coffee cooled, and Henry and Randy took turns sipping from the cup. They found the coffee extremely bitter, but they continued taking sips until it was finished. They both found that after drinking the coffee, their energy levels were higher. Henry said, "I can see coffee is like a medicinal tonic."

Henry got up to return their cup to the chuck wagon. As he handed the empty cup to the chubby man tending the chuckwagon, the man said, "Wait a minute. I got somethin' else fer you." He gave Henry a handful of green coffee beans, saying, "Take these beans, and when you need to be more alert, roast them over the fire, cool them, then crush them with the butt of your rifle on a flat rock. Mix the grindings with hot water, and you got a cup of coffee."

Henry was puzzled but managed to say as he stuffed the beans in his pants pocket. "Thanks, suh. But how do you know how to make coffee from such green beans?"

"Well, son, that's how the northern troops who traded us the beans told us how to do it."

Henry was surprised that this kind of trading could occur between warring sides. On his way back to where Randy and their stuff was, the man that recruited them rode up to him and said, "Come. Get your horses so we can go. We need to go as soon as possible to reinforce our troops at Ft. Smith. It could take us about ten days or more to get there, depending on the weather."

Henry could not believe his ears. They get horses besides the food and clothes they already got. He could not believe their good luck. The man on the horse saw on Henry's face an expression of happiness and bluntly said, "Look, we've a hard road ahead, and no amount of equipment and food we are able to give you can compensate you for your deaths in fighting for the southern cause."

The sergeant's sobering words brought Henry down to earth, and he promptly answered, "Yes, suh. Let me go get my brother and stuff, and we'll follow you to get our horses."

Henry and Randy carried all their stuff the best they could and walked behind the sergeant's horse. Before long, they came to a makeshift corral containing about a dozen brown horses. The sergeant said in a matter-of-fact manner, "We got some horses from Texas. These horses are freshly broken, but they're used to having a daily grain ration. We don't have any grain for them. We'll see how long they last without grain. This war will be won by whichever side has the most horses, and there are a lot of horses in Texas. Pick the horses you want."

Henry was curious about how they could get horses from Texas and asked the sergeant, "How did you get these horses from Texas?"

The sergeant responded, "I'm not quite sure, but I know our boys in Texas paid for them and the rifles with money made by the Confederacy smuggling cotton from the South to Mexico. Before, we were getting horses by impressing them from farmers all across the South, but there were many complaints, and farmers could not produce the food we needed to eat."

Henry was mulling over in his head the sergeant's words when the sergeant shouted. "Go on. Pick your horses. We got to be goin."

Spurred on by these no-nonsense words, they did not lose any time in choosing their horses. The sergeant called to some other men to bring out the two horses they had pointed at, saddling and outfitting them for assignment. Henry and Randy could not wait to load their stuff on their horses and start riding them. It had been a long time since they had ridden fresh horses, and they had seldom ridden horses so big. No matter. They thought it appropriate to ride Texas horses as they were still intent on going to Texas.

Once they were mounted, they had their horses trot a bit. The sergeant said, "I want you to find a place to do some target practice with your new Henry rifles while we finish outfitting a few more men. Let's go over to the edge of the woods and look for a good place to shoot your rifles."

They found a spot, and the sergeant dismounted and tied the reins of his sorrel horse to a bush. He gathered up some pinecones and set them on a log. He paced off thirty steps and told the boys to tie up their horses and come with their loaded Henry's. Henry and Randy followed as quickly as they could the sergeant's orders.

When they were alongside the sergeant, he commanded, "Kneel. Prepare to fire. Fire straight at the cones now."

Henry and Randy had never fired a repeating rifle before. They aimed at the cones and pulled the triggers of their rifles. Their bullets exploded out at lightning speed, and they both hit the cones at which they were aiming. There were still several cones remaining on the log, and the sergeant ordered, "Fire at will until all the cones are gone."

"Good shootin. I can see that both of you are good shots. With the Henry rifle, you can shoot faster than a dozen men can with a single-shot muzzle rifle. This gives us a real advantage unless the other side also has repeating rifles. We'll see how you do when the targets are real people at some distance away. Keep you rifles fully loaded with the twenty bullets they take. Be ready to use them at any time."

Both Henry and Randy said in unison, "Yes, suh."

The sergeant instructed, "Go and wait in the shade under that big black oak tree until I return with our wagons and the rest of our militia."

They waited under the big oak tree much longer than expected. It took a couple of hours before the rest of the militia, and three wagons showed up. The sergeant turned to address the men by saying, "It is a long way to Ft. Smith. Because of the wagons, we'll have to stick to the road, and we can't go faster than the wagons. The kind of progress we make will depend much upon the weather and how many water streams we have to cross. The good Lord willing … we'll reach Ft. Smith in a couple of weeks."

Henry could tell by the way the sergeant spoke that he was an unwilling participant in the war and an educated man. Yet, as a Southern patriot, he was obliged to fight for the preservation of his homeland. Henry felt like letting him know that he and Randy could read and write and were from one of the oldest of the elitist families in Virginia, but on the other hand, he thought it best to keep their background a secret.

Henry looked around, and he saw a ragtag group… not the disciplined fighting force he expected. They were strong now, but how would they be after going a couple of hundred miles? He was especially worried about the horses. They were fine now, but how would they be after a couple of weeks without a grain ration? Surely, they would have to stop at places with good grazing so the horses could rest. For him, keeping the horses healthy and well-fed was key. This was a must in spite of the delays it would entail.

The sergeant rode up to the front of the group of about fifty militiamen and the three wagons, saying in a loud, confident voice. "Fall in. Let's go. The sooner we can get to Ft. Smith, the sooner we can teach those Yankee bastards a lesson."

They were on their way and felt all-powerful, but deep in their hearts, they were scared, worrying they would never see their homes and loved ones again. They were happy about leaving but sad about all they were leaving behind. Perhaps Henry and Randy were the only ones looking forward to going to Ft. Smith. Their main concern was how they would detach themselves from their military mission and sneak away to Texas.

They had gone only a couple of miles up the dirt track when one of the militiamen dismounted because his horse was limping. The sergeant shouted, "Halt." And everyone stopped.

The sergeant approached the limping horse and its rider and demanded, "What's the problem? We need to go."

The man checked his horse's hooves and found that he was missing an iron horseshoe on his left back hoof. The rider looked up at the sergeant and said, "Why this hoss lost a shoe somewhere?"

The sergeant reacted in a loud voice so all could hear his words. "A horse without an iron shoe is no good to us. We got no shoes, so you'll need to walk the horse back to the base camp and see if you can find a shoe and somebody to nail it on. If you get this problem fixed, try to catch up with us."

The poor farm boy left the group, leading his limping horse. Both of them were not happy about going back to where they started, but they did not have a choice.

The sergeant rode to the front of the group and ordered, "Let's go. We've already lost too much time."

Observing this incident, Henry began to wonder how many of them and their horses would actually arrive in Ft. Smith. He made a mental note to check the shoes on their horses at the first opportunity. He could see if the South did not have enough iron for horseshoes, it could not win the war.

Meanwhile, the sergeant was worried that such an incident was a bad sign. He was ready to accept the hand that had been dealt to him, but he did not expect such a poor hand on his very first day. He was worried about the slow pace the wagons obligated his troops to move forward. Maybe it was folly to reduce the number of horses pulling each wagon from six to four, but they did not have enough horses to go around. And now they had already lost one good horse because of a missing horseshoe. He knew deep in his heart that the force he would arrive within Ft. Smith would make little difference in the overall war effort.

# Chapter Eight
# Little Rock Road

They started late in the morning on a sunny day. The sergeant rode up and down the short line of his militia cortege, saying, "Let's make hay while the sun shines and go as far as we can go before nightfall."

The sergeant tried to put on a happy face, but he could not hide his apprehension for what was in store for him and his raggedy band. He wanted to be a leader of men and not shirk from duty, but he was not sure that what he was fighting for was worth sacrificing his life and the lives of his men. He told himself that he must put such thoughts aside and concentrate on moving ahead on the bumpy dirt trail. He held out the hope that their situation would improve before they reached their destination.

The slow speed of the squeaky wagons held them back. The mounted men trotted their horses at a leisurely pace. Henry and Randy brought up the rear, riding side by side. Their nerves were on edge because of the slowness of their forward movement, but they were glad about going in the right direction in good conditions. They were thinking that maybe the slow pace was good for the horses because they would be less tired and not need to graze much. But they and their horses would have to drink, so they were thinking they had to camp each night near a stream.

There was no stopping until almost dusk. The sergeant indicated where they would camp for the night. He gave orders for laying out the camp and where the campfire should be. He had men tend to the horses and gather firewood. Many of the men needed no orders as they were used to making a military camp. The cook wagon was a central feature of their camp, and the tune sang softly by its master floated throughout the camp as he busied himself with cooking up some more grits.

The horses drank their fill of water in the nearby stream and were tethered in the grassy patch adjoining the camping spot so they could graze throughout the night. The men sat around the blazing fire, eating their grits and drinking their bitter coffee, when the sarge appeared in their midst and

65

gave a little talk. "Men, this is the first night of many nights we'll be on the trail. We'll follow this road until we hit the landing on the Arkansas River across from the Little Rock settlement on the south bank of the river, then we'll take the road to Ft. Smith. We need now to set up night watch sentinels and rotate them every two hours. Who wants to be first? Any volunteers?"

All the men raised their hands. This made it easy for the sarge to begin the nightly rotation by ordering four men to take up watch positions on each side of their camp. Henry and Randy were among this first group. They had no qualms about being the first to keep an eye out, but they did not have a good idea of what they were watching for.

Henry asked the sarge for permission to speak and said, "Suh, for what should we be on the alert?

The sarge was quick to reply, "Anything that moves. There are all kinds of bad people preying on those who travel this road. There are thieves of all sorts: deserters, bushwhackers, and renegade Indians. These are desperate times, and even good people are obliged to be bad, especially if they need food."

The sarge's words served to raise the fears of his men. The night had fallen, and the sarge said, "Be quick about you and take up your positions. When you think you have done your two hours, come back to camp and wake up someone who has not served yet. Let me know if you see anything suspicious. All men should sleep with their guns and be ready for action."

Henry and Randy went to their positions. For them, two hours were nothing. Their eyes were peeled, but they saw nothing in the dim moonlight. The thick woods limited what they could see. Their ears were keen to listen for any sound. They only heard the sounds of nightbirds and the distant wooing of an owl. Their two hours were about up when Henry started hearing a different sound. For a moment, he thought he heard the sound of a baby's muffled crying. Maybe his ears were trying to hear anything so hard that they were playing tricks on him.

Randy joined Henry and said, "We've done our two hours. Let's go and get somebody else to replace us."

Henry turned to go back to camp with Randy, and then he heard more distinctly this time, the crying of a baby. He stopped in his tracks and said quietly to his brother, "Did you hear that?"

Randy nodded in the affirmative, and they both turned around and started to move slowly through the underbrush to the spot the sobbing sound was coming from. They carefully parted the bushes, and there was a frightened, bedraggled woman with her newborn baby. This surprising sight left them speechless. They had expected many things, but they had never expected to see a mother with her baby.

Henry and Randy did not know what to do. Their first impulse was to turn and run, keeping what they saw to themselves. But Henry had second thoughts. He could not just leave them to die. As much he was ready to kill anyone who crossed him, he could not bring himself to abandon them in the woods. He bent down and said soothingly to the prostrate woman. "Ma'am, please do not be afraid of us. Can you walk with us back to our camp?"

The woman nodded and asked, "Please help me stand so I can follow you with my baby?"

Randy took the lead, and Henry followed as they slowly walked back to camp. They walked straight to where the sarge was sleeping. The sarge woke up, and Henry said, "Look what we found."

The sarge rubbed his sleepy eyes and quickly ran his eyes across the woman and her baby. He then jumped to his feet in a panic and yelled to the burly man in the cook wagon to sound the alarm. The cook began loudly clanking his irony triangle, alerting the men to grab their rifles and take up defensive positions.

The sarge was upset when he told Henry and Randy, "You, fools. Search the woman and be ready to deal with her companions."

Henry and Randy were confused by the sarge's reaction. They did not understand what they had done. Nonetheless, they promptly obeyed the sarge's orders. They ran their hands over the woman's calico dress and felt something hard. While Randy kept hold of the woman, Henry lifted up her outer skirt to find a double-barrel shotgun strapped tightly to her waist. All Henry could say was, "I'll be darned."

He unstrapped the loaded shotgun and handed it to the sarge, who ordered them in no uncertain terms, "Tie her to one of the wagons while we sort this situation out. Be prepared for incoming fire."

No sooner had they tied the woman to the wagon when bullets started splashing around them. They crawled under the wagon and aimed in the direction of the incoming fire. They waited until they might see a spark made by a rifle being fired, and then they fired with deadly accuracy.

After they fired, the camp was all quiet. In the middle of the night, they walked slowly with the sarge with their rifles at the ready to the spot where the incoming fire was coming from. Once there, they found two bloody bodies. The sarge took a quick look and said dolefully, "Drag them back to camp. I want the men to see why you can never let down your guard no matter how rightful it may seem."

While the sarge's head was turned, Randy quickly went through the dead men's pockets and found a wad of money that he just as quickly stuffed in his own pocket. Each of them picked up the limp legs of the dead men and followed the sarge back to camp. The sarge stopped near the campfire and ordered the men to assemble around the bodies. First, he said, "Put some more wood on the fire because I want you to see clearly what we are up against."

With the added wood, the fire blazed brightly. All could see the grisly scene of two dead men in bullet-riddled civilian clothes. The sarge cleared his voice and said loudly so all could hear. "You see here what we are up against. These two dead men are evidence that you can't trust anyone. We're at war, and the enemy can be anyone. There is no room for sympathy or pity. Cruel, yes. But that's how war is."

The men stood silently. Many averted their eyes from the dead bodies on the ground, but they knew the sarge was right. They had no friends, and their success could be measured by staying alive in a quagmire of dangers. If they wanted to increase their chances of coming out of the war alive, they had to cast aside all notions of compassion. They knew it would not be easy, but they had to harden themselves against all human feelings for the lives of their fellow man.

The sarge was not finished talking. "I want to admonish these two young men standing beside me. First, they made a huge mistake by falling for the trick of a crying baby and bringing the culprit into our camp. I understand how easy it is to succumb to human emotions. Secondly, I want to commend them for their excellent shooting in returning the fire of the scoundrels. Now, go get the woman and her baby to see if she is willing to identify these men."

Henry and Randy went to the wagon at a double-time pace and, untied the woman, and walked her back to their campfire. They were still in a state of befuddlement when the sarge said directly to the woman. "Do you recognize these two dead men?"

The woman was slow to respond but finally said in a remorseful voice. "That there is my husband, and that's his brother."

The sarge then asked her, "Are there any more where they come from?'

The woman replied, "No." But nobody believed her.

The sarge told Henry and Randy, "Tie her up. We'll decide later what to do with her. Now, I need some volunteers to bury these two dead men."

Several men reluctantly volunteered for this somber duty. The sarge returned to talk with Henry and Randy, saying to them, "I hope you've learned some lessons. Now we got a real problem on our hands. What are we to do with the woman and her baby? Any suggestions?"

Henry thought the best was to leave her where they found her. Randy disputed this with his brother because he thought it would be a certain death sentence for the woman and her baby to leave them behind. After further discussion with Randy, Henry suggested to the sarge, "Tie her inside the wagon and dump her with other people on the road or at the Little Rock landing."

A pensive sarge replied, "Okay. Take her to the stores wagon and tie her up inside. Position your horses so that you can guard the wagon and be on the lookout for any other of her accomplices. She says there are no others in her group, but I don't believe her."

The sarge was not finished in expressing his thoughts. "Keeping her does come with some problems for us. We'll have to feed her and stop every time she needs to go. The extra weight will slow us down. It would be a lot easier to just drop her and her baby somewhere along the road. We got over a week before we reach Little Rock."

Henry and Randy could easily see the drawbacks to keeping prisoners. Henry respectfully responded to the sarge's litany of woes by saying, "Let's keep her for now and see how it goes. We always have the option of dumping her anytime we want."

With the woman securely tied inside the wagon, the sun was beginning to peek over the eastern horizon, and the sarge gave the order to prepare to move out in twenty minutes. The men hustled to get their horses saddled and lined up in the road. As soon as the wagon horses were hitched, the sarge signaled to move out while yelling. "Forward."

Henry and Randy rode closely behind the wagon with the woman prisoner and kept a watchful eye out for any of her collaborators or any other unwanted intruders. They moved slowly through the hilly wilderness surrounding the Memphis to Little Rock Road that had been well traveled by military contingents and white settlers heading west. The road followed an old Indian trail and was one of the trails used to move Indians from their ancestral homes in the east to the Indian Territory just west of Ft. Smith and the Arkansas line.

The woman said she was hungry and to breastfeed her baby, she needed to eat something regularly. Henry rode up to the chuck wagon and explained to the cook the situation. The cook rummaged through his stocks and came up with some hardtack biscuits and some dried fruit. He also added small khaki paper packets of salt and sugar. He threw in a tin of beans. He hesitantly said, "Sorry, this is all I can spare for now. We're not set up to feed a nursing mother."

Henry put all the food items together and tied them up into a bundle with a ragged piece of old cloth. He mounted his horse and trotted back to his wagon and, flung open the canvas cover hanging on the back of wagon, and dumped the items on the floorboard in front of the seated woman. "This all we got."

The woman replied in a weak but resolute voice, "What about water."

Henry said, "Take our water pouch. We'll get another one."

It was tough for Henry and Randy to stay focused with the almost constant cries of the baby. Randy was tempted to look into the wagon to see if the baby was okay. But thoughts of how the woman had almost resulted in his death made such a kind gesture on his part seem foolhardy. Also, the words of his sarge were reverberating in his youthful mind. He had done a lot of growing up since they left Virginia over a month ago. He and Henry were not the same persons they were in Virginia. A world at war had obliged them to change fundamentally their nature.

Each time the woman had to relieve her herself and clean the baby, they had to stop while she did their toilet. These stops aggravated everyone because they slowed their progress toward their destination. The whole militia contingent was learning that it was no small thing to keep a woman and her baby prisoner, buy nobody saw a good alternative to keeping her and her baby in captivity.

Henry and Randy were finding it hard to adjust to their new situation. They tried to exercise patience. The cries of the baby were the most annoying. They tried to shut out these cries and keep observant. They had gone a few miles, and Henry noticed that Randy was dozing off on his horse, so he nudged him with the barrel of his rifle. Randy was startled to be poked in his ribs and, opened his eyes wide, and said, "Sorry. I guess the only way I can stop hearing the baby's cries is to put myself to sleep."

Henry nonchalantly said, "I know. It's maddening, but oddly, I have not heard the baby cry in a while."

A half hour went by, and when no baby cries were heard, Randy said to Henry, "The baby must be sleeping cause he hasn't cried in a long while."

Henry grunted in an assenting tone, and they kept moving along the trail to Little Rock. Another thirty minutes went by, and Randy could not help but say, "That baby sure sleeping a long time. Are you sure he's okay?"

For the hell of it and to give Randy peace of mind, Henry dismounted and walked behind the wagon. He flipped back the canvas cover and saw the woman sitting still, looking straight forward with tears in her eyes. The baby was lying hidden under her scarf on the wagon planks at her feet. She slowly turned her head, and looking straight at Henry, she said just one word while she pointed her finger at the baby. "Dead."

Henry immediately withdrew, mounted his horse, and told Randy with a shocked look on his face, "The baby is dead. I'll go tell the sarge."

Henry rode rapidly up to the front of the line and asked his surprised sarge for permission to speak, and said dutifully, "Just want to let you know the baby is dead."

Sarge did not take long to reply, "Another casualty among many of the war. We'll stop as soon as we encounter another group of refugees traveling along the same road and, bury the baby, and leave the woman to fend for herself."

"Yes, suh," said Henry as he saluted. He then rode quickly off to join his brother and relay to him what the sarge said.

They did not have to travel long before they encountered one of the many civilian groups seeking refuge in the West. The sarge called for his men to come to a halt while passing the word to stay alert. He dismounted to go talk with the leader of the group of weary travelers. After shaking hands, the sarge told the man about what had happened, and they needed to leave the woman with them so they could report as quickly as possible to Ft. Smith.

The leader said in a weak and distraught voice, "Okay, but we really don't need more people, particularly a woman. We barely got enough to make it to Little Rock. Bring the woman and the dead baby."

The elderly leader was dressed in black and looked like some kind of preacher traveling with members of his congregation. He had a small Bible tucked in his back pocket, and he had belted around himself a holster with a pistol. He believed that God had mandated the southern states to secede from the union because God had marked black slaves as inferior beings who should be subjugated by whites. For him, the mark of Cain condemned the Negro race to an inferior status.

The sarge signaled to Henry and Randy to bring the woman and her dead baby. They brought their female prisoner as instructed. She carried her dead baby in her one free arm. Her other arm was tied tightly with a strand of rope. The leader looked hard at her and, drew his pistol, and shot her at close range right between the eyes. The woman dropped dead in the middle of the road, and her dead baby rolled out of her arm to her side. The leader spat on her body and said in the most bitter tone, "That woman and her accomplices held us up at gunpoint a couple of days ago and took all our money and some food. She got what she deserved. Now we're all free from her devilish ways. Anyway, she didn't have any reason left to live."

The sarge, Henry, and Randy stood in shock of what just happened so quickly. They were speechless. They did not have to wait long to hear the leader say, "That's that. God's will have been served. We'll bury this rotten piece of baggage and her baby. Now, you boys, keep on moving. We need you to hold Ft. Smith against those Yankee bastards."

The sarge led the way as he returned to his troops. The sarge was hurting inside and said to Henry and Randy, "You see what the war has done to us? It has turned us against one another."

Privately, the sarge was thinking about his plans to marry a local girl back home and continue his studies. He had not anticipated that war would swoop down to shatter all his plans and cast him into a military role. He wished there had never been a war and his life could go on as before, but the harsh reality of the war stood firmly in the way of any hope of achieving better times.

# Chapter Nine
# Step at a Time

The trail to Little Rock cut through the verdant and wild wilderness. Henry and Randy brought up the rear, playing the role of good soldiers. They really had nothing to complain about. They had healthy horses, food, clothes, and the best of rifles. Yet compared to the rich life they had before the ravages of war, they had everything to complain about. The war had reduced them to poor teenage commoners fighting to survive.

Their short wagon train moved slowly forward. With about forty men impressed into military service, riding at close quarters two-by-two and three wagons, their convoy stretched along the trail for about a half-mile. In a good ten-hour day, they covered twenty to thirty miles, depending on the weather and the number of creeks they had to ford.

There were a couple of days when the rain came down so abundantly hard they had to take shelter beneath leafy trees. They all got soaked to the bone, and no fire could be made for a hot meal or coffee. They were thankful for the protection from the elements their frock coats and slouch hats provided them, but these new clothing articles were limited on what they could do to keep them dry. The few of their comrades had ponchos, so they fared better, but even they were unnerved by the downpour and the delays it caused.

When the sun did come out after such diluvial rainfall, the ground was flooded, making their forward progress on the muddy road even slower. Some creeks were flooded, and the water was too high to ford. There was nothing to do but to wait for the water to go down. They killed time by doing all they could to dry themselves, their horses, and equipment. They also collected deadwood to stack in the covered wagon to dry out for use in cooking fires.

The heavy rainfall also provided cover for a couple of their militia comrades to desert. Henry and Randy wanted to desert, too, but they were still too far from Texas. And what would they eat? They thought the best was to hold the course until they got to Ft. Smith before escaping from their military duties and making their own way farther west. Besides, they liked the sarge and wanted to help him.

Henry and Randy did note that a good time to sneak off was in the night when it was raining and there was no moonlight. They thought to do that, you had to have a good idea of where you are going. Also, you did not want to run into bushwhackers or other armed people who, at heart, were criminals and misfits. Henry was thinking that it was best to stay away from all sorts of people, even the sparse settlements they encountered here and there. Some settlers could also be real cutthroats.

Late one afternoon, after eight days on the trail, they finally made it to the Little Rock landing on the north side of the Arkansas River. They were warmly greeted by the large groups of people camped at this spot. They all said they were waiting for their turns to take boats which were ferrying people to the small settlement on the south bank of the river. They were grateful for the extra protection their small militia contingent provided them. But they were disappointed to learn that the troops would be moving on tomorrow on the trail to Ft. Smith.

The group of refugees were so friendly that the idea of joining them and their plans to make new lives for themselves in the Little Rock settlement appealed to Henry and Randy. Also, the eyes of young women in the group caught the eyes of Henry and Randy. They were not alone in thinking they could settle down in Little Rock and court one of these women, and live happy lives. The sarge saw the look in his men's eyes and cut through the jovial atmosphere by saying, "Men, let's move on and make our own campground at a spot upriver near the start of the Ft. Smith trail."

With the temptations of Little Rock behind them, they forged ahead, skirting the north side of the river. They found the Ft. Smith trail was more of a military road made for going and coming to Ft. Smith. Maybe it was originally traced by Indians, but since its use for the removal of eastern Indian tribes some decades earlier, it was almost strictly used by the military. And now the armies of the north and south vied for its use.

The river was never too far from the trail, so they always had an ample source of water for themselves and their horses. As it was spring, there were many spots covered with green grass for the grazing of their horses. In many ways, it was a bucolic scene, and you could be easily lulled into a false sense of happiness. If it were not for their fading homesickness and their sore butts from riding horses all day, Henry and Randy were enjoying the sights of the new scenery presented them and the adventure of exploring places far from their home surroundings.

Henry was riding alongside Randy when he broke their silence and said, "No matter how inviting these new places may seem, we must stick to our plan of going to Texas. That's what our mom wanted, and as far as I am concerned, she was right. We must get to Texas no matter what."

Randy said, "Texas or death, whichever comes first."

"We must never let anyone know of our plans. This is our secret and our private war," Henry added.

Henry continued, "We have learned a lot, but we got much more to learn about the ways of the West. Also, our bodies are adjusting to this more rugged life. That is good as we must be much more physically and mentally hard than we were to survive in the West."

Randy joined the conversation by saying, "We should also gain back some of the weight we've lost. We're still growing. We need more weight to maintain our strength and ward off sickness. We need to stay healthy and do all we got to do."

Henry nodded his assent and listened to some noise being made in front of them. They galloped forward and saw their comrades gathered around the broken-down stores wagon. Somehow, one if its back wheels had come off. They dismounted and heard the wagon master say, "Isn't dat the darnest thing? I just checked the wheels this morning, and they were okay."

Henry and Randy did not know anything about wagon wheels. They saw this as another learning opportunity. The sarge came and immediately ordered the men to find wood branches and stones to raise the wagon to a level position. He yelled at Henry and Randy, "You two start unloading the wagon to lighten its load."

The wagon master did not like for everyone to so see all his stores, but he had no choice but to allow his wagon to be unloaded. When his stores were stacked in the open on the ground, all could see that he had a bounty of food items. There was no reason for him to continue being so stingy about feeding the men. The wagon master could sense the rising anger among the men and hung his head low. They did not like learning they had been short-changed on their food rations for no good reason.

The sarge brought his motley band of men to order by telling them to get around the empty wagon and lift it while other men tried to wedge beneath it the limbs and stones they had found lying along the side of the trail. Once the wagon was propped up and stable, the sarge dismounted, and he and the wagon master tried to see why the wheel fell of its axle. They quickly saw that the pin holding the wheel on the axle hub was missing. He ordered the men to search the road they had just covered to see if they could fine the pin.

The men retraced the trail for more than a hundred yards, but they could not find the pin. Finally, one man spotted in one of the dirt tracks of the trails a broken piece of an iron pin. He ran up to show the sarge what he had found. The wagon master looked on and said, "We are doomed. My wagon can't move without a pin for this wheel."

At that moment, the rotund master of the cook wagon busted into the front of the group, and with a big smile on his beaded face, revealing his rotten front teeth, he blurted out, "Looky at what I got." He extended his hand to show off a new wheel pin.

An angry sarge said, "Why didn't you tell us before that you had a pin?"

The chuck wagon cook sheepishly said, "I wasn't sure. While you were working on this wagon, I was searching frantically through my wagon for an extra wheel pin."

The sarge quickly dismissed the cook and ordered the men gathered around to lift the wagon while other men shoved the wheel over the axle. He then handed the pin to Henry and told him, "Slip it through the axle hole and bend it with your pocketknife and insert the clasp so it will not slip off."

Henry had no trouble following sarge's instructions. He placed the pin and fixed it in place. The sarge ordered the men to set the wagon down gently and reload all the items previously offloaded. The men did as told, but they were tempted to pocket some of the food items.

Suddenly, the cook appeared with a gallon tub of hog lard and loudly said, "Smear this pig fat on the axle. It will help keep the wagon rolling smoothly and stop any rusting.

The men hesitated in doing what the cook wanted and looked at the sarge, who said, "He's right. Go ahead and rub the pig grease all over it."

Sarge rode back to the stores wagon to see what was going on, saying, "Get ready now to move out. We've lost too much time. Ft. Smith beckons."

They rode on. One day was as pretty as the other. The horses were tired and growing skinnier. They thought they would never reach Ft. Smith. The sarge sensed a decline in the morale of his men. He knew their enthusiasm for the war was waning, and they had mixed emotions about which side to fight for, if any. They knew that Arkansas was a Confederate State, but they knew little else about the conflict between the states. News was slow to arrive, and now they were isolated. And when they heard any news, they did not know if they were hearing the truth or a rumor. The whole world could have disappeared as far as they knew.

The sarge knew that some of his men were deserting, but he also knew he could not do anything about it. He certainly was not going to waste time searching for them and taking them as prisoners. He did give his men occasional pep talks and repeat the goals of their mission. He was fond of saying. *Keep your eyes on our mission. We have been ordered by our high command to reinforce our unit holding Ft. Smith so we can withstand any attack by Union forces. Don't think about anything else but achieving this mission.*

The wagon master, who was deeply embarrassed by the revelation of his ample food stocks in his broken-down wagon, gave the cook extra food supplies, saying, "The men deserve an extra ration tonight for all the good work they did today."

The cook smiled and then laughed, thinking more food was the answer to one of their main problems. He happily set up his iron tripod over the campfire and dished out extra rations of rice and beans from his big cast iron pot. He complemented this hot food with dried fruit. The extra food put the men in a good mood.

The sarge saw the men enjoying themselves and raised his hand to demand silence before saying, "I'm glad you're happy, but we still have days before we reach Ft. Smith, and anything could happen between now and then. Who knows if we are not being trailed by bushwhackers? We have to remain alert and never let our guard down."

The sarge's words served to calm the men down and prepare them for another night at top alertness. They ate until their stomachs were full, and the hot coffee flowed copiously. Many thought it was better to be killed on a full stomach than on an empty one. For sure, a full stomach put a rosier outlook on everything. Deep down, many of them knew they would not survive the war, so why not try to be happy? They were all young, but they had nothing to look forward to.

Most of the so-called militiamen were poor, illiterate farm boys from Tennessee who had lost everything. They did not know much but living poor had taught them to get by with little. And they knew how to handle a rifle and were good shots. They knew how to survive in the worst conditions. They were able to put up a fight when called on to do so, but they were not sure about what they were fighting for. For sure, all the fighting in the world would not bring back their previous lives.

Henry approached the sarge and asked for permission to speak, "Before I take my turn as a night sentinel, my curiosity is getting the best of me. How do you know Confederate forces are still in control of Ft. Smith?"

"I don't. But that is what was stated in the orders I received a couple of weeks ago. Things could have changed, but I don't think so. The Union does not care much about Arkansas. It has bigger fish to fry elsewhere."

Henry replied, "Thanks, Sarge, for such a good answer. Say, you mentioned fish. We could really use what fish and wild game can provide our diet. Why not take a day off to fish and hunt? There are plenty of fish in the river, and the woods abounds with varmints of all sorts."

The sarge quickly replied in a military fashion. "No. We have no time, and we want to save our ammunition. My orders are to get to Ft. Smith as quickly as possible."

"Sorry, Sarge, just an idea," Henry said apologetically.

The sarge decided to depart from his usually quiet self and say to Henry, "I know you've had a good upbringing. It is hard to hide that stuff from anyone. The way you carry yourself is a total giveaway to me. Keep that in mind for any future we may have."

Henry asked to be dismissed and left with a higher respect for the sarge. He decided then he would try to get to know the sarge more and help in any way he could. The sarge had become like a big brother to him. He did not want to fight for either side, but he would fight for the sarge because he wanted him to stay alive to realize parts of his dream.

The next morning, as the rising sun was peeking over the eastern horizon, the sarge assembled the men for another pep talk. He reminded them again in an inspirational voice, "It's our duty to move on. The road from Little Rock to Ft. Smith is longer than the road from Memphis to Little Rock, but I estimate we'll arrive in a couple of days. Now, let's do our duty and move toward Ft. Smith."

Henry related his conversation with the sarge to Randy, who said sardonically, "I thought so."

Henry continued by saying in a solemn voice, "When we get to Ft. Smith, we can start looking for a good way to leave and go west across the river. Only the Lord knows what awaits us in this lonely pursuit of our new lives in Texas."

Randy did not think it was worth saying anything, but he decided Henry's serious words deserved a reply of sorts.

"Let's take things a step at a time. Who knows what is ahead for us?"

# Chapter Ten
# Fort Smith

The sarge was right. After following the trail to Ft. Smith for two days, they arrived. They were one tired bunch, but their arrival at Ft. Smith did lift their spirits. They were careful not to be over-relieved by their arrival because they did not know what was ahead for them. And they were a long ways from home in unfamiliar territory. They did not know what to expect, and they all kept their trigger fingers on the ready.

They arrived late in the afternoon. They did not know which day or month it was, and they did not much care. They did welcome the warmth of the coming summer. The sarge called for making of camp outside of the small settlement of Ft. Smith. He wanted first to send a couple of scouts to the fort to make sure Confederates were still occupying it and, if so, inform its commanders that its requested reinforcements have arrived.

He chose Henry and Randy to ride up to the fort and inform its guards of their arrival and plans to move in early tomorrow morning. Henry and Randy did as ordered. They found a warm welcome awaited them and the news they brought. They were all ears as they listened intently to the fort's occupants. When these men finished telling them about their situation, they rode back to the sarge to tell him all they heard.

Henry was the first to speak to the sarge, but he spoke in a loud voice so all could hear.

"First, the Confederacy is in control, but most of the men in the fort rode off three days ago to join other Confederate forces in a big battle with Union forces some distance north of here. Only a dozen soldiers were left to guard the fort, so our arrival is most welcome. They want us to come forward now and camp within the old army fort."

The sarge interrupted, "Change in orders. Prepare to move into the fort."

The sarge then turned to Henry and said, "Is that all?"

Henry said, "No, there is more."

"Well, let's hear it."

"The men at the fort's gate said that most of their unit rode off with only three days of food rations in the haversacks and no rations for their horses. They wanted to travel light so they could quickly join their comrades in battle. They are worried because none of them have returned yet. What do you think happened?"

The sarge responded with his brow furrowed. "It is not for me to say, but it's probably taking them a little longer than expected, and they'll be back soon. All I know for sure is that the fort is still under the control of the Confederacy, and we have followed our orders and arrived to reinforce those still here. Let's go and fulfill our mission."

They filed through the main gate and were warmly welcomed by the troops who were left behind to maintain the fort. Everyone felt more secure within the fort's twelve-foot-high stone walls. Their heightened security put them more at ease. Their relaxed state made them feel almost human again. They were ready to rest and recuperate from their long journey.

One of the men in the fort played a welcome ditty on his fiddle, and all the men began to make dance steps in time with the music. The sight of the men dancing made the sarge crack a smile before hollering the order. "Fall out. Make camp and carry on."

After giving that order, the sarge turned to the uniformed corporal and asked again, "Your men are overdue. When do you think they'll be back.?

"Dunno. We ain't had any news from the north in days, but we're expectin' them at any time," the diminutive blond-haired corporal muttered.

The sarge asked dryly, "Do you have scouts and snipers posted?"

"No. We don't have any men to spare for scouts. But we do have snipers posted at points along the fort walls."

The sarge responded, "Well, as soon as my men get some rest and food, I'll send scouts north to see what's happening."

"Sounds good. Make yourselves at home. If you need anything, let us know. We got plenty of stores."

The sarge turned to tend to his camp and men. He rode up to Henry and Randy and said kindly, "I know I can count on you two. At first light tomorrow, I want you to ride north to see if anything is happening. Ride as far as you can but return here by dark and tell me what you saw."

Henry and Randy were hesitant but happy and a bit surprised to be chosen. This sign of trust prompted both of them to say in unison, "Yes, sir."

It was a riotous night in their camp on the fort's grassy courtyard. They were dished up a double ration, the fiddler played, and somebody introduced a bottle of whiskey, which made the rounds as one soldier after another took a swig of the devil's brew. Only two men did not drink any whiskey… Henry and Randy. They had never tasted whiskey before and wanted to keep their heads clear for their early morning mission.

The sarge came by to see how they were doing and to remind them of their scouting job tomorrow. He stared into their eyes to help him gauge the depths of his trust in them and gently said, "I've told the cook to prepare some vittles for you to carry with you tomorrow. Pick them up tonight so you are ready to go in the morning. Also, don't forget to fill your canteens with water. I look forward to hearing your report tomorrow evening. Good luck."

"Thank you, sir. We'll do our best," Henry quickly said in response.

The sarge smiled and said, "I know you will."

The camp gradually became quiet, and the blazing campfire died. All was quiet and dark. The only light was coming from the candles burning at the gate sentinels. There were also a number of outbuildings on the interior grounds of the fort, and some of them had candlelight. The darkness was sweet because it was covered with ample moonlight. The soft cooing of distant nightbirds filtered periodically through the cool night air. There was a sense of tranquility that the men had not known for several weeks.

Henry was snuggly wrapped up in his blanket, but he slept little because he was afraid to be late for their early departure. He wanted to follow orders and leave before the crack of dawn. Throughout the night, he kept checking for the first glimmers of a new day. He was up and ready at first light. He kicked Randy, who had been sleeping next to him, saying in a whisper, "Time to go and do our duty. I'll get the horses ready."

Henry carried his pack to where the horses were tethered for the night on the other side of the fort yard. He saddled both their horses. As soon as Randy arrived and tied his bundle to the horse, they mounted and rode toward the fort's front gate.

They saluted the sentinel at the gate and said, "Dixie." The password they were told yesterday.

The gate was promptly opened, and the guard said, "See you later. Good luck."

Henry and Randy rode out of the fort, not knowing exactly where to go. All Henry knew was to go northward, and to do that, he had to keep the rising sun on his right.

As the day got brighter, they could easily see a well-used trail leading north and followed it for some distance. Henry suddenly stopped his horse. Randy did the same. Henry whispered, "Things don't feel right to me. Let's get off the trail and walk our horses slowly north through the woods. Keep your ears opened and your eyes peeled."

They walked for several hours through and around thickets of woods and tall grass. Henry suddenly motioned to Randy to get down. They both hit the ground. Henry slowly raised his head and could make out a brown spot in the grass ahead of them. They crawled closer, leaving their horses behind, trusting that they would not run off. As they got closer, the brown spot turned into what was clearly a dead horse. The crept closer and could see that the horse was lying on top of a Confederate soldier in uniform.

They waited for some time before they stood up and walked slowly with the rifles at the ready to the spot where the dead horse and man lay. The sight they saw was a gory one. The horse had been shot down and had crushed the soldier riding him. They looked around, and they did not see anything. Then, they heard a moan coming from the man pinned beneath the dead horse. They kneeled down to get closer to the man's head to see if he could still speak.

Henry placed his face within a few inches of the man's face, and he said distinctly in a soothing voice, "We're scouts from Ft. Smith trying to find out what happened to our troops."

The man beneath the horse struggled to utter slowly a few broken words, "Go back. All men killed or captured. Go back now."

The man turned his head and went limp. Obviously, these were his last words. There was no doubt in Henry's mind on what their next move should be. For him, if they went farther north, they risked being killed, so they quietly withdrew to their horses. Henry indicated by using hand signs to Randy to mount and follow him back to where they came from.

They stayed off the trail and weaved their way back to Ft. Smith to deliver their news to the sarge. They were in a hurry, but they could only go as fast as the woods and underbrush allowed them to go. When the sun got high in the sky, they stopped to rest themselves and their horses and munch on some of their hardtack biscuits. Their teeth were not strong enough to break pieces off their biscuits, so they poured water on them and broke them into pieces by placing them on a stone and then crushing them with the butts of their rifles. They washed these pieces down with big gulps of water from their canteens.

Each relieved himself and then started their slow return to Ft. Smith. The sun was setting as they rode through the front gate of Ft. Smith. Their fellow militiamen were surprised to see them, as they thought Henry and Randy had deserted. Henry sat tall in his saddle as they rode directly to where the sarge was standing. He and Randy had a new sense of responsibility and were proud of being entrusted with the duty of scouts.

Henry and Randy dismounted and walked toward the sarge, stopping in front of him and after a semblance of a salute, Henry spouted out the following information, "They're not coming back. We found one man pinned under his dead horse, and his last words were they had all been killed or captured."

The sarge immediately said, "Did you see any Union forces?"

"No, sir. Nothing," said Henry.

"Well done. Be ready to testify more at an assembly tonight around our campfire. That's it for now. We'll talk more later."

By the time Henry and Randy had tended to their horses and returned to camp, the sarge was already talking to the assembled group of his militia and men stationed at the fort. The sarge stopped speaking when he saw Henry and Randy standing at the periphery of the assembly and said, "Here are our two scouts who reported back the information I provided. Do you have anything to add?"

Henry was not aware of what the sarge had already said, so he felt like he was being put on the spot. He had to say something, so he said loudly so all could hear, "We were told by a dying soldier from this fort that all his comrades had been captured or killed in a battle with Union forces. So, I guess we'll stop waiting for any of them to come back."

Henry's words set the assembly of men abuzz. The sarge called the men to order and said, "Are there any questions for these two loyal scouts?"

One fort soldier raised his hand high and said loudly, "Did you get the dead soldier's name?"

Henry quickly responded, "No. His dead horse covered his body, and all we saw was his head. We thought it best to get out of there and start on our way back here."

Another fort soldier had a question. "Any chance our comrades who escaped joined other Southern forces located farther south?"

Henry replied, "Dunno. I can only report on what I heard and saw. I did not see any sign of any forces."

The sarge interjected, "That's enough for today. We can sleep on what we heard tonight and see what actions we want to take tomorrow. Dismissed."

Henry and Randy were dead tired, but they could not sleep as their own next move was not apparent. They wanted to help the sarge keep the fort out of Union hands, but they also wanted to save their own skins and go to Texas as they had always planned. They decided to give it a few days before deciding what they would do. They were comfortable with staying a while in a place that was secure, well-equipped, and with plenty of food and forage grain.

So far, Ft. Smith was the best place they had stayed in since leaving home in Virginia over two months ago. And to go farther west, they would have to wade across the wide Arkansas River and make their way through risky Indian Territory. They had all they needed in Ft. Smith, but going farther west would entail some deprivations and additional dangers posed by places they did not know. They wanted to go, but staying for the time being seemed a better option.

The next day, they were told to report to the sarge. They scrambled and hustled to the office the sarge had set up in one of the outbuildings. They stood in front of the sarge's makeshift desk, waiting for him to speak. After a few minutes, the sarge said in a friendly tone, "Sit down and relax. I assume you haven't forgot how to sit in a chair."

Henry and Randy sat down on the hard but unstable wood chairs and waited for the sarge to say something. After a reflective pause, the sarge said, "I need you boys. I need your intelligence and schooled ways. I know you want to run off, but I ask you to stay here for a while longer. What do you say?"

Henry looked at his younger brother before saying in a reluctant voice, "We're staying."

The sarge knew that he could not trust any response from them, but he thought his chances were improved by appealing to their better nature. The sarge followed by saying, "Good. Now that we got that taken care of let me hear what you really think of our chances of keeping this fort out of Union hands?"

As usual, Randy kept quiet and looked to Henry to answer such a difficult question. To his surprise, Henry had an answer at the ready. "As long as the Union doesn't want the fort, you can stay here. When the Union forces do come, no sense in putting up a fight. You really have nowhere to go, so you might as well stay here."

The sarge responded to Henry's words by saying only, "I agree. Looks like we're stuck here for the duration of the war, alive or dead. Nothing left for us to do but prepare for and expect the worst. We'll need strong discipline to see us through this nasty ordeal. Maybe we'll be lucky, and maybe not. Time will tell."

# Chapter Eleven
# Surrender, Flight, or Fight

The sarge's effort to cultivate the close allegiance of Henry and Randy was working. Almost every day, they were called to his office and asked for their advice. The sarge knew they could read and write, so he asked them to help him with his daily log. It was not lost on the other men of this attachment of the sarge to Henry and Randy. They understood that these two young men were of a different class. They knew their elite status separated them from the rest of the group. They were just poor and unschooled farm boys, while it was obvious that Henry and Randy were from an educated upper class.

Henry and Randy found that they had to get to know better each of their fellow militiamen. They heard from each of them heartbreaking stories of how they ended up in the militia. The sarge's insistence that they write up a list with the names and origins of each man gave them ample opportunity to get to know each of their young comrades. This listing also allowed them to learn more about the cook and the stores wagon manager. They could easily see that they were in the same boat together.

They found in the barracks a stack of envelopes and writing paper so they offered to write letters from the men to their families. The men were eager to communicate with their families, but few had good addresses, and the postal system in the South had been interrupted by the war. They did not know how they would have the letters delivered, so they gave them to the sarge to try to mail when he got back to the eastern side of the Mississippi. It made the men feel good to write letters home even though their letters may never reach their families.

After a couple of weeks and the fort troops who went off to battle had not returned, sarge took over command of the fort. His first order was for his men to break camp in the courtyard and move to the barracks. The men delighted to be inside after weeks of camping outside. They could not believe their good fortune to have real beds to sleep in. Yet, some men were so used to sleeping on the ground that they put their stuff on their flimsy beds and slept on the hard floor next to it.

The fort had been something of a storage depot, so there was a warehouse full of food, feed, and ammunition. They and their horses ate well. There was also a water well on the fort compound, so they never lacked for water. They had everything they needed. The men and their horses put on weight. Many of the men had never had it so good.

They had everything they needed except meat. The shortage of meat prompted the sarge to allow his troops to hunt for game that was not too distant from the fort as long as the enemy was not nearby. The same applied to fishing in the river. These activities allowed the men to have almost nightly feasts on rabbits, squirrels, and catfish. The improvement in their diets lifted their spirits. They all hoped the Yankees would continue to leave them alone.

Henry and Randy continued their frequent scouting forays into the countryside. These forays included secretly scouting along the river to see where the best places were for crossing into Indian Territory. They also found a small cave in which to hide provisions they might use when they decided to cross the river and go on their way to Texas. They admired the site of the fort on a high bluff called Belle Point that was situated at where the Poteau River joined the Arkansas River.

One day, all the men were issued bars of soap. Henry and Randy took their bars and said they were going out to scout along the river. They rushed to a shallow pool in the river, stripped their clothes off, and washed themselves from head to toe. They also washed their ragged clothes. They enjoyed the heat of the blazing sun and spread their clothes on the tall grass near the riverbanks. They felt like kids again and played in the murky water.

When they returned to the fort, they headed for a comrade who cut hair. They both enjoyed haircuts and took the man up on having their faces shaved, even though their beards at their youthful age were scraggly. They presented themselves to the sarge, and he broke out laughing and said, "Why you two look like plucked chickens?"

Henry and Randy looked at each other and could not help but smile as they waited for the sarge to say something more. They did not have to wait long. "We need to start getting ready for staying here for the long haul. We'll begin by building stables for the horses and collecting firewood for the winter. I need you guys to help me draw up a plan for doing all that needs to be done to keep the troops busy."

Henry responded immediately, "Good idea. We need to develop a routine to pass the time and prepare for winter."

The sarge said, "Exactly. Maybe these maps of the fort and the surrounding area will be of use."

The sarge unfolded two old maps on his desk and inquired, "You do read maps, don't you?"

Although it had been a long time since they had saw any maps, Henry replied, "Of course."

They poured over the maps, and Henry said, "I think we should construct the stables along this south wall of the fort. They will be simple structures using tree poles to put them up and brush to cover them. We'll need to assign regular details to clean the stables, feed and water the horses, and take them outside to graze. These must be men who know how to care for horses."

The sarge took a moment and then looked intensely at Henry and said, "Very impressive words. If it were in my power to do so, I would promote you to the highest rank possible. You are probably the only one in the fort who can read a map and make comments like that."

The boyish Henry was not the type to get embarrassed, but he was lost for words. He finally said, "Shucks, that's nothing. Even my younger brother Randy could do the same. He's much smarter than me."

This prompted the sarge to ask, "How old are you anyway?"

Henry replied, "I reckon I'm seventeen by now, and Randy is two years younger."

"Well, you're big boys. You look much older."

Henry could not resist saying, "We had no choice but to grow up fast."

Henry continued by saying hesitantly, "While we are talking, can you tell us, sarge, what's your name and where you are from?"

The sarge happily said, "Sure. My name is Bill Bate, Jr., and I was born in Sumner County, Tennessee. If I make it through this war, I hope to return to my home state."

Henry and Randy looked at the sarge briefly and could see instinctively that he was a respectable, educated man of a tall but lanky build. No matter the many stresses placed upon him, he also remained cool, calm, and collected. They could see that he was a natural, true leader of men. The content of his character and his mannerisms attracted them to him and made them want to follow him. Their trust in him evolved to an unbreakable proportion. In many ways, his admirable attributes reminded them of their father.

Henry hesitated but could not help saying, "My full name is Henry Harrison Read, and my brother's name is Peyton Randolph Read. We're both born in Charlotte, Virginia. We only want to start new lives in Texas. There is nothing left for us back home."

There was much more that Henry wanted to say, but he did not want to give the sarge more information about them than he had already given. The sarge thanked them for the information and said tartly, "Well, you will always be Henry and Randy to me… the lost Virginia plantation boys. Now, enough talk. No sense in letting any sentiment get the best of us. Let's all do the work we need to do to stay alive and well."

At that moment, a fort guard stepped into the small room and said excitedly, "Sarge, you should come and see this."

They all rushed to the front gate to see a group of exhausted civilians gathered and trying to force their way into the fort. One man saw the sarge and blurted out, "Help us. We've walked from Little Rock, and we're starving. Union forces took over our town, and we fled for our lives."

The sarge stepped forward and looked over those huddled outside the front gate and forthrightly said, "The news you have brought us is important. We feel your pain that was caused by being uprooted by the enemy and your long walk. We can only spare three days of rations for each of you. Our military mission obliges us to tell you to try and look for help in the small settlement nearby."

After saying these words, the sarge gave orders to give them rations and walked briskly back to his office. Henry and Randy followed him. Once in the office, the sarge howled a loud noise and bitterly said, "We're trapped. There is no way out. The ways north and south are blocked by the enemy. It's going to be a long winter, and spring will likely bring our demise."

Henry and Randy let out long sighing breaths and bit their tongues. The sarge's words were slowly settling in, and it took them a while for the gravity of their predicament to sink in. After a few minutes of silence, Randy made a rare comment. "Sarge, why don't you come west with us."

The sarge immediately said, "I can't do that. That gets me farther away from home, and it probably is like going from the frying pan into the fire.

The Indians there are still mad about the suffering my people caused them by forcing them off their ancestral lands to a desolate reservation in Indian Territory. Some Indians and escaped slaves have joined the side of the enemy, and there is nothing worse than being caught by them. We might as well stay here and wave the white flag of surrender when the Union troops arrive."

Henry thought he should say something. "Sarge, come hell or high water, we're going west for better or worse."

The sarge replied, "Yes, I know. But you best stay the winter with us and cross the river before the spring rains."

Henry looked at Randy before answering. "Yeah. That sounds like a good idea. We'll need the time to become fit for our westward journey."

The mild winter passed peacefully, but its progressive monotony was unbearable. They and their horses had plenty to eat. The mounds of firewood they had collected in the summer and fall kept them warm even on the coldest day. Everybody had nothing to complain about, but boredom set in because of their isolation and the expectation that they would be attacked in the spring by an overwhelming Union force. The troops manning the fort did not know it, but the sarge had already confectioned a white flag of surrender. He figured there was no sense of

fighting or trying to flee. They would have to take their chances as prisoners of war. He thought this was the best option for him and his troops.

The men tried to pass the boring confinement placed on them by the winter weather by staying close to the fireplace in their barracks. They talked and exchanged stories until they did not have any more to tell. They played cards, checkers, and dominos until they were tired of playing their games. Those who had not already written letters home with Henry or Randy did so. When it snowed, and conditions were right, they had rowdy snowball fights. They were about at their wits end when the weather warmed enough for them to go outside and enjoy games of horseshoes. The boredom of winter proved to be the worst enemy they had encountered thus far.

On Christmas Day, their raucous party reduced the level of boredom. The fort fiddler was given some whiskey and played non-stop. The men jumped up and down and danced so hard that the floorboards were broken. Someone produced a bottle of whiskey, and it made the swigging rounds. The cook exceeded all expectations and produced a feast of army food, including something the men had never tasted before… johnnie cakes splashed with molasses.

A good time was had by all, and most of the men passed out and, for a brief time, forgot about the deathly predicament they found themselves in. They were surprised that they had not been fired upon by snipers or attacked by guerilla forces. They could not believe that the entire country was at war with itself and they had been ignored by all warring elements. They had been spared, but they realized that would end when spring caused the winter quarters to close, and men would once again be engaged in brutal and bloody combat.

The biggest crisis they faced that winter was that they ran out of coffee. They had plenty of tobacco, but there were no Yankee troops to trade it clandestinely for coffee beans. The cook

claimed the last time he had the opportunity to trade secretly tobacco for coffee with Union troops was months ago, and even then, he could not get all the coffee he wanted. Instead, he traded the rest of his tobacco for some knives and canteens. He had plenty of those items, but nobody among the men wanted those items. They wanted their coffee and were ready to do almost anything to get it.

As winter drew to a close, Henry and Randy began to get itchy. They both agreed that the time was drawing near for them to separate themselves by crossing the Arkansas River into Indian Territory. They both appeared before the sarge, and Henry spoke, "Requesting permission to speak, sir."

The sarge took a hard look at his beloved and faithful boys and emotionally said, "I guess the time has come for your departure. I can't say that I blame you. I'd go with you, but my responsibility is here, and I see this as my best chance to return home."

"We understand, but we want to give Texas a try. We're thinking that maybe you can order us to do some night scouting along the river."

"Okay. What night do you want to go scouting?"

"The next full moon."

"Okay. You got it. I'm going to miss you boys. I wish you best of luck. Now, get out of here before I get all teary-eyed."

Henry and Randy stepped outside and felt a sense of loneliness that they had not felt for some time. They asked themselves why they wanted to leave the comforts of fort life for the unknown wilderness and grasslands of Indian Territory. They only knew they had to go. For sure, they did not want to be captured by the Yankees, and to avoid capture, they had to head west no matter what. The words of their mother about going to Texas kept ringing in their ears.

The next day, the sarge assembled his men and surprisingly said. "Spring is almost here, and for sure, the Yankee troops will be coming. They will come with an overpowering force. We can either fight and die or surrender. I have decided the latter is the best course. As you know, we have nowhere to go. The Union controls north and south of here, and the Mississippi. The choice I have for you is stay here and surrender with me and be taken prisoner or take your chances by going off on your own. If you're not here, I'll know your choice. Whatever the case, I thank each and every one of you for your duty to the cause."

There was dead silence after the sarge gave his short speech. The men felt they were doomed any way you sliced it. They were mostly undecided as to what to do. Only Henry and Randy knew the choice they had made, and they thought that choice had prompted the sarge's speech.

# Chapter Twelve
# Texas or Bust

The moon shone bright over the land in the western sky, almost making the night look like day. Henry and Randy calmly walked their horses to the fort's front gate as if they were going on a routine scouting mission. The soldier guarding the gate had already been advised of their mission and quickly flung open the gate as soon as they arrived, shutting it quickly after they had passed through it.

As soon as they heard the clink of the gate behind them being locked, their hearts sunk as they knew there was no going back. Randy said in a low voice once they were out of earshot of the fort. "At least we could have said goodbye to the sarge instead of drifting off in the night like a couple of thieves."

Henry was quick to react, "No goodbyes for deserters. We care about the men we left behind, but our concern for them is not greater than our will to go to Texas. We are thankful for the help this episode in our lives was in getting us closer to Texas, but we must put all this behind us and forge ahead."

They went north along the river as they would usually do on most of their scouting missions. Their first stop was at the small cave where they had hidden some additional provisions. They loaded all they could on their horses and kept going along the left bank of the Arkansas River until they were almost in the southern outskirts of the tiny hamlet of Van Buren. Their previous sorties in this area had indicated that a shallow spot existed in the river where there was a sandbar to help them cross with their horses without too much trouble.

They made sure all was tightly attached to their horses before they led them into the water at the river's edge. The moonlight was reflecting off the river water's silky surface. The smoothness of the river's sandy bottom presented no problems with their arrival at the sandbar at about the middle of the river. They rested for a moment on the sandbar. Henry took a deep breath and said softly, "Let's move. Indian Territory, here we come."

As they waded into the cold water, their stress levels rose. They had no idea of what awaited them on the other side of the river. Their main fear was somebody had already seen them, and they were easy targets in the river. They began to think they should have stuck to their original plan and crossed the river during a dark, rainy night. Henry whispered to Randy, "When we get to the other side, avoid all settlements and people. Let's try to go as far as we can go without being heard or seen."

They reached the right bank, checked their horses, and led them to dry land on top of the bank before mounting them. They rode in a westward direction all night. Henry would check his compass in the moonlight to make sure they were going generally toward the west. The sun came up to slowly expose a broad expanse of grassland dotted with clumps of trees. They rested their horses and allowed them to graze, keeping a watchful eye out for any other human beings. They watered their horses every time they forded a creek. They rode all day, avoiding any trace of other humans.

When night fell, they tethered their horses on tree branches and collapsed into a deep sleep on the ground beneath the same trees. Fatigue had overcome their hunger or any resolve they had for continuing their westward journey. They did not know that for some time, they had been followed and watched by hidden eyes.

The sun peaked over the eastern horizon, and Henry felt a soft, feathery sensation on his nose. He brushed his nose with his hand, and then he felt the sensation again and heard a chuckle. His eyes snapped wide open, and he reached for his pistols. Randy heard the commotion and woke up. They sat up quickly to see they were encircled by the strangest-looking human beings they had ever seen.

One of the blanket-wrapped human figures stepped forward and said in a soothing but foreign voice, "Don't be alarmed. We mean no harm. We're surprised by your presence. What are you two boys doing here?"

Henry and Randy were relieved to see such plain English coming out of the mouth of such an alien being. Henry did not know what to say in response to the strange man and his colorful but odd group of people with differing facial features and darker complexions. To break the silence and to respond, Henry blithely said, "Is this Texas? We're going to Texas."

For reasons Henry and Randy could not fathom, all those surrounding them laughed loudly. Henry and Randy were puzzled as to why Henry's words were so funny. The man who first spoke gently replied after the hearty laughter had died down. "No, this is not Texas. This is Indian Territory. To get to Texas, you have to go farther south and cross the Red River."

Henry felt so small and weakly said in a sheepish manner. "I guess we need to head south. Thanks for the information."

His group had a good laugh again. For Henry and Randy, they seemed to laugh at anything. They did not realize that for the mixed group of Indians, they were quite an amusing spectacle. Then, their leader spoke again, "I didn't introduce myself and my Indian friends. My name is Jesse, and I'm leading these people so they can take refuge from all the troubles in the area of their capital of, Tahlequah. The war has divided the Indians in these parts, and we want none of it, so we're looking for places to camp until the war is over."

Henry said in the sincerest voice he could muster, "Same for us. We've come all the way from Virginia and been on the road since last spring to get out of this insane war. We want no part of it. We hope we can find peace and new lives in Texas."

Jesse then called to the others in the group, and they huddled together, speaking to one another in languages Henry and Randy had never before heard. Jesse stepped out of the group and said forthrightly. "We have decided to take you to our camp. Get ready and follow us."

Henry stood up and without thinking to say, "Wait a minute. Maybe we don't want to go with you."

Jesse made a scoffing sound before saying. "You do not have a choice in the matter. It is unwise to refuse Indian hospitality. And besides, you're in no shape to go to Texas. You must learn many things before you go."

Henry and Randy reluctantly untethered their horses and followed behind Jesse and his peaceful band of Indians. Henry walked closely to Jesse and asked in a worried voice. "Are we captives?"

Jesse laughed and said politely, "No. Consider yourselves as honored guests who need training in the ways of the West."

Henry felt relieved and tried to strike up a conversation with Jesse, inquiring first. "What language are you talking?"

Jesse sighed as if he knew to prepare himself from a barrage of questions from a tenderfoot. He replied as briefly as could explain a complicated subject, "I'm mostly Cherokee, but we have a mixed group of

Indians, so at times, we speak Choctaw or some other Indian tongue."

Henry continued to pepper Jesse with questions. "You said you're leaving Tahlequah because of the conflicts among Indians caused by the war, but I thought all the Indians supported the North because it was the Southerners who forcibly removed them from their ancestral lands in the east."

Jesse thought a long time about Henry's loaded question before responding, "It may seem like that, but it is not clear cut. It was Union troops who marched them west, so most Indians in these parts are against the Union. But the eastern tribes are not the only Indians in these parts."

Henry was busy in his head trying to put together the complex puzzle of the plains Indians when they arrived at a temporary campground of Indians of all ages. He and Randy looked at the site before them and decided it was best to remain quiet and open-minded. They were strangers in a different world where nothing was familiar to them.

Jesse said a stream of Indian words to his comrades, and they dispersed. He then turned to Henry and Randy and said, "First, I must introduce you to our chief, the oldest man in our group, and let him know we found you in the bush and you'll be staying with us for a few weeks."

Henry and Randy did not know what to say or how to act. They were brought before an old man, and Jesse explained to him in an Indian language about why these two young white men were present. The chief's head was bowed the whole time Jesse spoke, exposing a full head of long white hair. When Jesse finished speaking, the chief slowly lifted his head and looked deeply into Henry and Randy's eyes and, said a few words and waved his hand.

Jesse said, "Let's go. The Chief welcomes you. It is past time that we depart and continue our search for buffalo herds."

"What's a buffalo?"

Jesse laughed and said, "You really are greenhorns. For the plains Indians, buffalo are the difference between life and death."

Henry could not keep quiet. "I would sure like to see a buffalo. How can we help you find them?"

Jesse was not annoyed by their childish questions and said, "Be a keen observer of everything you see. Although you do not understand our language, you can learn much by seeing clearly how things are done. Do as they do and learn from their actions."

97

They continued walking west, following the direction indicated by their scouts. Jesse could see Henry and Randy were hungry and told them, "Try to munch on some of those hardtack biscuits in your saddlebags and drink some water from your canteens. No sense in trying to hide your hunger and thirst."

Henry and Randy did as Jesse suggested. Henry was curious about Jesse and wanted to know more about him. First, he wanted to know how he knew they had hard tack in their saddlebacks. Jesse answered this simple query by saying, "We searched your horses and baggage before we woke you with a dove's feather."

Henry knew his question had been a dumb one but kept trying to talk to Jesse. "What did you do before the war?"

"I was in the trading post business, but the war put a stop to all trading. When the war is over, I plan to trade again. Maybe you two boys can help me get back in business."

Henry retorted, "I doubt that. We don't know anything about business."

"Well, you got good rifles and lots of ammunition. In these parts, that can provide you with the kind of security needed. Also, those rifles of yours can help us hunt, and maybe they can kill a few buffalo."

Henry and Randy interpreted Jesse's words to mean that the main reason they wanted them to join their party of refugees was for added protection and food. That was all right with them, but they still wanted to go to Texas. They were willing to go along with Jesse and his group, but there would come a day when they would have to break away and go south to Texas.

They walked slowly for days in a zig-zag pattern through the tallgrass, making camp every evening near a creek or springs, without seeing any signs of life-saving buffalo. Henry and Randy were all eyes in observing how their Indian friends went about their lives. They learned a few words of their language, how to make fire without matches, and how to catch small wild animals in handmade snares.

Every evening, Jesse would come by their spot within the camp to check on them. He would usually say the same thing. "You boys okay? Don't worry. We have scouts posted in every direction, and at the slightest sign of any intruder, they will sound the alarm. Good to see that you sleep with your guns."

After days of looking for buffalo herds, Henry asked Jesse, "What if we don't find any buffalo?"

Jesse wasted no time in giving a curt answer. "If we don't find buffalo to live off of, we can't make it through the winter. This means we'll die."

Jesse's somber words shut Henry up. He could only see a dismal future for Jesse and his group. He did not realize the importance of buffalo to the lives of plains Indians. He still wanted to see a buffalo, but he and Randy wanted to go to Texas more.

They continued to follow scouts in their search for a buffalo herd to attach themselves to. The days passed, and still no buffalo. In his evening visit, Jesse shook his head and said, "Maybe we're doomed. With no buffalo, I don't know how we can survive the coming winter. Maybe the white man has killed them all off for their hides or sport. If so, they are killing the Indian way of life on the prairie. It's a real shame that ignorant outsiders can act in a way that condemns so many people to death."

Henry and Randy did not quite understand the gravity of his words. All they could think about was going south to Texas. They could see that the buffalo issue was serious for these people, but their destiny, for better or worse, was in Texas. With this thought in mind, Henry said to Jesse, "We appreciate the importance of buffalo to you, but we still want to try to find new lives in Texas."

Jesse understood their concerns and wanted to help them. and said, "Give us a few more days to locate some buffalo; if we can't find any, I'll guide you to a good place to cross the Red River so you can go to Texas."

More days passed, and still, there were no buffalo to be seen. Jesse did worry about the boys. They were coming too far west to turn south for them to cross at a good spot on the Red River. He discussed with the Chief the desire of Henry and Randy to go south to Texas. The aged Chief listened and said, "No sense in them staying with us to suffer in the winter. They don't belong here. Take a couple of braves and escort them to the river."

Jesse made his usual evening stop to tell the boys they would be leaving at first light tomorrow to go south toward the Red River and Texas. Henry and Randy could hardly contain their excitement. Randy blurted out, "Thank you, Mr. Jesse. We appreciate all you have done for us and your willingness to take us to the river."

Jesse smiled as if he were amused to hear Randy talk and said, "I don't know if I am doing you a favor. Texas is a rough territory full of meanness that could spell the end of even the toughest of men. For me, your chances of staying alive in Texas are next to nothing."

As Jesse faded away in the darkness, Henry was weighing in his mind Jesse's heavy words and quietly said to Randy, "Are you sure you still want to go to Texas?"

Little brother Randy did not hesitate to say, "Better Texas than staying here and freezing or starving to death in the dead of winter. At least, the weather should be warmer farther south. Our mom said go to Texas, and we're going no matter what."

All Henry could say was, "Soon, we'll be Texas boys."

# Chapter Thirteen
# Long Ride to Texas

Henry and Randy had trouble sleeping that night. Their anticipation of heading to Texas kept them thinking about all they could possibly encounter. Their efforts to get some sleep came to an end when Jesse woke them up and said, "Some of my people are sick with the white man's disease. Get ready, but we can't go until the situation of my sick people gets better. Stay put until I return."

Jesse's words had confused Henry and Randy. They did not know if they should do as Jesse said or run for their lives. They decided there was no escape; therefore, they had no choice but to stay put and wish for the best. Henry said in a bitter tone, "I'm sure they will blame us for making some of them ill. But that's not possible. We're not sick."

They waited for a couple of hours for Jesse to return. Henry and Randy were expecting the worst, but Jesse was alone, and they trusted him. Jesse could see the fear in their eyes and told them. "You have nothing to be afraid of. These people have been sick for weeks. But I have to stay here until they get better. Be patient. This delay doesn't mean you're not going to Texas, it only means a few days more before we depart. In the meantime, we should put the time to good use and do what we can to get you ready for Texas."

Jesse had some ideas. "Come with me to my trade wagon. You need to be outfitted to fit in better in Texas. My wagon is full of merchandise that I planned to trade for hides or sell before the war interrupted my life and business."

Henry and Randy did not know what to say, but they were eager to see what goods Jesse had. They followed him a short distance to a parked canvas-covered wagon. Jesse threw open the back flap and climbed into the jam-packed wagon, saying, "The first thing you need is clothes that make you look like you are from Texas. I got some clothes that might fit you."

Jesse handed some wool pants and some cotton long-sleeve shirts out the back of the wagon. "Try these on. If they are a little big, that's okay because you got some growin' yet to do."

Henry and Randy stripped down to their droopy undies and tried on their new duds. Their new clothes did not fit well, but it felt good to have new clothes. Jesse continued to rummage around inside the wagon. He tossed out the back a couple of items, saying, "Here's some leather vests for you. I think I also have some hats and big bandanas for you. Yep, here are a couple of hats and bandanas you can use. I reckon that's all I have for you. Not a bad start, but you'll need much more to fit in among those you'll come across in Texas."

Jesse stepped out of the wagon into the bright son, and for the first time, Henry got a good look at the man who was being so generous with him and his brother. He could see that this broad-shoulder man was of medium build, and his skin was a pale mahogany color. He could also see that his face had been weathered by the many forays he had made into the vast plains. The grayish black of his uncut hair and bushy matching mustache set apart this man, who must have been in his fifties. His hands were calloused from holding the reins of his oxen, horses and working hard outside for all his life. His greenish eyes sparkled. He was happy with his hard life, and he somehow made everyone who he came in contact with him feel better about themselves.

Jesse showed them how to tie around their necks their bandanas. He was proud to put their hats on, saying, "These hats are the latest models. They're worth their weight in gold. They're made from beaver fur. Their wide brims keep the sun out, and they help when it rains. They are fitted with rawhide stampede strings, so you can tie your hats tight in those Texas windstorms. Their flat tops also make you less of a target."

Henry and Randy were busting with happiness over their unexpected gifts and thanked Jesse repeatedly for his generosity. Jesse humbly said, "I wish I had more to give you because you need much more. When you are able, you should get some Texas boots. And if you ever work as a cowpuncher, you should get some stirrups that fit your boots. You could also get some new belts for your pants and one to go around your hats that matches your boots. You'll probably also need some chaps to protect your legs. Once you see some people on the open range in Texas, you'll see better what you need. You may also need a quirt. I've never been a cattle drover myself, so I really don't know all the ins and outs of being a wrangler. I can blaze trails for cattle to follow, but I don't know how to drive cattle to follow trails."

"And another thing. The kind of horses you have won't last long in Texas country. You'll need Mustang horses. These are wild horses that have been broken. They're able to handle Texas' tough conditions. You'll also need working saddles and so much more."

Henry and Randy were impressed by all the words Jesse was expressing and thought he had run out of words when he said. "I've been saving the best for last." He reached into the back of his wagon and pulled out a couple of finely woven ropes. "These are lassos with a fixed loop at their ends. You cannot live in Texas unless you know how to use a lasso. You always need a lasso attached to the saddle of your horses. It can be of many uses, but its main use is to rope and tie unruly steers. You got to learn how to use a lasso. Next to knowing how to use a gun is the use of a lasso. I'll give you a demonstration, and then I have to go and check on my sick people."

Jesse showed Henry and Randy how to hold the rope and twirl it over their heads before throwing it so it looped over a tree stump. Jesse expertly looped his lasso over the stump and pulled the lasso tight around it. He then asked, "OK, you guys try it."

Both Henry and Randy failed miserably at trying to lasso the stump. They had never done this before and were beginning to think they could never learn how to use a lasso. Despite many words of encouragement and interventions to correct their efforts at using the lasso, Henry and Randy could not lasso the stump. Their failure amused Jesse, who said after some time, "It isn't an easy thing to get the hang of. It takes almost daily practice for weeks. But, if you can't lasso, you can't brand cattle, and that is one of the main tasks of a plains cow hand."

Henry and Randy did not understand some of the words Jesse said. Their failure to lasso the stump prompted Henry to say, "Mr. Jesse, do we have to deal with cows?"

Jesse laughed and said, "No sense going to Texas if you are not going to be with cows. That's what they have the most down there. The Civil War shut down most of the markets for their cattle, so they have a surplus of cattle now, and the number of head of Texas longhorns will only increase as long as the war goes on."

"I'm sure there are other things to do in Texas, but we sure want to be among the best lassoers Texas has ever seen."

Jesse quietly laughed and said, "That's the spirit. Keep practicing while I go check on my sick people."

Randy asked Henry, "What should we do with our old clothes?"

Henry was quick to reply, "Save them. We may need them in case we have to change clothes."

Jesse walked back to the main camp while Henry and Randy kept tossing their lassos. This practice helped pass the time. When it became late afternoon, they went back to their spot to eat and, graze, and water their two horses. Night fell, and still no sign of Jesse. Their arms were sore from lasso practice. They finally wrapped themselves in their blankets to fend off the cool night air and went to sleep.

At dawn, Jesse hovered over them and softly repeated several times. "Boys. Time to get up and head to Texas."

Henry and Randy stood up, and Henry said, "Give us a few minutes to get ready. How are your sick people?"

Jesse cleared his throat and hesitantly said, "It is considered impolite to talk about those who are no longer with us. Suffice to say they are peacefully now in the spirit world."

Henry looked up to the mounted Jesse and saw his face distorted with grief. He wanted to express his sympathies for the departed but felt it would be unwise to do so. He was spared from bringing any words on this sad subject up again when Jesse said, "You should know that diseases brought by the white man have killed more Indians than wars or forced removals. The Indians have no resistance to cholera, smallpox, or any of the other maladies that the whites have brought to our country."

Muttering, Henry hung his head. "Sorry, Mr. Jesse. I didn't know that."

Jesse solemnly replied, "Son. There are many truthful facts that you and your brother don't know. You both have much to learn about the wrongs done to my people and to everyone else who doesn't agree with the greedy money class."

All Henry could say in response was, "Yes, sir. We got a lot to learn."

Jesse said, "Too much talk. Let's go now. I got two braves… one to lead the way and another to follow. Get on your horses and move south."

They trudged through the tall grass, avoiding clumps of trees and cockle burr patches. They kept going for hours across the wide valleys and up and down the low hills. They kept going south in spite of the penetrating rays of the sun. Henry and Randy were happy about how the wide brims of their new hats shaded their faces and how their bandanas protected their neck from the sun.

Jesse appeared to know where he was. He briefly talked to the lead scout, who trotted off on his horse until he could no longer be seen. Suddenly, Henry was startled and pulled his pistol and fired it instinctively into the tall grass. The noise of his shot brought everyone to an immediate halt, and the scouts came quickly back to see what had happened. Jesse stayed calm and looked around and saw, laying in the grass, a dead armadillo. Jesse looked at Henry and said with a serious look on his face, "Now, because of a dumb, harmless animal, the whole world knows of our presence. Never make such a loud noise unless your life is in danger. Let that be a lesson for you. Let's go."

Randy rode up alongside Henry to ask him, "What's an armadillo?"

Henry replied, "I don't know, and I'm afraid to ask. All I know is what I did was stupid. I need to control my impulses."

Night was approaching, and they made camp in a short grassy spot near a stream. The size of the moon in the night sky told Henry and Randy they had been with Jesse and his band of Indians for about a month. After they had roasted and eaten a couple of rabbits the scouts had caught by chasing them and hitting them over the head with their tomahawk hammers, Henry apologized to Jesse for the noise he made earlier in the day and timidly asked, "What's an armadillo? I never seen one before."

Jesse, in an untroubled and calm voice, said softly, "Don't worry, son. I understand. You'll be seeing plenty of armadillos where you're going. They are harmless creatures that mainly live off ants and termites. When attacked, they often roll up into a ball. The hard, leathery exterior protects them. Their name comes from the Spanish… 'little armored ones.' On that note, you need to realize that most of the Texas territory was under control of the Spanish, and many of the people you'll encounter are Spanish-speaking Mexicans. This was their land. Of course, they took it away from the Indians who have been here forever."

Jesse did not like talking too much, but he was not finished yet in giving Henry and Randy some background on the place they planned to settle down. He continued by saying, "So leave the armadillo alone. Other new animals you will see are prairie dogs. Best to give them a wide birth as the holes they make in the ground are bad on horses' legs. They usually make their homes in short grass areas."

"One more thing you got to know. You will run up against thorny mesquite trees in the Texas scrubland you must go through. Nothing you can do but wind your way around these nuisance trees. And where you find these trees, you'll also probably find patches of cactus. Avoid mesquite thorns and prickly cactus, as they both can do serious harm. Also, mean varmints and rattlesnakes like to make their homes in the snarl of thorny mesquites. Always have your guns at the ready when you're finding your way around the nasty mesquites."

Jesse paused for a few minutes, smacked his lips, and sighed before saying. "I'm sorry to see you go to Texas, but I have nothing to offer that can stop you. I feel like you are going to your deaths in Texas. Please don't die. I wouldn't want that to be on my conscience."

A pensive Jesse had more to say. "There is so much that can kill you in Texas. There are bandits, rustlers, renegade Indians, and numerous criminal cutthroat gangs. We especially fear attacks by vicious Comanche Indians. If you encounter a cruel war party of these Indians, you are as good as dead."

After Jesse said these somber words, Henry rejoined by saying, "Thanks, Mr. Jesse. I can see my brother, and I have a lot to learn. We have to learn to stay alive. Maybe we'll have some luck and survive."

Jesse exhaled a big breath and said, "Now, let's get some shut-eye. We got a long day's ride ahead of us tomorrow."

# Chapter Fourteen
# Red River

Daybreak came fast, cutting short Henry and Randy's deep slumber. Jesse and the Indian escorts, Wohali and Waya, were up and ready to break camp. Everyone was eager to keep heading south. They all wanted to see the Red River.

They continued to trek through the ups and downs of grassy land. Jesse became concerned when he spotted in the western sky a pile of scary storm clouds that were rapidly expanding and moving toward them. As the rumbling giant bank of clouds neared them, they grew darker and noisier. Henry and Randy had never seen such a furious buildup of storm clouds.

Jesse stopped to listen to the loud thunder and observe the lightning flashes. He was afraid the dry prairie would be set on fire by the lightning strikes. His biggest fear was that this kind of storm could spawn a tornado.

The wind picked up and started to blow to-and-fro, dust and natural debris were impeding their vision. As the wind speed increased, Jesse hollered, "Hurry. Let's look for a low spot to lay down in case a twister is in the works."

Henry and Randy did not know what Jesse was saying, but they could see that he was scared. They trotted their nervous horses alongside Jesse's horse to be more ready to follow his lead. The bright day turned dark as Jesse scanned the horizon for any suspected tornado funnels.

The wind blew harder, and it became more difficult to stay mounted. Jesse waved to the two scouts to take cover and guided Henry and Randy to a nearby culvert in which to hide until the storm passed. They made their horses lay down and prostrated themselves on the ground. Jesse screeched, "I see a twister comin'. Hopefully, we'll be safe here."

Henry and Randy were petrified. They had never experienced such ungodly weather. As they laid face down in the culvert with their hands over their heads, the roar of the wind above them sounded like a runaway locomotive. They were frightened out of their wits and thought they would all be killed. They held hands and said in hushed and strained voices their last goodbyes. Randy said in teary eyes, "Mom, we're about to join you."

Then, it was over much more quickly than it started. The storm rolled rapidly over them, leaving them unharmed. All was very still. There was a light drizzle, but soon that ended. The sun shone again brightly under a blue clear sky. Some birds were chirping their relief. Except for some sprinkles on the ground, it was like nothing had happened. The violent storm that had just traumatized them was like something they had dreamed.

Jesse sat up, smiled, and began humming a Cherokee song. He stood up and called in his language to see if his two braves were okay. They yelped back in a like manner to indicate they were okay and ready to continue toward the Red River. Henry turned to Randy and said, "They are sure risking a lot to show us the way to the river. Too bad we have no way to repay them. Sad that we may never see them again."

They continued their journey south. Henry and Randy could see they were now following old wagon tracks which followed an even older Indian path. They thought the Indian path must be overlayed with an animal path. Jesse could see that they were looking at the scratchy tracks on the ground and said, "Yes, this an old way to the river, and I've traveled it with my oxen-drawn trade wagon. I had hoped to set up a trading post on this side of the river, but the war came along to upset my plans. If the war is ever over, this will become a busy passageway, and people will need to buy the things I got for sale."

Henry and Randy were impressed with Jesse's entrepreneurship and the harm the war was doing to his plans to profit from the white settlement of the vast plains. Their views were adjusted when Jesse continued by saying. "My top priority is to trade with the Indians, but the size of the Indian population is growing smaller while the numbers of white settlers is on a steady increase. I fear that when the war is over, we'll be swamped by people coming west."

The dirt turned a reddish color as they approached the Red River. Jesse said, "Don't let the color of the earth fool you. This soil is rich. The river gets its name from the reddish color of its water. Not much for drinking because of its dirty and salty taste, but that's really not a problem."

The thirsty horses could smell the water and nervously quickened their pace. Henry and Randy were quiet as they spied the slowly flowing stretch of red water before them. They rode their horses alongside Jesse, who said,

"There's the river, and there's Texas on the other side. Maybe best to make camp here tonight. Tomorrow morning, you can cross the river, and then we can part ways."

Henry and Randy both nodded their accord as they looked for a good place to cross the river. Jesse could see they were worried about the crossing and simply said, "Don't worry. I know the best place to cross. The river is not too deep as it is coming around a big bend."

The two scouts hunted down several rabbits and skinned them, guarding the hides for possible use later. They built a fire with dead wood and some driftwood scattered around their campsite on the riverbank. It was something of a feast with roasted rabbit and a couple of tins of beans that Jesse had somehow come up with. He opened the tins, placed them at the edge of the fire to heat them. After they were finished eating, Jesse and the two scouts slowly did a little Indian dance around the fire while they chanted some Indian words.

Randy and Henry watched them dance and chant, but they did not have a clue as to why they were doing as they did. They suddenly stopped, and Jesse turned to the two teenage white boys and said softly, "That was for you. We called upon our ancestors to watch over you and protect you as you go alone into Texas. Now, let us sleep so you can get an early start tomorrow."

The first rays of daylight came all too quickly. It was time for Henry and Randy to lead their horses across the river and go alone into Texas. They were scared, but they could not stay. While they were entertaining staying, Jesse said, "I wish you could stay, but you can't. The winters here are terribly bitter, and if we don't find any buffalo and the winter is anything like the last one, we're all dead. Better you take your chances in Texas. Try to move as far south as you can to warmer weather before winter sets in."

Henry and Randy were speechless. Finally, Henry was able to say sincerely, "Mr. Jesse. We're thankful for all you've done for us. We wish we were in a position to help you and your band. We feel so helpless and lost."

Jesse replied, "Don't worry about any of that. If you want to do something for me, let all those you meet in Texas know of this river crossing and the trail that leads north. I'm thinking that the war will end some day and all the cattle in Texas will have to go to markets in the north. As far as I'm concerned, this is the best place to cross the Red and head north."

Henry and Randy knew this was speculation on Jesse's part, but they wished him well and assured him that if they stayed alive in Texas, they would spread the word about his crossing and trail. Jesse smiled and said, "Well, that's that. Get yourselves and horses ready to cross the Red and go to Texas."

Jesse followed Henry and Randy to the water's edge while the two braves stood on the bank, watching their every move. Jesse said his final goodbye to Henry and Randy and added. "You should be able to wade straight across without any difficulty. It doesn't look like that yesterday's storm dumped much water into the river. Watch out for holes and be prepared to swim if you fall into one. One never knows because the riverbed is constantly shifting. The most dangerous thing is quicksand spots."

Henry and Randy shook Jesse's hand and said their final goodbyes. They tied their boots around their necks as they began to tread the thirty yards or so across the river. They walked through the waist-high water, and all was going smoothly until Randy yelled, "I'm stuck."

Henry was alarmed by Randy's situation. Jesse, from his position on the bank, hollered, "Grab your horse's tail."

Randy quickly did as Jesse commanded, and he became unstuck and on his way. Both he and Henry reached the other bank and walked out of the water, turning to wave to Jesse and the two braves, indicating they were okay. Jesse and the two braves stood in their places until Randy and Henry disappeared into the Texas side of the great plains. When Jesse and his two braves could not see Henry and Randy anymore, they slowly started on their return to their home camp. In silence, they knew this unexpected chapter in their struggle for survival was over.

Randy took out his compass to see if they were moving south. Jesse had told them they should try to reach Ft. Worth and look for work. They only had the vaguest idea of where Ft. Worth was, but Jesse had told them they should find tracks leading to the Ft. Worth settlement. He had told them that the Army had abandoned its fort years ago, but some people were trying to make a town of the place. They estimated it would take them a couple of weeks to reach Ft. Worth.

Their eyes were on the lookout for other people and tracks. They looked in every direction for any signs of life. Their idea was to keep going all day and make camp while there was still some daylight. They continued in a southerly direction the best they could, but as Jesse had told them, they could not always go in the direction they wanted because of thorny mesquite tree and cactus patches.

They managed to move ahead all day and decided to make camp in a stream bed that was almost dry but with a few pools of water for their horses and them to drink. They filled their canteens and made a small fire, although they decided to munch on hardtack biscuits. They wanted their horses to rest and graze. They also wanted to try to catch some shut-eye and get an early start tomorrow.

Strange noises in the dark night perturbed their sleep. They could not wait for it to get light so they could be on their way. The spooky place they were in was not to their liking. Henry mumbled to Randy, "Our first night in Texas, and I'm uncomfortable as all get out. Maybe Texas takes some getting used to."

They welcomed the first rays of the sun in the eastern sky, and before the sun peaked over the eastern horizon, they were well on their way. They hoped to see some signs of tracks that would lead then to Ft. Worth. The midday sun bore down on them relentlessly. They were getting sleepy when rifle shots buzzed by their heads. They immediately jumped off their horses and pulled them down to hide with them in the tall grass. They had their rifles at the ready to defend themselves. They instinctively knew that when someone shoots at you, it is easy to shoot back, and if you survive, you can ask any questions later.

They heard horses galloping toward them. They had their rifles pointed in the direction of the pounding horses' hooves. They were ready to fire, but when the horsemen came into view, it was not as they expected. There before them were representatives of the Texas they were looking for. Two vaqueros sitting tall in their saddles with their rifles leveled at them.

They dropped their rifles and raised their hands above the grass. The two men on their horses rode up close to them, laughed loudly, and said words in a language Henry and Randy had never heard before. They could see that these men were surprised to find them and had many questions about how they got here, but they could not understand them. They stood up and were in awe of the sight before them… two genuine vaqueros.

They could tell they were different. They did not know if their skin color was tanned from the sun or if it were a natural color. The two men could see that Henry and Randy did not understand any Spanish. One of the men tried to say in the little he knew of English. "My Inglesa not good. Lo, siento to shoot at you. There are only bad Comanche Indians aqui. We vaqueros. Work at Palo Pinto Ranch."

Henry tried to cut through a tense situation by saying, "My name is Henry, and this is my younger brother, Randy. We're looking for Ft. Worth.

"Mi Carlos and este hombre est Juan. La pista a Ft. Worth ahi."

Henry and Randy had many more questions, as did the two men on horseback, but the language barrier prevented them from conversing. Henry could only say, "Thank you." He hoped they understood at least these simple words.

Carlos, who seemed to be the talkative one, said, "No hay de que. Nos vamos. Siganos. Vamos a ver la pista de Ft. Worth."

Henry and Randy did not understand his words, but they knew from his hand signals that they wanted them to follow. They mounted their horses and followed the jabbering pair, carefully examining their every move, how they were dressed, their Mustang horses, and all the gear that was on their horses. They trailed behind them for a couple of hours, listening to them talk… trying to pick up some of their words.

They halted, and Carlos turned to them and said, "Aqui est la pista de Ft. Worth. No se combien de dias por llegar pero yo se que est el rio Santa Trinidad est cerca de Ft. Worth. Buen suerte. Adios."

Carlos and Juan rode off quickly in a swirl of dust in the direction they had come. Henry looked at Randy and said, "They were really helpful. I wish we could have communicated because I'm sure they could have taught us a lot. Anyway, we now can see the way to Ft. Worth. Let's go."

# Part II: Texas Life

# Chapter Fifteen
# Fort Worth

They went as far as they could. They rode their horses along the fading tracks through sprouts of tall grass until their butts became so sore they dismounted and walked. Their saddle sores hobbled the pace of their walking. They walked as long and as far as they could before collapsing beneath the partial shade of a lonely oak tree.

They thought they would have reached the river mentioned by Carlos by now. They and their horses needed water. They were hungry, but they had little left to eat, and they were more tired than hungry. Their canteens were dry, and their horses were weak from thirst. There was no water anywhere around the place of their collapse, but they could not go on. They were totally spent.

They laid down on the ground and fell fast asleep. Their bodies were exhausted. They needed rest. Their horses also laid down while they tried to nibble on the sparse grass near them. Henry's last thought before he dozed off was that maybe this would be his last sleep on Earth.

Henry and Randy were startled awake by someone kicking them in their sides. They feebly screamed, "Please stop. We ain't dead yet."

The strange, tall dude who hovered above them with his horse and rifle said, "Sorry. You're an unexpected sight. You looked dead, so I thought I would find out if you were alive or dead, so I kicked you. Anyway, you two don't look like you should be here."

Henry struggled to utter some words. "Please, mister. We're almost dead from a lack of water and food."

"Well, I don't got much food, but you can have some of my beef jerky. As for water, there's a whole river not far from here."

As he handed some jerky to them, he said, "My name is Jake, and I'm hunting varmints to take back to Ft. Worth. There're a few people left in this tiny settlement, but they don't have much to eat."

Henry and Randy could not believe they were so near the river and that there was no food in Ft. Worth. The jerky was beginning to give Henry some energy, and he said weakly, "Damn. I thought we'd find plenty of food and some work in Ft. Worth."

Jake replied in an understanding voice, "Most people left Ft. Worth as the war cut off supplies and their business ideas sunk. The few that are left are scraping rock bottom as they try to survive in and around the old army stockade. There's nothing for you boys in Ft. Worth. How did you get here anyway?"

Henry reluctantly told Jake snippets of their story and introduced themselves. Henry then pleaded with the middle-aged Jake to allow them to travel with him to the river and on to Ft. Worth. Jake readily said, "No problem. Get ready to go. No good hunting around here anyway. Maybe your arrival will get the mayor to kill another one of his beef cattle. By the way, are you sure your horses can make it? They look plum worn out. It would be good to get them to the fort. It's been a long time since I ate horse meat."

Henry and Randy stood up on wobbly legs, and Henry tried to be strong and say, "Give us a minute, and we and our horses we'll be ready to go. We just need water, and we'll be okay."

They were only about thirty yards away from the narrow river. They all drank their fill and made sure their canteens were topped off. Jake kept an eye on them. He seemed to be amused by their foreign ways. He watched the boys and said, "Easy to see you boys are not from these parts and aren't used to life in Texas."

Henry was quick to reply, "That may be true now, but we're bound to adapt and become Texans."

Henry's words and the force with which he said them made Jake laugh. When he was finished with his smirky laugh, he said, "Well, I think there must be a place somewhere in this big land for you. Can you read and write properly?"

Henry was hesitant to reply. He looked to see what Randy thought. He finally said, "Yeah, we've been to school."

Jake said, "That's interesting. With your school learnin' and shootin' skills, there's got to be a place for you in Texas. Besides, we need more white people. Most of the people in Texas are Spanish-speaking Mexicans and no good Indian tribes."

"I guess that's the truth."

"Of course it is. We whites took this land away from Mexico after they had taken most of it away from the Indians. We're still fighting to conquer these peoples. Anyway, most people in Texas speak Spanish, so it is handy to know some Spanish words."

This prompted Henry to tell Jake of their encounter with Carlos and Juan and how they almost shot them because they mistook them for Comanche. Jake said, "Yeah. I've also met those two hombres. They're real Mexican vaqueros. They and their ancestors have been fighting the Comanche for generations. I know they fear the Comanche, and for good reason… they are the most savage of the Indian tribes. They're afraid they'll set the plains on fire. They have a lot of cattle at the Palo Pinto ranch west of here, but there is nowhere to market them. Maybe they'll round them up and try to take them west. I reckon their ranch is a two- or three-day ride west of here."

"We forgot to tell them that if they ever want to drive cattle north, they might want to use the trail we followed to cross the Red River," Henry added.

Jake said, "They may do just that if the Indians have been chased farther west and there is a market for cattle up north."

They waded across the narrow river as Jake said, "Once we are across the Trinidad, we can follow the trail to Ft. Worth. The old military stockade sits on a bluff above the Trinidad."

The water they had drunk had given them and their horses the renewed life they needed to make the remaining trek to Ft. Worth. When they arrived in the small settlement of Ft. Worth, they found mostly a ghost town. Jake took them to the old stone-wood stockade to report on his efforts to hunt some game and introduce them. The mayor was an elderly, well-clothed, bespectacled man of medium stature. He shook Henry and Randy's hands and said, "My name is Morton. Welcome to Ft. Worth. I regret that we do not have much to offer you except we have a surplus of lodgings. Most of our people left because there was no goods they needed to survive. Of course, as you know, this penury was caused by the war. Keep in mind that Texas is a Confederate state."

Henry and Randy thanked the mayor for his warm welcome, and Henry said, "Thanks for the lodging, but what we need the most is food for us and our horses."

Morton replied, "I guess we can butcher one more steer to celebrate

117

your arrival, but after that, you are on your own as far as food is concerned. As for your horses, they look like they are at the end of their rope. We can consider taking your horses in exchange for some surplus Mustangs we have. Of course, your horses will be for eatin.'"

After discussing with Randy, Henry said, "Mr. Mayor, you got yourself a deal."

Mayor Morton said, "Good. Glad to see some new people in Ft. Worth. We're not much to look at now, but we should be okay as soon as the war is over. Now Jake can show you a place to stay. I look forward to seeing you at our big beef celebration barbecue this evening."

Jake led then to a tiny house next to the stockade and said dryly, "You can put up here for the night. I'll be by later to go with you to our feast. At that time, I'll bring your new horses and take your old ones. We'll need to check if your old saddles fit on the Mustangs. See y'all later."

Henry and Randy looked inside of the empty two-room, rickety wooden house and started feeling lucky. They could not remember the last time they had slept under a roof. There was even a water well and a pit latrine out back so they could drink and wash up. They could not believe their good fortune... a place to stay, fresh horses, and real meat to eat. It was all too good to be true.

They unsaddled their horses and thanked them for their faithful services. It was sad to know their fate, but it was seen as a necessary step in their Texas adventure. Just as promised, Jake showed up with two shiny, well-fed brown mustangs with black manes and tails. They looked like twins. He attached their reins to hitching posts on the frontage road and said, "Here's your two new horses. They've been all checked out and fitted with new shoes by our local blacksmith. Now, let's see if your old saddles can fit them."

Henry and Randy dragged their old saddles off the front porch and put them on their new horses. They could quickly see there was no way they could fit. Jake said, "Just as I thought. Now, I got some lighter and wider cowboy saddles that'll be a good fit. I'll tell you what. I'll do you a favor and trade you two new saddles for your old ones. I'll bring my saddles later in my wagon for a look-see."

Henry and Randy took a quick look at each other, and then Henry said, "You got yourself a deal."

Jake grinned and said, "My new saddles are different from what you're

used to, but once you break them in, you'll find them more comfortable…
for you and your horses."

Jake then looked at their feet and shook his head. "That won't do.
Those old high-top shoes should be tossed on the trash heap. You need
western boots, especially since you are wearing the latest model hats."

Henry quickly retorted, "Can't argue with you there, but where in the
tarnation can we get some boots?"

Jake smiled and then said, "You know, before I came here, I was a
sutler following the Confederate troops of General Stand Waite in Indian
Territory. I lost money and goods in that effort. They paid me in worthless
Confederacy currency, and the Indians fought among themselves. I fled to
Ft. Smith, and there was nothing there, so I took the military road to Texas
and ended up here. I was attacked along the way by vicious guerillas and
lost a lot of goods. Somehow, I ended up here. I still have a lot of goods,
but there's no money here."

Jake was not done talking. "I got some fine western boots made by the
best cobblers in Kansas. I'm sure I got boots that'll fit you. But I can't give
them away. Each pair costs more than a month's pay. If you have any
money, I could part with them for what I paid for them."

Henry and Randy huddled together out of earshot of Jake to discuss
his boot offer. Randy reminded Henry that he still had the money that he
took off the guys he killed in Tennessee. Henry urged Randy to do the
bargaining with Jake. Randy turned to Jake and said in a business-like
manner. "It looks like you may have a deal, but it depends on how much
you want for the boots."

Jake replied, "I reckon I can part with them for ten Yankee dollars."

Randy returned to Henry, who agreed with the deal. Randy pretended
to go into the adjoining room to look for his money even though he always
kept his money deep in his pocket. He pulled the wad of bills out of his
pocket and pulled out a ten-dollar bill. He walked back to Jake and tendered
him the bill, saying, "Here's your ten dollars. Now, where's our boots?"

"I'll bring your boots later when I come to fetch you in my wagon late
this afternoon for our feast at the fort. Okay. You'll also need some spurs,
but I don't have any of those. Anyway, you'll learn as you go all that you'll
need to look the part you want to play."

Henry responded, "Okay. By the way, do you have any soap? We
would like to clean up before we gorge ourselves."

Jake could not help but laugh and say, "I got lots of soap. I have a couple of bars in my saddle bag that I can give you for free. It's lye soap. So be careful, as it can take off your skin."

Jake walked quickly to his horse to get the soap bar. He handed a bar of soap to Henry, saying, "See you later."

Henry and Randy quickly went behind the house and stripped down to wash themselves with soap. Taking turns, they poured water over themselves with an old wooden strapped bucket. They then debated whether they should wash their clothes, too, and if they would be dry enough to wear to the feast. They decided to wash their clothes and spread them on some nearby bushes in the sun to dry. They even washed their dirty muslin underwear.

They were having so much fun and feeling so good that they took turns in cutting off their dangling whiskers and cutting with Henry's pocketknife their lengthy strands of hair. They used an old horse brush to make their hair on their heads lay down and rid it of any bugs. They looked and felt like new men. They turned over their clothes on the bushes before wrapping themselves in their frayed blankets so they could take a nap on the hardwood floors of their shack.

They had trouble dozing as they could faintly hear somebody playing over and over a popular tune on a harmonica. Repeatedly, they heard a lively version of Dixie. The incessant harmonica music of this rousing tune finally stopped, and they drifted off into a deep sleep.

For them, it did not get much better than this. They had made it alive to Texas. All they needed now was something to do that paid them a living wage. This was the first day of their new lives in Texas, and they could not wait to see what tomorrow would bring.

# Chapter Sixteen
# On the Trail South

Jake's tall and lanky body frame hovered over the sleeping Henry and Randy. He kicked them both in the sides, saying wryly, "I never thought I'd have to wake you twice in the same day. Get up. Time to go."

Henry and Randy sprang to their senses from a deep slumber. They stepped slowly in their bare feet out the back door to fetch their clothes on the bushes and rapidly dress. Their somnolent antics made Jake laugh. They came back into the house with their woolen socks in hand to find their old high-top shoes. They slipped on their damp socks and were about to wiggle their feet into their shoes when Jake loudly produced a fake cough and said, "Wait a minute. I got somethin' fer you."

Jake ran outside to his wagon to fetch two new pair of western boots. He turned and quickly entered the house, displaying in each hand a pair of western boots. He proudly said, "Here you are. The best boots this side of the Mississippi."

Henry and Randy looked at Jake with wide eyes. They had almost forgotten the boots for which they had paid Jake earlier. Henry exclaimed, "Wow. Let's try them on now."

Jake handed the boots to Henry and Randy and chuckled while he watched them struggle to get their feet into them. It took some effort, but when they thought their new boots were sufficiently in place, they stood up and tried to take a few awkward steps. They wobbled to-and-fro. The boots hurt their feet, and they thought they could never get used to them. Nonetheless, Henry tried to sound upbeat when he said to Jake. "I think they're a good fit, but it will take some time to break them in. It's a done deal."

Jake had the satisfaction of saying, "Good. Now, let's go. Don't forget your hats and bandanas. With these and your boots, you are startin' to look the part. We'll take my wagon cuz there are many thieves lurking about. You better tie your new horses at the back of the house so you don't tempt anyone to steal them. You can ride with me. I hope you're hungry cuz we got a lot of food to eat."

Henry and Randy hustled to do as Jake asked and climbed onto the buckboard seat of his wagon to sit next to him. He grabbed the reins to his two mules, and off they went, quickly covering the short distance to the old stockade. Mayor Morton welcomed them and led them to sit near him in front of a huge campfire. Jake sat near them with a guy playing the harmonica. There must have been at least a hundred people gathered for the feast. Everyone was in a festive mood in spite of all their troubles. It was as if their gaiety had been spawned by the bleak circumstances.

Somebody sounded a metal gong, and the mayor stood to say a few words. "We are here tonight to celebrate the arrival of our two new guests, Henry and Randy. They are from the East, but somehow, they have found their way to our humble settlement. Now, let's toast to them our warmest welcome before we eat all we can."

Henry and Randy squirmed inside themselves as they stood to receive their welcoming toast. They had never been honored in such a way. There were calls for a speech. There was no way the introverted Randy could talk. The mild-manner older brother, Henry, had never been put in such a spot but felt the obligation to say. "Thank you for such a warm welcome. We've come a long way and endured much, but there is no doubt that tonight is the highlight of our travels. We can't think you enough."

The mayor said in a loud voice, "Let's dig in."

With the mayor's words, the man with the harmonica began to play vigorously his rendition of Dixie, and the few women in the group started passing out plates heaped with roasted beef. Henry and Randy ate with their hands and devoured the delicious meat. As guests of honor, they were also served full plates of cooked grits and greens.

They stuffed themselves to the point of throwing up. Out of somewhere, a bottle of whiskey began to make the rounds. The bottle was handed to both Henry and Randy and to their surprise, they both took hearty swigs before passing it on to the next person. Randy thought that this moment represented something like a rite of passage for them.

People began prancing around the campfire to the Dixie tune, singing loudly all the words they knew. Henry and Randy were invited to dance with them. They really did not want to dance, but they knew they could not refuse the invitation to do so. As they walked toward the fire to dance, the mayor watched them and chuckled when he said to Jake, who had come to sit beside him. "They sure walk funny."

Jake laughed and simply said, "New boots. Maybe all that dancing will help break them in."

Jake continued to talk the mayor, "You know me and my partner plan to be leavin' early tomorrow. There's no money here, and I still have a lot of goods to sell. They don't know it yet, but I plan to take those two boys with me. There's nothin' here for them. We need to go someplace where there is money. From the little I hear, the only place in Texas like that is the Cotton Road in the far south."

The emotional mayor had tears in his eyes when he reacted to Jake's words. "I can't blame you. If I were a younger man, I would leave too. All I can say is that I wish you the best of luck. Maybe I'll see you again after the war."

After spending a while with the mayor, Jake indicated to the man playing the harmonica that he was preparing to leave the party. He then went up close to Henry and Randy and said in a way he could be heard over the noisy crowd. "You boys about ready to go? Did you eat enough?"

Henry went up close to Jake and in an energetic voice, "Yes, siree Bob. We're feeling good. Just like well-fed wolves. When you want to go?"

Without hesitation, Jake replied, "Now, cuz we got an early start tomorrow."

Henry was perplexed over Jake's reference to their departure tomorrow and wanted to ask him what he meant, but instead, he called to Randy, "Let's go."

With feet made sore by new boots, they followed Jake to his mule wagon. They took their seats, and Jake turned his team of mules to exit the fort in the moonlit night. Henry could not contain himself and asked Jake, point blank, "What did you mean by we leave tomorrow?"

Jake replied, "I just decided that leavin' tomorrow is as good as anytime. There is nothin' here for us. The only place in Texas there is any good money to be made is along the Cotton Road, which is much farther south. Sorry, but my mind is made up. You can do as you please. Stay or come with me and my partner. We leave early in the morning. I'll come by with your new saddles. You can give me your answer then."

Jake stopped his wagon in front of their shack and said, "See you tomorrow at daybreak."

Henry and Randy entered their place, lit a couple of candles, and checked on their new horses. Neither of them said a word. They laid down to sleep, and Henry said softly, "Let's sleep on this one and make a decision when we wake up tomorrow."

Randy responded, "Okidoke."

They both lay awake for a long time. The Texas wind was blowing hard outside. It was as if the wind was telling them to go deeper into Texas and leave this refuge. They had to make lives for themselves, and it was not here.

Henry woke up early and saw that his younger brother was not sleeping either, so he asked, "What are you doing?"

Randy replied, "Getting ready to leave."

Henry spread a big grin across his usually dour face and exclaimed, "Yippee. On the trail again."

Jake was happy to see the two boys ready to leave when he rolled up in his trade wagon pulled by four mules. Jake yelled, "Get your horses ready and follow us. Sitting next to me is my partner, Elmer. Maybe you heard him play his harmonica. Let's go. The Waco Trail is calling us."

Henry and Randy hustled to get their horses ready and mount them for the first time to rush to follow Jake's wagon, which was already a good distance away. They easily caught up to Jake's wagon. They rode slowly their new horses behind his wagon. They thought there would be a stop for lunch, but Jake drove his wagon almost straight south for the entire day.

When they finally stopped in a shady place near a creek, Jake told Elmer to gather wood and start a fire to cook dinner. The word 'dinner' pricked Henry and Randy's ears. They were eager to get settled and eat. Elmer set a campfire ablaze and, cooked up some grits, and boiled some coffee. With full stomachs, all had found comfortable places to bed down.

There was a bit of a chill in the night air, but under their woolen sleeping blankets, they were comfortably snug. Henry and Randy had their bare feet sticking out of their woolen cocoons because the cool air felt good on the blisters caused by breaking in their new boots. In spite of their foot pains, they valued their boots and placed them near their heads and always ready rifles and Henry's old pistols.

Their main complaint was Elmer's repeated playing on his well-worn harmonica of the same song, Dixie. Henry became so irritated that he asked Elmer, "Don't you know how to play somethin' else?"

Elmer removed the harmonica from his lips and said, "I'd sure like to be able to play something else, but I don't hear any other music out here in the open range, and I have to hear it to play it."

Henry thought about Elmer's reply for a few minutes and said, "Okay. I understand, but maybe you can play a little more softly. After all, we don't want to attract unwanted visitors."

Elmer stopped playing after hearing Henry's words and said, "Goodnight."

Jake had a good laugh after this brief exchange and said, "Yes, goodnight. We got to get an early start tomorrow if we are to make more grassland tracks toward Alleyton and the Cotton Road."

Henry could not keep his mouth shut and just go to sleep. "Mr. Jake. I'm sorry. It's late, but I don't understand what you mean by the Cotton Road?"

Jake responded, "Son, the way I understand it, cotton is bought cheap from east Texas farmers and middlemen smuggling cotton from Louisiana by running the Yankee blockades on the Mississippi River and hauling it all the way across the border to Mexico, where ten times more is paid in gold for it. Sounds like a good money-making deal to me. And we get to see a whole another part of Texas."

Henry scratched his head and said, "I don't git it. What happens to the cotton in Mexico?"

"Well, I guess they ship it to Europe, which depends on cotton from the south for its cloth mills, but the war and the Yankee blockades cut the supply," quickly interjected Jake.

Now, Randy's curiosity was pricked by the exchange between Jake and his big brother. "So the wagons return empty after they unload the cotton in Mexico?"

Jake did not have a good answer for Randy's question but said, "I suppose they back haul arms and ammunition for the South with money made from the sale of cotton."

Randy sat up and raised his voice to say, "Who's they?"

Jake replied, "I don't rightly know, but with that much money at play, I bet there are a lot of hands I' greased."

Randy was getting frustrated and blurted out, "So this is really a scheme to get goods for the South so it can keep fighting against the North. It's like we're helping make the war longer while we are trying to get far away from the war."

Randy's words made Henry uncomfortable, and he said bluntly, "Yeah, by helping the cotton road, we're participating in the war on the side of the Confederacy."

These words agitated Jake, and he said, "I don't care what side it helps as long as I make a good profit."

Henry sleepily replied by saying, "I guess we're all guilty and ready to sell our souls to the devil for a few pieces of gold."

Elmer, who had been staying out of this conversation, popped up by saying, "Maybe you're right, but this is the best choice we have. Otherwise, we're all dead anyway."

Elmer had the final word, and they all dozed off into the gentle night to await the first sign of tomorrow's daylight. Henry and Randy were tormented deeply by the words exchanged and felt trapped in a situation they did not like. But they had no choice but to forge ahead toward Waco. They took things a day at a time, letting each day's experiences sink in and inform their judgements.

The next day came, and they were up at first light. They washed their eyes in puddles in the creek and went about their usual routines of checking their horses and saddling them, helping Jake fetch his four mules and hitching them to the wagon. Elmer took over, rekindling the fire and, cooking up some grits, and boiling a few cups of coffee. They spent little time for breakfast and were rolling south before the sun was fully up. They hoped to cover another ten or twelve miles before the sun went down.

In many ways, it was a solitary journey through the unending grassland and clumps of mesquite thickets and ornery patches of cactus. There were times Henry and Randy wondered if they had done the right thing to run away from their home territory. But they both realized it was too late to turn back, and the rest of their lives, for better or worse, lay before them and not behind them.

# Chapter Seventeen
# Fire on the Trail

This second day on the Waco Trail was just like the last. Henry was already tired of riding every day through the endless scrubland. His saddle was more comfortable, but the landscape was too monotonous. At their third night of camping on the trail, Henry said. "I can't wait to get to Waco and see some other people and stuff."

Jake hesitated and said, "I'm sorry, but we're not going anywhere near the settlement of Waco. Sure, there are more people there than in Ft. Worth, but that means there are more thieves. I can't risk losing my goods to thieves and wayward Indians by going into Waco. We'll be taking a trail that leaves Waco and the Brazos River to the east of us."

Henry was saddened to hear this news. He had counted on going to Waco and having a good time, and now Jake had taken that dream away from him. It was the thought of arriving in Waco that had kept him going. Now, he had to exercise true grit and bear the monotony of the long trail to Alleyton. He was not sure he and his little brother could endure another couple of weeks on the dusty trail under a sun that was increasingly hot.

Henry replied to Jake in a whiny tone, "I suppose we'll not see Austin either."

Jake replied, "Why, the trail we're taking goes way to the east of Austin. Even if we're going closer to Austin, I would avoid it like the plague … too many thieves and tons of runaway slaves."

"So, you tellin' us that we'll not see another livin' soul til we get to Alleyton?"

Jake curtly replied to Henry, "I hope so. Right, Elmer?"

Elmer rolled over in his bed to face the others and said blithely, "Yep. I've been this way before, and that is how it is."

Henry was not happy with Jake and Elmer's words, but he saw that he had no choice but to accept their situation. He told himself that he had to get used to the lonely trails in this vast country. Randy could see that Henry was not happy and said, "I guess we have to understand where we are and force ourselves to adapt to this new life."

Henry was in a bad mood and only said, "Yeah. Sure. Good night."

They were up early as usual and occupied with their morning chores when Randy asked Henry, "Do you smell something funny?"

Upon hearing Randy's question, Henry took a deep breath through his nose to see if he smelled anything strange. His nose told him something was burning. He thought this was the morning cooking fire. Then he looked up and saw gray smoke across the western horizon. He immediately ran to find Jake and said, "Look. It looks like the whole country is on fire."

Jake dropped his rope, scanned the western skyline, and yelled, "It's a prairie fire. Get ready to go east now."

Jake turned to Henry and said, "I was afraid something like this would happen cuz it has been such a dry spring."

An excited Henry said, "What could start such a big fire?"

"Maybe dry lightning."

Henry had never heard of such a thing, but he hustled to get ready to depart and stay out of the oncoming blaze.

Jake talked to Elmer and told everyone. "Head east to stay ahead of the fire. The wind is pushing it our way. Maybe we can cross the Brazos River. If we can, we'll be safe."

Jake told Henry and Randy. "Gallop east as fast as you can to see if there is any waterway of any kind. We'll follow your tracks. Save yourselves, and don't worry about us. Nothin' we can do to stop the fire."

Henry looked Jake and Elmer in the eyes and nodded to Randy before saying, "Let's ride east faster than the wind."

They rode for several hours until they came to a stream bed full of water. Henry studied the low watercourse in front of them and quickly said, "You stay here. I'm goin' to backtrack a bit to see if Jake and Elmer are comin.'

Randy wanted to object, but Henry was off in a swirl of dust before he could open his mouth. All of sudden, it was quiet except for a trickling sound of the water in the stream flowing gently over its gravel bed. It dawned on him this was the first time since they left Virginia months ago that he had been separated from his big brother. He felt especially lonely and so very alone in this empty spot on the plains of east Texas.

Henry rode furiously as he scanned the western horizon for some sign of Jake and his wagon. The farther he rode, the harder it was to see through the smoke-filled air. He and his horse were exhausted. He was about to give up hope of ever seeing Jake and Elmer again when he saw a dot coming toward him through the haze. He stopped his horse and waved wildly his hat in the direction of the dot.

Slowly, the dot came into focus, and a broad smile broke out on his face… it was Jake and Elmer lumbering toward him in their wagon. He never had thought he would be so happy to see Jake and Elmer, but deep down, he knew he needed them more than they needed him. He understood they were trying to help Randy and him find a life for themselves in Texas. From that moment on, he vowed he would never complain again.

Jake and Elmer came into plain sight, and their wagon came up alongside Henry, who exclaimed, "Boy! You're sight for sore eyes!"

Jake's eyes sparkled under his bandana when he said, "Aw, I didn't know you loved us so much."

His words made Henry chuckle before saying, "Follow me. There's water in the stream up ahead. Randy is waiting for us. We can easily cross the stream to safety."

Jake did not hesitate to say with a sense of urgency. "Let's stop wasting time and go. We got a fire lickin' at our heels. No time for chit-chat."

Henry slowed down his pace so the wagon could follow him. He watched carefully as he traced the way back through the tall grass. Within a couple of hours, they found Randy skipping stones across the surface of the stream's clear water. They were all happy to see each other. Randy felt like hugging his big brother but refrained from doing so because that would not be the manly thing to do.

They crossed the stream without any difficulties. They breathed easier, knowing they would not be burned by the fire. They looked back, and they could see that the fire was slowing down and moving in another direction. Jake said, "That's enuh excitement for the day. Let's make camp here and get ready for a long day tomorrow."

They needed to rest and recover from their fire ordeal. Their horses and mules also needed to rest, drink, and graze. The break for them caused by the fire was a much-needed respite from their daily routine. Jake put them all on notice by saying, "Be ready for an onslaught of varmints running to escape the fire, particularly be aware of rattlesnakes. Our campfire should help ward them off, but they are more traumatized than we are. Have your guns ready to shoot anything we can eat."

Henry retorted to Jake's comment, "Hey. I heard you can eat rattlesnakes. Right?"

Jake replied, "I'm not eaten any snake, particularly a poisonous one. But you're welcome to eat all the snake you can."

They were finishing their chores, and the varmints started coming toward the opposite bank of the stream. Henry and Randy killed all the rabbits they could eat. There were snakes, but they did not want to cross the water. Also, some armadillos stopped at the water's edge. The stink caused by skunks made them move their campsite away from the stream.

Once they were in a new campsite and all was settled, Henry stated, "Well, it's not that Brazos River you mentioned, but there's enough water to stop the fire."

The normally quiet Elmer replied, "Wrong. That was the Brazos. It had little water cuz of the drought. And if the fire came this way, it would've jumped the water and lit up the other side. But you did gud and now we can head almost straight south to the railhead at Alleyton."

Henry had more questions to ask. "How long do you think it will take us to reach Alleyton?"

Elmer had ready answers. "About two weeks if we have no problems."

Henry continued, "Tell us what you can about Alleyton."

"You'll like it cuz it is full of people. Lots of buyers and sellers of cotton. Also, lots of ladies trying to sell their favors. Warehouses bulging with big cotton bales and zillions of wagons vying for contracts to haul cotton. It is probably one of the busiest and noisiest places in Texas."

Henry thought a moment before saying, "Hard to imagine such a place. I'm surprised there's a railroad all the way to Alleyton."

"Yes, sirree Bob, the rail line goes through Houston and comes west to end at Alleyton. If it weren't fer the war, there would be trains going much farther west."

Henry finished their exchange by saying, "I can't wait to see it all. Sounds like a good place to find a job."

At that point, Jake said, "Yep, jobs shud be a plenty in Alleyton cuz all the men had went off to fight in the war. The only men left are young men like you who are under the age of conscription. With your school learnin' and guns, you should have no problem finding jobs."

"Thanks. Mr. Jake. That's encouraging. We sure look forward to seeing Alleyton with our own eyes and learning more about what this Cotton Road is all about."

On that note, Elmer pulled out of his vest pocket his harmonica. Henry's first reaction was to find some rags, tear off some small pieces, and stuff them in his ears. He could not bear to hear 'Dixie' again. He stopped his search for rags when he heard a different tune coming out of Elmer's harmonica. He immediately asked Elmer, "What's that? I thought you didn't know how to play any other tune except 'Dixie.' What's the name of what you are trying to play?"

Elmer removed the harmonica from his mouth, exposing several gaps of missing teeth, and said, "This is a tune I've heard only once. I was told it is called 'Yellow Rose Over Texas.' I don't know the words. I need to hear it again before I can play it good enough."

Henry tried to be humorous by saying, "I've yet to see a yellow rose or any kind of rose in Texas."

Elmer replied, "I think the yellow rose is not a flower but a woman. Anyway, I understand this tune is popular among Confederate troops."

They ate with gusto their roasted rabbit meat. Before turning in for the night, Henry was thinking about the yellow rose being a woman. He thought this sounded right to him because even the most beautiful woman was like a rose with thorns. His thoughts turned to Christ with His crown of thorns. For him, the Civil War was like a big thorn stuck deeply into the side of the country and the life he once loved.

# Chapter Eighteen
## Alleyton

There was nothing to do but keep rolling in a southernly direction across the empty plains in the hopes of running into a rail line. Once they found the rail line, they could follow it to its end in Alleyton. Henry was always on the lookout for any reflection the sun would make in the distance off the iron rails. He and Randy could not wait to get to Alleyton to get on with their lives. All they needed was something to do, which paid them and gave them some purpose in life.

As they got closer to the rail line, there were more wagon tracks. Seeing these traces of other wagons prompted Jake to say at their evening meal around the campfire. "All signs show we're getting close. So, we need to take some time to get ready for what awaits us in Alleyton."

Henry piped up, "But I thought we're ready and in a hurry to get to Alleyton."

Jake replied, "We're in a hurry, but I got to take a little time to organize my trade goods and talk to Elmer about how we goin' to do our business. You just don't go to a dance without making sure you know the steps."

Henry said, "I get what you're saying, but I tell you now that we're taking the first paying jobs we're offered."

Jake laughed and said, "Sure, enuh. You boys have to make a life for yourselves."

In those last days before they reached the rail line, Jake would stop early to talk with Elmer and arrange and re-arrange all the goods he had in the wagon. Henry and Randy would use this downtime to practice tossing their lassos over tree limbs they had planted in the ground. Jake saw what they were doing and said, "You're making progress, but it's one thing to lasso a post and another to be on a galloping horse and lasso a runaway steer."

Henry knew what Jake said was right, but he had to say something. "You got to start somewhere."

Jake chuckled and said, "Come over to my wagon. I found somethin' I want to give you, boys."

Henry and Randy curled up their lassos and tied them in their places on their saddles. They walked over to Jake, who was standing next to his covered wagon.

Jake spied them coming and smiled widely, adding wrinkles to a face already filled with unwanted stress crevices and pockmarks. In his hands were short leather belts. He happily said, "Here, I want you two boys to have these. I found them while I was organizing my stuff. No hat in Texas is complete without them."

Henry and Randy were not sure about what they were seeing, but they graciously accepted the gift of two short leather belts. Jake could see their eyes were deceiving them, and he said, "These are leather bands to fit around your hats. No cowpuncher's hat in Texas can be in style without these bands. You tighten the band around the base of the crown of your hat. I see you have stampede strings, but these belts can keep your hats from blowing off in a high wind."

Jake then proceeded to show them how to place the belts around their hats and adjust them for a comfortable fit. Henry and Randy held their belted hats before them, and both thanked Jake effusively. Henry spoke up for both of them, "Mr. Jake, we're mighty thankful for this gift and all you've done for us. These bands will make it so that we never forget you."

Jake had been hardened by his years of following many western trails, but hearing these words from two young men who were forced from their home months ago touched him, and tears swelled up in his eyes. He turned away from the boys so they could not see his teary eyes. He was full of emotion when he managed to say, "Go on now before you make me cry."

Henry and Randy were surprised by Jake's reaction. They did not know there was a sentimental side to Jake. In fact, they did not know anything about his previous life. For them, these were hard times, and there was no room for any sentiment for a life that could never be restored. They believed only those with the hardest hearts would survive. So far, they had enjoyed dumb luck by being spared death. All they had going for them was their youth and health. They intended to play their cards the best they could, no matter what hand they were dealt.

A couple of days later, Henry spotted a sparkling gleam in the far distance. He instantly became excited and debated with himself whether or not he should gallop back to the others to inform them of his sighting. He decided to ride a little farther forward to make sure that the sun's reflection was definitely off train tracks. He did not have to ride for long before he could say with certainty that the rail line was dead ahead of them.

He turned his horse and galloped back to the wagon, yelping like a wild Indian on the warpath. When Jake spotted the dust Henry's horse was churning up, he stopped the wagon and waited for Henry to arrive and tell his story. By the time Henry arrived, Randy had ridden up to the side of the wagon. They waited silently and impatiently for Henry's news. They could hear his yelping, but they did not know what he meant by his agitated state.

Henry arrived out of breath. He was perspiring profusely, and his horse was all lathered up. Henry stopped his horse and took a minute to catch his breath before saying as calmly as he could. "I saw the rails dead ahead."

As soon as Henry said the word 'rails,' Elmer pulled his harmonica from his vest pocket and started blasting out 'Dixie.' Jake felt like getting off the wagon and dancing. Even the studious and always serious Randy managed to crack a wry smile. It was time to celebrate, but Jake brought the gaiety of the moment to an abrupt end by saying loudly. "There are no rails until I see them with my own eyes."

Henry quickly enjoined by saying, "Let's go then. Seeing is believing."

They began heading south as fast as the wagon could go. Randy resumed his rear-guard position. Henry trotted well beyond the wagon, intending to arrive at the rails well before the wagon.

Henry saw up close for himself the train tracks and climbed on top the rail line to show his fellow travelers the point for which they should aim. He waited for over an hour before he could begin to clearly see Jake's wagon. He waved and yelled to indicate the point for which they should aim. It took about an hour for the creaky wagon to reach the rail line. Randy galloped forward to join them. Henry was about to say something when he spotted a train barreling along the tracks in a westward direction.

He and his horse jumped quickly off the tracks to avoid a collision with the oncoming train and joined the others. They all stood spellbound as they watched the long train roar by at top speed. Every boxcar of the train was stuffed with cotton bales. They watched in amazement as tufts of cotton floated in the air around them. The normally speechless Randy was the first one to say anything. "Golly. I've not seen many trains, but that train has to be the longest train I've ever seen."

Jake spoke, "Yah, a long train full of a valuable cargo. It's like seeing white gold speeding to make people rich. I hope I'm one of them. This is my last chance to make a fortune."

Henry could not keep quiet because he could not believe his eyes. "All that cotton, and that is only one train. They'll need a lot of people to offload and account for all those hundreds of bales. There's got to be a job in there somewhere."

Elmer thought it appropriate for him to add a few words. "By cracky, lots of money for me and Jake to make. Let's get goin' and follow the tracks east to Alleyton. It can't be too far away."

They turned right and followed west the train tracks. They did not know how long it would take them to get there, but they did know they were headed in the right direction. After a couple of hours, they encountered other wagons rolling along on a well-worn trail. It seemed like the whole world was headed to Alleyton to seek their fortune.

Jake noticed that he was one of the few older men driving a wagon. Most wagon drivers were in their late teens because most men in the area had left to join the Confederate army. Henry and Randy felt like adults compared to many of the teenagers driving wagons. They rode high in their saddles, trying to demonstrate an air of superiority. Henry rode up to the side of one of the wagons they were following to learn more and ask how far it was to Alleyton.

Henry greeted a freckled-face boy sitting next to a wagon driver. "Howdy, my name is Henry. What's yours?"

The boy was surprised to see someone on a horse and timidly replied, "My name is Pete, and this is my big brother, Ralph."

Henry continued to break the ice by saying, "My brother Randy is also with me. Where you guys comin' from?"

Pete looked at his brother before answering, "We had a farm near Houston and heard that good money can be made hauling cotton to Mexico. Our father and older brothers went off to war, and our mom needed money, so here we are."

Henry wanted to cut their exchange short and just said, "We've been on the road a long time, we're looking for jobs in Alleyton. How much farther do you think we have to go?"

Pete consulted with his brother and replied, "We reckon it is about fifteen miles away. Is this your first time to go to Alleyton?"

Henry rapidly replied, "Sure is. How about you?"

"Us too. This is the first time to be out of our home area."

Henry responded to Pete by saying, "I can well appreciate that. I better go back to our wagon now. Good luck."

"Wait a minute, mister. You talk funny. Where you from?"

Henry was hesitant because this was the first time he had been called mister, but he said, "We're from back East, so maybe we don't have the same accent as you folks, but we share the same goals. Later."

Randy said to Henry in a low voice. "I thought they talked funny. Do educated people in Texas talk like they do?"

Henry replied, "Well, I guess to fit in, we need to learn to talk like they do."

Henry rode back to tell Jake that he had talked with the wagon in front of them and was told how far away Alleyton was. Jake replied, "Dat's gud news. As soon as we get there, I'm goin' straight to a blacksmith to check out my mules, their harnesses and get advice on what is needed for the long trip to Mexico. I figure I'll need new iron bands on my wheels. For sure, my mules and your horses need some rest, water, and feed; otherwise, they can't survive the trip."

They continued to eat the dust of the wagon in front of them, using their bandanas to cover their faces. Gradually, Alleyton and the rail head came into view. Nobody was prepared for the riotous sight before them. There were hundreds of wagons and people jostling to be called by middlemen to load and sign for a heavy cargo of five hundred pound cotton bales.

There were many more people and animals than Henry and Randy had seen since they left Virginia. They were far from the ravages of war, but they were not out of its clutches yet. They were free to do what they wanted without risking too much their lives, but they could not live on freedom alone. They needed paying jobs.

As many bales as possible were loaded from warehouses piled high with cotton. Jake asked for directions to a blacksmith and headed off to get his mules and wagon tended. His plan was to set his goods out for sale near the blacksmith's place and use the money from the sales to pay the blacksmith. He was especially interested in catering to those returning from Mexico because they should have the money needed to pay his inflated prices.

Jake drifted away from Henry and Randy, and they rode their horses around the clamoring crowd to see what they could learn. As they sat on their horses, a smartly dressed man came up to them and said, "Don't be afraid. I mean no harm. Do you young men need work?"

Henry and Randy were not ready to talk about possible jobs so quickly after their arrival. Henry grudgingly answered, "Who wants to know?"

"Good reply. You sure have to know who you're dealing with these days. My name is Robert E. Cummins. You can call me Bob. I'm agent for Mr. Ford. Everybody in this part of Texas knows who this is. He's the man who is buying and selling most of this cotton. We need a couple of hands like you to escort his cotton to Mexico."

Henry consulted with Randy and then said, "What are the requirements, and how much is the pay?"

Bob chuckled before saying, "I can see that you two young men are tough customers. The pay depends on your abilities with a gun and on how much you can read and write. I see you have guns, and I assume you have ammunition for them. Now, can you read and write?"

Henry blew their own horn by saying, "We've had these guns for a long time and have learned to be good and fast shots with them. We've been to school and read and write better than anyone you can find in Texas."

Bob smacked his lips and said, "I guess you are just what the doctor ordered. We need one man with book smarts to keep track of the number of bales loaded in Alleyton for Mr. Ford and how many are unloaded in Mexico. We need another man to guard the wagons from banditos and anyone who tries to steal Mr. Ford's cotton."

Henry said a few words to Randy and, turned to look straight into Bob's eyes, and said, "Mister, you got yourself a deal, but how much do you pay, and can we get an advance?"

"That'll be ten dollars a week for each of you for the time it takes to get to Matamoros. Payment is in Mexican gold pieces. I can pay you upfront a week's pay. And I'll give you a couple of fresh horses. You'll need them to make the long trip to the border."

Henry and Randy tried not to show their excitement over getting some real money. Henry composed himself and said in a manly voice, "When do we get our money, and when do we start?"

Bob replied, "Well, we plan to move our wagon train out early tomorrow. Can you be ready by then? I can advance you some money now, but before that, we need to shake hands."

Henry and Randy dismounted and shook vigorously Bob's hand. While Bob was handing to them a few Mexican gold coins, Henry said reluctantly, "We were born ready. Tomorrow morning would be fine. Where do we report?"

"We should be the first wagon train to leave with our load of cotton, so we'll be out on the Cotton Road just west of here, ready to leave. I'm going with you, so I'll hold the train until you join us."

Henry's last question for Bob was. "Where's the blacksmith?"

Bob pointed to where the blacksmith was located and said, as he walked off. "See you tomorrow."

Henry and Randy were bone tired, but they could not pass up this work opportunity. They could not wait to see Jake and Elmer to tell them that they had jobs. They arrived at the blacksmith's, but they could not find them, so they asked the smithy about this pair of newcomers. The rotund smithy stopped what he was doing and said, "Oh, those guys. Well, they displayed their goods, but the prices they wanted were so high that the crowd of people around them became angry and chased them out of town. Of course, all their goods were stolen. They were lucky to leave with their lives. Why? You guys with them."

Henry and Randy tried to hide their shock over the smithy's news. Henry responded in a matter-of-fact manner, "No, we're not with them. We were just interested in some of their wares. Thanks for telling us what happened to them."

Henry and Randy slowly rode off in silence. A despondent Henry quietly said, "The Lord certainly works in strange ways. Sometimes you're damned if you do and damned if you don't. Surely, life is a continual struggle. You can never ever let your guard down. Anyway, a lot of good all that organizing of their goods did for them. Best we find an empty spot to bed down and see if we can buy any food for ourselves and grain for our horses. Tomorrow is another day."

# Chapter Nineteen
# Cotton Trail

Henry and Randy were happier than they had been in a long time. They were free, and the jingle in their pockets made by the advance of a few gold coins made them feel like kings of the world. They found that with just one of their coins, they could satisfy readily all their immediate needs. There were plenty of women selling food and a lot of guys selling grain for their horses.

Everybody was out to make a fast buck from the bustling cotton trade. Henry and Randy thought they had been cast into a bee-hive cauldron of economic activity. They had ever never seen money and goods change hands as fast as they were seeing it now. For them, Alleyton was the American epicenter of profit-making.

At the edge of the jostling mix of hundreds of people, horses, mules, oxen, and wagons, they found an open spot beneath a budding tree to bed down for the night. The noise of the crowd continued throughout the night. There was no ceasing of loading cotton bales on wagons and the dispatch of those wagons, and the passage of wagons headed east on the reverse journey with loads of guns, ammunition, medicines, and other items the South needed to continue the war. It was tough to sleep with all the non-stop commotion.

Henry was made nervous by all the ladies of the night who appeared out of the shadows. It appeared they could hear the coins jingling in his pocket and followed the sound they made. Henry turned to Randy and said, "I don't trust myself. Can you keep for me my share of our advance?"

Randy whispered to his older brother, "Sure, but you need to discipline yourself and stay out of trouble."

Henry nodded and said, "You're right, little brother, but you know that I'm not the sort to stay out of trouble. No matter how I try, my nature always puts me in hot water."

They both wrapped themselves in their blankets and tried to block out the noise of the thriving cotton exchange. They closed their eyes and told themselves they were asleep. They knew they needed to be rested to hit the cotton trail early tomorrow. They did not know how long that trail was or where it would lead them. All they knew was if hundreds of others could do it, they could do it too. Besides, what other choice did they have?

The chirps of the birds in the tree alerted them of the approaching morning. They got up, fed, and saddled their horses. They relieved themselves, checked their guns, and mounted their horses to search for a place to eat and drink something, wash their faces, and water their horses. They found a woman waiting for early morning customers, and she told them to take a seat on a wooden bench along a rickety, bare, splintered table and to help themselves to her water trough. She was quick to say how much her food and water services would cost and demanded payment upfront.

While they were savoring plates of cooked grits, Randy observed to Henry. "All the people in Alleyton seem happy because they're making money on all this cotton business which supports the Confederacy, but they don't seem to care what side of the war they're on. They only care about the money they can make."

Henry commented, "The money these people are making is chicken feed compared to what the people who buy and transport the cotton make. Those people are making fortunes while they keep the fighting going by selling cotton for Mexican gold and back-hauling for stuff the South needs. For them, I guess the war is a good thing in spite of the thousands who are being slaughtered."

Randy responded, "Best not to think of such things. Let's go look for Bob now and get started on our new jobs."

They rode to where they spotted a wagon train ready to depart and found Bob sitting up front in the last wagon. Bob looked up at them and said, "About time you got here. I think we're all set to go. To get you started, I got a few words for you."

Henry politely said. "Well, good morning, boss. We're ready to go to work. We're all ears to hear what you got to say."

"Okay, you make sure we're not attacked by any banditos. Keep a lookout in front and be ready to shoot anything that moves toward our wagons. As for your younger brother, I want him to take this little ledger book and pen to write down the number of cotton bales in each wagon. Keep an eye out for any side-selling or people sneaking off in the night with cotton. Report back to me about anything that looks suspicious. Now ride up to the front wagon and tell them that Mr. Cummins said its's time to pull out."

Henry and Randy had some other questions to ask Bob, but the boss just gave them an order, so they did what he asked. They rode upfront and told the lead wagon to start going. They noticed as they rode along the wagon train that it was formed by wagons of all shapes pulled by teams of oxen or mules. Randy found that different-sized wagons meant they carried various loads of cotton.

Henry rode out ahead of the wagon train, and Randy busied himself with getting to know each wagon and its contents. He introduced himself to the two drivers in each wagon and inspected

their cargo. He noticed that the drivers were either young or old. He assumed all men of conscription age were off fighting in the war. They were all eager to make money for themselves and their families.

After a couple of hours of visiting with each wagon and writing down in his little book the number of cotton bales each was transporting, Randy returned to report his findings and said, "It would be easier to keep track of things if I could number each wagon."

Bob replied, "That's a good idea. How do you think we can do that?"

Randy said, "I've been thinking about that, and the only thing I can come up with is a charred end of a stick."

"Yeah. Try that and let me know how it works. You may have to wait until we make the evening campfire. Anyway, the wagons are supposed to stay in the same position in line. Anything else?"

"As a matter of fact, my brother and I were wondering how many days this trip will take?"

Bob laughed aloud at Randy's simple query. "I thought you knew that before you signed up. This trip will take two to three weeks, depending on our luck. There's a long, hard road ahead us, but if we arrive alive, the payoff is big."

Randy was curious. "How long is long?"

Bob squinted and said, "I reckon it could be a thousand miles before we hit paydirt in Mexico. It's waiting for that damn ferry to cross the Nueces River and the tough slog through the big sands, which will slow us down before we reach Brownsville."

Randy did not know a thing about the geography of southern Texas and was afraid his queries would let Bob know that he had hired an ignorant tenderfoot. But his curiosity got the best of him, so he could not resist asking Bob. "Don't we have to cross another river to go to Mexico?"

Bob blurted out a response, "Yes, siree, that'll be the Rio Grande. No problema. Mr. Ford and his partners have flatbed steamboats flying Mexican flags, which can take us and our cotton to the Mexican side of the river. Once on the other side, we have then only a short distance to go to the small port of Bagdad on the Gulf Coast, where hundreds of ships from Europe are waiting to load cotton for their textile mills."

Randy was learning a lot and said, "Thanks, boss. It's good to know all this. You know we're not from Texas, and this is all new territory for us. I'll tell my brother what I've learned."

Just as Randy was finished talking, Henry rode up in a huff. Saying, "Mr. Boss. I don't know if I can lead the wagons along the correct trail. There are wagon tracks everywhere, and there doesn't seem to be a set trail to follow."

Bob laughed and said, "That's the way it is. They say in some places, the trail can be a mile wide. Just pick out as well as you can the best trail for us to follow. As long as you see tufts of cotton dangling from the bushes and hanging in the tall grass, you know we're headed in the right direction. Keep in mind that we're not the only cotton wagons traveling along this road."

Randy was hesitant to ask, but while they had Bob's attention, he said, "How long today are we to keep going?"

Bob cleared his throat of the blowing dust churned up by the wagons in front of him and said, "Usually, we go until the sun sets, but if there is a good moonlight and weather, we keep rolling some hours into the night."

Randy listened intently to Bob's words and said, "You mean we don't eat or drink?"

Randy's question irked Bob a bit, and he said, "We eat on the fly what we can. We all got to focus on the main thing, and that is to get our cotton load safely to the Rio Grande. Nothing else really matters. Besides, my wagon is chuck full of supplies, including food, feed, and water, which should carry us to a key stopover at Mr. Ford's ranch at Santa Rosa. When we get there, we can stock up with what we need, rest, and if need be, we can change our animals for fresher ones."

Henry added, "What if someone gets sick?"

Bob was quick to react to Henry's question. "Let's pray that doesn't happen, but if it does, too bad. We got to keep rolling no matter what."

Randy's head was spinning with all the information Bob had given him. He had other questions, but he would save those until later… after he had a chance to tell Henry all he had learned from Bob. There was a long pause, and then Bob mentioned, "Did you see the spare horses I've got tied to the back of my wagon? Those are for you when your horses wear out."

Henry said, "Randy and I will check them out, then we'll get back to work." They saw the spare horses, but the real reason they went behind the wagon was so Randy could tell Henry all that he had learned from Bob. Henry listened to what Randy had to tell him and said, "That's all good to know, but it really changes nothing for us. We're in this for the long haul … wherever it takes us. Gotta go now back up front."

Henry rode off at a gallop in a hail of dust. Randy pulled from his saddle bag his little book and read what he had written, making some edits. He then began making again the rounds of the wagon train. He said to Bob as he rode past him. "Back to work. See you later."

As the day wore on, both Henry and Randy found their jobs boring. They were passing over the same monotonous prairie. There was nothing that sparked their interest. And the hot sun was burning holes in their clothes and making it hard for them and their horses to breathe. Henry was out front of the wagon train, so the dust kicked up by the wagon wheels and the hooves of their teams did not bother him. Randy protected his nose by tying his bandana tightly over his face, but he felt like he was suffocating. They kept telling themselves they would get used to these rough conditions, but there was no getting used to it.

The wagons kept rolling along throughout the day and into the night. The men and their animals became exhausted. Randy was afraid that Bob was asking too much on this first day of the cotton drive. For him, there was no way they could keep up this pace. If they did not get some rest soon, they would never make it to the Rio Grande.

Randy rode back to Bob to express his concerns. Bob replied, "I reckon you're right. For sure, my butt is tired from sitting on this hard seat all day. Let's make camp at the next stream or water hole. Spread the word to each wagon so we're all ready to rest a spell. This is enough for the first day."

Randy sped off to inform all the wagons of the plan to stop soon. When he got to the lead wagon, he tarried and whistled loudly so Henry could hear him. Henry galloped back, and Randy told him that Bob had decided to rest for the remainder of the night. Henry replied, "I'll go ahead and look for a good place to camp. I hope the moonlight holds so I can see well the place."

Henry rode ahead a bit and found a water hole and then rode back to tell Randy who rode up to Bob to relay Henry's words to him. Bob said, "Okay. Sounds good. Tell everyone to hold tight until I've had a chance to inspect the spot that Henry found."

Randy rode up to each of the twenty wagons, telling them to stay put until Bob had a chance to see the camping spot.

Bob slowly guided his wagon and team of mules to the side of his wagon train, passing each wagon until he was in the front. He had a railroad signal oil lantern hung on the front of his wagon, making it easy for the others to see his location and come to a halt when he waved his lantern. After about an hour, Bob found Henry waiting for him, saying, "Here's the spot I found. It has some trees, and there is a water hole. What do you think?"

A pensive Bob climbed off his wagon with his lantern in his hand. "Let me have a look. It's good to stretch my kegs. Stay on your horse and follow me."

Bob worked his way through the tall grass and looked intensely at the water hole and its surroundings. He shook his head and looked to see if others had camped here previously. He found some evidence of the remains of a campfire, and almost hidden in the surrounding grass, he found two graves. He shook his head again and said in a low and troubled voice, "This place is no good. There are two people buried here. Maybe they were poisoned by the water in the hole. I also don't see any signs of critters drinking at the water hole. We can't camp here. Let's look for another place."

Henry was embarrassed about the camping place that he found not being suitable. He told himself that he would check out his next proposed camping site more thoroughly before recommending it for overnight camping. Whether Bob knew it or not, he had just learned a few things from him.

Bob said, "Let's get out of here before the snakes get us. They're always looking for warm bodies at night. We got to tell the others that we are moving on."

Bob climbed up on his wagon and called to Randy to tell him. "This place is no good for camping. Tell everyone that we got to move on a piece."

As Randy followed Bob's instructions, he noticed as he rode from wagon to wagon that the wind was picking up speed and the night sky was becoming cluttered with dark clouds, blocking the moonlight. Suddenly, the wind swept across the prairie at a high speed, blowing ferociously. It was as if the wind was intent on obliterating everything in its path.

Randy became alarmed and looked down the wagon train to see Bob's lantern waving wildly. He interpreted this as a signal to return to Bob's wagon as fast as he could. He galloped past the other wagons and got within talking distance of Bob, who cried out, "Have all wagons stop and brake. All people and cotton take cover. It may be a twister,"

Just as Randy was turning to warn the other wagons, Henry showed up and said, "It's too dark and windy to see anything."

Bob cracked, "Damn any campsite. We got to take cover from this mean weather. Give your brother a hand and warn the others."

Bob was holding on to his wagon as the wind tried to blow him into oblivion. Somehow, his loud words cut through the wind. Henry and Randy rode along at a gallop to shout at the other wagon drivers to take cover and button down their tarps. Some waggoneers piled on top of their cargo of cotton under cover of their canvas tops. Others secured their cargo and huddled beneath their wagons.

As Henry and Randy were turning to return to Bob's wagon, the wind died down, but suddenly, they were pelted with large balls of hail. The sky was full of angry bolts of lightning, which unleashed frightening rolls of thunder. They rushed back to Bob's wagon, tied their horses to the wagon, and dived under the wagon for protection against the hailstorm that was hammering everything. They were hoping that the pounding hailstorm would pass quickly.

They yelled at the top of their lungs to Bob to let him know they were under his wagon. As soon as the hailstorm began to peter out, Henry rushed out to get their blankets and check on the horses. It took a couple of minutes before he could return to snuggle up with is brother under the wagon when the rain began to come down even harder. It rained so hard that Henry and Randy became worried about flooding. Quickly, the bone-dry land was soaking up the deluge.

They also worried about the animals which were outside bearing the full brunt of the harsh weather. Overall. they were concerned about the safety of all wagons, their drivers, and precious cotton cargo. They worried all night about their rifles which they had left on their horses. They sat under Bob's low wagon all night long, leaning back-to-back with their blankets wrapped around themselves. They remained wide-eyed with worry for hours, and their butts became wetter as the water on the ground rose. There was nothing they could do but wait for the rain to dissipate and some daylight to appear.

They did learn something about themselves when hunched over in their refuge beneath Bob's wagon. They had grown and were still growing. Henry was already six feet tall, and Randy was close behind him. They were only teenage boys, but they considered themselves men.

# Chapter Twenty
# Five Notches

The rain stopped, and the skies cleared. At the dawning of a new day, Henry and Randy crawled out from beneath Bob's soggy wagon as soon as they could see their hands in front of their faces. In a groggy state, they rushed to see how their horses were doing and checked on their guns. They found there was nothing damaged that a little sunshine would not cure. They all needed to dry out.

They heard Bob stirring inside his wagon. He had weathered the night of rough weather spread out on top of his supplies. His head appeared from the front flap of his covered wagon, and with a big smile on his old, wrinkled face and, he said, "That was a doozy of a night. Randy, go as soon as you can and check the other wagons, and tell everyone to take a break. Henry, stay here with me as we plan our next move. No sense looking for a nighttime campsite so early in the morning. Besides, there is water everywhere now."

Randy visited on foot every wagon. The bunched wagon train was probably over a half-mile long. He wanted to ride his horse, but it was too wet and traumatized by the wild weather.

He was pleased to see that all had survived the night. Some wagons needed some adjustments to their wooden bodies. In some wagons, the parts of their cotton bales that were sticking out into the rain were wet, but they would dry out in the sunny weather that now prevailed. Everybody needed time to dry off their tack, unhitch their animals, and let them graze and drink. They also needed something to eat.

While Randy was away, Henry removed the saddles and blankets from their horses and spread them on nearby bushes to dry. He set his horses free so they could graze and drink from the many puddles of rainwater. He also helped Bob unhitch his mules so they could do the same. Bob had some dry firewood in his wagon so he could make a small fire on a bare spot near where they had stopped. He joyfully boiled some coffee and cooked up some grits. For him, life on the trail was his home.

Randy returned and wanted to give Bob his report, but before he could open his mouth, Bob called him over to eat. They sipped their hot black coffee and ate their grits. After a silent spell, Bob asked Randy, "What do you think?"

Randy tried some humor by saying, "I think I need to dry out before doing any thinking."

Bob and Henry laughed a bit, and Bob said, "Seriously, what do you think we should do now?"

Randy looked Bob straight in the eyes and gave him the answer he knew he was looking for. "After a break of a couple of hours, we should continue on our way south. After all, we have a valuable cargo to get to market."

Bob was pleased with Randy's reply and turned to Henry to say, "Your younger brother sure got a good head on his shoulders."

Henry responded with a quip, "I've known that for years."

Bob told Randy, "Go and tell all to get their business done so we can keep rolling on in a couple of hours. Get back here as soon as you can cuz we got to talk sums."

Bob then turned to Henry and asked, "How did he know we're headed in a southerly direction?"

"That's easy. The sun comes up in the east and sets in the west, and the setting sun has been generally on our right. But this old compass I've in my vest pocket shows that we are headed south."

"Compass? Never seen one. I've traveled back and forth over this land ever since the start of the war, but I've never used a compass. Can I see what you got?"

Henry scooted over to Bob's side, and as they both sat cross-legged on the ground. Henry showed him his compass and how it worked. Bob was mesmerized by the magical workings of the compass and acclaimed, "It sure is a wonderful thing."

Henry was curious and asked Bob, "You said you've been covering this trail since the war begun. Has it always been about moving cotton to Mexico and war supplies back to the south?"

Bob hesitated and then answered Henry's question abruptly, "No. Before cotton, thousands of cattle were driven this way and ferried across the Mississippi to feed the Confederate army. Mr. Ford and his partners made a pretty penny off those drives. It is only when Union blockades on the Mississippi cut off this cattle business that there was a switch to the trade in cotton."

Henry said, "So, let me get this straight. Mr. Ford is making a fortune off the war on the side of the South. What is he doing with all the money?"

"Well, for one thing, he bought a huge spread of land, which he has turned into one of the finest cattle and horse ranches in this part of Texas. You'll see that for yourself when we get to his Santa Rosita ranch. There, he has a well-stocked commissary and plenty of horses and mules. He also does a good business selling stuff from his commissary as well as raising his livestock and feeding wagon train hands. He's one hell of a businessman with a lot of fingers in the money-making pie."

"He sounds like somebody I'd like to meet someday."

Bob tried to finish this exchange by saying, "I'm sure you will. Hell, you're already working for him, and you're headed straight into his territory."

As they were concluding their conversation, Randy came sauntering up to them and cheerfully said, "All is well. Now, what's this about us doing our sums?"

To this, Bob said, "Get out your little book and writing instrument so we can figure out what we got."

Randy got his small ledger book and dull pencil and came back and sat down with Bob and Henry, ready to do what Bob wanted. Bob's first question was. "How many cotton bales do we have?"

"Well, we have twenty wagons of different sizes, but on the whole, we have sixty bales."

"Okay, how many pounds of cotton do we have if there are five hundred pounds of cotton in each bale?"

Randy scribbled in his book and said, "Well, according to my calculations, sixty bales times five hundred pounds per bale equals thirty thousand pounds."

As soon as Randy said this, Bob could not wait to say. "Now we're getting somewhere. Excuse all these questions, but my schooling is deficient. In fact, I've never been to school. Don't tell anyone. Most people think I'm a schooled man, but the truth is I can't read or write or do arithmetic. That's why I got you boys."

Bob continued to say things that Randy wrote down. "Now, we paid

149

three cents a pound for our cotton cargo, and it will sell for fifty cents a pound in gold in Matamoros. How much profit is that?"

Randy scribbled quickly, and when he was finished, he said, "Thirty thousand pounds at three cents a pound is nine hundred dollars. Thirty thousand pounds at fifty cents a pound is a total 15,000 dollars for a gross profit of about $14,100. Of course, the expense of transport and handling have to subtracted from this amount to get a net profit after expenses."

"Damn, son. You're too good. Don't worry your head too much. Mr. Ford and his partners are making money hand over fist. He has fingers into a number of money-making adventures, but the fact he and his partners are paid in gold in Mexico makes him wealthy. Gold pieces are worth more than any paper money you'll find."

Henry could not keep quiet. "What did Mr. Ford do before the war to make money?"

Bob was quick to respond, "Why, he was already a famous steamboat captain, operating boats to transport goods back and forth across the Rio Grande. He made his first fortune in the steamboat business, and when the war came along, he saw money-making opportunities in helping the South sell cotton."

Henry added, "He must come from the South to be so supportive of the Confederacy."

Bob curtly said, "No. He's from New York."

Henry was confused now and kept his thoughts to himself. It did not make sense to him that a Yankee from New York would risk so much for the Southern cause. He assumed Mr. Ford was willing to do anything to make a buck. He did find it odd that the richest man in Texas was from New York.

Randy was thinking much of the same thing and wanted to continue the conversation, but Bob felt he had already said too much. He got up, put out their dying fire, and started fussing with the cargo in his wagon. Obviously, he was in a silent mood and did not feel like talking any more.

Henry got up, turned over the blankets hanging on the nearby bushes, and walked into the tall grass to see how their horses and mules were doing. Randy also stood up and was wondering about what he should do when Bob told him. "Go tell the others to get ready to leave in about an hour. Make sure each wagon has checked its wheels and axles and applied axle fat if needed. All we need is for a wagon to break down because its wheel axles were not slickened up."

Randy began his walk to pass the message on to each wagon. He gave the message twice – once when going and once when returning. He returned to Bob to give his report. "All informed of our departure in about hour."

Randy joined Henry, and they worked together to lead their horses back to the wagon and saddle them up. They made sure their guns were ready to fire and helped Bob hitch his docile mules to his wagon. They then asked Bob if he had any rags and soap for them to clean up a bit in the puddles of water. Bob handed them a couple old rags and a used chunk of soap. As Bob handed to them the soap and rags, Henry said, "Thanks. We're going behind the tree to get ourselves ready for the day's long slog south. We'll be back in a jiffy."

Henry and Randy found a good place to hide behind the tree. They both looked for individual puddles near each other. They passed the soap back and forth as they washed and rinsed their faces in the cool and clear rainwater. Then they lowered their pants and drawers and, squatted carefully over the puddles, and had good bowel movements. They cleaned themselves with the rags. Later, when they were fully dressed, they washed the rags in separate puddles of water and wrung them out as much as they could. Their ablutions made them feel good and ready for hours on the Cotton Road.

While they were doing this, they noticed how hard and calloused their hands had become. They were also surprised to see how long their scraggly beards had become. They did not recognize the faces they saw reflected in the puddles of water. For sure, they were not the same teenage boys who had left their home in Virginia over a year ago.

"We're ready. Where do you want us to put these wet rags?" said Henry nonchalantly.

"I guess we should be going. Tie the rags on the wagon to dry. Randy, tell everyone that we're pulling out in ten minutes. I'll take up my place in the rear once every wagon has passed me," said a visibly tired and worn Bob.

Henry signaled that he was going to take up his place far in the distant front. And just when Randy mounted his horse to give the others their marching orders, Henry mounted his horse to go to the front. Bob hollered to both of them, "Well done. At least we don't have to worry about wildfires for a while, and we'll have lots of green grass for the livestock, but watch out for banditos."

Henry and Randy were out of earshot before Bob could finish his words. They both were surprised about how good it felt to be back in the saddle. They were enjoying breathing the fresh air and the greening of the trees, bushes, and grasses on this bright, sunny spring day. High overhead were two hawks flying in wide circles in search of prey on the wet ground.

The road was muddy but not flooded. The thirsty earth had swallowed up every raindrop. Wildflowers were getting ready to bloom. Trees were displaying their buds. The whole world seemed to be happy, as if blessed by the previous night's downpour. For a moment, in the middle of nowhere, Henry and Randy thought there was nothing better than to be on the Cotton Road at this time.

Randy kept riding up and down the wagon train. He stopped every time to tell Bob how he saw things going and what he was hearing, if anything, from the wagon occupants. On one of his stops at Bob's wagon, Bob said, "Well, the gully washer we had last night really made things look better. It is as if life has been given back to the earth and all living creatures. All we need is peace and smooth going, and we should be in Santa Rosita in a few days."

No sooner had Bob uttered these words when gunshots rang out in the distance. Without hesitation, Randy rode as fast as he could to join his brother in the front and see what had happened. As soon as he got within talking distance to Henry, he heard one word, 'Banditos.'

Randy unsheathed his rifle and aimed it in the same direction as Henry, who firmly said, "Fire if you see anything move. Whatever it was out there, they took cover when I fired a couple of shots."

Randy's first thoughts were that maybe they should take cover, too. Just when he was thinking like this, Henry rode toward where he was aiming to get a better look. Randy tarried at a good distance behind Henry, who kept riding slowly toward his target with his rifle on the ready. Henry got closer and said softly, "No, not banditos who want to steal our horses and cargo. Something else, but I'm not sure yet what it is."

They got closer to the gulley, where they thought the adversaries were hiding. Henry got as close as he dared and fired a shot into the air, which caused those in hiding to begin waving their hats and calling for a stop to the shooting. Henry yelled in a manly voice, "Okay. Come out with your hands up. Don't make any fast moves because I got a nervous trigger finger."

Slowly, two young Anglos stood up with their hands high in the air. They were unarmed and dressed in plain clothes. They stood in front of Henry and his rifle barrel, who said, "Okay, lower your hands. Now, tell me your story."

The oldest of the two caught his breath and said, "We have a load of cotton, but our wagon has broken a wheel, and we are stranded. We ran out of food and are starving to death."

Henry responded by saying, "Where's your wagon? I've got to see that before believing your story."

The older man said, "It is over yonder that way somewhere."

Henry told his brother, "Ride back and tell Bob about this and see what I should do with these two."

As Randy rode off at a fast gallop, Henry told the two, "Sit down on the ground, save your strength, and wait for my brother to return."

When Henry looked behind himself to see if his brother was on his way, he turned back to see one of the men with a pistol aimed straight at him. In a flash, he dismounted. In his panic, he dropped his rifle. Using his horse as a shield, he drew one of his pistols and shot around the horse twice, killing both men with headshots.

As soon as Randy heard the shots, he turned his horse around and galloped toward Henry's location. He did not go too far before he encountered Henry and blurted out, "What happened? I heard shots."

Henry said in a matter-of-fact manner, "Those two were not what they said they were. Anyway, they won't bother us again. And we won't have to share our food with them. They're buzzard meat. I don't know what they were up to way out here, but it could not be any good. No doubt they were troublemakers and deserved what they got. We got to be on alert because they could be only an advance party of a larger group of troublemakers."

Randy listened in silence. He believed every word uttered by his older brother, but he also knew that his brother had no qualms about using his pistols against anybody who crossed him. Henry said, "Go back and tell Bob I'm going to stay here and make sure there're not more coming from where those two dudes came from. Tell Bob that any shots he heard were about me trying to shoot a few rabbits."

"But that's a lie," ranted Randy.

"Yes, a lie, but can't you see that it is by lies and corruption that people are getting rich? Stick to the truth and honesty, and you'll not get anywhere. This is not the time to be so right unless you want to be dead," said Henry in a serious tone.

After Henry said these words, Randy did not know what to think. He feared that his mild-mannered older brother was becoming a cold-blooded killer. He concluded that it was best he remain silent and continue to live day by day. He turned his horse and slowly rode back to the wagon train.

As Randy rode off, Henry turned to scan the horizon. He stayed mounted but hid with his horse under the partial shade of a big mesquite tree, being careful not to be stabbed by one of the tree's thorns. All the time, he never took his eyes off the spot where the two men came from. He stared at the horizon for a couple of hours, but he did not see anything.

After a while, he rode over to search the two dead bodies to see if they had anything of use. He could not find anything in their pockets. The pistol that one of them had pointed at him was unloaded and broken. He could not see any tracks to trace from where they came from. He buried the pistol and left the two bodies where they lay.

When his wagon train caught up with him, Henry was some distance from the bodies and sitting quietly on his horse, carving with his pocket knife a couple more notches on the walnut grip of his old right-handed .44 pistol. He now had five notches. He wondered how many more notches he would carve before he would become a notch on somebody else's pistol.

# Chapter Twenty-One
# Dead Horse

The next day, Henry and Randy rose earlier than usual to be ready to guide the wagons across the shallow Guadalupe River. Each wagon crossed the river without any difficulty. Their high bottoms were well above the height of the water. The last wagon crossed and took up its trailing position in the long string of twenty wagons. Bob's wagon was the first to cross, and he brought up, as usual, the rear of the dusty wagon train.

Before Henry left to take up his place some distance ahead of the lead wagon, he asked Bob, "Any news?"

Bob scratched his head before spouting out, "What the hell are you talkin' about? How can I get any news out here? I don't even know if the war is still goin' on. You got to get use to not knoin' what's happening in the outside world."

Henry replied before riding off, "I hope no news is good news."

Randy was listening to this exchange and wondered why his brother would ask such an inane question. He agreed with Bob that they could not know anything about what was going on in the world in their isolated location. He often thought they were better off not getting any news. The main thing for them was to concentrate on getting their cotton to market and staying alive.

Henry could see from his point position the dust being kicked up by a wagon train in front of them. He conjectured that the dust being kicked up by their train was being seen by the train behind theirs. The trafficking of cotton from Alleyton to Matamoros was a big business, and everyone with a wagon was trying to get a piece of the profitable action.

Most were happy with this action to support the Confederacy, but all were after the good money they could make by transporting cotton to Mexico. Although their actions were prolonging the bloody war, they did not care about anything but making money. If they could make money while supporting the Confederacy, so much the better. They did not know by keeping this back door open to the cotton trade they were preventing the collapse of the economy of the South.

Henry returned to tell Randy to pass the word onto Bob that there was another train in front of them. In the course of making his rounds, Randy told Bob, and he reacted in a blast of words. "This whole country is covered by wagons hauling cotton. You ain't seen nothing yet. Wait until we get to the Nueces River Santa Margarita ferry crossing, wagons will be backed up for miles waiting for their turn. Good thing Mr. Ford has his own ferry boats for crossing the Nueces."

Randy listened to Bob and turned to continue making his rounds, chatting with those driving the wagons. He trotted alongside one wagon and relayed to the teenage waggoneers what Bob had told him. The first reply he got was, "How many more days before we git to the ferry crossing?"

Randy said, "I don't rightly know. We got a few more creeks to cross, and that should slow us down. I expect it will take us three or four more days to reach the Nueces. After that, it should take us a couple more days to reach Santa Rosita and Mr. Ford's ranch for a couple of days of rest before tackling the final leg of our trip through the Big Sands to Brownsville."

"We know all that. What we want to know the most is when we git our money?"

Randy was caught off guard by the simple question from one of the wagon boys and mumbled a reply, "I'm pretty sure you get paid when you deliver your cotton load to its owner in Brownsville. I think that is the way it's usually done."

One of the wagon boys stood up to stretch his legs, and Randy noticed his clothes must be handmade. The prompted Randy to grin and ask, "Where did you get your clothes?"

"Why my mama made these clothes from homespun cloth. You sure can't buy any cloth anymore. These clothes were hand-sewn by her. Wait. I got something else to show you that she made by hand. The boy reached down in the box beneath his seat and pulled out and unfolded a colorful flag."

All Randy could say was. "Wow. I never seen a flag like that before."

The boy reacted good-humoredly, "What? This here is a Confederate flag; I use it to let people know we're not Union sympathizers. My mama homespun and dyed the flag cloth from cotton yarn and sewed it by hand in the right way."

Randy was struck by the boy's use of the words, 'Union sympathizers,' so he asked the boy, "What if someone is identified as a Union sympathizer?"

The boy lost no time in responding, "They wud probably be strung up."

Randy swallowed hard. "I guess that's not much of a problem in these parts as Texas is a Confederate state, and we are transporting cotton for Mr. Ford, who is trying to help the South."

The boy did not want to argue with a schooled young man who must be a couple of years older than him, so he only muttered, "There's plenty of people in these parts who favor the Union side, but for their own safety, they keep quiet."

Randy acknowledged the boy's words and rode on to the next wagon. Deep down, he found the boy's last words disturbing. From that day on, he would look at everyone he encountered and try to determine which side of the war they were on. He knew he could not take anyone for their words, but he must consider their actions. There was more than money at stake, but money usually trumped loyalty and the truth,

In the couple of days ahead for them they did ford a couple of creeks without incident. They kept pushing on in their monotonous journey toward the Nueces. All were eager to cross the Nueces and be on with the journey to Santa Rosita, rest and refitting stop before heading toward Brownsville and the pot of gold that awaited them there.

Henry rode back to tell Randy that Bob should be told that there is a swarm of wagons ahead. Randy galloped back to tell Bob about the snarl of wagons. Bob said plainly, "That's the Nueces crossing. Pass the word to each wagon to halt and prepare for an overnight camp. I'll go to the front and signal to Henry to come for my orders."

Randy was puzzled and said, "Isn't it much too early to make camp?

Bob replied, "No time to explain now. Just do as I say."

Randy rode off quickly to pass Bob's message to bring the train to a halt and prepare for a night's rest. Bob re-confirmed the same message as he passed each wagon to get in front. When in front, he stood up and whistled loudly and waved his arms until Henry started on his way back. When Henry arrived, he said, "Saddle me one of the spare horses. We're going to go and arrange for our crossing."

Henry nodded and said obediently, "Yes, sir."

As Henry was removing a saddle from the wagon, Randy rode up and quizzically asked, "What's goin on?"

Without stopping what he was doing, Henry said, "Me and Bob goin' to ride ahead and arrange our Nueces crossing."

Then Randy rode up to Bob, who was in the process of climbing off his wagon, and asked, "What do you want me to do now?"

"Just stay here and get everyone ready to camp for the night in this spot. You can start by unhitching my mules and leading them to a grazing place. Too many wagons ahead for us to squeeze in and the place is barren of any grass. We can all drink our fill and wash tomorrow in the Nueces."

Bob's words were almost too much for Randy to take in. He decided to do as Bob said and not do any more questioning. Henry led the horse to Bob and handed him the reins. Bob mounted the horse and said, "Let's go."

Henry rode alongside Bob for almost a mile without saying a word. Bob was the first to talk, saying, "When we get there, you need to stay put while I search for Mr. Ford's crossing manager to let him know we have twenty wagons that need to go to the other side of the Nueces. We should have no problem in advancing through the crowd of wagons cuz Mr. Ford has his own flat bottom ferry boats."

Before Henry could respond, Bob had ridden off into the crowd and disappeared among the massive jumble of wagons and the teams. It took some time for Bob to return and say, "Let's go back. All is arranged for dawn tomorrow."

They turned and rode in the direction of their wagon train. Henry could not remain quiet and asked Bob, "What did you do to arrange things at riverside?"

"Well, as I said, Mr. Ford has his own ferries and place to cross. I found his manager, and he told me where to be at dawn. Most of the multitude of wagons you see are crossing in private ferries at the natural ford. Mr. Ford has his own crossing point. The manager will send out a scout early tomorrow to guide us to that point."

Henry thought about Bob's words for a while before saying, "So, only the cotton owned by Mr. Ford and his partners use his crossing. Who do the other wagons full of cotton belong to?"

Bob laughed and said, "I don't know for sure, but I reckon that cotton belongs also to Mr. Ford and his partners cuz they own almost everything in these parts, but they try to keep a low profile."

They arrived back to their train, and everyone was getting ready to settle in for the night. Bob told Randy to gather everyone because he wanted them to know what was happening and what was expected of them. Bob pointed at an old pecan tree and said he would meet everyone there. The tree gave scant little shade from the hot sun.

It took a while for all the wagon drivers to congregate in front of Bob. who began by saying, "Thanks for getting this far. We're about halfway to Brownsville. Tomorrow, we have to get moving before dawn as we're scheduled to begin our crossing at dawn. The ferries can only take one wagon at a time, so be ready to roll onto the ferry when your turn comes. The drought means the water level is lower, and the river is narrower than usual. We should not have any problems. Once we are on the other side, we'll keep on going as far as we can go. Any questions?"

One of the wagon boys spoke up, "How we know when to get started?"

Bob replied with a slight smirk on his face, "Why, one reason I hired these two fine young gentlemen was to get you up and on your way."

He pointed at Henry and Randy, who stayed mounted on their horses, and they both tipped their hats in accordance. After this gesture, Bob asked, "Any more questions?"

His query was met by silence, except some of the wagon drivers were saying to their comrades that they had done this before and this was how it was done. Bob closed the gathering by saying, "Okay. See you on the road before dawn tomorrow."

The group of waggoneers quietly returned to their respective places. Henry and Randy stayed mounted and stared at Bob, who said, "What's on your mind? Go ahead, get it off your chest."

Henry remained his usual silent self while Randy asked in a low voice, "How we going to get up so early to get everybody up and ready?"

Randy's innocent question gave Bob a good laugh before he said, "You two got to figure that out. I'm counting on you to do as planned."

Bob sauntered off to his wagon to begin preparing the evening meal while Henry and Randy looked for a good spot to bed down and graze their horses. They returned to Bob's wagon to unsaddle his horse and put it and his mules out to graze. Bob said, "Hang around to eat. I'm cooking up my specialty… hot corn grits."

They all had a good laugh over Bob's words. Then Bob said, "Let's all sit down around the little cooking fire I built and toast with our tin cups of coffee tomorrow's crossing."

Henry and Randy were happy to do as Bob requested. Everyone was in a good mood, and their adrenalin was running high in anticipation of crossing the Nueces tomorrow. Henry and Randy could not wait to see what all this Nueces business was all about and get to the other side so they could continue to Santa Rosita. They enjoyed eating their grits and drinking their hot coffee.

Dusk was enveloping them, and Bob was already sleepy, so he said. "Boys, I think I goin to turn in, but before I do, I'd like to know what you decided?"

Henry and Randy gave each other questioning looks. Neither of them knew what Bob was talking about. Randy said, "What do you mean?"

"How you goin' to get up so early?"

Randy quickly retorted, "Oh, that. Well, we really haven't talked about that yet, but I think we just going to stay up all night. Maybe we'll stay on our horses and do some patrolling to make sure no troublemakers are in the vicinity."

"Sounds good, but you have to stop using words like 'vicinity' cuz nobody in these parts will understand what you mean."

Henry and Randy laughed over Bob's words, and Randy only said, "Understood."

They mounted their horses and said good night to Bob, and Randy said to Henry, "How we really going to do this?"

Henry replied, "I thought what you said to Bob was a good plan. Anyway, I prefer staying on my horse than being on foot."

Randy said, "Okay. Do you want to take turns, or do you want to make the rounds together?"

"I'll make the first round. You get some rest."

Randy returned to their camping spot while Henry rode off to circumnavigate their wagon train. The moonlight gave him a good view of the lay of the land. He felt good mounted on his trusted horse. He rode slowly at some distance from the line of wagons, and all seemed well.

He was rounding the train for his return ride to their base camp when he felt a nick on his neck, and for a moment, he thought he was being attacked by an errant insect. But in an instant, he became fully alert and realized it was night, and most insects did not fly in the night. All of a

160

sudden, it dawned on him that he was being shot at. He had no time to think. He unsheathed his rifle and jumped off his horse.

He wanted to fire back, but he could not figure out from where the bullets fired at him were coming. He wanted to hide, but there was nowhere to hide except in the tall grass. He laid down and waited for the next shot at him. He saw a distant flash and forced his horse to lay down and took up a protective position behind it. As soon as he did that, the bullets came whizzing by fast and furious. He began to fire back, and there was quite a firefight for a brief spell.

The noise made by the exchange of shots woke up everyone in the wagon train, and quickly, Henry was not the only one firing back. With all the gunfire going on, everyone was in a panic mode. Randy was only worried about his brother. He saddled his horse and rode as fast as he could in the direction he thought he would find Henry.

Randy put himself in harm's way, but he did not care about anything but coming to the aid of his older brother. The shooting had died down, and Randy was hollering at the top of his lungs for his brother. He rode like a crazy man, oblivious to any danger. He finally spied a lump in the grass and yelled, "Henry, is that you?"

Henry heard his brother and yelled back, "Get down. We're being shot at.

Randy dismounted immediately and led his horse to where Henry was aiming his rifle across his horse. Upon seeing his brother, Randy gasped, "Thank God. You're still alive!"

Henry sighed. "Yeah, I was lucky this time. I think all the shooting from our side scared them off."

They both lay behind Henry's horse when Randy noticed how still the horse was. He felt around the horse with his hand and pulled his hand back when he touched a warm liquid substance. His hand was covered with blood. He did not have the heart to tell Henry that he thought his horse was dead.

Randy did not have to tell Henry this because Bob came walking up and said in a somber voice, "You guys okay?"

Henry and Randy replied weakly in unison, "Yeah."

"Well, that's fine, but it looks like your horse was shot dead."

Upon hearing Bob's words, Henry jumped up and screamed, "Oh God. That can't be true. I loved this horse."

While a tearful Henry was kneeling over his dead horse, Bob said, "The horse saved you, and you saved us all from the worst that Mexican banditos have to offer. I guess nobody is going to get any sleep this night."

# Chapter Twenty-Two
# Nueces

"Remove all from your horse and leave him lying. Randy, fetch a good spare horse and bring it to your brother. We might as well get ready to go. For sure, it's not safe here." Bob said as if it were hard to formulate words.

Everyone was scared that the banditos were not finished and would return with anger, kill everyone, and steal their cotton and all they possessed. Randy brought Henry a spare horse, and as soon as it was saddled, they rode off toward the wagon train at a gallop. Their nervous horses sensed that danger was near, and their nervousness communicated to Henry and Randy the urgency to get moving as quickly as possible.

The waggoneers worked as quickly as possible to get their mules harnessed and hitched and their wagons ready to move. Everyone had their guns at the ready. Bob's wagon was ready to go, and he took up a position in front. He told Randy to tell the other wagons to stay close to the next wagon in case they were attacked again so they would be better able to fight back. Henry rode alongside Bob and said, "What do you want me to do? Ride ahead, or stay back with you?"

"Stay here and keep an eye out. If you see any suspicious movement, shoot at it. We're lucky to still be alive."

Henry cradled his rifle as he rode slowly his horse while he said to Bob, "After that scary spat, I'm running low of bullets."

Bob quickly said, "Make all your bullets count cuz I got none to give you. Hold on until we get to Santa Rosita. You can get all you need there."

They rolled on through the soft moonlit night toward the Nueces crossing. Henry and Randy kept a watchful eye out on all sides of the wagon train while it moved toward the river. Bob got to a point where he asked Randy to take over the reins of his wagon while he used his horse to go with Henry to see if they could cross the river earlier than planned. Randy had never driven a wagon before, so he called to one of his wagon friends to help him. They did all this without slowing down the wagon train.

"Let's go, Henry. I got to see if I can find the same ferry manager I spoke to yesterday and see if we can cross as soon as possible. I'm sure he'll understand when I tell him we were attacked. I'll not feel safe until we're on the other side of the river."

Henry said, "I'm sure they'll be suspicious of anybody riding up in the middle of the night."

Bob replied, "Yeah, we got to be careful and approach the sentries I'm sure they have posted on the outskirts of the crossing. Keep your rifle sheathed so that there is not moonlight dancing off it. We sure don't want to invite incoming fire."

They headed toward the river and slowed their pace when they thought they were close enough to be seen by the nearest sentry. The kept their hands on their reins and scanned the horizon. They kept moving but at an even slower pace. Bob said softly to Henry, "I thought their guards would have appeared by now. Maybe they don't see two Anglos on horseback as a threat."

Henry added, "Or maybe they're asleep."

At that moment, they heard a shout coming from behind them. "Hands up. State your business and why you creepin' up this time of night."

Bob spoke rapidly in a flurry of words. "We're from Mr. Ford's next wagon train, which was just attacked by banditos."

The man behind them said, "Okay. Put your hands down and turn around so I can see your faces."

Bob and Henry slowly turned their horses around so they could see a short white man with his rifle pointed straight at them. For a couple of minutes, this man looked at him and then said gayly, "Bob, is that you?"

"It sure is, and is that you, Shorty?"

Henry had never seen two people so glad to see each other and stood idly by while Bob dismounted and gave the short man on the ground a bear hug. Bob exclaimed to Henry, "This is Shorty. We go way back. We were working for Mr. Ford when he was only a steamboat captain on the Rio Grande. Really a special sight, especially at this moment."

Henry tipped his hat and said, "Glad to meet you, Mr. Shorty. It's a relief to see you and Bob are such good friends."

Bob explained to Shorty their situation and asked where the ferry manager was so he could see him about crossing earlier than planned. Shorty was very cooperative and pointed to where Bob and Henry had to go to see the manager. In parting, Shorty said, "I cain't leave my spot, but you should do all right. Bob, it was good to see you again. Next time, the drinks are on me. Take care."

Bob gave Shorty a last bear hug and said tenderly, "You ol' SOB, stay safe and alive. I look forward to those drinks."

Bob re-mounted his horse and, with Henry, began their ride into the crossing camp. Bob reminisced at length about his brief encounter with his old friend, Shorty. He said in low but solemn voice, "It was quite somethin' to meet Shorty like that. He's been truly a dear old friend for years. I can probably count on one hand the people I knew when I first came to these parts some years ago. They either died or moved away. This is tough country to survive in."

Henry listened to Bob's sentimental side and said, "Where you from?"

"I was born and raised in Illinois. I drifted to these parts about six years ago. I did many jobs along the way, but I've been working with Mr. Ford and his partners in Brownsville and Matamoros for several years."

They arrived at the crossing camp, and it appeared that all were asleep. Bob slowly walked around, looking for the manager. He turned around one wagon to find a shotgun aimed at his face by a man who said, "Lookin' for someone?"

"Yeah. Where's the manager? We got a wagon train full of Mr. Ford's cotton, and we need to cross as soon as possible," Bob said nervously to the man holding the shotgun in his face.

Again, Bob was pleased to hear, "Why, Bob, is that you? Sorry for pointing a gun at you, but you never can be too careful, especially at this time of night when visitors to our camp are not welcome."

Bob excused this nighttime intrusion and explained his predicament to the manager and that his wagon train should be rolling in within the hour; therefore, his ferry crossing needed to start earlier than planned. The manager replied almost gleefully, "No problema, Bob. I'll wake up my people and tell them to get Mr. Ford's ferries ready to get you on the other side of the river as soon as possible."

Bob thanked the ferry manager and wanted to say his name, but he could not remember it. He felt bad about not being able to thank him personally but for the life of him, he could not remember his name. He felt especially bad because the manager was one of the few Hispanics Mr. Ford had assigned to a position of high responsibility. He was too embarrassed to ask anyone else his name.

Bob and Henry rode to the outskirts of the crossing camp to await the arrival of their wagon train. They heard the creaking sound of wagon wheels before they could see any wagon. Slowly, out of the nighttime obscurity appeared Bob's leading wagon with Randy sitting in front. Randy brought his wagon to a halt, where Bob and Henry were waiting on their horses. After Randy breathed a sigh of relief at seeing Bob and his brother, he asked, "Are the ferries ready?"

Bob replied, "Almost. Let's get all our wagons bunched up before I check on the ferries. You wait here and make sure all the wagons have arrived safely."

Bob and Henry rode down to the riverbank at the spot indicated for boarding on the ferries. Henry looked at the narrow and shallow clear river and asked Bob, "This is such a little river. Why don't we ford it just like we've done so many other water passages?"

Bob replied, "That's a good question. I really don't know. I think it is deeper than it looks and would leak into the bottoms of our wagons. Also, I hear there are some alligators in the river. If true, you sure don't want to be in water when they are lurking about. I never seen one, but I hear they're fearsome creatures."

"Oh. I thought maybe it was because of wagons falling in bottom holes and getting stuck or breaking their wheels. After all, our wagons are carrying heavy loads."

Bob's response was brief, "That too."

Just as they finished this brief exchange, three ferries were docking before them on the riverbank. The ferries quickly tied thick ropes to solid posts placed along the north riverbank and laid heavy planks of wood for the wagons to roll onto the ferry. One of the workers approached Bob and said, "We're ready. Where's your wagons?"

"There right here. Henry, ride back to Randy and tell him to start movin' the wagons forward."

Randy and his sidekick approached Bob's wagon, and Bob called them to a stop and said, "Okay, young man, come and get on your horse, and I'll take over. Have your companion watch how I drive the wagon onto the ferry so he can tell the others. Each ferry only takes one wagon at a time, so be patient as you wait your turn."

The three of them watched in silence as Bob rolled his wagon and mule team onto the waiting ferry, which pushed off from the bank as soon as Bob's wagon was fully onboard. Bob stood up and yelled back to the trio, saying. "Now hurry and have the other wagons cross. I'll be waitin' for you on the other side."

Randy mounted his horse and said to the wagon boy in an excited voice, "Go back to your wagon and get on the next ferry while I ride back to the other wagons to tell them all to move forward to board one wagon at a time."

The boy ran off, and Randy departed in a flash, leaving Henry alone with his thoughts on his horse at the river's edge. In a moment of silence, he asked himself. *What the hell am I doing here, and where am I going?*

He had no good answers to this moment of self-reflection. And, he had not time as the next wagon was at the water's edge ready to roll onto the waiting ferry. He figured his job was to help guide each wagon onto a ferry and that he would take the last ferry to cross. As he was watching the second wagon board a ferry, the first ferry was returning empty to take another wagon. Henry could see then that all twenty wagons would be across more quickly than he had thought.

The first sun rays began to peak over the eastern horizon. Before long, he could see the outlines of Bob waving that all was well on the other side about fifty feet away and that all was going well. It was plain daylight as Randy came riding up with the last wagon, and when it rolled onto the ferry, Henry said to one of the ferry workers, "Got room for two more on horseback?"

He and Randy got a hand signal to come aboard with their horses and squeeze in. Henry watched as a man on either side of the flat bottom ferry pushed off with long wooden poles and continued pushing the ferry across the river by shoving their poles against the river bottom. He could see that this crossing was a big deal but not as big as he previously thought.

They rode off the ferry and joined a grinning Bob, who exclaimed, "Welcome to Mexico."

Henry and Randy were puzzled how he welcomed them, prompting Randy to ask, "What do you mean? Aren't we still in Texas?"

Bob was in an ebullient mood because all the wagons had crossed safely the Nueces and, after a long guffaw said, "That's an old joke. The Mexicans wanted the Nueces to be their northern border, but Texans insisted on the Rio Grande being the border. It's still a sore subject with the

Mexican government."

"Enough fun time. Let's get this wagon train moving south toward our rest and re-fitting stop at Santa Rosita, which is about two or three days away."

Randy said in an urgent tone, "What about watering our horses and mules?"

"Dab gummet. Plain forgot about that. Good thing I got you boys to help me remember. Let's roll on a bit to get away from the river crossing and, take our animals to drink, and let them graze on any grass still standing. Ride ahead and tell all about our plan."

Randy rode ahead to pass the message while Henry looked for a good place to park their wagons. It was a good time to not only water the animals but to wash up, too. The wagon crews took turns at enjoying the life water gave them. They also found this was a good time to eat some breakfast and refill any water jugs they had.

They did not really feel like moving on, but after a couple of hours of their water break, Bob said, "We have to be moving on. We're losin' too much time. You'll get a longer break at Santa Rosita, which we should reach in a couple of days."

The waggoneers reluctantly gathered their mule teams and, hitched them in their places, and mounted their wagons, waiting until the signal was given to move out. Bob gave the order to move, and Randy rode by each wagon to make sure they were ready to head out. Each wagon was poised and ready to move as soon as the wagon in front of it was some distance from it.

Henry rode out to a distant point position and the lead wagon followed his horse's tracks that were among a multitude of wagon tracks. The lead wagon tried also to keep an eye on Henry and his horse, making sure that tufts of cotton were spread all along the wide way of the Cotton Road.

The grass on the rolling plains was becoming sparser and Bob commented. "This is the driest spring that I can remember. It is also hotter this time of year than I recall. This darn weather will increase our sufferings as we cross the big and desolate sands to Brownville. For me, getting through the Big Sands to the Rio Grande Valley is the toughest part of our journey. This is not country for sissies."

Randy listened to Bob and wanted to know more, but he did know enough to ask an intelligent question. All he knew was that he was on a great adventure to unknown parts, and he was a novice who still had a lot to learn. Before he turned his horse around and rode back to check on the wagons, he blankly said, "I don't know what is better or worse because this is my first time in these parts. I just take things as they are and hope for the best. I'm glad to have made it this far, and I look forward to seeing the Rio Grande."

# Chapter Twenty-Three
# Death on the Trail

Henry's thoughts repeatedly dwelled upon the blood dripping from his dead horse. He could not get over the fact that he owed his life to a horse that died while protecting him. His horse deserved more than being abandoned in the grass of the open prairie. Life was not fair neither for beast nor man.

Bob drove his wagon to the lead position, saying, "I want to be in front when we arrive at Santa Rosita to make sure we get a fair shake. I want Mr. Ford to see he can count on me."

Randy listened closely to Bob's words and asked him," Do you think we'll get to meet Mr. Ford?"

"Well, I plan on introducing you myself if I get the opportunity to do so. We'll see. He's a mighty busy man."

Bob continued talking, "We're getting' close. Mr. Ford can probably see our dust from his watch tower. They say he mounts the tower several times a day to see through his telescope the arrival of his cotton trains."

Randy said, "I can't wait to see Santa Rosita and take advantage of all its provisions."

"You got that right. If it weren't for the bounties of Santa Rosita, we couldn't complete our journey to Brownsville and deliver our cotton."

At that moment, Henry came riding in at a gallop and said breathlessly, "I'm beginning to see the outline of some buildings dead ahead. This has got to be Santa Rosita."

Bob replied instantly, "Yep. That's it. Randy, ride back and tell all that we should be arriving at Santa Rosita in a couple of hours. They should begin closing the distance between their wagons. Henry, you ride within eyesight in front of me in the direction of those buildings."

Randy rode off to spread the news to the other wagons. Henry rode in the front with his eyes glued on the horizon for any sign of buildings popping up from the flat horizon. Randy stopped to chat with a waggoneer near his age, and after he communicated his message, the young wagon boy said, "Yippee! I cud use a few days off. I cain't tell you how tired I'm for looking at and smelling mule asses all day, every day. There's got to be more to life than this. I feel like I've sold my soul for a few gold pesos."

Randy really did not know how to respond to the boy's assertion. He spouted out what he later would regard as a foolish phrase. "Don't worry. You're not sacrificing for yourself but for a greater cause."

Randy doubted the veracity of his words, but it seemed the right thing to say. Yet, there were rich people getting richer by helping the cause. He thought they were more interested in lining their pockets while they could than waging any war.

After informing the last wagon of their imminent arrival at Santa Rosita, Randy turned to return to his position alongside Bob's lead wagon. As he rode, he began to notice that Bob's wagon was not in line with the others. He rode a little farther and saw Bob's wagon meandering off to the side of the track. He whipped his reins across his horse to go fast as he could to the front.

When Randy arrived at the second wagon in line, the drivers shouted, "We don't know what's wrong with Bob's wagon, but it's sure not holdin' to its usual steady track."

Randy did not pause and continued at a fast gallop to see why Bob's wagon was off course. He arrived at the wagon and saw Bob slumped over on the wagon seat and the mule reins trailing on the ground. He yelled, "Mr. Bob. What the hell's wrong? Did you drop your reins?"

Randy words were met with stone silence. He dismounted quickly and grabbed the lead mule's halter to bring the wagon to a stop. He then rushed to Bob's side to see what was the matter with him. He found a lifeless body which fell to one side when he touched it. He shook Bob by his shoulders, but not a sound was forthcoming from him. He did not know what to do.

He looked forward in the distance to see if he could make out his older brother. Henry's eyes only looked forward, so he was not looking back at what was happening with the wagon train. At that moment, Randy decided to ride ahead and get his brother. Before he rode off, he told the second wagon, "Pass the word. Something has happened to Bob. We're stopping here until we get to the bottom of it."

Randy again rode as fast as the terrain would allow toward Henry. All the while, he was yelling at the top of his voice to get Henry's attention. Henry finally turned his horse to see what all the noise was about. He rode back at a gallop to join Randy, who blurted out, "I think Bob has passed away. We're at a standstill. Ride back quickly with me so we can decide what to do."

Henry was shocked by what Randy said and rode off as quickly as he could in the direction of Bob's wagon. Randy followed in the wake of Henry's dust. They arrived at the wagon. Henry jumped off his horse and climbed quickly up the wagon to check Bob's body. After a while, Henry said in a soft voice to Randy. "I guess he died of some kind of stroke. For sure, he's dead as a doornail."

Upon hearing Henry's words, tears swelled up in Randy's eyes as he whined, "What do we do now?"

Henry kept his emotions to himself as he said, "We got to move on. We're almost at Santa Rosita. Let's find some rope to tie him to the seat so all at Santa Rosita can see a well-known face. You drive his wagon the rest the way. I'll take your job and ride behind to inform the others of the sad news."

Randy was traumatized by the unexpected turn of events. In silence, he helped Henry tie Bob in place. He attached his horse to the back of the wagon, collected the reins, and climbed into the driver's seat. Henry said, "Okay, get started while I ride back to tell the others that we're approaching Santa Rosita."

Henry passed the sad news to the others and exhorted them to keep pushing on. By the time he returned to Randy's wagon, he was in a deeply reflective mood and said to Randy, "That's the first time somebody I knew and liked had died. That makes a difference. If it were a total stranger or an enemy, I wouldn't feel a thing. I wonder how the news of Bob's untimely death will be received in Santa Rosita."

Not a word was said by Randy as he sank deeper into a somber mood brought forcefully on by Bob's dead body sitting next to him. He could not imagine a sicker situation than the one he was in. He was learning the hard way – the only way… that life in the wilds of Texas was brutal and tough to the core.

Henry rode ahead as if nothing had happened. He did not know that he and the front wagon were in the sight of Mr. Ford's telescope. Mr. Ford saw that all was not normal with Bob and a white stranger who was driving his wagon. He immediately ran downstairs to order a posse of his trusted vaqueros to ride out an investigate the oncoming wagon train.

His Mexican force of a dozen men assembled quickly and rode at a gallop toward the wagon train. Henry saw them coming and rode back to the lead wagon. He yelled at Randy, "Stop moving. There's a band of armed men headed our way."

Before he could turn his horse around, their wagon was surrounded by a group of hard-core Mexicans with their pistols drawn. The first words they heard were, "Hands up! Captain Ford sent us to see what is wrong with Señor Bob."

The man who said these words said something in a language they did not understand to one of his sidekicks. They assumed he was speaking Spanish. The man that he spoke to sprang off his horse and climbed onto the wagon to see what was wrong with Bob. After checking Bob, the man looked at the mounted man and said a few words in Spanish. Henry and Randy assumed he was telling him that Bob was dead.

The leader of this fierce group of Mexicans said to Henry and Randy in heavily accented and broken English. "We'll escort you the rest of the way. You got a lot of explaining to do to the captain or one of his foremen."

Henry and Randy kept quiet and went along. Henry worked to keep his impulses in check. He was afraid that he would draw his pistols, and they would all end up dead. He had no choice but to accompany peacefully the wagon train to Santa Rosita.

Their wagon train came to a halt in the large compound of Santa Rosita. Randy could see nearby there was a substantial house that rivaled any of the best houses he had ever seen. It was remarkable to see such a house built in the middle of nowhere. He, Henry, and all the waggoneers were told to remain in their places until Captain Ford was informed of their arrival, and they received instructions as to what they should do next.

The train was enveloped by a somber mood. They had expected for days to celebrate when they arrived at Santa Rosita, but now, their tired bones were enmeshed in a funeral atmosphere. The lead Mexican returned from the big house and said, "Come along, and I will show you where to park your wagons and graze and water your horses and mules."

Henry and Randy were ready to follow the Mexican man when he said to them. "Not you. You go to big house. I'll drive the lead wagon and take care of Bob's body."

Randy mounted his horse and accompanied Henry to the big house. They dismounted and tied their tired horses to the hitching rail in front of the shaded wide porch of the big house. They stepped onto the porch and were ready to knock on the imposing front door when it opened wide, and a beaming Mexican servant said in perfect English, "Come in. The captain is waiting for you in the dining room."

The servant pointed the way to the dining room, where they found three Anglo men puffing on cigars and sipping whiskey in a well-adorned large room. They were thrown off guard by the luxurious surroundings and the latest dress the three men were wearing. The man at the head of the table told them in something of a New York accent. "Take a seat. Certainly, you've not forgotten your manners. I thought you should have some food in your bellies before you two tell us what you're doing so far west."

Henry and Randy could not remember the last time they had sat in a cushioned chair. They sat down in their chairs at the empty side of the table. Henry was surprised they did not ask him to remove his pistol belt. As soon as they sat down, servants appeared from a side room with a washing bowl. After washing their faces and hands, they were served food delicacies they had not seen since they had left their plantation in Virginia. They were also provided an assortment of drinks. The man at the head of the table said, "Eat up, and then we'll talk."

Henry and Randy's hunger did not need such a courteous invitation, and they gobbled up the food piled high on their plates like starving men. All the time they were eating, the other men were observing them carefully. They knew their eating manners would tell them a lot about the way they were raised. When they were cutting the last piece of steak off and placing it in their mouths, the man at the head of the table said, "I can see that you were not raised in a barn. We would like to know if you can read and write?"

Henry cleared his throat and, swallowed the cool water that was in one of his glasses, and said, "Thanks for inviting us to eat. We were mighty hungry. To answer your question, yes, we are schooled, and that is the main reason our dearly departed Bob hired us."

"So, Bob hired you to do what?"

Henry explained the best he could their jobs. Randy said, "If I can be excused for a minute, I'll go to my horse in front and bring my ledger book that Bob told me to keep notes in."

The man at the head of the table said, "That won't be necessary. Let's back up because we should do proper introductions. I'm Captain Ford or just Captain. These two gentlemen are my trusted foremen, Tom and

Moses. Their word is as good as mine. Now, what's your real names and where do you come from?"

Henry told them snippets of their story about how they got from Virginia to southern Texas. He asked his younger brother if he had anything to add. He shook his head in the negative. The captain spoke up, "That's an impressive story. You guys have been through a lot. It bolds well for you that you have survived to tell us your story. But are Henry and Randy your real names?"

Henry poked his younger brother in the side, indicating he should answer this question. Randy spoke loudly, saying, "My birth name is Peyton Randolph Read, and my older brother's name is Henry Harrison Read. That's the truth."

The captain smiled and said, "It's so refreshing to hear the truth. From now on, you're Henry, and your younger brother is Randy. Okay?"

At that point, the captain and his two foremen stood and raised their glasses in a toast to Henry and Randy, who also stood up and grabbed their glasses. The captain roared, "Welcome aboard!"

They put their glasses down and applauded the arrival of the newcomers who had blindly joined their team. When they finished clapping and were dismissed, Henry asked, "Aren't you going to ask about how Bob died?"

The captain was quick to reply, "We knew that old Bob had a bad heart and was liable to go any day. We're in mourning over the death of our dear associate, but we are happy that he died so near to Santa Rosita. My wife is not here, but I know she would insist on giving him a decent burial. If you like, you can join us in our small cemetery to bury him at dusk."

Henry did not like to talk much, but he had to say to the captain. "We have other questions. When can we ask them?"

The captain replied. "Your questions can wait. You're working for me now, and that is all you really need to know. Now, there will be somebody waiting to show you to your quarters. I'll give you instructions tomorrow. We all need to sleep on all this and re-visit where we are tomorrow."

Henry and Randy shook hands all around like real men and stepped outdoors, where they found a young Mexican man waiting for them. This man collected their horses and pointed out the features of Santa Rosita. He took them to the spring pool where their horses could drink their fill and explained that this location was selected because of the spring water. He said they had plenty of everything they needed. He took them to their bunkhouse and wished them a good sleep. He also said he would be back shortly to take them to the cemetery for Bob's burial.

Randy guessed this young and barefooted Mexican teenager was younger than him and said, "If you're goin' to be hanging around us, we should probably know your name."

Rafael said," I'll be back in about an hour."

Henry and Randy stepped into the bunkhouse and found their waggoneers already comfortably installed. They were all happy to see them. They had heard that Henry and Randy had been honored by being received by the captain. They considered that an exceptionally good omen. They became even more excited when they learned Henry and Randy had been invited to Bob's burial. One of them exclaimed, "Boy! The captain has really taken you under his wings."

Two beds had been reserved for Henry and Randy near the front door of the bunkhouse. They were beginning to feel like celebrities. They were laying in the comfort on their springy beds when Rafael showed up and said, "Time to go."

The sun was setting as they neared an opening in the prairie grass where a grave hole had been dug for Bob's final resting place. They had wrapped his body in a woven grass mat. Everyone near the grave removed their hats and bowed their heads as Bob's body was lowered into the grave. As soon as the ropes used to lower Bob's body were removed, several Mexican workers began shoveling dirt into the hole. Off to the side, a group of Mexican women began singing a song of mourning.

Henry and Randy did not understand a word of Spanish they were singing, but they were deeply touched by the tune. Just as the sun fell behind the western horizon, the singing stopped, and all those gathered for Bob's burial departed, going their separate ways. It was not the time for any talking. A life and the day had ended forever.

# Chapter Twenty-Four
# Home Away from Home

They enjoyed laying in their beds, but they could not sleep. It had been a long time since they had slept in real beds, but try as they might, they could not sleep. They thought their tired bodies were too filled with aches to permit sleep in soft beds. Randy thought maybe it was their way of mourning the death of Bob. He whispered to Henry, "I miss Bob. It's so sad he had to go in the way he did, and it's even sadder that he was buried without any family in attendance. Nobody even knows his next of kin. He's gone from everyone for good, whether they know it or not. It's like nobody cares. I guess if you venture into this uncaring country, you can expect to end up like Bob. Dead is more dead when it's alone and far away from home in the wild frontier."

Henry grunted his acknowledgment of Randy's words. When he looked at their worn boots aligned on the floor next to their beds, he instantly became startled and said, "Where's our rifles and saddles?"

Randy immediately responded, "That's a good question. I plum forgot about our horses and their tack. That fancy dinner in the big house must have lulled us into a false sense of well-being. It's night. There's nothing we can do about it now."

"Maybe so. But I can't sleep well without knowing if my horse, rifle, and saddle are okay. At least, I got my trusty old pair of .44 pistols hanging from their belt on my bedpost. By the way, I still don't understand why we were treated like royalty at dinner in the big house. Look at us. We're nothing but stinking, unkempt trail hands."

Randy thought a moment and replied to Henry's words, "I think it's our Virginia upbringing and formal educational level which causes Mr. Ford and his foremen to see something in us that we can't see in ourselves. I don't think he or any of the men at the table come from the best of backgrounds. But they got natural born smarts that are needed to survive in Texas."

Henry was always impressed with his younger brother's intelligence and only said, "I guess you have sized up the situation rightly. I would also add that we are big and strong white boys who have proven they can survive in the wilderness. Whatever the case may be, I'll feel more civilized after a full clean-up tomorrow."

Randy was quick to add, "I'm sure Rafael is taking care of our horses, rifles, and saddles. I think I'm going to sleep now."

Henry was up before dawn. He wanted to be ready to check on their horses and stuff at first light. Randy and all the waggoneers were fast asleep. Henry stepped out of the bunkhouse when it was getting light enough to see. He was surprised to find Rafael sitting on the step, looking out across the Santa Rosita station. Rafael was startled when Henry made a loud sound with the heels of his boots and said, "You up mighty early."

Rafael jumped to his feet and saluted Henry, saying, "Here early to serve you and your brother."

Henry responded, "Relax. We're here to serve, too. I guess we're stuck with you whether we like it or not. Maybe you can start by telling me where our horses, rifles, and saddles are?"

Rafael was quick to reply in broken English, interspersing his phrasing with some Spanish words. "Your rifles and saddles are in the barn building along with your rifles. Your horses have been put out to pasture. You'll get new horses."

Henry looked at Rafael and grinned. It was easy to like the earnest and helpful Mexican boy. Henry said, "I guess there's nothing for us to do except to eat, drink, and relax until we hit the road again."

Henry had no sooner said these words when a Mexican man came rushing up with two metal pots and stepped into the bunkhouse. He banged the two pots together, making a loud clanging noise and exclaiming loudly in Spanish that it was time to eat breakfast in the comedor. After saying these words, the man darted out of the bunkhouse and ran toward a building located close by.

Randy staggered sleepily out of the bunkhouse and found Henry and Rafael looking at him and trying not to laugh. Randy looked back at them and muttered, "I guess it is time to eat. What's a comedor, and where is it?"

Rafael laughed quietly and said, "A comedor is a place to eat, and it's next door. Let's go."

Henry and Randy followed Rafael along a well-beaten path to a nearby building. They stepped inside the wide entranceway to see a large room filled with long wooden tables with matching benches. Rafael instructed them to take a seat. No sooner had they sat down when waiters appeared with plates piled high with food and big mugs filled with water. Later, big cups were placed on the table, and another waiter came by with a steaming hot kettle of coffee and filled their cups to the brim.

They ate and drank with relish. Soon, the comedor was filled up with their wagon mates. They were served in the same manner. Although it was early in the morning, it was a joyous occasion. Nothing like good food to raise the spirits of the men. They all ate and drank as much as they could. One of Mr. Ford's foremen stepped into the comedor and said, "Please eat up. This spread, and those to come are in recognition of the hard road you have left behind and the tough road ahead. We expect you to be here for three days. During that time, you should make sure your mules and wagons are in good shape. Get at our commissary anything you need to cross the Big Sands and complete the Cotton Road to Brownsville. Most important. Make sure you have enough water for yourselves and your animals because there is no water in this final ten-day stretch. Any questions?"

The words of the foreman raised many questions in the minds of the waggoneers, but nobody asked anything. The foreman waited for a couple of minutes and left in a hurry. As soon as he left, three Mexican men wearing big sombreros entered, strumming on their guitars and singing in Spanish songs that Henry and Randy had never heard. It was all enjoyable, although foreign. The captivating music communicated to them that they were in a different country and had to learn new ways.

They were listening to the guitars and the singing when Rafael crept in and tapped on Henry's shoulder, saying, "Time to go to make the rounds."

Henry did not know anything about making any rounds and told Rafael, "Okay. But tell me first, what's the name of the song they are singing."

"Oh. That's a new song called 'Paloma.'"

Henry turned to Randy and said, "I like that song. It's called 'Paloma.'"

"Yeah, I heard what Rafael said. I wonder what paloma means in Spanish?"

Henry replied, "Let's go outside and ask Rafael what it means in

English."

As soon as they found Rafael waiting for them outside the comedor, Randy asked, "What does paloma mean in English?"

Rafael thought for a minute and said, "I don't know the word in English, but it is some kind of bird."

Henry and Randy would continue to be tormented by not knowing what kind of bird a paloma was and asked everybody they encountered. While making the 'rounds' with Rafael, they asked anyone who spoke any English for the precise meaning of paloma. Nobody had any idea about what paloma meant in English. Finally, one guy said paloma meant 'pigeon.' With that answer, Henry and Randy had thought they had solved the puzzle, but another guy who claimed to know more English than the guy that told them that paloma meant pigeon, came up to them and said, "I know more English than he does. I've been schooled by the Jefe's wife. Paloma means 'dove.'"

Henry and Randy thanked both men, and Henry said, "Does it really make any difference if it is a pigeon or dove?"

Randy chuckled and said, "No, it doesn't matter. I have not seen any of those kinds of birds since we left home. Right now, we need to see what Rafael is showing us."

Rafael had taken them to a large building and said, "This is our cotton bale warehouse. When there is any break in wagon train arrivals, we take bales from this warehouse. Sometimes, we assemble special super wagon trains with many mule teams so we can send more cotton bales to Brownsville."

Henry and Randy were surprised by how well Rafael explained in English the function of the cotton warehouse but assumed this was not the first time he had said all these words. They could see that the warehouse was full of cotton bales that had to be worth a fortune. The importance of the Santa Rosita Way station grew by leaps and bounds in their minds.

Rafael then took them across the earthen center of the ranch to a building about fifty yards away and said, "This is our commissary. You can get anything you want here."

Henry and Randy stepped inside the commissary to see floor-to-ceiling shelves stuffed with a multitude of goods. Randy asked Rafael, "We just take what we want for free?"

"No. It's not free. As you can see, an old Anglo man is here to write down every item you take and its cost. One of Captain Ford's associates will take into account this cost and deduct it from any money you're paid. The cost of operating this whole way station is considered a business cost."

They stepped outside, and Henry turned to Randy and said, "I'm starting to understand that Ford and his partners are making money coming and going on the cotton trade for the South. I guess we're part of his money-making schemes."

"No doubt about that, and it is likely we'll be playing a larger role in his schemes, whether we like it or not. It appears that he and his partners own everything in these parts, and there is no escaping their reach. We've no choice but to play along and get involved with war profiteering."

"Right, o. We would do the same thing if we were in his shoes," said Henry, as he looked behind them to see the multi-story tower hovering over the commissary building.

Rafael saw Henry looking at the tower and said, "That's our lookout tower that is manned around the clock with armed men with a telescope to see if banditos, rustlers, or renegade Indians are approaching us. When the Captain is here, he goes on top of the tower to see if any wagon trains loaded with cotton are coming our way."

Next, Rafael took them to the corrals to see a vast number of horses, mules, and oxen being fed high-quality grain and having access to the water of the spring-fed creek. Rafael beamed when he said, "As you can see, we have all the livestock needed to keep the cotton wagons moving."

Henry and Randy were impressed. Henry asked Rafael, "If we have finished making the rounds, we really need some things."

"Yeah, I know. You need to clean up. For that, we are going to my people's place at the edge of the station. Follow me."

They followed Rafael across a wide expanse until they arrived at a collection of mud jacal houses with many people busy with their daily activities. Rafael walked up to one humble dwelling built next to an old mesquite tree that provided some shade. Beneath the tree was a stool. Rafael said, "Sit here. I'll look for Pedro and tell him you're here for your haircut and shave."

Without hesitation, Henry sat down on the stool and waited for Rafael to return with Pedro. He was excited about getting a long overdue haircut and shave. Both Henry and Randy occupied themselves by gazing upon the myriad of activities going on in this Mexican community. Rafael returned with a smiling Pedro, who in one hand carried a bar of tallow soap and in the other a wooden bucket full of water. Rafael explained, "Pedro does not speak any English but knows how to cut hair and shave. He has all he needs to do a good job."

Henry smiled and said, "I can't wait. Let Pedro do his job."

No sooner had Henry uttered these words than Pedro swung into action, spouting out a stream of Spanish words. He placed an old, worn blanket around Henry and fastened it behind his neck. From somewhere, he picked up a sharp pair of scissors and a wooden comb. He began cutting in an expert fashion Henry's hair. When he finished cutting Henry's hair, he rapidly used soap and water to create a lather with, which he carefully applied to Henry's face. He then started shaving him with a sharp, straight-edge blade. He shaved Henry's neck and sides of his face and paused before shaving under his nose, asking Rafael something in Spanish before continuing.

Rafael interpreted quickly for Henry what Pedro had said, "He wants to know if you want to keep the mustache or shave it off."

Henry did not waste any time in saying, "Cut it off."

Randy told Henry, "I've noticed that everyone in these parts has a mustache."

"I don't care. I don't like a mustache." Thus, Henry would be an exception by remaining clean-shaven for the rest of his life.

Rafael explained why Pedro paused before shaving off Henry's mustache. "In these parts, we say not having a mustache is like eating eggs without salt. Of course, you're foreigners, so you may do things differently."

Pedro finished his job on Henry by splashing on his face some sort of alcohol-based tonic and rubbing it into his face and neck while softly blowing on it. He then untied his covering blanket and whipped it off with a flourish, saying simply in Spanish, "Done. Next."

He handed a face mirror to Henry, who looked at his head for the first time in months and said, "Best haircut and shave I've ever had."

Rafael immediately interpreted Henry's words to Pedro, who bowed low and said in Spanish, "My pleasure."

Randy was ready to take Henry's place on the stool and let Pedro work the same wonders on his lighter hair growth of his head. While Pedro was preparing him to do his job, Randy said with his tongue in cheek, "I like my eggs with salt, so you can leave my excuse for a mustache. Maybe it needs a little trimming, but I definitely want to have a mustache."

Rafael told Pedro what Randy had just said, and Pedro smiled widely, exposing many rotten black teeth. Henry popped up by saying, "I haven't seen an egg in months, and there is definitely no salt available."

Rafael sounded off by saying, "For sure, there are no chickens around to lay eggs, but I hear that the captain is also addressing the salt shortage by mining it on the shores of the ocean and selling it."

Henry replied, "I guess the captain has his fingers in many money-making pies."

Pedro finished cutting Randy's hair and gave him the same royal treatment that he had given Henry. They already felt like new men, but they needed to wash their dirty bodies and clothes. Henry told Rafael about their need to wash, and he replied, "You got to get new clothes while your old clothes are being washed. Let's return to the commissary so you can pick out some new duds."

They said goodbye to Pedro and walked behind Rafael to the commissary. While they were walking, Henry said, "I sure would like to give Pedro a big tip for the good job he did."

Rafael responded as best as he could, "Don't worry. All you do and buy here will be on your final bill in Brownsville."

Henry and Randy were encouraged by the buy now and pay later policy of Santa Rosita and took their time to try on clothes from the large collection on the shelves of the commissary. When they had collected the clothes they wanted, the old Anglo man marked everything down under their names in his ledger book. Rafael watched attentively and said, "What about soap?"

The Anglo man added the cost of two bars of soap to his list of items to be charged. All this time, the man was quiet. He offered nary a word nor a greeting of any kind. Henry and Randy thought he was deaf and dumb. It was only when Rafael said goodbye, and the old man raised his quivering hand did they know he could hear.

They again followed Rafael across the wide earthen compound and along the Santa Rosita creek until they came to a secluded pool in a wide arroyo, and Rafael exclaimed, "Here's the washing place. Take your time in bathing. You keep one bar of soap, and I'll take the other bar. Give me your old clothes so I can give them to women in my community to wash and dry. When you finish, you can wear your new clothes. I'll be back later."

Henry and Randy rapidly took off their clothes and gave them to Rafael. They placed their boots at the clear water's edge. Henry placed his .44's beside his boots. They both walked cheerfully into the chilly water. They felt like a new life was being transmitted to them. They shared the use of the bar of soap to wash every part of their naked bodies. After they had finished washing, they frolicked in the water, enjoying the cool reprieve of this idyllic sanctuary.

Bathing in the water served more than a much-needed hygienic purpose, it was also a miracle that made them forget all the trials and tribulations of their long and hazardous journey. They dared not think of their mother or how their father was faring fighting on the side of the South in the Civil War. Their past had to be kept closed and off limits to all thoughts. They were only open to thinking ahead. But their future remained unknown. At the most, they could only plan a day at a time.

# Chapter Twenty-Five
# Captain's Men

"*Que bueno*, so good," exclaimed Rafael.

Henry and Randy looked at each other, and then they looked at Rafael. Randy said, "I guess we look good because we feel good."

Rafael replied, "That's good, really good cause you been invited again to eat dinner later at the big house. But first I want to show you somethin."

They walked along the creek for a while. Rafael brought them to a place where all the livestock at Santa Rosita come to drink water. As far as the eye could see, there was a mass of longhorn cattle, horses, mules, and some oxen taking turns drinking before they disappeared into the endless grassland. Rafael noted, "As you can see, this is where the animals drink. Each year, the numbers of longhorn cattle increase cause, with the war, there is little market for them. We have lots of vaqueros ready to drive cattle to the market, but there are no markets."

Henry said with awe, "I've never seen so many livestock in one place. For sure, the cattle would fetch a pretty penny back East. How many head do you think are on this ranch?"

Rafael scratched his head and said, "I dunno, but more than ten thousand... maybe fifty thousand. More cattle comin in every day."

"What do you mean by saying more comin' in every day?"

"Well, I know for sure the captain is buying cattle in Mexico, and he's rounding up as many strays as he can. Also, every spring, each cow is having a calf."

"How do you know he's bringing in cattle from Mexico?"

"Well, I hear in my community that he bought all our cattle and invited us to move our village to Santa Rosita. All I know is here, but we came from south of the Rio Grande, or Rio Bravo as we call it."

"Thanks, Rafael, for that explanation. All good to know. By the way, where's our old clothes?"

"Oh. You'll get your old rags tomorrow after they're washed and dried. Now, I think you should go back to your bunkhouse to rest and check your other stuff."

Randy said, "Yeah, we should clean our rifles and saddles and make sure we have plenty of bullets. I understand things could get rough for us in the Big Sands."

Rafael added, "You call it the Big Sands, we call it the El Desierto de los Muertos."

"What's that mean?"

"I think it means in English, Desert of the Dead."

"Wow. And that is where we're going?"

"Yeah, it's a lot worse than here, which we call Wild Horse Desert because it's full of wild mustangs."

Henry remained silent but was digesting Rafael's every word. Randy acknowledged Rafael's words by saying, "Thanks for all the information. We're learning a lot from you. I can see we've a lot to learn."

"Maybe you can teach me about the outside world. I was born here, so I really know nothing of the world beyond Santa Rosita," said Rafael nonchalantly.

Randy replied, "You got a lot of world here and maybe you are better off not knowing anything about the world beyond Santa Rosita."

They arrived at the bunkhouse. On their way, they could see all their waggoneers were out and about, busying themselves so all their wagons and mules would be ready for the final stretch to Brownsville. Rafael ran off across the compound as soon as they were on the bunkhouse steps, saying as he left, "See you later to escort you to the Big House."

Henry and Randy carried their saddles outside and, with some old rags, carefully wiped every surface and the seams on their saddles. They also shook their horse blankets and hung them on a hitching posts. They checked and cleaned their rifles, doing an inventory of their rifle bullets. While Randy sat on the bunkhouse steps, looking across the compound at all the activity, Henry removed his pistol belt from his waist and meticulously cleaned it and his two heavy old .44 pistols before re-holstering them.

He also checked his stock of .44 bullets and muttered to Randy, "We better go back to the commissary to see if we can get more bullets. We may need it for this last stretch of the Cotton Road."

With those words, they both walked over to the commissary to see if there was the kind of ammunition they needed. The old Anglo guy was there and ready to serve them. They had samples of the kind of bullets they needed.

Henry said, "We want fifty bullets for my pistols and one hundred bullets for our two rifles. You got these in stock?"

The deaf Anglo man took the two sample bullets with him to the back of the commissary. Before long, he returned and slapped down on his sturdy counter small boxes of bullets and said in a convoluted way, "This should do you. I'll put it on your tab."

The Anglo man disappeared in the back of the commissary before Henry and Randy could try to communicate any thanks, so they exited and started walking back to the bunkhouse. Randy was thinking about the transaction they just made and said, "It doesn't quite seem right that we have to pay for the bullets we need to protect our convoy wagons."

Henry reacted to Randy's words in a bitter tone, "Well, the Captain has got us by the balls, and he knows it. We're captives in his world."

They sat on the steps of the bunkhouse, making small talk with the waggoneers who were coming and going. All of them seemed to be happy to be here. And they were all cleaned up and shaved. All agreed that this was a much-needed rest stop.

The sun was getting low on the western horizon when Rafael appeared carefully carrying their old clothes, saying, "Here are your old clothes early … all washed and dried in the hot sun."

Randy carried their old clothes inside and placed them on their beds. When he returned, Henry asked Rafael, "Did we miss lunch?"

Rafael laughed and said, "No, sir. No lunch. Only breakfast and dinner are served in the comedor. Let's start walking toward the Big House. Tonight, you're lucky to be the captain's special guests."

These words irked Randy, and he said, "We don't feel special, and we don't want any special favors."

"Sorry. But you're special no matter what you want. You're rare types who we've never seen before."

Henry and Ron mulled over Rafael's words. They wished they could blend in, but even on the surface, it was evident they were foreigners in this desolate country. They were misfits who would never fit in, no matter how they tried. Their youthful looks and refined Eastern ways set them apart. But, at the same time, their differences made them to try harder to adapt to the foreign life that surrounded them.

A servant came out the front door of the Big House to escort into the same vast, well-accoutered dining room and showed them to the same chairs near the front end of the long dining table. The captain sat at the head of the table, and two of his Anglo foremen sat across from them. The captain said in a loud voice, "Welcome, Henry Harrison Read and Peyton Randolph Read. Please take your seats, and let's eat while we talk business."

This was the first time in years that Henry and Randy had heard their full birth names. They sat down, and the waiters began to serve them fabulous food. They followed the examples of the others and ate their food with much gusto. Their good table manners impressed the captain. The captain cleared his voice and said with a smile on his ruddy face, "Are you guys sure you're the same guys I saw here a couple of days ago? My, my. You sure clean up good."

As the oldest, Henry thought he should speak first. "Yes, sir. We're the same guys that answer to the names you called out when we arrived."

For reasons not clear to Henry and Randy, Henry's words made the captain and the two foremen laugh. The captain further broke the ice by saying, "Enough small talk. Let's get down to business. We want you guys to work for me. From now on, you can say you work for Captain Ford. What do you say to that?

Randy fidgeted in his padded chair and said in response, "What you going to pay us?"

"Twelve dollars a month in Mexican gold coins."

When the Captain said this, Randy looked at Henry then he said, "You got yourself a deal. Where do we sign?

"No written contract. My word is my bond, and we have two witnesses to that word. Now, let's get down to tomorrow's business. We got too much cotton stored here, and to make more money, we need to send more cotton to Brownsville-Matamoros. Plenty of ready cotton buyers there."

The captain continued by rattling off quickly an outline of his plan to sell more cotton. "We got a couple of bigger wagons. We gonna harness twenty mule teams to these wagons and add them to your wagon train. That way, you'll be hauling many more cotton bales than you got now. What do you think?"

Neither Henry nor Randy wanted to say they had never seen a twenty-mule team before, but after giving a hard look at Randy, Henry said, "Sounds like a lot of cotton. Have you done this before?"

One of the Captain's foremen spoke up, "Yes, a lot of cotton, and yes, we've done this before. But now, there are more ships anchored off Bagdad than ever before to take our cotton to Europe. We need to move more cotton as fast as we can. We can never transport enough cotton."

Randy was impressed and said, "What can we do to help you move more cotton?"

The captain said in a matter-of-fact manner, "Just keep doing what you have been doing but on a bigger wagon train."

Randy had a lot of questions and began by asking, "Who's going to replace Bob?"

"I'm going to give you as your lead wagon driver my best vaquero, Juan Perez. He doesn't speak much English, but he knows all about driving wagons, and he's a good shot. He's an experienced hand who has crossed the Big Sands many times. Also, with each of the bigger wagons, you'll have two experienced hands."

"What about water? We hear there's no water in the Big Sands. With these extra mules, we'll need more water."

The captain responded, "Good question. An additional big wagon will carry nothing but big barrels of water."

The captain continued, "Be alert, but don't be afraid. Look at us. We've been back and forth to Brownsville a hundred times, and we're no worse for wear. And with the drought, you'll have less to worry about. You should have no trouble, but with a couple of twenty mule teams, it will take you a couple more days to make the crossing. If you do this, a big reward will be waiting for you in Brownsville."

All Henry and Randy could do after hearing the captain's words was to exhale heavily and say almost in unison, "You can trust us. We'll do our best."

The captain replied, "I know I can. Otherwise, I wouldn't have hired you. For sure, if you made it this far, you can make it to Brownsville."

Henry wanted to end things up and get out of the big house before it was dark outside. Randy still had a few more things he wanted to ask. He addressed the captain, "Excuse these questions, but there were a few other things bothering me."

The captain sat back in his chair. He was impressed with the well-mannered way Randy expressed himself and said, "Go ahead. Ask me anything you want, but please don't take a lot of my time. I'm a busy man."

The captain's words discouraged Randy from asking all his questions, but he began by asking, "Should we fear armed attacks by Mexican bandits, rustlers, and marauding Indians?"

The captain and his foremen chuckled before the captain replied, "I don't rule out anything, but I think any such attacks are unlikely because it is so dry. I think you got more to fear from the natural elements than any bad hombres. And besides, you have plenty of gunmen and Henry riding point."

Henry and Randy appreciated the captain's words, but they were not reassured by them. Randy decided to drop his other questions, but he had one he wanted to hear what the captain or one his foremen thought. Randy reluctantly said, "Just one more question. We understand the Spanish explored this land and left a lot of cattle and horses behind. The Spanish withdrew. The Indians were always here. Then the Mexicans arrived, and then there were Anglo settlers. Among those settlers are Germans, and now they are being hunted down because they support the Union. All very confusing to us. Can you help straighten us out?"

The captain and his foremen had a big laugh over Randy's words. The captain said, "Why, Son, we're confused too. You think too much. Just try to concentrate on the task at hand. As long as we can make good money, we don't pay much attention to the rest unless it gets in the way of making money. By the way, you didn't mention how the French are meddling in Mexico."

Randy's head was spinning, and he did not know what to say but. "Thanks, but I didn't know France was interested in Mexico."

Randy's reaction set the captain off. "Why France is waging war against Mexico and is threatening our cotton trading port of Bagdad. France's interference really complicates things for us."

Following a brief pause, Henry asked, "May we be excused? Looks like we have a big day tomorrow. My brother and I thank you for a good dinner and all your hospitality. We hope you can learn to count on us."

The captain said, "Welcome aboard. You'll be all right. I hope you learn to call this place home. I did. I'm from New York but came to Texas by way of Florida ten years ago, and now this is my home."

All stood, and they shook hands all around. One of the house servants showed Henry and Randy to the front door. As they exited the house, they could overhear the men talking. They were sure they were talking about them. They hoped they gave a positive impression. They were Captain's men now and thus had to behave in a way of which he would approve. Their newfound responsibilities made them feel taller and older.

Henry and Randy headed back to the bunkhouse in silence. They were about halfway there when Henry said, "Look around you. Do you think you could ever call this place home?"

Randy wasted no time in replying, "For sure, there's nothing here that's like our home in Virginia, but if I could make as much money as the Captain, I could call any place home."

Henry laughed and said, "Ain't that the truth? Tell me, is he called a captain because of his position in the Confederacy or because of his experience as a riverboat captain?"

Randy simply said, "I think it's the latter. He was a Captain before all this war insanity started."

They arrived at the bunkhouse to find Rafael waiting for them. Rafael said with a sense of urgency in his voice, "First thing tomorrow, you need to pick out and try your new horses. Then, you got to see how they are getting the big wagons ready to roll. You got to get everything ready tomorrow to leave at the crack of dawn on the following day. You got to show that you're Captain's men now."

# Chapter Twenty-Six
# Preparing for the Big Sands

Henry looked around the inside of the bunkhouse and murmured to Randy at his side, "Looks like everybody is here. I'll get their attention, and you tell them all they need to know to get ready tomorrow for crossing the Big Sands."

The presence of Henry tended to quiet the lively bunch of waggoneers. His big body frame, his quiet mannerisms, and the two big pistols strapped to his waist all worked to silence most men. Henry raised his right arm, and a hush fell over the crowded room. He softly said, "You know I'm not much for words, so I ask that you listen to what my younger brother has to say."

The waggoneers were all ears as Henry stepped away to give Randy the floor who was trying to think about what he should say to the big assembly of mostly teenage men. He cleared his throat and suddenly found himself speaking in a loud voice. "We're now working directly for Captain King. As you know, we're transporting his cotton. You are to be congratulated for making it this far with your cargo intact. We gotten more days to go through a sandy, dry, and treacherous territory before we can deliver our load of cotton in Brownsville. Since we are leaving at first light the day after tomorrow, you got to get everything ready tomorrow. Make sure your animals are well watered and fed before we depart. There will be not much stopping once we start. Also, Captain King is adding two additional twenty-mule team big wagons to our train. Any questions?"

Almost all the waggoneers had questions. But they were a bit intimated by the educated manners of the big boys from Virginia. Nonetheless, Randy wanted to hear from those young men who performed the all-important job of driving the wagons, so he recognized the young farm boy in the front who was not shy and holding his hand high.

"Who's goin to drive our lead wagon now after Mr. Bob has left us?"

Without hesitation, Randy answered, "Good question. The captain has decided that Bob will be replaced by one of his best and most experienced vaqueros, Juan Perez."

Randy then proceeded to answering another question about having enough feed and water. "Oh, yes. We'll have an extra wagon to carry water and grain."

There were a few other nitpicking questions which were posed more for the prestige of asking them than for any answers. Randy ended the session by saying, "Thanks for your attention. Get some rest. We got a lot to do tomorrow to get ready to get back on the move."

Henry was waiting for Randy at their beds and said with a big smile on his face. "Good speech, little brother. Keep it up, and I'm sure you will rise to the top of the captain's organization. With your smarts and my guns, I'm sure we'll go a long way."

Randy was thinking ahead. "Let's set a good example and try to get some shut-eye. Everybody needs to get as much rest as possible."

To their surprise, they slept fitfully until the crack of dawn. Henry was awakened by Rafael tugging on his blanket and whispering. "Time to go."

Henry was embarrassed that he was not yet up and about. He got up quickly and nudged Randy, saying, "Get up. Let's go. We've got a lot to do."

Once outside, the fully dressed Henry splashed water on his face from the horses' trough in front of the bunkhouse. Rafael watched him patiently and said, "Sad that this is my last day with you. Every night, I'm told of what to do with you the next day. Tomorrow, there will be only one thing for me to tell you, and that is goodbye."

Henry told Rafael, "Don't fret so much. I reckon we'll be back this way someday. Shucks. I've in mind to bring you a gift from Brownsville."

Henry's sympathetic words had Rafael beaming and saying, "Mr. Henry, I'll always be at your service."

Henry was softly patting Rafael on the head when Randy came out of the bunkhouse, saying, "What to do first?"

Rafael said, "Of course, first is going to the comedor to eat, then we can go pick out your horses."

They ate and drank their fill at the Comedor and then followed Rafael to the distant horse corral. There was plenty of horses for them to choose from, and one horse seemed as good as another. Rafael knew the horses better than they did, so they let him choose the four horses for them. Rafael pointed to two horses and said, "These two will be your main horses."

Rafael signaled to a couple of waiting vaqueros, and they rode into the herd of horses and, lassoed the two main horses for Henry and Randy, and brought them out of the corral. Rafael pointed to two other horses, and they were also lassoed and brought outside the corral. Rafael said, "Here's your two main horses and your two spare horses."

Rafael then said rapidly some words to the vaqueros, and they took the horses away. Rafael said, "They going to make sure they're well broken-in, have good shoes, and are well fed and watered before turning them over to you for a little test riding with your own saddles and tack."

Henry and Randy nodded in agreement to what Rafael said. Henry turned to Randy and said, "Did you see how easy they used their lassos? They reminded me that we need to practice more with our lariats."

"Let's go now to the warehouse to see the big wagons and their cotton loads," Rafael said in a business-like manner as he walked off in the direction of the warehouse.

Henry and Randy tagged along. Excited about seeing big wagons for the first time in their lives. They entered the huge warehouse and saw hundreds of cotton bales stacked from the floor to the ceiling. Even with the extra bales needed to fill the big wagons, their removal would hardly make a dent in this mass of cotton bales.

Rafael looked small next to the big wagons. Their wheels were much taller than him. Henry and Randy could not see into the wagons as they were so high. Rafael explained, "The Captain had these wagons special made up north before the war started at the same place his river boats were made. They are made of strong oak wood and can be loaded with a dozen cotton bales. That's two to three times as much as a regular wagon.

Randy said to Henry. "Impressive. All this cotton is worthless unless you can get it to market. The captain and his associates know this, and that is why they went to all the trouble and expense to get these twenty mule wagons."

The Captain's Mexicans were busy toting the heavy cotton bales and placing them snuggly in the big wagons. This was hard work, but somehow, the men did it with a flare and gaiety that Henry and Randy had not previously observed. Each time a man got near the wagon, they greeted Henry and Randy in a way they had not seen before. Rafael told them, "Now that you're the captain's men, you will be shown extra respect by all those in our community."

Meanwhile, Randy was doing some calculations. "Twelve cotton bales is equal to six thousand pounds of cotton. Therefore, each big wagon is carrying cotton worth at least $700 U.S. dollars or more. And payment is in gold, so it is worth more than that. White gold for yellow gold. We're part of a parade of riches. No wonder the captain wants to move and sell as much cotton as he can as fast as he can. This money-making scheme can't last long, but while it does, you can sure get rich fast."

Henry and Randy did not know how to climb up on the big wagons to look inside. It was hard to get a grip at the front of the wagon. Rafael showed them how to get on the wagon. Once on top, Henry muttered to Randy, "This is probably the first and last time I'll climb on a twenty-mule freight wagon."

Randy turned to Rafael and asked, "How they going to get the big lead wagon and its tandem trailer wagon out of here?"

Rafael hesitated in giving Randy a response but finally said, "Before dawn, they will use the whole team of mules to pull the main wagon and its trailer out of the warehouse. You'll see tomorrow. I don't have enough English to explain good."

They were happy to get out of the hot warehouse and breath the fresh but dusty air blowing across the dry coastal plains. They could see a dust devil forming in the open compound area. A procession of tumbleweeds blew aimlessly in front of them.

"Where to now?" asked Randy.

"I want to show you the extra wagon being added to your train to carry water barrels and grain feed. You need to check on everything."

They found the feed-water wagon filling its barrels with water at the main spring. The Captain's Mexican women were filling with buckets the big wooden stave barrels in the wagon. The women had formed a chain and were passing buckets back and forth. They appeared to be having a good time.

Rafael said, "When they're finished, they will drive the wagon to a shady place and care for its team of mules until putting them in line for tomorrow's departure. We've done this many times before, and we'll be doing it again when the next wagon train arrives."

As they followed Rafael, Randy said to Henry, "Looks like everyone knows what to do except us. Why does the captain need us?"

Rafael overheard Randy's remarks and interjected, "He needs more

Anglos, especially those who can read and write English. The war stopped most schooling, and all the Anglo men have gone to fight in the war. Anyway, he only has Anglos as true partners, even though my community is completely loyal and dependent on him."

Henry and Randy were not sure of what Rafael was trying to communicate to them, but in an awkward way, he had given them something to contemplate. They were now suffering from an overload of information. They could see that it would take them a while if ever, to absorb all they were learning. They were in a constant state of confusion, which obliged taking things as they came and not analyzing every bit of information. Someday the bigger picture may materialize, but for now, they had to get by with bits and pieces of the new reality they faced.

Rafael said, "Let's go and test-ride your horses. They should be waiting for you in front of your bunkhouse."

Henry immediately saw the horse he wanted and quickly placed his saddle on the horse and mounted it slowly while murmuring a sweet tune to the horse. Randy followed suit. They gently rode their horses around the compound, halting and going, turning right and left. Henry returned to where Rafael was standing and said, "This is a fine horse. I need to think of a name to give it. We don't need to test the backup horses. I'm sure they're fine too."

Randy said much of the same. They both dismounted, removed their saddles, and handed the reins to Rafael, who said, "These mustangs have been carefully broken in by my people. I will take them so they can feed and water during the night. I'll come back with them to the bunkhouse before the sun comes up. I'm going now. You guys should check all your wagons and make sure all the mules get all the feed they can eat and all the water they can drink."

Henry and Randy adjusted their hats and bandanas and lugged their saddles back to the bunkhouse. Randy said, "It's hot, and there is not a cloud in the sky, but let's go and check all our waggoneers to see what they got to say about the readiness of their wagons."

They walked to the area where the wagons were assembling for an early departure tomorrow. Randy recognized one of the wagon drivers and asked him, "All set for an early departure tomorrow?"

He got a quick reply, "We could have left yesterday. Our wagon and its cargo are in good shape. Our mules are rested, fed, and watered. I can't think of anything else. We're eager to get there and start the long trip back with the supplies the Confederacy needs to win the war."

Henry and Randy took a couple of hours to inspect the rest of the wagons. They chatted with the drivers, and they had much of the same to say as the first wagon driver. They traced their steps back, saying hello again to all the drivers, and headed back to the bunkhouse. They were about halfway back to the bunkhouse when Henry noticed the ground dirt being kicked up near them. At first, he thought it must be some kind of insect flipping dirt up, but when he saw the pockmarks in the ground, he became alarmed and said in a panicky manner to Randy, "It looks like somebody is shooting at us. Let's run to the nearest building and take cover."

Then they heard the loud ding-dong of a bell and looked to see where this unusual sound was coming from. They determined this sound was coming from the watch tower that loomed high above the commissary. They could see someone on top of the tower waving a red flag. Immediately, Henry said, "Oh my God. We're being attacked. We need our rifles to fight back, but our rifles are in the bunkhouse. My pistols are not enough to fight off the enemy at long range."

Randy tried to see where the shots were coming from and then said, "We just got to take the risk and run like crazy to get our rifles. We're sitting ducks here. Let's hightail it."

They ran to the bunkhouse as fast as they could. They grabbed their rifles and readied them to fire. But they did not know where to fire as they did not know where the shots were coming from. They crept outside the bunkhouse and looked in every direction, but they did not see anything out of the usual. They looked up to the tower to see no longer a flag waving and a bell ringing. Randy said to Henry, "Looks like whoever they were that, they are gone."

Henry replied, "Our first duty is to protect the boss and his interests. Let's hustle over to the big house to make sure the captain is okay."

With their rifles in hand, they jogged over to the big house and knocked loudly on the front door. A servant came to open the door, and Randy announced, "We're here to check on the captain."

A servant welcomed them in and escorted them to the captain's usual spot at the head of a long table in the dining room. The captain looked at them with some surprise and said, "You guys look troubled. What's the matter?"

Randy caught his breath and spoke up, "Well, there was some shooting, and we just wanted to make sure you are okay."

"Oh, that. That was nothing. Happens all the time. As usual, I sent out an armed band of my vaqueros to take care of these rustlers. No worries. Thanks for thinking of me. Good work. Make sure you pull out on time tomorrow because there is another wagon train arriving."

Henry and Randy were greatly relieved by the captain's words and almost embarrassed by their overreaction. They politely excused themselves and, went out the front door, and began walking in silence back to the bunkhouse. Henry started laughing first and then was joined by Randy in laughing heartily. When their laughing quieted down, Henry said, "Welcome to Texas, where a little shooting is no big affair."

Randy thoughtfully replied, "I guess you're right as long as you live to talk about it."

# Chapter Twenty-Seven
# Big Sands Trail

As they approached the bunkhouse, Randy said, "What are we going to do now? We still got a couple of hours before our last meal in the comedor."

Henry had at the ready an answer. "I don't know about you, but I'm going to make a deposit in the outhouse. After that, we'll see."

Randy followed Henry to outhouse row located behind the bunkhouse and entered one of the dozen stalls. They were both pleased to find stacked in one of the dark corners of their pit latrine stalls a pile of corn cobs. They felt like they were able to fully relief themselves in a first-class outhouse.

Randy waited for Henry, who stepped out of his stall and said, "No better way to start a long trip than with a good bowel movement."

Randy remembered some words from his course in French back on the plantation and said, "Sans commentaire."

Henry laughed and said, "What now?"

"I got an idea. Why don't we do lasso practice? To be real Texas hands, we have to know how to use a lasso."

"Good idea. Let's go get our lassos and find a post to practice on."

As they both walked back on the shady side of the bunkhouse, they encountered a couple of groups of their waggoneers playing mumbly-peg with an old pocketknife. One of them said, "You guys want to join us."

Henry stopped and watched them play as if he wanted to join in a game he had never seen before, but before he could make a decision, Randy said, "Thanks, but we got some stuff to do. Anyway, looks pretty risky."

Randy pulled Henry away, and they kept going to the bunkhouse door and went inside to get their lassos. They exited with their lassos and searched for an isolated post to practice. They found a distant post, and they thought they were in a place where nobody could see them. They paced off twenty steps and started trying to lasso the post. Only a few times did they succeed in lassoing the post.

No matter how hard they tried, they could not regularly lasso the post.

Their persistent failure at lassoing the post prompted Randy to say, "How we goin' to lasso a speedy steer if we can't even lasso a dumb post?"

At that moment, they heard a light laugh coming out of the tall grass. Henry yelled at the intruder, "Come out with your hands up."

Out of the grass rose Rafael, who said, "You guys sure can't lasso worth a darn. You have no technique."

Randy said, "Rafael. Why are you spying on us?"

"It is my job to know all that you do. You want me to show you how to use a lasso?"

Henry and Randy did not respond to Rafael. They just watched as he walked forward and took the lasso out of Randy's hands. He then proceeded to lasso the post with an expert flair, embarrassing Henry and Randy. Finally, Randy said, "Okay. Stop. Show us how to do it."

Rafael showed them how to hold and throw a lasso. His teachings had immediate effect. They lassoed the post almost every time they tried. They dedicated their lassos to Rafael and said, "Every time we lasso somethin', we'll think of you. Thanks for showing us how to lasso."

Rafael was happy to hear these words. He said, "The sun is going down. Let's go back to bunkhouse now and leave your lassos so we can go to the comedor and eat. There should be a special feast because tomorrow, before first light, you leave to cross the Big Sands."

As they walked back to the bunkhouse, Randy was curious and asked, "Does this mean we'll not be eating breakfast tomorrow before we leave?"

"Yes, you should keep any leftover food to eat while you're traveling tomorrow."

Henry mumbled, "I like starting off on a long trip with a full stomach, but I'm so eager to get movin' that I can easily make an exception this time."

Randy did not know if his older brother was trying to make a joke but said, "We'll make this trip, no matter what."

Henry liked his younger brother's way with words and said, "Let's hurry to get to the Comedor to get first dibs on the best food. We can use our bandanas to wrap up any leftovers. After all, we should get special treatment as newly minted Captain's men."

They ate their fill and then some. Any extra food they wrapped in their bandanas. The comedor was filled with excitement as they all anticipated the start of a long journey early tomorrow. They knew they would be crossing inhospitable territory, but they were eager to get started. They looked forward to meeting all the challenges of the crossing and arriving at their destination.

Rafael tip-toed into the comedor to remind Henry and Randy that they needed to get some sleep before waking up before dawn to get ready to head on. Henry and Randy were entranced by the music the guitarists were playing and the songs that were being sung. Henry asked that they play the *Paloma* again and was enjoying this song when Rafael crept up behind him. He heard what Rafael whispered and said quietly, "I'll be coming as soon as they end this song."

They exited and made their way to the bunkhouse. They told Rafael not to worry and that they were ready to leave at any time. They took their boots off and laid down on their beds. Most of the waggoners were also bedded down. They closed their eyes and tried to sleep, but neither of them could really sleep. They were too keyed up to get any real sleep. But they knew that tomorrow would not be easy, so they rested their bodies as much as they could.

It must have been around four in the morning when Rafael came softly up to their bunks and said, "I got your horses outside. Let's get them ready and then go and see how the big wagons are getting ready before waking your teamsters for the rough trip ahead."

Henry and Randy sprang from bed and slipped on their boots. Henry strapped on his gun belt. The lugged their saddles outside and dropped them while they splashed some water on their faces from the trough in front of the bunk house. They filled their canteens to the brim and fixed them on their saddles.

The stars shined bright in the cool night sky that had a piece of the moon dangling near the horizon. They were surprised there was no wind. All was still. The only sounds were the cries from night birds and the wailing howls in the distance of hungry coyotes. A few bats flicked wickedly through the dry air. All the world seemed to be in mourning for some unknown reason.

In tune with the melancholy night, Henry and Randy quietly saddled their horses, stuffing in their saddle bags bandanas full of food. They followed Rafael to the cotton warehouse, hitching their horses in front of the huge building. Inside the warehouse, there was a beehive of activity as a crew of Mexican men readied the big freight wagon and its tandem trailer to be pulled out into the open by a twenty-mule team. There men were being supervised by one of the Captain's Anglo foremen.

Lanterns were lit and placed about the warehouse where some light was needed. The foreman walked over to Henry and Randy and said, "Howdy. My name is Tom. I'm here to see if these wagons are properly arranged for their first trip south. I accompanied these wagons from where they were made in Ohio to here. If they work good on this trip, we might get some more. Lord knows we've plenty of cotton. But they're mighty expensive, and it takes a long time between when you order and delivery. I suppose that's because they have to season the oak wood used to build them."

Henry and Randy were impressed. Randy could not help but ask, "You mean this is the first time you have used these big wagons to haul cotton?"

Tom grinned and said, "Isn't that what I said? If this works to get more cotton to Brownsville, I'm sure the captain will try to get more big wagons as long as the cotton boom lasts and the profits keep rolling in."

Henry and Randy followed Tom over to the side of the big lead wagon. When they got next to the front wheel, Tom proudly said, "You see how big and tall the front wheels are. They are taller than we are and, are eight inches wide, and topped with iron tires. There are also iron axles. We came all the way from up north without a breakdown. These are strong wagons that are able to handle any conditions."

Randy studied the seven-foot-tall from wagon wheel and said meekly, "These are very strong wheels. I've never seen a wheel with eighteen spokes made from oak. Expert wheelwrights are needed to construct such heavy-duty wheels."

"Yeah, and we also think that the wideness of the wheel will keep them from sinking into the sand."

Rafael came up and tugged on Tom's vest and whispered, "The mules are coming."

Henry and Randy looked up to see a herd of mules gathering in the entrance of the warehouse. The men on the wagons jumped down to help the men with the mules maneuver each team of mules into position so they could pull a big wagon and its trailer. This was not an easy task. Tom muttered, "Don't worry. We've practiced this several times. A little messy at first, but it will all straighten out."

Henry and Randy were almost mesmerized by all the activity going on before them. Henry turned to Rafael and asked, "Where did they get all the mules?"

Rafael responded the best he could by saying, "We got a special corral where we breed male donkeys with our mares. So, we raise all the offspring mules right here. A mule is stronger than a horse, can put up with the heat, and go longer without feed and water. We're raising as many mules as we can."

Henry and Randy watched intently as the mules were lined up and attached from back to front to the big wagon. Randy thought he saw some horses among the mules and asked Tom, "Aren't the first two animals hitched horses?"

Tom said, "Good eye. Yeah, we got our two biggest and strongest horses at the front of the wagon. One man will mount the horse on the left. When this horse starts pulling, the mules will start going."

The hitching of the big front wagon was complicated business. Placing the reins and harnesses on each animal took some time. Each mule had blinders fixed on the side of its eyes. One long rawhide line ran all the way from the front mule to the seat in front of the wagon for the driver to hold and guide the team. Some little bells were attached to one of the front mules, prompting Randy to ask, "What are the bells for?"

Tom replied, "I'm not quite sure, but the guy responsible for making the wagons said that the mules liked to hear bells. He said as long as the bells are ringing, the mules keep goin'."

Henry wanted to say something, so he said, "I assume all your mules have been well-shod with high-quality horseshoes?"

Showing some annoyance at the question, Tom replied dryly, "Of course. We got some of the best blacksmiths in Texas working here for us."

The wagon driver signaled to Tom that they were ready to start going outside and get in line. The wheeler mounted the horse in front of the driver and gently urged the horses forward. The fully loaded wagon and its trailer started to move. All the slack in the lines had been taken up, and the movement forward was smooth. This was an exciting moment.

Henry and Randy walked at the side of the lead wagon, observing the wonder of a large team of eighteen mules and two horses pulling large loads. The driver and the wheeler exited the warehouse and turned the wagon expertly to be in front of the line of wagons headed south. These big wagons will set the pace for all the regular wagons. Much depended on these lead wagons in terms of the distance they would cover each day.

The man driving the big wagon also had in his hand a long rawhide whip, which he was ready to crack if need be. He mentioned the snake-like whip to Tom, who said, "Yeah, he has a whip to crack in case any of the mules show any signs of stubbornness. He also has sitting on the floorboards beneath his feet some tin cans filled with pebbles to throw at any mules not pulling their fair share."

When the big wagon passed them, Randy noticed a man sitting in front of the trailer and asked Tom, "What does that man do?"

"Why, that's the brakeman who will put on the brakes in the trailer if need be and stop the whole works. He's there, just in case. But you've mostly level land all the way to Brownsville, so I don't think he'll be needed much. If things go all right this time, we may add to the load next time."

Juan showed up driving the wagon Bob used to drive and introduced himself with a nod and the tipping of his sombrero. Henry and Randy acknowledged him in a similar fashion. By the looks of Juan, Henry, and Randy knew they had a lot to learn from him. After all, he was a native of this country and had been back and forth to Brownsville many times.

Henry and Randy mounted their horses and attached their spare horses to Juan's wagon, which was in front of the line. They could see the shape of a long line of wagons in the pale dawn light. Henry road to his position in the front, and Randy rode back to check all the wagons and then galloped back to tell Juan that the train was ready to depart. Juan replied, "Bueno. Let's go. Vamos."

Before the sun was up, they began rolling south in high spirits. Unbeknown to them, they were being watched by the captain through his telescope from the top of his tower. He was pleased to see them leave as he had a contract with the Confederacy to deliver many tons of cotton each month. He knew there were risks involved with moving cotton south through the Big Sands, but the risks compared to the profits to be made with the successful delivery of cotton were well worth it.

The big wagon kept up a good pace all day long in spite of the sand and heat. Henry and Randy were beginning to think on the first day that at this pace, they could arrive in Brownsville in a week instead of ten days. But they knew as the days wore on that the miles traveled and the heat would take their toll. There was a need to pace themselves, but at the same time, their supply of food and water was limited. They had to keep going, but they also had to be cautious.

It was easy to die in the Big Sands. If the boiling hot afternoon sun did not get you, there were a lot of deadly rattlesnakes around to finish you off. Of course, they always had to be on the alert for marauding Indians, vicious Mexican bandits, and uncaring rustlers who were out to steal anything of value they could lay their hands on by any means. The saving grace of this barren sandy land was that no living human being could survive for long in it. Mainly for that reason, the Desert of Death was to be avoided if at all possible. The desert had taken its toll on many human lives, and it was not finished yet.

# Chapter Twenty-Eight
## Desert of Death

They wanted to wait until later in the day to eat, but the sun was burning their necks, obliging them to gobble the food they had wrapped in their bandanas so they could use them to protect their necks. It was the hottest weather Henry and Randy had ever endured. They expected their horses to drop any moment from the excessive heat. But even if they dropped, the sandy, dry ground was hotter than the air. As far as they could see, there was no shade to rest under. The fact that this was their first day on the trail worried them the most. If the first day was too tough, how would they make it through many more days?

They had no choice but to keep their mouths shut and bear the best they could the duress. The only way for them to get by was to develop the delusion that they were some place nice and all this was a dream. They trudged on in a changed mental state, but this first day of moving south with a wagon train full of cotton under the blazing sun was more challenging than they expected. They kept telling themselves that all they had to do was get through this first day.

The wagons kept moving in spite of the ferocious heat and the dryness of the land. They followed the sandy tracks that wove their way through the clumps of brasada thornbush and cacti. The drought had been so severe that even the leaves of the heartiest chaparral were curling up. The innumerable scrub and short bushes were wilting under the intense heat. Henry and Randy could easily see why this was called the Desert of the Dead.

The wagon train had no choice but to continue moving forward. There was no going back. They had to forge ahead no matter what. Hopefully, they would make it to Brownsville just like many had done before them. But nothing was certain, and they knew they could as easily lose their lives as make it to their destination.

Given the life-threatening duress of their circumstances, it was irritating to Henry and Randy to see Juan acting as if there was nothing the matter. He seemed oblivious to his surroundings. He kept guiding his team of mules along the sandy tracks, appearing as happy as a lark. When Randy got a chance, he told Henry, "Look at him. He doesn't have a care in the world. He seems to be enjoying what makes us suffer so much. No doubt he's in his element."

Henry replied, "I don't know if it is possible, but we got to get like him if we want to thrive in this God-forsaken corner of America."

Randy knew deep down what his older brother was talking about, but he also knew they could never be like Juan, who was born and raised in this territory and had made this trip many times. After a long pause, he said to Henry, "We can never be like him, but there's a lot we need to learn from him. Learning from him will be tough because he speaks little English."

Henry was fast to reply, "At least, we can learn some Spanish from him. For sure, we'll need all the Spanish we can get where we're going."

Randy nodded his agreement as they separated ways. They rode their horses slowly. The extreme heat waves shrouded them in an envelope that resisted quick movement. Everybody was quiet, and their mouths were closed to preserve their saliva. It was all they could do to keep their wagons on track and moving southward. The big wagon seemed to be faring better than the smaller ones. So far, it was meeting all expectations.

Gradually, the long-awaited disappearance of the sun on the western horizon occurred. Breathing became easier without the relentless sun beating down on them. They felt some life restored to their dehydrated bodies, but there was no stopping. Juan kept the wagons rolling into the dark night before calling a halt to rest, eat and, feed, and water the mules and horses.

Juan whistled loudly through his hands. Henry and Randy interpreted this as a signal for them to come. Juan lit and hung out the same big lantern, just like Bob used to do. The lantern illuminated a bright spot around Juan's wagon. Henry and Randy stopped at the edge of Juan's wagon to hear him say some words in Spanish. As they both shook their heads sideways, Juan could see they did not understand any Spanish, so he struggled to piece together in a profoundly serious manner the following word fragments in English.

"Use little water and food. Tell everyone. There's a lot of desert ahead of us."

Henry and Randy easily got what he was trying to communicate and rode off to remind everyone to minimize the water and food they used this first night for them and their animals. They could see that everyone was busy unhitching their mules and allowing them to rest. The removal of harnesses from the mules pulling the big wagon and its trailer was onerous but had to be done so the mules could rest and eat and drink some mouthfuls. The time they had to spend with their animals would mean less time for themselves.

Juan was busy making a small campfire when Henry and Randy rode back to tell him by hand gestures they had passed the word. Juan responded by using other hand gestures, telling them to dismount and take care of their horses, including the spare ones attached to the back of his wagon. Juan concluded by saying, "Entiendan."

Randy surprised himself by saying, "Entiendo."

Juan grinned widely after Randy said this Spanish word, meaning 'understand.'

Randy excitedly told Henry, "Did you hear that? I just spoke in Spanish."

Henry chuckled as much as his dry throat would allow. "Good going, brother. Keep it up. We'll need more than one word of Spanish in the days and weeks ahead. We should have learned more from Rafael."

They took care of their horses and joined Juan at is little campfire. He offered them some cooked grits and small cups of coffee from the tin kettle boiling on his fire. Randy pointed at items around him and asked Juan to tell him how to say the name of the object in Spanish. Juan laughed but played along with Randy. After several word exchanges, Randy told Henry, "I think I should go get my notepad to write all this down."

Randy was about to stand up, but Henry reached over to stop him, saying, "No, we got to get in our heads what he says so that it sticks. If we can't remember the meaning of any of his words or how to say them, we can ask him again. This is a good way to pass the time, and we have plenty of that."

Randy was ready to ask Juan the names in Spanish of other items, but Juan began a long spiel in Spanish that they could not grasp. Randy asked him a number of times to repeat his words by politely saying in Spanish, "Por favor, repite."

Juan repeated his words several times. Henry said, "I think I know what he is saying. I know that horse in Spanish is Caballo, and he is talking about some kind of horses."

Juan was losing patience, but he wanted Henry and Randy to know what he was saying. Juan accompanied his words with many hand and arm gestures. Randy kept hearing the word desierto, and that told him he was talking about the 'Wild Horse Desert' they were leaving behind them. It finally dawned on Henry and Randy that he was happy about getting away from the Wild Horse Desert and the menace of its stampeding herds. Juan repeated the word, 'estampida,' and Henry and Randy finally figured out that he was relieved to be out of the territory where stampeding wild horses can wreck a wagon train by charging into them.

Henry and Randy made Juan happy by showing him they understood what he was saying. Randy was a quick learner and told Juan they were also happy to be deeper into the Desert of the Dead because it is less likely that banditos and Indios would come this way. Randy spent some time to make sure Juan understood what he was saying. While he was talking to Juan, he suddenly closed his eyes and tipped over to lie on the ground. Juan's loud snoring signaled with much surprise Henry and Randy that he was fast asleep.

They both took some time to look at the sleeping Juan. The saw lying on the ground before then a middle-aged, bronzed colored Mexican man with a big black mustache. He really did not have any distinguishing physical features, but they both knew he was a man to be reckoned with. Henry was the first to speak, "There you have it. Time to get some shut-eye. We got to learn to sleep like Juan."

Henry doused the fire and turned down the lantern before spreading his blanket near his saddle. Randy did the same. They bedded down to get as much sleep as they could. They thought they had only rested a few minutes when Juan was up and tapping on the soles of their feet. He said some words in Spanish. There was no need for any translation. Henry and Randy knew it was time to get moving.

They got up and tried to wipe the sleep from their eyes. They felt like they were sleepwalking and only going through the motions in alerting the others of their impending departure. Everyone stumbled around in the darkness, doing the necessary to get moving again. Juan whistled loudly through his hands, and all knew that that meant to get moving.

Henry and Randy did not feel like doing again what they had done the day before, but they had no choice but to trudge on. The wagons were strung out for about a mile, but they were all moving forward at a pace set by the big wagon. The sun peeked over the eastern horizon, and the light was welcome, but the sandy desolation of the landscape was not welcome. As the sun rose, a deep sense of foreboding swept over all living beings who dared venture into the devil's sandlot.

Henry rode point, but when the sun was at its zenith, he could not see far ahead. The sun's rays danced of the hot, lifeless plains, and in the distance, they bounced off the baking ground in a shimmering that mimicked steam and watery marshes. Henry was so tired of seeing mirages that he covered his eyes with his bandana and only peeked out to see if he were still on the southern tracks. Suddenly, Juan's loud whistling jarred him from his somnambulant state. He turned and forced his horse to gallop back to Juan.

When Henry arrived at Juan's wagon, he saw in the distance Randy waving for him to come toward him. Juan pointed to where Randy was located, so he galloped toward his brother. When he neared Randy, he readily saw that the problem was caused by a wagon that was not moving forward as it should. He got close to Randy and asked, "What's wrong with this wagon?"

"I don't rightly know, but one of the mules closest to the wagon refuses to budge."

"Well, whatever it is, we got to fix it so the wagon train keeps moving forward."

Henry and Randy jumped off their horses. Henry asked the wagon boy, "What the hell is wrong with your mule? We got to go."

"I don't know. He just stopped in its tracks and said, 'nothin' I did got him movin'."

They approached the ailing mule to see what was wrong with him. Henry spotted immediately that the mule was lifting his left back hoof off the ground. He took a quick look at his hoof and said, "The mule can't work cause it doesn't have shoe on his hoof. He lost his shoe somewhere, and now he can go no farther."

The wagon boy scratched his head. "You got to be kiddin.' We checked his shoes before leavin, and all was okay. What we goin to do now?"

Henry huddled with Randy to discuss the situation. Meanwhile, Randy was signaling all the wagons trailing this one to go around and keep going.

After talking to Randy, Henry returned to ask the wagon boy, "Can a horse replace a mule?

"I s'pose so, but I never tried it before."

"Well, we're thinking that one of our spare horses could substitute for your lame mule. What do you think?"

"It's worth a try. Otherwise, we're stuck here."

Randy road off to fetch one of the spare horses and explain to Juan what was happening. He told Juan rapidly what was going on. Juan understood English better than he spoke it. He simply nodded his head to attest that Randy was taking the right action. Regardless of what Juan thought, Randy believed this was the only action they could take. Otherwise, they would be obliged to abandon the wagon and its load of cotton.

When Randy returned to the wagon with the lame mule, he found that Henry and the wagon boy had already unhitched the injured mule and were ready to replace it with the spare horse. They tried to make this swap as quickly as possible so the wagon could catch up with the rest of the train, which kept moving south.

The spare horse did not like being hitched up with a pack of mules. The horse had never worked as part of a team, and it had never before pulled a wagon. No matter how much the wagon boy whipped the horse, it would not cooperate. The horse knew that this was not its place, and it refused to move forward.

After some effort, Henry said, "This is of no use. It won't work. Let's unhitch the horse."

Randy said. "I'll take the horse back to Juan's wagon and ask him for advice as to what to do."

Juan laughed loudly when he heard what Randy had to say. When he finished laughing. He stopped his wagon and told Randy to tell all the wagons to stop and take a break. Juan jumped off his wagon and, mounted bareback the spare horse, and rode back at a gallop to see for himself the wagon in distress. As soon as he got there, he instructed firmly in Spanish the wagon boy to unhitch his team from the wagon. The wagon boy somehow knew his intentions and scrambled to unhitch is team.

Once the team was free of the wagon, Juan signaled to take off one mule and re-hitch two mules to the wagon. The wagon boy did as Juan indicated but said indignantly, "A two-mule team can't pull this wagon load."

Juan then told Henry and Randy to get into the wagon and roll off one bale of cotton. They did so, and Juan told the wagon boy, "Go now. Catch up with the train. We'll attach your two mules to the back of your wagon."

Henry and Randy were perplexed. They could not just leave a bale of precious cotton behind. Randy said to Juan, "What about the cotton bale? We can't leave it."

Juan smiled and said in broken English, "Of course. The cotton is going with us. Tie your lassos around it and use your horses to drag up the bale to the side the trailer of the big wagon."

Henry and Randy did as Juan said, but they did not understand what they were doing. They did as they were instructed and slowly towed the cotton bale over the sandy trail. They arrived alongside the trailer, and Henry asked Juan, "Now, what?"

Juan replied in a garble of mixed English and Spanish words, and he called in Spanish for those on the big wagon to come help them lift the cotton bale onto the top of the trailer. It took all of them to lift the bale onto the tall trailer. Then, once on top, it had to be tied down so it would not fall off. Randy turned to Henry and said, "That's pretty smart. One more bale should not make a difference to the big wagon."

Juan did not waste any time in getting back to his wagon, and he told Randy, "Break over. Tell everybody that we're pulling out."

And that was that. The cotton train kept moving south on the sandy track. Henry and Randy had learned some lessons, but the main thing they retained was that cotton came first no matter what. It was all about getting cotton to market and, making money for its owners, and giving the South the means to fight.

# Chapter Twenty-Nine
# Brownsville Arrival

They continued to push on. They wanted to quit, but there was nowhere to go. Everywhere in the Desert of the Dead was the same. They had to stay with their wagon train loaded with cotton if they wanted to stay alive.

The blazing sun beat down upon them with such ferocity that they wanted to hide in a shady spot, but such spots were rare in the desert. They stretched their large bandanas over their necks and face in an effort to ward off the burning rays of the sun. It was all they could do to stay on track and forge ahead.

One day was like another until they saw some furry critter dart across their path. Henry thought he was seeing things. So far, he had seen no living creature in this wide-open desolate land. He looked behind himself to see if Juan had seen anything. When Juan saw him looking his way, he signaled Henry to come near him so he could be heard.

Henry rode back to Juan, who said, "Do you smell it?"

Henry did not smell anything different and said, "No, but did you see it?"

Juan chuckled and said, "Yes, I saw the little ocelot scamper across the trail. Another sign proving what I smell?"

Henry took a deep breath through his nose again, but he still did not smell anything but the suffocating aridity of the desert. Juan breathed deeply again and said, "Such a beautiful smell."

An exasperated Henry blurted out, "Okay. Tell me what you smell that's so beautiful?"

"The smell of the Rio Grande Valley. All goin' to change soon as we get closer to the big river."

Randy rode up to see what was going on between Henry and Juan. Henry told Randy, "He says he smells the Rio Grande. I don't smell anything. Do you?"

Randy took a few deep breathes and said, "I don't smell anything different, but if Juan says he smells the river, I'm ready to accept what he says."

Then Henry told Randy about the wild creature he saw run across the trail. Randy hesitated but said, "Keep an eye out for any changes in the landscape. I trust Juan's nose, but maybe it's because I want it to be true."

Juan popped up. "My nose never lies. Tell all to watch their animals cuz they can smell water from a long distance, and they will start actin' up."

Randy gave a blank look at Henry and rode back to tell each wagon to be on the alert for their thirsty animals to become unruly as they neared the Rio Grande. His words were received with disbelief because they did not see or smell anything different in their surroundings. But his words did encourage them that in the next day or two, they would be enjoying the sights and sounds of Brownsville.

Henry rode out in front of the train farther than usual to see if there was any change in the landscape. He did notice some minor changes. Where there was once a soil composed of sand, there were patches of short mesquite grass. As insignificant as these small changes were, he was encouraged and rode more quickly forward.

The gradual downward slope of the land was noted by Henry. He looked out across the vast delta plain before him and became convinced that they were indeed coming to the end of their passage across the Desert of the Dead. He rode back to tell Juan. "Your nose is right. Soon, we'll be heading into the valley."

Juan snorted. "My nose is never wrong."

Henry was joined by Randy. Juan instructed, "Tonight we camp, so we get into Brownsville at Sunup tomorrow. Be on special alert... there are many banditos out to steal our cotton in these parts."

Then, Henry smelled it. A slight but fresh southern breeze gently caressed his face. The tantalizing sensation restored life to his body and put a smile on his face. Uncontrollably, tears swelled up in his eyes. He paused a moment to better appreciate the sheer goodness of the breeze and all that it foretold.

He was jarred out of his momentary trance by the noise made by another creature rushing by. He did not know what it was, but Juan also saw it and said, "You should have shot that one. Javelina meat tastes as good as a pig."

Henry assumed that a javelina was some sort of wild pig. He replied to Juan by saying. "Next time, I'll make sure any javelina gets to know the wrong end of my rifle."

Juan said something in Spanish in response to Henry's words and then he said in English, "Look ahead for a good place to pass a good part of the night. We want to roll into Brownsville early tomorrow and go straight to Mr. Ford's dock to have our cotton unloaded on his steamboats for crossing to the Mexican side."

Henry rode off to search for a good place to spend the night. It was dusk when Henry returned to tell Juan that there was a good place not too far distant. Juan replied, "Thank God. This has been a great passage. We're very lucky. No serious breakdowns and the big wagons have performed perfectly. And no attacks. We are truly blessed. This is the easiest trip I ever had to Brownsville."

Henry thought his last words were added to irritate him. As far as he was concerned, this week on the trail had been the toughest in his young life and this was not an experience he would ever get used to doing. If he never crossed the Desert of the Dead again, it would be too soon for him.

Randy rode up, and Juan told him to pass the word about stopping to spend most of the night before rolling into Brownsville early tomorrow. A gleeful Randy rode back to spread the news that they were almost there. His news animated all the teamsters and all of a sudden, what had tested them severely had become a trivial game. With the end in sight, their battered mental framework was amended, and their spirits were upbeat.

Juan signaled the train to stop and rest themselves and their animals for the night. He instructed Randy to inform all the wagon drivers to provide their mules with the last of the grain they had, if any, and give some good swallows of water. They also should unhitch all their mules and allow them to roam freely nearby to rest and graze on any grass they could find.

Doing all this involved a lot of work, but it was negligible given that excitement levels were high in anticipation of the arrival in Brownsville tomorrow. Everyone was busy making sure they, their wagons, and mules were looking as good as they could. They all wanted the people in Brownsville to look at them as if their journey had not required any unusual effort.

Juan tried to make that last night on the trail a jubilant one. He hauled out the last food items and tried to make the evening meal a festive one. Henry and Randy enjoyed eating their fill and listening to Juan rattle off stories in Spanish. They acted like they understood, but they really did not comprehend what was being told to them. They pretended to understand and laughed along with Juan, but his monologue only communicated to them how much Spanish they had yet to learn. Anyway, they thought it was good to get their ears used to hearing Spanish.

As usual, Juan woke them early, and they got their horses ready to hit the final leg of the long trip. Henry and Randy sprang into action, and the wagon train moved toward Rio Grande. As the sun peaked over the eastern horizon, Juan gesticulated wildly. Henry and Randy rode up near him to see what the matter was. Juan repeated in Spanish one word over and over that they did not understand. Repeatedly, Juan happily said, "Tortuga."

Henry and Randy did not have a clue about what he was saying, but they could see that he was ecstatic. Juan could see their ignorance of the importance of what he was saying and pointed to an item in the distance. Henry and Randy strained to see what was making him so happy. At last, they spotted a terrestrial animal that, for them, looked like a hefty land turtle. They had never seen such a turtle before, but they could not fathom why the sighting of this creature made him so happy.

Juan could see the puzzlement of their faces instead of the joy he expected to see. He was prompted to blast out in the best English he could muster. "Seeing a Tortuga is good luck. This is the first time I've been so blessed."

Henry and Randy looked at each other and restrained themselves from laughing at Juan. Instead, they joined him in rejoicing over this piece of luck. The jubilation of the moment made them all feel better. They were all glad that the sighting of the turtle promised them good luck for their onward journey. From then on, a Texas turtle would be for them be a sign of good luck and cause them to remember Juan forever.

They edged along in the riverine area, appreciating the increase in ground vegetation and trees. They arrived in Brownsville without fanfare. The streets were bustling with people who were used to passing wagon trains. Even the big wagons in their train did not attract attention. Their train had to go slow as the streets were congested with people, horses, mules, and wagons. Yet, they headed without hesitation to the river port.

They encountered wagon trains going in the opposite direction full of imported supplies for the Confederacy bought with money earned from the sale of cotton. These wagons were overflowing with guns, ammunition, food, and medical items. It was clear to Henry and Randy that cotton trade over the border with Mexico was key to the survival of the South.

Henry could see that their horses and mules were becoming rambunctious as they approached the river, and they would need watering as soon as they unloaded their cotton. There was something of a traffic jam as they reached dockside. It appeared as if everyone was vying to get their cargo to the dock for transport across the river to Matamoros. Although there were several flat-bottom river steamboats working around the clock to get all the cargo they could over to the Mexican side, the movement of goods to the other side of the river seemed to go all too slow.

Randy was busy doing his calculations. He could see that the captain and his partners were making huge profits by selling and transporting cotton and other goods. With all the money they were making, these 'foreigners' were buying up huge tracks of land to convert into ranches. Randy turned to Henry and said, "If they survive the war, they're set for life as some of the wealthiest people in these parts. They have put to use their entrepreneurial know-how where most people would not see money-making opportunities. I guess we're too young and arrived too late to take advantage of these profit-making opportunities."

Randy continued, "The way I understand it, the river is counted as international waters, and it is pretty nifty that the river steamboats are flying Mexican flags. Therefore, according to international law, the Union can't touch these boats unless they want to go to war with Mexico."

Henry interrupted his younger brother by saying in a loud outburst, "What's that?"

Henry and Randy looked at the strange creatures being led past them loaded with two bales of cotton. They had never seen such four-legged beasts of burden. They both looked back at Juan and gestured in a way to ask him what in the world they were seeing. Juan simply answered, "Camello."

"Now we know what the words are for turtle and camel in Spanish. I can understand turtles in Texas but, for sure, the camels had to be imported. Who would have ever imagined camels in Texas? I wonder from where they come from."

All of sudden their wagons were swarmed by mobs of Mexican workers who were hellbent on unloading cotton bales and carrying them to the steamers waiting at dockside. When the steamer was stacked high with bales, it would be untied from the dock and head to the other side. As soon as one steamer was on its way across the river, another would take its place. Evidently, activity continued like this night and day.

Now that their wagons were empty of their cargo, Henry and Randy were at a loss as to what they should do next. They felt lost among the crowd in Brownsville and did not know where to go. They turned to Juan, and Henry said, "What do we do now?"

Juan laughed and said, "You boys are chosen ones. You get to cross the river. The Jefe wants you to help out on the Mexican side. You should go with your horses on the next boat. You'll meet an Anglo men on the other side who will take care of you."

Henry and Randy were dumbfounded by Juan said, and Henry asked, "Why didn't you tell us that before?"

"I didn't think it was a good idea to let you know that your journey did not end in Brownsville. Of course, if you don't want to go to Matamoros, you can go with us back to Santa Rosita once we get loaded with our return cargo."

Suddenly, going to the Mexican side seemed like a good option. The very thought of crossing the Desert of the Dead again made the Mexican option attractive. Henry and Randy turned to say something to Juan, but before they could say anything, Juan waved his hand and said in Spanish, "Que vaya bien. Nada mas es necessario."

Juan turned his head away from them while waving for them to go. Henry and Randy interpreted the way Juan was acting that there was no need to say goodbye to their wagon mates. It did not feel right, but Henry motioned to Randy to follow him onto the dock so they could catch a ride across the river.

They waited for a while, and then one of the men working on a boat gave them a hand sign to move onto the flat-bottom steamer. They did not dare look back. They knew that what was behind them was gone. They looked ahead with some trepidation to unknown territory and a whole different country. They could see already that some deference was afforded them because of their white skin. Somehow, everybody knew they were the captain's new young men.

Randy had one question. "Say, when do we get paid? We spent ten days crossing the Big Sands, and we were not paid anything."

Henry huffed and replied, "Good question. We got to ask that of whoever is waiting for us on the other side. Lord knows we need money for new clothes and to clean up."

Randy added, "And to eat."

# Chapter Thirty
# Bagdad Port

They led their horses off the boat and were caught up in a beehive of activity. Many men were frantically working to load oxen carts with cotton bales, and swarms of people of all types were milling about. Henry and Randy were lost in the tumultuous crowd as soon as they stepped on the dock.

They worked their way to the edge of the dock and were ready to enter Mexican territory when they heard a deep voice with a pronounced Texas drawl. They both turned to see the person speaking in such tones and found a tall Anglo man with his right hand extended. The man was obliged to shout so he could be heard above the din of the crowd. Henry and Randy were sure of his words. "Welcome to Mexico. You must be the two young guys I was told about."

Henry and Randy released their grip on their horses' reins and shook vigorously the hand that had been extended to them. They got closer to the man, who said, "My name is Jeff. Like you, I work for the captain. My station is here at the Matamoros dock. We'll need you to start work immediately. Okay?"

Henry replied, "I guess so. What do you have for use to do?"

"We need you to go with the ox carts with your load of cotton to the Bagdad Port and stay with it until it is safely loaded on a ship bound for Europe. That way, you can see how the operation works from start to finish. The port is not far… only about twenty miles."

Randy was about to ask a question when Jeff said quickly, "I got to get back to work now. You go, and when you return, you can give me a full report."

Since Randy could not get a word in edgewise, he turned his pockets inside out so that Jeff could see they had no money. Jeff got Randy's meaning and said as an afterthought, "Excuse me. I forgot to give you guys your pay."

Jeff dug into his deep right pocket and pulled out a leather pouch full of Mexican gold pesos. He counted out a number of coins and handed them to Henry, saying, "That should more than cover what we owe you. Don't spend it all in one place, and be careful of pickpockets. There are thieves everywhere, and everybody here is out to get as much money as they can. I got to go now."

Henry handed the coins to Randy and said, "Keep these in a safe place. I don't trust myself with so much money."

The next thing they knew, some scruffy, short Mexican guy came up to them and bowed after taking off his sombrero and said, "I'm Carlos. Sr. Jeff said I should go with you to Bagdad."

At first, Henry and Randy thought they were being scammed, and they looked toward where Jeff was, and he yelled, "Carlos is okay. He's my man."

Carlos beckoned them to follow him off the dock to a spot where oxen carts full of cotton were being lined up for the trek to Bagdad Port. Carlos signaled to them to water their horses and get ready to leave. He showed them a place to water their horses and where there was some cut hay for them to eat. He also showed them a food stall where they could eat their fill of tortillas and fried beans. Henry and Randy had never before eaten this food, but it tasted good to them, especially since they were desperately hungry.

Carlos indicated to them that they should pay for their food and the feed for their horses. Randy held out to Carlos a handful of coins and let him take whatever was needed to pay for what was eaten. Randy made a mental notes to study later the coins, their inscriptions, and their value in terms of exchange. They were in a new world, and everything was not the same as they had ever experienced before.

They mounted their horses and fell in behind the last oxen cart. They waited to see Carlos join them on his horse, but he said, "I'll walk. If I get too tired, I'll jump on one of the cotton carts."

Henry and Randy were impressed, especially since Carlos was barefoot and the ground was rough and hot. They were also impressed with Carlos's English. Randy told Carlos, "Your English is good. Where did you learn it?"

Carlos was quick to answer, "My mother was Mexican, but my father was an Anglo. We spoke mostly English at home. I always spoke English with my dad and Spanish with my mother. I'm what they call a 'mestizo.' A lot of people here speak English and mix Spanish with English."

Carlos' response prompted Randy to ask, "Do your mom and dad live in Matamoros?"

"We lived on the Texas side along the Nueces River. When I was six years old, our small jacal was raided by Comanches, and they killed my mother and father and captured me.

I was just a young boy. I tried to run away, but the Comanche burnt the soles of my feet, so I could not walk. They wanted to hold me for ransom. Since that time, I don't like to wear shoes.

After a few years, the Indian camp I was being held in was attacked by a group of Anglo settlers, and I managed to escape. Since then, I've been mostly under then care of the captain and his partners. Like you, I work for the captain, and my job now is to make sure this oxen train of cotton gets loaded on some of the dozens of ships waiting off Bagdad Port."

Henry responded, "That's quite a story. We're happy to have someone like you to show us the ropes. By the way, how old are you?"

"I'll be fourteen next week. Please excuse me. I talk too much."

"Remind us next week to celebrate your birthday. You can talk all you want. We got a lot to learn."

With a big smile on his face, Carlos ran off to tell all the oxen cart drivers to start going to Bagdad. There was no time to lose because time was money, and the Confederacy needed all they could get. Carlos came back and said to Henry and Randy that their main job was to show that this oxen train had armed guards. They nodded, and Henry rode up to the front while Randy took up the rear guard. Both of them had their rifles ready to deal with anyone interrupting the forward progress of the procession of oxen carts full of valuable cotton.

Carlos ran back and forth so he could be seen, saying encouraging words in Spanish to all the cart drivers. There was probably not a cart he did not jump on to have a wordy dialog with each driver in Spanish. The more Henry and Randy observed Carlos at work, the more they were convinced of their good luck in being associated with such a person. Seeing Carlos in action was a delight to them, and they could not wait to benefit more from him.

As far as they could see in front and back of them, there were long lines of oxen carts. They were all headed to the Port of Bagdad. It did not take more than three hours to reach the docks of this unlikely port. Henry and Randy were surprised to see that adjoining the port was a thriving town of thousands of people and dozens of shops and saloons. It appeared that people have been drawn to Bagdad to partake of the money generated by the cotton trade.

As they neared the docks, Carlos tried to explain the operations of the port. "We unload the cotton bales in our oxen carts onto small flat bottom boats which cross the ocean shallows to transfer the bales to the ships anchored beyond the sandbar. Those ships come from many countries, mostly European, to get cotton for their textile mills. They all have agents onshore."

Henry and Randy had many questions. Randy began by asking, "Why have a port here in a place where ships can't even get near?"

"I guess because it is as close as you can get to the source of cotton and remain beyond the reach of the Union Navy. Without cotton, there would be nothing here."

Henry could not wait to ask. "There are many oxen trains full of cotton. Do they all belong to the captain and his partners?"

Without hesitation, Carlos simply replied, "All."

Henry and Randy could see they were at a large floodplain at the mouth of the Rio Grande. They could also see that among the merchant ships anchored around five hundred feet offshore were some gunships. This sighting prompted Randy to ask, "Why are there some warships out there?"

Carlos quickly answered, "To protect the cotton ships from the Union Navy, which is located nearby."

Henry and Randy scanned the wide ocean horizon, but they did not see any Union Navy ships. Carlos said, "We got to get ready to load our cotton on the flat bottom boats that go out to the big ocean-going ships. You should go with these boats to see how the bales are loaded onto the ships and how the reverse cargo is loaded on the boats for the return trip. I'll stay here and take care of your horses."

Reluctantly, Henry and Randy stepped onto the boats, grabbing hold of some cotton bales. They had never been on salty ocean water. Three boatmen lost no time in shoving off into deeper waters. One man steered the boat's rudder, and the other two worked on each side of the boat with long poles, pushing them against the shallow sandy bottom so the boat would go toward the ships anchored off the wide sandbar.

When they got close to the waiting ships, a long rope would be thrown out to them, and the boatmen would tie it tightly to an iron hook on their boat. Men on the ship would then pull on the rope so the lighter would come alongside and be secured in a stationary position by attaching more ropes. As soon as the lighter was secure, dozens of men from the boat would busy themselves to unload onto the ship its cargo of cotton.

Henry and Randy stood motionless as they observed the intensity of activity around them. They had never seen anything like this and kept their mouths shut to disguise their ignorance. In particular, they were awed by seeing such a big, fully-masted ocean-going ship. They could easily see that it would take many lighter loads of cotton to fill one ship this size.

As soon as the cotton bales were lifted onto the deck of the ship, the return cargo of rifles and ammunition was loaded onto the lighter. As much of this war material was loaded onto the lighter as was possible, then the lighter was detached from the ship and pushed toward the shore. The lighter was adrift, floating slowly with the tide and gentle sea waves pushing it toward the shore. When they arrived at a spot where their long poles could reach the bottom, the polemen began working earnestly to return the lighter to its home dock.

They looked about, and the delta bay was strewn with lighters taking cotton to the ships offshore and returning to shore with items needed to keep the Confederacy alive. Each ship had raised a colorful banner so it could be identified by the lighter designated to deliver cotton to that ship. They docked on the shore, and Carlos clapped his hands and said, "You see, that's not so bad. It's spookier at night. As you know, we work around the clock if the weather permits."

Henry said, "I guess everyone wants to keep the cotton and war supplies moving as much as possible. This northern strip of Mexico seems to be fully under control of the Confederacy and its interests."

"Yes, that is true, but everyone wants to get their fingers in the pie. We've had the French, revolutionists, and local jefes demand part of the receipts. Control of the Bagdad Port is complicated and changes hands frequently. The port is a big honey pot, and everybody wants a share."

The war cargo carried by the lighter was rapidly transferred to the empty carts, which had been turned around and were ready for the return trip to Matamoros. Randy scribbled a few notes in his writing pad so he could give Jeff a thorough report. Carlos checked all the oxen carts and gave the hand signal to go. He jogged back to Henry and Randy and said, "You guys are the only ones I know who have done all of the cotton road. I wish I could know faraway places."

Randy said, "Look, we're not much older than you. I've seen a lot of country, but my favorite place is home. Now, we just have to be happy with what we got and stay alive for another day. For sure, the grass is not greener on the other side of the fence, especially with a war goin' on."

Henry spoke by saying, "We're going back already without seeing how Bagdad town is?"

Carlos quickly responded by saying, "You're not missing much. The town is full of drunkards, desperados, whores, and bandits who are out to get your money. Sadly, cotton money has attracted all the worse types. Besides, we have to get back before dark, and you'll probably get to know Bagdad more than you want."

Suddenly, some men rode by at a gallop. After the dust stirred up by this group of horsemen settled, Randy asked. "Who were they?"

"Southern soldiers. They're probably looking for Union sympathizers. For sure, they are checking on the flow of cotton and the backhaul of war goods for the South. They know that this is a lifeline for the South. Also, I heard there are some German immigrants from Texas Hill country who are held up in Bagdad waiting for a ship to take them to a northern state. A lot of them have already been killed, and if they keep up their Union tendencies, more will be killed."

Carlos' lengthy reply had Henry and Randy scratching their heads as they digested their new experiences and all the information Carlos was giving to them. They did not dare ask more questions. They had already received more information than they could handle and feared an overload. But, whether they were ready or not, they spotted Jeff waiting for them on the river dock and knew he would have more for them to do.

Jeff was easy to spot in the crowd because of his height. He stood head and shoulders over all others on the dock. Before they could dismount, Jeff spoke, "I see you're back already, so I guess I have to deal with you. Anyway, it's a good time cause some problems with the next boat have obliged us to take a break."

Henry and Randy dismounted, and Jeff said, "Follow me to see where you can bunk."

Randy looked around himself and saw all of them squatting and not sitting on the dock. He asked Jeff, "Why don't they sit down and rest til the next boat arrives?"

With a puzzled look on his face, Jeff looked at his workers and said, "They are resting. That's the way they sit."

Randy replied, "I could never sit like that."

"You got to start young. There are many things in the Mexican way of living that are different than the way we were brought up."

"I reckon we've a lot to learn about Mexican life."

"You sure do. This is only your first day on the Mexico side. It will take you months to fully digest this mixed-up place. This is a border boomtown that has attracted some of the worst elements from both sides. There's so many people here from the states that they have a newspaper in English. But don't trust anybody, regardless of where they come from. Everybody is here to make money, and many people will do almost anything to line their pockets. If the day ever arrives where there is no market for cotton, much of this place will die."

Jeff's words gave Henry and Randy so much to mull over they forgot to say goodbye to Carlos. This prompted Henry to ask, "When will we see Carlos again?"

Jeff laughed and said, "He's probably waiting for you and your horses at your shack. He'll care for your horses and do anything else you want him to do. You guys and him will be a team to oversee the transport of cotton to Bagdad. That's the job the captain wants you to do… make sure his cotton gets loaded on the ships at sea."

Henry was not sure of his reaction but said. "That should keep us busy for a while."

"Yep. As long as the cotton keeps coming, you'll have good-paying jobs."

# Chapter Thirty-One
# Matamoros

Their wooden, tin-roofed shack was small, bare-bones but adequate. Inside the shack were two narrow beds with mattresses and a plain wooden table with two wobbly chairs. On the wall were a few rusty nails for hanging their clothes. Attached to the outside back wall was a place to wash up. Also in the backyard was an open well and a bucket attached to a long rope. Hidden in the brush behind the shack was a makeshift outhouse constructed over a pit latrine. Their favorite part of the shack was its covered front porch.

Jeff showed them quickly around and, just before leaving said, "It's not much, but it will do. I live in a similar shack next door. You guys take the rest of the day off. Carlos should show up soon. I got to tend to something. We'll talk later."

Randy looked at Henry and said, "He's right. It's not much, but it's a roof over our heads. Now we know how our slaves lived in their shacks on our plantation."

Henry replied, "Well, we got to get used to it cuz we could be here for a good long time. I think as soon as Carlos shows up, we should spend some of our money to get cleaned up and to buy some new duds."

"Yeah, good idea. We need Carlos to show us where to go in this bustling town."

They were moving their two chairs to the front stoop when the energetic Carlos showed up and said, "I've got to take your horses to be checked out, fed, and watered. Let's take off their saddles and get goin'."

Henry said, "Okay, but we thought we should clean up a bit."

"No problema. Near the stable is a place you can get a hot bath, shave, and haircut. Not far is a store with all the clothes you want. Not far from there is a place where the finest ladies in Mexico will take care of your every need."

Uttering this last sentence caused Carlos to burst out in laughter. Henry and Randy were not quite sure how to interpret Carlos last words, but Henry managed to say, "Let's go. It's getting dark."

They followed Carlos and their two horses. Carlos was in his typical talkative mode and said, "Don't worry. You'll be well taken care of. And Matamoros never sleeps. You can stay up as late as you want, but Jefe Jeff expects you to be present bright and early tomorrow."

They dropped their horses off at the nearby stables. Carlos communicated a stream of Spanish words to the Mexican caretaker of the stables. He then turned to Henry and Randy and said, "Let's go to the clothes store first so you can have new duds to wear after you get cleaned up. Follow me."

They wove their way through the crowds in one of Matamoros' main streets. Everywhere they went, there were attractive ladies eyeing them in a way they had never seen women do before. They could not dodge how they were flirting with their eyes. Carlos noticed the discomfiture the ladies were causing Henry and Randy and said, "Pay no mind to the ladies. If you want one, fine. But, if you don't want, that's okay too. Anyway, there will always be women."

They climbed up the steps of the boardwalk leading to a store with a large sign stating, 'Johnson and Sons, Best Clothes in Mexico.' They entered the store, and the shop clerks acknowledged the presence of Carlos with winks and immediately put themselves at the service of Henry and Randy. They brought a wide selection of pants, shirts, vests, bandanas, undergarments, etc. All appeared to be in their sizes. They brought much more than Henry and Randy could ever buy and wear.

There was a side room hidden behind a thin, flowery, floor-length cotton curtain where they could try on the clothes they liked. When they had dressed in what they thought was best for them, they called Carlos to see what he thought. Carlos was impressed by their selection and said, "Looks good to me. You'll look even better when you've cleaned up. The main thing lacking is new hats for both of you. I'll take you to a hat store after this."

The clerks wrapped their new clothes in brown paper and tied the bundles with strands of sisal string twine. Carlos carried the two packages of clothes. Randy gave Carlos some money to settle their bill. He went up to the store manager standing behind a counter, and they could see him counting out the gold coins. Carlos saw out of the corner of his eyes that Henry and Randy were looking at him. Henry and Randy noticed that the manager gave him back some money.

When Carlos re-joined them, he said one word, "Propina. It's the custom here that you are given a tip for bringing buying customers. Every place we go, and you spend money, I get my share. Dats just how things are here."

Henry and Randy now realized the reason why there as such a big smile on Carlos' face and why he was so happy to show them around. They did not object to this kind of behavior. For them, this was how things were done in this part of the world. Anyway, they had little previous experience to go by in such situations. They were content to be in the capable hands of Carlos, who knew all the ins and outs of a chaotic Matamoros.

Their next stop was at a nearby haberdashery store. There were all kinds of hats, and Henry and Randy did not know what was best for them to wear south of the border, so they asked Carlos to choose for them. He chose for them the latest model of a wide-brimmed felt hat that was called 'The Boss of the Plains.' These new hats were expensive, but Carlos asserted that it was important that they have such hats to impose their positions as the captain's men.

Carlos said, "The very fact that you can afford such a hat adds to your status and makes people forget about your young ages. This is the kind of hat Anglo men should wear. It's got a wide brim, a hat band, it's light and it's waterproof. It will last you a long time. Try it on."

The moment Henry and Randy placed the new hats on their heads, they were sold. These hats made them feel older and more manly. They knew they were costly, but they had to have them. They dished out the money to Carlos so he could pay and get his finder's cut. They strode out to the street with their new hats on, and all heads turned. They had entered the store as teenage boys and came out as men.

Randy asked Henry, "Why is everyone looking at us? Is it our new hats or those old .45 six-shooters that you insist on wearing?

Henry smiled and said, "Why, of course, it's the hats. They've seen plenty of six-shooters in these parts, but it is rare to see two young Anglos in these latest model hats."

Carlos added, "You see. People look at your hats and know you're boss, men, and should be treated accordingly. Now, let's go and get you cleaned up so you can put on your new clothes."

They arrived at a place on the outskirts of town that had an abundance of beautiful Mexican women. They were greeted enthusiastically in Spanish. Carlos explained in Spanish to the head woman what they wanted, and the other women immediately swung into a flurry of action. Carlos turned to Henry and Randy and said, "Go behind those curtains and, remove all your clothing and hang them over the curtain rod. Your old clothes will be washed and ironed. Take your packages of new clothes to dress in after they have given you hot baths and scrubbed you from head to toe."

Randy replied, "Fine, but what about our haircuts and shaves?"

"I'm going to fetch the barbero man who does that while you soak in your hot baths. Don't worry. By the time the sun goes down, you will be just like newborn babies."

After they had stripped down, Henry and Randy continued buck naked into an adjoining shack to find two tin bathtubs full of water and soap suds. They touched the water in the tubs and found it too hot to submerge themselves in, so they waited until the water cooled and then slid slowly into their bathtubs. They had not been in a bathtub since they left their Virginia home. They had almost forgot how good it felt to take a hot bath,

As soon as they were settled into their tubs, a bevy of women wielding an assortment of hard bristle brushes descended upon them and began scrubbing every part of their dirty bodies. They scrubbed so hard that it hurt. Just when they thought they could not tolerate any more scrubbing, a couple of women carefully used a washcloth on their faces and began washing their hair with a strong-smelling soap. All the time, the women were smiling and humming a song. Henry and Randy were impressed. They were genuinely happy with what the women were doing.

The head woman entered a side door, and all the women who were tending Henry and Randy quickly exited through another door. The head woman carried several drying cloths and laid them on adjoining stools. She only spoke Spanish, so she used hand signals to indicate they should get out of their tubs, dry off, and wait for the barber to come to cut their hair and give them shaves.

They sat on their stools with their drying cloths wrapped around themselves when a dapper Mexican man burst into the room exclaiming with much exuberance in a mixture of English and Spanish. "I'm Antonio, and I'm here to give you the best haircuts and shaves you have had in your lives."

After presenting himself to the wide-eyed Henry and Randy, he took a deep bow and removed from his leather satchel the instruments of his profession. He said, "I'll start with the oldest first."

His scissors whirled snappily around Henry's head in a rapid, methodical fashion. It was apparent that Antonio gave good haircuts. Henry looked better than he ever had. Antonio finished Henry's haircut and then removed a leather strap, straight-edge shaving blade, small soap dish, and shaving brush from his bag. Antonio used the water from the tubs to dampen the soap in the shaving dish and filled his brush with soap foam, which he firmly swirled over Henry face and neck.

When Antonio began shaving the whiskers from his face, Henry said firmly, "Cut it all off. I don't want a mustache."

Antonio understood what Henry was saying, but he did not agree with him. All men in these parts have at least a mustache. Antonio looked at Randy, hoping to get his intervention to preserve Henry's mustache. Antonio's dilemma prompted Randy to say, "Do what he says. Shave it all off. As for me, I want to have a mustache."

Antonio finished shaving Henry by applying a stimulating perfumed tonic to his face and neck. He withdrew from his bag a hand mirror and handed it to Henry so he could admire his new look. He turned to begin giving the same hair and beard treatment to Randy. Henry had not looked at himself in a mirror for over a year, and he was surprised to see a grown man looking back at him. He spent a long time looking at his face and was lost for words but finally said, "I feel like a plucked chicken, but this is the best haircut and shave I ever had. Gracias, Antonio."

Randy was pleased that his older brother was happy with the services they were getting. Randy was also satisfied with the work Antonio was doing on his head and praised him for it. Antonio was sweeping up the hair on the floor and looking for a waste bucket when Carlos stepped into the room to see how things were going. He was impressed at how good the transformed Henry and Randy were looking and exclaimed, "Mama Mia. Fantastico. You look so good."

Henry and Randy stood up and prepared to bid farewell to Antonio and put on their new clothes. Antonio said, "I'm leaving a scissors behind so you can cut any unwanted hair on your private parts."

As Antonio was leaving the room, Henry looked at Randy and said, "I guess I can do with a little trimming downstairs."

When Carlos saw what they were about to do, he said, "Excuse me.

I'll be back shortly. Don't get in a hurry. You'll still need to get your finger and toenails fixed."

Henry replied, "Oh. Okay. We didn't plan on that. How we goin to pay for all this? We don't have much money left after buying our hats."

Carlos quickly responded, "La verdad, but you can always pay later. Your credit is good here."

Just as Henry and Randy finished trimming their pubic hair and wrapped their drying cloths around themselves, a group of women entered the room and told them to sit down while they gave them manicures and pedicures. They had a woman at either side of them to work on their fingernails, and sitting on small stools, they had two women working on their toenails. This was a totally new experience for Henry and Randy. They did not know whether to cry or laugh.

They had never felt so clean. The nail team withdrew graciously, and Henry and Randy thought it was time to get dressed in their new duds, but before they could standup six women came into the room carrying two basins filled with water. They sat the basin at their feet and begin scrubbing vigorously their soles. This hurt their sensitive feet, but they bore their pain because they believed the women knew what they were doing. They also thought that it was good for them.

After scrubbing their feet, they gave them a soothing massage of their calves, which took off the sting of the foot scrubs. They thanked effusively this group of attractive young women. Randy said to Henry, "My feet have never been so clean. It's almost a shame to put our feet back into our dirty old boots. Let's get dressed in our new clothes."

They slowly put on their new undergarments, pants, belts, shirts, vests, and blue bandanas. Just as they were admiring their new looks, Carlos sprang into the room and exclaimed, "You look so different! It's like you aren't the same two guys who I knew before we came to this place. Really, this is an unbelievable change. Put on your new hats so the transformation is complete."

Henry and Randy stepped outside to show off their new personas to the world. All the ladies who had attended to them were lined up on either side of them to observe the miraculous transformation they had wrought on these two young men. The women softly applauded. It was a joyous occasion that almost brought tears to the eyes of Henry and Randy.

They waved and thanked again all the women. They offered a special thanks to the older gray-headed woman who was at the end of the line. They headed back to their shack, following closely behind Carlos. Henry broke the silence by saying quietly to Randy, "I'll be back."

# Chapter Thirty-Two
# Bagdad Town

An excited Carlos rushed up to the front stoop of Jeff's shack and yelled, "Come see two new Anglo hands I brought you."

He waited a couple of minutes for Jeff to appear. When Jeff did not come out of his shack, he knocked forcefully on the door. His noisy knocking was met with silence. He walked back a short distance and said to Henry and Randy, "Jeff, is not in his shack. He's probably at his girlfriend's house and nursing a glass of aguardiente."

Henry immediately responded, "He has a girlfriend?"

"Yes, he has a beautiful local woman. You can have one, too, if you want."

Randy jumped into the conversation, "What was that word you said … agua… somethin'"

"Dats the local clear and pure alcoholic drink made from sugar cane juice. It's very powerful and addictive. Jeff is addicted and almost refuses to drink anything but aguardiente. He says water rusts his pipes. He's been doing this for years, but it's not sure how much longer he can go. As long as he has his girlfriend and his bottle of aguardiente, he's happy."

Randy responded by saying, "He seems to do a good job regardless of his off-duty habits."

"Don't get me wrong. He's a good man and totally loyal to the captain. He doesn't let his habits keep him from getting the job done right and on time. Speaking of time, let's go to a roadside eatery, and then you guys have to get some shuteye so you can show up at the dock bright and early."

Carlos continued by saying, "Take your saddles off and put them inside your shack. The stables is on the way, and I'll drop your horses off."

Henry and Randy did as Carlos said and placed their saddles next to the beds. Henry closed the door of their shack behind him and said to Carlos, "It's getting dark. What's to keep the thieves out of our shack?"

"Did you lock the door?"

"No, I didn't know if you could lock it."

"There should be an old key on the top inside of the door frame."

Henry reached up and felt the key. He took it and stepped outside, inserted it in the keyhole, and turned it twice so the door was solidly locked. He handed the key to Randy for safekeeping and said, "I guess that'll help keep the thieves out."

Carlos said, "I wouldn't worry about thievery. Everyone knows that this is where the captain's men stay, so the thieves stay away cuz they know what will happen to them if they mess with anything that belongs to the captain."

Henry and Randy got the meaning of what Carlos was saying. His words had reinforced again their special status. Carlos took the horses to the stable, and they walked a short distance to the roadside place to eat. Night had fallen, but there was some light cast off by the smelly candle flames placed on the long table. They took a seat on the wooden bench. Carlos said something in Spanish, and quickly, they were served heaping plates of tortillas and fried beans with a dash of some sort of sour cream.

They watched how Carlos would tackle his plate. They saw him gorging himself by using the tortillas to spread the sour cream over the beans and then to scoop up the beans to his mouth. They followed suit, and Carlos observed. "You guys are eating like real Mexicans."

Randy smiled and said, "Yeah, but I need some water to wash it all down."

Carlos said something quickly to the barely visible corpulent woman serving them, and immediately, she placed mugs in front of them and a big pitcher of fresh water. Randy filled their glasses and offered a toast. "To Carlos for making this such a spectacular day."

They laughed heartily. When their plates were scraped clean, Henry asked, "How much do we pay?"

A grinning Carlos said, "You don't pay anything. You guys made me a lot of money today, so the food is on me."

Henry replied, "We are thankful for the meal and all you have done for us today. Someday, I hope we can repay you. But next time, tell us in advance that you are paying, so we'll eat more."

They all had a good laugh over Henry's last words. They were in a good mood as they walked back to their shack. Randy asked Carlos as they neared the shack, "What's on tap for tomorrow?"

Carlos replied with a straight face, "More of the same as today."

"How long is it goin' to be like that?"

"As long as there is cotton to transport and ship out."

After a pause, Randy said, "I guess we are locked into this job for the duration."

Henry joined the conversation by saying to Randy, "What do you mean by 'duration'?"

"As long as there is a war and the South needs to market its cotton in exchange for money and war material."

"I wonder how long that will be? We could be stuck here for years," uttered Henry.

Carlos added, "You got anything better to do? Best you stay on this side of the border until the war between the States is over."

Henry responded, "I guess we'll never be free. We'll always be beholden to someone or somethin'."

Both Henry and Randy nodded their agreement with Carlos' words, but they were uncertain about their future. For the time being, they were willing to take things a day at a time. They arrived at their shack, and Carlos said, "Get some sleep. Be ready to go at sunup. I'll be here with your horses, and we'll go together."

Henry and Randy shook Carlos' hand and thanked him again for all his help. Just as Randy was turning the key in their front door, Randy turned and asked Carlos, "Where your place?"

Carlos sheepishly responded, "Right here." He pointed to a hammock attached to two nearby trees.

Henry and Randy were surprised to see that Carlos slept outside while they slept inside. Carlos could see their puzzlement and said blankly, "Here, I'm considered a Mexican, so sleeping outside if okay. You are boss men, so you sleep in beds. Dats just how it is."

Randy said, "Okay. Understood. What do you do if it rains?"

"It doesn't rain here much, but if it does, I snuggle up on your front porch. I got my blanket and pillow. I don't really need any more."

Henry and Randy looked at each other. They both knew they could not change the culture of the place even though there were some practices they did not like, especially as this was only their first day in Mexico. They bid Carlos good night and were stepping inside their shack when Carlos said, "If you need light, there should be some candles and matches next to where you found the key. See you at the crack of dawn tomorrow."

Although they had plenty to say, they were too tired to talk. They locked the door behind them and lit one of the candles to lighten up their dingy room a bit. They dripped some wax from the candle onto the table and secured it so it could burn freely. They took their clothes off and laid them neatly across the table. They did not want to take off their new hats, but they could not sleep in them. They gently placed their hats on top of their clothes.

They tiptoed out the back door to relieve themselves in the bushes. They took turns washing their mouths out by swishing water from a jug and spitting it out. They returned to the shack, locking the back door behind themselves. They crashed into their beds. They were eager to go to sleep. Randy used his last wakeful breath of the day to say, "Not enough hours in the day."

They immediately dozed off, and before they knew it, there was a gentle knock at the door. They heard Carlos muffled voice saying, "Time to go."

Henry and Randy hollered back in unison, "All right. Coming."

As they got their tired bodies up and tried to shake off the deep state of sleep they were in, Henry managed to say, "Not enough hours in the night."

They slowly dressed and opened the front door to let Carlos in. They stepped out of their room located on opposite sides of their front porch with their water jugs and poured water into their hands to vigorously wash the sleepiness out of their eyes. They then swirled water around in their sour mouths, spitting it out as far away from the shack as they could.

They saw their two horses in front of their shack, and this reminded them to carry out their saddles and prepare their horses for a day's work. Henry went back into the shack to strap on his old .44's and get their two rifles. He locked the front and gave the key to Randy. He then turned to Carlos and said, "I guess we're now ready to go. Did Jeff already leave his shack?"

Carlos said in response, "Jeff never came home. He rarely sleeps in his shack. We'll find him at work on the dock."

Henry and Randy were starting to understand that Jeff was a real character who was totally dedicated to his job. He worked almost night and day, even when he did not feel like it. His top priority was to please the captain. For him, there was no future except with the captain. He was with the captain for better or worse.

They mounted their horses and slowly followed the barefoot Carlos to the dock. They found Jeff directing the loading of cotton onto a line of waiting oxen carts. There was cotton stacked high on the dock. He spotted Henry and Randy out of the corner of his eye and turned to face them, exclaiming, "Wow. You guys look radically different. You sure clean up good. I hope there is nothing in your new appearance which keeps you from working all out on this fine day."

Henry dryly replied, "We're ready to do as you command."

Jeff chuckled and said, "Your job is the same as it was yesterday and the same as it will be tomorrow. Get to work."

Carlos stepped up and said, "Let's get this loaded oxen cart train moving toward Bagdad."

Randy rode along the line of loaded oxen carts, noting in his pad how many carts and bales. Carlos ran up and down, telling the oxen cart drivers in Spanish that it was time to move out. Henry and Randy took up their usual positions.

Henry and Randy did not think their jobs were really useful to keeping the cotton flowing to Bagdad ships. They wondered if their presence really made a difference. If a group of bandits attacked the oxen cart train to steal the cotton, what would they do with the cotton? Their presence was to ward off bandits, but where were the bandits to ward off?

When Carlos showed up, Randy queried him on what they were doing. Carlos listened to Randy's doubts about the necessity of their jobs and said, "Yes, what you are saying is true during these peaceful times, but you can never let down your guard. There have been cases where renegade Union sympathizers try to burn the cotton and threaten the ships anchored offshore."

Randy waited until Carlos finished talking. For the lack of something better to say, he muttered, "Thanks. We'll keep an eye out for all those who want to damage or take our cotton. I can see that in these parts, cotton is indeed king."

Carlos had more to say on this subject. "It is the return trip when we're loaded with war material that we are more likely to be attacked. These items are much more marketable in Mexico, and such goods can change hands quickly."

Randy replied, "Sounds right to me. I'll tell my brother. We'll up our guard on the return leg."

They arrived at the Bagdad landing, and the operations were just as yesterday. Carlos said, "You don't have to go out with the lighters if you don't want to."

Randy said, "What we going to do while the lighters are loading cotton onto the ships?"

"Why don't you go into Bagdad town and explore what it offers. It's a lively place with mobs of people and lots of shops. Be sure to be back in time for the return trip to Matamoros."

Randy rode over to his older brother and said to him, "Carlos said we should take this time to get to know Bagdad town. What do you think?"

"Sounds like a good suggestion. Let's go and take a look-see."

They rode slowly into the adjoining Bagdad town. They were surprised by all the people and activity they saw. It was like there was a carnival in town, and everyone was trying to get into the act. Of course, they were all attracted there by the large amount of money in circulation. This was the place to be if you lived in the South and wanted to get away from the war.

Henry and Randy did not know that Bagdad and Matamoros were two of the busiest and most prosperous towns in the world. All they knew was that they were being swallowed up by an urban whirlwind. The sights and sounds were overwhelming. Henry guided them to the side of the Main Street to get out of the way of the riotous flow of traffic of all sorts. They saw in front of them a saloon. Henry suggested that they tie up their horses and take a look inside.

They stepped inside the swinging gate doors and saw a crowded, smoky room that smelled of tobacco, whiskey, and cheap perfume. A burly Mexican man inside the door said to them, "I'll take your arms. You'll get them back when you leave."

Henry was ready to object, but Randy convinced him that was normal practice. Anyway, Henry replied to the man, "You mean our rifles and my six-shooters?"

The man said in a more serious tone, "Especially your pistols."

Henry ran his eyes over the big and muscular Mexican man who was bigger than him and said meekly, "Okay. Be sure to take care of my babies and our rifles."

The man grunted and said in Spanish, "Of course."

Henry sauntered through the dense crowd up to the bar with Randy in tow, Randy whispered to Henry, "Why you goin' to the bar? You don't drink."

"I know, but that is where the action is."

Randy was uncomfortable in such a place filled with more low lifes that he had ever seen. He wanted to get out of the place. He said to Henry, "Let's get out of here. This no place for us. We're probably not old enough to be here."

Henry acted like he did not hear Randy and squeezed his way forcefully up to the bar. He noticed that everyone in the place was giving them curious glances, wondering who these two young newcomers were. Nobody caused them any trouble because their hats marked them as important dudes. As soon as he got to the bar, he almost stumbled over a brass spittoon. He grasped the shiny wooden bar to keep from falling on the dirty floor. A short Mexican man behind the bar saw him coming and asked him, "What will it be?"

Henry did not know what to say and looked to each side of him and said, "I'll take the same as him."

Henry was served a small jigger glass of rye whiskey. He gripped with his right hand the tiny glass and looked to either side of him to see the kind of people with whom he was drinking. He pretended to drink by bringing his glass up to his lips, but he never drank. He was happy being among the men at the bar.

Of course, the men at the bar were speculating on who the young stranger was among them. They could see that Henry was a big and strong young man. They were impressed by his new clothes and the cleanliness of his look. One man next to him said, "You're new here, aren't you? What brings you to these parts?"

Henry turned his head toward the bearded man and simply said, "I work for the captain."

The man passed Henry's words along. After that, he got no more questions. Henry turned to see what Randy was doing and was surprised to not find readily find him. Randy had moved slowly, weaving his way through the crowded room to its back wall. He was standing with his back to wall, watching a group of men sitting around a table playing cards. He was attracted to the game they played and, thus, was trying to learn all he could. But he did not want to risk any of his money. Someday, he thought he would play when he had money to lose.

While Randy was leaning against back wall, observing a card game, a young, attractive woman rubbed up against him and whispered through a veil of perfume, "Youngster, you want a poke?"

Randy was thrown off his guard and became flustered. All he wanted to do was to flee and get away from the woman. He darted as fast as he could to the exit. He asked the man for their guns and went outside to wait for Henry.

He did not have to wait long. Henry caught a glimpse of Randy making his way out the exit. He told the guy next to him. "Somethin' has come up. I got to go. Here, you can have the rest of my drink."

Henry walked out of the saloon into the bright sun to find Randy waiting for him beside their horses. Henry was concerned about his little brother and said, "What's wrong? It can't be time to leave already?"

Randy did not reply until he was back in the saddle. Then he said in a bitter tone, "I didn't like the place. I'll never go there again."

They both rode back to the Bagdad docks without saying a word. When they arrived, Randy said, "After more thought, maybe I'll go back when I have more money."

Henry did not know what to think of Randy's words. He saw the saloon as representing the real world that they needed to know if they were to become accustomed to all the dimensions of this historical melting pot.

# Chapter Thirty-Three
# New Values in a New Land

"You're back just in time. We got this ox wagon train loaded and all ready to go on the return trip to Matamoros. Remember what I told you about being extra vigilant," said Carlos upon seeing at the dock's edge the mounted Henry and Randy.

Carlos came closer to Henry and Randy and, looking up at them, asked, "How did you like Bagdad?"

Henry replied, "It was all right, but we need more time to know it better."

"You'll be back here many times, so you'll have the chance to know the town better."

Randy was deep in thought and nodded to Carlos. He rode up to the train to count the carts and their cargo. He was thinking about being in this same job for the duration of the war. He did not like their situation, but he could not do anything about it. This was the hand this new life had dealt them. On the other hand, he had never had a paying job before, so maybe this is what working was like. Anyway, having a job was better than having none.

Henry took up the point position with his rifle at the ready for any sign of trouble. Randy had told him that the carts were loaded with repeating rifles and their ammunition. They both knew these were hot commodities on the local market. The Mexican government would pay a lot for these items to help it in its war against French forces and other unruly indigenous elements in Mexico. They knew that their jobs were risky ones and they could be injured or killed by marauding bands of banditos. They could do nothing but hope for the best and be ready for the worst.

They stood tall in their saddles, on the lookout for anybody hiding behind the bushes or in a nearby gulley. Their idea was to shoot first at anything that looked suspicious. They wanted to discourage any attacks on any of the carts. Sometimes, they fired into the air so that any outsiders planning to attack their ox train would think twice before doing so. They knew that their shots in the air would indicate their locations, but that was a risk they were willing to take to protect the captain's cargo.

And then it happened. Volleys of shots came from both sides of the road. Obviously, armed banditos were hiding in clumps of bushes on either side of the road. It was the kind of ambush that was the worst fear for Henry and Randy. They immediately fired back in the direction from which the bullets were coming. At some risk to himself, Carlos was running wildly along the train, yelling in Spanish for the drivers to take cover beneath their wagons or in a nearby ditch.

Henry and Randy reloaded their rifles and poured shots into the clumps of bushes where the banditos were hiding. They stopped firing and waited to see if there was any more firing coming from the bushes. After a period of silence, Henry motioned to Randy to cover him while he inspected the offending bushes. He rode over to one clump of bushes then crossed the road to see what was still in the bushes.

The expressionless Henry rode back to Randy and, with a deadpan face, said, "Tell Carlos to get the wagon train moving again."

Later, after the train had gone some distance, curiosity overcame Randy and he rode up to Henry and asked, "What did you see in the bushes?"

Henry answered in a matter-of-fact manner, "Two poor Mexican men dead on each side. There were probably others, but when they saw our bullets coming their way, they hi-tailed it.

"We did our job. You can write that in your book. Anyway, they were bad dudes and got what was coming to them. No remorse."

Randy drifted back to his hind position. On his way back, he passed Carlos and told him what he had heard from Henry. Carlos exclaimed, "Good job. When Jeff hears about this, I'm sure you'll get a bonus."

Randy looked deeply into Carlos' eyes and said, "Yeah, but it could have gone the other way. We're lucky this time."

They rolled up to the Matamoros dock. Carlos ran ahead to tell Jeff about their ordeal. Jeff listened intently and said, "After that scare, I guess you guys are not ready to go back to Bagdad with another load of cotton."

Henry overheard Jeff's words and loudly said, "Why not? Can't let a little shootout keep cotton and war material from flowing to their buyers. We're just doing our job."

Jeff smiled widely and said, "That's the spirit. Take a break and get ready to go back to Bagdad. I'll make sure your mornin' deeds are passed along. I'm sure you'll be rewarded."

Henry and Randy turned their horses over to Carlos and joined a group of local men eating at a roadside table located under a shade tree. They ate and drank their fill. They also filled their canteens before joining Jeff on the dock. Henry said in a perfunctory manner, "Reporting for duty."

The good-humored Jeff laughed and said, "Good. Get yourself ready to go."

For Jeff, the sight of a clean-shaven, educated young man was amusing. Henry and Randy were oddities in these parts and stuck out like a sore thumb. Any dealings with them was the cause of some delight.

Randy was interested in staying a little while longer with Jeff to get to know him better. He thought a way to do this was to offer him a sip of fresh water from his canteen. He tried to hand Jeff the canteen and was met by these words. "Thanks, but I don't want to rust my pipes."

Randy was a bit stunned by this response. But he remembered Carlos' words about Jeff's addiction to the local white lightening. He could not understand how a guy could go all day in the hot sun on the docks without drinking water. He responded to Jeff by saying, "Okay. Say, how long you been in this job?"

Jeff did not feel like talking, but he made an exception for Randy and said, "Since the war began and, cotton started rolling this way."

"What did you do before that?"

Jeff did not like talking about himself, but he answered Randy by saying, "I worked for the captain at his ranch."

Randy dared to ask Jeff one more question. "Where you from?"

Jeff replied, "Nowhere."

Then he walked off. He considered Randy's questions as impertinent and impolite. He knew Randy was new to these parts. In time, he would learn not to ask somebody on the edge of the frontier those kind of questions. Their pasts made no difference in their present lives. Many were here because they were trying to start their lives over. They wanted to forget their past lives. Their previous lives paled in comparison to their current reality.

Henry and Jeff collected their horses from Carlos and checked their guns. They mounted their horses and signaled to Carlos to get the train moving toward Bagdad. Before Randy left to

take up his position in the rear, Henry said to him, "Let's hope all goes smoothly so we can be back before dark."

They made the uneventful trek to the Bagdad docks. Although this was among the first of hundreds of trips they would make to Bagdad, they were already bored and restless. Carlos saw the forlorn looks on their faces and said, "Why don't you go into Bagdad Town while we ferry the cotton out to the waiting ships and load the return cargo. I'm sure once you get to know the place better, you'll find somethin to your likin'."

Henry replied, "Maybe you're right, but doin' Bagdad right takes money, and I'm flat broke."

"No problema. I'll loan you some money."

Randy joined the conversation, "Carlos, you don't need to do that. I got enough money for both of us."

They rode back into town and looked around but ended up in the same saloon. At least they knew the place, and most of its patrons had seen them before. Henry gravitated to the bar and ordered a whiskey even though he did not drink. He also did not chew tobacco, so he had no need to position himself at a spot along the bar that was near a spittoon. Henry did not talk much, but he enjoyed being among the rowdy group of people who were around the bar.

The younger Randy did not like the bar side of the room and placed himself near the back wall where he could observe how cards were played. He was interested in the card games, but he had never played. He wished he were old enough to play. He followed silently the habits of each player and learned what were good and bad hands. When one of the player's was about to play a wrong card, Randy involuntarily made a groaning sound like he was in some sort of visceral pain.

The five players at the table immediately folded their cards and cast spurious looks his way. There was no doubt that Randy was in some sort of trouble because of the noise he made. Randy stood petrified, hoping this moment would pass and the game would continue. The man who was playing removed his cigar from his mouth and said to Randy, "Young man. If you think you can play better, take my seat."

The man's words set off a round of raucous laughter around the table. Then another man who appeared to be running the game said, "Why not? His money is as good as anyone else's."

The man with the cigar promptly stood up, saying to Randy, "Take my seat. You can't do any worse than me."

Randy was in shock and pleaded with the man, "Please sit back down. I've never played cards before in my life."

The man quickly replied, "No matter. The best way to learn is to play poker and risk your money."

Randy was shoved into the man's empty chair. Before he could object again, the cards were gathered up and shuffled. The dealer said, "I think everybody agrees with me that the new person should cut the cards."

Randy had watched enough card games that he knew what was involved in cutting the cards. Hesitantly, he cut the cards and was quickly dealt a seven-card hand along with the others. He tried to understand his hand and decide if he had a bad or good hand. The dealer told him to keep his best five cards. When it was his turn to bet, he could not sit on the fence any more and reached in his pocket and tossed in enough money to match the previous bet and stay in the game. As a newcomer to the game, any play he made came across as akin to a bluff. He thought

maybe he should fold and not risk his money, but he wanted to see if his hand was strong or weak.

They all continued to play their hands to the hilt, waiting to see who would drop out. They kept adding to the pot. Randy was running out of money, but he believed he had a strong hand and was determined to hang in there. Foolish thoughts begun to creep into his head, but he believed it was worth taking the gamble and betting all the money he had.

Randy was surprised when his main competitor folded. He was followed by all the other players. The dealer looked Randy straight in the eye and said, "Show the hand you bet the store on."

They were all startled by the hand Randy exposed. Two aces and three jacks … a full house. The dealer looked at the other players before saying, "Go ahead. Scoop up your winnings. Dab gum it all. This has to be the biggest case of beginner's luck I've ever seen."

Randy played on. He was fully absorbed with learning how to play the game. He won some and lost some. Overall, he was well ahead when he asked, "How long have I been here,"

The surly dealer replied, "About a couple of hours."

Randy immediately said, "Oh my. I'm late. Please excuse me. I got to fetch my older brother at the bar. We have to get back to our jobs at the docks."

His fellow card players wanted to object seeing him leave the game with so much of their money. The dealer spoke up forcefully, saying, "Let the boy go. Can't you see he has important business to tend to?" Randy stood up and filled his pockets with money he scraped from the table into his hands and said, "Thank you. I'll be back another day."

The dealer said, "Your money is always welcome here."

Randy walked off into the standing-room-only crowd in the direction of the bar to find Henry. He was followed by a number of young women who knew he had money to burn. Randy left in his wake a gossipy group of card players who were having a good time laughing about having such a tinhorn play with them. The dealer stopped cold all their humorous speculation about Randy by saying, "He may be young, but he's smart and from a world we could never set foot in. And did you see his hat? A man does not get a hat like that unless he's important."

Randy looked up and down the bar, but he could not find Henry. He finally returned to the spot he usually stood at the bar and asked a drunken old man, "Have you seen a clean-shaven guy with a hat like mine?"

"Yeah, I've seen him. Now, if you buy me a drink, I'll tell you where he went."

Randy felt he had no choice and handed the man a coin. The old man smacked his lips and said, "You see those stairs? He went up there with one of the ladies who works here. I guess he needed his horns trimmed."

Randy did not know what to do. He did not want to make a scene, so he waited at the bottom of the stairs for his brother. When there was another woman going upstairs, he asked, "Can you check on my brother? We got to go?"

The woman stuck out her hand with her palm turned up and said, "Sure, but that will cost you one gold piece."

Randy dug one gold coin out of his pocket and placed in the smooth hand of the woman, noticing the thick makeup on her face and the low cut of her blouse, which exposed the ample

cleavage of her breasts. The woman went up the stairs and turned to ask Randy in a sweet voice, "Are you sure you don't need a little tender love and care, too?"

Randy avoided direct eye contact with the woman and said, "No, ma'am. I just need my big brother."

Randy was intrigued by the woman's complexion and accent. She was lily white and had an East Coast accent. There was a sweet and sour smell about her. He wondered how she ended up in this life here. He would later find that the population of Bagdad and Matamoros was made up of people from all corners of the world. Mexicans were the majority, but there were thousands of foreigners trying to get their hands on all the money flowing through these two towns.

Eventually, Henry came gently down the stairs. His boots barely touched the wooden steps, and he portrayed a dizziness as if he had his head was in the clouds. He approached Randy, who asked him. "What's wrong with you?"

Henry answered in a dreamy tone, "I've been to heaven to lose my virginity. I wish I could go back for seconds, but I know we have to get back to work. Give me some money so I can pay the woman upstairs."

Randy reluctantly dished out some money to Henry. He did not like how Henry was behaving, but he had also sinned by gambling. He recognized that they would have to drop some of their standards in order to fit in. He also knew they were growing. For sure, they were in a different and rougher country where few of their old values applied.

# Chapter Thirty-Four
# Back to Texas

The days and months passed. Henry and Randy became accustomed to the same routine each day. They accompanied ox carts full of cotton form the Matamoros landing to its loading on flat bottom lighter boats at the Bagdad dock for transport to ocean-going ships waiting offshore. They let Carlos oversee the loading of the lighters with cotton and the loading of return cargo of war material. While Carlos did this, they assumed their usual positions at Bagdad's main saloon, *Port of Call*.

Henry went to the saloon to meet his woman, Aurelia. He could not get enough of her and did not mind her profession, which meant he had to share her with other men. As long as she was happy, he was happy. And she was always happy to see Henry and his money. There would have been no relationship if Henry had no money. Aurelia was a beautiful Mexican half-caste woman from Guadalupe, and she was in Bagdad for the money.

Randy was focused on learning to play well the poker game of cards. He obtained his own deck of cards and spent all his spare time playing with them. He always sat in the same chair at the back table of the saloon. His fellow players and all those gathered around the table to watch him play were impressed with his poker acumen. He could never get enough of playing poker, and his winnings were piling up. His reputation as the kid who could not be beat in poker grew.

Port of Call was not the only saloon in Bagdad, but it was the biggest and the most popular. All the women had hand fans, and to take an edge off the intense heat, the floor-to-ceiling windows were left wide open to catch as much of the sea breeze as possible. Every poker table had two young Mexican lads waving up and down crowd fans. Some other lads were running around swatting flies. All the fanning helped keep the pesky flies moving. For the most part, people got used to the heat and flies and carried on as if these nuisances were absent. Even on dusty days, they preferred keeping the windows wide open. The air with dust was better than no air and no dust.

The saloon was always crowded with people from all over the world. There were agents from each of the couple hundred foreign ships anchored offshore. They were intermixed with every type of con artist from north and south of the border. Each person tried to outdress the other by donning the latest fashions. It was a wild crowd tinged with a wave of electrical excitement that was unknown elsewhere on the globe. It was the kind of place where anything could happen and usually did.

At night, the saloon was even a more attractive magnet. It was lit up with a hundred smelly oil lamps and candles. It was a well-lighted beacon that drew people in from miles away. Its lights could be seen by the ships at sea, and all the crews dreamed of following the lights. The crews begged their commanders to take turns to go on shore to take advantage of all that Bagdad had to offer. They were all welcome, and their money was especially welcome.

Nobody thought about the terrible war that caused them to be in Bagdad. They knew that the profitable trade they were participating in helped the South continue its battle again the North, but that was not their concern. For them, the war was good for business, and the longer it continued, the better for them. The rich lives they were living depended on the continuance of a distant war between the states.

Many of the people were determined to collect enough money to return home after the war to build a house for their families and start a business. Even though the money they gained was stained by the blood of the hundreds of thousands killed in the war, for them, it was a chance of a lifetime. Money made by the cotton trade along the border was a future investment in the development of the country.

It was all about getting much-needed cotton to textile mills in Europe. And sometimes, some of the cotton cargo would find its way to mills in northern states. Cotton was considered a strategic commodity and was in high demand across the world. War or no war, cotton was king, and anyway you could get it was justified. Thanks to Bagdad, the textile mills in Europe were kept running.

Henry and Randy kept up this routine until the end of 1863, when an unprecedented freeze hit the south coast of Texas. For the first time in living memory, there was ice on the Rio Grande and the bay at its mouth. All cotton trade operations stopped for a few days while the winter returned to its normal warm ways, not long after that, Henry and Randy were given a few days off to celebrate Christmas and New Year. Both of them felt it was strange to be riding to Bagdad to spend their holidays.

After the holidays, they rode back to the Matamoros dock, and Henry approached Jeff with a big smile on his face and said, "Reporting for duty."

It was all Henry could do to keep from laughing, but he saw immediately that Jeff was in no laughing mood. Jeff turned to face Henry and Randy and said, "I got some news for you. You will not be going back to Bagdad."

An alarmed Henry spoke up almost immediately, "I have to go back to Bagdad."

Jeff interrupted Henry and said loudly, "Why? To see that whore, you've been cuddling?"

Henry was thrown into a tizzy by Jeff's rough language and was ready to draw his pistols when Randy stepped in and quietly said, "Why in the world can we not go back to Bagdad?"

Jeff reacted quickly, "Oh. You can go, but you'll not be working for the captain any more."

Jeff's words gave Henry and Randy reason to pause and think. For sure, if they did not have money, Bagdad would be a different place for them, they both realized that it was their money that did most of the talking for them in Bagdad. Randy timidly said, "What other job do you have in mind for us?"

Jeff calmly said, "It's not me. I'm only passing on instructions from the captain. The way I heard it is the Union has taken control of Brownsville and is hassling our cotton supply line, so we can no longer receive cotton here. The captain says the cotton wagon trains have to try to go farther upriver to, maybe to Laredo or Eagle Pass, to unload their cargo."

Henry had calmed down and said, "Wow. That really changes things. I guess you want us to go upriver to one of those towns?"

"Nope. I got a different set of orders for you two. The captain wants you two to go to his ranch and oversee its repairs and then go to San Antonio to bring his family back to his ranch."

Both Henry and Randy sighed when they heard this news because the last thing they wanted in the world was to cross the Desert of the Dead again. Henry was upset and demanded, "Where's the Captain. We want to hear this from his mouth."

Jeff responded, "You can't see the captain. He's in hiding after barely escaping with his life. Union troops attacked his ranch home and did a lot of damage. He fled, but he's still wanted as a rebel agent. I guess the Yankees got tired of seeing cotton traded under their noses."

Henry and Randy let the reality of their new situation sink in, and after a brief pause, Randy softly said, "Nothing is forever. When do we leave?"

Jeff, without hesitation, replied, "As soon as you can. Is now too early?"

Jeff's reply gave Henry and Randy an idea of the kind of urgency that was attached to their new assignment. Randy looked at his older brother and said, "Well, we'll leave at first light tomorrow morning. This will give us time to say goodbye to Carlos and tie up some loose ends. What about our horses?"

"You'll get fresh horses. Carlos is arranging that now. I'll be here at the dock for your early morning crossing."

Randy commented, "So Carlos knows."

"He knew before you did. But I'm the one who had to tell you. I know this is too much to handle, but there isn't any other option but to do as the captain says. Go on now and do what you have to do to get ready to go early tomorrow."

Henry and Randy rode slowly back to their shack in silence. On the front porch of their shack, they found Carlos quietly waiting for them. Carlos could tell that they had received the news about their new job. He did not know how to talk to them and just hung his head. Henry and Randy dismounted, and Carlos looked up at them and said with tears in his eyes. "I'm goin' to miss you guys."

Henry was as full of emotion as he could get but managed to mouth some words by saying, "We goin' to miss you too."

Carlos tried to change the subject by saying, "I got some fresh horses for you. As soon as you take all your stuff off your horses, I'll take them and exchange them."

Henry and Randy undressed their horses and turned them over to Carlos. After Carlos was out of earshot, Henry turned to Randy and said in no uncertain terms, "Give me all the money you can. I want to send some money to Aurelia with Carlos with the message that I will be back someday."

For Randy, his older brother's words were pure nonsense. It was the height foolishness for him to give his brother any money for his whore. Henry could see the quandary he had put his little brother in and added the sobering words. "She told me she is pregnant, and the baby is mine."

Randy was surprised by these words and pulled out handfuls of gold coins to give to his brother, and said, "Here. Take it. That's all I got."

Henry thanked Randy effusively and told him he would repay him someday. Randy did not tell Henry that he had only given him what was in his pockets and had not touched his stash, which was hidden deep in his saddle bags, He was saving that money for a real emergency. He only said to his brother, "When you goin' to tell her when you will be back?"

"When the war is over and, we can settle down."

Randy kept his thoughts to himself. Telling Henry what he thought would serve no purpose. He did not have the heart to tell his brother that when the war was over, there would be no need to send cotton this way, and thus, there would be no Bagdad. He realized that he and his brother, and everyone else in these parts, were living wartime lives that would disappear when the war was over.

Randy also felt some guilt himself. After all, gambling was also a vice, and he was addicted to playing poker. He told himself that at least his vice was done with his head and not with his heart or part of his below-the-belt anatomy. His brother was thinking and feeling more with his heart than with his brain. Maybe his heart was right for its own reasons, but his heart knew nothing of the ongoing war and their temporary situation.

Henry was trying to regain his focus and said, "Look. We got to think about what lies before us. We got to get ready to cross some rough territory."

Randy said, "By all means. I'm thinking of the water we'll need as well as the food. We'll be on horseback, so we won't have any wagons slowing us down. Maybe we should take a pack mule to carry grain, food, and water."

"Then we'll have to feed and water the mule. I think we should try to tough it out and travel at night as fast as we can. It should not take us more than four or five days to reach the ranch."

"Traveling at night is a good idea if there is enough moonlight. I hear Carlos coming back now. We should ask him for advice."

Carlos was in a somber mood and did not want to talk, but after Randy asked him what he thought, he rattled on at length about all the measures they should take for their journey north. He thought riding at night was a good idea, but he was afraid they would not be able to detect the new way stations in the darkness. He explained, "Since you came across the Big Sands, way stations with food, water, and grain have been set up every twenty miles or so. So, if you run out of these basics, you can help yourself with what you need."

Randy interjected, "How to we recognize these places?"

Carlos replied, "That's easy. Anytime you see alongside the road a big wooden box, go and open it lid and see what there is. Anyway, as you will have only a couple of days of water and rations, you'll need to get what you need from these boxes before you get to the ranch."

Henry was tired of being his silent self and said, "Maybe we'll travel by night for the first two nights and do the rest in the daytime so we can see their boxes. Don't worry. We'll get to the ranch one way or the other."

Henry called Carlos to the side of the front porch and said in a low voice, "I got an important job for you to do as soon as you get to Bagdad. You see this old bandana. I've tied tightly a lot of money in it. I want you to go to the Port of Call in Bagdad to give this to Aurelia and tell her I've been called away, but I will be back. Comprende?"

Carlos took the bag of gold coins and assured Henry he would do as instructed. He told Henry, "I will guard this bag with my life and give it and your message to her as soon as I get to Bagdad tomorrow. Sin falta. You can count on me."

When Carlos had finished speaking, a tearful Henry hugged Carlos and said, "I knew I could count on you. I hope you are here when we return."

Carlos was lost for words. He had never seen Henry so emotional. Randy was also affected by the emotion displayed by his older brother. He, too, felt the emotion of the moment. He had not felt like this since he had to leave his mother behind in their burning plantation home in Virginia. Just like then, he felt they were entering a new chapter in their lives. Only God knows what life lay before them.

# Chapter Thirty-Five
## Snake Meat

It was still dark when they heard a light tap on the front door of their shack. The tapping paused, and they heard the voice of Carlos. "Buenos dias. Time to get up and get ready to go. I got your fresh horses."

Henry groggily replied, "Okay. Give us a minute,"

Henry sat up on the edge of his bed and reached over to nudge Randy, saying. "Let's go, little brother. Time to rise and get out of here."

Randy groaned to indicate he had heard Henry, who was getting dressed. After putting on his pants and boots, Henry unlocked the front door so Carlos could come in. Carlos grabbed a saddle to start the process of fitting it on a new horse. As he was dragging a saddle out the door, he said, "You got two fine horses, and I've brought extra food and water. Your horses will be loaded as much as possible, but they will still be able to move along at top speed."

Henry replied, "Sounds good. I'll give you a hand as soon as I finish getting dressed and go out back to wash my face and take a piss."

Carlos was busy getting all the tack sorted out, but he said, "No problema. And don't worry. I'll take care of delivering your package and message to Aurelia. Right now, it looks like our main problem is getting your brother out of bed."

Henry looked at Randy, who had gone back to sleep and slapped him hard on his shoulder, saying, "Get up now. Enough beauty rest for you."

Randy rapidly sat up on the edge of his bed and said in a sleepy voice, "What's the rush? It'll be some time before I sleep in a bed again. My body wants to stay right here."

Henry cut him short by saying, "Enough wishful talk. Get up, and let's get going."

Carlos had dressed the horses. Henry came out to check them. He went under the horses and cinched up a notch on the saddle belt. He rubbed his hands all over the horses and placed his head on their heads. He softly mumbled some words to them and waited to see their reactions. He then turned to Carlos and said, "I'll take this one. As usual, I will not give him a name because I don't want to become too attached to him. Anyway, these horses are probably only good for this trip, and then I'll get another one. Right?"

Carlos scratched his head and replied to Henry by simply saying, "Probably."

Randy staggered out of the shack, rubbing the sleep out of his eyes, saying assertively, "Ready to go."

Randy saw in the pale light of pre-dawn the fully loaded horses. He noted the extra saddle bags and water bags strapped to the horses. Carlos saw the way Randy was glancing at the horses and said, "You should have enough food and water to last for three or four days. If you need more, don't forget to check for those ration boxes."

Henry made it clear which horse he was taking. Randy did not care. Each of the black Mustang horses looked the same to him. They both mounted their horses to get a feel for their saddles. The short distance they rode to a nearby roadside food stand gave them a good feel for their new horses. They sat with Carlos on a wooden bench in front of a low table made of scrap lumber. Tin plates heaped with tortillas, boiled rice, and fried pinto beans were placed in front of them with big mugs of clear water. Through the flickering light of smokey candles, Henry and Randy could see a beaming smile on Carlos' face. Randy asked him, "Why are you so happy?"

"I'm happy every time I see such good food. For me, food is life, and I know that this food will keep my life going. Dig in. This one is on me."

They all ate with much gusto and licked their plates clean. Carlos said something in Spanish to the obscure woman who had served them. The stomachs of Henry and Randy were so full they had difficulty mounting their horses. They followed Carlos to the Matamoros dock. They spied Jeff overseeing the last cotton bales being loaded on oxen carts bound for Bagdad.

Jeff saw them coming, and as soon as they were close enough, he said loudly, "Go right on the boat. We got to get going while the going is good."

Henry and Randy sensed the urgency in Jeff's voice. They wanted to dismount to hug Carlos and thank him for everything. But there was no time for the kind of goodbyes they had in mind. They weakly waved farewell to Carlos as they were hustled onto the boat for the crossing to Brownsville.

Jeff went along with them and said, "We'll be landing upriver a bit west of Brownsville to avoid any trouble. You need to find the trail north as quickly as possible. Be ready to ride off fast as soon as we hit the bank."

The fuss Jeff was going through put Henry and Randy on high alert. In fact, they were becoming afraid they were getting mixed up in something, not of their liking. Jeff noticed how fear streaked across their faces and said in a straightforward manner, "Stay calm, but have your guns at the ready. You got to hi-tail it north and get far away fast from Brownsville and its bands of Union troops. If they catch you, you'll be made prisoner or conscripted. Also, be aware that roaming Confederate troops are about, and they can conscript you, too. You might have noticed that all the young men in these parts have been conscripted."

Jeff's strident words made Henry and Randy acutely aware that they were in deep and there is no getting out of their predicament. They unsheathed their rifles and checked their stock of ammunition. Henry checked the old .44 pistols he always wore belted around his waist. He looked at Jeff and said, "We're ready. Tell us when to jump our horses off the boat."

The flat-bottom steamboat skimmed rapidly over the shallow river water, edging ever closer to the southern bank of the Rio Grande. Henry and Randy were mounted and ready to jump their horses off the boat as soon as they got the signal from Jeff. As they neared the bank, Jeff said, "I'm not one for saying goodbyes... too many people have come into my life and left. So, I'll say goodbye and good luck. I may never see you again. We're moving our two steamboats and the whole operation to Laredo tomorrow. We're determined to keep the cotton moving as long as we can. Too much money at stake to do otherwise. But the day is coming that the Union will choke off the cotton trade. When that day comes, all this will be gone."

The boat jammed hard the bank, a tailgate was slammed down, and Jeff waved Henry and Randy forward and told them to jump their horses as far as they could. They did their best and rode off once on tierra firma at a fast gallop. They followed the tracks north and planned to go all day at a fast clip. They still feared the Desert of the Dead, but they saw it now as a place beyond the grasp of military troops.

They rode all day through the wide Rio Grande valley and entered sandier land that indicated they were at the start of the desert part of the Big

Sands. Night fell, and they walked their horses off the wide road forged by unending trains of wagons hauling cotton. They found a clump of mesquite trees and tethered their horses before undressing them. They fed a few handfuls of grain to their horses and poured some water into their tin plates for them to drink.

After tending to their horses, they crawled under a big mesquite with their bedding and a little food and water for themselves. There were creepy night noises all around them, but they were too tired to notice. They fell fast asleep with their guns beside them. It was late morning the next day before Henry woke with a start. He sat up and looked at Randy at his side. Randy opened his eyes and saw that Henry was sitting bolt upright on his bedroll and said while still half asleep, "Shouldn't we be goin."

"No. Not now. Get some rest cause just like we said we're traveling by night."

After hearing Henry's words, Randy turned on his side and prepared to get as much rest as he could in the daytime. Henry crawled out from beneath the mesquite to tend the horses, making sure they were well and in the shade. It was early morning and winter, but it was unseasonably warm, and Henry could feel some sweat on his brow and the slow trickle of drops of perspiration running down his back. He took off his shirt and vest and hung them on a branch of the thorny mesquite.

Henry wanted to rest too, but he also wanted to keep his eyes and ears open for anyone or thing approaching their hidden campsite. He was ready to crawl back under the mesquite tree to lay down when a panicked Randy came scrambling out. He turned around and followed Randy outside the tree's canopy. He asked Randy, "What the hell is the matter?"

Randy was so scared that he had difficulty responding to his older brother. Henry grabbed his little brother's shoulder's and shook him, saying, "Settle down and tell me what's wrong?"

Randy took a few deep breaths before he was able to softly mutter one word, "Snake."

"Is that all that caused you to act like some big crybaby?"

Randy took offense at his brother's words and tried to act calm when he said in an even voice, "Why, it was staring at me right in the face and making a rattling noise with its tail."

Henry became more alarmed and quickly said, "Sounds like a poisonous rattlesnake. If it had bitten you in the face, you would be good as dead."

Henry drew his right .44 pistol from its holster and cocked it. "No snake goin to kill my little brother."

Henry crawled back beneath the mesquite with his pistol at the ready. He knew if he shot his pistol, the noise of the firing would give away their location to anyone within earshot, but he had to rid themselves of the rattler if he could get a good shot at its head. He crawled slowly to their shady camping spot and immediately spotted the fat rattler curled up on Randy's bedroll. He made a soft clicking noise with his tongue, and the snake lifted its head to meet an oncoming bullet from Henry's six-shooter.

The snake was blown away. Henry picked up the dead snake and crawled with it to where his brother was standing. He stood up and brandished the snake in front of his brother, saying in a gleeful tone. "Is this the snake you were so damned afraid of?"

"Yeah. That's the one. I'm happy he's dead. For me, the only good snake is a dead one, whether they are poisonous or not."

A smiling Henry said, "That's what some people say about Indians. I just hope no unsavory types heard my shot. We need to be on the lookout for any intruders."

Henry threw the headless snake on the ground. They waited silently for a while to see if anyone was coming to see where the shooting noise came from. After a while, Randy said, "I heard they skin, fry, and eat this kind of snake and that its meat tastes just like chicken."

"You don't say. Maybe I can skin this snake with my pocketknife, and we can cook it over a small fire. What do you think?"

After some thought, Randy said, "Go ahead and give it a try. I'll collect some dead branches to make a small fire. Maybe I can find a straight stick we can use as a spit."

Henry used his pocketknife to remove the snake's skin while Randy made a small fire. Henry peeled the bark off the straight stick and speared the snake lengthwise. They took turns tuning the spit stick over the fire, roasting the snake over the fire. Henry laughed as he asked, "How do you like your snake meat cooked? Medium well or well done?"

They both laughed louder than they had in a long time. Henry pulled crispy snake meat from the fire. After it had cooled, he tore off half and gave it to Randy. He ate the meat straight from the spit stick, finding it tasty and to his liking, after swallowing a bite, he said to Randy, "Go ahead. It tastes really good and gives us the extra boost we need to make it across the desert."

Randy stuffed a small piece of his share of the meat into his mouth and was pleasantly surprised by its good taste. "You're right. Tastes good. Maybe we should look for some more rattlers. That's probably the only thing that can survive in the desert."

"I'm sure we'll come across some more rattlers if we are on the lookout for them. They'll probably come after us in order to square things with their relative I killed and ate."

They had a good laugh over what Henry said. Randy said hesitantly. "Maybe we should bring our stuff out here with the horses. Our mesquite nest seems to be a haven for snakes and other critters."

Henry nodded and said, "You have a good point there. Anyway, we should stay near our horses. We're dead men without them."

They dragged their stuff from deep inside the mesquite clump to its shady fringes. Their new campsite was not as cool, but they were safer from ornery unwanted visitors like snakes. Henry said, "It's warmer here, but a few degrees higher temperature is a small price to pay for tranquility. Let's try to get some rest. We got a long night ahead of us."

They both laid down on their bedrolls, propping their heads up on their saddles. Their rifles were at their sides, and Henry always had his pistols ready for action. The daytime temperature was stifling without any wind but cooler than what they previously experienced. There were dancing mirages appearing across the wide sandy plain. Henry mumbled, "At least, by traveling at night, we can't see the desolation that surrounds us."

Randy replied, "Thank God for small blessings."

They never thought the day would end. They tried to sleep, but it was hard to sleep in the daytime, and the temperature was so high. The sun finally set on the western horizon, and Henry got up and said, "Thank God. The day is finally over. Let's get ready to ride as far as we can by daylight tomorrow."

Randy responded, "Yep. We got a lot to thank God for. Mostly, we should thank Him for still being alive. I hope we can keep it that way, but the odds are stacked against us."

# Chapter Thirty-Six
# Big House Boys

The farther they rode north, the more the weather became uncomfortably cool. Yet the cooler weather made the going easier for them and their horses. They made mental notes to go to the commissary at the ranch to see if it had any jackets. They were making good time, and that put them in high spirits.

Day was breaking when they came across the first ration crate. It was huge and well-constructed of lumber hauled in for the purpose of building these strong big boxes with a hinged top door. They looked around themselves, making sure they were not being observed. They dismounted and opened slowly the crate as the sun was peaking over the eastern horizon. They found the crate full of food items. They took only what they thought they needed to reach the ranch.

Next to the crate were wooden barrels filled with water. They and their horses drank their fill. They topped off their canteens and water bags. Randy said, "It is really a good idea to have such ration boxes. It removes a lot of the fear of crossing the Big Sands. Let's camp nearby so we can get some more water before we take off again."

They found a place near a mesquite clump not too distant that looked like a good site to bed down. They stretched out on their bedrolls after making sure their horses had a shady place to rest. The chill in the morning air prompted them to wrap up in their blankets. They tried to sleep, but they were not accustomed to sleeping in the daytime. Also, the anticipation of arriving at the ranch and what they would do there when they arrived gnawed on them.

It was just past noon when Henry said, "I can't take it any more. The hell with resting. Can't we eat somethin' and get back on the road?"

"I was waitin' for you to say somethin' like that. After I munch on a few hardtack biscuits, drink some water, take a piss, I'll be good to go. Maybe we can ride all the way to the ranch."

"That's my brave little brother talkin'. Let's do as you say and make tracks."

They got their horses ready to go and led them to the ration box to let them drink again. They also topped off their canteens. Their horses also seemed bored and ready to go again as they mounted and headed north on the well-traveled cotton road.

After going a few miles, they encountered a cotton wagon getting ready to stop for the night. Randy engaged in a conversation with the driver of the lead wagon while Henry kept a lookout. Randy found that they knew about them coming to help fix all that was broken by the raid of the Union troops. They said the word about them was being spread by one of the captain's foremen who had arrived earlier in the week from Matamoros.

News of their arrival was only a small part of the information the foreman brought with him. Randy listened to all the drivers had to say so he would be up to date in all the news and gossip that was circulating. He learned that the Union troops had left as fast as they had come, leaving the cotton bale warehouse and the commissary intact. The damage done by these troops was focused on the big house where they broke and stole many items. Furthermore, they shot and killed the trusted vaquero chief whom the captain had left behind to care for his wife and children.

The house lay barren now. The captain's wife and children traveled north to take refuge in San Antonio. His wife had another baby in San Antonio. All this talk reminded Henry and Randy that they had been told to help fix the house and escort the captain's wife and kids back to the ranch once the house was fixed. Of course, they could never replace the items broken or stolen by the Union troops, but they could make the house livable.

Randy passed on to Henry all he heard. When they were saying their goodbyes, Randy mentioned to the lead driver, "You know not to go to Brownsville. You got to make your way all the way upriver to Laredo to unload your cotton. By the way, how soon do you think we'll arrive at the ranch?"

The driver responded loudly, "We know all that. We have no choice but to move forward and see how it goes. If you keep riding on horseback, you should be at the ranch tomorrow."

Henry and Randy tipped their hats and rode off in a swirl of dust and sand. They could not wait to get to the ranch. It would be something of a homecoming for them. They would have ridden until they got there, but their horses needed rest. It was not daylight yet, but Henry said, "Let's rest near here and get goin' again early so we arrive there before dark."

They tended to their horses and got a few hours of rest lying down but with their guns always at the ready. When there was enough daylight, they made all ready for going the last miles before entering the ranch's grounds. All was quiet, and the weather was cool and crisp. They both thought they were getting used to this kind of job and maybe they were becoming true Texan hands. About a mile before their arrival at the ranch, they were greeted by a familiar face. There was Rafael yelling like a wild Indian. It was evident that Rafael was almost overcome with emotion at the sight of Henry and Randy. Rafael kept repeating, "I knew you would come back. I's so happy to see you."

Henry and Randy rode up close to where Rafael was standing in the road, and both of them smiled widely as Henry said in a gleeful tone, "Good to see you too. Are you the Rafael we left last year? You've grown so much."

"You guys look different too. You left here as two Anglo greenhorns and returned as Texas men ready to tackle anything the frontier throws at you. It's so good to see you're doing so well."

Rafael mounted behind Randy on his horse. There was still a mile or so before they got to the ranch. Rafael yammered nonstop the entire time. He tried to bring Henry and Randy up to date since the time they left the year before. Rafael repeated himself to make sure he was reciting all they should know and then some. Sometimes, Rafael switched to Spanish because he thought certain parts of his spiel were better told in Spanish, even though Henry and Randy's knowledge of Spanish was still rudimentary.

When Rafael was about out of breath, he asked them, "How was Mexico?'

Henry and Randy really did not know how to reply to this question. Randy replied in a matter-of-fact way by saying, "We really didn't see much of Mexico as we were stuck pretty close to the mouth of the Rio Grande the entire time."

Henry added with a grin on his face, "We learned a lot. I got my horns sheared, and Randy learned how to play poker."

Rafael laughed when he heard Henry's words. His laughter caused Henry and Randy to join him with hearty laughter, which put them all in a good mood. When their laughter ended, Rafael commented, "You know my people come from a village south of the border. The captain bought all our cattle and asked all the people in the village to start anew on his ranch. My people gladly came north into Texas to serve the captain. We're all dedicated to satisfying the captain and his big ranch work."

Henry and Randy thought it was an audacious move by the captain to ask the inhabitants of a Mexican village to move over two hundred miles north to his ranch land, but this arrangement seemed to be working well for all parties concerned. The captain got the people he needed to make his ranch work, and the destitute people got all that he afforded them. One could not survive without the other.

They arrived at the outskirts of the ranch, and Rafael said, "Go directly to the big house. The foreman will need to know of your arrival and tell you what to do next."

Before going to the big house, Randy asked Rafael, "Are we dressed okay?"

"You look good to me. You must have bought some new clothes, and your expensive new hats really set you apart from run-of-the-mill wranglers."

Standing on the front porch of the big house was a tall Anglo man puffing on a hand-rolled cigarette. They stopped their horses in front of him. Rafael slid off Randy's horse and disappeared. The foreman was the first to speak, "What took you so long?"

Henry replied, "We came as fast as we could."

The foreman took a puff on his cigarette and said dryly, "Plans have changed. You're gonna stay here and not go to San Antonio. We've already sent a team to fetch the missus and the kids. The house is ready for them. The captain wants you to stay and work here."

Henry and Randy were surprised by the change in plans but somewhat relieved that they did not have to go to San Antonio. The foreman's words had perked Randy's interest, and he asked, "What job we goin to do here?"

The foreman chuckled and stamped out his cigarette butt with his boot before saying in a pronounced Texas drawl, "You goin' to help us round up and brand the excess of cattle we have on the ranch. The war has already blocked us from marketing our cattle, and then the bitter cold weather forced many more cattle to move south onto our ranch. We got to establish ownership over these thousands of longhorn before we try to market them."

Henry digested the foreman's words and said, "Understandable, but we have never rounded up cattle and branded them."

The foreman shot back, "I know that, but you'll learn all about it from our vaqueros who know well how to do all this. The captain wants you to learn how to be true cowpunchers before he assigns more responsibilities to you."

"When do we start?" an anxious Randy wanted to know.

"As soon as you are rested and equipped. This equipment will include pencil and paper so we can get a good idea of the size of our herds."

Henry asked, "What other equipment do we need?"

"For starters, you'll need horses that are accustomed to this kind of work. You'll need chaps and spurs. And you'll need slickers in case it rains or to ward off the cool northerners we can have this time of the year. You'll also need to know how to use your lassos. Don't worry, the vaqueros will show you how to do everything, and you'll have plenty of time to practice."

Henry said, "Is that all? We're mighty tired right now. I guess we'll head to the bunkhouse now, and as soon as we're able, we'll go to the commissary to get the things you mentioned."

The foreman interrupted Henry to say, "Hold on a minute. You'll be staying in the foremen bunkhouse behind the big house and taking your meals in the big house with me. I've been charged with keeping an eye on you and following your progress. Of course, I'll send regular reports to the captain. He sees a lot of potential in you boys, and he's willing to invest in you the money and time to get you up to snuff. I guess he's got big plans for you boys."

Henry was too tired for more words, and the overload of information made him even more tired. He managed to say, "Thanks to you and the captain for your confidence in us. Can somebody show us where we can sleep?"

The foreman loudly clapped his hands, and a manservant appeared from within the house. The foreman asked him in Spanish to show them to their beds. The foreman then turned to Henry and Randy and said, "Again, welcome. Good to see you boys. I look forward to working with you. You'll find everything you need in our bunkhouse. By the way, my name is Rudy. Now go on and get some rest. I'll have somebody call you when there is food on the table. Get some rest because we start at first light tomorrow."

Both Henry and Randy said in unison, "Yes, sir."

They followed the manservant around the big house and were quietly shown their new quarters. There were six springy beds in the bunkhouse, and they could see one bed was occupied. They assumed this is where Rudy slept. On the opposite side of the large room, they saw two beds with all the items Rudy had mentioned laying on top of them. They assumed these were their beds.

They stepped outside their bunkhouse to find Rafael removing the saddles and all the tack from their horses. Rafael said with a sad voice, "Take your saddles inside with all your other stuff. I'll be here early tomorrow with your new horses. After that, I won't be seeing you much."

Randy was curious as to why Rafael said he would not see them much, so he asked, "Rafael, why do you say you'll not be seeing us much?"

Rafael said rapidly, "You're big shots now, living and eating in the Big House. I got no place here, and soon you'll be out with the vaqueros, and I got no place with them either. I'm happy for you but sad for myself."

Randy exchanged looks with Rafael and Henry and let the conversation with Rafael come to an end because at that moment Rudy appeared and Rafael disappeared. Rudy wasted no time in saying, "You all settled in? Food is on the table. Oh, say, here's a couple more items you'll need for your new job."

Rudy tossed on their beds two pair of leather gloves and then said, "Follow me."

They followed Rudy around to the front of the Big House. There was a house servant holding the door open for them. They went into the large dining room and took their places with Rudy at the long table. Once they were seated, servants exited the kitchen and placed on the table a variety of sumptuous food. Rudy lost no time in saying, "Dig in."

Henry and Randy took ample helpings of each food item, washing it all down with the big mugs of fresh water placed near their plates. They ate until they were ready to bust. Rudy watched them eat like a pair of ravenous dogs. Rudy smiled and said, "I guess you boys were hungry. It's good you eat up cuz you'll need all your energy tomorrow. Clean your plates, and then get some rest. Breakfast tomorrow morning will be simple and quick."

Henry thanked Rudy for both of them and asked to be excused. Rudy responded, "See you bright and early tomorrow. The wash house and latrine is behind our bunkhouse. Try to get all done before nightfall. It gets dark earlier this time of year. I'll be there to help you get ready for your first day as a ranch hand. Oh, I'd say wear your old hats and save the ones you're wearing for special occasions."

Henry and Randy left Rudy sitting at the long table smoking a cigarette. As they exited the Big House, they could hear Rudy laughing in a peculiar fashion aloud. They wondered if he was laughing at them or with them. For sure, their new jobs were no laughing matter.

# Chapter Thirty-Seven
# Godliness and Cleanliness

They were too tired to wash up and threw on the floor the items on their beds so they could collapse into their beds. Nothing mattered except getting some sleep. The night passed by quickly, and before they knew it, Rudy was hollering at them to get up and dressed so they were ready to go.

They stumbled around in the dark. Rudy had lit a candle, but it did not provide enough light to see clearly. Randy tripped over his chaps on the floor. They both ran out to the back of their bunkhouse to piss and splash water on their faces. They returned on the run and finished dressing. They helped each other put on their chaps and spurs. They stuffed their gloves into their pockets and folded their slickers so they could be tied to their saddles.

Rafael made a snorting noise, so they knew he was waiting outside with their horses. They dragged their saddles outside and, with the help of Rafael dressed their horses. Both horses looked and acted like twins, so there was no squabbling over the selection of horses. Rudy appeared and said, "Come and eat and drink some coffee. You got a long and hard day ahead of you."

Henry and Randy were in a daze. Their bodies unwillingly followed Rudy, and they ate some breakfast and sipped some coffee. Rudy got up, and they followed him to the front porch, where there was a Mexican man waiting for them. Rudy exchanged some words with the man in Spanish. Then Rudy introduced the man to Henry and Randy, "This here is Humberto. He knows all about our cattle and rounding them up for branding. He speaks a little English. But you should do as he does and not as he says."

Humberto was of a medium, wiry build and looked as tough as nails. His hands were gnarled and scarred from years of work on the ranch. He had a big mustache which covered half his face. His eyes were snakish but twinkled. He extended his right hand to shake the hands of Henry and

Randy. They shook his hand and discovered that he had a painfully tight grip. They could not wait for him to release his grip. At the same time, they hid their pain and pretended that nothing was amiss.

The most noticeable thing about his worn apparel was his sombrero … it had a wide brim and set just above his shaggy eyebrows. Henry and Randy could see that he was a true ranch hand and a force to be reckoned with. Humberto said something in Spanish and, revealed by his big smile, rotten black teeth. Henry asked Rudy what Humberto said. Rudy said, "He says welcome, and he's glad to make your acquaintance. He's pleased to make you guys experts in the ways of cattle ranching. After a few months with Humberto, you'll be able to work with the best of cow hands. The captain wants you to have that experience and knowledge. Go now and follow Humberto's lead."

"Wait a minute. We've got to get our hats in the bunkhouse, and I got to take one last piss," interjected Randy.

Henry and Randy ran to the back of the house to get their old hats and pee. Randy managed to say to Henry as they ran, "I don't know about this cattle thing. Maybe we're getting in over our heads."

Henry replied, "I know what you mean. Maybe Humberto and his cows will look different in broad daylight. Anyway, we don't have any choice but to obey the captain's wishes."

They raced past Rafael and their two horses. Randy told Rafael, "Wait for us. We'll be right back."

They went into the dimly lit bunkhouse to fetch their old hats. Henry was tormented because he knew his pistols would be in the way, but he felt undressed without them so he buckled then around his waist. They put on their hats, grabbed their rifles, and relieved themselves in the outside bushes. The found Rafael where they had passed him and mounted their new horses. They rode smoothly back to the front of the house to join Humberto and Rudy.

Humberto mounted his horse and said in Spanish, "Nos vamos rapido. No hay tiempo para perder."

Humberto tipped his sombrero to Rudy and took off quickly in a swirl of dust. Henry and Randy were almost caught off guard and urged their horses to follow Humberto. They had no time for parting words with Rudy or Rafael, who had disappeared into the shadows. They did not know what they were getting into, but they knew they were in for a long day of doing

Humberto's bidding.

The sun was just peaking over the eastern horizon when some other Mexican men joined them. Humberto led then to a distant corner of the ranch. Henry and Randy could see there were plenty of longhorns grazing calmly in this patch of the vast prairie. They stayed close to Humberto and tried to imitate his every move. They could see that the idea was to round up several hundred cattle and herd them into a holding pen about a mile away.

They watched the other men maneuvering on horseback so the cattle could be herded toward the pen. Humberto said in Spanish, "Follow me and do as I do."

Henry and Randy did their best to help Humberto get the cattle moving as a group in the right direction. Some cattle were stubborn and needed prodding to go the way Humberto and his men wanted. They could see that this task demanded lots of persistence and patience. The men surrounded the cattle herd and drove them toward the pen. It was not an easy job to get cattle to do what they did not want to do. They did not want to go into the pen, but nonetheless, they followed Humberto to the wooden corral.

Once a few cattle had entered the enclosure, the others followed. Henry and Randy assumed this was herd instinct at work. The long horns of these beasts were dangerous. Henry and Randy could see why they should wear gloves and why Humberto had so many scars on his hands. They also saw how their chaps protected their legs from horn tips and mesquite thorns. And they learned their spurs were handy to get a horse to pursue an unruly longhorn.

After all the cattle had been jammed into the corral, Humberto led them to a second, adjoining corral. They could see that this is where the hard work of branding was done. There were other men ready with a hot fire and branding irons. A gate was opened to allow a few cattle into the branding corral. Men on their horses had their lassos ready to ensnare each animal around the neck, and another man would lasso its legs to bring it down. Once an animal was down, the men tending the wood fire hustled to bring a hot iron to burn the captain's indelible brand into the animal's hide.

Henry and Randy stayed mounted on their horses, observing all that was taking place before them. Randy said, "I guess I should note how many cattle for which the captain has taken ownership.

"Yeah, and this is only day one. There were thousands of cows out there before the harsh winter forced thousands more onto the captain's vast ranch. No reason to put up with so many if there is not a market for all this beef."

Randy replied, "And this is only a few hundred head. It will take us months to round up all the unbranded cattle flooding the ranch. If he does not find a market soon, his ranch will be overgrazed."

Henry said, "I can see that these longhorns are tough and well-adapted to the Texas plains. They represent a legacy of the Spanish. The important people and cows in these parts are not native to these lands. I wonder if all had been left to the local Mexican and Indian populations if these lands would have ever developed."

Randy changed the direction of their conversation by exclaiming, "All new smells. The smell of frightened cattle herds, burning cow hides, and a smoky fire irritate my nostrils. I don't think I can ever get used to these smells.

Their conversation was abruptly interrupted by Humberto, who rode up to them and said in English, "Now you try."

Henry and Randy understood Humberto but were not sure if he wanted them to try lassoing or branding. Humberto then removed his lasso from his saddle horn and indicated that they should do the same. Henry and Randy took their lassos in hand, but Randy objected by saying, "We have never lassoed any cattle before."

Humberto laughed and said something like, "Not important. What's important is that you practice now."

Humberto indicated to the man at the gate that Henry would try to lasso the next cow. Henry positioned himself and said to Randy, "I guess this will give everyone a good laugh."

Out came a big longhorn, and Henry chased it with his open lasso but failed miserably to get his lasso to fall around its horns. And sure enough, all the vaqueros laughed at his first attempt at lassoing a longhorn. Randy had the same experience. Humberto came up to them and held up five fingers, indicating that every fifth longhorn let into the branding pen was for one of them to try to lasso.

Henry and Randy spent the day trying to lasso a longhorn. They were embarrassed by their failure to lasso a single cow. They watched how the vaqueros lassoed with ease and tried to imitate them. But what was second nature to them was all new to them. They had grown up in this ranch life, but Henry and Randy were aptly called greenhorns. They had everything about wrangling cattle to learn. They could see that the road ahead of them would be long and challenging, but they were determined to learn and perform well all the tasks of a ranch hand.

The last longhorn entered the branding pen, and Henry attempted to lasso it but failed. The arms of Henry and Randy were sore from their many attempts to lasso a longhorn. The sun was setting in the west when Humberto rode up to them and said in broken English, "Thanks for giving us laughs. You'll do better tomorrow."

It was a tired bunch who rode back to the ranch houses. Henry and Randy parted ways with Humberto, who said, "Manana temprano."

They rode on to the big house and found Rudy smoking a cigarette as he sat on the porch. Rudy wryly said, "I've been waiting for you. Your plates of food are on the table. I've already eaten, but I'll join you to hear all about your first day as ranch hands."

Out of nowhere appeared Rafael, who said meekly, "Gimme your horse, and I'll take care of them and your stuff. I'll meet you back here before dawn."

Henry and Randy dismounted and handed their reins to Rafael, who scurried off before they could thank him. They patted their clothes to knock the dust off before they entered the house. Next to the long table were wash basins where they could wash their hands and rinse their faces. They sat down at the table and began gobbling the food on their plates, washing it down with ample swallows of water. Rudy watched them eat, and once their hunger was ebbing, he said, "Well, tell me about your day."

"Not much to say," replied Henry between bites.

Randy added, "Judged on our performance this first day, we're the worst ranch hands in the world. We can never match the cow-handling skills of your vaqueros."

Rudy smiled and said, "It's only your first day. You got to give it time. You can and will learn all you need to know to be regular cow punchers."

Henry said, "Don't get us wrong. We're not giving up. I know for myself I'm gonna lasso a longhorn tomorrow if it kills me."

Rudy laughed and said, "That's the spirit. Now tell me how many cows did you brand today?"

Randy quickly answered, "Three hundred forty-four."

Rudy said, "That's a good start. When we get up to three thousand head, we'll have enough to drive to market, wherever that may be."

Randy asked, "How many cows do you have on this ranch anyway?"

"Don't rightly know, but it has to be over fifty thousand. If we don't find a market soon, that number could grow to over seventy thousnd. With calving alone, we got too many cattle. A real shame because up north, there is a real hunger for beef. Down here, a cow is worth three or four dollars, while in the north, a cow can fetch forty dollars. Texas could be rich if it could get a market for its cattle."

Randy was curious and asked Rudy, "Excuse my ignorance, but I'm confused about the definition of what is a cow. I hear other words like bull, heifer, and steer. Are they all cows?"

Randy's words made Rudy laugh aloud before saying, "Why, son, you're asking questions that only a few experienced cowhands can answer. They're all cows to us, but a cow is really a heifer that has had a calf. A bull is a man cow, and when it is castrated, it is a more docile steer. I hope that makes things clearer."

Henry joined in by saying, "From what I can see, you got too many bulls and not enough steers. I sure don't want to help drive a bunch of bulls to market."

"Excellent observation," exclaimed Rudy.

Rudy continued talking, "After you finish branding enough cattle, we'll need to castrate the bulls, only leaving a few bulls for breeding purposes. The idea is to get enough cattle ready for a long drive in the spring."

Randy asked, "Why don't brand and castrate at the same time?"

"Too much stress on the cows, and they all need branding, but only part of them need to be castrated. Two different operations. But we have to get our brand on all our cattle to make it harder for rustlers to steal our cattle, and there are plenty of cattle thieves in these parts."

Henry and Randy were struggling in their minds to get their heads around the enormity of the job of getting three thousand cattle ready to be driven to an unknown market. It was like having your pockets full of money and nowhere to spend it. Nonetheless, they were determined to gain all the knowledge and skills needed to demonstrate that they were high-performing wranglers.

They excused themselves to Rudy, saying they expected to see him before they headed out before dawn the next day. Rudy replied, "You betcha. I'll be with you all night in the bunkhouse and see you off just as I did today. Now you boys get rested and washed up. I'll join you shortly."

Henry and Randy walked slowly around the big house to their bunkhouse. Randy was doing some calculations in his head and said to Henry, "Three thousand cattle at forty dollars a head is a one-hundred and twenty thousand dollars. Even after deducting all your expenses, that's a colossal sum. The captain could be the richest man in the world if he can get his cattle to a northern market."

They took turns pumping water by hand into a bucket to take a bath in the darkness of the stall next to the latrine. They found a bar of lye soap in the stall and washed their entire bodies with some sort of native sponge they found hanging from a rusty nail. It had been a long time since they had felt so clean. They both remembered what their mother would often say, *Cleanliness is next to Godliness.*

For sure, God was gone from their lives, and they were rarely clean. Living on the frontier in southern Texas was a rough, Godless, and unclean existence. They were thankful to be alive, but they were not sure about what they were living for. They were taking it a day at a time. They were both thinking of how they would lasso a longhorn tomorrow.

# Chapter Thirty-Eight
# Cattle Drive Canceled

One day was like the next. There was an endless number of cattle which needed branding, and many of them had to be castrated. There were also some ornery cattle which needed their horns cut. No matter if there were high temperatures and winds, hailstorms, and rain, the cattle work continued day after day. Henry and Randy learned if the cows could handle the weather, a true wrangler could, too.

Henry and Randy became accustomed to the routine. They learned something new almost every day. After weeks of practice, they were finally able to lasso a cow for branding. They were determined that they would someday be able to lasso with the best of the vaqueros. It was a harsh life, but one that they were making their lives.

They found that part of their lassoing problem was due to their horses, which were not used to being in a pen chasing after cows. Once their horses became used to their new circumstances, they helped Henry and Randy with their lassoing. In fact, their horses adapted to cattle work quickly.

Henry and Randy were proud of their horses and made sure they got the best of care. Both of their horses were recently broken mustangs of a dun coloration. For Mustangs, they were well formed and tall... at least fifteen hands. The thing that Henry and Randy liked the most about the horses was that they only needed a slight touch of their jingling spurs to do what they wanted them to do. They both were convinced they should hold on to their horses as long as possible.

They preferred the stench of burning hides with a branding iron than the ugly process involved with castrating young bulls and turning them into more docile steers. Only a few of the best bulls were spared castration. These bulls were kept separate and used for breeding with the most promising heifers and cows. All these cattle had one thing in common – the ranch's brand that showed they were the property of the captain.

A special, super-sharp castration knife was used to cut off the testicles of young bulls that had been immobilized by being lassoed in their front and back. Among the vaqueros were specialists at doing this nasty work. Henry and Randy bit their tongues as they observed these men rob young bulls of their sex. After watching many times this ugly operation, the knife was handed to Henry, indicating that it was his turn to try to castrate the prostrate young bull lying on the ground before him.

Henry hesitated, trying to decide if he needed to go this far to become a wrangler, but he grit his teeth and quickly did the nasty task. He then handed the bloody knife to Randy, saying. "Next."

Henry walked away from the castration area to get his bearings. He did not want to watch his little brother do the same dastardly deed he just did. He was sorry they both had been put in this situation and felt like running away. He was soon joined by Randy, who said, "If doing another castration is what it takes to be accepted here, I'm out of here."

Henry nodded to agree and said, "Yep, that is one step too far and really not necessary for us."

Humberto rode over to where they were standing and indicated by hand signals and touching his eye that there was something else he wanted them to see. They climbed over the boards of the castration corral into another pen where some vaqueros were cutting the horns off some of the more aggressive cattle. They watched the men saw off horn tips as Humberto tried to explain that this was being done to keep them from injuring other cattle. Also, once cattle were dehorned, they behaved in a more peaceful way.

Humberto pointed to some men who were preparing a gum made from the agave plant that would be placed on the spot where horns used to be for antiseptic purposes and to ward off flies. The same gum was also used for the same purposes on the wounds left on the castrated young bulls. Henry and Randy were impressed with the medicinal properties of this local traditional remedy.

Henry and Randy could see they had much to learn about all the ins and outs of ranching. They could see that castrated and dehorned beef cattle were a good way to go, but they preferred that all the cattle be left in their natural state. After all, they were all destined to be eaten one way or the other.

Humberto chalked it up as normal for two young Anglo greenhorns to not like castration and dehorning, but he insisted that they participate in all parts of branding cattle. If they wanted to work on the ranch, branding all their livestock with the ranch's recognized symbol was of the utmost importance. If there was not any brand on an animal, anyone could claim ownership and put their own brand on it.

One night, Henry and Randy were having their usual talk with Rudy, and he said, "Looks like you got about three thousand head ready for the long walk to markets in Missouri. It's good that our brands don't look too fresh so we can avoid being accused of stealing cows. You two think of all you need to be on the trail for a few months. As you're novices in herding cattle over such a long distance, you'll be assigned to drag positions."

Randy quickly asked, "What's drag?"

Rudy chuckled and said, "Why drag is the tail end position in a cattle drive? You ride behind the herd and eat their dust and breath their smells. It's the worst place to be in a cattle drive, but that is where any beginners are placed in spite of their race and background."

Henry made a snide remark, "Sounds like fun. When do we start?"

"Cattle drives are no fun, and it is even less fun returning home after delivering your cattle. Many men don't make it back to their home base, and those who make it back are often broke because they spent all their money having a good time at their destination. It takes a special kind of man to do a cattle drive."

Randy reacted to Rudy's comment, "I guess we'll find out if we belong to that group of special kind of men. Again, when is our first drive likely to occur?"

"Well, we're thinking you can get everything assembled and start right after the first spring rain. You'll need good pasturage and the rain will give life to new grass. Of course, too much rain will swell the many creeks and rivers you have to ford, but we're bettin' on an average season."

Henry said, "Maybe you can tell us more about what this 'drag' position is all about."

"Sure, the two men riding drag behind the herd are responsible for encouraging any stragglers to move ahead and rounding up any strays. You also got to keep an eye out for cattle thieves, any marauding Indians, and Mexican wolves. Keep your rifles at the ready. Take at least one extra bandana to cover your faces because of all the dust the herd kicks up. You'll get the hang of it fast enough."

Randy says, "Sounds like a dirty job we can handle. Anything else you can tell us about riding drag?"

"Your biggest fear is anything that causes the herd to stampede. You got to keep an eye on the herd and constantly measure its pulse. You'll be in the saddle for over twelve hours each day, and it is slow going… at the most twelve to fifteen miles each day. There is no time off. Your stamina will be tested to the limit. As I already said, you also got to be always on the alert for cattle thieves and wild Indians. To be a true wrangler, you got to know not only about cattle, but you have to be ready to fight anyone who threatens your herd."

Rudy added, "You'll be part of a team of around eight people plus the cook and another guy to tend to the spare horses. We call that a remuda. You'll need to use several horses to complete the drive. The trail boss will tell you what to do after he gets to know the herd. Do what he says, even though you don't agree with him."

Henry asked, "Who is our trail boss?"

"Don't know yet. We need to get a guy who has worked on other cattle drives to Missouri. Anyway, get yourselves and your cattle ready to go."

Henry and Randy separated from Rudy, and as they walked back in the dark to their bunkhouse, Randy said his final remarks of the day by saying, "It'll be hard work, but at least we get the experience, paid, and food to eat."

They both laughed until well into the night. Before they knew it, Rudy was hollering at them to get up. They readied themselves for another day with Humberto. Rafael was out front of the bunkhouse with their horses ready to go. Seeing the faithful Rafael always made them happy. They wished he could come with them on the cattle drive to Missouri. He was really helpful, and they wanted his help to continue.

Rafael spoke up, and his words cut short this kind of thinking, "I wish I could go with you, but I'm too young. Besides, I can't leave my mother. She is all alone. My father was killed last year by rustlers attempting to steal some of the captain's cattle. You guys will be all right. Better to be on the trail than be hanging around here. Oh, I forgot I also have to tend to the captain's wife's rose garden."

Henry and Randy expressed their deepest sympathy for the passing of his father, and Randy reminded Rafael, "We'll be back, and you will be older. We should have many cattle drives ahead us, and one day, you will go with us."

Henry could not resist making a wisecrack, "If you believe any part of what you just said, you're more of an optimist than I thought was possible."

The next day, they got more of a taste of a cattle drive than they bargained for. Humberto wanted to round up all the cattle they had prepared for the drive and herd them to the northeast corner of the ranch so they were ready to start the long drive to Missouri. All of the about three thousand head of cattle were rounded up and herded toward this distant corner.

Henry and Randy were fascinated by the assorted coloration of the longhorns. A lot of them were a reddish brindle color, but the multi-colored black and white coloration was also common. There were many colors – black, brown, cream, dun and gray. Some had speckled spots all over them like they had been peppered with spices. If they would have been dogs, they would be called mixed-breed mongrels. One thing they all had in common was their remarkable long span of horns and their hearty nature, which allowed them to thrive on the dry prairie.

For Henry and Randy, the longhorns were all cattle mutts descended from cattle the Spanish left in these parts centuries ago. It was something of a miracle the way they had adapted to this

austere land and multiplied their numbers. Much of the same could be said of the Mustangs. There were thousands of mustangs which still ran wild on the open range. The longhorns and the mustangs were all part of foreign imports, which changed this land forever.

Without being told by Humberto, Henry and Randy placed themselves behind the large herd in their drag places. The herd stretched out for about a mile, and it was several miles to where they were going. When they got to where they were going, Humberto told them to keep any cattle from wandering and that he would send a group of his people to camp here all night to keep watch on the cattle, making sure they drank from a nearby waterhole and grazed. The preparations for a big cattle drive were exhausting.

Days passed, and this big herd of cattle was cooped up in the same spot. Henry and Randy asked Rudy every day, *When are we going?*

Rudy always had the same answer, *As soon as the trail boss arrives.*

After a few days of getting the same answer, Randy sounded off, "We can't keep these cattle in the same place forever."

Rudy did not respond to Randy's comment and walked away. Randy told Henry, "I'll keep saying the same thing to him until I get a decent reply."

Henry chuckled and said, "Go right ahead, but no matter what you say, it won't change anything."

Several more days passed, and they had their daily encounter with Rudy. But this time, he was not alone. There was another tough old Anglo man standing next to him. This new man was of medium built and his skin was weathered and deeply wrinkled from spending most of his life outdoors. He was the kind of guy you were leery of but respected just from the way he looked. His shaggy white beard and unshaven face were enough to get your attention.

Rudy said dryly between puffs on his cigarette, "This here is your trail boss. His name is Hank. He's got some news for us."

Hank cleared his throat and spat some phlegm on the ground before saying in a deep voice, "You can't go to Missouri."

Henry and Randy were shocked by his words, which really pulled the rug from under all they had been doing over the past few months. An upset Henry blasted loudly out, "Why not?"

"Now settle down, son. I don't like giving this news any more than you like hearing it. I just returned from Missouri, and I can tell you that I'm lucky to be alive. If you still want to drive your cattle to Missouri after hearing me out, prepare yourselves to lose all your cattle and meeting your master."

Hank's sobering words tempered Henry and Randy's irate reaction, but they did not end their questions. Randy could not wait to ask. "Why can't we go to Missouri?"

"Well, it's simple. They don't want to see any Texan longhorns coming their direction. All the communities and farmers in those parts are up in arms and ready to kill on sight any Texan cattle and their drivers."

Henry could not believe what he was hearing and interjected, "Now, why in the world would they want to do that?"

Hank was not a man who liked talking, so he simply said, "Tick fever."

At that point, Rudy chimed in, saying, "The people up in those parts claim that our longhorns carry ticks which infect their animals with a deathly fever. They've taken the matter into their own hands and shoot any longhorn entering their land and anyone driving longhorns in their direction. If we do as we planned, it is possible that we lose our herd and some of you. We got to find another way to get our cattle to market."

Rudy's words stunned everyone into silence. After pause of a few minutes, Rudy said, "We just got to wait for the war to be over and the railroads to come farther west and south."

Randy sputtered a few cynical words, "When will that be?"

"I dunno. Maybe next year or the year after," Hank replied.

To the surprise of all, Rudy offered his opinion, "The war will be over when the South can no longer sell cotton. We're helping prolong the war by continuing our profitable cotton business. This has to end so we can begin our profitable cattle business."

What Rudy just said sounded logical to Henry and Randy, but this did not diminish in any way their eagerness to hit the trail with all the cattle they had helped prepare for a long drive through the open range. Henry said half-heartedly, "I know a trail north. My brother and I came into Texas last year from Indian Territory, and a man showed us a trail. I don't know where that trail leads, and I don't know anything about railroads, but I know there is another way north besides going to Missouri."

Rudy responded to Henry by saying, "We'll take all that into account. I'll have to communicate with the captain and discuss with other ranchers. This may require me going to Brownsville. There has to be a way to get our cattle to some markets. After all, Texas is only rich in cattle if those cattle can make money."

Hank had some words to add to what Rudy said, "Yeah, and those cattle are Texas longhorns – the only breed of cattle tough enough to make a long drive. Hell, they can go two days

without water and eat the grass that the buffalo used to eat. They got by for a couple hundred years, surviving on the prairie without us. I'm sure they can get by a little longer."

Rudy ended the conversation by saying, "I've got to go see Humberto. You guys go ahead and eat your dinner. Hank, there is a bed for you in the back bunkhouse. Henry and Randy can show you the way."

Nobody felt much like eating after the cancellation of the drive to Missouri. All Henry and Randy could think about was what to do with the three thousand head crowded into the northeast corner of the ranch in preparation for the drive to Missouri.

# Chapter Thirty-Nine
# Change in Plans

Henry and Randy were up early. They were eager to see what Humberto was going to do now that the drive to Missouri had been canceled. They did not expect Humberto and his fellow vaqueros to head in the opposite direction from where the three thousand head were located. Henry galloped up to Humberto and excitedly asked, "Where you going? The herd is the other way."

Humberto jabbered some words quickly in Spanish, saying, "Forget those cattle for now. We got to get another herd ready for the long drive to market."

Henry was dumbfounded. He rode back to Randy and told him what Humberto had said. Randy thought for a moment and then said, "I guess we'll be branding, castrating, and dehorning cattle for the duration."

Henry asked Randy, "What do you mean?"

"I reckon there is nothing we can do except get more cattle ready for a market that won't exist until the war is over. So, we need to get used to what we are doing for some time yet."

Henry furrowed his brow and asked Randy, "How long do you think we'll be marooned in this same place doing the same things?"

"One or two years, maybe less, maybe more. But sooner or later, we'll hit the trail."

Henry was still fuming and expressed his state of mind by saying, "I was really looking forward to seeing all there was to see between here and Missouri. I like moving around, and now we're confined to this ranch. I imagine our situation is like a ship lost at sea, except our sea is the stretch of prairie grass the spreads as far as the eye can see in every direction. I don't know if I can endure staying in the same place doing the same things."

Henry's words worried Randy, but he had no choice but to say, "Hang in there. We got to do what we got to do. After all, were the captain's men."

Not surprisingly, Randy's attempt to mollify his older brother did not work to lower his anxiety. Henry kept talking to himself and his horse, trying to rid himself of his disgruntlement. But Humberto was not giving them enough time to think. He signaled to Henry and Randy to join him in his lead position, where he was pointing to a large number of longhorn grazing peacefully. He indicated they were going to round up these cattle and drive them to the distant branding pen.

Henry and Randy were in no mood to get more cattle ready for an unknown market, but they reluctantly played along and did their jobs. They were much better now at handling cattle, but their hearts were not in this kind of work. On the contrary, this was the only work the vaqueros knew how to do, and they tackled their jobs with much zest. Randy looked at Henry and said in a soft voice, "Why they got us here? The Mexicans can handle well enough this job. We're just in the way and the butt of their jokes. We know enough to be trailhands. This additional experience adds nothing to the skills needed to be a trailhand."

Henry had settled down and was in a reflective mood and said, "I agree. We're best suited to work as trailhands. But let's go along for a while to see where this repeat job leads."

They did what they had to do and herded as many cattle as they could to the distant branding pen. They understood the importance of branding, dehorning, and castration, but they did not know why they had to continue doing these things if they already knew how to do them. They got busy with preparing another herd for the market, but they were not happy. Their discontent was visible to all who associated with them. After several days of this routine, Henry raised the issue with Rudy by asking, "Is this it for us? Are we going to do what we're doing for a year or two more?"

They were surprised by Rudy's quick answer, "No. We got somethin' else for you to do. I heard from the captain, and he wants you two to explore the northern route to Kansas to see if it leads to a market for our cattle. Henry mentioned the other day that there was a trail in Indian Territory. We want to see if that is a viable trail for a cattle drive."

Henry and Randy were speechless. They did not expect to hear such a thing. But for them, this was good news. They saw it as a way of being relieved of their mundane daily duties and a chance to make a real contribution. There was much they wanted to say, but Henry kept it simple by saying, "Good idea. When do we leave?"

"Well, it will take a few days to get all organized. We want you to travel with a supply wagon. In that way, if the wagon can make it, we can be surer a cattle drive can make it."

Randy wanted to make sure that Rudy knew he was fully onboard and said, "I'm pleased you are entrusting us with such an important mission. We'll do our best to not let you down. But you realize that going there and returning could take around six months or more?"

"That's all right. We don't expect to move any cattle north to market until the war is over, and that could take a long time yet."

Randy tried to bring the conversation to a close by saying, "You've given us a lot to think about. We need to talk things over. Maybe we can meet tomorrow to go over some of the details."

Rudy replied, "Okay, you guys talk it over and sleep on it. We'll meet tomorrow right after breakfast. I'll let Humberto know of your new job."

Rudy added, "By the way, the captain's wife returned from San Antonio with her newborn baby and two of her children. So, we'll be taking our meals in our bunkhouse."

Henry was curious and asked, "Will we be meeting her?"

Rudy quickly replied, "That depends on her. Right now, she has her hands full caring for her kids. And she has to recover from her long trip over rough trails."

It was hard to contain their excitement as they walked to their bunkhouse. They were bubbling over with the news that soon they would be on the move again. They knew it was not an easy task being assigned them, but anything would be better than staying put and handling cattle day in and day out. Although it was rough, there was something about following the trails across the vast open prairie that appealed to them. Maybe it was because they were used to being lost in unknown lands.

The next day, after they had finished their breakfast, which was delivered to them on trays placed on a rickety old wooden table just outside the front door of their bunkhouse. Rudy and Hank joined them. They all ate and drank in silence. Hank looked up to see a Mexican man approaching and said, "Here comes the answer to all your questions."

The middle-aged man dressed in clean clothes removed his large sombrero and said politely, "Ernesto, at your service."

Evidently, Hank knew the man, and Rudy praised him to no end before saying, "This is Ernesto. The best man we got to go with you on your long trek to Kansas and back. He knows all about cattle and is also an excellent cook and wagon driver. He's the kind of man who has always got your back. Treat him good and he will treat you better."

After that glowing introduction, Henry and Randy stood and shook vigorously Ernesto's hand, saying, "Pleased to meet you. Looking forward to working with you."

Rudy pulled up an extra chair and asked Ernesto to take a seat, saying, "I guess this is as good of a place and time to start going over your needs for your great northern adventure."

Ernesto timidly and respectfully joined them around the old table, saying, "My English may not be good enough to express all my ideas for this trip. But thanks for asking me to go on such a long journey north. I'm honored."

The unsentimental Rudy said firmly, "Enough small talk. Let's get down to planning this trip."

Hank said, "Yeah, you'll need a whole lot to make this trip, including a lot of luck."

All eyes were on Ernesto, who reluctantly and softly said, "We'll need a good wagon full of food, feed, and water. This wagon will have to be pulled by horses used to doing this kind of work. The first step for me is checking out the wagon and its horses."

Rudy had a ready answer for Ernesto, "Go to the cotton warehouse and check out the small, covered wagon there. The horses which go with it are in a corral next to warehouse. Have one of our blacksmiths check out the shoes on these horses. If the wagon and horses are okay, go with it to the commissary and fill it with all you need for the trip, including any grease and spares you might need for the wagon."

At that point, Hank looked at Henry and Randy and said, "You can't take the horses you got. You'll need several horses to get you there and back."

Rudy interrupted by saying, "Go to the horse corral and select the mustangs you want. Lord knows… we got plenty of horses. You can use two, and the others can tag along behind the wagon. If you need help with anything, call on your pal, Rafael."

Henry and Randy wanted to add their two cents worth, but they thought it best to conclude this initial session by Henry saying, "Yes, sir. We're going to the horse corral now."

Rafael was standing quietly in the nearby shadows to their short conversation about what they will need to travel across the endless prairie. He was ready to accompany Henry and Randy to the horse corral. After a few minutes of silence, Rudy piped up and said, "What are you waitin' for? Get goin'."

Henry and Randy got up quickly from their chairs and headed on foot at a fast pace toward the horse corral, which was about two hundred yards north of the big house. It was mostly located downwind from the house to prevent its bad smells from blowing in the house's direction. It was next to the spring-fed creek that ran through part of the ranch. Thanks to this creek, the horses and all the animals on the ranch had a plentiful water supply even during times of drought.

Rafael hurried to catch up with Henry and Randy, saying, "Wait for me. You can't choose horses without me."

Randy, "Come along, friend. You're essential to our picking the best horses."

Henry uttered, "I really don't like the idea of giving up our horses for different ones. I really liked my horse, and I'll miss him."

Randy replied, "This is not time for you to get sentimental on me, big brother. We got to do as told. Anyway, a horse is a horse. You just got to get used to the steed you ride. It is just like a poker game… you got to play the hand dealt you."

They arrived at the corral and climbed up on the boarded enclosure. Rafael joined them and said immediately, "I know these horses. Let me choose for you."

Henry replied, "Okay. Go right ahead. Like my little brother said, a horse is a horse. And there are dozens to choose from."

Rafael yelled in Spanish to the two vaqueros to alert them that they were here on the orders of Mister Rudy to select some horses. They responded in the affirmative, and Rafael began to point at the horses he esteemed as being the best for the long round-trip north. The vaqueros gently guided the horses selected by Rafael to an adjoining corral where they could be examined more closely.

They all went into the adjoining corral to look at the horses. Henry and Randy petted them to calm them down. They carefully examined every part of their bodies. They looked in their mouths and spent a lot of time looking at their hooves while Rafael tried to hold them still by jerking on their manes. They mostly judged a horse by the temperament it displayed during this thorough examination.

After they finished their appreciation of the six horses selected by Rafael, Henry said, "These horses look fine to me. Keep them here until we can come back tomorrow to give them test rides. Let's go to the cotton warehouse to see how Ernesto is doing."

They walked slowly over to the big warehouse and found Ernesto busy at work, meticulously going over every aspect of the wagon. Henry and Randy stood back, watching Ernesto at work. Rafael had slinked into the shadows but kept a watchful eye out. Ernesto turned to Henry and Randy and said, "This will do. Let's go outside to the wagon corral to check the horses."

Ernesto went through the drill that Henry and Randy had done previously with their selection of horses. Ernesto examined his selected horses from A to Z before saying to Henry and Randy, "Perfecto. No hay problema."

Henry and Randy did not understand much Spanish, but they had no problem in understanding these few words spoken by Ernesto. And his words made them all happy. They all felt they were making good progress. Ernesto was eager to get started. He caught Henry and Randy off guard by saying, "Help me get two horses over to the wagon, and let's try to hitch them up."

They slowly removed the horses selected by Ernesto and walked them over to the inside of the warehouse. They followed the best they could Ernesto's instructions to hitch the horses so they could pull the wagon. Ernesto was happy as a lark when he climbed up to the wagon driver's seat, took the reins in hand, and said, "Climb aboard. Let's test this rig out. If all goes well, we'll go to the commissary."

Henry climbed into a spot on the seat next to Ernesto while Randy hopped in the back bed of the covered wagon. Ernesto gently urged the horses to move forward, and once outside of the warehouse, he drove the wagon all about the center of the ranch. After a long ride, he said again, "This will do. We can go to commissary now."

The old man at the commissary acted like he was expecting them. He catered quickly to every request from Ernesto. He sat all the items in a growing pile on the floor. When Ernesto was done asking for stuff, he asked Henry and Randy to help him load it all into the wagon. He went inside the back bed of the wagon to receive and place every item in its place. While he was going back and forth inside the wagon, he said, "It's important that I know where each item is so when it comes time to use it, I'll have no problem with laying my hands on it."

It was getting dark by the time they returned to the cotton warehouse to park the wagon and put the horses back in their corral. They had been so busy they had forgotten to drink and eat. They separated from Ernesto and walked back to their bunkhouse to eat, drink, wash off, and go to bed. They waved off attempts by Rudy and Hank to talk with them. All they wanted to do was sleep. Henry managed, in spite of his exhaustion, to say. "There is not enough hours in the day. Manana."

Hank chuckled and said softly to Rudy, "Those boys are really tired. I guess they know what trail-tired is, and that's being more tired than they are now."

# Chapter Forty
# On the Trail North

Today was the day they could finish getting ready for their big trek north. They knew that Rudy would have to give his blessing before they could depart. They walked over to the cotton warehouse to check things with Ernesto. He was ready to head north. They checked their horses and found them fit for the long journey. All they needed was the okay from Rudy, but he was nowhere to be found. Henry asked Ernesto, "Where's Rudy?"

Ernesto replied, "Dunno. No, see today."

Then, it dawned on Randy that Rafael was also not around as usual. The only place they knew to inquire about Rudy was the Big House, but they were reluctant to go to there since the captain's wife and kids had returned from San Antonio. They approached the house but stayed a polite distance away from it. They looked in every direction, but they saw no other living soul. They became afraid that something sinister had happened. They felt vulnerable because they had left their guns in the bunkhouse.

They felt all alone as they stood there in the dusty courtyard of the Big House. The wind had picked up, and tumbleweeds were blowing across the open land. They had only one question on their minds. *Where's Rudy?*

They were concerned that something bad had happened to Rudy and Rafael. Where could they be? The eerie silence increased their fears. They were at a loss as to what to do. For sure, Rudy and Rafael were not present as they had been every day for weeks. They asked themselves, "Why was today different?"

Just as they were about to give up on finding any trace of the whereabouts of Rudy and Rafael, they heard a loud cry coming from the side of the Big House they had never seen. They walked quickly to peek around the corner of the house. They saw Rudy, Rafael, and a matronly woman standing in the middle of a large rose garden. Rafael was squealing and waving his bloody finger in the air. "You see, I was stuck by a thorn."

Henry chuckled quietly and whispered to Randy, "Roses are beautiful, but they do have sharp thorns. Just like you can get wounded deep in the heart by a beautiful woman."

Randy retorted, "You should know. Just like you can't tell a book by its cover. But I guess that common saying doesn't apply in these parts because I've never seen a book in Texas."

"It took the territory back home a couple of hundred years before every plantation had a book library. This is the wild frontier... civilization has not yet arrived this far west.

Rudy also was laughing at Rafael's antics while the woman remained expressionless. The woman said something to Rudy and Rafael, and she walked back to the house. Henry and Randy assumed the woman was the captain's wife. When she was gone, they stepped out into the open and walked toward the rose garden. Rudy saw them coming toward him and said, "I guess you boys missed me. The Missus has upset my usual schedule by demanding that her rose garden be tended to. Above all, she loves her garden. For now, on, Rafael will need to devote all his time to tending roses."

Henry and Randy were busy marveling at the large assortment of rose bushes. There were roses of all colors. Rudy turned toward Rafael and said in his Anglo-Spanish, "From now on, you got to be in or close to this garden. Make sure all the rose bushes are pruned and that the roses get plenty of water and the manure they need to grow. You know how much the Patronna loves her roses. I'm counting on you to keep her happy."

Rafael acknowledged Rudy's words and began immediately to slowly walk down a row of rose bushes. He knew what to do and how often to revitalize the Patronna's rose garden, which thrived in the dry climate. All he had to do was make sure the soil was worked, enough water and manure were supplied, and they were pruned as needed. It was a lot of work, and he was sorry that he had neglected to do all he could do with the garden while the Patronna was away.

Rudy turned to Henry and Randy and said, "Forget about asking for any help from Rafael until he gets this rose garden back in shape. Now, I suppose you want me to see how you've done in preparing for your big trip north. Let's go see."

They marched across the wide, dusty courtyard to the cotton warehouse. They found a wagon train that was loading cotton to haul to the Rio Grande. Off to the side was Ernesto and his smaller wagon, which was chock full of provisions. Rudy looked inside the wagon and walked all around it. He made a clicking sound and said, "Looks good to me. Where are the horses to pull this rig and for you to ride?"

They walked out to see the horses that were in the adjoining corral. They all climbed over the corral fence, and Rudy checked the horses out from head to hoof. He took his time in doing this, saying in a serious voice, "Without good horses, you're as good as dead. As far as I can see, you've made good choices of the horses, which will help keep you alive."

Rudy was not finished talking yet and said, "Follow me. Let's find a shady place so I can give you my final words of advice."

They walked around the cotton warehouse to its shady side. Rudy pushed his hat back and said in the most serious tone Henry and Randy had ever heard come out of his mouth. "Listen up. I feel like I'm sending good men off to a battle from which they won't return. Don't get in a hurry. There is no hurry because we can't market cattle until the war is over, but when it is, we want to be ready to market our cattle surplus. Stay away from people as much as you can. Find a trail to drive our cattle north and get back here to tell us about it."

Ernesto was bubbling over with words meant to convey to Rudy that he was ready and willing to travel as far north as they could and then return after this pre-drive scouting mission. It was beginning to sink in for Henry and Randy the importance of their mission. Given all the dangers they would face over a number of months, they both thought they had a fifty-fifty chance of returning.

Rudy turned to Henry and Randy, "You work as a team with Ernesto. He has been as far as Fort Worth. After that, we're counting on you to get across Indian Territory. Stay away from any settlements or any place where military troops are stationed or passing. Keep in mind that you can be conscripted by both sides or put in prison. Don't do anything reckless, and minimize your risks. Take plenty of ammunition and be ready to fight if necessary. I'll be giving you a hundred dollars in gold coins for the trip. Keep this money hidden and use it wisely."

Henry and Randy looked at each other and sighed deeply. They were lost for words. They were deeply impressed with the great responsibility being assigned to them. They felt like they had aged a few years in several minutes. Rudy saw that they were digesting his heavy words and said, "See you off tomorrow at first light."

That was it. Their perilous mission was a go. They stood without moving for a while, letting the realization of the gravity of their mission sink down to the core of their beings. They checked and re-checked all again. They helped Ernesto fill large water barrels that were strapped to the side of his wagon. Whether they wanted to go or not, their departure was nearing. They felt like a noose was tightening around their necks, but they could not do anything about it.

They ate as much as they could. They tidied the spaces around their bunks and assembled all they would take with them. They made sure their guns were clean, and they had plenty of ammo. They wanted to get a good night's sleep, but thoughts about the trail ahead kept them awake. They finally decided to get up and ready, waiting for the pre-dawn time of their departure.

They were surprised when Rafael showed up in the dark morning with a pack mule, saying, "Help me load your stuff on the mule, and then we can join Ernesto in the cotton warehouse to sort everything out."

The old mule snorted as if in acknowledgment of what Rafael said. They stumbled around in the dark, but after several goings back and forth, they were able to pile their saddles and their other belongings on the mule. Rafael kept busy tying their items on the mule. They walked slowly with the mule to the cotton warehouse. As they walked, a pale light began to shroud the land. When they got to the warehouse, they knew they had to work fast to beat the first rays of the sun creeping over the eastern horizon.

They found Ernesto busy hitching horses to his wagon. Rafael disappeared to bring all the horses which would go with them. He chose the two he thought Henry and Randy should ride first and tied the others to the back of the wagon. They saddled their horses and placed all their tack. They talked to them soothingly while stroking their necks before mounting them. They rode them around in circles, smiling at each other, their satisfaction with their new mounts.

The early light of the morning made Rudy's image look larger than usual when he stepped inside the wide warehouse door. They all gathered at the side of the wagon. Rudy executed a cursory inspection and exclaimed in an unsentimental fashion, "Get goin' before the sun is up."

Rudy signaled to Henry and Randy to dismount and step outside with him. They did as they were told and stood face-to-face with Rudy, half expecting to hear sympathetic words from him. But Rudy was not that type.

He simply said to them, "Ernesto knows the trail as far as Ft. Worth. After that, it's all on you to find a way across Indian Territory and a cattle market in Kansas. I expect to see you back here in six months. Here's your money. Hide this leather pouch in a place where it can't be found. Happy trails."

With those words, Rudy walked off and never looked back. Rafael brought their horses, waved goodbye, and scampered away with tears streaming down his face. He disappeared into the shadows where nobody could see him. Ernesto was all set. He gently slapped the reins against the backs his wagon team of two horses and headed out the warehouse door, turning north. He had no words for Henry and Randy as he passed them, but they naturally fell in behind the wagon.

The sun was breaking when they were some distance out of the ranch grounds. Henry told Randy he was going to ride point about a half mile in front. Randy nodded and said, "As usual, I'll take up the rear."

Henry passed Ernesto, who was sleepily guiding his wagon along a barely visible northern trail. Henry signaled to him that he was going in front, and Ernesto nodded and said, "Bueno."

Their first day dragged on so much they thought it would never end. They had not seen one living thing. It seemed that no one was using this old trail. They were not sure they were on the right trail, but if Ernesto said this was the way to go, that is the way they would go. For sure, they were off the beaten path.

On the third day, they crossed the Nueces River at San Patricio and kept heading north to the east of San Antonio. They crossed a number of creeks and gullies. The weather was exceptionally dry, and consequently, the ground was hard, and their passage stirred up much dust. They looked for signs of wild animal life, but there were none they could see.

All day, each day, they rode across the vast grassland, avoiding mesquite-cactus outcroppings and prairie dog villages. Henry and Randy barely talked with Ernesto. They stopped when and where he wanted. They had no complaints about him, but they wished he would talk to them more and not stay so wrapped up within himself. They were grateful that he did seem to know where he was going and kindled a small fire every evening to fix them some food. He was good in everything he did, but he was a hard man to get to know.

The days wore on. They skirted to the west of Austin and headed straight north. After a couple of weeks, they passed the west side of Waco.

293

They were making good time, and in another couple of weeks, they had pass to the west of Ft. Worth. Henry and Randy entertained the thought of going into the fort to see if any of the people they once knew were still around, but they concluded that would be a bad idea. After all, the chance that the same people would be there were slim, and Ernesto would go nuts if they diverted from their northern track.

They forged on. They forded the Trinity River, and once they did that, Ernesto's wagon came to a surprising halt. Henry and Randy rode up to his wagon to see what the matter was. Ernesto looked at them and said, "That's as far as I know. You got to lead for the rest of the way."

Henry replied, "Okay. We'll do our best, but we're not sure of anything. We got to get to the Red River and then cross it to get into Indian Territory. It should take us about a week to see the Red. I'll stay close. Follow me."

Henry scanned the ground for old traces of tracks leading north. He called to Randy to help him find any semblance of a trail. They knew that they had been here before, but it was like the first time for them. Randy rode back and forth, trying to find some tracks. He was so engrossed in finding some marks on the ground that he did not pay attention to the prairie dog holes around him. All of a sudden, his horse bellowed and fell to the ground. He was lucky that his horse threw him before it fell with a hard thud.

Randy ran to his horse and could see it was in much pain from having put one of its front legs into a prairie dog hole. Henry rode rapidly up to see what the problem was. He looked at the scene before him and said tersely, "Your horse is done for. Its front leg is broken. Remove all your stuff, and I'll do the necessary."

Henry signaled to Ernesto to come closer with his wagon. Randy tried to calm his horse as he struggled to take his saddle off it, as well as all other tack. Henry dismounted and helped Randy carry his stuff over to the wagon, saying, "Pick another horse and get it ready to ride."

Deep down, Randy knew what Henry was going to do, but it was not until he heard the shot that he knew his horse was dead. He paused a moment as he thought of his horse and all they had been through together. Henry returned to help Randy get another horse ready and explain the situation to Ernesto. Upon hearing what had happened, Ernesto suggested, "Maybe we should butcher the horse and take some of its meat with us."

Henry looked wide-eyed at Randy and said, "Little brother, what do you think of Ernesto's idea?"

Randy was quick to spout out, "No way. I could never eat meat from a horse that was my friend unless I was starving to death."

Henry looked over to Ernesto and said, "There you have it. Let's get out of this place. Leave the dead horse to Mother Nature."

Ernesto snapped his reins, and the wagon rolled in a northerly direction. Randy mounted his new horse and stared at the ground to make sure there were not any prairie dog holes. Henry looked back at the dead horse lying hidden in the tall prairie grass. But its stench had no such camouflage. Already, the smell of blood and death had signaled to the buzzards that it was a good day for them. As they pushed on, they could see in the blue sky above flocks of black buzzards flying gayly in circles over the horse's dead body. Dead was dead, but seeing the buzzards gather made death seem a lot worse.

# Chapter Forty-One
# Kansas Cattle Market

They arrived at the south side of the Red River. They sat on their horses on the right bank of this fast-flowing river, trying to figure out how they would cross it. They rode along the river upstream until they found a familiar deep bend in the river. At this bend, the river narrowed, and its current slowed. They determined this was the spot they had crossed before in the opposite direction.

Ernesto drove his wagon to the spot where Henry and Randy indicated they would cross the Red. He leaped off his wagon seat to get closer to the river's edge. He removed his wide-brimmed sombrero, scratched his head, and said, "Too deep. Horses can cross, but not the wagon."

Henry and Randy understood what Ernesto was saying… the horses' hooves could reach the bottom of the river, but the wagon wheels could not. This posed a problem which had them stumped. They had to move ahead, and they could not go without their supply wagon.

For lack of a better alternative, they decided to unload the wagon and pack as much of the wagon items on the horses and then guide the horses across the river by swimming with them. They emptied their water barrels and floated them across to the other side of the river. After several crossings, all their stuff was wet but on the north side of the river. They spread all the items out in the sun to dry.

They continued to be stumped by how they would get the empty wagon across the river. Ernesto came up with the idea of pushing the wagon into the water and then pulling it with lassos firmly attached to their horses. The wagon would float a bit, but the horses would pull it to the other side. Henry replied, "Let's do it."

They all got into the river water again and swam with two horses to the other side. They attached one end of their lassos tightly to the wagon and the other to their horses. Randy guided the horses back into the water while Ernesto and Henry pushed the wagon into the water. They kept pushing as long as their feet touched the riverbed while the horses kept the lassos taunt by moving forward.

Their efforts were successful, and the wet wagon arrived safely on the other side. They all agreed to make camp at this spot while they waited for all their stuff to dry. They re-filled their water barrels with river water and strapped them back in their places on the sides of the wagon.

All was going well until dark clouds blew in and dropped large hail balls and raindrops on them. The high winds carried off much of their stuff, and the deluge soaked everything. They were in a panic as the river rose. It was at the end of the day, and they frantically tried to gather all their effects and horses to move to higher ground.

As the sun set in the west, they were all huddled together in a clump of sheltering bushes. They were shivering and in a miserable condition. They were unsure how they would make it through the night. They were drenched to the bone. They wanted to flee, but there was nothing they could do but wait for the rain to cease and the first rays of daylight.

They sat back-to-back with their legs extended. It was dark, and all was soaked by the heavy rain. They grit their teeth as they tried to survive the night on the muddy ground. The only time they were able to find peace was when they dozed off in spurts of sleep. The night did not seem to want to end. They looked often toward the eastern horizon for any signs that a new day was dawning.

After a long and wet night, day finally broke. They immediately got up and began to search for all their belongings, bringing what they found to a central location. They also lost no time in checking on their horses to see how they survived the rainstorm. They were exhausted, but happy all was intact under bright sunny skies.

Randy was especially happy because he found the pouch with their money in its place at the bottom of one of his saddle bags. All they needed to do was get everything dried, load their supplies, feed the horses, eat something, and check their guns and ammo. Doing all this took several hours. Nonetheless, they were eager to get started north again. They knew this was Indian Territory, so in spite of their level of fatigue, they were keen to cross as quickly as possible this unexplored land.

Ernesto mumbled some words that Henry and Randy interpreted as, "Good thing we crossed the river yesterday. Look at it now."

The gravelly stretch they had used to cross the river had disappeared beneath a raging current of a much deeper river. If they had waited until today to cross the river, they would still be on the other side. Ernesto crossed himself and thanked God for getting them to this side of the river.

Randy said in a hushed tone to his big brother, "I don't see how you can drive thousands of head of cattle across the river to a distant Kansas market. I really don't know how anyone in Texas can get their cattle to market. But I think if you don't sell cattle, there is no future for the state."

Henry only grunted his acknowledgment and said, "Let's get out of here and go as far north as we can before nightfall."

Henry saddled his horse and talked to Ernesto. After their brief conversation, Ernesto hitched up his horse team to his loaded wagon and pointed it north. Randy was on his horse and ready to go. Henry checked his old, rusty compass to make sure they were headed in a northerly direction and then gave a hand signal to move out.

They were pleased to find some semblance of a trail north. There were hoof and wagon wheel traces hidden among the tall grass that covered the rolling hills of this empty but enchanting land. Henry and Randy were convinced that the fading markings on the reddish ground were left by the passage of Jesse's trading wagon. They hoped to see Jesse again. They wondered if he and his Indian band ever found any buffalo. They also wondered about how they survived last year's bitter winter.

They could not keep their eyes from scanning the plains for Jesse's band and any signs of buffalo. Ernesto noticed how they were looking across the plains and said, "If you're looking for buffalo herds, there are none. They have all been killed for their hides by white buffalo hunters. No buffalo means no Indians."

Henry and Randy were surprised by how well Ernesto spoke and were impressed by his analysis. Randy told Henry, "Ernesto is right. The Indians living on the plains depended on the buffalo for their survival."

Henry added sardonically, "Yeah, that's correct, but many Indians were killed by Union soldiers sent to tame the West and by diseases the increasing numbers of settlers brought. Many of those Indians who remained were forcefully moved onto reservations. We're in Indian Territory, which is mostly a reservation set aside for Indians from various parts of our country. When the war is over, I'm sure more white settlers will come this way, spelling further doom for the Indians."

Without the Indians and the buffalo, they were all alone on the wide-open plains. Henry and Randy hoped they would cross paths with Jesse, but they kept their sights on heading north to Kansas. They traveled across the grassy plains for several days. They thought they were already in Kansas, but they were not sure until they met another group of travelers heading south. Although they were reluctant to meet and greet others, they were also relieved to see other human beings in this vacant world of grass.

The group of three men said they were headed to New Mexico, and they wanted to cross the Red River and head west. It was about dusk, and Ernesto said quietly and surprisingly to Henry, "Invite them to eat with us. It would be good to hear about where they have been."

Henry turned to the three strangers and extended the invitation to camp overnight with them. Since the sun had already set, they scurried around to find an agreeable campsite. They all found places to lay down their bedrolls and gathered around a modest campfire made by Ernesto, who was busy preparing food and coffee. He handed full plates to their guests first, who began eating immediately. Obviously, they were famished,

Randy started a long conversation by asking, "Are we in Kansas?"

All three of their visitors laughed, and the youngest among them said, "Yep, this is Kansas. We're coming from Wichita. Our food has mostly come from the rabbits we shot along the way. Why you want to go to Kansas? There ain't nothin' there."

Henry replied, "Maybe so, but we come from Texas cattle country, and we're lookin' for a place to market our excess of cattle."

The same young guy thought a moment and said, "In Wichita, I heard that they are building a rail line to a place called Mud River in northern Kansas."

Henry replied, "I guess that is where we want to go. We got lots of time because nothin' goin' to happen til the war is over."

Henry and Randy wanted to continue their conversation with their guests, but they were beginning to mistrust them. He noticed that the youngest, who appeared to be the leader, carried openly a much-used pistol in his holster belt. They began to think they were dealing with bandits on the run. They looked at Ernesto and could see that he was also suspicious of these men.

Henry brought their conversation to a halt by stretching his arms above his head and yawning. He sleepily said, "Excuse me. I need to check on our horses and get some shut-eye. Maybe we can talk more in the morning."

299

Randy quickly inserted, "Me too."

The young leader of the group got up and said, "Getting some shut-eye is a good idea. We need to sleep so we can get an early start tomorrow."

Everybody went to their individual sleeping places and made themselves comfortable. Henry and Randy could see that Ernesto had already crawled under his wagon to sleep. They pretended to care for their horses so Henry could talk to Randy in a place where he could not be heard. Under his breath, he told Randy, "I don't trust these guys. Keep an eye out and your trigger finger on the ready. I'm sure they're not up to any good. I'll be sleeping with my pistol and one eye open."

Henry was wide awake before dawn. Through eyes barely open, he spotted Ernesto making a small campfire. While he tried to lie still, he turned his eyes toward where the three intruders had made their beds. He did not see anything, so he opened his eyes wider. He saw nothing and jumped up to see if the three outsiders were still among them. He walked rapidly over to their sleeping places and saw that they were gone with their horses. He approached Ernesto and sleepily said, "Where are they?"

Ernesto had trouble speaking English so early in the day but managed to mutter, "They left during the night. Muy bien."

Henry said with a smile on his face, "Good riddance. I didn't trust them at all."

Ernesto wiped the coffee from his lips and said in bits and pieces, "The law must have been after them. They looked like banditos to me. I'm glad we were nice to them. I did overhear one of the men call the younger one Billy, so if the law comes this was we can say Billy and two others came this way."

Henry retorted, "I don' trust the law either. Best we don't say nothin' and get movin' from this place."

Henry woke his little brother, and they hustled to eat and get their horses ready for another long day heading north through the prairie. They ate what Ernesto had prepared for breakfast without caring what they ate. They swizzled their cups of black coffee and helped Ernesto hitch his team. They were moving northward while the sun was just peaking above the eastern horizon. In every direction they looked, they saw nothing but tall grass. Somehow, they were happy in not seeing anything in this vast sea of grass waiving to and fro in the constant wind.

They did see lots of rabbits and wanted to shoot and skin them. They could use meat of any kind in their diet. But they were afraid of the noise made by shooting rabbits would attract unwanted intruders, so they left these furry creatures go about their natural business. Randy wished they were able to run the rabbits down and club them like their Indian comrades did when they were last on these lands.

They kept driving north through grassy knolls and low-water creeks. They came to a well-watered valley with undisturbed green grass. Their first thought was what a great place for a cattle herd. They camped in this place and explored it for a couple of days. Randy said, "This is an ideal place for cattle. Too bad there is no way to get to eastern markets from here."

Ernesto also found this spot agreeable and did not want to move from it. He spied on the hills surrounding the valley a trail of dust and pointed out his sighting to Henry and Randy. They were intrigued by the dust and wanted to go and see what was making it. Ernesto looked at them and said, "Go ahead and see what makes the dust rise."

When they approached the ridge, they dismounted and quietly walked through the tall grass to find wagon tracks cutting through the prairie. After careful examination of the tracks, they determined they were going from east to west and back again. Henry said to Randy, "I got to see where these tracks are coming from. I'm goin' to ride east for a few miles and see if there is anything to see. You go back to Ernesto and tell him what I'm up to."

They did not like splitting up like this, so it was with some hesitation that Randy rode back to inform Ernesto what his older brother was up to. He and Ernesto waited all day for Henry to return. Randy was the first to spot Henry riding at a gallop across the prairie, making some dust of his own. He was pleased to see that his older brother was safe and sound. He stood at the ready to take the reins and hold the bridle of his brother's horse while Henry dismounted.

Henry was obviously excited and could not wait to share his news with Randy and Ernesto. Henry caught his breath and the spouted out, "There's a stagecoach stop not too far from here. It's called Mud River. The people there told me they're building a railroad toward them, and it should be finished next year. When the rail line reaches them, they goin' to change the name of their tiny settlement to the more respectable Abilene."

Ernesto and Randy listened intently to Henry but wondered why he was so worked up over such little news. Randy asked, "Is that all? You were gone all day, and that is all you have to say? Was there a trading post there?

Henry replied, "You don't get it. If there is a railhead, then cattle can be marketed. We got to get ready to get our cattle here so they can be shipped to eastern markets."

Ernesto felt he had to say something, "What about the Guerra? There can be no cattle marketing until the war is over."

Henry replied to Ernesto by saying, "The people in that place said the war is going badly for the South, and they expected it to end soon. Anyway, we got to get our cattle to this place, so as soon as there is a rail line, we can ship them back East. I say next spring we go on a long cattle drive and hold our cattle here until the railroad is operational."

Randy interjected, "If that's the case, we can start heading back south tomorrow. But maybe we can buy a few things in Mud River before leaving. What do you think?"

Ernesto replied first, saying, "Si, we need to stock up before we go home."

Henry said, "Of course. We'll buy all we need and then start the long journey back to the ranch in southern Texas. We'll come back this way with over three thousand head of tough Texas longhorns, and as soon as the train arrives, we'll be the first in line to market our cattle."

Randy wanted to have the last word and said, "I wish it was as easy as you make it sound."

# Chapter Forty-Two
# Goners

They broke camp and headed a few miles east to Mud River. There were probably no more than a couple hundred white settlers from the east in this tiny community. Most of the settlers had built from lumber hauled in by wagon modest wooden houses topped with dirt roofs. All their houses were near the main activity in the tiny wide spot in the rutted dirt road. This activity consisted of a stagecoach station and a trading post.

Everybody depended on these two operations. For certain, they would not be here if these activities did not exist. Some people tried to coax a living from farming the land. All were pioneers trying to survive in an unfriendly environment. The men in this hardscrabble hamlet banded together to hunt small game and to fish in the nearby streams. It was springtime, but they all had an eye on the coming harsh winter and were trying to build their food stocks and put away enough firewood so they could stay alive during the coldest season.

It was a life filled with hardships and much hard work. They were obliged to struggle to get by with little. Some saw their limits and left to go back east, where creature comforts were readily available. The stagecoach from Topeka and Kansas City usually came weekly. Lately, the number of stagecoaches had increased as there was an effort to reach farther west because gold had been discovered in Colorado.

When a stagecoach arrived, most of the people in Mud River came to see the people and goods the stage was carrying. They all thought that Mud River had potential for growth but believed that would never happen as long as the war continued. The war between the states was a setback in more ways than one for the whole country.

They all thought the rail line being built that would hook them up with the rest of the country would be a huge boost for their hamlet, but it might be over a year before they would see their first steam train locomotive. Henry and Randy were always impressed by how people survived against all odds in these small settlements, but none of their stories really struck them because they were only interested in what they were about. They were focused on marketing cattle.

Ernesto went into the small rustic trading post to see what he could buy that would be useful for the return trip to their home ranch in south Texas. At first, the gruffy, overweight, barely sober, bald-headed white man in the store did not want to deal with a Mexican. Randy followed Ernesto into the store with his leather pouch full of gold coins. Randy saw that the store manager did not want to deal with Ernesto, so he rattled his pouch, opened it, and poured a few coins into the palm of his hand. The demeanor of the store manager changed immediately, and he was all smiles from that point on.

Ernesto carried a couple of baskets of goods out of the trading post, and Randy paid the manager without saying a word. Henry helped Ernesto load the items he had purchased in the post into his wagon. While Ernesto and Randy were in the post, Henry was getting their horses checked out at the blacksmith's shed and stable, which were attached to the main stagecoach station. The blacksmith was glad to check out the shoes on the horses, give them a small burlap sack of feed, and was eager to talk with anyone from the outside world. Henry asked for a gold coin to give to the swarthy middle-aged smithy with a full head of red hair and a bushy beard.

They were all set to begin their long trek south when Henry told Randy, "Maybe we should try a different way back. The smithy told me there was another trail that, before the war, was used to drive cattle up from Texas, and that trail was clearer and faster. He recommended that we take that trail at least as far as the Red River. What do you think?"

Randy scratched his head and said, "I don't know. Sounds kind of risky. Was the war the only reason they stopped using this trail for cattle drives?"

"No, there was also something about farmers in Kansas and Missouri complaining that Texas Longhorns carried ticks which made their animals sick with the fever."

Randy replied to Henry, "If it's faster. Let's give it a whirl. Maybe after the war, it would be good to know another way to get our surplus of cattle to market."

Henry had heard more, but he was reluctant to say more but felt obliged to tell his little brother more. "There's one other thing. Parts of this trail are used by the military from both sides, so we have to keep an eye out for any troop movements and hide when they get close."

Randy thought for a moment and said half-heartedly, "Thanks for telling me. We got to be careful. Either side of the military will likely arrest us for being deserters. After all, all young men have been conscripted to fight in the war. Better tell Ernesto we are going a different way back. He might have something to say."

Henry turned around and walked over to Ernesto, who was sitting on his wagon seat, to tell him of their change in plans. Ernesto's reaction was plain and simple. "For me, faster is better. But you guys are taking a risk. Nobody gives a damn about us poor Mexicans."

Henry returned to where Randy was standing and said, "He's okay with a different trail. Let's go. The smithy said head straight south, and we'll join up with an old trail in a couple of days."

Henry and Randy mounted their horses and signaled to Ernesto that they were going. They followed tracks on the south side of Mud River and kept heading straight south across the rolling hills of the vast grassy prairie. Henry checked his compass to make sure they were headed in a southerly direction. Nothing seemed to be too different from the part of Kansas they had already gone through, but they thought this part of Kansas was more scenic and watered.

They were in their usual formation… Henry in front and Randy bringing up the rear. Ernesto was humming a song from his home country as Randy rode up to check on him. Ernesto looked at Randy and said, "Conejo. I can't think of what you call them in English, but they are here, and we could eat them."

Randy did not know what 'conejo' meant until a rabbit crossed in front of the wagon, and Ernesto pointed excitedly and said, "See, conejo."

Randy responded, "Si, I see the conejo, and now I know what you mean. Let me talk to my brother to see what he thinks about shooting us a few conejos for dinner."

At a fast gallop, Randy rode up to his brother and asked him. "Okay, if we shoot a few rabbits for dinner?"

Henry replied nonchalantly, "Just the thought of tasty roasted meat makes me want to kill the next rabbit I see. Let's wait until about dusk when we make camp at a creek before we start hunting these furry creatures. We got to make sure every shot counts to conserve our bullets and shoot as few times as possible so as not to attract the attention of anyone within earshot."

It was near the end of a long day when they came to a low-water creek, and Henry signaled to Ernesto that this would be a good place to make camp for the night. Randy rode up close to Ernesto and said quietly, "Make your fire. We goin' to hunt conejos for you to skin and cook."

Upon hearing Randy's words, Ernesto let out a loud yelp of pleasure. Henry and Randy unsheathed their rifles and rode into different parts of the endless grassland to scare up some rabbits. It did not take long before they had fired two shots each at cottontails darting through the tall grass. They hit their targets in their heads… right where they aimed. They both dismounted to fetch their kills and strap them to their horses so the blood would drain out of their head wounds. They rode back to Ernesto, full of chatter, debating on who was the best shot.

Ernesto untied the four rabbits from their saddles, got his sharp knife from the wagon, and walked briskly to a spot on the creek bank to skin and gut the dead rabbits. He could not wait to smell the rabbit meat roasting on his metal spit over a fire which was already burning. That night, they only ate roasted rabbit meat, and their full stomachs gave them a brighter outlook on life. They could not believe how good the rabbit meat tasted, and this made them want to take the risk again of shooting a few rabbits.

The days wore on, and they easily found a well-worn trail south. They met a few solitary families struggling to go north in search of a civilized settlement. They confirmed that, indeed, this was the Texas Road, and soon they would be in Indian Territory. They were told to avoid, if they could, any Indian groups and go straight to the Red River and cross it into Texas. They said they were leaving these parts because of the battles among various Indian tribes. Some tribes sided with the north and some with the south, but they were all fair game for the plains Indians, especially the Comanche. Evidently, the plains Indians did not like other Indian tribes from farther east being moved onto land that had traditionally been theirs.

Henry and Randy listened to their stories they told in haste because they wanted to get far away from Indian Territory. After listening to their stories, they doubted the wisdom of taking the faster old trail back to Texas. Henry said tersely to Randy, "This trail is faster if you stay alive. It is certainly more dangerous. The sooner we cross the Red River into Texas, the better."

They continued on their way and increased their level of vigilance once they were in Indian Territory. They went as fast as they could go from dawn to dusk. They were making good progress and expected to see the Red River soon. Then, all of a sudden, they were surrounded by an armed foreign group that appeared out of nowhere.

They did not have time to talk, Henry and Randy were quickly pulled off their horses and gagged with their own bandanas. They were thrown to the ground, and their hands tied tightly behind their backs. Their ankles were also bound together with rawhide strands. They heard the strange men talking to each other in a different language. Although these men wore parts of a Confederate Army uniform, they assumed they were Indians collaborating with the South.

They picked them up and tossed them like distasteful waste into Ernesto's wagon. There was no sign of Ernesto. It was assumed that he had been killed and his body discarded into the tall grass. They could see that this was a mean group of Indians, and if they offered any resistance, they would gladly kill them. There was nothing they could do except accept their awful fate.

The worst part of being treated in such a rough manner was not being able to talk to each other. The wagon turned and was headed in an easterly direction. For two long days, they bounced around in back of the wagon. They were given neither food nor water. They could not help it, but they were obliged to defecate and urinate in their pants. It was like those who captured them wanted them dead.

The wagon finally stopped, and they could hear somebody talking in English. The back flap of the wagon was thrown wide open, and a Confederate soldier in full uniform said in a curious tone, "Well, looky here. What do we got?"

He then turned and barked an order, "Take them into the fort and toss them into the stockade."

Henry and Randy were totally at the mercy of those who captured them. They were weak and almost delirious. They were at the point of passing out when they were carried into their cell in the stone stockade. Later, a bucket of water and plates of fried beans were placed on the floor of their cell. After a while, they awoke enough to drink a little of the water and nibble a bit of their food. They were in a daze and wondered if they would survive this ordeal.

A couple of days passed, and they were more awake but in miserable condition. A uniformed, well-shaven white man appeared in front of the bars of their cell and said in a business-like manner, "Welcome to Fort Waschita. Unless you can convince me otherwise, you are deserters and will be punished by a firing squad. However, before any action is taken on your case, we need more information from you, and I've got to get the clearance of my commanding officer in Arkansas. Now, are you boys ready to talk?"

With much effort, Henry managed to say silently, "We need to clean up before we talk."

"Okay. I'll give the order to untie you and take you to the wash house. I'll come back in the afternoon to hear anything you have to say."

Almost as soon as the military man left, a couple of young Indian men opened their cell and untied them. They then led them out into the bright sunlight and across the fort compound to the wash house. They tried to look around, but all was fuzzy because their squinting eyes made it difficult to see their new surroundings in the brightness of the day.

They were provided with two buckets of water and a bar of soap. They entered a washhouse stall and took off their clothes. The washed their bodies from head to toe and their clothes. They were given flimsy cloths to dry off and wrap themselves in while their clothes dried on a nearby rope line that had been strung between two tall poles. Their two-armed Indian guards kept a close eye on them.

They had no thoughts of escaping because they could see no way to escape from a fort where everyone was armed except them. Henry was concerned about where his pistols were and had a mind to bring up the whereabouts of their goods with the military man when he came back to talk to them. All Randy wanted to know concerned the well-being and whereabouts of Ernesto.

When they were returned to their small cell, they used part of their energy to discuss with the southern military man. Their dried clothes were brought to them, and they dressed the best they could. They tried to maintain some composure and conserve their energy for the talk they knew was coming.

They did not have to wait long before the spiffy uniformed man return and began his brief session with them by asking in a formal manner their names, birthplace, and why they were in these parts. It was decided beforehand that Henry would do all the talking. Henry told the man their real names, about their Virginia origins, and that they were scouting a trail to market Texas cattle. Henry finished his brief spiel by saying, "And that's the truth."

The spiffy military man was scribbling on some papers he held in his hands and said, "And who are you working for?"

Henry told him about the big rancher they worked for, and the man nodded approvingly and said, "It's good you are working for someone who has been of great help in marketing cotton for the South."

Upon hearing these words, Henry was prompted to say, "Our father, Captain Clement Read, is fighting for the southern cause in the Confederate Army. He was already gone when we left home two years ago."

"That's good to know. I'll put all you said in my report, which will go to Ft. Smith."

When Henry and Randy heard the words, 'Ft. Smith,' their hearts sank. After the man left, Randy turned to Henry and solemnly asked, "What's the penalty for desertion."

"Death."

Randy looked at the floor and said in a sad voice, "We're goners."

# Chapter Forty-Three
# Escape from an Ending War

The days tuned into weeks and months. Henry and Randy spent the hot summer days and the frigid winter cooped up in a dirt-floor cell with thick iron bars on the entrance and on the small high window. On good weather days, they were escorted outside to walk back and forth freely on fort grounds as long as they did not talk to anyone. Every few days, the military man would come by their cell and say he was still waiting for word from Ft. Smith. Until that word came, they remained locked up as deserters from the Confederate Army.

It was cooler in their stone-walled cell in the summer but too frigid in the winter as the stone walls absorbed and emanated the bitter cold of winter. They joked to one another that their cell was smaller than the inside bathroom of the plantation home they grew up in. Sometimes, they would cry when they thought too much of their plight. Randy was sniffling when he said half seriously, "A faster way ended up being the slowest way possible. In hindsight, I prefer the slower but safer way."

Henry replied, "I write it all off to bad luck. I hope we can shake off this bad luck and get out of here alive."

One day, the military man passed by and talked longer than usual. He glumly said, "I see you boys as good southern boys working for a man who helped the South, so I hope my commanding officer takes it easy on you so when I get his order, I can release you so you can join my small band of southern soldiers."

Randy's curiosity got the best of him, and he interjected, "Small? Seems to me that you got a lot of people in this fort."

"Oh, I was referring to our regular forces. Most of the people you see are Indians. The Choctaw and Chickasaw tribes have allied with us and are good fighters. It was a group of Choctaw warriors who captured you. Some Chickasaw braves are in charge of helping the manager of our stockade. The manager is a sergeant who you have probably not seen because he lets the braves take care of prisoners while he keeps an eye on the front office part of the jail."

Henry asked a question, "How many prisoners do you have?"

"Just you two. Nobody dares venture into these parts these days. We're always on guard for attacks by Union forces."

Henry had to ask another question, "What about the other guy that was with us."

"What other guy? Our Indian collaborators only found you two and an abandoned wagon."

His response indicated to Henry and Randy that Ernesto had somehow managed to escape. But his chances of survival were almost zero because he did not have a horse or anything to eat. They assumed that Ernesto was dead.

Randy just had to ask, "Any news on how the war is going and when it might end?"

The polished military man sighed and said, "We don't get much news, but the last I heard was that it's not going well for our comrades in arms. I don't think the war will end anytime soon. The Yankees will have to kill every last one of us for that to happen."

With those words, the military man walked off in silence. After that, it was a long while before Henry and Randy talked. They did not know it, but it was Christmas time. For the first time, the scruffy jail manager sergeant came to the front of their cell to wish them a Merry Christmas and to inform them that they would be escorted to the fort's mess hall for Christmas dinner. He also tossed into the cell a worn deck of playing cards, saying, "You guys have been here for months, so here somethin' to help you pass even more months. The way things are goin', I doubt if your case will ever be resolved. I'd let you go, but there is nowhere for you to go. Besides, you're safer in here than on the outside."

The jail master left, and Randy said to Henry, "If we're goin' to the mess hall for Christmas dinner, we need to be lookin' for a way to escape."

In an angry tone, Henry replied, "Get out of your head any ideas about escaping. There's no escape. We're inside a fort in the dead of winter amidst bands of Indian warriors who would easily hunt us down and kill us. The only thing that can possibly save us is the end of the war, but I'm not even sure about that."

They enjoyed the Christmas feast in the mess hall with the regular troops. For a moment, they almost forgot they were prisoners. The ate and drank their fill and partied with the others. But then, the harsh reality of their confinement descended on them like a heavy and cruel blanket of nightmares. They were marched back to the stockade in freezing weather and blowing snow by armed guards.

They welcomed in the New Year by playing a game of cards they had invented. They played cards unceasingly for weeks. They played until the cards became so worn that the numbers were no longer visible. When it no longer made sense to play with ragged and faceless cards, they used them to take turns in attempting to build a house. They would do anything that would help to pass the time.

When the cards were no longer good for anything, they went back to passing the time by watching a spider build its web in an upper corner of their cell. They felt like the spider was trapped in its own web. They studied the spider's situation and applied it to their own. They were indeed entrapped in a situation of their own making. They wished they had taken the same route south they had used to go north. It was their own decision to take a different trail that put them in this cell. They felt very stupid and immature.

They also passed the time by befriending a tiny mouse that had taken refuge in their cell. They fed the mouse crumbs of their food and tried to build a place for him to stay with their used cards. Their ambition was to train the mouse to perform acts like standing up and rolling over. Spending time with the mouse demanded a lot of patience. This was all right for them because all they had was time and patience.

They tried to enter into a conversation with the young Indian men who brought them food and carried out their slop bucket, but either they did not speak any English, or they chose to keep their lips sealed. Henry and Randy wanted to learn a few words in their language, but they never heard a word from them. They felt they did not want anything to do with them, and they were just there to do their job.

Early one morning, they were preparing for another session with the tiny brown mouse when they heard a lot of noise outside. Henry hoisted Randy so he could look out the small window in their cell to see what all the commotion was about. Randy could not see anything from his vantage point. While Randy was looking at the window, the jailer came, unlocked their cell, and said, "Yankee troops are coming, you better get out of here.

We're trying to save ourselves… you should do the same."

Henry and Randy were stupefied by his words, and it took a few minutes for them to comprehend what was being said. Then, it dawned on them that they were free to go. They rapidly gathered the little they had and swung the door of their cell wide open so they could run to the front of the jail. They could not believe it, but they found all their stuff neatly assembled in the front office. Henry was happy to strap on his pistols and grab his rifle. Their saddles and all their horse tack was in the neat pile. Henry said, "All we need is horses to get as far away from this place as possible."

With their loaded rifles in hand, they exited the jail to see a fiery scene of pandemonium. The few people left in the fort were running about in a panic as they looked for the best way to escape. Members of the regular Confederate troops had set all the main buildings of the fort on fire, and the flames were raging. The spare horses had broken loose from the fort's corral and were looking for a way to escape the flames. Henry told Randy, "We need to hurry and catch us a couple of horses, saddle them, and get the hell out of here before the Yankees get here."

They went back into the stockade to get their lassos and ran outside to catch a couple of horses. After a number of struggles in a smoky atmosphere of sheer chaos, they were able to lasso two horses and tug them toward the stockade. They tied the horses to posts in front of the stockade and rushed into its front office to drag out their saddles. The hustled to put their saddles, bits and bridles on the horses the best they could. They both knew they would need to stop later and adjust their saddles, especially cinching tightly the saddle belts.

With flames licking at their heels, they headed south at a fast gallop, trying to reach and cross into Texas before the Yankee soldiers arrived. Certainly, the Yankees would find Fort Washita a burnt ruins as the retreating Confederate troops did not want to leave anything behind that would be of use to their northern adversaries. But none of this concerned Henry and Randy. They were only interested in staying out of the war and somehow getting back to their home ranch in southern Texas so they could drive cattle to Kansas.

Not far from Fort Washita, they found a place to cross the Red River. They looked around and saw that they were all alone. They assumed those who once called Fort Washita home fled to the east to avoid Union troops and in the hopes of joining up with other Southern comrades. The water in the river was cold and deep. They tied their boots around their necks and rode their horses into the river water. Their horses barely could make it across the river. The got to the other side and decided to keep going as long as there was daylight in spite of their wet clothes.

They were lost but thought sooner or later, they would pick up a trail heading south. They were worried about food for themselves and their horses. They did have full canteens of river water. Their high adrenalin levels kept them going. Their horses were also motivated to get as far as they could from the conflagration.

The sun was setting when they slid off their horses and decided to camp in place. They unsaddled their horses and tied them in a place where they could graze. They did not have any energy left to do much more and collapsed on their bedrolls with their heads on their saddles. Sleep came fast, and they slept like the dead all night long. It was good to be free, but they did not feel safe. It was tough to balance freedom with security in such circumstances.

The first rays of the sun woke them. It took a while to get their bearings and realize where they were. Hunger was gnawing holes in their stomachs. They knew they had to eat, but they did not know how they would get any food. Their surroundings seemed devoid of any kind of food.

A thought then crossed Randy's mind to check his saddle bags. He expected all that was in his bags had been pilfered, so when he dug into his bags, he was surprised to find their contents intact. He held up some hard-tack biscuits and exclaimed to Henry, "We are saved!"

Randy then decided to search both his saddle bags and was pleasantly surprised to find his leather pouch with the gold coins. He grinned as he told Henry, "I didn't think it was possible. but we got our money. Those were sure some honest Indians."

Henry replied, "It's good we have our money, but what good is it if there is nothing to buy?"

They munched on the tooth-busting hard biscuits. Even though they soaked them with water from their canteens, these cast-iron biscuits were difficult to stomach. As they were eating, Henry said, "I think our escape from jail and these hard biscuits indicate our luck has changed. All we got to do is to keep heading south. I hope we make it. But, if we do make it, it'll be too late in the year to do a cattle drive to our spot near Mud River. We'll have to get all ready for a drive next year. It would really help things if that damn war could end."

The endless prairie swept before them. They looked across the sea of grass and felt at home, even though they were lost. But the ancient scenery was distorted by their growing hunger. They did not know what to do. There was nothing to eat as far as they could see. They figured they would go as far in a southwesterly direction that their tired horses could take them. They rode through the night under the full moon and into the next day. They rode until they could not go any farther.

Their spirits wanted to continue on. But their exhausted bodies slid off the saddles to the dry ground. They laid prostrate with their heads down. Somehow, the warm earth relieved a bit the hunger aches in their bellies. Their horses wondered off to graze on some green grass. Both of them passed out, thinking this was the end and there was nothing they could do about it.

Hours passed, and the buzzards circled high above in anticipation of dead meat to feast on. Fate was not on the side of Henry and Randy, but a miracle did happen. A lone hunter was following their tracks, and when this back woodsman came about their bodies, he stayed on his mule and stared quietly at their bodies for some time. He eventually eased himself off his mule and slowly walked up to where Henry was lying and kicked gently the sole of one of his boots. He was ready to do the same to Randy when he heard a slight moan from Henry.

This sound told him that they were still alive and he should try to give them some water and food to revive them. He took his canteen off his mule and, turned over Henry's body, and wet his lips with water. He did the same for Randy. He had a small bottle of molasses, and he put some drops of this sugary substance in their mouths with his finger. He repeated this practice several times. He stayed with them through the rest of the day and night. He was intent on bringing them back to life so he could know what the hell they were doing out in this desolate land.

In the evening, the pioneer of the prairies made a small fire and cooked up some bean soup. He used his wooden spoon to give Henry and Randy small sips of this nourishment. After a few sips of this soup, Henry and Randy were able to sit up on their own. A few more sips of this porridge, and they could say some words. Henry looked at their unbecoming savior, and his first words were, "Where are we?"

The man who had saved their lives guffawed and said gleefully, "Mighty glad to hear you talk. Well, you're in the middle of nowhere. I left Ft. Worth a couple of days ago in search of a new life somewhere on the open range. I wanted to get out of the way of all the people coming west to avoid the post-war uproar."

Henry and Randy thought their weakened bodies were causing their ears to play tricks on them. Henry struggled to ask the man to repeat himself. The man said the same thing again, and Randy interrupted him in order to say, "Did you say post-war?"

"Yeah. That's the big news. The war is over, and the Yankees are coming to run our lives. That's the reason me and others are looking for new lives in the west where the war and its aftermath were not so unsettling. By nature, I'm a loner who stays away from people, but I made an exception in your curious case."

The news that the war was over gave a spark to Henry and Randy's will to live. They stayed another day in the same spot so they could recover and get more news from the man, Rick, who saved them, swapping stories about their lives. Henry was prompted to say, "Rick, would you like to help us get back to our ranch and join us in a cattle drive?"

The bearded Rick was all smiles when he said. "Why not?" I got nothin' better to do. I might as well get in front of the line cause thousands of men will be coming to these parts looking for work now that the war was over."

Henry replied, "Welcome, Rick. I think you'll make a good drover. All we got to do now is get back to our big ranch with its huge surplus of cattle. I think we're headed in the right direction, but gettin' there could take us some weeks."

# Chapter Forty-Four
# Saved for San Antonio

In the days ahead, Rick proved his worth. Henry and Randy believed he was more than a lifesaver. He was a real blessing sent by God. Rick did everything. He was used to surviving in the wilderness and an expert marksman. His jovial nature made him a good companion. Although he had never before ventured out on the vast open range, he felt quite at home in the Texas grassland. The only drawback to partnering with him was the slowness of his beloved mule, Sally.

Rick loved his mule and talked to her all the time. Somehow, he would ask the mule a question and hear it answer. His conversations with Sally were real head-scratchers for Henry and Randy. Before long, they started greeting Sally every time they got near her. Staying on Rick's good side meant staying on good terms with his faithful and hard-working Sally.

They made good progress in crossing the prairie in the direction of San Antonio. There was a drought, so they easily forded creeks and gullies. They dodged prairie dog holes, cactus patches, and mesquite trees. Rick was always able to find water holes for filling their canteens. In spite of the noise, Rick hunted daily enough rabbits to add ample meat to their diet. He always had food for them to eat when they made their camp each night. He was careful to find campgrounds that afforded patches of grass to their horses and his mule could graze on. It was like he could smell water, so they and their animals were never excessively thirsty.

With Rick at their side, Henry and Randy thought they could go on forever, but they knew San Antonio was drawing near, so Henry told Rick, "We need to take a day off so we can clean up. We can't enter San Anton' looking like somethin' the cat dragged in."

Rick was quick to answer, "Good idea. We'll stop at the next big water hole so we can wash up. I got an old bar of soap that will make us shiny clean."

Henry chuckled at how readily agreeable Rick was. His good humor was infectious. It was hard not to be in a good mood when you were around Rick. Henry enjoyed striking up a conversation with Rick and said to him. "You said you heard in Ft. Worth that the war was over. When was that?

Rick wrinkled his brow and said, "I don't rightly know. As you know, there are no calendars in these parts, and it takes a few weeks for news to reach even an outpost like Ft. Worth."

Henry thought a moment and said, "Yeah, the news travels slow in these parts. They're probably still fighting in Texas. What month do you think this is anyway?"

"I can't say for sure, but I guess it's May."

When Rick said that, all Henry could say, "We're too late."

Henry's words perplexed Rick, who questioned, "Too late for what?"

"The annual cattle drive," Henry reluctantly said.

"Why is that? I thought you said there's a surplus of cattle on your ranch."

Henry cleared his throat and prepared to tell Rick some of how cattle drives work. He told gently the amicable Rick, "The best time to start a cattle drive is in the spring after rain has greened up the prairie. It can take us over three months to drive three thousand head of tough longhorns to a market point in Kansas. We got tens of thousands of cattle and they are overgrazing the ranch. We got to find a way of moving some of them out. We've seen that the way is clear to Kansas. All we're waitin' for was the end of the war. Now, the war is over, and we're not ready to drive cattle north. What a kick in the head."

Rick listened intently to Henry, lapping up every word he said. After a few minutes, he mumbled, "I never saw three thousand cows let alone the tens of thousands cows, you say you have on the ranch you work for. That's a big operation."

Henry was quick to impress upon Rick some more facts but simply said, "You can't ride across the ranch in one day."

"Wow, that is big. Does just one person own all that?"

Henry thought about how much he should say in his answer to Rick's question. He finally said, "Yep. One person and he has taken refuge on the other side of the Rio Grande in Mexico. Now that the war is over, I expect he'll come back and take over the reins of directly managing his ranch."

Rick hesitated a bit before saying, "Excuse me. I got to see if I can find a place for us to clean our bodies, clothes, and stuff so we can look respectable when we arrive in San Anton'.'"

Henry spotted something on the distant horizon and replied with a sense of urgency in his voice, "That's a good idea. You see those whiffs of smoke in the distance? I'm thinking that's San Anton'."

Rick scanned the horizon and said excitedly, "By cracky. I think you're right. I better get goin.'"

Rick saw that his words were not heard by Henry because he had already galloped off to tell his brother what he saw. Randy saw Henry coming fast to join him. He thought if his brother was coming so fast, there must be a problem, so he unsheathed his rifle and readied his trigger finger. When Henry was near, he said, "What's the problem now?"

Henry smiled and loudly said, "No problem. Put your rifle away. Look at the horizon. We're almost in San Anton'."

Randy studied the blue sky in the distance, where it joined the grassy earth and saw the puffs of smoke, and excitedly said, "By golly. We're almost there."

Henry and Randy were full of joy. The sight they beheld lifted many burdens from their shoulders and gave them hopes for a brighter future. They knew San Antonio would be a delight, and from there, back to the ranch was an easy stretch to cover in a few days. They were more than ready to clean up and, taste the life of San Antonio, and get to know the Alamo.

Rick found a big waterhole, and they made their camp under a mesquite tree next to it. They were eager to pass the night and get up at daybreak to begin cleaning themselves and all their meager possessions. From somewhere, Rick came up with a brush with stiff bristles and said, "Looky here. I've carried this brush with me ever since I left home in Kentucky years ago. It's great for scrubbing your ragged clothes. It can make those fancy hats of yours look new. All you need is a little of my soap and some elbow grease."

After hearing Rick out, Randy turned to Henry and said, "I think we need to buy ourselves some new clothes in San Anton'. Maybe we should give Rick some money. After all, he did save our lives and has taken good care of us."

Henry said, "I agree, but while you're handing out some money, give me some too. I'm sure they have saloons in San Anton' in which you can dally."

Randy smirked and said, "I know what that means."

Henry responded, "Yeah, but it has been a long time, and I want to see if I still have what it takes. Don't you want to risk some of our money playing cards? Maybe our luck will carry over to your gaming table."

A thoughtful Randy changed the subject a bit, saying, "On second thought, maybe our clean up tomorrow should be minimal. The three of us could use a full bath, shave, and haircut in San Anton'. Then we go buy our new duds. After that, we can see the sights and have fun. Of course, we'll have to take first our horses and Sally to the livery to be checked out and cared for. I can't wait. I'll tell Rick about our plans."

Randy informed Rick of the money he had and their plans for using some of it in San Anton'. Rick had almost tears in his eyes when he responded to Randy, saying, "Well, dats mighty nice of you. I'm sure glad you fellas survived, and I joined forces with you. Otherwise, I'd be wondering, lost somewhere in the Texas prairie."

Randy looked sympathetically at Rick and said, "We owe you our lives, so there is nothing we can do for you that is too much."

They all had trouble sleeping that night under a full moon and brilliant starlit sky. The anticipation of arriving in San Antonio had their minds racing. They had never been in a place with so many people. Henry's last words that night were, "Maybe San Anton' has more people than cattle on the ranch."

Randy sleepily responded, "I don't think that is true, but with the war over and all, we should see more people on the trail leading to San Anton'."

They welcomed the first rays of the sun and did their best to tidy up. Instead of the full cleaning planned, they packed their gear and were on their way to San Antonio before the sun had crested the eastern horizon. Needless to say, they were eager to get to San Antonio, which was considered as something of a beacon of civilization.

As they got closer, they could see many people heading to San Antonio from all directions. They saw so many people and wagons that they thought there would be no room left for them. It was obvious that with the war over, people were flocking to this old town on the prairie. They were comforted by the thought they would no longer be conscripted and could enter San Antonio without that worry.

They guided their steeds down the narrow and crowded streets, jostling with others who were eager to find a place to settle. After spending months in jail and weeks on the open range, there was more than their eyes could take in. They were on the lookout for the first places they saw that would care for the mounts and give them the clean-up they needed.

It did not take them long to find a livery and stables for their horses and Sally. The lingua franca was Spanish. Henry and Randy were pleased that they could understand this language enough to follow directions to a nearby place where they could get a haircut, shave, and bath. They marched off to this place and waited their turn to get royal treatment.

It was a different and better world for them. They could not believe all the expert pampering they were given by the cluster of attentive Hispanic workers. Once they paid in advance the boss of the swanky establishment, they were given the best haircuts and shaves that they ever had. Following that, they were escorted into an adjoining room with tin bathtubs full of hot water.

It was evident what was expected of them. They cast all modesty aside, undressing rapidly and getting into their tubs filled with soothing water to soak their tired bones. After a while, specialized female attendants swarmed around them with soap and brushes to scrub every part of their bodies. They had never been so clean… they hurt all over from the hard scrubbing that had been given to them.

When they were finished with the washing tubs, they were asked to immerse themselves in other tubs of cooler water to rinse themselves. They observed that their old clothes had disappeared, and Henry asked in broken Spanish where their clothes were. The response he received was that they were being washed and dried.

While they were still in their rinse tubs, new clothes, boots, and hats of all sorts in their respective sizes were put on display on wooden shelves located on the side of the washroom. With their old clothes being washed and their naked state, they felt pressured to buy the new clothes and undergarments offered to them. The only choice they had was to pick new clothes from those on display.

Doing this was not fair, but they were trapped in a situation not of their making. They played along in a good-natured way, but deep down, they did not like having their choices limited. Henry wondered if the clothes were covered by his initial payment or they were a separate and additional charge.

They were told to get out of their tubs, dry off with the cloths provided them, and get dressed in the new clothes that had been chosen. There was no time for exhibiting any modesty. They dressed rapidly and looked at

321

each other to see how they appeared. Henry and Randy kept their old and expensive hats but dressed in all-new outfits. Rick delighted himself with his new set of clothes and said with a big smile on his face. "I never had it so good. You guys look terrific. It's hard for me to believe you're the same guys I came into this place with."

Rick's words caused Henry and Randy to laugh aloud, and Randy said joyfully, "I don't care what it costs. It doesn't get any better than this."

Henry strapped on his pistols and said to Randy, "My pistol belt and holsters don't go with my new duds, but I'll never part with my pistols."

Randy replied tersely, "I get that. You'll always be identified by your pistols."

Henry exclaimed, "I feel so good. All we need before seeing more of the town is to eat a good meal. Let's get out of here and find out where we can go to get some good grub."

They were all on the same page with Henry and tromped toward the exit in the adjoining room. At the door, they found the boss with his hand extended. He not only wanted to be paid extra for the clothes they had selected, but he believed a handsome tip was in order. Randy kept hidden all the money he had but fished into his pockets for a few gold coins. He handed these coins to the man and said bluntly in Spanish, "No hay mas dinero."

Randy was ready to argue with the boss, insisting he was now broke because of his excessive charges. He feigned being out of money and tried to convey that in Spanish, in spite of his looks, he was not new to these parts and, thus, a person to be reckoned with. He told the boss 'Gracias' and walked out the door. He was followed by Henry and Rick, who acted like they had no choice but to agree with Randy.

Once out in the street, they were pounced upon by a large assortment of street vendors who saw them as men of means. Randy shook off the vendors as here returned inside to confront the boss, saying in a no-nonsense manner, "What about our old clothes? Where are they?"

The boss said blankly, "No worries. They're drying. Come back in a couple of hours to pick them up."

Randy replied in a cutting voice, "You betcha. I'll be back later."

Randy could not shake the feeling that the boss was ripping him off. He could see that he could speak good English. He did not buy that he was a poor, meek Mexican acting in a way to get sympathetic treatment. One thing Randy had learned from his experiences over the last few years was that no one deserved to be treated in a charitable fashion. To survive in these parts, it was a dog-eat-dog life.

He exited again the personal grooming salon to find Henry and Rick surrounded by street vendors and shouted to them, "Come with me. Let's go eat."

His shouting had more to do with extricating Henry and Rick from the overbearing vendors than anything else. He had no idea of where they could get a bite to eat or how much it would cost. He did want to go to a nice place, particularly since they were all dolled up.

They wove their way through the crowds of people, and then Henry saw a big sign on the front of an old adobe building that stated in big letters, *La Mejor Comida en San Antonio.*

"Look, that's where we should go. I'm hungry, and that sure looks like a place to fill an empty stomach," said Henry while licking his chops and walking across the street toward the sign.

Randy and Rick followed Henry, who appeared to be attracted by some magnetic force to the restaurant across the street. They arrived at the front door, and before opening it, Henry declared, "Here it is. Nothing like a good meal to put a positive perspective on our lives. Let's go in and eat all we can."

Henry threw open the door and beheld a view that opened new vistas for him. All was better than he expected. He was in a kind of heaven that he did not deserve. He, Randy, and Rick were full of 'ou's and ah's'. Rick said in a dreamy voice, "I can't read, but I know a good thing when I see it."

# Chapter Forty-Five
# Hello and Goodbye, San Antonio

It was dark inside. Their eyes took a while to adjust to the soft illumination of the large restaurant room. When their eyes could see, they saw a place of luxury. They also saw several well-dressed patrons. This made them wonder if they were suitably dressed for this palatial restaurant. Henry suggested they leave, but at that moment, a glamorous Hispanic woman appeared, all decked out in expensive traditional Mexican clothes. She said sweetly in perfect English, "I'm Doña Tomasita. Welcome to my restaurant. May I seat you?"

They were all aglow as they followed Tomasita to a well-accoutered table. Oddly, there were no windows, and the place was lit by hundreds of sparkling candles and oil lamps. The thick adobe walls and high decorative ceilings made the dining room cool. On the walls were hung tapestries representing scenes from the long history of San Antonio. The dishes and silverware were antique and of the highest quality. A group of mariachis filled the air with music. There was no doubt that eating at this place would be costly.

Tomasita handed them menus and said softly, "Take your time to select your food. I realize this may be a special occasion for you."

Randy reached over to turn Rick's menu right side up. A nervous Rick reminded Henry and Randy that he could not read and added, "I never been in a restaurant before. If the food is as good as the place looks, I'll be happier than a pig in shit. By the way, what is our special occasion?"

Henry chuckled and said, "We're celebrating our arrival in San Anton.' It's good to be back to civilization."

Henry and Randy studied the Spanish menu, noting the high prices, and wondered if they could afford to eat in this place. A beautifully adorned Hispanic beauty arrived at their table to fill their glasses with cool water. She asked them if they were ready to order. Henry was ready to order because he wanted to keep her a little longer at his side. Randy told the waitress, "Please give us a little more time to decide."

Randy then turned to Rick and said, "What do you want… meat, chicken, fish or pork? And do you want spicy? All the dishes come with fried beans, tortillas, and sour cream. What'll it be?"

"I can't remember the last time I had chicken, so I guess it will be chicken for me," said timidly Rick, who undoubtedly exhibited some shyness in these unfamiliar surroundings. He watched Henry and Rick and tried to mimic their good manners.

It had been years since Henry and Randy had eaten outside their plantation home in Virginia, but they had no problem in applying the best manners in this high-class restaurant. The only problem they had had so far was the deposit of their guns with a guy guarding the front entrance. Dona Tomasita assured them this was normal practice and their guns would be returned to them when they were ready to leave.

Henry said he was ready to order. Randy looked at the menu for a few more minutes and then beckoned to the lovely waitress. He ordered for Rick a big plate of chicken with boiled rice, and for himself, he said he would take the specialty of the house. Henry piped up that he would have the same his little brother had just ordered. The waitress asked, "What about drinks?"

Rick squirmed in his cushioned chair. Henry and Randy did not know that he liked alcoholic beverages. Randy hesitated before saying politely, "Bring us your specialty drink made from the hibiscus flower."

The charming waitress smiled and disappeared into the shadows of the back. She returned with three big glasses balanced on a small shiny board. They could not wait to taste the sumptuous-looking red-colored drink with floating lemon slices. They lifted their glasses and clinked them together in acknowledgment of their good fortune. Rick was the first to take a sip and exclaimed, "This the best drink I've ever tasted. It really hits the spot."

They slowly nursed their drinks, especially Randy, because he was worried about how much the drinks and their food would cost. Without much delay, their food began covering the table. It was truly a feast fit for a king. They thanked the waitresses and sat for some minutes admiring the food spread out before them. Henry was the first to break their silence by saying, "It looks too good to eat, but I'm too hungry to wait any longer."

Before Henry could finish his sentence, they had all began eating like starving dogs. They had trouble slowing their gobbling, but the gradual application of their table manners obliged them to eat more slowly with the utensils placed next to their plates. Randy had to remind Rick to not eat with his hands but use the fork at the side of his plate. Rick was enjoying digging into his food, forgetting to wipe away the dribbles from the side of his mouth with the soft white cloth napkin provided him. Randy tried to slow Rick down and place the napkin on his lap, but he did so reluctantly because Rick was beaming with happiness as he devoured the delicious food in his own way.

Between bites, Henry exclaimed, "I don't know what I'm eating, but it is sure good."

Rick took time out from eating and, with his mouth half-full, declared, "If I were rich, I would come here to eat every day."

Randy was quick to reply, "Well, we're not rich, and this could be the first and last time we eat in such a fancy place."

They ate every crumb of food on their table and finished every last drop in their drinking glasses. Rick licked his plate clean and belched before saying, "Why, that was really good. I'd eat the fancy tablecloth if it was on the menu."

They all had a hearty laugh after they heard Rick's words. They sat a while to let their food digest. Then there was nothing but silence because they knew paying the tab would cost a pretty penny. Randy cleared his throat and said, "Why don't you guys get our guns and wait outside for me while I settle up with Tomasita."

Henry and Rick exited, leaving Randy alone to deal with Tomasita, who did not waste any time making her way to their table. She said forthrightly in the King's English, "I see your friends have left. Are you ready to pay the bill? Or would you like a cup of our imported coffee and try one of our fine Cuban cigars?"

Randy could see that Tomasita was a strong businesswoman, trying to milk as much money as she could out of him. There was no sense in trying to bargain with her, so he politely asked, "How much do we owe you?"

Tomasita told him firmly the cost of their meals, and Randy nearly fell off his chair … it was much more than he expected. He tried to maintain his composure when he inquired, "How many Mexican gold coins is that?"

Tomasita was fast to answer, and Randy felt he had no choice but to dig deep into his pocket for the amount she cited. He handed her the coins she asked for and said, "Thank you. Great food for hungry men just off the trail."

326

He was about to stand when Tomasita asked, "No tip for my girls?"

Randy handed her a couple more coins, saying, "That's all we got. We'll be back after we strike it rich."

Tomasita could see that Randy and his comrades were potentially good customers and said with a big smile on her face, "You're welcome here anytime. Please come again."

Randy exited and found Henry and Rick standing at the side of the cobblestone road that passed in front of Tomasita's place. Henry was the first to talk, "We've asked passersby's and learned that one of the best saloons in town is just down the road. Let's go."

"Yeah, let's go to the saloon. You go for the ladies, and I'll go for lady luck at the card table. If I'm not lucky, we'll be headed back to the ranch with empty pockets. That place we just ate in cost us an arm and leg. I hope you still have the money I gave you."

Randy's words on their money-shortage problem took the wind out of their sails, so they walked toward the saloon with much lower expectations. Rick knew he needed money to enjoy a few rounds of whiskey, and Henry knew without a few coins jingling in his pocket, the ladies would not get anywhere near him. Randy knew he needed all the money he had left to make a decent effort to win more money at the card table.

They entered the crowded and smoky saloon in a gloomy, make-or-break mood. The riotous atmosphere in the saloon suited them. It was relief to be in such a lively place with so many people. Henry went up to bar to find a spot. Rick needed no introduction to the saloon. He also took a spot at the end of the bar. Randy gravitated to one of several poker tables and waited for his turn to try his luck.

Everybody was happy, but their money shortage problem dampened their spirits. They did not have enough money to enjoy fully all the delights of the saloon and San Antonio. This was not how they wanted to spend their day in San Antonio before hitting the trail again and going home to the ranch. Henry and Rick stayed at the bar longer than usual. Rick drank much slower than usual his favorite muleskinner drink. They felt like poor people in a rich man's paradise.

After a few hours, Henry felt a jab in his back. He turned around, and it was his little brother who urgently whispered, "We got to get out of here pronto."

Henry could see fear in his eyes and knew instantly that this was not the time to ask him to explain himself. He gave the guy next to him his drink, telling him he had to go. In a hushed tone, he said to Randy, "Let's go outside and talk."

They wove their way through the crowd, grabbed their guns at the exit, and walked a short distance down the street. Randy broke their silence by saying, "I won a lot of money. The last pot was a good one. Lady luck shined on me. I had the best hand. There was another guy at the table who lost everything in that pot. He thinks I cheated. He and his buddies are tracking me. They will do anything to get their money back."

"You really got yourself in a pickle. Start walking home now, and I'll make sure you're not being followed. What do you say?"

"Good idea. If I'm being followed, shoot you rifle into the air to let me know and attract attention. My plan is to work my way back to the store to get our old clothes and then to the stables. We'll sleep with our horses and head farther south tomorrow morning at the crack of dawn. We got to get out of town before the sore loser and his friends find me."

Henry appreciated the hurry his little brother was in and told him, "Don't worry. I got your back. We've come too far to be bumped off over a card game."

Randy was turning to get lost down the busy street when Henry said, "Say, you shouldn't be walking around with all your winnings. Me and Rick could use some money."

Randy stepped into the shadows, dug into his pockets, and pulled out some money for Henry, saying, "Here is your share. Be sure to give Rick some. Don't stay up too late cause we got to get out of town at daybreak tomorrow."

"What about seeing the Alamo?"

"That will have to wait until our next visit. It's been there for over a hundred years, and I'm sure it'll be there when we come this way again," said Randy quickly.

Henry was happy to receive the money. He could not wait to spend it on one of the attractive senoritas inside who were ready share their feminine favors with men of means. It was Henry who was now in a hurry, and he told Randy, "Go now. I'll make sure you're not followed."

Henry watched with his rifle and pistols at the ready as his little brother disappeared down the street. After he was satisfied that no one was following Randy, he re-entered the saloon and checked his guns. He spied

Rick at the end of the bar and jostled the crowd as he walked in a beeline toward Rick. He slapped a few coins on the bar in front of Rick and said, "Here's some more money. Drink your fill. I got some business to take care of, and then I'll be back to fetch you."

The half-drunk Rick raised his glass and said in slurred words with watery, bloodshot eyes, "You're too good to me. I'll be right here."

Henry then walked through the crowd and sided up to a woman who was talking to a group of men and whispered in her ear, "Don't we have some business to take care of?"

With those crisp words, Henry turned and walked over to the back door to wait for the woman. The woman politely extricated herself and walked over to where Henry was standing. Without saying a word, she withdrew a key from her bodice and opened the locked door. Henry followed her into a narrow, dark hallway, and she locked the door behind her.

It was all he could do to keep his hands off of her. He felt as if he had an itch, and nothing could get rid of it except her. She led him into a tiny room, and as soon as she closed the door behind them, he ravished her in ways that cannot be described. All the months of wanting a woman were poured into this one sensual act.

He could not get enough of this woman, but he had nothing left to give her. He threw all cares aside and exhausted himself. He knew then that he had to get himself a full-time wife. The voluptuous woman could speak only a few words of English. She let her body and experience with men speak for her. She took all Henry had to offer, including all his money. She was delighted that she could give him such pleasure and make so much money.

Henry got dressed and recovered his bearings as to what he would do next. For a brief time, he had forgotten where he was and what he had to do. She guided him down the hall and unlocked the door. He quickly said, "Goodbye. I'll be back."

He quickly found Rick in the same spot at the bar. Rick was soused, and Henry had some difficulty guiding him to the exit and keeping him quiet. They had a long way to go to the stables, and he did not want anyone to take too big a notice of them. Rick was barely able to walk, and Henry had to support him by placing his left arm over his shoulder. Rick was singing unintelligible ditties. Henry acted drunk and joined him in singing.

He did this so it would appear to all they encountered that they were harmless drunks on their way home after having had one too many.

They arrived at the livery and explained to the night manager that they were going to sleep with his brother near their horses and Rick's mule because they had to get up early and hit the southern trail. It was not easy finding their way around the inside of the dark stable. Rick's inebriated state made things even harder. They stumbled in the dim natural light given off by a pale half-moon.

At last, they found Randy, and Henry said softly, "Is that you, little brother? All okay?"

"Yeah. But it is not good for us to separate like that."

"I agree. We've got to stick together if we're goin' to survive, but when it comes to women, I can't help myself."

"We've been through a lot together, and it is not over yet. Now, get some shut-eye so we can leave at first light."

Randy paused a moment before saying more, "Where's Rick? We can't forget about him."

Henry was busy arranging a place to lay down in the empty stable next to where their horses were being kept, but he took a moment to reply with a grin in his face, "Listen and hear Rick snoring. He's already passed out and on his way to the land of a thousand winks."

# Chapter Forty-Six
# Return of Ghosts

It was still dark when Randy got up. He waited until the first light of day made things around him vaguely visible. His plan was to get out of town and far away from San Antonio as early as possible. He did not want any trouble from the men he won the money from last night. He kicked his brother's leg and said, "Get up. Time to go. Get ready and get Rick up. I'll settle with the livery master."

Henry did not feel like getting up, but he knew their break was over, and they had to hit the trail south and get out of town. He moaned, "Can't we stay a little longer? San Anton' has got everything we need."

Randy shot back, "You know we can't. We got to get back to the ranch and show them we're still alive and ready to drive cattle north to Kansas. Anyway, I'm more used to living on the open prairie than being in a bustling town. This is not a place for us."

Henry got up and staggered over to the horse's water trough and washed his face. He then sauntered over to where Rick was fast asleep. He had to kick Rick several times before he stopped snoring and opened his eyes. He loudly commanded Rick, "Get up. We got to go."

Rick sat up and rubbed his eyes. He took a few minutes to orient himself. His head was pulsating, and he did not know where he was. Standing up was a feat he could not do. He grabbed the wood panel of a stable stall he was sleeping in and managed to pull himself up to an almost vertical position. Henry watched him stumble about and laughed, saying, "I guess it will take some time for last night's binge to wear off."

Rick did not know what Henry was talking about. He could not remember anything about a saloon or drinking too much. But he was concerned about why his body was not functioning. Henry helped him get the saddle on his mule, making sure he had not left anything behind. It was a big job to lift him onto his mule, but once Rick was sitting atop his mule, Henry said, "Here's the reins. Hold steady, and don't go anywhere until

Randy and me are ready."

Randy returned and said, "We can go now. Let's get our horses saddled and get out of here."

Henry led Rick out of the stable onto the front dirt road. Randy followed and said, "The livery master told me the trail south can be found at the end of this road. So go that way to the end of town."

They headed down the road out of town, but their gentle ride was slowed down by a big swirl of dust headed their way. Randy said with a sense of urgency in his voice, "Let's get off the road at the next empty lot so whatever is comin' can get by."

Luckily, an empty lot was nearby, so they could get out of the way of the herd that was barreling toward them. In the midst of the oncoming dust, they began to make out men in blue riding horses furiously into town. They cowered on the side of the road in their empty lot as the group of mounted troops passed swiftly by. They watched spellbound as the Union soldiers passed them by in a rumbling flash.

The troops paid no mind to them, but their minds were fascinated by what they were seeing, particularly they could not believe that the last rows of the troops were darky men. Randy looked at Henry and said in a low voice, "You see what the world has become."

Henry was lost in thought but managed to say, "Did you see that guy on a horse in the last row nearest us? I swear it was Jo. What do you think?"

"I only think that it is a good thing for us that the war is finally over. If it wasn't, we probably be dead. Besides, it has always been hard for me to tell one black person from another."

Henry was still in a thoughtful mood. "That was Jo, all right. Glad to see he's still alive. It's amazing to me that he was once a slave on our Virginia plantation, and now he's a soldier in our new nation's army."

Randy was in a hurry to move on as soon as the dust settled but added, "The world has changed for Jo and us. He's in the army, and we're searching for a home on the open range of Texas. Nobody would have thought any of this was possible five years ago. Now, let's go."

Rick was starting to come to his usual senses and, despite an awful hangover, was able to formulate a few words, "Yeah, let's go. Let me experience the new world that awaits me. I'm tired of this old world and ready for a change."

They rode out of town. Their steeds were rested, watered, and grain-fed and happy to be back on the trail again. The main difference this time was the number of people on the trail. It seemed like in this post-war period, everyone wanted to go and find a place to settle in the West, making the frontier gradually disappear. Randy muttered after seeing so many wagons full of settlers, "We better hurry while there is still an open range to drive cattle across."

The trail south was well-traveled and, thus, easy to follow. They made good progress without incident. The weather continued to be dry and hot. The farther south they went, the hotter it got. They lived off the land and the stash of rations they had in their saddlebags. They ate and bought more food as they crossed at San Patricio. Once they crossed the river, they felt like they were almost back to where they started over a year ago.

Although it would take them a couple more days to reach their destination, they were increasingly becoming giddy at the prospect of getting back to Santa Rosita. They rode as long as they could, pushing their mounts to the limit. They could not wait to tell their story to Rudy and maybe even the boss himself, Captain Ford, if the Union government had allowed him to return from Mexico.

They were eager to see familiar faces on the ranch, particularly they wanted to see Rafael. It was already good to be in familiar surroundings. Their expectations grew as they got closer to the ranch. Rick could not see anything but an empty, vast grassland and, thus, wondered what all the fuss was about. It was the sober and clear-eyed Rick who spotted on the distant horizon some buildings popping up magically out of the prairie. He softly said, "You see that?"

Henry and Randy were beside themselves when they saw the same thing as Rick. When they started to see bunches of longhorn cattle and, Henry excitedly declared, "We're here."

They wanted to ride off at a gallop, but it was late in the afternoon, and Rick advised, "Better to wait until tomorrow morning and ride in as nothing had happened."

It was tough for Henry and Randy to make camp while they were almost knocking on Santa Rosita's door, but they accepted Rick's advice as the best course of action. It was a sleepless night for them as the anticipation of their arrival had their adrenalin flowing, they were up before dawn and ready to go. Rick had also been infected by their excitement and mounted his mule and said, "Let's go. I'm sure that there are people ahead who will be surprised that you're not dead."

Randy slowed things down by saying, "Not sure what awaits us at the ranch as we've been away a long time. Let's enter slowly and see how we're received. We don't even know if the same people are there or what. A lot can happened in a year, even in a place where not much happens."

"You got that right. We might have been replaced by the new hands flooding into these parts from the east after the war's end. They might not be interested in what we got to say about driving cattle to Kansas."

Randy chuckled and said, "I don't think so. Look around you. As far as the eye can see, there are cattle looking for grass to eat. These cattle represent Texas' riches, and now that the war is over, they need to be sold at a market which will ship them to people back east who are hungry for beef. The era of big cattle drives is just beginning, and we're in a good position to spearhead that era. All we got to do is play our cards right."

Henry could not match the eloquence of his intelligent brother. The unschooled Rick kept is mouth shut. He was not so stupid as to say anything. His instincts told him to keep quiet and only speak if he had something important to say. They silently entered the wide dirt courtyard of the ranch and stopped to see who would spot them first.

They did not know it, but a hundred hidden eyes were peering at them from behind windows, doors, and bushes. Everyone ran away and hid when they saw strangers riding in. They were all waiting to see if these strangers were bad or good. Although the war was over, there were many armed men who had banded together to form criminal gangs which were capable of the worst kind of trouble.

Henry said, "I'm sure they're seeing us, but they do not know who we are. We look different than the two guys who left here over a year ago. Let's ride closer to the house and take off our hats so they can see clearly who we are."

They rode to the front of the big house and, removed their hats, and made sure their guns were out of sight. A few minutes passed, and there was no sign of life from within the house. Finally, Henry called out, "Rudy, are you there."

Almost immediately, a man came out of the house with his rifle aimed straight at Henry. The man with the rifle said tersely, "How do you know my name?"

Henry was overjoyed to see Rudy and said, "Why, Mr. Rudy? It's us.

Henry and Randy. And this is our friend, Rick."

Rudy replied harshly, "Dats not possible. They're dead."

A perplexed Henry said, "How do you know that? It's us in flesh and blood."

"Ernesto told me you were dead."

A breathless Henry quickly said, "Ernesto. He's alive?"

Rudy lowered his rifle a bit and said, "Look behind you and see Ernesto. Ernesto, can you tell me if this is Henry and Randy, who you said were dead."

Ernesto was speechless. He could not believe his eyes, but he had to reply to Rudy, "Si, señor. It's them. I guess it takes a ghost to see ghosts."

Rudy put his gun down and said, "Unbelievable. I was sure that after such a long time away, you were long dead. You got a lot to explain once you get settled. In the meantime, welcome back. We're really glad to see you and can't wait to hear your story."

Randy felt like he should say something at this momentous occasion and said, "Yeah, we want to hear about everything that has happened here while we were away. In particular, we'd like to know how Ernesto survived."

Rudy hesitated but said, "I'll meet all of you in the back bunkhouse in a few minutes so we can talk this through."

Henry and Randy got off their horses and gave Ernesto big abrazos. A teary-eyed Henry said to an ebullient Ernesto, "You old son of a dog, how did you do it? Is it really you... the guy we last saw months ago in Indian Territory?"

Ernesto was so excited he had trouble speaking in English, but Henry and Randy listened intently to any word that came out of his mouth. They were able to make out of Ernesto's incessant jabbering that as soon as they were captured by Indians, he jumped off the wagon and hid in the tall grass. He said the Indians were more interested in capturing his wagon and all that it contained than finding him, an old Mexican.

Ernesto explained how he crawled through the grass and then ran away as fast as he could. He walked night and day until he swam across the Red River. He survived by eating bugs, lizards, and snakes in their raw state. Sometimes, he would find old pecan nuts under trees and would eat them. He ate anything that would not make him too sick to keep walking south.

Surreptitiously, he entered the Ft. Worth settlement at night and stole a horse and some food. He headed as fast as he could toward San Antonio, where he rested and was able to be fully provisioned by sympathetic Mexicans for the week that remained for him to get home. All in all, it took him about three months to get back to Santa Rosita. He claimed that the thing that kept in alive was the desire to rejoin his family at Santa Rosita. He spoke of his glorious homecoming and how some people ran away when they saw him because they thought he was a ghost.

They slowly walked with their horses to the back of the house while they listened to Ernesto talk about how he survived. Ernesto was eager to hear Henry and Randy tell all about their long absence. They waited in front of the bunkhouse under the shade of a tree until Rudy joined them. Rudy walked up in a hurry and said, "Let bring some chairs out of the bunkhouse and set them down under the tree. It may take us some time to get the whole story from these two ghosts from the past."

Chairs were brought out, and they all sat in silence, waiting for someone to talk. It was obvious that Rudy was overjoyed with seeing Henry and Randy and just wanted to stare at them so he could start believing they were alive. After taking a deep breath, Rudy smiled and said, "Okay. Let's hear it. Take your time, and do not leave out anything important."

As the oldest brother, Henry spoke first in a meek voice, "There's a lot to tell, but I don't rightly think I can do justice to our story. My brother is much better at words than me, so I let him tell our story."

Randy had an idea that Henry might pass the buck to him. He tried to keep their story short so they could get down to the real business of marketing their surplus of cattle. He simply said they were captured by the Indians and taken to a fort controlled by the Confederate Army and held in jail as deserters. They spent months incarcerated, and they were able to escape when the fort was abandoned and burnt. They headed south, crossed the Red River, and kept going until they could not go any longer. They lay in the trail face down like dead men until Rick came along and saved them. He finished by saying, "We owe Rick our lives and hope he can become a cattle drover."

Rudy was ruminating, taking in every word said by Randy. "Very interesting. You boys are lucky to be alive to tell is this story. Now, is there anything you can tell us that will help get rid of our excess of cattle?"

Henry could not wait to reply, "On that score, I'm sure Ernesto has already told you... there is a place in Kansas which offers good pasture for cattle while we wait for the railway to arrive and haul our cattle to the eastern markets."

Rudy stopped Henry from talking by saying, "Yes, Ernesto told us that, but we were waiting for you to confirm what he said, and then it became too late to send cattle north."

Henry felt obliged to make a bold assertion. "We take three thousand head now and head north, and if the train is not yet there, we can keep them in a well-watered valley near where the railhead will be. That way, we will be the first in line to ship our cattle by rail to eastern markets."

Rudy rubbed his chin before saying, "It too late in the year to drive cattle north. We'll have to wait until next spring."

Henry was fast to disagree with Rudy, "I say take the risk and go now. Now that the cotton trade has stopped, you need the money, and you got too many cattle for this big ranch. What do you got to lose?"

A thoughtful Rudy replied, "I see your point. It would be good to remove three thousand head from the ranch as our pastures our overgrazed and our water sources are limited. But this is a decision bigger than me. I'll have to send a message to the boss, who is still in Matamoros, for a final decision. That may take a couple of weeks, but I would say get rested and get ready to drive cattle north to Kansas."

Rick, who had sat behind Henry and Randy, meekly said, "What about me?"

Randy chuckled and said, "Don't worry, Rick. Where we go, you go. You're our lucky charm, and we don't want to lose you."

# Chapter Forty-Seven
# Miracle Celebration

There was someone hiding behind the tree. Henry drew his pistol and said, "Show yourself before I blow you into your next life."

A young Mexican man stepped from behind the tree. It took Henry and Randy a while to recognize the person standing timidly before them. Suddenly, they started rejoicing because, without a doubt, it was Rafael. Randy hugged him and said, "Is that you, Rafael? When we left, you were a boy, and now you're a fine young man."

Henry gave Rafael a big hug, too. A sobbing Rafael fell to the ground as if he were prostrate with grief, but it was the opposite. He was bowled over by the living presence of two men he believed dead. He pounded the ground. Every time his fist hit the ground, he thanked God in Spanish for doing a miracle and bringing Henry and Randy back alive. Henry and Randy lifted him gently up and sat him down, soothingly telling him, "Your worries are over. We're back and well. You were always in our thoughts, and we're beyond happy to see you again."

They all sat quietly while they waited for the emotion displayed by Rafael to die down. Rudy joined the group and said, "You three can sleep here with me, Señora Patronna is here with the kids, so we'll eat here. As soon as you feel up to it, get your herd ready to drive north. I'll send a message about this to the boss. We should have his answer within a week or two. Anything else for now?"

Randy was curious and asked, "What's new here? Bring us up to date with all that has happened over the past year."

Rudy looked Randy straight in the eyes and said in a boring tone, "Nothing has changed except we got more cattle than we can handle. As you know, the war is over, and the way is open for driving our cattle to market. We've been waiting for the boss to get his presidential pardon so he can return."

It was Henry's turn to be curious, "Presidential pardon? What's that all about?"

Rudy cleared his throat and said, "The way I understand it, he has to be pardoned by the U.S. President before returning to this country."

Randy interjected, "Why does he have to be pardoned? This is his ranch, and it's in this country?"

"My understanding was the U.S. government named him a rebel agent, and that is treason. He wrote a letter to the president explaining his situation, and now that the war is over, he should be free to come to his home in Texas."

After hearing Rudy's awkward explanation, Henry said, "Whatever the case may be, we have to get cattle to the market. That's all we care about."

With Henry's words, Rudy got up and said, "Let me show you your bunks. Maybe you should get rested up. I'm sure the community will be having a big fiesta at dusk to celebrate your return."

Randy commented, "Wow. A celebration for us. That's too much. It's good that you still have a place for us. We were afraid that you had already hired new hands to replace us."

Rudy replied, "Well, we had a lot of men returning from the war looking for work here, but until we can market our cattle, there's no work for anybody. Maybe we'll hire a couple more drovers when the first herd is ready to go north. You boys get sorted out while I attend to some other matters."

After Rudy left and they were alone, Henry and Randy jumped up and down on their beds like a couple of crazy schoolboys. The idea of sleeping in a bed had Rick stunned into silence. After Henry and Randy finishing bouncing on top of their beds, a bashful Rick said, "I never slept in a bed before. This will be a new experience for me."

Henry and Randy looked at Rick and laughed heartily. Rick wiped the tears from his eyes and laughed with them. He said, "Boy, I'm sure glad I met you guys."

They continued in this joyful mood as they removed all their tack from their horses and mule and confided the care of these trustworthy animals to Rafael, who was standing by to be of any help... just like the old days. Henry and Randy did not know it, but Rafael was determined to never leave again their side. Wherever they would go, Rafael had decided that he would go too.

They took long bucket baths in the bunkhouse stalls made for this purpose. Rafael took their clothes to be washed and dried and returned them before sundown. They told one another that they had to wear their new San Antonio clothes for the evening fiesta in their honor. They wrapped themselves in their drying clothes and lay peacefully on their beds. Rafael came in to say, "I brought a barber to give you a trim and shave. You got to look your best for the big fiesta."

Henry went first for the barber to work his magic on him. Randy followed, and then Rick sat for his tidying-up session with the barber. He could not believe his good luck. His allegiance to Henry and Randy grew in leaps and bounds. At last, he had found a place he could call home.

The homecoming fiesta was much more than they expected. The Mexican community really went all out to show how grateful they were for the return of Henry and Randy. After all, it was not every day that they got to celebrate a miracle.

A big circle was formed with lighted fire torches, and cushioned chairs were assembled on a carpet in the place of honor. The mess hall musicians played loudly, and some people were dancing in time with the music. A woman sang a beautiful song in Spanish, which was only half intelligible to Henry and Randy, and its meaning was completely lost on Rick.

The jefe of the Mexican community gave a long speech, partly in Spanish and partly in English, that was interrupted many times with lengthy and loud applause by the hundreds gathered for this joyous occasion. After the speech, ladies dressed in festive Mexican costumes served big trays of food, drinks and large quantities of food of all sorts. They piled their porcelain plates high with food they had not tasted for a long time and ate as only hungry men fresh off the trail can do.

The quality of their plates prompted them to look around in the dim light. The spied for the first time the boss' wife sitting quietly with her children a short distance from them. Randy whispered to Henry, "Maybe we should pay our respects to the Patronna and her family."

"Yeah, later. At the end of the fiesta."

Every person in attendance passed by to shake hands with Henry and Randy, crossing themselves after a handshake. Some women could not hold back their tears and bowed as they passed. For them, it was truly a miracle. Nobody thought in their wildest imagination that they would see Henry and Randy again. They all believed that they were once dead, and now they were alive. They were witnessing a true miracle.

They celebrated for hours. The men, women, and children started drifting back to their community. Henry nudged Randy and said, "I guess it's time we said hello to the boss' wife and family."

Randy quickly replied, "Too late. She and her kids are already gone."

Henry looked over to where the Patronna was sitting and saw empty chairs. "I guess we missed that one. I'm a little surprised that she did not come over and say something."

"Not knowing her is all right with me. I'm sure she knows who we are and what we're about. Her coming here tonight tells me a lot."

At that time, Rick, who was sitting behind Henry and Randy, coughed to draw attention to himself and said, "Swell party. Best time I ever had. Maybe you guys should die again so we can enjoy such a glorious ceremony. I feel like I died and went to heaven."

Randy harped, "Have you been drinkin' again?"

"No, I purposely stayed away from the hard stuff so I wouldn't make a fool of myself at such a great ceremony."

Henry interjected to this brief exchange, "Good. We'll all need to be clear-eyed in the morning when we discuss all that needs to be done to get three thousand head from here to Kansas."

Randy said, "You got that right. Let's go and get some shuteye."

At that moment, Rudy appeared from the shadows and said, "Party is over. Get some sleep. I'll need the best of your thinking when we meet tomorrow after breakfast."

As usual, Rudy was way ahead of them and already planning their departure with a large herd. Rudy walked off, and they followed him to the bunkhouse. They went to bed without saying a word, but their heads were spinning in preparation for their meeting tomorrow morning with Rudy. It was time to get serious about driving three thousand head to Kansas.

# Chapter Forty-Eight
# Cattle Drive Preparations

The next morning, they met for breakfast again, and Rudy was full of information. Rudy began by saying, "I checked with the jefe of the vaqueros, and he'll begin today rounding up all the cattle he can find that you prepared for the drive before. He'll herd all these cattle up to the north pasture. Other cattle can fill any shortfalls."

Henry said, "You make a big job sound simple."

"Well, it is not simple and will take a week or more. It's so dry that cattle will resist moving away from a water source. We may have to haul water out to them. We'll see. I reckon you can be on your way in two to three weeks."

Randy spoke up, "What about the other guys who will be goin' with us?"

"That's still up in the air, but Ernesto told me to give him a couple of days to select from the community who was best suited to make the long drive to Kansas."

Henry said, "Sounds like we got to wait a few days before we can be sure of anything. Let's know when there is somethin' for us to do. Otherwise, we'll be restin' up for the long ride north."

Rudy reflected a bit and then said, "Our first concern is security... for you and the cattle. You can't let your guard down. There are still some bands of wild Indians and cutthroat rustlers. I'm tryin' to get you some newer model rifles with lots of ammunition."

Henry said, "I like my rifle fine, but if you get somethin' better, that's fine with me. As for my trusty old .45 six-shooters, I'll never part with them."

Rudy said, "That does it for me. Be thinkin' about anything else you'll need before you hit the trail north. I got to go see Ernesto and see what we goin' to do about the chuck wagon and the extra hands for the drive of a big herd of cattle north."

Rudy left Henry, Randy, and Rick with a lot of downtime they were not used to having. They really did not know what to do. They could not rest, yet there was nothing for them to do. For them, it was better being on the trail and making their way across the open expanse of grassland.

They were at their wits end when Rafael sauntered into their bunkhouse space and said, "Let's go see the horses I've picked out for our long drive north."

Henry was the first to say, "Good idea. Let's go."

They all jumped up to follow Rafael, who had given them an escape from their irritating idleness. Rick gladly tagged along but was annoyed by the mention of only horses, so he asked Randy, "Does this mean I can no longer use my old mule, Sally? I hope not, as it will be mighty hard for me to part with Sally. We've been together for years."

Randy replied, "Maybe so. In this life, you got to get use to changing mounts. I never give names to my horses because I don't want to get attached to them. As good as horse may be, I know that someday I'll have to get another horse. I don't like attachments. For me, one thing I've learnt is there nothin' in this life worth getting sentimental over."

Randy's final words struck Rick like a gut punch. He then knew he had to harden his natural jolly self so he could make it in the days and months ahead. He began to have doubts on whether or not he was cut out for the life of a drover. He wanted to be true to his inner core, but the life he was embarking on required that he be tough inside and out. He counted his lucky stars, and he had no choice but to continue on the path he was on, but his inner soul told him he could quit and go his own way at any time.

Rick's allegiance to Henry and Randy gave him the discipline he needed to stay on the straight and narrow, but deep down, he did not like it. He wanted to be free to wander as he felt like. He knew his wanderlust was a failing, but he could not help it. He was sorry that Henry and Randy counted on him. He knew that was a mistake as he was unreliable and ready to follow his instincts.

Randy pointed out to Rick the buildings they were passing as they walked toward the corral next to the former big cotton warehouse. They climbed up on the corral fence, and Rafael indicated which horses he thought would be good to start with. Rafael said, "You know we'll need to use several horses to make it all the way to Kansas and back. Dat's why we'll be taken a lot of extra horses with us. All the horses you see here will be goin' with us."

Rick had an unhappy look on his face and could not help but ask, "Where's my darlin mule, Sally?"

Rafael replied, "Oh, that old mule. She's with our other mules. She's so old and tired you're lucky that she got you this far."

Rick did not know exactly why, but he felt anger swelling up in him when he heard Rafael's words. He did not like anyone talking bad about Sally. He buried his true feelings and said, "Can I see Sally? We've been together for years."

"Of course. Follow me."

They followed Rafael a short distance to the mule corral. Rick spotted Sally and, ran up to the fence, and climbed over it in a state of excitement. The others looked on as Rick approached Sally. It was like a man finding his true love after a long separation. Rick hugged Sally and whispered sweet words into her big ears. He knew in his inner self that Sally was communicating to him. After stroking Sally in a loving manner, he walked slowly back to the corral fence and said, "It's okay. She told me it was time she retired and be with her own kind. Take good care of Sally. She's the only family I got."

With those words, a sad Rick wiped tears from his eyes and climbed over the fence to join the three others, saying, "It's okay. I'm ready to become a drover."

They walked back to their bunkhouse in silence to find Rudy sitting under the tree with two new shiny rifles. Rudy could not wait to hand the rifles to Henry and Randy, "Thanks to our Confederate friends, here are two new Henry repeating rifles for you courtesy of the Patronna. We got plenty of ammunition in stock. With these rifles, you'll be masters of the prairie. A Henry for Henry and one for Randy."

Rudy was full of good cheer as he handed over the rifles with small boxes of their .44 caliber ammunition. Henry and Randy did not know what to say. They examined closely their new rifles and Randy asked, "Will we get a chance to thank the Patronna in person for this great gift?"

Rudy snapped, "I doubt it. She is a very private person, and for all matters concerning the ranch, she only deals with me while her husband is away."

Henry said, "I can't wait to do some target practice with our new rifles. I assume they will shoot straight and true."

"Yes, siree Bob. You get sixteen shots without reloading. Now that's real progress."

Rick reluctantly said in a meek voice, "What about me? I sure could use a new shooting iron."

Rudy acknowledged Rick by saying, "I'll see what I can do. As far as I'm concerned, every man going on this drive should be equipped with a Henry repeating rifle."

At that point, Rudy stood up and said, "I got to go see Ernesto to continue our discussion about our big drive north. There are a lot of details to get ironed out. I should be ready to go over things with you guys tomorrow morning."

Henry, Randy, and Rick had time on their hands. Henry said, "This is good as time as any to see how our new rifles shoot."

They took their rifles and ammunition to an isolated spot in the open prairie some distance from their bunkhouse. There was nothing to shoot at, but Randy said, "Look for a wildflower, and we'll shoot at that."

They found a lonely flower amid the grassy plain and, with the sun behind them, began taking shots at the pretty white flower. It did not take them long to obliterate with a few bullets the flower. They wanted to find another flower to practice shooting, but in the interest of saving their ammunition, they stopped shooting and walked back to the bunkhouse. Henry said, "Well, we know our rifles work good enough against a defenseless flower."

They passed the time by telling stories about their childhood in Virginia to Rick, who could not relate but listened intently. Henry and Randy told these stories to remind themselves of where they came from, but they knew their distant memories of their lives on the plantation in Virginia were over for good, and this life was theirs now. They almost wished the past was fully dead and beyond their capacity to remember. Deep down, they knew they would never see Virginia again.

Supper was served, and they ate quietly and then went to bed. They were bored and tired of resting. Rudy came in late and went straight to bed. He was up early and waiting with breakfast for the others in front of their bunkhouse under the tree. After they were seated, he began talking quickly in a no-nonsense fashion that compelled a high level of attentiveness, "Listen up. I spent several hours talking with Ernesto, and this is what we decided."

Henry replied, "All right, lay it on us."

"First, Ernesto changed his mind, and he's goin' to be your chuck wagon master. He said that he had talked it over with his family, and they all agreed that it best he accompanied the miracle boys. For me, it's good that he's goin.' You guys need to get his advice on all that you do. All we got to do now is find a good team of oxen to pull his wagon and make sure his wagon is fully stocked."

Randy smiled when he said, "That's good news. Having Ernesto along with us makes the tough job ahead a lot easier."

Rudy continued, "Now, you guys know giving you the job as trail chiefs is a big deal. Normally, such a job would not be given to guys as young as you are, but you have been there and back, and this is an experiment to see if long drives to Kansas work. If you have any questions along the way, ask Ernesto."

Henry said, "We understand. You can trust us."

"Randy, maybe you should get your pencil and notepad to write all the details we're going to discuss."

Randy ran inside the bunkhouse to fetch his writing material. Rick used this brief interlude to scoot his chair closer. Rudy said, "First, Ernesto says you need ten men instead of eight. That's two in front... the trail boss and the point rider... that's you two. Then, you need two men on each side of the herd. Then, there is the drag rider bringing up the rear. I assume that is Rick."

Randy was scribbling furiously in his notepad. Rudy waited a minute before continuing, "Ernesto says it's best that Rafael be the wrangler who takes care of all the spare horses you got to take with you. We call this herd of horses the remuda. You got to take at least three horses for each rider, so that is at least thirty extra horses. The wrangler will work closely with Ernesto, who wants Rafael to learn all about operating a chuck wagon, especially the cooking part. Any questions?"

Randy laid down his pencil and said, "It seems you know a lot about cattle drives. Where did you learn all this stuff?"

"It's true, son. I've been on a few cattle drives east. Before the Yankees blockaded the Misissip,' we drove cattle to barges and crossed over the river to New Orleans and sold our cattle to the Confederate Army. Those were good days, and we made a lot of money."

Henry said, "I'm not surprised. It's good to have someone like you tellin' us what we need to do to get these cattle to market. By the way, when we sell the cattle, how are we paid?"

"Good question. We prefer you be paid for the cattle in gold coins. If you can't get and carry that many coins back, try to get at least half in gold coins and half in a draft drawn on a good bank. Don't accept paper currency. Our biggest concern is you comin' back with the money. Don't get robbed and get back here with the money. Of course, it's the money made on this risky venture is what we are most interested in."

Henry said, "What about the men? When do we pay them?"

"Pay them as soon as you can after you get paid."

Randy said, "How much do we pay them? I want to write that down."

"It's basically like this. We have generous terms. You guys get $200 per month, and the rest of the trail hands get $60 a month. The wrangler get $50 a month, and the chuck wagon master gets $80 per month. We figure it should not take you more than three months to get there and sell our cattle, but that depends on the harshness of the weather and any other misfortunes which you may have on the trail. You'll be able to come back much faster … maybe in less than two months if your horses hold up. That leaves a lot of money left over to bring back here."

Henry was lost in all these numbers and said, "Anything else? There's much more to driving cattle than meets the eye."

Rudy said, "Yeah, There's plenty more. My main advice is to not get in a hurry. The cattle need to have time to graze and drink when they can. Our longhorns are tough and can go two days without drinking, but don't push it. Keep in mind it's about one thousand miles to where you're going. It's the job of the trail boss and the chuck wagon to find a good place to camp with good grazing and water sources. Also, you can't leave the herd unattended at night. You got to work in shifts to keep an eye on the cattle at night."

Randy was busy taking notes, so he didn't have time to ask all the questions he wanted, but the information he was getting from Rudy was more than he expected. He asked, "Anything else? That's already a lot."

"Yeah, there's plenty more, but anything I tell you will not be more important than firsthand experience on the trail with a big herd. There are many dangers, but for me, the most dangerous is a stampede. If your cattle stampede, you lose control, and you got to do all you can to settle them down so you can herd them again."

Henry was seized by Rudy's scary talk about stampedes, and his fear was palpable. Henry had to say, "I've never experienced a stampede. Why would a herd stampede?

"That's a good question for which nobody has a good answer. A sharp, loud sound can set them off. Thunder or pots falling out of the chuck wagon can set them off. Sometimes, their leaders just take off. Best to avoid any loud sounds at night and keep the herd well-grazed and watered."

Randy said, "If we ever get ourselves in a stampede situation, we'll be sure to get Ernesto's advice on what to do."

Rudy replied, "Yeah, good to get Ernesto's advice on everything, but a stampede is an exceptional event for which no man really knows how to handle. My only advice is to always keep your cattle content. If they get agitated for any reason, they are more likely to stampede, and that makes for one hell of a big problem."

With those words, Rudy excused himself and drifted away. Rick was dead serious when he said, "Boy, I hope we don't have any stampedes. I never thought of stampedes before, but now they're my worst nightmare."

# Chapter Forty-Nine
## Big Cattle Drive North

The next morning, they had their usual meeting with Rudy. He told them how Ernesto was breaking in a new team of oxen and making sure the commissary had all the items he needed to fill his chuck wagon to the brim. He also noted all the items they would need on the long trail and emphasized they had to make sure they had all they needed. He cited good boots, leather gloves, spurs, bandanas, chaps, lariats, slickers, wide-brimmed hats, and an extra set of clothes. He said, "If you don't have these items, go to the commissary and get them."

Randy was busy noting in his pad all the items Rudy mentioned and said, "Thanks. I guess we'll spend some time today at the commissary."

Rudy appeared distracted and said, "Excuse me. I need to scrounge up a Dutch oven and drinking water barrel for Ernesto. I also got to check on Rafael and his horses."

Henry noted, "We already saw the horses with Rafael... all looked good."

"Some of those horses are still too wild and need to be broken in to be ridable. That is what Rafael is concentrating on now. I want to see how he is doing. I also want to check in with the vaqueros to see how they are doing in rounding up your herd of cattle."

Randy said at that juncture, "Don't worry about us. By the time all is ready, we'll be rarin' to go."

Rudy laughed at the youthful exuberance displayed by Randy and said, "I hope this works. We're countin' on you guys to show us how our cattle surplus can make us money."

Henry said, "One thing for sure, you can count on us to make every effort to get the cattle to the Kansas market and to get the money exchanged for them back to you."

"We know all that; otherwise, we wouldn't be sendin' you. By the way, I think I may be able to get my hand on a new rifle for your sidekick.

Give me a couple of days."

Rick's ears were pricked by Rudy's last words, and in a meek voice, he said one word, "Wonderful."

Rudy left and went about his business. They walked slowly across the wide compound to the commissary, dodging tumbleweeds and being sprayed by dust picked up by the gusting south wind. It was hot and would get hotter. There was not a cloud in the sky, and the merciless spring drought continued. Henry sighed and said, "I hope there is some rain where we're goin' cuz we and our cattle need to drink. Let's hope that up north it's rainin' more than here."

They entered the commissary building, and after they shook the dust off, they spied leaning on the weathered wooden counter the same old man in charge. The man saw them and said, "Bout time you came. I've been expectin' you. I got three piles of stuff for you behind the counter. Come and see what I got for you."

It was a short walk to go around the counter to its backside. They found there the piles of stuff for them. Henry said, "I guess it's okay for us to bundle up this stuff and carry it back to our bunkhouse. We'll bring back anything we don't need."

The Anglo-elderly man responded in a long phrase in Spanish. They thought his use of Spanish was to show them he had been in these parts for a long time. His fluency in Spanish indicated to them that his wife was probably Hispanic. Anyway, they got his first few words. "No hay problema."

They took turns in loading their stuff on outstretched arms, calling on the manager to help them. They stumbled out the door that was held open by the manager, who said, "Que vayan con Dios."

They knew what those Spanish words met, but they were not sure if he was giving them a blessing for their return to their bunkhouse or if he was saying these words as a benediction of their long trek north. Whatever, they accepted his words to apply to both situations.

The manager's words quickly slipped their minds as they were trying to keep their loads balanced as they walked extra slowly back to the bunkhouse. Keeping a tight hold on their stuff in face of a stiff wind was a chore. They crashed into their bunkhouse... eager to spread their goods on their beds and see up close what they got and trying on the clothing items. For them, it was like having Christmas in June.

Henry closely examined his gifts, storing them neatly. He said, "Looks like I got everything I need. I don't know about you guys, but I'm ready to hit the trail for better or worse."

Randy and Rick stepped back to admire their gifts, and Randy uttered, "Me too. The sooner we get on the trail, the better for me."

Rick did not know what to say, but he had to say something, so he said, "I was born ready, and I love the open range."

Henry and Randy laughed heartily over Rick's words. After a bit, Henry said, "We should ride out tomorrow and check on how it's going in rounding up the herd we're goin' to drive north."

Randy and Rick grunted their assent, and Rick said, "Yeah. Good idea. This will give me a chance to check out the horse I'm goin' to have to ride. It has been a long time since I rode a horse, and I've never rode a mustang."

Rick's words added to the good mood that Henry and Randy were enjoying. They laughed again, and Henry said, "We better see Rafael about our horses and tack and riding out to the north pasture tomorrow. Of course, we'll need to tell Rudy."

They sat on the edge of their beds. Silence enveloped them as they all were in deep thought about the long trail ahead of them. They knew they were being assigned a big responsibility and that it would be a tough job to get their herd of cattle to a distant market. Randy wandered if they were really up to herding three thousand cattle across the prairie for nearly a thousand miles. He knew if they were lucky, it could take them three months or more to get to where they were going. He hoped that work on railway was progressing well and all would be in place to ship their cattle back East.

They did not look like much. Randy had doubts they could even successfully escort a large herd for months over such a long distance. He looked around himself, and he was less confident that they could do the job. His older brother was a steady hand, but this task and all the responsibility that went with it could break him. His brother was fine specimen of a man, always clean-shaven. He was tall with a muscular build and always polite but with an anxious trigger finger, ready to shoot first. He could do the work but was easily distracted and did not brook well anyone who crossed him.

The bearded and unshaven Rick had never driven cattle before and was a wanderer at heart. Before this job, he did as he pleased and went where he wanted when he wanted. He listened to his own drummer. He had been lucky to survive this long and was worried his life's changing circumstances would change his luck. He was a middle-aged, happy-go-lucky man who followed his own rainbows. He was not a drover and never would be.

Randy thought about himself and what he really wanted in life now that the war was over. He was in his late teens, and already, he was feeling the urge to settle down. He believed he belonged in an office setting somewhere back East instead of helping herd cattle in Texas. He should be putting his schooling to use. There were plenty of guys better than him for this job, and more were returning every day from the war. He looked at his lanky frame and, touched the straggly beard on his baby face, and told himself that he was miscast. He was convinced he could do better elsewhere, but he felt trapped by his current circumstances.

Randy thought it was folly for the ranch to entrust so much to them, but he could not say that. He was ready to try something else, but the world was changing so fast he did not know where to turn. Staying put and on course was the only option he had, but he had dreams of something better for him. For now, he did not want to bite the hand that fed him.

Henry broke the quiet interlude by standing up and saying, "Let's go see Rafael and our horses."

They moseyed across the wide dirt compound to the horse corral next to the big cotton warehouse. Rafael had separated his herd of horses into two groups… those broken and ready to ride and those which needed more breaking in. Henry greeted Rafael amicably and told him about their plan to ride out to the north pasture right after breakfast tomorrow. Rafael knew immediately what brought them his way and said, "I'll be there in the morning with your horses. This is a good way to test-ride your horses and tell me if you have any misgivings. You're getting the best of the lot."

Rafael was like all the other vaqueros. This was the only life he knew, and he wanted to be good at what he did. Henry and Rafael were envious of all his skills and wished they could match them. They were convinced you had to be born into this life to be really good at it. They felt like they were foreign interlopers, trying to meddle in areas that were best left alone. The main things that differentiated them from the dedicated vaqueros were their ability to read and write in English and the trust the boss had in them.

Henry and Randy were elites on the ranch, but they did not like their status. They did not consider it fair that because of their pale white skin, education level, and origins, they were trusted more than the people who would lay down their lives for the boss. For them, these loyal people had more to offer than they did. This was more their land than it could ever be for Henry and Randy. They saw it as a case of the 'outsiders' ruling over the indigenous people.

Henry and Randy knew thoughts like this were not productive and that they best accept things like they are and make the best of things. The whole world was out of kilter, and there was nothing they could do to restore balance, especially after a brutal civil war and its aftermath. Deep down, they wanted to go someplace far away where none of this mattered, but they did not know of such a place. There was no escape. It was all about accepting their current situation and satisfying expectations.

Rudy came barging into the bunkhouse to say, "I hear you goin' out to the north pasture tomorrow mornin.' Right?"

Henry quickly replied, "You heard right, but we can only go if you approve."

"I'll go with you. We got to agree that the herd is ready to go."

Randy, "That does it. We three we'll be ready to go with you tomorrow mornin' after breakfast."

The morning came fast, and breakfast was served earlier than usual. They were all in a good mood and eager to ride the few miles to the north pasture to see the herd they would help drive north. Rafael came to deliver their horses and said gleefully, "I brought an extra horse cause I'm goin too."

They finished their coffee and relieved themselves in back of the bunkhouse. Rafael handed the reins to Henry, Randy, and Rick. They quickly mounted their new horses. Rudy was already mounted and ready to go. When Rafael mounted his horse, Rudy took off in a whirl of dust. The other horses instinctively followed.

They did not try to catch Rudy. They were too busy trying to get used to their new horses. Rafael stayed appropriately at the back of the pack. Rick trailed even farther back. Rick was so far back that Randy turned his horse around and galloped back to see if anything was wrong. He yelled at Rick, "What's wrong?"

Rick yelled back, "Nothin' really. This horse is good, but I'm not used to goin' so fast. Sally was slow but sure. On this horse, I feel like I'm racing."

Randy laughed, "That's okay, but don't lose sight of us. Anyway, as our drag rider, it's good you get used to eating dust. You should've brought a bandana to cover your face."

"Don't worry about me. I'm right behind you. Anyway, it's not far."

Randy turned his horse around to gallop up to be alongside his brother. He liked the feel of his new horse. It felt good to be mounted again and out in the open. He said as much to Henry, who replied, "You got that right. This is the best I felt in a long time. I really hope our herd is ready to go because I'm more than ready."

Within an hour, they began to see gaggles of cattle which were part of their herd. They road slowly through the herd at Rudy's side. Rick had caught up with them, and Rafael was within earshot. They all liked what they saw... cows ready to move steadily north to market. Rudy was all smiles and stopped to say, "All looks good to me. Once you are on the move, the herd will sort out its leaders and followers. Just coax them to go in the direction you want to go. Let me know if there is anything that will keep you from startin' your drive in the next day or two."

Henry responded by saying, "All looks good to me, but I would like to hear from the men who will be goin' with us."

Rudy replied, "I thought you would say somethin' like that, so I've called a meetin' late this afternoon of all the men who will be on this drive. We'll be meetin' in the old cotton warehouse."

Henry smiled and said, "Great. We'll be there."

Randy did not know if this was a good time to bring up a subject that had been weighing on his mind, but he said anyway, "What about money? When are you goin' to give us some money just in case we got some expenses on this drive."

Rudy said, "Before you leave, is this not the right time to talk about this subject?"

As soon as Rudy said these words, he galloped off, saying, "See you back at the ranch."

Henry told Randy and Rick, "Look around you. These are our babies for the next few months. We got to get to know as many of them as possible. Take in their smell and get used to it. A lot depends on them to make our marketing scheme work. We lead on the trail while the vaqueros do all the work. We need to prove ourselves as drovers."

They arrived early for the meeting with their fellow drovers in the cavernous cotton warehouse. The vaqueros came as a group led by Ernesto, who held Rafael's hand, treating him like a son. The sat on the ground with their legs crossed or squatted. They formed a circle, which included the wooden bench Henry, Randy, and Rick sat on. It was quiet until Rudy appeared in the wide-open door, and all the vaqueros applauded his arrival. Rudy stepped into the circle and was given a big welcome in English and Spanish. He then said, "My Spanish is not good, so I will speak in English, and Ernesto will translate as necessary. I think all of you know the job that lies ahead of you. This meeting is mostly about introducing your trail leaders and to answer any questions you may have. I also want to set the date for your departure."

After a brief interlude while Ernesto made sure all the vaqueros understood what Rudy had just said, he introduced as young old timers, Henry and Randy, as the two men they had entrusted this drive to. He underscored that they knew the way as they had been there and back. He also noted that Ernesto could vouch for them because he had been with them.

After the clapping had died down, Rudy turned to Rick and said, "This is a man who is new to you. He knows the plains but has never been on cattle drive before, so we have put him in the drag position. By the way, he also saved the lives of Henry and Randy."

Rick was amazed at the applause he got. He could not believe the vaqueros were so endeared to him. He wanted to say something in acknowledgment of their loud applause but kept quiet.

Rudy said a few words about how rugged and long the task of herding three thousand cattle to Kansas would be. He emphasized how much he, the boss, and his wife were counting on then to deliver these cattle to market and return safe and sound before winter.

The group remained silent as Ernesto repeated in Spanish all that Rudy had said. When Ernesto was finished, Rudy asked, "Are there any questions?"

The vaqueros did not have any questions, so Henry broke in and said, "Looks like there is nothing more to discuss except our departure date."

Ernesto replied, "We are ready to go when you are ready."

Henry said, "We're ready."

Rudy ended all discussion by saying, "That settles it. You leave the day after tomorrow at the crack of dawn."

The vaqueros sang and danced. They were happy to be hitting the trail. Their happiness spread to Henry, Randy, and Rick, and they joined in the dancing with the vaqueros. Rudy drifted back to the bunkhouse, thinking. *Poor devils. I'm sure glad I'm not goin' with them. They really don't know how tough it is to drive a big herd of cattle across such treacherous territory.*

# Chapter Fifty
# Stampede

The cattle sensed something was up. Before the sun peaked over the eastern horizon, there were men on horseback and an oxen-drawn wagon in their midst. Vaqueros were taking up positions to herd the cattle to form one large group so they could begin pushing them north. The cattle did not want to budge, but, at the urgings of the vaqueros and their horses, they began to move, and one followed another.

Henry and Ernesto rode far in front of the herd to set the direction and search for the best way to join with the northern trail. Rafael followed Ernesto with his herd of horses. Randy stayed a healthy distance in front of the herd, trying to get the lead cattle to follow him. Rick was stuck in the back, keeping his eye out for any strays and potential dangers to the herd. The large herd was kicking up some dust, but he knew the dust coming his way would get worse when they hit the dry sections of the open range.

It took the better part of the first day to get the herd organized into a vast mass that moved slowly north. They found a safe pace at which to move forward. Their objective was to go twelve to fifteen miles a day. At that pace, they should be at the Nueces River in a few days. From now and until then, they practiced at herding cattle so they would be ready for a couple of months on the trail north, crossing nearly one thousand miles through Texas and Indian Territory, going into the heart of Kansas.

They arrived at the Nueces and crossed it without any mishap. All was working well, and the men, their horses, and the cattle were settling into a good rhythm. But as soon as they crossed the Nueces, a huge and turbulent storm blew rapidly in from the west, and they were drenched by heavy rain and pelted by large hail stones. Men and animals suffered. All movement ceased. All was thrown into disarray, and the vaqueros fought against the odds stacked against them to maintain order in the herd.

All the men donned their slickers, but they did little good against the cloudburst. Ernesto, and Rafael, and his horses sought refuge under a patch of mesquite trees. The cattle dispersed in all directions, seeking shelter from the hell delivered by the heavens. Henry and Randy huddled together under the flimsy branches of an old mesquite tree. Rick stood his ground in spite of the deluge, but he did not know if that was what he was supposed to do. He tried to console himself by thinking at least he did not have to be covered in dust.

Overall, it was a chaotic mess, and would take a change to better weather to get all the cattle together again. Any way you looked at it, this was a setback that would take them a couple of good weather days from which to recover. The men were hungry because they had not eaten, because Ernesto could not light a fire and cook for them as usual. They expected hard times, but not so early in the drive. Some of them entertained thoughts of quitting and going home before they were too far away from the part of the country they knew.

Ernesto struggled to maintain discipline and obedience to a greater cause among the vaqueros. He borrowed one of Rafael's horses and rode around to each vaquero, telling them that this kind of weather was to be expected, and they owed it to their manhood to stick with it and do the job they were assigned. Quitting now would stain them with shame for the rest of their lives.

Over the next couple of sunny days, they worked hard to find stragglers and put the herd back together. Henry estimated that they had only lost a few head. Nothing to worry about compared to the losses he expected on the long trek ahead. For sure, they would arrive with less than the three thousand head they started with, but the drive would still be lucrative. No matter what, he was determined to get to Kansas so he could show that it was possible to cross the great plains with a large herd and market them for a handsome profit. All else paled for him next to this goal.

They were all set to keep moving north. Henry gave the signal to Ernesto and his fellow drovers to move out. He spoke briefly to Ernesto before taking up a position far ahead of the herd. Henry said, "Let's keep movin. We got to do this."

Randy overheard Henry's brief remarks and muttered to himself, "Yes, we got to do this."

While he said these words to himself, he reached down to check if all the gold coins Rudy had given him the night before he left the ranch were deep in his saddle bag. He had wrapped them in his extra bandana and put other items on top of this heavy bundle. This was their trail money, and he was bound to guard it with his life. He told no one... not even his older brother... of the existence of this stash of money.

Within a few days, they had re-captured their rhythm and were moving the herd steadily north. Over supper, Ernesto expressed his concern that the heavy rains would make the crossing of some creeks perilous. Henry replied, "We'll deal with that the best we can when we have to."

They did not have to wait long before Henry could see what Ernesto was talking about. They had arrived at a swollen creek that was too deep to cross. Randy scouted up and down the creek, looking for a good place for them and their herd to cross. He found no good place to cross. His negative report prompted Ernesto to suggest that they camp here for a couple of days until the water went down. Henry saw no alternative, so he agreed with Ernesto, saying, "Okay. Let's camp here and take advantage of ample water and green grass for the cattle to graze on."

For the vaqueros, they kept working, tending to the herd, making sure each cow was given the attention it needed, rotating groups of cows to drink at the water's edge. Their work continued night and day. They worked in shifts, so there was always one or more of them overlooking the welfare of the cattle. Henry, Randy, and Rick were impressed at how expert they did their work and how they did it with much gaiety. They did not want to admit it, but they were learning much from the vaqueros.

After a couple of uneventful days camped on the creek bank, Henry and Ernesto decided the water had receded enough to allow for safe crossing. Their main concern was getting Ernesto's wagon across the fast-moving water. They chose a spot for the crossing and decided Rafael should cross first with his horses to test the depth and the solidity of the riverbed. Rafael said he could swim, if necessary, and it would be normal for his horses to swim.

Rafael and his horses struggled against the creek's current but made it safely to the other side. This was a good sign, and Ernesto drove his wagon into the water. When the wagon and its oxen were fully in the creek, they found that the wagon wheels could not touch the bottom, and the wagon began to float downstream. Rafael jumped into the creek grabbed ahold of the wagon, trying to settle it. He cried for help, and two vaqueros removed their boots and dove into the creek to steady the wagon.

Henry, Randy, and Rick watched helplessly as the wagon was carried by the current downstream. They could see items coming out of the wagon to join the flotsam. Luckily, there was a bend in the creek bed where the brown water was shallower, and the wagon stopped drifting. Ernesto guided the water-soaked wagon onto the opposite bank. Rafael and his fellow vaqueros were busy trying to fetch the items that came out of the wagon.

Henry swallowed hard after regarding this spectacle and said, "We're lucky. Give Ernesto a day to dry out, and we'll be on our way. Nobody said this drive would be easy. Now, let's get these cattle to the other side."

Upon Henry's hand signal, the vaqueros began pushing the herd into the water. They knew once they could get some of the cattle started, the others would follow. Once some cattle reached the other side, the rest quickly followed. Some cattle lost their footing, or they could not touch firmly the riverbed and drifted downstream. Some vaqueros were busy tracking these cattle and saving them from drowning by lassoing them and pulling them to safety.

Randy tried to help but found he was of little help. No doubt they had lost some head in this hazardous crossing. Each head lost meant less money to take back to the ranch. He assumed that Rudy would understand that these losses were expected, given the multitude of challenges they faced on the long trail.

After all the cattle were driven to the other side of the creek, Henry, Randy, and Rick tied their boots around their necks and rode their horses across the creek without any difficulty. Their smooth ride to the other side prompted Henry to say, "We should have waited another day for the water to go down. Oh well, you live and learn."

Ernesto and Rafael were busy taking everything out of the wagon and spreading it on the grassy ground and mesquite bushes so it could dry. Ernesto saw Henry ride up and said, "Give us this day to dry out. We'll be ready to move early tomorrow. Meanwhile, the vaqueros can hunt rabbits and any varmints they come across to add some meat to our diet."

Rick eagerly said, "I've hunted my whole life to stay alive. I'll also spend the day hunting for anything with four legs that moves."

The childish way Rick said his words got them all to laugh, and Henry said, "Well, what are you waitin' for? Go hunt."

Some vaqueros were arranging the large herd, which stretched almost a mile long for tomorrow's leg of the long drive. Henry rode around, checking on the men and the cattle. It was finally beginning to sink into him that this was a big, complicated, and risky job. And there was a lot of money on the line. These cattle were worth next to nothing in Texas, but if they could sell them for markets that catered to the meat-hungry Easterners, they were worth $30 to $40 a head. Thus, he was responsible for a herd worth around $100,000. An astronomical fortune!

Henry was not good at numbers, so he related his thoughts to Randy, who could run the numbers in his head. Randy said, "I'm way ahead of you. I've done these calculations in my head over and over. If we can sell these cattle for the Eastern market, we'll make our boss super-rich. Of course, his dealings in the cotton trade already made him rich. I hope he gets his presidential pardon so he can enjoy his wealth, which will grow with the more cattle he sells."

Henry said, "I'm curious. How much will the boss net after he pays all of us?"

Randy quipped, "We're gettin' chicken feed compared to what he's makin.' We do all the work and take all the risks so he can roll in deep clover. I estimate that after he pays all of us off and miscellaneous trail expenses, he gets ninety-five percent or more of the cattle sales receipts. Somethin's wrong here. But they're his cattle, and without the cattle, we wouldn't have a job."

"Henry, you'll get no argument from me. What we get is a pittance compared to what he gets. Maybe it's a good thing the men have not done the numbers, so they don't know how much they are gettin' screwed. I wonder how many cattle drives it will take before they wake up. It's like we're sacrificing and putting our lives on the line so a rich man in the big house gets richer. I guess that is how life is… nothing fair about it."

The hunting was good. They ate all the roasted rabbit meat they could stomach. All was in order to move out early tomorrow morning. During the following day, they regained their rhythm and were entering a dryer land on the open range. This land was suffering from drought in spite of the rain clouds that passed overhead. They could see these clouds dropping some rain on spots in the distance. In some instances, they witnessed bolts of dry lightning streaking to Earth in the distant blue sky.

Henry spotted a plume of black smoke on the horizon. He assumed that the lightening had set the prairie ablaze. He knew they were no match for a wildfire and frantically rode back to confer with Ernesto about what they should do. It did not take long for Ernesto to respond. "Let's go east and see if we can dodge the fire or find a creek with water. We got to get out of the fire's path."

Henry immediately signaled to Randy to guide the big herd east. He pointed to the smoke on the distant horizon so he would know why they were heading east. In turn, Randy signaled to the vaqueros to begin turning the cows eastward. They all knew that turning a large herd to go a different direction was not an easy thing to do, and it would take time and a lot of effort. But staying clear of fire was well worth it.

Henry rode far out to keep an eye on the fire. He was pleased to see that the menacing fire was burning itself out. He rode back to tell Ernesto that it appeared the fire was no longer a threat. Ernesto suggested they bring the herd to a halt and allow the cattle to graze before continuing. Henry replied, "Good idea. Let's do it."

They made their camp, and Ernesto and Rafael whipped up some hot food and coffee. The sun was setting, and there was a gentle westerly breeze. Night was falling. The men made their bed rolls as they watched the lightening in the west. They could see quite a storm developing in the distant west, but all was calm where they were. The thing that disturbed them the most was the cattle were made nervous by the loud cracking sound of thunder made by the lightening.

All the vaqueros were busy with trying to calm down the herd. The lightening and the thunder it made were getting closer. The vaqueros feared the cattle would stampede if the thunder continued. A stampede was their worst nightmare, representing life-threatening dangers and cattle losses. They silently prayed while they attempted to calm the herd, especially its leaders.

They wished there were some moonlight so they could see better. With each flash of lightening, they looked fast to see where action was needed. Ernesto was up and nervously watching the lightening. He told the others still in camp, "Get up and have your horses ready to go. We got to be on a high estampida alert."

Everyone in camp did as Ernesto said while watching the lightening and hearing the loud roll of thunder. Suddenly, Ernesto yelled at the top of his voice, "There they go. Every man got to try to stop them, or we'll be left with nothin'. Rafael, keep your horses calm. I'll make sure my oxen don't join in the hysteria."

Henry, Randy, and Rick took off toward the herd upon hearing

Ernesto's words, but they did not have a clue about how to stop a stampede. They saw the cattle charging at a fast clip and spotted a few vaqueros riding erratically within the herd. They did not know what to do. Even if they got close to a vaquero, none of them spoke English. All they knew is that the stampede had to be stopped, or all was lost.

Ernesto turned over his oxen and the camp to Rafael and rode out to join the frightened and perplexed trio. He said, "You got to get out in front of the herd and turn them back. It's a hard and dangerous job, but it has to be done."

Henry and Randy took off as soon as Ernesto finished speaking. Rick stayed behind, saying, "I hardly know how to ride a horse, so how can I get in front of a running herd?"

Ernesto said, "That's okay. Two men and the vaqueros should be enough. You stay with me. If they're successful in slowing the herd, we can help do clean up."

Henry and Randy raced alongside the fast-moving herd and did their best to join two other vaqueros who were working feverishly to turn the herd and stop the stampede. They were all thankful that the lightning and thunder had ceased. It appeared that the stampede speed of the herd was slowing, and the vaqueros were having some success in turning the herd back into itself.

The herd was beginning to settle down. Henry looked around for Randy and did not see him. He backtracked, looking for his brother, but could not find him. When Ernesto and Rick rode up and in a panic, he said loudly, "Where's my brother?"

They shook their heads, and Ernesto said, "We don't know. We'll have to wait for daylight to look for him and see what all this estampida has cost us."

"I got to find my brother. For me, he's worth more than all the cattle in Texas."

Ernesto replied sympathetically, "I understand. Finding him will be our top priority once we have some light. He probably fell off his horse and is lying somewhere in the tall grass. If so, we risk our horses stepping on him."

"I can't lose my brother. I got to stay close to him. I'll stay here all night, looking for him on foot. Go and make sure the cattle are all right. I'll stay here with my brother. He's the only family I still got."

# Chapter Fifty-One
# Licking Wounds

Henry walked about through the tall grass all night long, looking for his brother. He found his horse hiding near a mesquite stand and still shaking in fright. He was exhausted, but he had to find his little brother. Daylight began to erase the darkness of night. Henry could see more clearly now, but his brother was nowhere to be seen.

He feared his brother's body had been mashed into the ground by the stampeding herd. His fears mounted, and he was worried about his own life … he did not think he could live without his younger brother. He called out incessantly for his brother, hoping for some response, but all his frantic calls were met by silence.

He was losing hope of finding his brother when he heard a slight whimpering sound coming from behind himself. His instincts told him to turn cautiously to where the sound was coming from. There, about ten yards from him was the image of his brother. He could not believe his eyes. His brother stood weakly before him. Randy was bloody and bruised, but he was alive.

Henry rushed to his brother's side and had him put his arm around his shoulders so he could help him walk back to camp. His brother looked like he had been in a fight for his life. Randy was too weak and beat up to talk. Henry told him, "Take it easy. Don't try to talk. Let's get you back to camp so you can rest, and we can doctor you."

The important thing for Henry was getting his younger brother back to camp so Ernesto could check him over and administer any remedies he had at his disposal. It took them a good while to hobble back to camp. A couple of times, they had to sit down so Randy could rest his hurting body. As they approached the camp, Henry called out to Ernesto, "Help. I'm comin' with my injured brother."

There was no reply to his call. They limped into camp to find Ernesto huddled in prayer with his head bowed with most of the vaqueros. He placed his brother on the ground near Ernesto's wagon and walked slowly over to the group to see what they were praying about. He peered through the circle of men to see lying on the ground next to a grave hole the body of one of the vaqueros.

He took off his hat and stood behind Ernesto with his head bowed. He wanted to concentrate on the dead man's funeral, but his grief for the dead was overcome by his worry about his brother and the continuation of their cattle drive north. With the herd scattered, a vaquero dead, and his brother severely injured, what hope was left?

Henry waited patiently for the man to be given his last rites and laid to rest in a hastily dug shallow grave. The men erected a crude cross on top of the grave confectioned from some dead mesquite branches. For him, the man's death was caused by the stampede and should be mourned deeply by all. On the other hand, he knew no one would care to hear this sad story because the man was Mexican.

When Ernesto turned, Henry expressed his profound condolences for the death of the vaquero and then said with a sense of urgency, "I found my brother. He's hurt somethin' terrible. Please check him out. I laid him down next to your wagon."

Ernesto did not say a word. He walked quickly to Randy's prostrate body and began checking him over. He completed his inspection of Randy's bloody, scratched body and somberly said, "He's lucky to be alive. I've got to clean his wounds and bandage him where needed. Let's gently undress him and bed him down so I can work on him."

They carried Randy's semi-conscious body to a shady spot beneath a mesquite tree. Henry slowly removed his clothes. Ernesto came with a bucket of water, soap, and his medical kit. He began washing every wound and applying some kind of salve. He applied bandages on the deeper wounds. He whispered to Henry, "He's beat up pretty bad. He must have fallen off his horse and been dragged by his horse for some distance. What did he tell you?"

"He hasn't said anything yet. He can't talk. But we can talk a little when you're finished doctoring him."

Ernesto finished working on Randy and returned to his wagon to find Henry waiting for him. Ernesto said, "Let him rest. When he comes to, I'll feed him some of my special rabbit stew. He'll heal, but it will take some time."

"What do you think? Is this drive still doable? My brother can't work, and one vaquero is dead. And our cattle are scattered. How can we continue?"

Ernesto hesitated before he replied to Henry, "True, this is a serious setback, but we have no choice but to keep moving north with the cattle we have left."

"But how?"

Ernesto had already thought about all the angles and said, "Your brother will sit next to me in the wagon until he's well. One of the vaqueros on the flank will replace him on point. We'll stay here for a couple of days so we can lick our wounds and our cattle have settled down."

Henry mulled over Ernesto's words and said, "Okay. That makes sense. But it's a shame that all this had to happen so early in our drive."

Ernesto, in a nonplussed fashion, commented, "I hope it doesn't happen again, but it could, so we got to be prepared for anything."

Henry said, "Let's see how many cattle the vaqueros are able to round up before we decide on too much. By the way, has anybody seen Rick?"

"Nope," replied Ernesto.

"Well, I'm goin' to find my horse and look for him. He should have been safe in his drag spot."

"See you later. Don't worry about your brother. I'll keep a close eye on him."

Henry walked to the spot where he had left his horse. He took the reins of his horse in his hands and saw his brother's horse nearby. He knew his brother was hiding money on his horse, so he also took the reins of his horse and attached them to his horse. It was best that he not let his brother's horse out if his sight.

He mounted his horse and rode south to look for Rick, with his brother's horse trailing behind them. He looked far and wide for Rick and did not see him until he called aloud his name. Rick came out of the eastern sunlight, herding a dozen or so stray steers. When he got close enough to Henry, he said excitedly, "Boy, that was somethin'. I never saw cattle run so fast in my life. The whole herd disappeared in front of me. I was lost until daylight. Not knowing what else to do, I stood my ground til I could see and rounded up all the strays I could see, but where's the herd?"

Henry explained to Rick all that had happened. After hearing what Henry had to say about their calamitous situation, Rick had trouble expressing himself but said, "I guess riding drag is lucky. Any other position could have meant my death. I'm startin' to like drag."

In spite of everything, Rick's words made Henry chuckle before he said, "Let's herd these strays a bit farther and go to camp for some grub."

"Good. I'm mighty hungry."

They rode into camp to find Ernesto and Rafael busy around a cooking fire. Ernesto looked up and saw Henry and Rick coming and said, "Come and get it before the flies do."

Henry and Rick did not waste any time finding places to tether their horses where they could graze. The rushed to grab their plates of food and ate like starving men, which they were. Ernesto observed the gusto with which they were consuming their food and said, "Eat up. There's more from where that came from. The vaqueros are eating in shifts. Your brother is healing well. I fed him some soup. Maybe he can talk to you now. We should be able to leave with our smaller herd now."

Ernesto's last words stung Henry's ears, and he asked, "How many cows do you think we lost?"

"Maybe a couple hundred."

Henry replied, "Well, that's a lot of money, but we still have a big herd for the Kansas market. I'm goin' to see my brother now."

Rick had finished licking his plate clean and said, "Seconds?"

Henry dropped to his knees to talk with his convalescing little brother, who's first words were, "Where's my horse?"

"Don't worry. Your horse and all its tack is safely in the camp. Now, tell me, what happened to you?"

Randy slowly explained, "I don't quite know. My horse was bumped hard by one of the stampeding steers. I fell off the saddle but caught my foot in the stirrup and was dragged through the grass for a while. I guess I was knocked cold cuz I didn't hear anything til you began calling my name."

"Get some rest and get better fast. You'll sit next to Ernesto in the wagon til you feel well enough to take up your point position again. See you later. I got a few things to take care of."

Ernesto and Raphael were still hovering over the cooking fire. Henry asked Ernesto, "What time we leavin' tomorrow?"

"Let's try to leave at sunup."

"That suits me fine. We got to make up for lost time. Still, a lot of

Texas to get through before we cross the Red River into Indian Territory."

"This is only our second week on the trail north. We got maybe another month before we see the 'Red'. Let's hope nothin' else bad happens to us and the herd."

Henry ended the conversation with Ernesto by saying, "I'll ride out and check how the vaqueros have rounded up our herd and pass the word about our departure early tomorrow."

Henry rode out of the camp to do his job of trail boss. He spent several hours going around the big herd and greeting the vaqueros. He tried to say the best he could that they planned to leave at dawn tomorrow. The vaqueros acknowledged his position of authority by tipping their sombreros. They did not understand his English, but they knew Ernesto would tell them about the same thing in Spanish.

As planned, they got the herd moving north early the next day. In spite of all their travails, they were happy to be moving forward again in the hot and dusty open range. Each day was the same. As long as they moved steadily ahead without mishaps, they were content with the progress they were making.

After a few uneventful weeks driving the cattle northward, they came to the Red River. Randy had healed enough to take up his point position again. He and Henry rode up and down the 'Red,' looking for the bend where the shallower waters that would make easier their crossing.

They camped on the south bank of the 'Red' for a couple of days, allowing their animals to graze and drink water. Henry and Ernesto talked and decided if the next day were clear, they would cross the river into Indian Territory and keep heading north to Kansas. The word was passed around about the crossing so everyone would be ready tomorrow.

As usual, Raphael crossed first with his horses. He was followed by Ernesto and his oxen-drawn wagon. Then the vaqueros started urging the herd leaders to go across the 'Red' to its north bank. It took all day, but the herd came across in a natural way. Henry and Ernesto were pleased by the crossing.

The last bunch of steers were being guided across the fast-flowing waters of the 'Red' by a couple of vaqueros on horseback when one of the vaqueros screamed the Spanish word, "Socorro," for help. His horse was stuck and sinking. Evidently, his horse had stepped into quicksand.

Raphael was quick to grab his lasso and one of his horses. He rode as far as he dared into the edge of the water and tossed the lasso to the stuck vaquero, asking him to attach it to his horse so he could pull them both to safety. This should have worked, but it did not.

The horse kept sinking. The vaquero jumped off his saddle into the water while holding on to the taunt rope. He reached under the water and pulled on his horse's stuck front legs as hard as he could. At the same time, Raphael and his horse kept pulling on the lasso. Every time the vaquero pulled on his horse's legs, he signaled to Raphael to pull harder.

It was with some relief for everyone that the vaquero and his horse started moving through the red water to the north bank of the river. Ernesto turned to Henry and said, "It's time to celebrate. I've been saving back some specialty food items for just such an occasion."

"Sounds like a good idea to me. Let's set up camp and get on with celebrating our crossing of the 'Red' and arrival in Indian Territory."

While they were all sitting around the campfire listening to one vaquero playing a melancholy tune on a guitar that Ernesto had stored in his wagon, they munched on roasted rabbit meat and some small fish the vaqueros had caught in the river. It was a joyful occasion. One vaquero stood up with his sombrero in his hand and thanked God for getting them this far and asking Him to bless the remainder of the journey.

Henry, Randy, and Rich sat side-by-side, enjoying immensely the moment. Randy asked Henry if could remember the first time they had crossed the 'Red', and Henry retorted, "Of course, I remember being led to the river by Jesse and his Indian companions. Boy, it would really be something if we ran into him again. After all, we are doin' what he said to do... follow his trading trail."

Randy said, "I wonder if he and his people ever found any buffalo. If they didn't, I don't see how they survived the winter."

"Maybe it's better we don't think such thoughts and concentrate on the tasks we have to do to get this herd to the Kansas marketplace."

Randy said, "You're right. No sense in reminiscing over the past. What is past is past. We should know that better than anyone."

They all slept comfortably on their bedrolls. It was a beautiful starlit night. They were soothed by the sound of the river water flowing by and the gentle wind blowing across the endless prairie. They were eager to get on their way so they could see if they could drive a large herd of cattle to a place in Kansas where there was a new railroad spur for the marketing of Texas beef to the satisfaction of the appetites of eastern consumers.

# Chapter Fifty-Two
# Freezing to Death

Indian Territory was kind to them. It was hot, and the drought continued, but the great plains spread out before them with a variety of grasses that were all edible by their cattle. There were an increasing number of creeks which were easy to cross but with enough water for their herd to drink. Near the creeks were also growing different kinds of trees. There was also more wild game to hunt to supplement their diet. Somehow, they found the rolling plains of the Indian Territory more pleasant than the huge flat expanses of the open dry range in Texas.

The going in Indian Territory was so much easier than they had experienced in Texas that Henry was prompted to say to Ernesto, "This is easy compared to Texas."

Ernesto replied, "Don't let this country fool you. It can unleash some harsh surprises in a spur of a moment. Don't forget that we are in tornado country."

Henry had never heard the word 'tornado' before, so he asked, "What's a tornado? Is it the same as a twister? I've been scared in this same territory by one of them."

"I can't explain it. You have to see it to understand what I mean. If a tornado drops from storm clouds, it can kill us all. Bein' in the path of a tornado is worst thing that could happen to us."

It was hard for Henry to imagine anything worse than what they had already experienced, but he took Ernesto at his word and, scanned the clear blue skies, and said, "No tornadoes in the sky. I count on you to tell us what to do if a tornado crosses our trail."

"I'm counting on us being lucky and entering Kansas in a few days. Encountering a tornado would be the kind of bad luck that we don't need."

"Well, I'll add the word, 'tornado', to my vocabulary," said Henry as he returned to a distant point in front of the herd.

After a couple weeks of sitting with Ernesto, Randy was well enough to return to his position as the full-time point rider. They all had changed horses, so their mounts were fresh and energetic. Raphael had done a good job of managing the remuda.

While they had hoped to cross Jesse and his band, they crossed into Kansas without even knowing it. A passing frontiersman told them that this was Kansas. When they got to the sandy banks of the Arkansas River, they knew for sure they were in Kansas. The wide, shallow river with murky water was easy to cross. They were careful to avoid any quicksand and keep the herd moving across the river. They also avoided any of the small settlements which were cropping up across the prairie. Farmers and sheep herders did not mix well with a large herd of Texas cattle.

They were almost giddy over the prospect of arriving in the valley near Mud City in a couple of weeks. It was hard for them to believe they would be at their destination after a little more than three months on the trail. The day arrived when Henry told Ernesto, "I'm goin' to ride well ahead to scout out the territory and to make sure we're on the right track. If I'm not back by nightfall, don't be concerned."

Ernesto grunted his assent, and Henry took off at a gallop to find the well-watered valley with thick grass cover for their cattle to graze on for days if needed. It was the next day before Henry returned to tell Ernesto and his companions. "We're almost there. Straight ahead is the promised land. There's only one big catch... the rail head has not yet reached Mud City. Therefore, we'll have to camp out with our herd until it does. The rail head should be finished in a couple of months. Then, we can ship our cattle back East and start the long trek back home."

Henry's words caused quite a stir. Randy was the first to react, "We didn't count on the railroad not being finished and thus obliging us to spend extra time outside Mud City. Is there no one who would like to buy our cattle so we can get our money and go back to our ranch?"

Henry eyed his younger brother in a way that indicated his displeasure over his question and simply said, "That's something I got to look into."

The vaqueros were disgruntled, and it was all Ernesto could do to quiet them down and assure them the cattle would be sold and they would get their pay. Ernesto turned to Henry and said, "Please don't make light of the fact that the railroad has not reached Mud City yet. With no link to the railroad, we can't sell our cattle. We have proven that we can drive cattle this far, but what good is that if we can't sell our cattle?"

Henry scratched his head and said, "Where there is a will, there is a way. We'll sell our cattle at a good price and be well on our way home before winter sets in. The rail line is coming, and when they know we're waitin' for them with lots of cattle, it will come faster."

Ernesto listened to Henry's words with a look of incredulity on his face and said dryly, "I hope you're right and not just saying a lot of wishful garbage to get me and the men to go along."

Henry sensed Ernesto's rancor, but he was not discouraged and said, "Don't worry. We'll sell our cattle, pay the men, and go home."

Henry put on a happy face, but deep down, he was worried. He felt like a fool. He had helped drive at great sacrifice a cattle herd almost a thousand miles to a railhead that did not exist. He was counting on the rail line spur to be completed quickly so he could sell his cattle to a willing buyer and start heading south with his men. His fate and that of his men depended on the speed with which the new rail line was constructed.

The grassy valley bordered by a river was there as expected, but the rail line needed to haul their cattle to eastern markets was not there as planned. Their cattle were worth a lot, but they were worth nothing if you could not sell them. They could fatten their cattle up on the good pasture, but for what purpose if there was no market for them.

Henry tried to raise the spirits of the men by telling them the railroad was coming. In anticipation of the arrival of the Kansas Pacific Railway, the settlement of Mud City was growing, and new buildings were being constructed. He told the men they should be proud of being the first to ship cattle east on the new rail line.

Privately, Ernesto told Henry, "The men are tired and want to go home, so your pep talks are falling on deaf ears."

Randy also pulled Henry to aside and said, "We got to get rid of our cattle and start heading back to Santa Rosita. Waiting here for weeks is more than any of us bargained for. We got to find a buyer for our cattle, even if we have to sell them for a lower price per head."

Every day, Henry rode into Mud City to get the advice of the people living there as to what he should do. Nobody had any good ideas about what he should do with his cattle. Some people thought he should drive the cattle east toward Kansas City, but Henry was afraid to do that because he would meet resistance from farmers of this more heavily populated area. He would also be in violation of the quarantine boundary established by the state government that prohibited Texas longhorns because of the ticks they carried. The last thing he wanted was to get local farmers up in arms because tick fever was killing their livestock.

Another idea was to sell some head to the military if it could release men from Fort Riley to herd the cattle to the places they needed them. Henry was thinking of going to Ft. Riley himself to see if this were possible. He was ready to do anything to be relieved of the responsibility for such a large herd, but he could not go home empty-handed.

None of these ideas were practical. There was nothing for Henry to do but wait for the rail line to reach Mud City. His worries increased as much cooler weather set in, and winter was just around the corner. He turned to Randy and desperately said, "Any ideas about what we can do to get out of this jam?"

"None."

"I've asked everyone except Rick. Maybe I should ask him. You never know what he has to say."

"Forget it. He's gone."

"What do you mean?"

"He said this drover life is not for him, and he sneaked off alone several days ago. He was afraid to tell you and didn't want to argue with anyone. He just wanted to leave and enjoy the freedom he had before to roam about as he pleased. He didn't care about the money, but I gave him a few coins. I also let him keep his horse."

"I can't believe that Rick left just like that without saying goodbye."

Randy reluctantly said, "If you were not my brother, I would have gone with him. I don't blame him for leavin'. If I had known we were herding cattle all this way for no good reason, I would have left a long time ago."

Henry did not like being on the outs with his brother. After a long period of silence, Henry asked Randy, "What are we going to do? Winter is coming. We got to get out of here, or we and our cattle will freeze to death."

Randy replied, "I've thought about this a lot, and I don't have an answer. It's like we're damned if we leave, and we're damned if we don't. I don't think we're ready yet to abandon our cattle."

As they talked around their dying campfire, it was getting much colder. The men had never been in such cold weather before. Henry knew he had to do something to keep his men and cattle from freezing to death. He didn't know what to do about the cattle but assumed many head would perish in the cold weather.

The men needed the warmth that they could get only from fire. They collected wood and built a bigger campfire for them to sleep around. But they did not have clothes for the kind of bitter cold winter that was known in this part of Kansas.

The cattle huddled together for added warmth. They had never experienced such cold. The men almost leaped into the fire to get the warmth their cold bodies needed to stay alive. Henry arranged a deal with the owner of the stagecoach depot to allow his men to stay inside his small station house. He got some money from Randy to pay the owner for sleeping privileges and the burning of firewood in the iron stove that was installed in the depot house.

The men almost slept on top of each other. They stayed warm and ate all their meals inside. When they had to relieve themselves, they rushed outside and returned as quickly as they could. They found it excessively boring to stay cooped up inside for days, but it was better than being outside in the freezing cold.

They could not believe they were trapped by a severe Kansas winter. On clear days when the wind died down, they would take turns checking on their cattle and horses. When a man returned from the cattle pasture, he would tell Ernesto how many dead cattle he had found. Ernesto would then pass the word on to Henry. This time, he said, "I estimate that at least one-third of our herd has frozen to death. We'll be lucky to have more than a one thousand head left come spring."

"This means we will have lost two-thirds of the herd we started with. This is so sad. I don't know how I can ever explain this to Rudy. I'm sure he and everyone else at Santa Rosita are wondering what happened to us and our herd."

"Yes, sad as can be. It almost brings me to tears when I think of how many of our cattle have frozen to death. On the next clear day, I'll go out myself and try to understand better the herd we have left to work with. I feel sorry for the cattle. We brought them all this way only to freeze to death."

The scruffy middle-aged owner was happy to rent out his store. It was a real windfall of money for him. Normally, he got little business in the wintertime, and now he was able to rent his station house, get money for firewood, and sell some food items he had in stock. He was sad for the drovers and their cattle, but their folly was good fortune for him. He was the only winner in this sad episode.

A clear day with no wind and blue skies prompted Ernesto to venture out to do a sort of damage assessment. A shivering Raphael saddled a horse in the adjoining stable and brought it to Ernesto so he could quickly mount it from the front door of the store. He handed the reins to a waiting Ernesto and ducked back into the much warmer inside.

Ernesto had his blanket wrapped around him and wore all the clothes he possessed. He began his lonely trek through deep snow for the mile or so to the wide valley where they had left the herd. He saw a lot of cattle carcasses lying in the snow, but he knew there were more carcasses hidden beneath the snow. The cattle still standing surrounded him, thinking he brought the care and feed they needed.

In spite of the cold sinking into his old bones, Ernesto was determined to get a better picture of what remained of their herd. He crisscrossed the valley and was heading back to the station store when a huge winter storm swept in behind him. He had been caught unawares in a blinding blizzard. He could no longer see where he was going. He became lost as the driven snow sent him and his horse to their deathly fate.

Ernesto did not know he was freezing to death. He thought it was normal not to feel the exposed parts of his face. He became worried when he could no longer feel his hands or feet. He fought to stay awake and keep moving, but his old body succumbed progressively to the deathly grip of the bitter cold.

The weakened and half-frozen Ernesto fell to the ground and was covered by the unrelenting snow. His horse waited for him to re-mount, but when he did not, the horse also fell to the ground to be frozen stiff by the snowy onslaught and the below-zero weather. They both had frozen to death and would lay where they fell until their bodies were revealed by the melting snow.

When Ernesto did not return to the stage house before the end of the short winter day, everyone became alarmed. The vaqueros were besides themselves. Rafael turned to hide his face in a corner to sob. Henry and Randy were overcome by the monumental loss of Ernesto. They knew this was the end of the most respected and oldest member of their crew.

375

It was a sleepless night for all of them. The vaqueros were organizing a search party. They were at their wits end. Henry worked to stop them from venturing out by saying aloud, "Look outside and see how deep the snow is, and the storm has not stopped yet. Even if Ernesto is still alive, you won't be able to find him, and you put your own lives in danger."

Raphael translated into Spanish what Henry said and told Henry and Randy what they said, "We don't care. For Ernesto, we give our lives."

Randy muttered to Henry, "We're lost. All is lost. We started as giant killers with good intentions, and we've ended as the lowest of the low. Maybe we should flee this life like Rick did."

# Chapter Fifty-Three
## Selling Out

The bad smell in their small log station house was intolerable. The seven men crammed into the room for weeks had created an awful odor. They tried to keep the front door open a crack to allow for some ventilation and dampen the smell of dirty bodies and clothes, but doing this provided little relief and let the frigid air in.

When they went outside to relieve themselves, they stayed as long as they could stand the bitter cold weather, but that did nothing to reduce their high level of misery. Since the disappearance of Ernesto, they no longer checked on the welfare of the herd. They only cared about getting out of their frozen confinement and heading back home in southern Texas.

Rafael stepped in and cooked instead of Ernesto. He also continued to tend to the remaining horses and the stable attached to the rustic house. He gave the care of the horses a high priority because, without horses, they could never escape from their frigid prison and make their way home. Rafael was the busiest of the vaqueros and had become a man in his own right.

Henry and Randy did not know what to do. They were in a miserable state and scraping the bottom of life itself. They knew it was about time for Christmas and the New Year, but they did not have the strength to do anything to distinguish these special days. The entire tiny community was hunkered down in their dirt-roofed abodes, waiting for a warm break in the winter weather.

They had a good supply of firewood, but as the stack of wood dwindled, they worried if they would have enough to outlast the unusually cold and prolonged winter. Then it happened suddenly. The snow stopped blowing, and the sun appeared in a clear blue sky. The sun's rays melted some of the snow, and the icicles hanging from their house began dripping. They interpreted these signs to indicate that the worst part of the winter season was over.

Henry threw open the door so they could breathe fresh air and air-out their dumpy, foul-smelling a little room. The spirits of the men rose with the expectation they would soon be on their way home. Rafael sought out the station store master and began seeing what products he could sell them so he could re-stock his chuck wagon. The improved weather had given them hope of returning home.

Henry observed the happier spirits of the vaqueros and feared interfering with their happiness, but he had to say so all could hear. "What about the cattle?"

There was animated chatter among the vaqueros that Henry and Randy did not quite follow. They turned to Rafael for interpretation, and he said, "In brief, they no longer care about the cattle. They only care about going home and re-joining their families at Santa Rosita."

At that moment, a tall and slim Anglo man appeared at the door. He was dressed in black, which made the crew think he was some kind of preacher. He took off his black hat and said in an accent they had not heard before, "My name is Franklin Peters. You can call me Frank. I've come all the way from Chicago via Kansas City to see what progress has been made in connecting the railroad with the settlement. I'm ready to invest in making this a center for the shipment and marketing of Texas cattle to beef-hungry customers back East."

His words served to hush the men. The room was covered with a pall of silence and shock. Rafael quietly tried to say in Spanish what the strange man had said. Randy was lost for words, and before Henry could say anything, Frank continued by saying, "The harsh winter has delayed the construction of the railroad spur to Mud City, but all should be set early next year to ship cattle back East. I hear you cowboys came from Texas with a large herd only to find that the train had not arrived yet. I'm here to buy all your cattle, but I have one condition."

Henry's attention was perked up by Frank's words, and he tersely said, "How much per head can you pay? And what's your condition?"

"That depends on how many head you have to sell. My condition is that you promise to come back here next year with a large herd and spread the word far and wide that there is a ready market for Texas cattle in Mud City."

Randy was quick to reply, "We don't rightly know how many head survived the winter, but we're going to check over the next couple of days.

Can you come back the day after tomorrow so we can discuss terms?"

"If the weather holds, I'll be back."

Before Frank could leave, Randy said, "By the way, we never heard before that word, 'cowboys'. Is that what Easterners are calling us now?"

"Well, you got a better word for guys who herd cattle?"

"I guess not. That's probably good as word as any."

Before departing, Frank said, "You cowboys stink of somethin' bad. As soon as you can, you should wash up. See you in a couple of days to talk about how many cattle you got to sell me now."

Henry said to Randy and Rafael, "Let's get saddled and ride out to check to see how many head survived the winter. Rafael... how many vaqueros are willing to go with us?"

Rafael was quick to reply, "All of them because they also want to look for Ernesto's body, and if the ground is unfrozen enough, dig him a decent grave."

"Good. Let's get ready as fast as we can. I hope we find some cattle still alive 'cause we need the money."

Henry led the mounted crew out to where the herd was supposed to be. They saw many dead cattle carcasses, but to their surprise, there were still many head still alive. They crisscrossed the wide pasture, and the numbers of cattle still standing were provided to Randy. When all was said and done, Randy said to Henry, "We've about eight hundred head for sale, give or take a few."

"Well, I wonder what Frank will pay us for eight hundred head. I also wonder how in the hell he's goin' to market them."

Rafael rode up to them and said, "Follow me."

Henry and Randy did as requested and rode to a distant place to find the vaqueros off their horses and standing around the stiff preserved body of Ernesto. They had cut the grass near the body with their long knives and traced the outline of a grave they would dig with a couple of crude shovels they had taken from the stable. At first, the ground was frozen hard, but once they had broken through this hard layer, the digging of the shallow grave became easier.

They carefully lifted the body of Ernesto and in silence gently placed it gently in silence in the shallow hole. They said some prayers and slowly began to cover the body with the earth they had dug out. The men encircled the grave, removed their sombreros, and said more Catholic prayers. Some men held rosaries tightly in their right hands.

It was getting late. The vaqueros promised the dead and buried Ernesto that they would return tomorrow to give him a proper grave... one that was covered with stones and topped with a wooden cross with his name carved in it. There were tears, and the mood was solemn. Nearby was Ernesto's dead horse. They removed all its tack and left it to the hungry buzzards, which were already circling overhead.

While the vaqueros prepared to return the next day to decorate Ernesto's grave site, Henry and Randy prepared for the return of Frank. They decided they could not go lower than twenty dollars per head. Of course, if he offered to pay more than this, they would readily accept. Their discounted price was calculated in the knowledge that if the railroad had been completed, they could have been paid up to forty dollars per head.

The vaqueros paid no heed to Henry and Randy's discussion about the price for selling their remaining cattle. They concentrated on doing what was needed to demonstrate their high honor for Ernesto's grave. They gathered all the stones located in or near the settlement and placed them on a blanket they would hitch a horse to and drag them to the grave site.

A couple of vaqueros were busy hacking with their knives a flat surface on a firewood log. On this surface, they would carve Ernesto's name. They would tie it with strands of rawhide to a sturdy post for implanting deeply in the ground at the head of Ernesto's grave. No matter that the post was stolen from the stable.

The next day, the vaqueros rose early to go with their stones and the grave cross marker to pay Ernesto their last respects. Henry and Randy stayed behind to wait for the promised visit of Frank. They sat on a log in front of their station house, and Randy said, "I hope we get the low price we have in mind cuz we need the money. I spent the trail money I had for our prolonged stay. We're flat broke. We need any money we can get."

"Okay. I understand, but we don't want to come across as being desperate when we discuss with Frank. We need to be firm in our asking price and hide our dire plight."

"Okay. Here he comes. Let's do all we can to get the best price for our cattle."

Frank dismounted and, after the usual greeting, sat down on the log next to Henry and said, "Are you cowboys ready to do business?"

Henry replied, "Yes, sir. We scouted our herd yesterday, and we found about eight hundred cows alive. That's all we got left from the three thousand we started with. No matter how you slice it, we got a big and shameful loss to report to our bosses."

Henry thought it would be helpful to his case to add. "We lost so much money that it would be surprising if any Texas rancher would drive cattle this far after hearing about our sorry experience."

Frank wanted Henry to know he perfectly understood their situation and, therefore, was willing to do all he could for them, keeping in mind the promise of selling thousands of head of Texas cattle starting next year. Frank cut to the chase by saying, "I don't know what I'll do with them, but I can offer you ten dollars per head sight unseen."

Randy blurted quickly out, "What? That can't be. That's half of the lowest price we had in mind. We can't go back to our ranch in Texas with so little money."

"Well, son, I understand, but that is the best I can do. I'm sorry cause I'm countin' on you to be among my future customers who will receive top dollar for their cattle. Take it or leave it."

Henry asked Frank, "Excuse us as I step inside to discuss this matter with my younger brother."

"Alrighty. I can see you guys are well-bred and educated and not from these parts, so I will not trifle with you."

Henry and Randy stepped inside, and Randy said in a whinny voice, "He really has us over a barrel, and he knows it. He's got a winning hand, and there is really nothing we can do but to accept it and get out of here."

Henry quickly mulled over Randy's words and said, "Looks like we have no choice. Let's take his money and go back to Santa Rosita with our tails between our legs."

They rejoined Frank, and Henry said, "You got yourself a deal. When do we get our money?"

Frank stood up, and they followed suit. He shook their hands and said, "I got to get my strong box. I'll be back in a giffy."

As Frank rode off, Randy said, "I hope we're doin' the right thing."

Henry replied, "We're doin' the only thing we can do. Let's get our money and get out of here as fast as we can."

"Yeah. You're right. I sure wonder what he's goin' to do with eight hundred head."

"Ask him when he gets back."

Frank came back, pulling a mule behind him with a strong box. He was accompanied by two other armed men. Frank dismounted and said, "I got eight thousand dollars for you in my strong box. Now, where are the cattle?"

Henry said, "Let me get my horse and show your men where the cattle are located. While we're gone, you can pay my brother so he can begin settling our expenses. Okay?"

Frank said, "That should do. I trust you. When you get back, I'll have a paper for you to sign saying you sold eight hundred head to me for ten dollars apiece."

Randy did not like being separated from his older brother, but he knew he had to concern himself with the business side of their operations, and he said, "No problem. You show them the cattle while I take care of the money end of things."

Henry rode off with Frank's two men, and Randy said to Frank, "For starters, show me the money."

"Well, help me carry the strongbox inside, and we'll count out the gold coins there."

Randy spread a blanket on the ground and, stacked the gold coins in 1,000 dollar piles, and said, "That's what you agreed to pay us."

"Yes, that's it. I trust my men will see at least eight hundred heads. If not, I'll be back here after they return. If I'm not back, that means are deal is done, and you can go on your way."

"Understood. I've got to separate the money out to pay us and our vaqueros and then save the rest to give to our bosses. By the way, where you goin' to sell all these cattle anyway?"

"Well, just between you and me. We're going to herd the cattle east to Ft. Riley, and if any are left, we'll sell them to the railroad workers in Kansas City. After paying bribes to some farmers and local officials, I don't expect to make anything. I consider this as an investment in the future business I will do with your ranch and others."

Randy was a bit confused and said, "With all due sincerity, after our vaqueros pass the word about the disastrous experience they had in Kansas, I doubt if any of them will want to return. They're the real cowboys, and I don't see driving big herds north without them."

"Son, when they hear the railroad is built and how much money they can make by selling their surplus of cattle in Kansas, they will come.

Besides, with all the young men returning from the war, there will also be a surplus of men who want to become cowboys. Everybody will be looking to make money, and I plan to give them the opportunity to make a fortune."

A thoughtful Randy said, "I think you're right. The main resource Texas has is its cattle, and if it is going to stay afloat as a state, it must sell its cattle. The end of the war and the advancing railroad should result in somethin' of an economic boom for Texas.

# Chapter Fifty-Four
# Back at the Big Ranch

Everybody got their money, even those who had died. Money helped heal some wounds, but nothing could heal the loss of close comrades, especially the highly respected Ernesto. Everyone was eager to hit the long trail home.

Rafael worked with the local smithy to make sure all the horses were well-shoed. He gave special attention to the pair of wagon oxen. He knew they needed healthy horses and oxen for the long journey home. His chuck wagon was full of useful items, mostly food products that he had managed to buy from the store tended by the stagecoach station master. He was ready to leave, and the men were more than ready to get going.

There was still the crunch of snow under their feet and hooves to remind them that winter may not be done with them yet. Each step urged them to go as fast as they could farther south to warmer climes. Henry and Randy could easily sense that the vaqueros wanted to head home now. To help calm them down, Henry said to the crew, "We leave tomorrow at the first light."

Rafael happily interpreted in a loud fashion Henry's words. The vaqueros broke out in song and did a little dancing. There was little sleeping that night as the anticipation of heading south tomorrow gnawed at them. At long last, they could escape their confinement and head to the place where their hearts were.

Henry and Randy lay next to each other, talking about how they would explain their long absence to Rudy. There was really no way to describe their ordeal and all it cost in terms of lives and money. They knew they would forever be blamed by the Vaquero community in Santa Rosita for the death of Ernesto. They dearly missed Ernesto and wished they had never let him go check on the herd in such frosty weather.

On another subject, Randy asked. "Do you think Frank will make more money than he paid us, or was he just doing us a favor so we could leave and bring back more cattle next year?"

Henry replied, "I think he'll be lucky to make any money. But he's a businessman, and maybe he's got ways to make money that we can't know. Anyway, I think we're lucky because, thanks to him, we're getting out of here. Getting rid of our cattle gave us the freedom we needed to leave."

"But what do we say to Rudy?"

"The truth in as much detail as he wants. There's no way we can sugarcoat our awful experience. Of course, we need to emphasize that the railroad will be waiting for us next year. We have proven this can work if there is a railroad to ship our cattle back east."

"Sounds like you've already committed ourselves to another drive."

"Got to if we are to redeem ourselves and show that long cattle drives can be real money-makers."

The night passed slowly. All were up early. They could not wait to be on their way. Raphael made breakfast, which they devoured immediately, and washed it all down with tin cups of black coffee. The vaqueros waited outside with their horses. Some of them helped Rafael clean up and hitch the oxen to his wagon. When Henry and Randy appeared, their hearts sang as they knew it was only a matter of minutes before Henry would give the signal to head out of Mud City.

The station master and a few dowdy townspeople gathered to see them off. Henry looked to see if Randy, Rafael, and his wagon were ready to roll. Just as the sun was peaking over the eastern horizon, he signaled with his arm and hand in the expected manner to go south. The vaqueros reacted with loud whoops and galloped out of Mud City so fast they did not see the feeble hand waves of the people gathered to see them off.

Henry was the last to leave. He turned his horse to face the small group of Mud City residents, tipped his hat, and said, "See you next year when you got a railroad."

Deep in his heart, Henry knew he never wanted to see Mud City again, but he hungered for the satisfaction of driving a large herd over a thousand miles for their sale and shipment via the railroad. Nothing could be worse than what he had already experienced, and he knew the way and how to do it. He thought that his bosses should place a high value on him and the men who had held the course in spite of great sacrifice and against considerable odds.

Randy found himself waiting for his brother to catch up. He rode alongside Rafael and his wagon. Rafael was struggling to keep up with the vaqueros who had ridden far ahead. They made good time… much faster than when they were obliged to tend to the needs of a large herd. At their current pace, they thought they could be home in two months instead of the three months it took them to cover the same ground with a herd of cattle.

Henry caught up and asked, "Where's everyone else?"

Rafael said, "They rode far in the distance. I assume they'll settle down once their stomachs are hungry for the food I'll cook this evening."

Henry replied, "I hoped they would stay in at least eyeshot. We're safer if we're together. They got to understand that we cannot go faster than your wagon."

Rafael said, "They know that. This is just the first day. Let them have their fun. We got a long row to hoe."

"I reckon you're right. Let's be patient and enjoy as much as we can being on the trail south in the wide-open prairie under the big sky."

All Randy had to say was, "Amen. Let's pray for smooth goin'."

One day was like another. Going home was smoother than expected. They made good time, and there was no major mishap. The main difference they noted was that more settlers were making their way west in search of peaceful and productive places to homestead. The vaqueros saw them as a passing oddity.

Henry and Randy knew better. They saw them as signs that the times were changing for good. Already, the massive buffalo herds have been decimated. With the demise of the buffalo, the Indians had been dispersed and killed in battles with the white newcomers, or they succumbed to diseases transmitted by the whites. Most of the remaining Indians had been rounded up by the army and placed in reservations. Land that was once theirs to roam freely was now firmly in the grips of white outsiders, and their number was growing rapidly.

When Henry spotted a group of settlers on the distant horizon, "He said to Randy, "Times are changing. I guess there's plenty of land for everyone. Not sure if there is enough water to go around. I'm sure a lot of these people won't be able to tame this tough land to their likin'."

"Yep. The only thing that has not changed is the prevalence of mesquite trees and prairie dog villages. There is also the constant wind and all the dust it carries."

Randy's comment elicited a few chuckles from Henry then he said, "We need to take advantage of the time we got to herd more cattle to a railhead in Kansas before this place is filled with settlers."

"I think you and me that we've more time than we need. I don't think we plan on spending our whole lives doing what we are doing. Maybe we should go farther west or go back to where we started in ol' Virginie."

Henry ruminated a bit on Randy's words and said, "Maybe you're right. I'm sorry, we're the men for the big job of herding thousands of cattle from southern Texas to Kansas. I wish we could do somethin' else, but I don't know what that would be. But you're right about movin' on at some point."

Henry wanted to continue the conversation with his brother, but he did not know what to say. After a while, he said, "Times are changing so fast it is best not to think too far into the future. Let's take things a step at a time."

They exited Kansas and crossed into Indian Territory without incident. The Red River was lower than it was when they came. The spring rains had not yet flooded it, and maybe this year, there would be no spring rains. They crossed the Red and moved into Texas to the cheers of the vaqueros.

They moved across the wide Texas plains as fast as they could without wearing out their horses. The vaqueros were sometimes in their saddles for up to eighteen hours. There was no more taking shifts to keep an eye on the herd; all they had to do was to ride. The only thing holding them up was the wagon and the evening meals that depended on its contents.

With the vaqueros speeding ahead, there was no need for Henry and Randy to distance themselves from Rafael's wagon and spare horses. Once they crossed the Nueces River, there was no stopping the vaqueros. They rode for two days and nights until they reached Santa Rosita. Their arrival sparked a joyous outburst from the Santa Rosita community, including Rudy, who was happy but puzzled and said, "We thought you were all dead. Did Henry and Randy make it?"

One vaquero attempted to reply to Rudy in broken English, saying, "They come."

Rudy waited on the front porch of the big house well into the night. When he saw that they had still not arrived the next morning, he organized a team to ride out with him to search for them. They rode for about a half day and found Henry, Randy, and Rafael gathered around a broken-down wagon. Rudy could not hide his joy and was the first to speak, "Damn. You guys are a welcome sight. You sure took much longer than we expected to herd cattle to Kansas and come back. We're beginning to think that you all died. Glad to see you still alive and kickin'.'"

Henry tried to hide his happiness over returning and said, "Yeah, it's us, but maybe we're more dead than alive. We got a lot to tell you, but we don't know what to do with the busted wheel on this wagon."

Rudy said, "Forget about the wagon. I'll send a team out tomorrow to fix it and bring it and its oxen in. It's on ranch land, so nobody should bother it. Let's head to the ranch. By the way, I see Rafael and some of his horses, but where is Ernesto?"

Randy was waiting to see how his brother would answer this question. Henry gave Rudy a short answer, "He didn't make it."

This sad news deeply affected Rudy. He could only say, "Let's go to the ranch so I can hear all about it."

They rode in silence for the rest of the day. The news of Ernesto's death put a huge damper on any conversation, and Henry and Randy believed this was not the time or place to tell their story. Rafael parted with them when they reached the ranch's big courtyard. He was also eager to park his horses in the corral and go see his family.

Rudy sat under the shade tree in front of the bunkhouse and said, "I know you boys are tired, and talking is the last thing you want to do, but you better tell me the whole story before the vaqueros spread their version like wildfire."

Henry and Randy sat down across from Rudy, and Henry reluctantly began by saying, "I don't know rightly where to begin. I just want to say first that herding cattle to Kansas can be done but should not be done unless a railroad exists. We learned the hard way that there will not be a railway until next year, and we should return with a large herd."

Rudy was a bit exasperated by Henry's words and said, "What do you mean? There's no railhead in Kansas? If the railroad is not there, what did you do with our cattle?"

Randy thought he would spare his brother from Rudy's grilling. "That's right. There's no railroad yet in Mud City, but they're building it, and it should be there next year. It will be ready to receive and ship back East Texas cattle."

Rudy quicky said, "Okay. I get it, but you didn't answer my question."

"We sold the cattle remaining after the stampede and freezing winter to a local buyer at a rock bottom price."

"So, you not only lost men, but you also lost us money."

Henry came to the aid of his brother. "We had no choice. We had to get out of there to report back to you. We did our best, and we're sorry if that is not good enough for you. We promise that next year will be better."

"Maybe there'll be no next year. We'll see what the boss has to say. Come for breakfast in the big house tomorrow and tell your story from start to finish. He wants to hear all the details, so be prepared to spend several hours with us. Get some rest. You'll need to be in top shape for tomorrow."

Randy popped up, saying, "Wait a minute, we thought the boss was still in Matamoros waiting to see what the decision was on his request for a presidential pardon."

"Well, he got his pardon, and he's back and fully in charge. Be ready tomorrow morning to tell him why he should herd some more of his cattle to Kansas."

Henry then said, "Well, it was not a total loss. Randy, get your saddlebags with the gold coins.

Randy set his saddlebags down on the table with a loud clank. He emptied their golden contents on the table for Rudy to count. Rudy looked at the pile of shiny gold coins and said with a smile on his face, "Well, that certainly takes an edge off things. By my count, this money represents about what we could've sold all the cattle for locally."

Randy was perturbed and thought it pertinent to add. "That's assuming you could sell the cattle locally. There's still too many cattle on this ranch. Perhaps more important than the money is that we've proven that it is possible to drive a large herd to Kansas and learned the status of the railroad. I believe the main question for the boss tomorrow is whether or not we get a herd ready to go north to Kansas next year."

Henry wanted to bolster his brother's argument and said bluntly, "There's no local market, and even if there were, you can make a multiple of any local proceeds for cattle in the Kansas market. I guess it is a choice of having more cattle than you need or selling the surplus where they will get top dollar."

Rudy wanted to save all their breaths and simply said, "Tell all you have to say to the boss tomorrow morning. He's the one who decides. Not me."

After saying these words, Rudy got up and walked away. Henry and Randy used the little strength remaining to them to unsaddle their horses. They stumbled into the bunkhouse with their gear and collapsed on the beds. All they wanted to do was sleep.

# Chapter Fifty-Five
# Meeting the Big Boss

They arose early to get ready for their meeting with the big boss. They crept quietly outside so they would not disturb Rudy. To their surprise, they encountered Rafael and another Mexican man in the pre-day morning darkness. Rafael greeted them and said softly, "I heard you had a meeting with the patron this morning, and I knew you would have to clean up, so I brought with me the Barbero. He will give you shaves and haircuts."

Henry and Randy smiled, and Henry said, "I don't know what we'd do without you. You've seen us through the worst of times, and now you're helpin' us get ready for our big meeting with the boss. Aren't you tired?"

"I'm plenty tired, but this meeting is important, and you got to look good. Now get your haircuts and shaves."

"Wait a minute. How's he goin' to see to do his work?"

"Don't worry, he can shave and cut hair well in the dark. What clothes you goin' to wear?"

Randy said, "I dunno. I guess we'll wear our old clothes. Those are the only duds we got that are halfway clean."

Rafael said, "I guess you don't have any choice. Let me at least brush off your old clothes and help make them look presentable. Everyone knows you just got off the long trail and had no time to spruce up."

Henry said as he began to sit on a chair for his haircut and shave, "You got that right. I almost got saddle sores from those long days on the trail. But, you know what? I miss already not riding a horse on the open range."

Randy went back inside the bunkhouse to fetch their old clothes and came out just as the first-morning bird was announcing daybreak to hand them over to Rafael for inspection and brushing. He then waited his turn with the barbero. Henry finished with the barber, thanking him for his good work, and Randy took his place. Henry excused himself to go to the washing stalls behind the bunkhouse. He stripped down and entered a stall to give himself a thorough washing, from head to toe, with lye soap.

Henry stepped out of the stall and dried off with a cloth hanging on a nearby mesquite tree. He felt like a new man as he wrapped the cloth around himself and tip-toed while carrying his boots back to the front of the bunkhouse where Randy was finishing his round with the barber. He said to his younger brother, "Your turn. The cold water is a real waker-upper."

By the time Rudy appeared outside, Henry and Randy were all cleaned up and dressed, waiting for him. Rafael and the barber had long departed. Rudy gave Henry and Randy a hard look and asked, "Are you the same guys who rode in yesterday?"

Henry replied, "Yep. We're all cleaned up and ready for the big meeting with the boss."

"The cleaning up sure made your youth shine through. But I guess you're older than you look cause you've done the miles and been to Hell and back more than once. You're more men than men twice your age."

Randy said, "Yes, sir. You can call us cowboys. That's what they called us in Kansas."

"Hmm… I like the sound of that word, and it seems fitting. I believe I'll introduce you to the boss as our first cowboys. I bet he'll like that."

Henry, "Well, we never planned to be cowboys, but that is what we are now."

Rudy said, "Let me go and see if the boss is ready to meet with us. When I spoke with him yesterday evening, he said he wanted to see you for breakfast."

After Rudy was gone, Henry said, "We got to put our best foot forward when trying to convince the boss to send more of his cattle north to join up with the new railroad. We have proven that it can be done. All that is needed is a railroad to ship them back to meat-hungry Easterners."

Henry was ready to continue laying his arguments out for the boss when Rudy appeared and beckoned to them to follow him. At last, they would be able to see the boss of it all and tell him of the great promise the railroad had in Kansas for marketing his surplus of cattle. He and Randy were more excited than they expected.

Their excitement went through the roof when the boss himself was on his front porch to welcome them with open arms, saying, "And here they are. Our courageous cowboys who have returned from the cold winter of Kansas to join us again on our cattle ranch."

Henry and Randy were so intimidated by the stature of the tall man and the force of his words that they forgot themselves as they shook vigorously his hand. They were ushered into the big house and its cavernous dining room and treated like victorious conquerors returning home from the battlefield. The boss was joined by his wife and then said, "Behold the two men who have shown us that herding cattle to Kansas is possible."

They tipped their hats to his wife and immediately removed then and placed them on the floor next to their cushioned dining chairs. They sat down when the boss did. After this loud introduction, he said. "Let's eat first and talk later. Please forget all protocol and dig in. This is a big moment for us, this ranch, and all of southern Texas."

Henry and Randy were blown away by the magnanimity of the boss, but this did not slow down their eating. They took huge proportions and heaped them on their decorated white porcelain plates until they were overfilled. Their large coffee cups were constantly filled by servants who hovered behind them. It was an early morning breakfast ceremony like they had never seen, and they were deeply grateful.

They had cleaned their plates, and their stomachs were bursting at the seams. The boss slid his chair back at the head of the expansive table, lit his morning Cuban cigar, and said, "I've heard already your story and all its details from Rudy, but I want to hear from you about herding more cattle to the Kansas market."

The boss looked at Henry with the expectation that he would respond. Henry hesitated and cleared his throat before saying, "You got to get your cattle to market, and there will be a big market in Mud City, Kansas, as soon as work on the railroad is completed next year."

Randy felt like he should add some words and said, "Maybe you can get three dollars a head for a cow here, but in Kansas, you can get thirty or forty dollars per head for cows shipped east on the railroad. Any way you look at it, it's a lucrative deal."

Henry added, "My brother has said it all. You have little to lose and a fortune to make."

The boss said in a booming voice, "I like you boys. In my eyes, you have already proven yourselves. You're right. I have too many cattle, and there's money to be made from sellin' them in Kansas. I have confidence in you, boys. I have a hunch you're going to make me rich. I say get another big herd ready for a long drive north next year."

The boss then turned to his wife and asked her if she had anything to add. She only nodded to give her assent to what had been discussed. There was a brief pause, and then she said one word, "Bonuses."

The boss captain said, "Oh yes. I forgot to say that I'm given every man, alive and dead, who participated in your drive a twenty-dollar bonus. That should encourage them to go on the next drive."

Henry and Randy were pleased to hear about the bonus. The boss was not finished and said to them between puffs on his cigar, "As for you two cowboys, you not only get a bonus of thirty dollars each, but I'm puttin' each of you on our permanent payroll at one hundred dollars per month."

This was welcomed news for them. They could not hide their joy at being accepted in such an unexpected manner. With those words, the boss stood up and said, "I got some other business to tend to. You can discuss with Rudy gettin' ready to drive another herd north. Maybe I'll see you tomorrow at the memorial ceremony. For now, it's goodbye."

Henry and Randy hustled to say their goodbyes. Henry looked the boss straight in the eye and said, "You can count on us."

As the boss was leaving the dining room, he said, "I know that. Otherwise, I would have not been so generous."

As soon as they exited the big house, Randy asked, "What memorial?"

Rudy replied, "Our Mexican community is having a ceremony and wake in the honor of our dearly regretted Ernesto. Everyone misses him. He was a pillar of the community and one of our most respected hands. It will be tough getting by without him."

Thoughts of Ernesto's passing put everyone in a deep funk. Rudy did not feel like talking but said, "Let me talk to some of our vaqueros, and I'll get back to you. Take the next couple of days to rest before starting to get more cattle ready for the drive north. As the boss said, the only profitable market for our cattle is in Kansas, and we need to get ready to drive big herds north."

Rudy left them standing beneath the shade tree, looking at each other. They did not know what to do next. It had been so long since they had any time off. They had forgot how to deal with freedom. Henry suggested, "Let's sit down while we figure out our next move."

They sat in silence for a long time. Neither of them knew what to say. Randy finally broke the silence by saying, "You know, I thought the boss would talk about his time on the other side of the border and his presidential pardon."

"Well, we're only his favorite cowboys and not members of his family. I'm sure he only speaks to his wife about such matters, but I'm not even sure about that. He probably wants to forget about that chapter in his life. Anyway, if he hadn't got the pardon, we wouldn't be here, so we should be thankful he got it."

"I'm glad he returned cuz this land needs someone like him to tame it and use it. How'd he get all the land anyway?"

"I rightly dunno. I heard he bought it from several Mexicans whose families have claimed ownership for a couple of centuries but did not live here and did nothing to improve the land. For me, the land should belong to those who work it."

A reflective Randy changed the subject a bit by asking, "Were their Indians here before?"

"Of course, all this land was home to lots of Indian tribes. The Indians were here for thousands of years. Why, even where we come from, there were Indian tribes before the arrival of the white man. This is their land. We took it away from them."

"Where are the Indians now? Seems like such a big land for so few people."

"There were more Indians before, but their numbers were greatly reduced by the white man's diseases and their outright forced removal and killing by the white man. Those Indians still left are being killed or rounded up and placed on a reservation."

"I guess this is a part of the great American manifest destiny we studied in school. I guess the war ended slavery for the blacks, but I'm not sure if it did anything to end the oppression of the Indians."

"I've had enough of this highfalutin' talk that has nothing to do with us. We got to stay focused on our lives and the job they depend upon. We're employed to get a cattle ready for the Kansas market and drive them to that market. I know this is simpler said than done, but our survival depends on it."

"Yep. No sense on trying to solve the world's problems when we got our plate full right here. Staying alive and well comes first in this dog-eat-dog world. If we don't look after ourselves, who will?"

This was the first time in a long time that the two brothers had taken stock of their situation. They both thought this was what 'free time' was for. But they really did not have all the facts at their disposal. There was nothing to read, and the news traveled slowly, if at all. It was easier to focus on the task at hand. Besides, they were out of touch with the outside world. Their whole world was about getting cows to the Kansas market.

They were silent as they looked at each other and thought about how far they had come since fleeing their plantation in Virginia four years ago. They were boys then. Now, they were young, experienced men and among the first Texas cowboys. There was no going back. They had to make the best of their current situation.

Randy took a good look at his older brother. He was tall, over six feet two inches, with broad shoulders. He had a muscular build and liked to have all facial hair shaved, and this made him an exception among men who mostly grew beards and mustaches. He liked to keep his sandy brown hair combed. His face was distinguished by the deep furrow wrinkles on his forehead and his penetrating deep blue eyes. He was generally mild-mannered but was quick to draw his pistols and shoot anyone who crossed him.

While Randy was looking at his older brother's physical appearance, Henry was also sizing him up. Randy was lanky and maybe six feet tall. He was not muscular, but he was strong. He was book-smart and had been forced to become 'life-smart' by the obligation to stay alive under the most difficult circumstances. He also had the same sandy hair, but he had a matching mustache. There was nothing about his hazel eyes to set him apart, but anyone who engaged with him was quickly impressed by his keen intelligence. He looked young but was older than his years.

They both had in common their deep love for each other. This love obliged them to do anything needed to help the other. Their bonds were deep before they fled Virginia and grew deeper as they overcame many trials to get to Texas and find a new life. Neither of them could live without the other. For better or worse, their lives were intertwined and inseparable.

Henry interrupted this silent, reflective pause by saying, "That's enough. As our mom used to say, 'The idle brain is the devil's playground.' We're not cut out for this downtime. Let's mosey over to the corral to see if anything is going on."

"Yeah, I'm with you. Let's go and see if we can learn something we don't already know."

# Chapter Fifty-Six
# Final Goodbye to Ernesto

They did not find anybody at the corral. There were not even any horses. The same emptiness was found in the big cotton warehouse and the twenty-bed bunkhouse. The commissary was locked. They walked back to their smaller bunkhouse behind the big house to wait for Rudy.

After several hours, Rudy came walking up to their shady place beneath a tree and said, "You boys enjoying your rest?"

Henry was eager to reply, "No. Restin' is not for us. We're used to keepin' busy all the time. We need somethin' to do."

"You'll be plenty busy soon. Tomorrow is off, so we can attend a tribute to Ernesto. Everyone on the ranch will be there, even the boss and his family. You guys can go with me."

Randy replied, "That's good, but what do we do now? We're tired of restin'."

"I don't know what to tell you. There is nothin' to do now. But I could tell you about the vaqueros' plans to get herds ready for your next drive north."

"Henry sat up in his chair and said, "Now, you got our interest. Go ahead and tell us. We're all ears."

"Well, I talked to the vaqueros, and they're goin' to start workin' this week to get a big herd ready to go north next spring. You boys can help them just like you did to get the three thousand head ready to go last year."

Henry excitedly said, "Now that's good news. We can't wait to get started."

Rudy had more to say about his meeting with the vaqueros. "Another thing. We got so many cattle, they are thinkin that it is good to get two big herds ready for the long drive north. I think that's a good idea, but I've not yet figured out how to do it. You guys got any ideas?"

Rudy's comment gave Henry and Randy pause. After some minutes in deep reflection, Randy said, "Well, you shouldn't send the second herd until it's sure the railroad is there."

Rudy said, "Yeah. That's the point I'm stuck on. It'll take a couple months to hear back about the experience of the first herd. It would be foolish to send a second herd until we know how it went with the first herd."

Henry concluded this conversation by saying, "Give us some time to think about this one. One thing is, are you goin' to be able to find enough cowboys to herd two big herds north? I don't think the vaqueros who suffered such a long time with us in Kansas will want to go again. And they've probably spread the word about their experience."

Rudy said, "You're right, but money talks louder than words. And we get some guys asking for work every day. They're returning from the war and eager to work. For the most part, we're looking for guys who know how to shoot a gun and ride a horse and who are willing to make the long drive north."

Randy said, "That's all well and good. Just let us know about the guys who we will be working with us on the first drive. Of course, we expect Rafael will be running the chuck wagon and will have a strong say on who will take care of the remuda. All we need is seven more good men."

Rudy said, "I got ya. I think we can find you those seven men and ten more for the second herd. We got to make this work. It is the only way to keep the ranch afloat. Of course, we could split you two up, and you could both be trail bosses for a second herd, but I reckon you wouldn't agree to that."

Randy said firmly, "No splitting us up. Don't even think about it."

Henry added his two cents. "Well, I'm sure you'll let us size up first any men you have in mind to hire for our drive. We want to be able to trust their abilities and character."

Rudy asked, "Do you care about their skin color? We've had some blacks lookin' for work."

Henry rapidly replied, "We don't give a damn about the color of their skin, but we do care about the quality of their skills as drovers."

Randy added to his brother's comment, "Yeah. And they have to be a good fit and get along well with the rest of the crew."

Rudy said, "I guess that does it for now. I'll let you know of anything new I learn. Be ready to go with me early in the morning to attend the ceremony for Ernesto. Somebody should be bringin' you food shortly."

Randy said, "Wait a minute. Have you recovered our chuck wagon, and do you have another one for the second drive?"

"Yep. Your chuck wagon has been rescued, and it will be repaired. We're goin' to get a second chuck wagon and find a cook to drive it. Be thinkin' of anything else. We got time to get this right."

Rudy walked off and left them to sit in silence as they allowed their thoughts to ramble far and wide. Randy was worried that he could not see well his mother's face when he thought of her... as he often did. He mentioned this to Henry, and he replied, "That's a sign that the present is replacing the past. In my mind, I can still see her face, but I know I can't allow that to distract me from the matters at hand and surviving in Texas as she instructed us to do. Anyway, the past is past. We got to live in the present and work for a better future."

"I guess you're right, but sometimes I feel the world is changing so fast that it is leaving us behind. There's a flood of settlers coming west, and there is no denying they are changing the landscape. They're all looking for a better life and are willing to make many sacrifices to get that life. It seems like settling the frontier has become popular, and everyone wants to go west no matter what."

Henry replied to Randy's rambling thoughts by saying, "You think too much. We got to stop thinking so much and find somethin' to do to keep our minds off the ways of the world."

To this, Randy said, "Maybe you're right, but this is the time we have to think and discuss. All right, I just have one more question. If this is the frontier for settlers, what is it for Indians?

Henry was dead serious when he looked into his brother's eyes and replied with one word, "Home."

Randy scratched his head and said, "So we are taking their home from them. That doesn't seem fair."

"Nothin' is fair. One big lesson we have learned is life is not fair, and it never will be, especially for the Indians and blacks. Life is about making choices, and a lot of those choices are cruel."

Randy was impressed. These were the most profound things he had ever heard his older brother say. His older brother had certainly put a stopper in his train of thought. He was convinced more thinking along these lines would be troublesome and not change anything. He got up and went into the bunkhouse and came back with a deck of cards and asked, "Deal or cut?"

They played cards to while away the time until their food was served. Randy said, "I've got to stay sharp. If this cattle trading scheme goes as planned, they may have a saloon someday in Mud City."

Henry replied, "I hope so. If this cattle business booms, they'll have all they need to cater to cowboys at the end of a long cattle drive. As long as it is not winter, Mud City should be in store for a real facelift."

"You know that three thousand head at forty dollars a head results in a huge sum. Even after paying expenses and our crew, that's too much money. I'm not sure how we goin' to carry this money safely back to the ranch."

Henry nodded and said, "You worry too much. Don't count your chickens before they are hatched. But it is good to keep your thinkin' cap on and note the things we got to talk over with Rudy."

They ate their food and played cards under the dim light of an oil lamp well into the night. Rudy returned and, without saying a word to them, headed right to his bed in the bunkhouse to get some shut-eye. The thought they should do like Rudy so they would be ready at dawn to follow him to Ernesto's requiem ceremony.

Rudy was up early and called, "You boys got to get up if we are not goin' to be too late for Ernesto's final farewell."

Henry and Randy got up, dressed and washed their faces, and presented themselves in front of the bunkhouse. Rudy took a look at them and said, "Let's go. It's good if we get to the Mexican community public place before the boss and his family does."

They accompanied Rudy, who was walking with long strides at a fast pace. What they encountered in the community was nothing like they expected. A Mexican band was playing joyous music, and young people were dancing. Those who could not dance were sitting and talking animatedly. Everyone was dressed in colorful clothes that they had acquired for this special occasion. Everywhere was decorated with prairie wildflowers. Even the weather made an effort to contribute to this special day by being overcast and cooler with a lower temperature.

They were shown to seats in the circle of honor. It appeared that all the important Anglo whites were held in reverence by the Mexican community. Henry and Randy enjoyed hearing the music and seeing so many people having a good time. Suddenly, a hush descended over the rambunctious crowd, and they turned their heads to see what caused such silence to replace all the loud noise.

It was as if Jesus in the flesh had graced their presence. There he was … the patron and the patronna with their three children. The community worshiped them and was eternally grateful to be taken out of Mexico and transplanted to the patron's ranch. There was not a man in the community who was not ready to lay down his life for the patron. The patron came today because he had a high respect for Ernesto and the undying loyalty of every member of the community.

After the boss and his family stepped forward, the master of ceremonies stepped forward and took his hat off to say in Spanish, "We're here today because we lost one of the most respected members of our community. We mourn our dearly departed Ernesto in the way he would have wanted. His importance to us and this ranch is reflected by the presence today of our patron and his family. We've already prayed for the peaceful final rest of Ernesto. It is time now to celebrate his life with the biggest fiesta and feast this community has ever seen. But before we continue with the festivities, I must turn to our beloved patron for a few words."

The several hundred people… men, women, and children… gathered for the glorious event applauded in an uproarious fashion. They all became stone quiet when the boss stood to say his piece. He spoke in bits to give the Mexican man standing by his side time to translate his words into Spanish. The patron spoke softly and said, full of emotion, "Ernesto was the best man I had ever known. He possessed all the qualities I admire in a man. He was hard-working, smart, and absolutely trustworthy. I join with you in missing him dearly and honoring his life today by holding this huge fiesta. Thank you."

The thunderous applause of the people after the patron had spoken was loud and long. The presence and words were unprecedented. This was the first time the community could recall the patron coming to the community, speaking to them in such an eloquent and emotional manner, was truly exceptional. There was no doubt in their minds that this day would be the subject of much talk for days to come and enter in one form or another into the annals of the community oral history. This was a day that no one would forget, and it would be talked about by future generations.

It was only when the band struck up a lively tune that the applause died down. A long table laden with food and drink of every type was prepared beneath a huge oak tree. Plates heaped were served to each of those in the circle of honor. After the guests of honor were served, the people clamored around the table and filled their plates with food and their cups with their preferred beverage. Everyone ate and drank their fill. It was a sight to behold.

The patron and his family got up and were escorted by trusted members of the community back to the big house. Rudy, Henry, and Randy tarried to bask in the glory of the moment. As the sun was dipping behind the western horizon, the music was going nonstop, and the young people were dancing up a storm. Rudy had drunk so much homemade aguardiente that he was unable to stand. Henry, who did not drink, and Randy, who drank little, suggested to his brother to support Rudy as they walked him the thousand feet back to their bunkhouse.

It was almost dark when Henry and Randy bid their hosts farewell and grasped Rudy on either side of him to help him walk back. This proved to be a much larger task than they thought because Rudy was near passing out and was more violent in his inebriated state. It took them longer than they had planned to get him back to the bunkhouse and in his bed.

Henry and Randy stepped out into the cooler night air and saw shining above them a bright full moon. Henry said, "Another full moon and the promise of a better future. All we have to do is get a herd ready to drive north. We've done that before, so it should be easier this time. Hey, do you think Rudy will be okay in the morning. We can't make a move until he tells us to."

"I'm sure he won't remember anything about our walk back, and he will be up as usual. For me, tomorrow is a workday, and we got to start getting our herd ready for our big drive north."

With a tinge of an excitement, Henry replied, "Yep. It's all work and no play from here on out. We got time, and by spring of next year, we should be more than ready. I think I can like the cowboy way of life now that I got the hang of it."

Randy wanted to say something, but he thought it was best to remain quiet. For him, the jury was still out, but he was thinking now that this was the way he wanted to live.

# Chapter Fifty-Seven
# Working the Herd

They got up early to check on Rudy, but his bed was empty. Rudy was nowhere to be seen outside. They thought he would be along shortly and went about doing their morning toiletries. As the sun crept over the eastern horizon, there was sufficient light to widen their search for Rudy. Still, he was nowhere to be seen.

A servant brought their breakfast trays and gently set them on their old wooden table that quivered when the slightest weight placed on it. There was only breakfast for the two of them, so they assumed Rudy had already eaten or was eating in the big house. While they were gobbling up their breakfast food and guzzling their hot cups of black coffee, Rudy came marching forcefully into their bunkhouse haven and sat swiftly down hard as if he wanted to break the wobbly wooden chair and said forthrightly, "Good morning, cowboys. Are you ready to hear the latest skinny?"

Henry replied, "It's good to see you. Go ahead. Lay on us all the news you have."

"I just had breakfast with the boss, and we talked about you boys and the drive you'll lead to Kansas. He's agreed with you goin' on your drive as soon as spring arrives. He also wants to send two herds … one a month after you leave. He's a risk-taker. He expects that high risks mean high gains. He's really countin' on you boys."

Randy said, "He can count on us to get his cattle to the Kansas market in the first drive, but he'll need to find another trail boss for the second herd."

"Of course, but he wants you guys to work with the vaqueros to get the two herds ready for the long drive deep into Kansas."

Henry cut into the exchange by saying, "We're all set to start today working with the vaqueros to begin rounding up cattle for the drives north. We're just waiting for you to tell us where to go. We're ready to start today."

Rudy appreciated the boys' eagerness to get started, but he had to say, "Hold your horses. Give the Vaquero community time to recover from yesterday's festivities. Maybe you can start tomorrow."

"I understand, but maybe we can least ride out and see where the cattle are on the ranch to get an idea on how we can round a herd up."

Rudy responded to Henry by saying, "No harm in doing that. But I don't think you can find a horse because Rafael is also knocked out for the day. Be patient for another day. The vaqueros know what they have to do, and they will do it when they're good and ready."

The usually reserved Randy said, "Okay. No problem. We're ready to go when the vaqueros are ready to go. But are you sure they'll be ready to go tomorrow? We're restless. They should be ready. Look how quickly you recovered."

Rudy was surprised by Randy's final words and said, "Recovered from what? I feel just fine today."

Obviously, Rudy did not remember anything about his drunken state of yesterday. Henry and Randy smiled at each other, and Henry said, "Never mind, my brother. The important thing is that we're fit as a fiddle and ready to do our job."

Rudy replied, "Good. Now I'm goin' to walk over to the Vaquero community and see if any of its leaders are free to talk to me about the big roundups for the drives. You boys get some more rest. You'll need it in the busy days ahead."

Randy added, "I'll take busy over restin' any day. We're tired of restin,' but one more day won't kill us."

Rudy said, "I got to go." And disappeared around the corner of the big house.

Henry chuckled and asked Randy, "Don't you think he's acting strange? Where's he got to go?"

Randy answered by saying, "I don't know, and I don't care. I do care about how we are to spend another day with no work."

With those words, Randy pulled out of his pocket a well-worn deck of cards and said, "I'm ashamed of myself. The things I know how to do well are to herd cattle and play cards. I was hopin' my life would amount to more. Anyway, let's play."

Henry knew his wily younger brother would win any hand of any game they played, but playing cards was better than doing nothing. Randy slapped the deck down on the table and asked, as usual, "Deal or cut?"

They played cards for several hours, taking breaks to relief themselves in the nearby bushes. Randy won every game. He was honing his gambling skills and could not wait for the opportunity to play again with some real card sharks. During one of their breaks, he picked up some small sticks and broke them into even smaller pieces. They used the stick pieces like make-believe chips to add some reality to their rounds of card games.

Henry finally threw up his hands. "You're too good for me. I'm probably the poorest card player you've ever known. No sense in me continuing to play with you… losing every time. Besides, I've only hung in there this long because you want to play. Let's figure out somethin' else to do."

"All right. What else can we do to pass the time?"

"Well, it's hot, dry, and sunny, but let's walk around and see what there is to see."

"Let's go. Which way you want to go? It all looks the same to me no matter what direction you go… open prairie on all sides dotted with cattle as far as the eye sees."

"Well, I never been west, so let's take a little stroll that way. Get your rifle in case we run into anything to shoot. I got my guns. If anyone asks us where we were, just tell them we went huntin.'"

They trudged through the tall grass, circumventing mesquite clumps and cactus patches. They walked thought gullies that would be filled with water if it had rained. They came to a wide gulley, and since it was easier and more interesting, they walked along the gulley bed. A bevy of prairie chicken were scared into flight by their intrusion. Suddenly, they heard voices speaking a language they had never heard.

Their wanderlust turned quickly to shroud them in fear. Stopped in their tracks, they became silent. They automatically put their trigger fingers in place and were ready to fire their rifles at the slightest provocation. They crouched down and walked slowly around the bend in the gulley to peek at who was talking and laughing.

When the voices were near, they crawled stealthily beneath some underbrush, being as quiet as they could be. Randy followed Henry, who briefly saw what was happening and signaled to Randy to backtrack. After they were a safe distance away from the voices, Henry gestured to Randy to maintain his silence. It was only when they were far away and almost back to their bunkhouse that Henry spoke about what he saw. He said tersely, "It was Injuns, and they were slaughtering a couple of our cows. There were six in the gulley, but I suppose there were plenty of others I didn't see. For sure, these savages outnumbered us. We got to get back and tell Rudy."

They picked up their pace and returned to the ranch's center to look for Rudy. The sight of Indians slaughtering cattle was not something they expected to see. Henry wanted to find Rudy and get a group of well-armed men on horseback to go back and rout the Indians. For Henry and Randy, the Indians were the enemy, and they should not be stealing and butchering ranch cattle.

They looked everywhere for Rudy, but they could not find him. The situation demanded quick action, but they could not act without Rudy. They paced back and forth in front of their bunkhouse, waiting for Rudy to appear. Footsteps were heard approaching. It was Rudy. They both began jabbering profusely, so much so that Rudy gave them both a hard look and said, "Stop. Settle down. Just one of you tell me why you are so up in arms."

Henry took the lead in speaking angrily for the two of them, "They're wild Indians butchering cattle right on our ranch. We need to get some men quick and ride our and teach them a lesson."

Randy added, "We got to go fast and hard and show them that they can't do what they are doin.' We need to go now to stop them once and for all."

Curiously, Rudy laughed when he heard them so passionately spout out emotionally charged words. With a wide grin on his face, he said, "Settle down. There's no problem. Those are our Indians. We made a peace deal with them… they don't attack us if we allow them to butcher two steers each month."

Henry and Randy were astonished by what they just heard from Rudy. They could not believe their ears. How could such a deal with cutthroat savages be trusted? While Henry and Randy were stunned, Rudy continued talking, "There's much more to this story. There's been a small band of renegade Comanche Indians camped out near the western limits of our ranch for months. I had a long palaver with them and we came to terms. In fact, I'm blood brother with their leader. I just saw him to give him the okay to go ahead and take two beef."

Henry responded acridly by asking, "Are you sure you can trust them?"

"Hold on boys. You got this band of Indians all wrong. They're our friends and they give us the added protection we need on the western side of our ranch. It's a good deal and the captain approves every move I make to keep the peace with them. They're defeated people who have lost everything. It's sad to me to see them like this. No better than beggars in a land where they were once lords for generations."

Rudy's sympathetic words served to calm Henry and Randy down, but they both scratched their heads about the peculiar arrangement Rudy had with the Indians. They did not know or even guess that Rudy had any soft spots in his heart. They had never heard him say so many words filled with such passion and sincerity. After a long pause, Henry said, "Thanks for telling us this. Sounds like a good deal for all the right reasons. Now, what about our big round up?"

"Glad you brought that up. Be here at sunup tomorrow ready to go. Rafael will bring your two new mounts and we'll ride with some vaqueros out to the south pasture and see what cattle we want to get ready for the big drive north."

Thoughts of Henry and Randy's brush with Indians subsided. They were replaced by new thoughts of getting back on horses and riding to begin the preparation of healthy cows for the long trail north. They could not wait to get out on the prairie and start separating out those cattle fit to go on a three-month walk. They were surprised at how eager they were to get started with this round up and get back on the trail. Maybe they had become true cowboys.

Early the next morning they were up and ready to go as soon as they ate breakfast and Rafael showed up with their horses. They swallowed their last cup of coffee when a smiling Rafael showed up. Although it was early and the sun was barely peaking over the eastern horizon, it was a joyous occasion. Henry and Randy felt like hugging Rafael but, instead, did all they could do to show their happiness at seeing him. It was good to be with the faithful and able Rafael who had been through a lot with them.

They were genuinely pleased to see him and went out of their way to welcome him. They invited him to sit with them and drink some coffee, but Rafael decline politely the invitation. He knew his place. It would not be proper for a young man from the Mexican community to associate so closely with the Captain's Anglos. Rafael occupied himself with getting two horses ready for a long day on the range.

Rafael's hesitancy to join them prompted Randy to say softly to Henry. "I don't understand it. They could not operate this ranch without the Mexicans, but they are treated like a lower class. They're separate and not even equal to Anglos. No matter if the Anglos are less able and willing to work, they are the bosses. Smacks of oppression to me. But there's nothing I can do about customs that are so deeply ingrained."

Henry said, "I'm glad you said the last part. We're not here to change the way things are. Live and let live is my motto and give priority to your own survival."

Rafael had finished dressing their horses and stood quietly for them to mount and ride off to the southern range. Rudy came riding up in a swirl of dust and hollered, "Come on you guys. We're waitin' for you. Daylight is burning."

They all mounted and rode off at a gallop to catch up with Rudy and the vaqueros who were waiting for them. As soon as they caught up, they rode at a fast pace to the southern pasture to identify and separate cattle out for the long drive. There was a lot to do and every man was busy separating and rounding up cattle. It would take them weeks to get three thousand head for the drive rounded up and worked on to get them ready for the long trail north.

They tried to take only the healthiest cows, castrating young bulls and dehorning the ornerier cows. They made sure that for the herd there were lead cattle which would be followed by the herd. Each cow had to be branded with a fire hot iron. All this work for such a large herd took several months to perform.

Henry and Randy had done all these tasks before so this time they fit in better and the vaqueros were pleased to see Anglos skillfully do the work that was normally attributed to them. One day Rudy came riding up to Henry and Randy and said, "When you get this big herd ready to go, you can start working on a second herd."

Henry said, "Are you sure?"

Rudy pulled a sheet of folded paper from his vest pocket and said, "Read this and tell me what you think."

The paper was a flyer advising that Texas cattle were welcome at the train stop in Mud City. The last words on the printed flyer were. *Get the best price for your cattle.*

Randy saw the writing on the flyer and said, "I guess they're making progress on the railroad and want to drum up business so they will have lots of cattle to haul back east. If that be the case, they can take all our cattle."

Henry agreed by saying, "Let's get busy. We got our work cut out for us to keep a steady stream of cattle moving north to the Kansas market. By this time next year, the boss should be rolling in money."

# Chapter Fifty-Eight
# Shipping Texas Cattle East

Henry and Randy threw themselves into getting the herd ready for the big drive north. They wanted to show they could be counted on and perform well all the tasks normally done by a vaquero. They used all they had learned in their previous experiences as novice cowboys to round up cattle suitable for the long drive. Their active participation in branding each cow, castrating those young bulls which needed it and dehorning any ornery cows was much welcomed. The vaqueros were impressed and praised the skills of their Anglo bosses.

Months passed as they helped get their herd ready and the next one. Rafael made sure the chuck wagon was in good shape and well-provisioned. He also recruited a fellow Mexican to care for and oversee the horse remuda. They were all set well before the spring rains arrived and in a hurry to get going. Rudy came by with a handful of flyers and said, "Everyone is getting the same flyer, so the train is there this time. If you're ready to go, you can go. Looks like we'll have a lot of competition. Every rancher has received these flyers and is gettin' cattle ready to drive north to the new money-making market in Kansas. Sellin' cattle is now the quickest way to get rich."

Henry was quick to say, "That is good news, but who is willing and ready to go with us? We need a capable crew."

To Henry and Randy's amazement, Rudy said, "Well, you got the same vaqueros who came back with you last time, plus a new one or two."

Randy said, "That's hard to believe. We thought that they had such a bad experience on our last drive that they would never do it again."

"They do it cuz they know they can do it and the money they earn doin' it. Of course, they have a certain amount of affection for the trail and its freedom. Doin' this also gains them a lot of respect in their community."

Henry said, "Whatever it is, they're welcome. Nothing like havin' a tried and tested crew to trust. Give us three days to get out of here. Pass the word we're leavin' with our herd at sunup three days from now."

The excitement levels at the ranch rose as the word was spread about the imminent departure of the first herd. Everyone's step was faster than before as they anticipated the sound of thousands of hard hooves of cattle being driven north for sale at the Kansas railhead in Mud City. A certain amount of special pampering was allotted to those going on the three-month drive.

The three days went by quickly as all those concerned made sure repeatedly they had everything they needed to cross a one thousand miles of the Great Plains. Henry and Randy were checking out the horses corralled for the drive and the chuck wagon and its oxen team in the big warehouse when Rudy approached them and said, "Tonight is the last night before you head north with the herd, so the big boss and his wife have invited you to their house for an early dinner. See you there."

Randy asked, "What time is that?"

"About two hours from now."

Henry wanted to ask Rudy something else, but Rudy walked off in a hurry. So, he turned to Randy and said, "Well, we better return to our bunkhouse, wash up and put on our best duds."

"I guess we'll wear our new trail clothes that we got yesterday from the commissary. That's the best we got."

Henry replied, "No doubt about it. Maybe we'll try to clean our good hats a bit."

The time passed quickly, and they were all ready for the big 'do' with the boss. They looked at each other and mutually adjusted their clothes a tad. Their boots were the same ones they had worn for a long time and were deeply scuffed. For sure, the boots did not go with their new trail clothes, but the boots were like a part of them, so there was no changing them until their soles were worn out.

Rudy was already at the front door of the big house when they arrived. When he saw them coming, he snapped his fingers, and a Mexican servant opened the door wide so they could pass. They took off their hats and were escorted to the opulent dining room. They found the boss and his wife already seated. After the appropriate courtesies, they were shown their seats next to Rudy's and across from the boss' wife.

Before any words were said, a bevy of servants began circulating and serving heaping portions of delicious food and pouring water into their glasses. Once they were served, the boss' wife spoke. She said, "Bow your heads while I ask God to bless this food and the great drive you are about to undertake."

This was the first time they had heard the boss' wife speak and it had been ages since they had bowed their heads at a dinner table. They had almost forgotten the manners of their elite youth in Virginia. Randy wanted not to bow his head so he could use the time to study the appearance of the boss' wife, but he was afraid to do so. He and Henry listened to her words and tried to gain a sense from them of the role of the woman who spoke to them. They wanted to know what role she played in influencing the decisions of the boss.

After the brief prayer delivered by his wife, the boss said crudely, "Dig in. This is the best meal you'll see in months. Enjoy all you can."

Henry and Randy had no trouble obeying the words of the boss. They ate until they could not eat any more. The boss eyed their every move while his wife demonstrated the best of table manners and stared straight ahead. When the boss saw that the boys had finished eating, he lit a cigar and said, "Rudy tells me you are the best men to trust with driving three thousand head of my cattle north, selling them, and coming back here with lots of money for me, so I guess I don't have much to say except happy trails."

Rudy was feeling good and clapped at hearing the boss' words and said, "Yes sir, these boys can and will do the job. By the end of the year, we'll all be sittin' pretty."

Henry spoke softly, "We're mighty appreciative of the trust you have in us. We won't fail you. You can count on that."

The boss took a few puffs on his cigar and said, "There is just one thing I need to tell you. I've hired a security guard to go along with you. His job is to keep any robbers and renegades at bay, but on the way back, his main job is to protect the strong box with all the money. The strong box is already hidden underneath stuff in the chuck wagon. The security guard's name is Burt. He's a war veteran and a well-armed sharpshooter. Any questions?"

Henry and Randy has some questions, but all their thoughts had been pirated by the news of Burt being added to their crew. After a long pause, Henry said, "No questions except when we meet this Burt?"

Rudy took over the conversation by rapidly saying, "He should be in the bunkhouse tonight. I'll introduce him as soon as he shows up. He's a solitary character, so don't expect to chit chat with him."

Rudy's words made Henry and Randy more uncomfortable with adding Burt to their crew at the last minute. They thought this trusted confidant of the boss would spy on them and all they would do. The boss suspected Henry and Randy were thinking like this, so he said, "Don't worry about Burt. You're in charge. He's only there to help give you extra protection for the huge sum of money you'll bring back. Speaking of money, Rudy will give you all you need for your trail expenses. Now, I suggest turning in early so you can get a good start tomorrow. Good luck. I look forward to seeing you in five or six months."

They politely excused themselves and said their polite goodbyes. Once outside with Rudy, Henry said, "We look forward to meeting Burt. I hope he's all you said he is. And why did you wait until the last minute to spring this on us?"

Rudy laughed and said, "It was not my idea… it was the boss'. I didn't learn about it until today. The boss is nervous about you travelin' with such a huge sum and wants to take added measures to protect his money. Don't read anything more into it."

Henry and Rudy were both thinking the same thing… they would size Burt up when they met him. Henry wanted him to know that he was the trail boss and Randy was his point rider. He had better stay out of their way and, add value to the drive, and not be a problem for them.

They were up early to get all ready to start their big drive. All was ready to start heading toward the trail that they would follow to Kansas. Although meeting Burt weighed heavily on their minds, he was nowhere to be seen. Any way they were fully occupied with getting all in place to begin moving their herd in the right direction. Henry took his place as the trail boss well ahead of the herd, and Randy took his place as point rider near the front the herd. Henry gave the hand signal to move out and Randy passed this on to the vaqueros at the sides of the herd, who in turn let the new rider in the drag position know they were heading out.

Everything went well. The mood of the men and the cattle was good when they stopped for lunch. Rafael had found a good spot to park his chuck wagon and prepared a fire to cook a meal for all the drovers. The horses in the remuda and their caretaker were also accepting the movement toward new horizons. The weather was dry and clear with the usual prevailing wind. Henry thought if these conditions held, they could make at least twelve miles on the first day.

There was a guy who showed up to get his plate of food. He did not say anything to anyone and went away with his plate when Rafael served him. Henry asked Rafael, "Who was that?"

"I dunno. I thought he was with you."

Henry turned to Randy and said, "I guess that was Burt. What do you think?"

"If that is Burt, he's much younger than I expected. He was wearing an old Confederate jacket, so I guess he's a Civil War survivor. For sure, he's a loner and wants nothin' to do with other people."

"Yeah. I agree with what you say, but he needs to know who I am, so I'll mosey over to him and introduce myself."

Henry walked slowly in a non-threatening manner to where Burt was eating his food some distance from the central camp. Burt had his head down and pretended to not know that Henry was coming to see him. Henry cleared his throat so Burt would know he was near him. Henry said, "I know you don't want to be bothered, and we don't want to bother you, but I wanted to make sure that you are okay and know who I am."

Burt continued eating his food and did not look up, remaining silent. Henry did not know what he should do next and was about to leave when Burt said in a deep Texas accent without looking up, "I know who you are, and I knew you would come. If I don't do my job, tell me. If I do my job, don't bother me. Other than that, leave me alone."

Henry was perplexed by Burt's words and hesitantly said, "All right, have it your way."

He walked briskly away from Burt and sought out Randy to tell him what Burt said. Randy laughed and said, "Sounds to me that he's suffering from some kind of war trauma. He probably experienced horrors that we can't imagine. I say leave him alone as long as he doesn't cause any problem."

"Yeah. He's so different than what I expected. He could be my age or younger. I sure didn't expect a shock of blond hair and wild-lookin' blue eyes. We may never know anything about him. He doesn't look like much. I think the best way to treat him is not to deal with him at all."

"Just do as he wants and leave him alone. Now, the cattle have grazed a bit, and it is time we moved out."

Henry mounted his horse and told Rafael to break camp and get ready to move on. Rafael clanged his tin plates together to indicate that the break was over and it was time to get back in the saddle and do their jobs. All the vaqueros vanished in an instant and were back herding cattle, nudging them to get moving in the direction they wanted. Randy made sure the lead cattle were at the front of the herd. He knew that once they moved, the other cattle would follow.

They had many more days, like the first day on the trail. They wove their way through the ocean of grass, avoiding mesquite out-croppings, cactus patches, and prairie dog villages. There were the usual hazardous gulley, creek, and river crossings. They were rained and hailed on hard, but this was to be expected. All these hazards were considered part of the job. The one thing that truly frightened them was a stampede. For them, this drive was blessed because there was no stampede.

All along the way, they ate lots of roasted meat because Burt dropped off every day with Rafael some rabbits he had killed with his trusty Henry rifle. Rafael would always thank him, but Burt never said a word or even looked at Rafael. Burt was in a world of his own, and he was not sharing any of it with anyone. He did not want people to know of the deep pain he harbored within himself.

The weeks went by without a major mishap, and magically they found themselves in Kansas in the grassy, well-watered valley next to Mud City. Henry rode into Mud City to find the railhead had been completed and stockyards built. It was not the same place he remembered. The small settlement had expanded, and there was the outline of a real town.

While Henry was taking note of all the changes that had taken place in Mud City since the last time he was there, he heard a loud voice, "I knew you boys would be back. We're all set now. All we need is your cattle."

Henry turned his horse around to see Frank. He had a big grin on his face, but he was genuinely a sight that Henry was delighted to see, saying, "You want cattle to buy. You got em."

"That's what I wanted to hear. How many head you got to sell?"

"I reckon we lost about two hundred during our long drive from southern Texas, so that leaves us with about twenty-eight hundred head."

"That's a lot of cattle. I'm ready to take them off your hands. Let's go talk terms in the new saloon."

Henry got off his horse and walked alongside Frank the short distance to the saloon. Henry smiled when he saw the name, Alamo, of the saloon. He followed Frank through the swinging doors and he, led him to a corner table, and said, "What will it be?"

"I don't drink, but I'll take anything wet that does not have alcohol in it."

A waiter appeared, and Frank said, "One double whiskey for me and a cool glass of water for my Texas friend."

Then he turned to Henry and asked, "What is your asking price for a head?"

Henry replied, "My brother takes care of the finances, but we discussed this, so I know our price range. What are you willing to offer?"

"I'll give you forty dollars for each healthy head."

Henry almost choked on his mouthful of water. He quickly cleared his throat and said, "You got a deal. When do you want us to drive our cattle to your loading stockyards?" (His brother had told him to accept any offer above thirty dollars per head.)

"Is tomorrow too soon?"

"Not if I leave now to inform my crew that we sold our cattle."

"Well, let's shake on it so I can let you go."

Henry stood up and said, "See you tomorrow."

Frank said, "We'll get a good count of your cattle in the stockyards. Then we'll meet up here for paperwork and payment in gold."

Henry was already gone as he hurried back to his cattle camp. Frank was not sure he had heard what Henry just said. Never mind. Tomorrow, he would make history by loading Texas longhorns into his boxcars and ship them to lucrative markets in Chicago and New York City.

# Chapter Fifty-Nine
# To Mud City and Back

Their cattle had been loaded and counted. They were ready to do business with the trusted Frank. They sat at the corner table with their empty, strong box and waited for Frank to arrive with their money. Honest Frank showed up at the appointed time. Two men struggled to carry in his strong box loaded with twenty-dollar gold pieces and set it down on the floor next to Henry, and quickly hustled out of the premises.

Frank spoke first. "Here's your money and bill of sale to sign for your two thousand, eight hundred and twenty-six head of cattle. At forty dollars a head, that makes a total of $113,040. It's all there in my strong box if you want to check it. Maybe best that we just exchange strong boxes. You give me your empty one, and I give you mine that is full of gold coins in payment for your cattle. Okay?"

Randy took the lead in the discussions with this wily entrepreneur from back East. He said, "Sounds like you have considered all the angles of our deal. We need to look into your strong box before we sign any papers. We trust you, but we just want to be sure all is like you say it is. After all, these cattle belong to our boss, and we have to give him an accounting."

Without hesitation, Frank flung open the strong box and said, "All right, see for yourself. It is all there."

Henry and Randy stared at the open strong box for a few minutes before Randy said, "Okay. It looks like it is all there. If it is not, you'll never buy cattle from us again. Let's sign the papers."

Frank smiled and said, "Here, sign at the bottom of the page. I'm in a bit of hurry cuz there are more herds approaching Mud City. My flyers worked to get all the Texan cattle ranchers to drive their cattle to this railhead. Business is starting to boom and will continue to boom as long as people back East hunger for beef, and there are Texas cattle."

Henry signed the paper and said, "Pleasure doing business with you. If our boss in Texas likes the deal, we'll be back next year with more cattle, and there is probably already a second herd en route from our ranch in southern Texas."

Frank stood up and said, "I look forward to doing business again with you educated cowboys. Tell your boss that he needs to get a bank account so I can send him a bank draft transfer. That's better and safer than hauling around strong boxes of gold coins. Now, I got to make sure your cattle are being shipped so my stockyards are ready for more cattle. Keep your money well-guarded. Happy trails back home."

Henry and Randy sat in silence. They were not sure what to do with the money. Randy said, "I can lighten the load by taking the money out that I need to pay ourselves and all members of our crew."

"Go ahead. Take what you need to cover the costs already incurred, and we'll store the rest away in Rafael's chuck wagon."

Randy removed from the strong box handfuls of shiny gold coins and placed them on the table. He then proceeded to count out the amounts he needed to pay each man. While he was counting, Henry got up to look outside to see all their trail hands waiting to be paid. Rafael was also there with his chuckwagon. Not far away, under the shade of a tree, was standing the ever-vigilant and stone-silent Burt.

Henry told Randy that the men were waiting outside to be paid and said, "When you're ready, I'll call them in one by one to get their money. I fear that when they get their money, it will be hard for them to act in a civilized manner, and Mud City will never be the same after they get done havin' their fun. Nothin' worse than guys who had been on the trail for months to get money in their pockets. I'm even afraid that I will not be able to control myself."

"Yep. As our mom used to say, money is the root of all evil. I'm ready. You can start calling in the vaqueros to receive their payment."

Henry went to the front entrance and called in Spanish and English, "Venga, come."

The vaqueros arranged themselves in a line according to seniority and removed their sombreros. They stood in line respectfully until Randy handed them their payment, and then they turned and ran out to the street to do a little jig. When all had been paid, they assembled as a group to purchase a funeral wreath from the house of the elderly woman who made them. The wreath was for Ernesto's grave site. They rode out to his burial site and solemnly laid the wreath on his grave. After a few minutes of silence and prayer, they rode back to Mud City to taste the hamlet's liquor and see if there were any loose women around. They had money, and they wanted to use some to do all the things they could not do when they were on the long trail.

Randy gave Raphael his money and the money owed to his man caring for the remuda. Even after all these payments, the strong box was almost full. They shut and locked the strong box. Randy was about to put the key to the padlock on the strong box in his vest pocket when an open white hand with palm up appeared at his side.

Randy looked behind himself to see Burt standing ominously over the strong box. It was clear that he wanted the key. Randy did not want any trouble and placed the key in Burt's palm. Burt slid the key into his pants pocket and then grabbed ahold of the strong box and lugged it out front to Rafael's chuck wagon.

Henry and Randy followed Burt out to the street and watched him put the strong box into the chuck wagon. Henry asked Raphael if Burt had said anything to him, and Rafael replied, "Yes, he said 'Come' and another word, 'Wait.' I was scared and did as he said."

Henry said, "It's okay, Rafael. Now that we're paid, we can start heading home."

Rafael said, "Home sounds good to me. I'm eager to get started, but I need some money to buy some provisions."

Randy said, "I got some money for you. Get ready to leave as soon as possible. Give the men a couple of days to work off their end-of-the-trail horns, and then we'll go back to Santa Rosita. It could take us a couple of months. For me, the open range has become my home, and I'm only at home when I'm in the saddle."

Rafael asked in a low voice, "Is that Anglo goin' to be stuck to my chuck wagon like a flea on a dog all the way home?"

"I'm afraid so. Where the strong box goes, he goes. Get used to it. There is nothing I can do about it because there is nothing I can do with him."

Rafael climbed into his wagon, sat down and, grabbed the reins leading to his sturdy oxen, and slowly moved out. Burt was on his horse and followed closely behind the chuck wagon. Henry and Randy stood still as Burt passed. So far, Burt had shown no signs of acknowledging their presence. Henry wondered if he even knew he was the boss. For sure, Burt worked for a different master and lived according to a different set of rules.

Henry and Rafael stood with their horses in the road, and Henry said, "I guess we're free men for a couple of days. Let's check our horses into the livery and then see what there is to do in this wide spot in the road."

Randy said, "The first thing for us to do is to get cleaned up. There's gotta be a place where we can get a haircut, shave, and a bath. After we get all that done, we should look for some new duds. Then we can see if this place has anything else to offer."

"Why don't we start at the new hotel next to the livery. It should offer all you said, and if it doesn't offer these things, they better have plans for them because more herds are headed this way."

They trudged into the hotel and found all they needed offered. After seeing the place, they decided to take rooms for a couple of nights to pamper themselves. They were offered rooms with comfort or without comfort. Henry took the former, while Randy took the latter. Rooms with comfort meant a female roommate would be added to the bill.

Their haircuts and shaves made them feel like new men. The long soak in a tin hot tub and soap suds in the bathtubs made them feel even better. Henry was thinking that they better set up many more places like this if they wanted to deal with the onslaught of cowboys coming their way.

Randy was enjoying his hot soak when he said, "You know I've been thinkin', and anyway, you look at it, we're getting screwed out of a lot of money. We do all the work, and the boss gets almost all the money. It cost him about two percent of the total he receives to get his cattle to market. Doesn't seem fair."

Henry said, "You got a point, but it's his cattle. And that is the way things are."

"Anyway, things need to change. He gets too much, and his trail hands get too little. If the vaqueros knew all the details, I'm sure they would revolt in spite of their loyalty to the boss. It would be in his interest to pay more."

"You think too much. Leave good enough alone. Right now, I'm worried about gettin' some new clothes to cover my clean body."

At that moment, a bathhouse attendant showed up with some new clothes for them. He said, "These clothes are all we got. I hope they fit you. At least, they should be better than what you came in."

Henry and Randy were rinsed with buckets of warm water, dried themselves with the cloths provided, and got dressed behind blanket stands.

They did not like their new outfits, but they were better than their soiled trail clothes. Their hats, boots, and belts had been cleaned up. Henry said, "I guess we look decent enough to eat in the adjoining restaurant."

It was good to be served a regular meal in a well-lit place. They felt so good that it was as if all those months on the trail were worth this reward at the end of the trail. It was like they were prairie sailors, and they had crossed a wide ocean of grass and made landfall. If they had complaints, they had forgotten what they were.

"If it is all right with you, I think I'll go to my room to see what kind of comfort I get."

A smiling Randy replied, "Go right ahead. I hope your expectations are met and you don't get more than you bargained for. I see some guys playing cards at a table in the corner. I'm goin' to mosey over there and see if I can join them."

They stayed much longer in Mud City than they thought. Henry said he was married to the woman assigned to his hotel room and did not want to leave. Randy was doing well playing poker. Rafael was worried and came to look for them to remind them that they had jobs to do and they had to get on the trail to go back home. Henry and Randy reluctantly left their hotel, gathered their crew, and headed south, leaving Mud City behind them.

They felt good in Mud City, but they felt at home on the open range. It was only when they were in their saddles and looking across the immense expanse of grassland that they felt peace and a sense of belonging. They made good time and were back at the ranch where they started almost six months ago. Rudy was there to welcome them and said, "I can see from the strong box Burt already turned over to the boss that this was a successful drive. Did you see the second herd we sent out a month ago?"

Henry thanked Rudy and said, "What second drive? We didn't see anything, but that don't mean nothin' cause the trail is more than a mile wide, and it is gettin' plenty of use now. By the way, who did you get for drovers."

"There's plenty of good southern boys returning from the war to pick from. It was easy to get a crew together who knew the basics of heading cattle on horseback. As long as the money keeps rollin' in, we plan to send two big herds a year to the Kansas market. We hope you boys will be ready to prepare the next herd and to drive it all the way to Kansas. Take a few days to rest and then get to work getting the next herd ready to go."

Randy was busting to ask something, "Given all the money you are makin,' shouldn't you raise the wages of your cowpunchers?"

Rudy could not hide his ire at Randy's words and said dryly, "Noted. We'll take that under consideration."

Rudy walked off, and Henry turned to Randy to say, "We're southern boys too, and to give us more money, they'll have to give everybody more money, and I don't think they are ready to do that."

Randy furrowed his brow and asked, "How long do you have to be in Texas before you're a Texan? I feel more Texan now than Virginian. I don't think we'll ever see Virginie again. Once a Texan cowboy, always a Texan cowboy."

"Well, when you get a better idea of what we should do, let me know."

As Henry said the words, the mysterious Burt walked by them as if in a trance. When Burt was out of earshot, Randy said, "Seriously, I don't like him. I don't care if the war made him like this. I hope he's not imposed on us again."

Henry and Randy rested a few days before getting with the vaqueros to start rounding up cattle for their next drive early in the spring. They would normally wait for the spring rains to turn the prairie grass green so their cattle could graze to maintain their weight. This type of annual activity became routine for them. And the boss did raise their wages … they made an extra five dollars a month.

They knew they were trusted by the boss and had jobs as long as they wanted them. Their main complaint was that Burt was assigned to accompany them every time. They also worried about the changing landscape. More homesteaders were coming all the time, and the railroad was advancing farther south. Their whole way of living seemed to be at the mercy of rich men back East and the railroad moguls. The open range was not so open any more. They felt like trespassers on a land that they had once roamed freely.

# Chapter Sixty
# Fleeing Texas

Randy said to Henry, "I've been doing some calculations. Even with our raise in salary, the total costs to the boss are less than three percent. Still not fair."

"That is the way things are. Like it or lump it. There's nothin' we can do to change the balance of things. Let's just do our jobs and not get involved with the finances of our cattle drives."

For Henry and Randy, getting ready for the drives and doing them became deeply rooted in their way of life. They drove herds up to Kansas every spring and came back to Santa Rosita to do it again. They knew how to drive cattle and all the treacheries that could occur on the long trail. Their reputation as being among the most experienced cowboys in Texas spread far and wide.

Henry was impressed by the developments in Mud City and planned to marry his woman there and settle down. Cattle trading had definitely made Mud City a bustling Cowtown, but activity diminished there when the railhead moved farther south. They were happy that this made their drives to Kansas shorter, but they missed the contacts they had made in Mud City.

They had done a half-dozen drives when a new invention started to spell the end of the open range. Cowboys referred to this invention as the devil's rope, but its inventors called it barb wire. Ranchers and farmers found it useful for fencing in their land. In particular, ranchers were interested in marking their land so homesteaders would stay out.

Barb wire fencing was a volatile subject and the cause for violent conflicts between ranchers who wanted to keep the range open and those who wanted to demarcate their land. Cowboys were particularly enraged because barb wire fencing threatened to put an end to their livelihoods. The advent of sheepherders in search of good pasture prompted cattle ranchers to fence off their large patrimony of land to safeguard their grazing rights.

All this fencing prevented cowboys from herding cattle freely as previously done on the open range.

After suffering many encroachments on his vast land, the boss decided to invest in the resources to erect fences along the distant outside boundaries of his prairie kingdom. Henry and Randy were given the big job of overseeing this huge fencing operation. They were quick learners of this work, but they felt they were working against their best interests. Erecting fences meant they could not go on long cattle drives any more.

It was not surprising that they had mixed feelings about their fencing job, but it was the boss' call, and they made the same pay as they did as cowboys. There were gates for allowing the passage of cattle to the railhead, which was not so far away. There were sheepherders and rustlers who would cut the barb wire fences so they could graze their sheep or steal cattle.

This fence-cutting problem did so much harm that the boss requested via Rudy for Henry and Randy to undertake night patrols of the fence lines. With guns ready, Henry and Randy rode out to where the problem was most acute. They split up. Henry went one way along the fence line, and Randy went the other way. The full moon gave them ample light to see any intruders.

Suddenly, Randy heard some gunshots and turned his horse around to gallop along the fence in the opposite direction. He wanted to cry out the name of his brother, but he thought it best to remain quiet so any intruder would not hear him coming. Randy rode quickly in the direction of his brother and found him sitting quietly on his horse with one of his pistols still drawn and looking down at a body lying in the tall grass.

Randy got off his horse and walked gingerly up to the body and gasped as he said, "Why it's Burt. You killed one of our own men. Why?"

Henry spat on the ground next to the body and said, "He tried to shoot me first. I guess he didn't like me seeing him cut fence. Anyway, I never liked the SOB."

Randy was in a state of shock and did not know what to say. After a while, he said, "Dead is dead. Nothing we can do about that. Let's find his horse so we can take back his body. I'm sure Rudy will understand that it was a case of to either kill or be killed."

The remorseless Henry holstered his pistol and said, "I saw his horse over there. I'll be back with it in a jiffy."

When Henry returned with Burt's horse in tow, he said dryly, "Let's lift him up and lie him across his saddle, and then we can tie him."

After Burt's body was secured, they began to ride the several miles back to the ranch. Randy noted the break in the fence and said, "We'll have to send a team tomorrow to repair this stretch of fence."

It was near dawn when Henry and Randy arrived at their bunkhouse with Burt's body. They dismounted and waited for Rudy to get up. Rudy stepped out of the bunkhouse and immediately spotted Burt's dead body. Henry and Randy were amazed at the high level of anguish expressed over Burt's death. Burt was the most unlikable person they had ever met. Rudy's first words were, "Oh my God. Burt is dead. The boss ain't goin' to like this. How did this happen?"

Henry wanted to lie and say they found him dead, but he decided that the best policy was to tell the truth. He cleared his throat and looked into the eyes of Rudy and said, "I found him cutting fence wire. He pointed his rifle at me, and I involuntarily drew my pistols and shot him."

Rudy said with much ire in his voice, "I don't get it. Why was one of our own cutting fence?"

"I don't know. Maybe he was upset about closing the open range. Anyway, it didn't have to come to this."

A curiously unsettled Rudy said, "I have to go now and try to explain all this to the boss. Stay here until I get back."

Henry and Randy sat silently while they waited for Rudy to return. They did not have to wait long. In less than ten minutes, Rudy was back on the run and blurted out, "The boss is beside himself with anger and grief. He does not know how he's goin' to give the sad news to Burt's father. He's already sent a messenger to the father to come and collect the body of his son."

Randy could not believe all the fuss that was being made because of Burt's death and asked, "Who's the father?"

"The father is the boss' best friend and former partner who owns the next ranch over. I'm sure he'll not rest as long as the killer of his son walks this Earth."

Henry was worried by Rudy's last words and said in a pleading tone, "His son cut the fence and was about to kill me. Does that truth make no difference to his father?"

Rudy said after a bit of reflection, "No matter. Burt was his son, and he'll seek vengeance. If I were you, I would lay low until this matter blows over. Too much passion now to make rational decisions."

Randy meekly said, "I guess to be on the safe side, we'll go back to monitoring our fences."

"Good idea. Meanwhile, I'll go and try to cool down the boss. Leave Burt's body like it is. His father should be here by nightfall."

Rudy returned swiftly to the big house, and Henry said softly but firmly to Randy, "If there is anything you want in the bunkhouse, go and get it now. We got to get out of here now."

Randy was confused by Henry's words, but he could see that the subject was not open for discussion, so he ran to bunkhouse to see what he wanted to take with him. Henry did the same, but all he was interested in was getting extra ammunition. Henry told Randy, "Make sure you take all the money you have."

Randy found Henry already outside, mounted on his horse. Henry said, "Let's go east and keep goin.'"

Randy figured he had no choice but to follow his brother. His mind was racing to grasp what was happening. They reached the perimeter of the ranch and, cut through the fencing, and kept on going. Other than going east, they did not know where they were going. They rode day and night. They followed stream and gulley beds in an effort to cover their tracks and stay unnoticed.

They only stopped because their horses needed to rest, graze, and drink. Night travel was the best, but they needed to know where they were going. Henry stated his idea, "Let's follow the old cotton road to Alleyton and then take the train to Houston. When we get to Houston, we can figure out our next move."

A troubled Randy asked in a trembling voice, "Why we leavin' anyway? I had plans, and none of what we're doing fits into my plans."

"I know that, but plans are no good if you're dead. These big-shot Texans will never stop until they get their man, no matter how much it costs or how long it takes. They always get their man even if it is the wrong man for the wrong reason."

"I never thought that our days of being Texas cowboys would end so abruptly. At the very least, I wanted to say goodbye to Rafael. Now we're gone, and we don't know where we're goin'."

"Hey, look. I was ready to settle down with my woman in Mud City and become a family man. Now, I'll never see her again. Don't get in your mind that I like our situation."

"I'm not sure where we're goin', but we have to get as far away as possible as quickly as possible. We just got to stay beyond the reach of Texas Rangers. Think about it. When we get to Houston in a few days, we'll decide where we can go."

They found the old cotton trail and followed it for ten days at some distance away at night. No one saw them, and they did not talk to anyone. Their horses were tired and in need of a long rest, but there was no rest until they got to Alleyton. They planned to sell their horses and tack in Alleyton and buy a train ticket to Houston.

It was a struggle for them to get to Alleyton, especially as they only had to eat some hard-tack biscuits stashed away in one of Randy's saddle bags. The main thing they had on their minds when they got to Alleyton was to eat. They sat down at the first outdoor kitchen they came across and ordered a heaping plate of food. Their hunger trumped all their other needs.

Once they filled their bellies, they started asking where they could sell their horses. They ended up at the town's livery and sold them and their saddles to a blacksmith who thought he could make money off the horses. Henry and Randy took the money from the sale of their horses to the train office, and Henry bought two tickets. Randy asked, "Where we goin?"

"Well, we got to get out of this state, so I bought tickets to New Orleans. When we get there, we'll see if we can go farther."

Henry replied, "Oh. We're just visiting family. We'll be back in a couple of weeks."

Randy said, "We should disguise ourselves and don't let people get a good look at us. We got to change the way we look. If anyone is looking for us, it would be easy for someone to know it was us who came this way. As it is, we're sticking out like a sore thumb."

"You got a point. We should change into new clothes and get different hats. You got the money for that, don't you?"

They went to a store and bought new eastern duds and shoes that would not make them look like Texas cowboys. They changed quickly in a side room and dashed to catch their train.

They boarded the train and took their places on a passenger bench next to the window. The conductor came by and punched their tickets. He looked at Henry and Randy and said, "You boys sure you want to leave Texas?"

Randy lied and said, "Oh. We're only goin' to visit some relatives livin' in Louisiana for a couple of weeks. Now that the war is over, it's time for us to have a family reunion."

When the conductor left, Henry laughed and said, "Now that was biggest piece of croc shit chat that I've ever heard, but my hat's off for such devious words. We got to be prepared to live lives full of ways to hide our identities and the places where we've been. This applies particularly to me as I'm the one they're after. I've got to do all I can to throw them off my trail."

Their train crossed the Mississippi River and pulled into the New Orleans station on time. Henry said, "Let's get off so everybody thinks we are goin' to New Orleans. I'm goin' to buy tickets for us for the next train leavin' to go farther east."

"But I thought we were goin to New Orleans. Where's the next train headed?"

Henry replied, "I dunno, but wherever it goes, we go. I don't care as long as it throws those who are followin' us off our track."

Henry got some money from Randy and rushed to buy two tickets on the next train headed east. They headed out of the station, acting like they were going into the city. They hid behind some nearby trees for a while and then re-entered the station just in time to board the other train.

They took their bench seat side-by-side as usual, and Randy asked, "Where we goin'?"

"I dunno exactly, but it is somewhere in northern Florida. Here's your ticket. Now, I'll find another seat. We should not be seen together. Makes it easier to identify us, and I'm the one they want. Now go on and sit somewhere else and act like you don't know me."

This unexpected arrangement puzzled Randy, but he thought it might be for the best. As he got up to look for another place to sit, Henry said, "One other thing, my new name is Charles. Never use 'Henry' again. My new last name is Bonard. Therefore, from now on I'm Charles Bonard. Henry Harrison Read is dead and buried. Now, for your own good, get away from me."

Randy could not believe his ears and asked with much irritation, "Where in the hell did you get such a name?"

"I just saw a sign out the train window that had the name of Charles Bonard and Sons. It immediately dawned on me that that is the name I should adopt if we are goin' to be successful in covering our tracks."

Randy hesitated, but he said before he left, "That's fine and dandy, but I don't think a name change will do much. After all, how many big guys are there who are clean-shaven and who carry two pistols. If the law is after you, it is not your name but your physical description that will lead them to you."

Henry looked fondly at his younger brother and said, "Are you done yet? Anyway, you don't know me. Go away."

Randy ended their exchange facetiously by saying, "Okay, Charles, have it your way."

# Part III
# Florida

# Chapter Sixty-One
# Escaping to Ocala

Clickety-clack… this sound and other train sounds reverberated in the ears of Charles and Randy. The wood-burning locomotive made a constant racket and rattled unceasingly the rickety wooden passenger cars it pulled. The putrid smoke enveloped the entire train. When its whistle blew off some steam, the noise it made woke up all the passengers, penetrating deeply into all crevices, human and non-human. The clang-clang of the bell on the locomotive alerted all that they were nearing a station stop and they should all get their tickets out for verification by the conductor, who always cried the name of the stop and all going there should get off. He could also loudly say, "End of the line. All get off."

The train noises and smells were a far cry from the silence and odors of the open range that Charles and Randy had grown to love over the past twenty years. They suffered from having their lives abruptly uprooted for the second time in their young lives. Their minds were mostly blank as their long train rides took them farther away from Texas and deeper into an unknown future.

They missed being on a horse and being cowboys. Their fancy clothes did not suit them, and they wanted to be free to dress in the way they wanted. Above all, they wanted to return to Texas, but deep in their hearts, they knew that was out of the question. They were lost and did not have a clue about what was in store for them for the remainder of their lives. They were unwillingly back in a basic survival mode. And their blue-blood upbringing on their old plantation in Virginia was a distant memory with no application to their current lives.

They did know they wanted to settle down, get married, and have a family. To do all this, they knew they had to get jobs that paid a livable wage and save some money. Charlie was in his thirties, and Randy was a couple of years younger. It was time for them to settle down. For them, Florida was their last chance to have a life.

The trains rolled on. In a zig-zag fashion, they headed to Florida, thinking if any men were trying to track them down, they would not guess they would go to Florida. They stopped at multiple stations, and Randy always bought tickets that would get them closer to Florida. Charles would hide in the bushes at a safe distance from the station and would make a hissing sound when he saw Randy walking his way. Randy would quickly hand Charles his ticket, and then he would relieve himself in the bushes and quickly return to the station platform. Charles would wait in the bushes until the train arrived and was ready to depart. They did everything possible to give the appearance that they were not together.

Their money ran out, and the last tickets they bought were for a new line to Ocala. This new train had a different sound, and when it moved on its smoother and more solid steel rails, the joints between each rail made less the clickety-clack noise. Randy lamented this fact because he had become accustomed to the sound made by old cast iron rails. Anyway, their money had run out, and the railroad did not go farther south in Florida than Ocala.

They deboarded separately in Ocala. Charles went one way, and Randy headed in another. Randy found a boy named Tyke in the street who could take a verbal message to Charles for a small payment. He did not give Charles' name… he gave only a snippet of a description. His first message followed his advance pay at a livery on the outskirts of Ocala, where he landed a job as a stable hand.

Tyke came running back and told Randy that he found the man he described, and he said that he was okay and had a job in a new store in town. Every two to three weeks, they exchanged messages in this way, keeping secret their relationship. Randy was thinking it was a good thing there was no resemblance between them. Randy was lanky and much shorter than Charles. He also had a full beard and was usually unarmed. Randy was a regular guy; Charles was not.

Although Charles changed his name, his physical appearance stuck out like a sore thumb. His six-foot, two-inch muscular frame set him apart from most men, but the big giveaways to his true identity were his clean-shaven looks, his distaste for alcohol, and his excessive politeness. Of course, his insistence on wearing his two old .44 pistols handed down years ago by his father made him a dead giveaway.

Charles liked Ocala and saw it as growing quickly economically. New buildings were being constructed all the time, and with the influx of former black slaves and the Seminole Indians, there was plenty of labor available. The leaders of Ocala were all white southerners who had moved farther south instead of staying in their home areas to rebuild after the Civil War. They felt freer and far from the worst aspects of the U.S. government's post-Civil War reconstruction policies. Everybody in Ocala was from somewhere else, but all desired to put down roots and make a new future for themselves. For Charles and Henry, this was an ideal place for them to get a new start on life.

They both had heard of someone starting orange orchards, and they wanted a piece of the growing citrus fruit action. They needed to buy some land and get their hands on orange tree seedlings to plant. All this required money. They skimped and saved part of their salaries, saving after some months a tidy sum. They had been in Ocala for about a year and were ready to buy a small plot of land in Randy's name to plant the seedlings they planned to steal from a local nursery.

They paid two darkies to break into an orange tree nursery on a moonless, rainy night to steal a batch of seedlings. With about twenty seedlings, they created an orchard in a distant and isolated area and paid a small sum to their two darkies to camp out on their land and tend to their fledgling small orchard. They were excited about their future prospects and ready to celebrate with their respective patrons on Thanksgiving Day 1883. On this day, Charles was ready to participate in the grand opening of the new building where he worked.

Randy was ready to leave the livery where he worked when three men rode quickly up in a whirl of dust. They did not dismount when they confronted him. They claimed in a deep Texas drawl to have ridden for weeks all the way from Texas. They made it clear they were desperately looking for a guy named Henry, who fled Texas after murdering the son of an important cattle rancher.

Upon hearing they were searching for a man named Henry, Randy fought to control an upsurge of emotions occurring within him and keep his wits about himself. He shyly played dumb and said, "I've been living in Ocala for almost a year, and I never heard of anyone by that name. Can you describe the man you're looking for?"

They quickly gave a description that fit his older brother to a 'T'. He was doing his best to remain calm when one of the men said, "Can you take care of our horses while we go into town and ask around about this guy and see if there is a place where we can eat and clean up?"

Randy, who by then went by the nickname of Buck, took their horses and led them to the back of the stables, where he quickly stepped outside and beckoned for Tyke to come on the run. In a hushed voice but with a clear sense of urgency, he told the boy, "Run quickly and tell Charles that three men from Texas are in town and looking for him."

Tyke ran as fast as he could on the muddy street, passing the three men, and ran into the new Bartlett building to deliver the message to Charles, who politely excused himself from the boy and left his store unattended while he went quietly upstairs to his room to fetch his pistols which were always loaded. Tyke ran off in a hurry to confirm to Randy that he had delivered his message and to get his payment. Randy reminded him that their transactions were private and none of his business. Randy's final words of warning to Tyke were, "If you know what's good for you, keep your mouth shut."

Tyke humbly said, "Yes, sir. As long as you keep paying me, I'm nothing more than a dumb errand boy."

Randy smiled at these words, and Tyke ran off. Randy busied himself with getting two of the tired horses belonging to the Texas men ready in case they would need them to get out of town fast. He fed the horses and watered them. He removed their saddles and brushed them before re-saddling the best two horses. He wanted to be ready in case his older brother survived his encounter with the three Texas men. He was hoping they could stay put, but he knew that the deck was stacked against him and his older brother.

The three men had been told by a couple of people they met on the main street that there was a guy who worked in the Bartlett building who fit the description of the guy they were looking for, but they said he went by a different name. They also said that they highly doubted he was the man they sought because he was just too nice. Charles was sitting calmly in the shadows of the stairwell when the three Texas men entered the dry goods store where he worked. He waited until the men were well inside the store. One of them yelled out, "Henry, if you're here, show yourself."

Charles immediately stepped around the bottom of the stairs with his pistols blazing. He fired rapidly three shots, killing instantly all three men with deadly accuracy. He then bounded upstairs to his sleeping room and

434

used the oil lamps next to his mattress to set the building on fire. He waited until the flames were roaring before he stumbled out of the building with his handkerchief covering his face, saying to the gaggle of confused people gathered outside in the street, "I was upstairs when I smelled the smoke. I feel lucky to still be alive. What can we do? Maybe I should go back inside to try to save some goods."

The townspeople ran to and fro, but nothing could be done to stop the fire from spreading. The wooden building was easily consumed by the fire, and it spread to nearby buildings. In the panic, Charles disappeared and drifted toward the livery on the outskirts of town to hook up with his younger brother. He spotted Randy standing quietly beside two horses watching smoke bellow into the sky from the middle of town.

Charles said in an even and quiet voice, "I knew I could count on you. Mount up and head south. I'll tell you all about it later."

They rode fast out of Ocala and kept going at a gallop until nightfall. They were unprepared for this dastardly turn of events. Charles briefly described to Randy what had happened. They stopped in their tracks, unsaddled their horses, and tethered them to nearby bushes. Before exhaustion and the dark night drove them to lay down on the trail to get some shut-eye, Charles turned his head to face Randy, who was laying down beside him, and said softly, "Happy Thanksgiving."

# Chapter Sixty-Two
# Fleeing Farther South

"Damn you."

Randy repeated these words over and over with a tint of rising anger in his voice. The body of his older brother was aligned with his on the two-track dirt road. He heard Randy every time he said these words, but he did not know what to say in response. He had never heard his younger brother utter such angry words, so he was a bit surprised. Whether he liked it or not, he felt obliged to reply and said only, "You're right."

His words set Randy off, and in a torrent of words, he related to Charles his frustrations. "You ruined everything for us in Texas, and just as we were getting a foothold in Ocala, you ruined that too. Now, here we're down and out with our bellies stuck to our backbones in the worst shape ever. It will take a miracle for us to survive."

Charles heard his brother loud and clear and cleared his throat as the sun was beginning to peak over the eastern horizon. And said a few words, "I can't deny anything you say. I'm a curse to you and all you want to become. You're much better off on your own. After all, I'm the one they want to kill and not you."

Randy was struck by the meaning and frankness of his brother's words. They had been together a long time and were inseparable, but he could see the time coming when they would have to go their own ways. He wished his older brother the best of luck and always wanted to help him, but it was best that he strike out on his own.

For him, it was only a matter of time until they would go their separate ways. Now was not the time. They had to work together to figure out how to survive. They had nothing to eat and no money. They sucked the dew off the grass and searched for something edible in mother nature's cupboard. This was unfamiliar territory for them, and they did not know one plant or tree.

To make matters even worse, it began to rain. And it was not the kind of rain they knew in Texas. They did not see the rain coming, and before they knew it, they were drenched. The rain gave them water, but they needed more than that to survive. With their last bit of energy, they saddled and mounted their wet and exhausted horses and headed at a slow trot down the road.

They had gone only a short distance when they heard a sound coming from behind them. They were soaked to the bone, but they managed to hide behind some bushes on the side of the road and waited to see who was headed their way. From the sounds they heard, they knew it was the creaking of a wagon that was making the noise they heard. They waited, and sure enough, in the early hours of the day, a small covered buck wagon pulled by a team of two mules was approaching. As far as they could tell, only the driver was with the rig.

Charles was debating in his mind whether or not to shoot the driver and steal whatever he possessed. Randy was afraid of this side of Charles and rode onto the road to greet the driver, who replied in a cheerful manner, saying, "I never expected to see anybody else in these parts. Good to meet you, my name is Hank? What's yours?"

Randy smiled in spited of the pelting rain, saying, "My name is Ron, and I'm with another fella I met on the road. His name is John."

At that moment, Charles guided his horse onto the road. "Howdy, pleased to meet you. And yes, my name is John. Where you comin' from?"

"Ocala. I've been goin' all night to get out of that place. When I left, it looked like the whole town was going to be burnt to a crisp. Right then I made up my mind to go to Peace River to mine phosphate. I'd been thinking about that a long time, but when I saw that fire. I knew it was time to leave. Where you guys headed?"

Randy replied, "Don't rightly know. Anywhere we can get jobs. We're down on our luck and ready to accept anything we can get."

Hank thought for a few minutes and then said, "Why don't you join me. I could use the company, especially in case I'm attacked by runaways and renegade Indians. I can't pay you anything, but I can feed you. You seem well-armed, and it's safer to travel in a group. What do you say? Want to tag along with me?"

Charles was the first to speak up and said, "As far as I'm concerned, you've got a deal."

Randy quickly chimed in, "Count me in." He quickly added, "We're mighty hungry now."

Hank happily replied, "I can see you guys are hungry. I plan to have breakfast as soon as this rain lets up."

Charles and Randy were pleased that as soon as Hank said these words, the rain stopped. At the first wide spot in the narrow road south, Hank parked his wagon and started rummaging around in the back for dry firewood and something to eat. He said, "No worries. I got plenty of vituals for all of us. Here's some wood and some matches. Maybe you can help me start a fire."

Randy got ready a place on the ground ready for a fire, and Charles stacked the wood in a pile and lit it. Hank declared, "I don't like to brag, but I'm a good cook."

With those words, Charles and Randy were ready to be dazzled by Hank's culinary magic, but all he cooked was a plate of grits for each of them and boiled some coffee. They did not care. This was no time to be fussy. For them, the grits were a Godsend and the coffee washed away their remaining stomach pangs.

"That was some fire in Ocala," popped up Hank. "The whole center of town was burnt down. All the legal records and the old newspapers were destroyed. Too bad. I was startin' to like Ocala and thinkin' of settling down there, but I left while the smoke was still risin'."

Randy was fast to respond, "Gee. You think they'll ever find the cause of the fire?"

Quickly, Hank said. "Well, many people think the fire was started by a couple of guys who worked in the Bartlett store and slept on mattresses in the upstairs room above the store."

Charles felt he should say something, "I bet the townspeople are ready to lynch those two guys."

Hank interjected in a matter-of-fact manner, "Nope. Those guys died trying to put out the fire. There are some people who observed guys going back into the Bartlett building when it was up in flames and they found three bodies burnt to a crisp in the smokin' ruins of that building."

"Story tellin' over. We best be on our way," said Hank as hustled to put out the cooking fire and return all back into the wagon, check his mules, and start pulling out. His two friends with fake names followed his wagon.

Hank hollered, "If we go all day, we can make Orlando. Let's make tracks."

Charles and Henry trotted their stolen horses behind Hank's wagon. Charles whispered to Henry, "I guess I covered my tracks really good and I died doing so. I can't see how they can continue to pursue a man who died in Ocala. For the first time in a long time, I feel like a free man."

Randy heard his brother's words but remained silent until Charles asked, "What do you think? Cat got your tongue?"

Randy hesitated a bit but finally said with a tinge of bitterness on his spare words, "I think they'll never give up until they get their man."

Charles was put off by Randy's words and clammed up himself. He knew once Randy made up his mind, there was no changing it. He separated from Randy and rode ahead to make small talk with Hank. He asked, "How far to Orlando?"

Hank replied, "I reckon we should be there by sunset. We'll need to find a campsite on the outskirts of Orlando and then head farther south to Peace River. If we see anyone on the road, we'll ask them if they know where we are. It could take us several days to reach the river, especially if Florida has its regular downpours."

Charles thanked Hank for the information and said, "As long as you feed us, we got your back. I'm goin' to ride ahead and make sure there is no trouble waitin' for us."

Hank said simply, "Sounds good. By the way, where did you say you're from?"

With a puzzled look on his face, Charles said, "Why, I don't think we said anything about where we're from. I hail from Virginia. You'll have to ask the other fella where he is from."

Hank replied innocently, "Okay. No problem. I was just curious because you got a Texas accent."

One thing Charles could not tolerate was anyone who denoted anything Texas about him. He stilled his impulse to pull his pistol and shoot Hank dead on the spot. He fought to control himself. He did not want to do anything to upset Randy. He rode back to Randy to tell him that he thought Hank was on to them because of their Texas accent. Randy replied tersely, "That's your problem, not mine. Just don't kill him."

When he said those words, he knew Hank's days were numbered. He told himself that he had to get away from all the violence and killing if he were to get anywhere in life. Charles was deep in his own thoughts about what his little brother had said. He was wondering why both of their accents were not a problem. They were both silent for the rest of the day as they tried to figure out where they stood on their long-standing, inseparable, brotherly relationship.

The sun had almost set on the western horizon when Hank stopped his wagon and unhitched his two mules. Charles and Randy knew without saying a word that this was the spot they would eat dinner and stay the night. They unsaddled their horses and tethered them in places that would give them access to graze on the ample green grass that covered the well-watered land. They both noticed that the lay of the land was different from what they knew in Texas. It was warmer and much more humid, and the farther south they went the weather became hotter and wetter. Adapting to their new surroundings was indeed a challenge for them. They were trying to decide if saying goodbye to winter was necessarily a good thing.

Charles did not perspire much, but Randy was always drenched in his own sweat. This fact was not lost on Hank, who thought Charles' sweatless condition fit him. Hank opened the conversation around the evening campfire by saying, "Yeah, it's hotter and more humid here, and you sweat more, but you don't have to deal with much cold. But some people adjust better than others and altogether it's better than dealing with freezing winters."

Charles and Randy nodded their assent, not knowing what to say. They kept quiet and allowed Hank to ramble on with what he had to say. Hank had plenty more to say. "Orlando is destined to become a great citrus fruit center. A lot of money is coming in to set up large orange groves. The appetite for oranges in the North is high. It's quite a novelty up North to get oranges to eat in the dead of winter. The railroad is coming father south… all they need to get their oranges to northern markets is more freight trains."

Charles and Randy marveled at Hank's talk about the growing market for oranges and all that is involved in getting the industry going and to keep it going. Charles admitted in a few soft words, "I recall once when I was a boy in Virginia, there was an uncle who brought us some oranges that he bought from a ship docked on the east coast. This was the first time we ever saw an orange, and didn't quite know how to eat it. My uncle showed us how to peel it and eat the inside. It tasted so good that we saved the peelings to eat a few months later."

Charles' last words caused Hank to laugh. Randy felt he had to say something, "I've seen an orange tree, but I've never seen or eaten the fruit. Sounds like these parts will have a booming orange business once the

440

railroad arrives."

Hank replied, "Yesiree, Bob. Many years ago, I almost came south to get involved in the orange business, but there was a panic in the financial markets, which interfered with investors. But that is all in the past now, and the future for the orange business looks rosy. Anyway, the discovery of phosphate in the Peace River is promising, too."

Randy said, "Interesting talk, but I need some shut-eye. See you the first thing in the morning. By the way, Hank, is grits all you have to feed us?"

Hank sheepishly replied, "I'm afraid that's all I got."

Randy rolled out his bedroll near Charles' sleeping place as he had done countless times. When Charles came, he pretended to be fast asleep. He wanted to think clearly about his situation and what was best for him to do. He was in his early thirties and it was time for him to make a life for himself. He spent a sleepless night dealing with all that tormented him.

Charles slept fitfully, and when he awoke, he was surprised to see his younger brother on his horse and ready to go. Hank was still asleep, so he could not figure out where Randy was going before the sun was up. He did not say anything. He stared at his brother with an incredulous look on his face.

When he was sure that his older brother was wide awake, Randy said with tears in his eyes, "I'm going now. I'll be in touch once I get settled. Take care and good luck. Stay safe and out of trouble. I'll be okay."

With those few words, Randy rode off toward the center of Orlando, leaving his older brother whimpering like a dog which had just received a hard kick to the gut. Charles had never felt so alone. He and his younger brother had been to Hell and back many times over twenty years. The deep bonds they had cemented over so many years were permanent. For him, this was only an interlude. He was certain he would be back together with his brother, and things would again be like they had always been.

# Chapter Sixty-Three
# Randy on His Own

Randy felt in the depth of his being that his existence had been cut in half. By habit, he kept turning his head to see his older brother, but he only saw an empty space. He could not help thinking he had made a mistake. Many times, he thought he should turn around and re-join his brother. It took all the discipline he possessed to stay alone on the muddy trail to Orlando center.

He experienced fits of anger within himself. These fits were always followed with convulsions and much sobbing. He profoundly missed his brother! He felt like a baby in need of the love and guidance of an older family member. It was like being lost on the vast Texas prairie without a horse and not knowing which direction to take. He knew it would stress every fiber in his body to stay on his unknown course.

This was the first time in his life he had been on his own and separated from his brother. He found himself asking his brother in his head for advice at every turn. Maybe he could live without the physical presence of his brother, but he could not live without the pervasiveness of his spirit. He was lost alone and only was able to keep going because he strongly felt his brother's spirit within himself. He knew deep down that he had to learn how to go it alone and not be dependent on his brother's presence. He had chosen a new path in life and had to learn to live with it.

Randy was deep in thought and so full of emotional turmoil that he did not see the mounted guy stopped in the trail ahead of him. He was about to run into this guy when he brought his horse to a rapid halt. He raised his head to stare straight into the eyes of the elderly stranger who had turned to say, "Howdy. My name is James Murphy. What's yours?"

Randy heard the man's question but did not know how to reply. He hesitated because he did not know whether to give his real name or a fake one. He struggled to say softly, "Randy Read. Pleased to meet you."

James talked like a man who was in a hurry and quickly asked, "Can you read and write?"

Randy found this an odd question but said, "Yes."

James said, "In that case, come along with me if you don't have anything better to do. I'm in a hurry to get back to my orange grove. I can use a schooled man like you."

Randy did not know what he was getting himself into, but in the absence of any other options, he said, "Okay, but what do you have in store for me.?

James rode off and Randy followed at a slow trot. As they rode, James explained, "I need somebody who can record all the oranges I'm harvesting and how many I shipping to northern markets. I'll pay you the goin' wage and you can sleep and eat at our packing station."

Randy was counting his lucky stars and said, "Did you mention eatin'? I'm mighty hungry now."

James replied, "Well, we'll get you some grub and get you squared away on our operations."

Randy was curious and asked, "What were you doin' out alone on the trail north so early in the mornin'?"

"That's all right. Ask me anything you want. I was out looking for people like you. I thought there may be some travelers on the road and I want to get some of them to come and work for me. I was lucky to find you," said James.

"I'm the lucky one because I was headed to Orlando to look for a job in the orange business. I didn't expect to get a job so fast," Randy asserted.

James could not wait to say, "The citrus fruit business is booming. We're getting top prices from northern buyers who can't get enough of our product. We're trying to expand to meet the demand, but we need more workers and fruit trees. A lot of work opportunities in Florida so the competition for workers is stiff. Look in front of you to see the largest orange grove in these parts. We're almost there. All we need is for all our trees to be old enough to bear fruit."

Randy walked his horse slowly behind James' horse. He thought it was remarkable that James was unarmed. They slowly trotted through the young trees. Every time they encountered anyone James greeted them with exceptional courtesy. He saw that Randy was bemused by the excessive manner of his greeting people regardless of their race and station in life. This observation prompted James to say, "I believe in treating everyone like

443

a royal king or queen. I find that it's good business to do so. If you want to retain workers and get the most out of them, you got to treat them right."

Randy could see that James was highly respected by everyone he met and that James held a high position in this orange grove farm operation. They came upon a complex of wooden buildings and James said, "Let's go to the kitchen and get you some grub."

Randy followed James' example and dismounted in front of one building and tied the reins of his horse to a post. They stepped inside the front door and were warmly greeted by a comely woman who said, "Come on in. I've been holdin' your breakfast. I now see I'll have to make two plates."

The woman disappeared into a back room. James and Randy sat down on sturdy chairs placed around a small table. As Randy sat down, he was thinking he had fallen into a heavenly spot and soon his stomach pangs would be satisfied. Before he could complete his thoughts, the woman darted out of the kitchen with a tray of two plates heaped with a variety of food and two big coffee mugs. As the woman was taking items off her tray and placing them on the table, James cleared his throat and said, "I would like to introduce you to my daughter, Maud. Maud, this is Randy. I've hired him to work for us. Please put him on the payroll and make sure he gets an advance on his salary."

Maud said, "Pleased to meet you, Randy." And surprised Randy by extending her right hand to shake his right hand.

They shook hands vigorously. While Maud was gripping his hand, he felt dizzy. For him, it was a magical event that ended too soon. She released his hand and all became normal. It was like she had some special powers over him. He could not dwell upon this subject because his stomach was urging him to devour the food in front of him.

Maud turned to James and briefly said, "I'm glad that Randy is on board. Dad, you did a good thing."

Maud rushed back to the kitchen and James said, "Dig in before it gets cold."

James also ate, but he was watching closely Randy's table manners. He could see that he was a little rusty, but he had basic good table manners. James looked straight into Randy's eyes and asked, "Tell me your whole story so I can know better who is working for me?"

Randy finished his generous plate of food and was on his second cup

444

of coffee before he was able to give him a brief sketch of his life. He told him the partial truth about his life as a boy on a wealthy old-time plantation in Virginia and how they had escaped with his brother and the ended up in Texas where his brother was killed. Since his brother was killed, he wanted to get out of Texas and go to Florida to take advantage of the post-Civil War economic boom. He finished by saying, "Running into you and getting a job in an orange grove farm is for me like a dream come true."

James listened intently to every word Randy uttered while he drank his cup of black coffee. He wiped off his bushy gray moustache, which amply covered his cragged face, and pushed his narrow brim brown hat back on his forehead before responding forthrightly to Randy's spiel with his own story. "You got an interesting background. I look forward to knowing more. As for me, after the war, I came here from Thomasville, Georgia where I had a successful dry goods business. I invested every penny I had in this orange growing business. I hope it will pan out with this next harvest. Much depends on you and how you fill in the gaps in my business. You might say that I bet the whole kit and caboodle on you."

Randy took a deep breathe at hearing these words. He was too tired to be put in such a high position of dependence and struggled for the words to reply. It was too early to throw all this on him. He could only say, "I know next to nothing about the orange business. I can only promise to do my best and learn as much as possible as quickly as I can."

James was quick to reply, "I can't ask you for more at this stage. Maud knows this business inside and out, so I suggest that you start by putting yourself in her hands. She has my utmost trust. Now, can you excuse me while I tend to some other matters?"

The short-statured James limped out the exit and Randy found himself alone. Before he realized it Maud was sitting across from him and saying, "Now, tell me all that my father told you?"

Randy could not readily find any words to answer her forthright question. There was something about her that put him on edge. He thought maybe it was that he had never dealt with a woman at such close proximity. He stammered as he tried to formulate a response. Her patience was short and she said in a feisty manner, "Come on and tell me. I don't have all day. What's wrong? Cat got your tongue?"

Randy finally blurted out, "He told me you would tell and show me all I need to know about your business."

Maud's infectious smile accompanied her reply, "Now were gettin' somewhere. Now I know I got to tell and show you everything from scratch. When do you want to start?"

Randy found his voice and said meekly, "As soon as I get settled in my sleeping quarters. By the way, can you tell me who James is? Is he the foremen?

Maud laughed aloud at Randy's last remarks and said, "My dad owns the entire works here and what he says goes. He's got more business smarts than all of us put together."

Randy felt foolish. He now thought he should have never asked such a silly question. He promised himself that from now on he would never make again such an inquiry. Before he could finish thinking along these lines, the boisterous Maud loudly volunteered, "You're probably wondering why we don't look anything alike. I'll just say that the Seminoles killed my real parents, but I was rescued when I was just a toddler. My dad saw me in an orphanage and gave me a home, raising me as his own. No need to say anything more."

Nonetheless, Randy felt that to be polite he should say something. "Mr. James did a good deed. I'm sure he and his family love you very much."

Maud could not help herself. She giggled and said, "He had a wife and children in Georgia, but they died and he came here. I'm the only family he's got. Now, let me go get this apron off and get on my work shoes so I can show you where you sleep and as much as you want to see on your first day."

As Maud walked quickly by him, he could see that by any accounts she was an attractive woman. She had all the physical attributes he liked in woman. She obviously had big breasts, a tight waist and a bouncy bottom. She had a clear facial complexion, sparkling blue eyes and narrow but strong forearms. Most of all she was intelligent and had a gift of gab. Her long red hair put her in a class by herself. She was a bit short in height, but her bubbling, captivating personality had swept Randy off his feet and she had not even tried to rattle his cage. Randy was afraid of her and realized that he was vulnerable to her charms, which may only be apparent to himself. Anyway, he told himself that he did not worry because such a woman was probably already married and with children.

She hustled back in an all-business manner, saying, "Let's go. Your room is next door."

Randy acted as if her presence did not affect him in the least of ways. On the outside he appeared unaffected by her, but his insides were churning. He tried to write off the affect she was having on him by attributing it to his long time away from members of the opposite sex. He tried to relax and concentrate on the business at hand.

She showed him his room. It was small and adorned with only the basics, but it was all his. She also showed him the outside latrine and washroom. A short distance away was what she called the front office. When she arrived there, she said in a no-nonsense manner, "Go and liberate your horse and take him to our nearby corral where he will be given good care. Put your saddle and all your stuff in your room and come back here to join me for a full tour of our operation. I expect you back here in thirty minutes."

Randy turned and sped away. He was thinking that she was testing him, therefore he did all she asked and found his way back to the office. He found her just inside the small office with two other people. She turned to look at him and said with a smile that revealed her shiny front teeth. "Good job. I would like to introduce you to Amy and Frank who keep things running smoothly for our entire operation. For the time being, you'll need to report to them at least daily and adopt any suggestions they have."

Randy shook hands with Amy and Frank and said, "I look forward to working with you. Please treat me like a baby because I know nothing about the growing and selling of oranges. I have everything to learn about your business."

Frank replied in an amical tone, "No matter. We've been told that you are an educated man and a quick learner. We're here to help you."

Randy said, "Thank you, you can count on me to be back to learn more from you."

Randy was surprised by the loud slap on his belly and Maud saying, "Here's a sheave of papers and a pencil for you to take notes on and record all the oranges we ship out of here and the prices we sold them for."

While Randy was nodding his good receipt the items brusquely given him, Maud went out the office door with the words, "Follow me."

Of course, Randy did as Maud requested. They did a fast tour of their ten-acre spread to see orange trees in all growth stages. They walked down each row and in between rows. Maud talked a mile a minute and it was all he could do to keep up with her. When they had almost completed their rounds of the grove, Randy asked a question, "How many oranges have shipped out?

Maud quickly answered as if she anticipated this question, saying, "None."

Her one-word answer had him scrambling to wrap his head around her reply, but he did not want to upset the friendly atmosphere, so he bit his tongue, Maud rushed by the many workers without introducing him saying, "No time now to introduce you. Seeing you with me should be enough introduction for now. But you need to get to know all these people well enough so you can address them by their names."

Maud stopped in her tracks when they encountered one person, making an exception to her first-day introduction rule, she introduced Randy to Jasper, the chief grove agronomist, saying to him, "This is Randy. In the next few days, you need to get together with him and start educating him about all that an orange tree requires to grow and what it needs to stay healthy and keep growing."

Randy shook Jasper's hand and said, "I'd like the chance to talk with you as soon as you find the time."

Jasper smiled widely and said, "Any time. You can always find me wherever I'm needed in the grove. Right now, I'm spending a lot of time in the tree nursery."

Randy did not have any more time to say anything to Jasper and waved goodbye as Maud marched on to the end of this first tour of the grove. When Maud stopped, he said, "I have a lot of questions."

Maud answered, "No time right now. Write them down and ask me tomorrow."

Randy was perspiring profusely after the brisk walk around the orchard in the hot and humid Florida weather. He noticed that only a thin film of perspiration was on Maud's forehead. He wanted to look at her more, but she said, "Tour over. I have to go now. Get some rest and be ready for a full day tomorrow. If you get hungry, go to the kitchen. They can serve you at any time."

Randy was about to say something, but Maud did not give him a chance and rushed off. As she went rapidly her way, her hand brushed against his, sending a tingling impulse that spread over his whole body. Randy was trying to figure out if her hand touched his intentionally as he

448

raised his hand to his face and was pleasantly surprised that it smelled like a rare flowery fragrance. He asked himself if it were possible that her perspiration smelled like a sweet scent or was his imagination playing tricks on himself. He vowed to never wash this hand again as long as it smelled so heavenly.

Randy was overcome with many thoughts. He was thankful that his dominant thoughts about Maud and the orange business made deep inroads into his thinking about his older brother. As always, his brother's spirit pervaded all that he did. He knew he could not tell anyone about his brother who was dead to everyone except himself. He constantly wondered how his brother was doing and where he was. He was grateful that the positive events of today helped him to re-focus his thoughts and get on with living his own life, but his brother would always remain central to his being.

# Chapter Sixty-Four
## Orlando Oranges

"Bong, bong."

This repeated loud banging sound awoke Randy from a deep sleep. At first, he tried to figure out where he was. It took him a few minutes to realize he was sound asleep in his new bed in orange heaven and somebody was pounding on the door of his small room. He staggered to his feet, wrapping his thin blanket around himself, and took a couple of wobbly steps to unlock his door. He immediately saw in the dim dawn light that it was Jasper who had been hammering with his fists. Jasper said with respect and hat in hand, "Sorry Mr. Randy to knock so hard on your door, but it's late and we got a lot to do today."

Randy's facial expression was one of abject shock. All of a sudden, he remembered where he was and all that he needed to do. He said apologetically, "Excuse me. I lost my bearings for a moment. Give me a few minutes to get dressed."

True to his words, Randy appeared fully dressed to Jasper in the briefest possible time and he begged his pardon for the delay and humbly said, "I got to have some breakfast and coffee before spending the day with you. I hope you can be delayed a little longer and join me for a cup of coffee."

Jasper grinned and said, "I can wait a little longer, but I can't join you for that coffee."

Randy was about to ask Jasper why he could not join him when he realized that Jasper was black and the color bar applied in this part of the deep South. He felt bad that Jasper could not join him, but he had to eat, so he sheepishly said, "I understand. Please excuse me while I eat as fast as possible."

Jasper lowered his head and said quietly, "Go ahead, Mr. Randy. I know all too well my place."

Randy found waiting for him a cold breakfast plate and cup of coffee on the table nearest the door. He gobbled the food rapidly and washed it down with his mug of cold coffee. He ate and drank as fast as he could because he did not like that Jasper had to wait for him. He swung open the outside door to the kitchen to see the short-statured Jasper standing, patiently waiting for him to appear. He looked straight into Jasper's eyes and said, "Let's go. I got a lot to learn from you."

Jasper, "Yes, sir, Mr. Randy."

They walked at a fast clip toward the grove farmland. Randy said, "Jasper, my name is Randy and I don't need or want to be called mister or sir."

Jasper said after some hesitation, "Okay. But I'm accustomed to saying those words to a white man."

Randy again said, I understand the post-Civil War times we live in, but if I had my way our roles would be reversed and I'd be addressing you in these respectful terms. After all, you are older than me."

Jasper laughed at Randy's words and saw that he could talk freely to him and said, "A bloody war was fought to end slavery, but barriers have been put firmly in place by white people to keep people with my skin color separate and far from equal."

Before they arrived at the place they were headed, Randy wanted Jasper to explain how he could speak English like an educated white man. With the utmost sensitivity he asked Jasper, "How is it that you speak English better than I do?"

The good-natured Jasper chuckled again and then said with tears in his eyes, "My owner was a highly educated man and he saw that I was gifted and he took me under his wing and taught me all he knew. He was a good man. He experimented with wild orange trees. Of course, I could not go to school, but he taught me how to read and I devoured all that was in his books. But mostly I learned by doing and re-doing under his tutelage."

Randy was lost for words and only could say, "Wow. Where's this man now?"

Jasper answered fully in a somber tone, "He went off to war and got killed. His wife died over the stress of his death. His kids went back to Georgia to live with relatives. His death and the collapse of his family left me and my family to survive on our own. If it hadn't been for Mr. James, I'd probably be dead."

Randy felt he was getting more information than he needed on this first full day of work, but he asked Jasper, "Where were you born?"

Jasper had an odd look on his face and said, "Why, I was born right here in Jernigan."

Randy was curious, "Where's Jernigan?"

Randy's simple question made Jasper openly laugh and answer, "Right here. Orlando was called Jernigan when I was born."

Randy wanted to ask more personal questions of Jasper, but they had stopped in a big field, and Jasper wanted to switch the subject to the business at hand. Jasper also had questions for Randy, but he did not want to pry. Mostly, he wanted to know why Randy's voice sounded like he was from Texas. Jasper pointed to the vacant land and said, "This is where we'll transplant orange tree seedlings from our nursery."

Before Randy could say anything, Jasper continued by saying, "You should have seen this field before we cleared it of its natural vegetal cover. It was a big job to chop down the undergrowth and burn it. I've still got scars on my hands from the cuts I suffered from the saw palmettos, which keep trying to come back."

Randy was impressed but could not imagine the work it took to clear the several acres of land. He was sad because he knew such manual labor could not be done without ex-slaves. He also knew that Florida's economy was fortunate because of the Spanish who came to Florida over three hundred years ago and left cattle and oranges which were today the mainstays of the state's post-war economy. All Florida needed were the trains to ship these commodities to northern markets. Thus, the arrival of the rail network to Florida was a make-or-break deal.

Jasper continued his instructive monolog. "This land may not look like much now, but with mature orange trees, it will be a money-producing marvel. My job today is to cram you with as much knowledge as possible about the care of orange trees, from the beginning of tree growing to harvesting oranges for the market. It's good you brought along your note-taking papers."

Randy said, "Sounds good. Treat me like a child because I know next to nothing about growing orange trees and selling their fruit."

Jasper said with something of a grin on his face, "Well, by the time I get done with you, you might wish you had never met Mr. James. I will say that Mr. James is a good man. He pays us three-quarters of what is paid a white when most white masters only pay us half of what white people make."

Jasper continued talking, "I'll save what happens in the nursery until we get there. Right now, let's concentrate on turning this patch of land into a thriving orange grove. First, we need to do a sketch map that depicts the layout of the grove. I want to give you information that will allow you to participate intelligently in the drafting of this field map."

This was much more than Randy was expecting. He gulped, then exhaled heavily, and then said, "Okay. Let's give it a whirl."

Jasper was more than ready to describe the process of creating an orange grove and said without hesitation, "You have your field map in hand, so you know where to dig the holes to plant your seedlings. The placement of the holes is measured and marked. The holes are twenty-two feet apart, so you can plant around one hundred trees on an acre. Each tree has to be tenderly planted by hand and cared for daily until it takes hold. Even under the best of conditions, they'll take several years before they start producing oranges. When they're five to six years old, a healthy tree can produce several hundred oranges, so a mature one-acre orange grove can produce thousands of oranges. Any way you slice it, if we can get these ten acres productive and ship the orange bonanza to northern markets, we'll have a lucrative business."

Randy was scribbling wildly on his papers. He wanted to note all the details that came out of Jasper's mouth so he could study and digest well part of Jasper's knowledge about oranges. Randy had one question, "When do we transplant?"

Jasper responded, "Good question. Planting season begins in April. In the meantime, we have to maintain this field to make sure it's ready for the planting of orange tree seedlings. We have to keep the brush cut back in this hammock land and observe how the rainwater lays on the land. Orange trees thrive in our hot and humid climate, but they don't like a lot of water. We have to make sure there is no puddling around our tree holes. In other words, we have to make sure the soil around the trees is well-drained."

Randy now had more information than he could digest and said, "Is that all?"

Jasper replied, "This work is more easily explained than done. This positive scenario precludes any pest, disease, or weather problems. Also, mature trees require pruning and other care. Every day, there's always work to do. It takes a couple of hundred of hired hands to keep this place going, and we've not even reached the stage of packing and shipping yet. And we're competing with other growers. The sooner you get up to snuff, the better. Don't be afraid to ask any questions. I know it's a lot to take in on your first day."

Randy was keenly stressed by Jasper's last point and said, "Thanks to you, I'm learning a lot on this first full day. I hope in the days ahead, I can prove my worth. Excuse me, but I've one observation."

Jasper said, "Well, what is it?"

"I see some large trees on the land. Why were they left standing?"

Jasper replied quickly, "When clearing the land last year, we left the live oak trees standing to give some needed shade to our orange seedlings. Now, let's go see the nursery."

They walked about three hundred feet to the other side of the operation to the nursery station, which was a beehive of activity. Dozens of people of both sexes were tending to orange tree plants in a various stages of growth. Randy was all eyes. He spotted Maud busying herself with hands dirtied from working the soil used to fill clay pots for the young plants. Jasper noticed that he was looking Maud's way and said, "Yeah, that's Maud. She's dynamite. Without her and her work, this place would not exist. She's quite a woman. She'll not ask anyone to do any task that she wouldn't do herself."

Randy was a little embarrassed that Jasper had noticed that he was looking at Maud and tried to cover up his feelings by sticking to the subject of how to produce orange trees, saying, "How did you get all these seedlings?

Jasper was quick to answer, "Most come from grafts on the dozen or so mature trees we have. Others come from budded seedlings that Mr. James was able to buy from other orange farmers. We try to be careful not to mix orange varieties so as to maintain the taste of our navel oranges."

Randy had a question, "How do you graft a mature tree."

Jasper replied, "That is not an easy question to answer. You have to see it so I can begin to explain it. When we finish here, we can go over to our experimental plot, and I'll show you."

Suddenly, Maud stopped her chores, cleaned her hands, and came over to greet Randy. Everyone observed her movements because they could see that Randy became increasingly petrified with every step that brought her nearer him. Randy remained stiff and nervous as Maud said, "I see that

Jasper is giving you the introductory course on orange growing. We missed you at breakfast. I see you're in good hands. Back to work for me."

Randy overcame his fear of her enough to tip his hat as she excused herself. He feared her because of the way she made him feel. Her close physical presence upset his insides and made it hard for him to think. He hoped nobody noticed the effect she had on him.

His thoughts on that score were nullified by Jasper daring to say. "Are you okay? Looks like Maud really affects you. Of course, we've never seen her close to a white man before. Anyway, let's go see those grafts."

Randy interjected, "Wait a minute. What about the foundation stones I saw next to the nursery station?"

Jasper replied, "Oh, that. That's where we plan to build the packing house for the oranges we plan to ship out."

Randy, in a reflective mood, said, "Oh, yeah. A lot to do when we get to the stage of selling our oranges."

Far in an isolated corner of the farm were a dozen or so mature orange trees that had each been grafted multiple times to provide seedlings that could be removed and planted in nursery pots. Jasper said, "Here, you can start to see a glimpse of our future. We could grow new trees from seeds, but it's much faster to graft buds onto a branch of a healthy, mature tree. Grafting buds is complicated and is usually best done by women who have much experience with grafting. I can try to explain the process, but you can only understand it when you see it done a few times."

Randy inquired, "When can I see grafting done?"

Jasper replied, "You'll have to wait until grafting season in April – May when the weather is warmer. Come back then, and you will see our grafters at work. For me, the most important step of many is that they have sharp knives that have been disinfected so they don't introduce any plant diseases."

Randy could relate only to castrating bull calves, but he did not dare bring up that subject. He asked innocently, "You have to cut the tree branch?"

Jasper chuckled and said, "Of course. You have to clean the branch you want to graft and cut it with an upside-down 'T,' and insert a sanitized bud in the cut, and wrap a bandage around it to hold in place. In a couple of months, the bud may develop sufficient growth so it can be transplanted to the nursery. I oversee grafting, but I've never done it myself. I don't trust myself to do it. It's a job best left to those who have done it."

Except for the last part, Randy was taking notes on all that Jasper said that he could review later. Randy had a lot of questions. He could not believe how fast the day had gone by. He looked at Jasper and said, "When do we break for lunch?"

Jasper responded with a hearty laugh, "Lunch? Don't you know? There's no break for lunch. Anyway, the day is almost gone, and it will be time for supper soon. Come. I'll walk you back to your kitchen."

They arrived at the kitchen, and Randy turned to thank Jasper for a good day, but he had disappeared in the last glimmers of the sun. Randy went to the washhouse to relieve himself and get cleaned up for supper. He walked back to the kitchen and timidly opened the door to see James and Maud seated at a table. James spied him at the door and said loudly, "Come on in and sit with us. We've been waitin' for you."

Randy politely greeted both of them and sat next to James and across from Maud, who said, "Excuse me. I got to go to the kitchen to get our food ready."

Randy turned to James and asked, "There's nobody else comin?"

The elderly James replied, "No, we're it. That is to say that we're the only whites. As you saw today, all the other workers are black."

James was not done talking and said, "We can't afford yet any more help. That's one reason we're countin' on you to prove yourself a good worker. If it weren't for Maud's good work and initiative, I would just die an old poor man. Thanks to her, I have a chance to die an old but rich man."

Randy did not know how to reply and said, "I can see Maud is a force to be reckoned with,"

"Yeah, but I worry about her. She should be married and raisin' a family of her own, but she has no time because she is married to this orange farm and determined to make it a success. The next few years will make or break us."

The tireless Maud came prancing back into the dining room, holding a tray piled high with food and drinks. She was in a festive mood and served James and Randy with much gaiety. Randy was intimidated by her and the party atmosphere she tried to create. James smiled and winked. Randy finished eating his food. He feigned fatigue so he could be excused and go to his sleeping room early. Maud looked at her father and Randy and said, "Well, if you two are not going to talk, I am. Tell me, Randy, how was your day with Jasper?"

Randy felt compelled to reply and quietly said, "It was okay. I learned a lot. I need to study my notes before I dare say more."

Maud aggressively said, "Well, if that is all you got to say, I might as well collect the dishes and wash them. Goodnight."

Maud left the table in a huff. James smiled and said, "I think she likes you. Pay no mind to how she just acted. I could be wrong, but I think you two will make a nice pair."

James' words made Randy feel uncomfortably nervous, and he asked, "May I be excused? I need all the sleep I can get."

"Sure. Go on. Go to bed. We'll have plenty of time to talk once you get well settled."

Randy left James sitting alone and went directly to his room. He could not wait to dive into bed. He promised himself that he would show the world tomorrow that he was an early riser.

His head was spinning with thoughts of his day and his encounters with Maud. Before he faded away into the land of nod, feelings of guilt slowly crept over him. He felt guilty because he had not thought of his older brother all day. He wondered how he was doing, what he was doing, and if he would ever see him again. He escaped from his mental torments by falling asleep in the depths of a remorse that only he could know.

# Chapter Sixty-Five
# Death in Orange Heaven

Randy got up early and was seated at the breakfast table before the kitchen was open. James eventually joined him, greeting loudly, "Good mornin,' early riser."

James, in his usual jovial fashion, continued by saying, "Let's talk while Maud is fixing our breakfast. I thought a lot last night about what to do with you, and I decided the best use of your talents is for you to concentrate on the packing, shipping, and selling sides of our orange business. What do you think?"

Randy did not know how to reply, but he had to say something, so he said as politely as he could, "I don't know squat about this business, and you want me to oversee parts of the business that I know nothing about? Is that what you mean and want?"

James smiled and looked at Randy straight into his eyes and said, "That's basically right. You got a good head on your shoulders, and you've been to school. I've faith that you can figure out all that needs to be done. Besides, there are people around whom you can learn from and get good ideas. What do you say?"

Randy mulled over James' words for a few minutes and said, "Okay. Why not? But I have a condition."

James said sharply, "What is that?"

"That's easy enough said. When I screw up or when you think I'm headed in the wrong direction, don't hesitate to tell me so."

At that moment, Maud came carrying breakfast and sat down with them. They busied themselves with eating and did not say a word. Their silence prompted Maud to say in her feisty manner, "If the cat's got your tongues, that does not mean you got to clam up on me."

James responded, "Well, I can't say much until I've had my mornin' coffee."

James then repeated to Maud what he had told Randy and how Randy had replied. When James finished talking, Maud said, "Sounds good to me. Maybe Randy should tag along with me. I'm goin' to the nursery, and we can talk about building a packing house on the land beside it."

Randy gulped at Maud's suggestion. He had never been alone with her and was afraid that her presence next to him would push him over the edge. James said, "That's a good idea, Maud. You two need to work in a close partnership if we are goin' to make this orange business a success. I'm too old to do much except give advice and the funds you need."

As James said his final words, Maud got up and went to his side of the table to give him a big hug. Randy blushed at the love Maud was showering on James. He was fearful and envious at the same time. The last time he had been hugged by a woman was when his mother put her arms around him when he was a child. He was starving for feminine affection, but he did not know it. He steadied himself by thinking of his place and the work at hand. He knew that spending the day with Maud would be an overwhelming challenge for him.

They arrived at the nursery after a brisk walk from the kitchen. Randy found he had to walk fast to keep up with Maud. She walked around the piece of ground where the packing warehouse was to be built, hollering out her thoughts, which Randy was quick to write down on his papers. When she was finished sharing her thoughts, she turned to Randy and said point blank, "What do you think?"

Randy was stumped. All he knew on this subject was what she said. His long silence irritated her, so she repeated her question more loudly. Randy finally found some words to say, "I think we need to find someone who has built somethin' similar and get an estimate of what he would charge to do the work we want."

Maud looked at Randy wide-eyed and declared, "You're smarter than I thought. That is a good idea. I'm sure Jasper knows somebody who can do this job. Let's go look for Jasper and ask him to find somebody reliable to build us a packing house."

Randy breathed a sigh of relief because Maud had accepted his idea. From that time on, he felt more relaxed around her. And she gained more respect for him and his hard work to make their orange farm work. They spent most days together, working on various aspects of the orange farming operation. Randy learned a lot from her, and she was happy to see him apply his lessons well. Little by little, they became good friends, and no job on the farm was done without their approval.

They found Jasper, and sure enough, he knew a guy who could build a dandy packing house for them. Once they were given an advance, this guy and his crew lost no time in erecting a spiffy packing house. Of course, James was asked to give his blessing to everything they did. He was old, but he was no fool. He was a fountain of information and controlled all the finances. Maud and Randy were aware that he was almost scraping the bottom of his funds; thus, they were in a hurry to make their orange operation profitable.

Every morning, they ate breakfast together, and they did the same for supper. They would pick James' brain as much as they could in these daily sessions. Randy always had his paper and pencils with him, and one evening, he asked James, "How much do you think you can sell one orange? I want to do a business plan for our operation, but I need to know how much we can sell our oranges for."

James was quick to reply, "If we get access by the train to northern markets, I reckon we can sell our oranges at least at four cents apiece and maybe more in the Christmas holiday season."

Randy jotted this price information down and said, "Now, I got to calculate how many oranges we'll produce per tree and deduct all of our operational costs to see what our profit margin is."

James added, "Don't forget to include all the money I invested in this farm to get it up and running. Also, include all the back salary we have not paid you."

Randy was quick to react, "Why, Mr. James, you house and feed me; that's more than enough. Anyway, there is nowhere to spend any money. I think there is only one or two stores in the hamlet of Orlando. Hell, if I had any money, I'd probably risk it at a poker game in Orlando's only saloon. Of course, there's a lot of 'ifs' here, and we're a long way away from me having any time off and money in my pocket."

James could not help but chuckle at Randy's words and say, "I didn't know you were a poker player. We'll have to play sometime. In my youth, I was known as a good player of cards."

Maud came with the food and, as usual, joined them. James and Randy were quick to change to a more business-like subject. James repeated what he had said to Randy about the selling price of an orange and asked her what she thought. She replied by saying, "Our oranges must be consistently of the highest quality, so we earn a high reputation as a good place to buy oranges. With such a reputation, the buyers will compete among themselves to get our business. That means we'll be paid the top price for our oranges."

James smiled at Maud's business acumen and said, "Maud, you got that right. Reputation is everything. We got to grow the finest oranges in Florida and deliver them in good shape and on time to the buyer."

Randy excused himself from the table, saying, "Please excuse me. Now that I know how much an orange can be sold for, I want to retire to my room to do some calculations."

James said, "Go ahead. I look forward to knowing the results of your calculations."

Maud smiled sweetly and said, "Me too. It will be of interest to know whether all our efforts were worth it."

Randy tipped his hat and, flung open the kitchen door, and went straight to his room. He lit his kerosene lamp and turned up the wick so he could see well the calculations he was making on paper. He could not wait to see the numbers he came up with. There was no stopping him once he got started with his calculations.

He basically figured that at a selling price of four cents per orange, a mature tree produced five hundred oranges. and if there are one hundred trees per acre, and they have ten acres, that would result in five hundred thousand oranges total, and at four cents per orange, that would be twenty thousand dollars. Even if they paid half that in expenses, they would still net ten thousand dollars for each annual harvest, and that was a minimum profit.

Randy re-did his calculation several times, but he always came up with fabulous profit of around ten thousand or more dollars. He could not wait until tomorrow morning to tell James and Maud of the results of his rudimentary calculations. He was excited. If all goes well, riches are just around the corner.

It took Randy a long time to get to sleep. He was rehearsing his calculations in his head so he could recite them perfectly to Maud and James at the breakfast table. The next morning, Randy was almost floating in the air when he opened the door to the kitchen dining room. He found James already sitting at a table and exclaimed, "I got good news for you. There is a handsome payoff just around the corner."

Randy thought his news would be received by James ecstatically with open arms, but James remained still and slumped over the table. He timidly placed his hand on James' shoulder, and there was no reaction. He shook James gently, but he remained as still as a stone. Randy then checked to see if there was any air coming out of his nostrils. It then dawned on him that James had passed away. Involuntarily, he let out a loud, blood-curdling scream.

Maud came running from the kitchen to see what the matter was. She looked at Randy, who was in a frightful state, and then she cast her glance on James. When she saw James collapsed on the table, she knew the unthinkable had happened. Randy was shaking when he said, "James is no longer with us."

Maud was deeply affected by Randy's words and started bawling while she cried out, "This can't be. Not before our first harvest. I can't live without him. What can we do?"

Maud became inconsolable and sat on the floor, sobbing buckets of tears. Randy felt deep inside of him the horror of the moment. He wanted to be strong for Maud, but he was no match for this sad situation and buckled also into a dark pool of remorse. He crawled over to be at Maud's side. She felt him near herself and embraced him as if her life depended upon it, saying, "Now, you're all I got."

After a brief while, he untangled himself from Maud's tight embrace, saying softly, "I'll go look for help. Please try to be strong in this most trying of moments."

Randy stepped outside and began walking with a dark gloomy cloud over his head toward the nursery. He stopped the first person he saw. He tried to convey in a non-alarmist manner, "Go fetch me, Jasper. Tell him to meet me at the kitchen."

Despite Randy's effort to show an even demeanor, everybody knew something was amiss, and the alarms spread like wildfire for all those who worked on the farm. Jasper came running and almost overtook Randy before he got back to the kitchen. The gasping Jasper said, "What's wrong?"

Randy could not formulate the words that would not divulge his deep grief. He finally uttered words he did not want to say, "Mr. James died."

"What are you saying? That's not possible," said Jasper in shock.

One look at Randy's teary eyes told Jasper the truth... Mr. James was dead.

Randy had much difficulty saying, "What do we do now? His body is inside. You got to come inside to help me handle the body."

Jasper wiped away his tears and followed Randy inside. Maud was still sprawled out on the floor in the throes of grief over her great loss. They lifted James' body out of the chair and placed it on the floor. They wrenched his arms to his sides and pulled his legs into a straight position. They covered the body with the flimsy tablecloth. Randy turned to Jasper and said in a low voice, "What do we do now?"

Jasper scratched is balding head and said softly, "You take care of Maud. I will go into the settlement to get help and start making the funeral arrangements."

Jasper exited the room rapidly, and Randy tended to Maud, who lay prostrate on the floor. He whispered in her ear, "Maud, you must go home. It's best that you mourn the loss of your beloved father there. Please take my arm, and I'll lift you up and escort you to your house."

Maud's house was a clapboard dwelling a short distance away. He entered the shaded living room and sat her down in an upholstered chair. He left her to go sit on the front porch, waiting for news from Jasper. It was still morning, and Jasper was nowhere to be seen. After a couple of hours, Jasper appeared and said, "Arrangements have been made for his burial in the local cemetery late this afternoon. Everybody on the farm and in Orlando knows and will be there for the burial."

Before he could ask Jasper anything, he was gone in a flash. Randy did not know what to do. He felt like he had been set adrift and no longer had a rudder in his life to direct himself. He decided to go inside the house and check on Maud. To his surprise, Maud was up and about. She pointed to some clothes she had laid out on a couch and said, "These are for you. He would have wanted that you look nice for his funeral."

Randy looked at the clothes and knew they had belonged to James. He did not like the idea of wearing a dead man's clothes, but he needed clothes to wear to his burial, so he said, "Thank you."

Maud displayed her methodical thinking by saying, "You need to get the horse and buggy ready for us. The buggy is parked at the side of the house, and the horse is in the corral. Get all ready so we can lead the funeral procession."

Randy nodded and said, "No problem. I'll get it all done. You don't have to worry about anything."

Randy went to fetch the horse and made sure all the tack for the buggy was clean and in place. He sat on the front porch again, trying to decide to dress first or get the buggy ready to go. He decided to go inside and find a place to try on his duds. Maud was out of sight, and he imagined she was readying herself in her bedroom. He found another room to try on his dead man clothes. He was surprised that the clothes fit him well. He also borrowed one of James' hats that was just his size.

All decked out in his new clothes, Randy went outside to maneuver the buggy into a shady spot under a tree. In this way, all could be ready as soon as Maud gave a sign for their departure.

While Randy was waiting for Maud to appear, in the distance he spotted on the dirt, dual-track road a wagon heading his way. As the wagon got closer, he spied a lonely wood coffin in its bed and knew it was carrying James' body.

Maud came out of the house and walked to board the buggy. Randy picked up the reins and sat down beside her. The oncoming wagon went in front of them, and its driver said follow him. Randy slowly drove the buggy behind the wagon carrying the casket. He briefly glanced behind himself, and he saw the entire farm workforce walking behind him in their best attire. They were softly singing a Negro spiritual.

When they passed though the small settlement of Orlando, they saw all its inhabitants had formed a group to follow the procession to the nearby graveyard. In the overgrown tiny graveyard, a hole had been dug and James' coffin was carefully lowered into it. Orlando did not have a preacher yet, so no words were said to send his remains off for all eternity.

Workers began covering his grave and people from James' grove broke into spiritual songs. The sun was setting in the West and the crowd dispersed. Maud stood silently beside James' grave with tears streaming down her cheeks. Randy stood at her side, prepared to do her bidding. When it was almost dark, Randy said quietly to Maud, "It's time to go home. We can come back tomorrow if you want."

Maud turned and walked slowly back to the buggy. They boarded the buggy and were some distance away from the graveyard when Maud said, "It's over. I just wish he had not died so unexpectedly, so suddenly. I'm not ready for this. Nothing is forever. In his honor, we must make his orange business a success."

# Chapter Sixty-Six
# The Great Freeze

Dusk brought the bats swooping and diving as they chased errant night insects. Randy watched the spectacle displayed before him in the darkening sky, but his thoughts were all about how they could do without James. His thinking was at a dead end when Jasper, like a ghost in the evening mist, came close and said in barely audible words, "What do we do now?"

Randy looked at Jasper and could see that he had been crying. He hesitated as he tried to find the words to reply to Jasper's question. His tongue felt like it was inflated and stuck in his mouth. He freed his tongue to say simply but awkwardly, "Take three days off to mourn, then back to work."

Jasper silently disappeared into the night air and Randy continued to wait for Maud to show herself. He knew there would be no supper tonight. That was okay. His concern was about whether there would ever be another meal.

He waited for Maud for a couple of hours and was at a loss as to what he should do. He finally entered the house silently and tippy toed up to the closed door of her room. There was no sound coming from the room. So, he tapped lightly three times on the door and whispered, "I hope all is all right. I'm leaving now. See you tomorrow."

Immediately Maud flung the door wide open and said painfully with tears in her eyes, "You can't leave me alone. Go stay in our spare room."

Just as quickly as she opened the door, she closed it with a clack. Randy felt he had no choice but to look for the spare room. He stumbled across the sitting room to find a kerosene lamp to light. There were two doors on the opposite side of the small sitting room. He opened one and could see instantly that this had been James room. The other door had to be the bedroom where he would try to sleep.

The room was tiny but clean. There was a feather mattress covered with a colorful quilt. Randy took his clothes off and lay down to try to get some shut eye. His head was aching from the thoughts that churned incessantly about the impact of James' death on the orange operations. The hunger pangs growling in his stomach also made it impossible to sleep.

Randy closed his eyes and pretended to sleep. He told himself that he had been in worse situations. Yet, he recognized that in those situations, he had always been with his big brother. He did not want to dwell upon his brother at a time like this. There was enough worry and grief on his plate.

Although his eyes were closed, Randy could clearly hear the wailing call of the night birds and the untiring chirping of crickets. He told himself he would get up at the first crack of dawn and make himself a cup of coffee. While he was waiting to see a little daylight pierce through the cracks of the wooden shutter window of his room. There was a loud bang on his bedroom door and he heard distinctly Maud's voice, "Time to get up. Come out."

Randy was in a state of shock but hurried to get dressed and obey Maud's surprising but much welcomed command. Evidently, she had ceased her deep mourning for James and was ready for a fresh start. Despite his sleepless night, he was excited and could not wait to see Maud.

He quickly stepped out of the door and found Maud waiting for him in the dim light of the early morning. She was surprised to see her still dressed in her black funeral clothes. Without turning around to face him, she said sweetly, "Be a dear and unfasten the back of my dress."

Randy had never done such a thing before, and these words of Maud were totally unexpected. She stepped backwards so he could see better the small metal clasp at the top of the backside of her dress. At first, he was afraid his strong, rough hands would break the clasp. He struggled for a bit before he was able to unclasp Maud's dress. His embarrassment was great when the dress suddenly fell to the floor around her feet.

Randy wanted to turn away, but the beauty of her curvy, smooth body riveted his focus on her nudeness. He was not only fascinated by her beautiful womanly body but by the skimpiness of her undergarments. Before he could turn around, she turned and fully embraced him. He wanted to escape from her grasp but found that he was helpless in her arms and ready to do anything she asked.

No words were exchanged. She held tightly his hand as they walked slowly to her room. She removed her undergarments and signaled to him to do the same. Randy was shaking and perspiring lightly but strange forces were moving him to undress and get into bed with her. Once he was alongside her in bed, nature took its course to the satisfaction of both.

Randy laid on his back wondering about what had just occurred and what it meant for his life. Maud did not give a second thought to what had just happened and bounded out of bed saying in an even tone of voice, "I'll get dressed in my work clothes and go to the kitchen to fix us some breakfast. Are you comin'?"

Randy could not believe how lively and rational she was after what they had just done. For him, it was big deal. She appeared to make what they had done as a routine matter. He was confused by her behavior but assumed that what they had just done was as important for her as it was for him. As he swung his legs over the side of the bed, he replied. "I'm right behind you."

She came out of the kitchen with a tray piled high with savory breakfast food and a pot of hot coffee. She served Randy and ate all the food on her plate. Not a word was exchanged between them until they were sipping their cups of coffee. Maud began a long conversation by saying emphatically, "We got to make this work. We must carry on and make James' orange business a success. Right?"

Randy unhesitatingly exclaimed, "I'm all in for the long haul. We can do this."

Maud smiled and replied, "Good. Let's go."

"Wait a minute. I told Jasper to give all the workers three days off to mourn."

Maud said, "That's okay. Let's walk around and talk about how we'll turn this farm into a productive orange grove in the years ahead. We got a lot of work to do to stay on track."

Randy's spirits were running high when he said as he stood up, "Let's go. We can do this. I can't think of a better team than you and me. We'll make this work and, in few years, 'James' Oranges' will be a household word."

They walked around the entire ten acres while they talked a mile a minute about their plans to turn this farm into a highly productive orange grove. Randy could not have been happier, and Maud was ecstatic. Yesterday they were down in the deepest dumps while they mourned the passing of James but today their proverbial cup of hope for a better future runneth over.

Their walk ended at the nursery and the spot they wanted to erect a packing house. Randy said, "I see as my priority task to get the work started on the packing house and see what must be done to get our oranges to market. I'll follow up with Jasper as soon as he comes back to work."

Maud said, "Don't worry about money. Worry about doing what is right for our business. Just ask me for money when you need it. By the way, James had already been in contact with the lumber mill that started operations near Orlando about building crates in which we can pack our oranges. You may want to see the operator of this mill."

Randy responded, "That's a good idea. It's somethin' that has escaped my mind completely. I'm sure the mill will do a good business with all the pine trees around and the demand for lumber to construct buildings must be high."

Maud said, "We not only need suitable crates, but we also need brown khaki paper to wrap each orange in, so it won't be damaged during shipment."

"I never thought about that, and I don't have a clue about where we can get wrapping paper. And, even if I did, I have no idea about how much it costs."

Maud added, "I'm more worried about how we goin' to find all the workers to pack and ship our oranges."

Randy exhaled heavily and said, "Whew! A lot of details to work out. Good to think ahead, but we got to take things a step at a time. After all, we are only two people."

On that note, Maud said, "It has been a long day. Let's go back to the kitchen and I'll fix somethin for us to eat."

They walked toward the kitchen in silence. Maud took Randy's hand into hers. This made Randy feel as if he were a permanent part of her. Already he did not think he could live without her. When they arrived at the kitchen door, she released his hand and he said, "Excuse me for a minute. I need to go to my room to get my papers and pencils so I can take some notes."

Maud said in the sweetest voice, "You do that while I'm in the kitchen cookin' somethin' nice for us eat. We can talk more business while we eat. Later."

Randy rushed to his room to get his writing materials. It felt good to be free of Maud, but he could not wait to get back to her. He did not know why, but he felt more complete when he was with her. Reluctantly, he admitted to himself that she had easily become the center of his life.

Supper was a festive occasion. They laughed and their bonds grew as they each told stories about their lives. Randy was careful not to mention all his years in Texas were with his older brother and they had come to Florida together. Maud yawned and Randy could see their joyous day and evening together was coming to an end. He waited nervously for her to say where he was sleeping.

Maud ended the evening by saying pointedly, "If there is anything you need in your room, go and get it while I tend to our dirty dishes."

Now it was time for Randy to smile and say without hesitation. "Yes, ma'am. Are you sure?"

Maud was quick to reply, "I can't stay in that house alone. Besides, I like you. We're partners. Aren't we?"

Randy grinned widely. He resisted the impulse to go and hug her. He just said again, "Yes, ma'am. I like you too."

Randy rushed to his room to gather up his belongings and was back in the kitchen long before Maud had finished washing the dishes. He sat at the table, scribbling on his paper while Maud was doing her work in the kitchen. When she was ready, they walked arm-in-arm the short distance to her small house, Randy opened the front door and said, "Please, after you."

She was not used to getting such royal treatment and said, "Thank you my darling."

They entered the parlor and Randy lit a lamp. She said, "The night is for sleeping, so I am goin' to bed. What about you?"

Randy was a little confused and said, "I'm tired too. I think I will go to bed in my room."

Maud looked at him coyly and said, "You're always welcome in my bed, but I don't want to oblige you. But you better come because I like to have you close to me."

Randy liked being close to her too but was uncertain about her welcome. He followed her to bed, and she went fast to sleep after putting his arms around her just below her nude breasts. Her last words before dozing off were, "This is how the good Lord intended things to be. We can't argue with destiny."

Last night Randy could not sleep alone after the funeral of James. Now, he was not alone, but also could not sleep because he was near the woman of his dreams. From now on, they would always be happy because they knew at night, they would be together in bed, enjoying the forces of nature.

The days passed. The workers were happy because they saw them as a match made in heaven. This caused them to raise their work efforts and exhibit more zeal in turning the James farm into a top-notch orange grove.

Everything was going smoothly. With each year, they got closer to their orange bonanza. Randy was pleased that the lumber mill was able to use its scrap lumber to build sturdy crates in which to pack oranges. The owner, Harvey, of the lumber mill also referred him to a guy, Ozzie, who had just started a general store in Orlando for his wrapping paper. This guy was able to order a huge role of khaki paper.

Randy was pleased with the packing house structure, and he found that he was good at construction work. Jasper helped him hire a bevy of women to wrap and pack in wood crates plenty of oranges. When they got a wagon load full of orange crates, they hauled them a couple of miles to the train station, where they were loaded onto box cars for the trip to northern markets. They developed solid relationships with key buyers in the north.

As their trees reached maturity, they produced large numbers of juicy large oranges that fetched top price in the marketplace. The price per orange soared at Christmas time. Northerners loved filling their Christmas stockings with oranges when there was snow outside. Oranges became a seasonal novelty gift. It was amazing to be able to get a tropical fruit in the middle of winter.

The years passed and the money rolled in. Randy and Maud built a new brick house much larger than the old wooden Florida cracker house they had. The house was furnished with the most fashionable furniture available. There were also enough bedrooms so each of their two children could have their own room. They could not be happier with what they had achieved.

Of course, they realized that their achievement of a successful orange business was largely due to the diligent efforts of their workers. They did not care about local customs and paid their workers a premium wage in recognition of their much-appreciated labor. They received a lot of criticism for the treatment of their workers as equals, but they did not care. Besides, they found that this was indeed good business practice.

It took ten years of hard and smart work, but they were wealthy beyond their dreams. Although they had never been married by a justice of peace, everyone in this part of Florida had the highest respect for them as a couple and what they had achieved. Furthermore, all that was involved in mounting a successful orange business and raising a family, made Randy's memory of his older brother grow dim.

All was moving nicely like clockwork until December 1894 when temperatures dipped below freezing, killing all the oranges on the trees. Maud and Randy had to dig into their savings to cover the cost of losing this annual harvest of oranges. They sadly had to write the year off as a total financial loss. Their northern buyers also lamented Florida's unusual cold weather.

As they were reeling from the loss of their 1894 orange crop, another cold snap blasted Florida in February 1895. This cold spell was worse than the last one that occurred a couple of months earlier. The temperature dropped so low that the bark split on their orange trees, killing them forever. With only dead orange trees to deal with, they no longer had a highly productive orange grove. In more simple terms, they were out of business. It was a catastrophe of large proportions, and it affected all citrus fruit growers in the area. Suddenly, growing oranges in the Orlando area became a losing proposition.

Maud and Randy walked through their dead grove and wept. There was nothing they could do but start over. But, for them it would be foolhardy to start over in the same place. After all, there may be another unholy freeze in this area. They decided they would move farther south to avoid any such freezing weather in the future.

Moving was traumatic for them, their children, and their workers, but they had no choice. All they knew was the orange business. They sold their farmland at a fraction of its pre-freeze value. Jasper and a few of their workers said they were going with them. They packed all their belongings into rented wagons and traveled over rough roads for three days before reaching the Lakeland area. It was in this area that Randy said he knew about some land available for sale.

Maud and Randy worried that they did not have what it took to start all over again. For sure, after what had happened, their children wanted nothing to do with oranges. The kids could see that their parents were hooked by orange business, but that was their business not theirs. Maud and Randy were middle-aged and wondered if it were not too late to get a new start in life.

# Chapter Sixty-Seven
# Riches to Rags

They bought some land and a little house to live in. They felt like they had moved from penthouse to the outhouse. The whole family and the few workers who came along with them were in a deep state of depression. They were scraping the bottom of the barrel.

Randy sat on his front step looking across the unruly hammock land around himself and could not picture turning it into an orange grove. Even if he could clear the land of its thick undergrowth and deal with all the snakes and other varmints hidden in nature's green tangle, where could he find orange trees to plant? And, how many years of toil, sweat and headaches would it take. His two kids would be grown and gone before he and Maud were able to turn this ugly sow's-ear piece of land into a productive orange grove. And, if they had a God forsaken freeze again, all their labors would be for naught.

Maud joined Randy on the front step, and he said to her in a hesitating manner, "I don't think I have it in me to help you create an orange bonanza from scratch."

Maud scanned the unruly brush around her and said to Randy, "Me too."

Randy was surprised by Maud's response. He took Maud's hand into his and said, "My dearest. What are we goin' to do?"

Maud replied, "I don't know, but whatever it is it must make us some money soon because our savings is growin' thin."

Randy did not want Maud to fret about this subject and said, "Don't worry. I'll find some way to make enough money to keep our heads above water. I think I will go into the small Lakeland settlement and nose around."

Maud did not know that Randy had once been a talented poker player. This is something Randy kept a secret from her. What he really meant about going into Lakeland to look around was he wanted to see if there was a saloon with a poker game. He was rusty at playing cards, but he was confident he could multiply the small amount of money he had in his pocket.

Randy bid farewell to Maud and walked the mile into Lakeland. Sure enough, one of the few buildings was a rundown building housing a standard saloon which was the main watering hole for these parts of Florida. The billboard sign on the saloon was almost as big as the place itself and its huge letters left no doubt about its name, *Lakes*.

Randy timidly entered the saloon and was loudly welcomed by the dozen men who were there. Everybody who was anybody in this wide spot in the unimproved dirt road was present, but that was not saying much. Sure enough, Randy spied out of the corner of his eye a card game going on at a small table in the corner of this tiny one-big room saloon.

Each man shook his hand and welcomed him. He was asked by the obese man tending the makeshift bar, "What would you like to drink? First drink is on the house."

Randy looked around at the other rough men in the saloon to see what they were drinking. What he saw confirmed that they would find it unbecoming for a man to order anything but hard liquor. To their utter disappointment he replied softly, "Sarsaparilla."

His reply elicited some 'teeheeing' from the guys around him, but as uncomfortable as that made him feel, he revolted against the idea of changing his drinking habits. He tried to size up the men in the saloon and could see most of them were refugees from the southern states north of Florida. A lot of them had come to this area to take advantage of the land boom and establish farms and ranches. Some were like him… former orange growers looking to start all over in a frost-free environment.

With his big non-alcoholic drink mug in his hand, he went around the room to briefly talk with every man. He got the impression that with the arrival of the train this place would grow in leaps and bounds. Some of the men had big plans for their farms and ranches, but they were stymied over their need for the construction of buildings. These men did not look like much, but, for the most part, they had money but were constrained in how they could invest it productively.

After a while, he arrived to where the poker table was located and stood silently observing the cards being played. One man got up to leave and he was asked to sit down and try his luck. Another man said, "Don't worry, we play for the lowest stakes."

Randy acted reticently, saying, "Well, I don't know. It's been a long time since I've touched a deck of cards. I guess I've a little money to lose."

At first, Randy lost every pot for which he thought he had the winning hand. The other men expressed regret over taking his money, but they were glad to take it. Progressively, Randy remembered how he used to play, and when he won several pots consecutively, the other men at the table folded their hands and said they had other business that needed tending. They all said the same thing to Randy, "You got beginner's luck. Just you wait. Next time will be my turn to win."

Randy was stuffing his winnings into his pockets when one of the men he was playing with said, "You know anyone who can give me a hand with constructing some buildings on my farm."

Randy looked at the man and said point blank, "You're looking at the man who can help you."

They entered into a long and animated conversation which only ended with Randy agreeing to meet him early the next day so he could take him to his place to see what he needed. Randy walked home in an excited mood. He could not wait to tell Maud of his good fortune. He wanted to show her the money he had won, but he did not want to tell her how he won it. On this subject, he felt like he was caught between a rock and a hard place. He thought that maybe saying the truth was the best way to go.

Randy went into the house and pulled all the money out of his pockets and dumped it on the dining table so the family could see. Maud exclaimed, "What did you do, rob a bank?"

With a sheepish grin on his face, Randy said, "Lady luck shined her light on me and won all this dough in a little game of poker."

Maud could not hold her scolding tongue and said, "Shame on you, Mr. Read, but we can really use the money."

Randy's wide-eyed nine-year-old son, Henry, said, "Gosh, Dad, does this mean we're rich again?"

Before Randy could reply, his seven-year-old daughter, Annie, giggled and said, "I guess this means I can get that baby doll I want."

They all had a big laugh. Later, Randy took Maud aside and said, "More important than the money is this conversation I had with a guy about constructing some outbuildings for his farm. I'm sure I can do what he wants. I'm gonna go see him early tomorrow. I'll take Jasper and his crew with me. If this job goes forward, I want them to help me."

Maud was happy to hear about this and said, "My darling husband, a construction foreman. Don't that beat all? I guess our life on the James Orange Grove was not a total loss."

They both enjoyed a good laugh then Maud said in an offhand fashion, "You go right ahead. This is the first day since we lost our orange grove that I have felt we have a bright future ahead of us. Really your news helps restore my hope in the future, I got plenty to do in keeping this place up and caring for our children."

Randy took her in his arms and as he kissed her on the cheek, he said softly in the most endearing tone he was capable of, "My love for you and the kids is unbreakable. I won't stop at anything to make you happy and give you a good future life."

Jasper and the other hired hands who accompanied him were briefed at length on the good impression they wanted to make. Randy emphasized to them that he was going to present them as experienced construction hands. He would do all the talking, but they were there as backup. Every effort would be expended to make the buyer believe they could do the construction job he needed as he desired at a price he could afford.

Randy did not get much sleep that night because he was busy rehearsing in his head how he would go about convincing the man that he was the one to do the job he needed done. He was convinced that all he needed was this opportunity to prove himself. Maud observed that Randy's mind was working overtime and tried to reassure her beloved husband by saying, "Keep in mind that I'm behind you one hundred percent. You can do this."

The next day, they walked to town to meet the man Randy had agreed to meet. Randy's main problem was that he could not remember the name of the man. He was worried that if the man did not show up as agreed, he did not know how to find him. He forgot all his worries when a big, burly man rode up on a well-groomed horse and had another horse in tow. He greeted Randy, saying in a forceful manner, "Pleased to see you again. I forgot to give you my name yesterday. It's Vince Goodman. I brought for you a horse to ride. Your crew can walk behind us. My place is only two miles away. Mount up."

They rode slowly to his place. Vince did all the talking. He wanted to grow oranges and raise cattle because both were money-makers now that trains ran as far south as Lakeland. He had made a lot of money selling goods to both army sides of the Civil War and now he wanted to invest in businesses in Florida. For him, it was all about being in the right place at the right time.

Randy listened intently to Vince and could not wait to get a word in edge wise and say, "I know all there is to know about the orange business. I had a successful grove in Orlando. The Great Freeze wiped us out and sent us packing in search of warmer climes."

Vince said, "That's good to know. Maybe you can give me some advice,"

Randy did not mince his words when he quickly said, "Maybe, but I left the orange business for good, and now I'm all about building construction."

Vince replied, "That's good to know. Almost everyone I know in these parts wants to construct some buildings. And more people are arriving every day, and they all need housing."

Randy was delighted to hear Vince's words and said, "Spread the word, 'Read Construction' can build the way you want at the price you can afford."

Vince grinned and told himself that he was glad that he had run into Randy. He was ready to do business with him even before they had discussed any business. Vince halted his horse and said, "Here we are. Not much to see because we are just getting started. All you can see is workers clearing the land. I'll show you what I want constructed and where."

Randy struggled to keep himself composed and put on a professional appearance. Vince walked him to various places on the grounds and asked him what he thought of erecting a certain type of building in this spot. Randy's replies to Vince's queries were mostly the same. Invariably, Randy said, "No problem. This can be done to your satisfaction."

It was only when Vince came to a spot where he wanted to erect an orange packing shed that Randy's answer changed, "I've done that and I can do it again."

When they had finished tromping around Vince's newly bought land, Vince said, "What are your terms and when can you start?"

Without hesitation, Randy said confidently, "Half upfront and half when the job is done. We can start as soon as we have delivery of the materials needed."

Vince shook Randy's hand and said, "Mount up. We can talk while

476

we go back."

Vince was the first to talk, "I know I'm taking a chance on you, but I like you. If you can do the job well for me, I'm sure others will be knocking on your door. I'll meet you in town tomorrow about this time to take care of the financial arrangements."

Randy dismounted and tied his horse to the back of Vince's and said, "See you tomorrow at the same time in the same place."

Randy was tempted to go to the saloon to celebrate, but he saw that Vince was headed in that direction, so he joined Jasper and his crew to hurry home. He turned to Jasper and said excitedly, "We're in the construction business now. Maybe you can send word to Orlando that we need more workers here, particularly those who have had some experience in carpentry, masonry and roofing. Anyone who has worked in building anything is welcome. Tomorrow, I'll sign a contract with Vince and get an advance. We got to make this work."

Maud was standing in the front doorway. Randy spotted her and waved wildly and began to step more quickly. She saw how animated he was, and this told her that his mission had been a success. He got close to her and exclaimed, "It worked. We're in the construction business now."

He embraced her, lifting her into the air, swinging her around, they both laughed uncontrollably. The children came running to see what all the commotion was about. They jumped for glee and ran circles around their parents. Little Henry stopped after making a few rounds and asked, "What are we celebrating anyway?"

Randy set Maud down, and she took her children in her arms and explained, "We're celebrating Daddy's new construction company. He just started, and it will take a lot of hard work, but our future looks better than it has in a long time."

The sun was setting, and Randy was in a hurry to get cleaned up, eat, and get ready for his big meeting with Vince in Lakeland tomorrow. He could not think of anything except how he would conduct himself at this meeting. His nerves were on edge as he waited for the sun to rise.

With the dawn's early light, he had a cup of coffee and, kissed Maud goodbye, and said, "Wish me luck. I'm goin' into Lakeland early, so I'll be there when Vince arrives."

Maud said happily, "Good luck. I'm sure all will go just fine."

Randy arrived in Lakeland early in the day, and the only place open was the Lakes. He decided to wait for Vince in the Lakes. As expected, the place was empty. But he was surprised to see a few men sitting at the poker table playing cards. He stood close to the table, observing how the cards were played. The obese man who tended the bar yesterday was one of the players. This man gave him a curious look and said, "There's an empty chair if you want to join us."

Randy replied, "Don't mind if I do, but I don't have much money to gamble."

A tall guy with a big mustache and well-dressed was seated across from the obese bartender said, "No matter how little your money, we'll take it."

For Randy, those were fighting words that made him want to show off to the other players by winning all the pots. His raking in several pots caused the tall man to say, "You're a good player. It's good to have a worthy opponent who is new on the scene and knows nothing about me. Just so you know, I'm coming from Tallahassee, and I'm headed to Arcadia to see my sheriff. I decided to stop over in Lakeland to try my luck in a poker game."

Randy thought he should say something after this introduction by a man who appeared to be important, so he said, "I'm Randy Read. I'm coming from Orlando to start a construction business in this area. I've never been to Arcadia. Maybe I should check it out. By the way, what is the name of the sheriff of Arcadia. Maybe he could be a good contact for me and my business."

The tall man laughed heartily. He loved being with people who did not know who he was. After the cards were dealt, the tall man said, "I'm laughing because I'm probably the best contact for you. Be that as it may, the sheriff's name is Charles Bonard."

Hearing this name was like the roof falling on his head. Randy could no longer think straight and mis-read his hand and lost to the tall man a big pot. He could no longer play and feigned an upset stomach and asked to be excused. The tall man said as he was getting up from the table, "I hope you feel better quickly. Sorry to take all your money."

Randy staggered outside. His head was spinning. Could his older brother be a sheriff? This question made him dizzy, and he struggled to keep his balance. He could see Vince arriving on the road, and he knew he had to his act together.

Brusquely, the tall man exited the saloon and, came up to him, and said, "Sorry to win your money. Here, take your money back. You need it more than I do."

Randy felt small in front of this giant of a man, and being reimbursed his losing wagers made him feel even smaller. Although he felt like he was standing in a hole, he wanted to shake hands and thank the tall man, but he was gone inside in a flash. Vince came up and said, "That's impressive. You didn't tell me that you know Zebulon Ford."

"I don't know him. Who's he?"

"Well, for starters, he's one of the richest men in Florida. He owns everybody and everything in south-central Florida. It's rumored that he has fifty thousand head of cattle. You're lucky to have met him. Now, let's get down to our business."

# Chapter Sixty-Eight
## Arcadia Charles

There was little shade provided by the lonely pine tree he sat under to get his thoughts together. He did not care about the heat, humidity, and protection from the blazing mid-day sun. His head was spinning out of control. He held onto the tree trunk to keep falling into a deep emotional hole of his own making.

It was not his business dealings with Vince that put him in the devil's doldrums. Although it was tough on him, he managed to not allow the alarm bells riveting his being too upset his discourse with Vince. He was on the verge of fainting right in front of Vince, but he drew upon inner forces he did not know he possessed to conclude his important business with Vince. Thoughts of his family's interests helped keep him on track.

Vince noticed that Randy was not himself and something was troubling him, but he carried on in the belief that Randy would recover his senses and do the job for which he was hiring him. Vince entrusted Randy with a large sum of money, saying, "Here's what you need to order supplies for our building job. I have no idea of where you can get all the construction materials you need. That's part of why I hired you. Why don't we meet in a couple of weeks to see where things stand?"

Randy was in a daze, but he shook Vince's extended hand and said, "That's a good idea. You can trust me. See you in a couple of weeks to give you an update."

Randy staggered down the sandy dirt track toward his home and collapsed under the first roadside tree. Many questions tormented him. Repeatedly, he asked himself if Sheriff Charles Bonard of Arcadia could be the older brother he had not seen in almost a decade? Another question that whirled around in his mind was, *How could a cattle baron in southern Florida have same last name as the cattle baron he worked for in southern Texas?*

He knew that he had to see, no matter what if the sheriff in Arcadia was his brother. He thought of what he would tell Maud about why he had to go to Arcadia. He had never heard of Arcadia before today, and now he desperately needed to go there. He would lie to Maud, telling her that Vince said he could get some construction materials in Arcadia.

Maud was not fooled but went along for the sake of peace and for the deep love of her husband. She did not want Randy more out of sorts than he already was. She went along with his ruse, but her woman's intuition told her that her husband needed to go to Arcadia for other reasons.

She did leave a small window in her mind open, thinking that maybe he could find some construction supplies in Arcadia, but she wrote that off as wishful thinking. Yet, she had heard that a lot of companies had moved into the Arcadia area since the discovery of phosphate in the nearby Peace River. She kept trying to justify her husband's motive. Anyway, she knew he would not do a two to three-day horse ride to Arcadia for nothing.

Maud looked at her frazzled husband and tried to help him settle down by saying in loving voice, "When do you plan to leave? I'll help you with all you need for your trip to Arcadia."

Randy sensed his wife wanted to be helpful, although she did not want him to go to Arcadia. He tried to give her a satisfactory answer by replying, "I was thinking of leaving on the trail south first thing tomorrow morning."

"You'll have to take some food and water with you. I'll get those items ready. I hope our only horse is up for the trip. I'm so afraid you'll be attacked by bandits who will shoot you dead and steal all your construction money."

While her worries were justified, Randy tried to make light of them. "Don't trouble yourself so. Nothing is going to happen to me. I expect to be back in a couple of weeks or less. Now, if you'll excuse me, I've got to go see if Jasper is in his shack out back so he can check on our horse. I also need to talk with him about what construction supplies I can find in Arcadia."

Now that his Arcadia trip was set, Randy's nerves quieted down. He wanted to be on his best behavior with Maud and their children so he could depart in a calm and happy way. He told them, "With this new construction business, I'm likely to be away from you often with these kinds of trips. I don't like it, but it is what I got to do to make this business a success."

Tomorrow's morning came fast. Maud was up early to fix breakfast and pack Randy's saddle bags full of food he could snack on. Jasper was in front of the house with Randy's horse, all ready to go. Randy looked approvingly at the fully loaded horse and said, "There's one more thing I need to get."

Randy retrieved from the corner of his bedroom closet his old rifle. He also grabbed a small box of bullets, collecting dust on a closet shelf. As he attached his rifle to his horse, he said, "You can never be too careful. I'm a big believer in preparing for the worst even though it's unlikely to happen."

Randy hugged and kissed Maud and his two sleepy-headed kids. He mounted his horse, waved goodbye, and rode in the direction of where the trail south should be. Although it felt good to be back in the saddle, leaving his family did not feel good, especially as he was not telling the truth as to why he was going. His older brother was already getting him to obscure the truth contrary to the upright life he wanted to live. He felt sorry for his inability to tell his beloved Maud the real reason he was going to Arcadia. He damned his brother for doing this to him.

The long ride to Arcadia was uneventful. The sub-tropical, moist, and flat landscape made Randy wonder why anyone would want to settle in these parts. The daily deluges were too much for him and his horse. When it rained, he decided to let himself get soaked because he would dry out in this sunny climate. Deep down, he had a vision of where he wanted to live, and this was not it. This land was a far cry from his childhood memories of the rolling green hills of Virginia. There were many days he just wanted to go back to where it had all started and start all over again.

There was a man walking on the dirt road, and he asked him, "Where's Arcadia?"

The man said, "Just keep ridin'. It's a few miles ahead."

It was late in the day. Randy decided to camp on the outskirts of the settlement of Arcadia and, first thing tomorrow, ride directly up to the sheriff's office. He would just say he's looking for the sheriff without saying the true nature of his business. The very thought that the sheriff of Arcadia could be his long-lost brother made his hands tremble and made his heart overrule his head.

He broke camp at the first rays of the sun. He rode slowly into town and planned to ask the first passerby where the sheriff's office was. When he came across the first person, he could not get the words out of his mouth and ended their encounter with a tip of his hat. He steadied himself and asked another passerby on the settlement's main road. He cleared his throat and asked, "Where's the sheriff's office?"

The answer he got. "Oh. He's got his office and jail in the front rooms of the general store up the street on the left side."

Randy's first reaction was to turn his horse around and get out of Arcadia. Maybe it was better to avoid the truth and go home to his wife and kids. But he had to know for better or worse if his brother was still alive and kicking. Maybe he was worried about nothing, and it was just some guy with the same name that his older brother adopted. After all, his brother was the volatile type, and those types were not known for their longevity. And there was no way in hell that this type could become a sheriff.

His breathing was cut short as he tied the reins to his horse to a post in front of a store that was marked as the sheriff's office. He walked slowly up to the office door and took a deep breath before opening it. Once the door was opened, he spied a man hunched over some papers at a nondescript desk and inquired meekly, "Is the sheriff in?"

Without lifting his head to look at him, the seated man said tersely, "Who wants to know?"

"Peyton Rudolph Read."

By saying his full name, Randy knew that if the other man was his brother, the man would jump out of his skin. Sure enough, the man rose quickly. He took a few steps forward to size up the person standing before himself. In an instant, he grasped Randy in his strong arms and hugged him so tight that he thought he was going to squeeze the life out of him. Tears rolled down the cheeks of both brothers. This was an unbelievable reunion.

Charles released Randy and said, "It's so very good to see you. We got a lot to talk about, but you cannot be seen here alone with me. You got to act like your reason for seeing me is about sheriff's business. Go stay at the boarding house on the corner. Ask for Lula Mae and tell her Charles sent you. See you later. Now, go."

Randy had a million questions for his brother, so it was tough separating from him only after a brief encounter with him. But he did as his brother instructed and went to the nearby boarding house to get a room for the night.

Lula Mae was standing at the door of her boarding house as Randy hitched up his horse. She came out and loudly greeted him with a deep southern accent, "Welcome. What can I do for you?"

"Well, Sheriff Bonard said I could find a room here."

"Yes, sir. I can rent you a room by the night, feed you, and wash your clothes if they need it at a price so low you won't believe it."

"You got yourself a customer."

"Unpack you horse, and I'll call someone to tend to it."

Randy removed his saddlebags and rifle from his old horse and walked the couple of steps to Lula Mae's two-story boarding house. She opened the door to her place and said, "Watch out for the little ones. Ever since Charlie and I got married nine years ago, we seem to have a kid every two years. We got three now, and I think another one is starting to grow in my stomach."

The talkative Lula Mae did not know she was overwhelming Randy with information. He could not believe his brother was married and the father of three. He had been true to his word. "I'll marry and settle down with the first woman who wants me."

Randy was lost for words. He tried to keep the conversation going by asking, "Are you the owners of this place?"

"No, but it's like we are. The same wealthy man who gave Charlie his job bought this place for us when we married. He sent word that it was a wedding gift, but as far as I know, he still owns it."

Randy thought the true owner was the tall, wealthy man he played poker with briefly in Lakeland. He said to Lula Mae, "Never mind. Where's my room?"

"You can take the room at the top of the stairs on your right. If there is any problem, let me know. I got to check on the kids and get lunch prepared for Charlie. I'm sure he'll want you to eat with him. See you later."

Randy entered his room and closed the door behind himself. He dove into the big spring bed with a soft feather mattress. He wanted some privacy so he could dwell on the things he had learned in the last hour. The sheriff was indeed his brother, who was married to Lula Mae, and they had three children. More than ever, he wanted to know more how his brother got from where he was to where he is now. He wondered if he would ever have enough time with his brother to learn all he wanted to know. Of course, his brother would want to hear his story, too. They had a lot of time to make up.

There was a soft tap on his door. He got up to see who it was. He opened the door a crack to see it was Lula Mae. She said, "Your lunch is ready. If you come now, you can join Charlie."

"I'll be right down. Go ahead and serve me at Charlie's table."

Randy washed up and sped downstairs to start hearing from his brother what he had been doing since they separated about ten years ago. He took a place at Charlie's table, respectfully greeting him as he would stranger. As they began to eat, the normally silent but always courteous Charlie told bits and pieces of his story.

Between bites and gulps, Charlie tried to bring Randy up to date. He said he made it to Peace River and was about to pick up a pick and shovel to work as a phosphate miner when a guy rode up to him and said his boss was looking for someone like me. My response to him was, "What's so special about me?"

The man on the horse said, "Well, you got all the attributes we're looking for... your big, you have guns, and you know one end of a four-legged animal from another."

At first, I thought he was looking for someone to wrangle cattle, so I told him, "I know how to herd cattle, but doing that in these parts would take a lot of skills I don't have. The cow hunting skills needed here and the use of a whip are much different than I know. Besides, I don't want anything to do with cattle. Of course, if you want to give me some cattle, I'll put my brand on them."

The man then said, "The job we have to offer you has nothing to do with cattle. The boss is looking for somebody to take the records from the old county seat of Pine Level to the courthouse in the new county seat of Arcadia. If you do a good job at transporting these records, I'm sure the boss will offer you more jobs."

I asked, "Who's the boss?"

The man answered, "Zeb Ford, the wealthiest man in Florida, and he owns almost everyone and everything in these parts."

Charlie continued to tell snippets of his story and said, "The man offered me an interesting sum of money, and I quickly decided to work for Mr. Ford. I provided security for the records and oversaw their delivery to their new location in Arcadia. Then, I was offered the job of sheriff and accepted it. I met Lula Mae, and we got married quickly and had one kid after another. I love her and my family. Now, that is about it for me. What about you?"

Randy noisily cleared his throat and proceeded to say, "Well, I was lucky in Orlando and found good work creating a successful orange grove, got married, had two kids, and became wealthy. But we lost it all to the

Great Freeze and moved farther south to the Lakeland area to start all over again. But we changed our minds, and I'm trying to start a construction business. It was in Lakeland that I heard your name mentioned by a tall man from Arcadia. When I heard your fictitious name, I knew I had to come and see if it were really you."

In a low voice, Charlie said, "We can't talk here too long. Lula Mae will become suspicious of our association. Nobody must know we are brothers and that we spent a long time together in Texas. We must devise a plan to meet secretly at regular intervals."

"It's okay. I'm keeping secret our relationship. For the first time, I lied to my wife. I told her I was going to Arcadia to look for construction supplies."

"Well, tell her you did not find any supplies, but you found other construction job opportunities. There's a lot of money pouring into Arcadia for the development of the phosphate industry. Moreover, we need a lot of government buildings. For example, our courthouse is made of wood and too small. We need a new brick courthouse. The state government will give us the money to build a new courthouse if the old courthouse is unusable. I could set fire to the old courthouse and then make sure you get the contract to build a new one."

Randy could not believe his brother's willingness to commit a crime and said emphatically, "I don't want to be involved with any illegalities."

"Okay. But I've found that's the way it's done, and most people go along because that's the only sure way of getting ahead."

Randy smiled. He could see that much of what he remembered about his brother was the same. He would always be his brother, and he would always want the best for him, but ten years was a long time to be separated, and they had followed separate lives and had different values. They were born of the same mother, but they were not the same and had different lives. They would always care deeply for each other, but they had divergent destinies.

# Chapter Sixty-Nine
# Living Life

Arcadia was booming economically and growing fast. The new railroad network facilitated the arrival of newcomers and goods and allowed for the export of huge quantities of phosphate being mined from the bed of the Peace River just west of town. Cattle ranching and citrus growers were also experiencing success. The future of the town and its inhabitants looked bright.

Randy was so impressed with the town that he thought of moving with his family from Lakeland to Arcadia. On second thought, he determined that would never work. He could not live in the same town with his older brother. He hungered to see his brother but seeing him could spell trouble for both of them.

Even now, he wanted to spend time with his brother, but he was afraid that their blood association would be noticed. He agreed that any meeting between them had to be in absolute secrecy. It was time for supper, and he was hesitant to go down to the dining room because his brother might be there. He was thinking that it was okay to eat with him and say goodbye for now.

There was a gentle tap on the door. It was Lula Mae. She handed him a sealed envelope and said, "Charlie was called away, but he wanted me to give you this message. I'll be serving your supper shortly."

Randy quickly opened the closed envelope, which read as follows. *On the road home, about halfway to Lakeland, you will see an old oak tree. Meet me there at night on this day next month. If I'm not there, try again the next month.*

Randy folded the scrap of paper his brother had written into a tiny square and stuffed it into his right pocket. He did the same with the envelope and shoved it deep into his left pocket. His plan was to burn it at his first opportunity.

It was strange to stay in his brother's house and near his wife and kids.

He wanted to be close to them but was forced by the circumstances to act like a total stranger. There was no option but to leave. He gobbled up his plate of food and told Lula Mae, "I'll be leaving early in the morning, so I'd like to settle up now."

"Okay, but won't you be havin' breakfast?"

"No. I'm sorry, but I won't have time. I got to finish my business and head back to Lakeland."

Lula Mae was curious and asked courteously, "What's your business?"

"Why, ma'am, I'm in the construction business, and I'm here to nose around for construction supplies."

"Well, you may want to see the manager of our new sawmill. I assume you'll need lumber for whatever you are doing."

Randy thanked Lula Mae for all she did to make his stay comfortable and paid her with an overly generous tip. He found his horse tied up outside and gave the boy standing by his horse more than the cost of one night's boarding at the local livery. He asked the boy, "Where's the lumber mill?"

Without hesitation, the boy told the generous stranger that it was located just out of town near the banks of the Peace River. The boy pointed in the direction he should go, and Randy placed his saddlebags and rifle on the horse and mounted up for a slow ride in the direction of the sawmill. He passed in front of the storefront marked *Sheriff's Office* and wondered if his brother were there.

He thought it was a real shame that he could not drop in and say hello to his brother. It took all the courage in the world to pass his brother's office without stopping. He was sorry for his action, but he knew that was how things had to be. His life was doomed to always have the dark shadow of his older brother hanging over it.

The sawmill was a busy place with pine tree logs on an elevated stand being cut by hand into rough planks by two men on each end of a long saw. Randy dismounted and hitched his horse. He started to walk around when a blond-headed guy in coveralls stopped him in his tracks and said, "Hello, my name is Sam. I'm the manager of this here Sawmill. How can I help you?"

They shook hands, and Randy told him briefly about his business in Lakeland and the need for lumber to build an orange packing house. Sam quickly answered, "You've come to the right place. I know exactly what you need. Just tell me when you want it and how you goin' to pay."

Randy was a little taken back by Sam's aggressive behavior but said, "I used to have an orange grove and oversaw the building of a packing house. I have in mind a building of the same type for my customer. Any lumber I buy here must be delivered to a farm near Lakeland. I can be contacted through the Lakes Saloon in Lakeland. Can you do that?"

Sam was ready to reply without mincing his words, "No problem. But, of course, you have to pay for the delivery costs. Should I call my secretary to draw up a bill of sale?"

Randy nodded his assent and followed Sam to a tiny shop he referred to as his office. Seated in this office was a young black woman. Sam pointed to her and said, "Her name is Helen. She's my secretary. It ain't right, but she's the only one among us who can read and write."

They agreed on the size of the order and the timing and terms of delivery. In silence, Helen showed exceptional penmanship in dutifully drawing up a bill of sale, which Randy signed with a flourish and dated. Two copies were made. One for Randy, and one for blue-eyed Sam, who had a peculiar signature. Randy looked at his squiggly signature and told himself a chicken could scratch the ground better than Sam could sign.

All Randy cared about was getting delivery in a couple of weeks for the lumber for which he paid. Although he was put off by the wild-eyed antics of Sam. He asked him if there was any place in or around Arcadia he could look for other construction materials. Sam replied in his usual curt fashion, "No, not that I know of. Everybody I know here gets their supplies out of Tampa. Sorry, you'll have to go north instead of south to get what you need."

They shook hands to seal their deal, and Randy folded nicely his copy of the bill of sale and placed it in one of his saddle bags. He mounted his horse and waved goodbye, happy to be on the road home. He was especially happy because he could show Maud the bill of sale for the lumber he bought in Arcadia, thus proving he had indeed gone there to look for construction supplies.

Going all the way to Tampa for the rest of his construction supplies was disappointing to him, but he was prepared to do anything to get his business going. He told himself he would check out if he could take the train to Tampa. Right now, he wanted to concentrate on the trail back to Lakeland and especially had his eyes peeled for the big oak tree where he was to meet his brother at night in a month.

About halfway to Lakeland on his second day on the trail home, he noticed a majestic old oak tree on the side of the road. It was so big he wondered how he had not noticed it on the way to Arcadia. He stopped in front of the tree and made a mental note of its whereabouts. After a brief pause at the tree, he continued to Lakeland.

The next afternoon, he rode into Lakeland center and went straight to the saloon to catch up with the latest news and ask how to get to Tampa. He went up to the heavy-set bartender and asked for any news. This man replied, "Nothing new since you asked me last week. As far as I'm concerned, no news is good news."

His reply was as Randy expected, so he asked, "How do I get to Tampa?"

The bartender, Bart, laughed and said in a teasing way, "Well, you get on your horse and point it in the direction of Tampa, and you'll get there in a couple of days."

"Only two days? It took me three days to get to Arcadia."

The jolly bartender laughed louder and said, "Well, Arcadia is farther away than Tampa. And Arcadia is hotter than Tampa and less developed. I don't know why anyone would go south to Arcadia instead of going almost straight west to Tampa."

Randy felt like a dummy, and he could not reveal the real reason for going to Arcadia. He hoped Maud did not know that Tampa was closer than Arcadia. He was afraid to ask any more questions, but he asked, "Can you take the train to Tampa?"

"Only if you want to go all over the state to get there. There's no direct line to Tampa. It's easier to go there by riding your horse, and you'll need a horse to get around when you're there."

Randy thanked the bartender and said hello to the three guys playing poker, saying, "I'm too tired to play. Some other time. See you later."

He was eager to get home to Maud and the kids. He especially wanted to show Maud the bill of sale for the lumber he ordered in Arcadia. He would rest up and wait a couple of days before he would tell her of his need to go to Tampa. Right now, his thoughts were all about embracing Maud and their two children.

It was deeply satisfying to be at home with his wife and kids, and all was well until he announced he had to go to Tampa to search for more construction materials. Maud looked at Randy tearfully and said dolefully, "We don't want you to go, but we understand that you have to go to keep your business going and our family afloat. I'm behind you a hundred percent. I couldn't ask for a better husband. When are you leaving?"

"Well, I wanted to talk to Jasper first about getting a couple more horses. We can't get by with only one horse. But that shouldn't take long, and I expect to leave tomorrow or the next day."

Maud said, "I'll do my part to see you off in the best of conditions. Spend all the time you can with the kids, letting them know that you are only away for the good of our family."

Jasper told Randy that he would locate a couple of good horses while he was away, and he said the horse they had was good enough for his trip to Tampa. Everything was set, and Randy told Maud, "I will be leaving for Tampa first thing tomorrow, so if you can have an early breakfast for me, that would be great."

The early morning goodbyes were said, and Randy rode west to pick up the sandy two-tracked road to Tampa. He was surprised to see quite a few travelers going and coming. It seemed everybody was on the move and looking for a new place to settle.

There were so many people on the road, Randy had to look hard for a bare spot to make his camp for the night. He had nothing against camping beside other people, but in his past experiences, he mostly camped alone. Besides, for him, people could cause trouble, and he wanted to travel in peace so he could do his business.

There were more people than he had seen in a long time loitering about the road as he entered the outskirts of Tampa. Randy tried to think of the last time he had seen so many people in one place. He thought that it was in San Antonio, but that was a long time ago, and his memory had become fuzzy about his previous life.

A brief view of Tampa Bay also reminded him that he missed seeing the ocean. He did not know which way to go, so he stopped at the first hotel he spotted and asked for a room for a night or two. The hotel said it was full up, but he could try another hotel down the road. The second hotel had a room, and although it was a little pricy, he took it when they offered to take care of his horse at a nearby stable.

His room in this hotel was spacious and well-furnished. He locked his room door and went out to the front veranda to join those seated who were watching the people, wagons, and horses passing by. His restlessness overcame his tiredness, and he wanted to know where to go for the construction supplies he needed. He asked the well-dressed guy sitting next to him, "Where do you think one can find building materials?"

The guy did not hear him. As Randy thought the clamor from the road was blocking his hearing, he repeated more loudly his question. This time, the guy responded, "I have no idea. Maybe you can find where to start your search in this daily newspaper."

He handed the newspaper to Randy and left to join the crowds in the main road into town. It had been many years since Randy had a newspaper in his hands. He hardly knew how to handle a newspaper, but he easily read its name on the top of the first page, *Tampa Tribune*.

The newspaper only contained five pages, so he quickly leafed though it to see if there were any ads that would lead him to a place to begin his search for construction materials. On the second page was the name of the author of an article that stopped his perusal of the newspaper. That name was Clement M. Read.

He squirmed in his chair and patted his forehead with his handkerchief to absorb the droplets of perspiration. He tried to stay calm, but he felt like choking. Could that name be for his long-lost father, Captain Clement Melanchthon Read? He thought his father had died in the war fighting for the South. There was no doubt in his mind about where he had to go immediately… the office of the *Tampa Tribune*.

The woman at the reception table gave him directions, and he hustled off in a daze. After walking some distance, oblivious to all that was going on around him, he arrived at a building that had splashed in large letters, *Tampa Tribune*. He entered rapidly and asked the first person he saw inside, "Is Mr. Read in?"

The young man who answered him said, "Yes, he's in, but he only sees people by appointment. Do you have appointment with him?"

"No, but I think he'll be happy to see me."

"Okay. I will tell him. I need your name."

"Peyton Randolph Read."

The young man went to the back of the crowded room and spoke with an elderly man who immediately rose and came hurriedly to the front to look at who was saying the name of his son who had been lost for over thirty years. He stopped a few feet from Randy and looked at him from head to toe. He could not believe his eyes and with tears rolling down his cheeks he tried to say in front of others in a way that befit the occasion. "Thank the good Lord for bringing one of the jackleg boys to me. Where's the other one?"

Randy said only one word, "Dead."

It had grown silent in the room and all eyes were on the two men embracing each other. After holding each other tightly, Clement held Randy's hand up high and said in a thunderous voice, "Behold. I'm proud to announce to the world that this is my long-lost son who I have not seen since the war started. This is indeed a day for rejoicing."

When he said these words, everyone in the office stood and clapped. Randy was stupefied and lost for words. Clement escorted his son back to his table so they could have a little privacy. After they were seated, Clement asked softly, "Where's Henry?"

He knew his dad always put a lot of stake in his oldest son and he did not know whether to tell the truth or lie. In this case and in keeping with his promise to Henry, he said simply, "He died years ago when we were in Texas."

He hated to lie, especially to his dad, but he believed it was the best way to go in this case. At the same time, he was telling himself what a shame it was because Henry was in Arcadia masquerading as Charles Bonard. If his dad ever found he had lied to him about Henry, there would be hell to pay. But he was obliged to bury deeply the truth about Henry.

Clement reacted, "All these years, I thought both of you were dead. The war took a heavy toll on all of us. Hell, I fought on the losing side. I was wounded and interred in a prisoner-of-war camp. I lost everything that was bequeathed to me by many generations of great American patriots."

Randy could see that his dad, even at an advanced age, had not lost his keen intelligence and his gift for articulation. He did not know what to say to a father he hardly knew and did not grow up with, but he allowed a few words to flow from his mouth. "Dad, all these years, I thought you were dead... killed in the war."

Clement took Randy's hand in his and whispered into his ear, "God has brought us together at long last. This is not a place we can talk. I wish you could come to my place to meet my wife and children, but it's hard to find. Where are you staying?"

Randy told him the name of his hotel and Clement said, "I'll meet you there in the dining room tomorrow morning for breakfast. We got a lot of ground to cover. Right now, I've got to finish an article I'm working on for tomorrow's edition."

They embraced, and Randy stumbled outside into the road. At first, he did not know which way to go and could not recall where he was or why. Seeing his father after so many years had thrown him off course. Suddenly, his father was in his life, but he did not know how to fit him into his current reality.

# Chapter Seventy
# Looking for the Exit

The cotton tablecloth was of a common red and white cross-hatched design. What distinguished each table in the cramped breakfast dining room was the peculiar small vases made of beach shells that contained a fresh magnolia flower. Randy was admiring the flowers when his father strode in with a flair that only someone of his age and background could duplicate.

Randy stood and stepped away from the table to welcome his elderly father with a handshake and a hug. He was impressed by how spry and mentally acute his father was despite his age and all that he had been through. After the expressions of the morning, Randy said, "I told the woman who runs the kitchen to serve us breakfast as soon as you arrived."

Clement retorted, "Thank you, but all I need is a big cup of hot black coffee to get started on my day. We have no time to lose to tell our stories and then I need to go to the office to make sure my article is printed exactly the way I wrote it. I'll start."

Randy could not believe how active his dad was and that he was still working at his advanced age. He must be in his early seventies, but he acted like a man twenty years younger. Randy replied, "I can't wait to hear how you sum up the last thirty years."

"I already told you that I was injured in battle in the war and taken prisoner. I went back home after I was released and healed, but there was really nothing to go home to, so I moved next to kin in North Carolina. I re-married there to a lovely woman, but our house burnt down with her in it. Some months after the fire, I heard of the newspaper job in Tampa, so I moved here. I'm so glad about my move to Tampa because if I had never made that move, I would have never met you. I'm so glad we met. Of course, I'm sorry for Henry's death, but we got to accept the hand life deals us. Now, your turn."

Breakfast plates and black hot coffee had been served while Randy was spellbound, listening to his dad recite in a few minutes the highlights of his life over the past few decades. He could never be as articulate as his dad, but he started by saying, "War was consuming our plantation, and the house was on fire. Mother told us two boys to flee and go west to Texas. I will not go into the details, but by some miracle, we made it to Texas after around a year, and we kept going south until we got jobs with a big cattle rancher who was also supporting the South by trading cotton in Mexico. We then became expert cow hands and drove large herds to Kansas markets. Barb wire spelled the end of the open range. After Henry was shot and killed, I got out of Texas and took the train to Florida, where my wife and I created a successful orange business outside of Orlando. We lost everything in the Great Freeze and moved to the Lakeland area to start all over again, but I switched to construction work, and that is what brought me here. There you have all those years in a nutshell."

Clement listened intently, trying not to get emotional while he swallowed in measured gulps his steaming coffee. There was a pause of silence before Clement said, "That's quite a story. Sorry to learn that my son had to suffer so much, but I'm beside myself in happiness to see that you lived through all these trials and tribulations so you can be here today to tell me all about it. You're truly a survivor."

Randy could not help but spout, "You're the most spectacular survivor I know."

Clement could see that there was no sense in differing with his son and said solemnly, "We're both among the survivors of a horrific war that turned life inside and out for millions of people while it turned our country upside down. We all must start all over and make the best of things."

Clement's erudite words sunk deep into Randy's being. Although he was intimidated by his father's presence, intelligence, and high education, he mustered a simple reply, "Yes, we all must carry on the best we can."

"Speaking of carrying on, I got to go to the office. We must meet again for a longer time to fill in the details of our stories."

Randy was taken aback by his father's abrupt departure. He did not want to see his dad leave his life again. He had to think fast and said, "By the way, do you have any leads as to where I can procure materials for my construction business?"

Clement was quick to answer, "Yes, I certainly do. 'Jacob Barnes and Sons' is where my office did a lot of business. He can find and deliver anything you want. I highly recommend him. I can meet you there at three

496

this afternoon and introduce you to him. He's a great guy to do business with and I'm pleased to be of service to you. That's that. See you this afternoon."

His dad stood up and was ready to dash off when Randy was obliged to ask, "How do I find this place?"

As his dad was leaving, he said, "Ask anybody from Tampa. Everybody knows where this place is. See you later, my son."

It was comforting for Randy to see his real father, hear his voice and hearing him call him son brought tears to his eyes. He immediately asked the kitchen woman how he could find the Barnes and Sons store so he could get there early. He did not care if he had to wait all day for his father to arrive and get his business off to a good start.

Randy got good instructions about how to find Barnes' place. After sitting at a small table on the front veranda for a while, listing on a sheet of paper exactly what he thought he needed to complete the job of building an orange packing house for Vince, he joined the many pedestrians and headed in the general direction of Barnes' place.

He enjoyed walking through the busy streets of Tampa and discovered he could use with many of the people the Spanish he had learned in Texas and Mexico. His Spanish was rusty and of a different dialect, but he found that it was mutually understandable with the many people he encountered who were from Cuba. In many ways, this had been Spanish territory for centuries, and they bequeathed to Florida two of the mainstays of its economy... cattle and oranges.

The streets got tighter, and the walking more constrained by all the people and wagons in the streets. It was slow going, and he had to ask a few people along the way for directions, but there was no doubt left in his mind when he arrived because of the large sign that proclaimed, *Barnes and Sons.*

One of the workers asked what he wanted, and he replied that he was waiting for his partner before doing any business. In the meantime, he got out his pencil and paper that listed all his needs. He added a bunch of hand tools to his list. When he was all done, he folded the paper and, put it in his back pocket, and stored his pencil in his front pocket. He then hopped on the wood barrel he had been writing on to sit down and wait for his father. While he waited, he observed the brisk business going on in this mecca of construction hardware.

His dad came prancing up to the place exactly on time. He greeted

Randy and said, "Let's go see Jacob. I assume you know what you need and when you need it."

Randy replied, "Yes, sir. I got it all written down."

"Well, in that case, we only have to show Jacob the list and ask him how much and when it all can be delivered. We're lucky that Jacob can read."

They found a bearded man sitting on a stack of lumber, puffing on a corn cob pipe. The short-statured Jacob jumped up when he saw Clement, saluted, and said, "Captain, Corporal Jacob Barnes at your service."

Clement and Jacob shook hands vigorously before Clement said, "This is my son from Virginia."

Jacob was excited by this news and said while giving Randy a long handshake, "Pleased to meet you. It is a great pleasure and honor to meet my Captain's son."

Clement casually said. "You'll have to forgive Jacob for some of his language. We served together in the great army of the south, and for him and lots of others the war is not over."

Randy said, "I understand. No problem as far as I'm concerned."

He was thinking that the war would never be over for a lot of people. The war had left deep scars on the country, and those scars still divided the people, perhaps forever.

As usual, Clement was in a hurry and said to Randy, "Show Jacob your paper so we can get on with business."

Jacob withdrew from his shirt pocket his reading spectacles and Randy handed him his paper listing the items he wanted. Jacob read over the paper and said, "No problem. When do you want all these items"

Randy answered, "As soon as possible – delivered at a work site near Lakeland."

"We'll have them there in a couple of weeks. I assume the usual terms: half now and half when delivered. Of course, as the captain's son, you are eligible for a hefty discount. Is a handshake enough, or do I have to draw up a bill of sale?"

Randy looked at his dad and saw him slightly nod his head, so he said, "Under the circumstances, a handshake is good enough for me."

Clement said, "Son, if you have any problems, just send me a word, and I will come over here and beat up Jacob."

They all had a hearty laugh and parted company in high spirits. Randy would have soon everything he needed to do his first construction job, and he owed this to the unexpected blessing of finding his father. They walked into the street, and Clement took Randy aside and said, "I hate to tell you this, but I've got to get back to the office. I'm thinking the best is to accompany with my family your construction supplies to Lakeland and stay for a few days. What do you think of that idea?"

Randy replied respectfully to his dad, "That will work. I can't wait to tell my wife. Having you and your family at our house will be the high point of my life. We'll count on seeing you and your family at our place in Lakeland in a couple of weeks."

Clement hurriedly replied, "Good, it will be a great day for the Read family. Don't worry. We'll be there. I'll let Jacob know. Safe return to Lakeland."

Randy watched his dad dash off until he became lost in all the crowds of people congregating in this busy section of town. He slowly found his way back to his boarding house and immediately told the woman that he had concluded his business and would be checking out. He knew his late afternoon departure meant riding in the night, but the moon was full, and he could not wait to tell Maud the great news of meeting up with his father.

He rode as far as he could before catching a few winks by lying down on the side of the road. His intention was to ride straight home without stopping, but when he got to Lakeland, a strange man hollered at him, "Stop. I believe you're the guy I need to talk to."

Randy halted his horse and said, "Who are you?"

My name is Dexter Mills, and I represent Southern Railways, and we heard that you're in the construction business. Can I have a few minutes of your time? I've a proposition to offer you. Let's go have a drink in the saloon."

Dexter looked like a decent guy, so Randy agreed to talk with him in the saloon. They entered the saloon, and Bart, the bartender, immediately said to Dexter, "That's your man."

They sat down at one of the small side tables, and the dapper Dexter asked politely, "Do you want anything to drink?

Randy replied, "I just rode a long distance, so a glass of water would be welcome."

"For me, it's rye whiskey. Bartender, did you hear our orders?"

Dexter continued, "I don't have much time, so I'll ask you point blank:

Can you build us a new train station in Lakeland?"

Randy could not believe his ears and said, "I thought you already had a train station in nearby Acton."

"Yes, we did, but it burnt down last week, and the company decided to move its operations here."

"I guess I can oversee the building of your train station if you have the plans. This will be a big project for me, but I can do it."

"That's all I needed to hear. Now I got to ride out of here to tell my bosses. If you are the selected contractor, I'll be back with a contract for you to sign."

He gulped his half-glass of whiskey, ran out the door, mounted his horse, and was off in a whirl of sandy dust. Randy drank his glass of water and greeted the guys at the poker table. As he was about to exit, one of the guys said to him, "The courthouse in Arcadia also burnt down, and I hear your outfit was on the short list of companies being considered to build a new courthouse."

Randy said, "Thanks for that news. If I'm going to build a new train station in Lakeland, I don't see how I can also build a new courthouse in Arcadia."

He knew he could not say anything, but he was sure that it was his older brother who burnt down the courthouse in Arcadia. He did not know about the mysterious fire that burnt the train station to the ground in Acton, but he could imagine that his brother was behind that fire, too.

He galloped all the way home. He could not wait to tell Maud and the kids all his exciting news. Not only had he met his dad in Tampa, but he also had more construction work than he could possibly do. He thought when it rained, it poured. His whole being was saturated, inside and out, with many blessings.

Maud and their kids were waiting for him in front of their house. He was exceedingly happy to see them. He jumped off his horse and ran to kiss and hug them, saying, "Let's go inside. I have a lot to tell you. It's all good."

Randy sat close with his family and told them in a rapid-fire fashion all that had happened in Tampa and since he got back to Lakeland. He looked at his kids and said in earnest, "Your grandfather, my father, will be coming to visit us in a couple weeks. For me, that's the best of my news."

He sat on the couch with his arm around Maud and said ecstatically, "I'm could not be happier. I found my father, and he's coming with his family. Our life is more complete and better than ever."

Maud was speechless. She could only sob over the joy her husband had brought into their house. She was already thinking of the feast she would prepare to welcome her father-in-law and his family. She helped her husband take his boots off. Once things had settled down, Randy dozed off into a deep sleep. She lugged him into the bedroom, put him in bed, and cuddled up beside him… satisfied that her children were already in their beds. They all needed rest so they could fully bask in the glow of the great success of Randy's first trip to Tampa.

Maud awoke the next morning to find Randy already up and talking with Jasper outside. Jasper was showing him the two horses he had found that were for sale, and Randy was relaying to him all that had happened on his Tampa trip. Jasper was really impressed that he had found his father and began praying immediately to thank God for making this happen.

When Randy was telling Jasper about his two big construction opportunities, he said, "We're going to need more laborers, so get the word out that we'll be hiring in a couple of months. If we are going to go big time, we need more workers."

The next several days passed tranquilly. Out of nowhere, a guy came riding up to the house, stopped his horse near the front door, and asked loudly, "Does Peyton Randolph Read live here."

Randy stepped out of his house, "Yes, he does. Who wants to know?"

The reply he got was. "The city council of Arcadia. It wants you to come next Thursday at two in the afternoon to a meeting on building a new courthouse. Come with all your smarts and be prepared to say all you can about building us a new courthouse. I got to head back to Arcadia. Message delivered. Bye."

Randy knew his brother was behind all this. It was convenient that next, Wednesday night he was scheduled to meet his brother at night at the old oak tree. He now had a reason to tell Maud for his next trip to Arcadia. He would take the two horses Jasper acquired to test them out and have his brother check them out.

The next few days went by peacefully. Maud got all ready for Randy's trip to Arcadia. Randy left early on Wednesday, saying, "I want to get there early to put my best foot forward."

Randy arrived at the old oak tree. Dusk came, and the dark night fell like a black cloth curtain. He waited for his brother to appear out of the darkness. The thuds of the hooves of a horse pounding the sandy ground were getting closer. He hid in nearby bushes to see whether or not his brother was approaching. His surprise was great when he saw that the person on the horse was wearing a skirt.

A woman's soft voice further startled him. "Randolph, are you there? Charlie told me you would be here."

Hearing these words compelled Randy to step out and get up close to the female rider. He was shocked that it was Lula Mae who said in a desperate voice, "Hurry. Follow me back to Arcadia. We don't have a minute to spare."

Randy did as she said, but he did not understand what was going on and why she was in such a flutter. His adrenalin was flowing off the charts. He had to know what was happening. He rode alongside Lula Mae and demanded, "Stop and explain."

She stopped and blurted out quietly, "Charlie is locked up in his own jail cell. He got put there because his boss accused him of continuing re-branding after his boss had signed a treaty ending the cattle wars. But now there are three men from Texas looking to kill him. The boss wants him to escape from jail before these men find him. Please, we got to go and help Charlie escape. It's good that you brought extra horses because Charlie will need them to make good his escape. Let's go fast."

Randy knew more about the urgency of his ride, but he was still confused and at a loss about what to do. They arrived on the outskirts of Arcadia. He followed Lula Mae at a much slower gait in the shadows of the night on a circuitous route around the town. When they reached a dark place next to a building, Lula Mae dismounted and whispered to Randy, "Stay here. I'll get Charlie out of jail and give him his old pistols."

A nervous Randy stood like a shadow of himself and kept his horses quiet. Lula Mae came back hand-in-hand with his older brother. They embraced briefly, and Charles mounted Lula Mae's horse and looked at his brother, saying softly, "Thanks. I knew I could count on you."

Lula Mae attached the two spare horses to the back of Charlie's horse. Charlie rode off and quickly disappeared in the darkness. Lula Mae said, "I got to go home to my children. See you tomorrow."

Randy sat down and tried to get his head around all that was happening. Suddenly, he felt a tight noose around his neck and a rag stuffed in his mouth. A rough voice said in his ear, "We know what you just did, and you're goin' to help us catch Henry."

It was clear to Randy that the man who talked was from Texas, and he was not alone. He could not believe that after all these years that, Texans were still in pursuit of his brother.

They roughly threw him on a horse and tied him to the saddle. Another man said, "We're taking you with us in case Henry is holed up somewhere. We're thinking that when he hears your voice, he'll show himself."

All of Randy's thoughts were gone from his head. He was in a real, unusually cruel, heart-stopping mess from which he could not even imagine escaping. The three Texans rode night and day, stopping periodically to check the trail and ask people if they had seen a lone horseman riding in a rush. The Texans purposely kept Randy hungry and thirsty. They wanted him weak but able to speak. The also threatened to kill his family if he did not cooperate.

After several days, their long ride north took them to Stateline. One of the Texans said, "Well, get our man or die trying."

They reached the small town of Thomasville, Georgia. The Texans asked around, and one guy said there was a man fitting their description who had rented a one-room cabin on the edge of town. The head of the three said, "That could be our man. Let's wait until nightfall before we close in. Meanwhile, get Randolph ready to talk."

They took the rag out of Randy's mouth, warning him to be quiet if he knew what was good for him and his family. He drank a little water from a mug held up to his mouth and was spoon-fed some grits. When he finished getting this little nourishment, the rag was again stuffed in his mouth, and he was blindfolded. Also, the rope around his neck was tightened.

Deep in the dark night, they quietly approached the lonely cabin. The head Texan stepped up to the door and knocked on it loudly. Not a sound was heard from inside, although the Texans knew somebody was inside. As they drew their pistols, the Texan knocked again more loudly. They then heard a muffled voice from inside, "Who's there?"

The head Texan signaled to his associates to take the rag out of Randy's mouth. Randy had already been coached on what he was to say if he wanted to see his family again. They shoved Randy closer to the door, and he said with tears running down his face, "It's me, Randy."

Upon hearing his little brother's voice, Charles opened the door. The head Texan immediately shot him point blank in the face, and he fell dead in the doorway. Randy was horrified and went mad. He managed to loosen his bounds and ran off screaming into the dark night.

The head Texan said, "Set the place on fire."

Another Texan said, "How do we prove that we got our man?"

"Take his guns. Nobody but him carries such old pistols any more."

The flames burned brightly, and the fire consumed the cabin and all its contents. Not a trace was left of Henry Harrison Read (aka Charles Bonard). The wind blew his ashes into oblivion. His life was erased and gone forever.

# POSTSCRIPT

### Henry Harrison Read (AKA Charles Bonard)

His body was never found. A man with the last name of Beaty came to Arcadia to inform Lula Mae Blanche that her husband Charles was dead. Beaty stayed in Arcadia and eventually married Lula Mae, helping her raise the four Bonard children. No record of Beaty can be found. Lula Mae's tombstone has her name as Lula B. Beaty. She died on November 12, 1937.

### Peyton Randolph Read

He returned to Lakeland to join his family. They later moved to Houston, where he made a lot of money in the construction business. He lost his business and money in the Great Depression. He moved back to the Lakeland and Arcadia area. He died on December 31, 1955, a successful owner of a large orange grove and a construction company.

### Clement Melanchthon Read

He continued to write articles until his death in Tampa on August 18, 1919, five months before his hundredth birthday. He was the last of the line of the highly educated generations of blue-blooded Virginians who could trace their lineage back to the founding fathers of America with the arrival of their first ancestor, Nicolas Martiau, at Jamestown, Virginia, in 1620.